ALEXANDRA RIPLEY is one of America's most highly praised writers of historical fiction. She is the author of *From Fields of Gold* and four national bestsellers: *Scarlett: The Sequel to Margaret Mitchell's Gone With the Wind*, *Charleston*, *On Leaving Charleston*, and *New Orleans Legacy*.

ALSO BY ALEXANDRA RIPLEY

Charleston
On Leaving Charleston
New Orleans Legacy
Scarlett: The Sequel to Margaret Mitchell's Gone With the Wind
From Fields of Gold

ALEXANDRA RIPLEY

A Love Divine

WARNER
VISION
BOOKS

A Time Warner Company

WARNER BOOKS EDITION

Copyright © 1996 by Lafayette Hill, Inc.
All rights reserved.

Cover design by Diane Luger
Cover and illustration type design by Iskra Johnson
Book design by Giorgetta Bell McRee

Warner Vision is a registered trademark of Warner Books, Inc.

Warner Books, Inc.
1271 Avenue of the Americas
New York, NY 10020

Visit our Web site at
http://warnerbooks.com

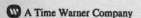 A Time Warner Company

Printed in the United States of America

Originally published in hardcover by Warner Books.
First Printed in Paperback: October, 1997

10 9 8 7 6 5 4 3 2 1

THE
BEGINNING

This book is dedicated to
my mother,
Elizabeth Johnson Braid,
and to the memory of
my father,
Alexander Joseph Braid

ALBION

BELERION

Itkis

GERMANIA

GAUL

PANNONIA

DALMATIA

Marseilles

Rome

SPAIN

Ostia

ITALY

Puteoli

Cadiz

PILLARS OF HERCULES

Mediterranean Sea

N
W — E
S

THE WORLDS OF
JOSEPH OF ARIMATHEA

In a small town
in the southwest of England
there is a tree, not very tall,
that blooms twice a year,
at Christmas and at Easter.
This is the story of how it got there
and the man who brought it.

ACCORDING TO THE RECKONING OF CALENDARS MANY CEN-
turies later, it was the year 6 C.E., or 6 A.D., the date: April 8.

The stone walls and streets and houses and palaces of
Jerusalem were rose-gold beneath the high blue sky and afternoon sun. Light breezes floated the scent of spring from
the hidden gardens of the ancient city across the open marketplace on its Western Hill.

A small group of men were standing near the cityside
end of the agora, as the marketplace was called. Their appearance proclaimed their status. They were dressed in the
long belted tunics and loose open-front cloaks that were
worn by all men, including the indentured servant or slave.
But the clothes of these men were made of silk, or fine
wool, or thick, smooth linen of the finest weave. They were
richly colored and richly ornamented with designs in embroidery or braid. Fringe and tassels trimmed their cloaks.
The four blue tassels on the corners of the cloaks identified
the men as Jews; the decoration was ordered by the Law of
Moses.

The man talking at the moment was the shortest in the
group, by at least half a head. He was not thin; nor was he
bulky, but strong muscles made up the vigorous body be-

neath the elegant silks. He was clean-shaven, as were his companions. Thick wavy black hair made his head look especially big on his small body. Large, slightly protuberant ears added to the impression of disproportion. His eyebrows were shaggy and dramatically arched. They called attention to his dark eyes, which had extraordinarily clear whites. At some time in the past, his nose had been broken, and it had not healed well. Two bumps gave it a slightly comic appearance. In repose his face was quite ugly.

However, his face was seldom immobile. He was a man of dynamic energy. He spoke rapidly and emphatically; he even listened with energy, leaning toward the speaker, reinforcing his statements with expressive, encouraging movements of eyebrows, eyes, and mouth.

When he smiled, observers forgot that he was ugly. He had strong, large, evenly spaced white teeth in a mouth that stretched wide and seemed to be hungry for life and enjoyment.

This was Joseph of Arimathea.

Joseph was in mid-sentence, but he stopped speaking for an instant when the fragrance of lilies overcame the strong odor of spices that dominated the air. Then the sweetness was gone, and he completed the words he had half said.

". . . cargo by ship costs a tenth for transport and arrives ten times faster than by caravan. Winter is behind us, and the seaports will soon be open."

"Open and perilous," said one of the men in the group around him. "With guards against bandits, a caravan is certain to arrive. Your ships are at the mercy of the wind and storm, Joseph. I'm too old to start gambling."

A third man laughed. "Except with dice, you mean, Eleazar."

All of them laughed, including Eleazar. Springtime was always intoxicating. A man could put his worries behind him and believe that only good things lay ahead. Even when experience told him otherwise.

On this beautiful, fresh day there was truly reason to

hope. Prince Archelaus, the incompetent, abusive ruler who had oppressed them for ten years, was gone. A new system would soon be in place. True, the Romans were now openly in control. Before, when Archelaus' father, King Herod, ruled, the power of Rome was largely unseen. But, at least, there would be stability again. Peace. For businessmen like Joseph and his friends, peace meant prosperity and security after many years of uncertainty.

Joseph could not remember a time when the teeming agora rang with so much laughter, and even the faces of the beggars wore smiles.

"Father," said a voice behind him. Joseph turned, smiling, to greet his son Aaron.

The boy was scowling, his handsome young face distorted with anger.

"Now that I've had dice dangled before me," Eleazar said, "I feel a thirst that can best be satisfied at the Greek's wineshop beside the Hippodrome. Will anyone join me for a cup and a few throws?"

"Aaron." Joseph reminded his son of his duty.

The boy bowed to each of Joseph's friends; he was trying to smile politely, but he was unsuccessful. The men nodded recognition and moved away.

"Don't worry, Joseph," Eleazar murmured with a sly wink. "My Malachi was exactly the same at that age. Later he gave me four fine grandchildren." He hurried to catch up with the others.

Joseph faced his son. He had to look up into Aaron's eyes. Only twelve years old, the boy was already taller than his father. It was a source of secret pride in Joseph. He was glad that his son would not ever need to know the misery of being shorter than other men.

"Come, Aaron," he said. "Let us go to that bench in the sunlight, and you can tell me what is troubling you." Proud as he was of his strong, tall son, Joseph saw no reason to get a cramp in the muscles of his neck.

When they were seated, a glance told him that Aaron's

hands were still clenched fists. Joseph braced himself. "What is it?"

"It was a boy at the temple."

Joseph looked away from his son, across the rooftops of Jerusalem to the glittering trimmed roof of the shining white marble temple, center of Jewish worship of the One God. All power and all knowledge resided within the mystery of that holiest place. Some day, Joseph hoped, his son would be one of the priests there.

"Who is this boy?" Joseph asked.

"A nobody, a nothing," Aaron said, hot with anger. "I was with the others of my class, listening to the teacher Hillel."

Joseph nodded encouragement.

"And then, Father, this boy, a nobody, interrupted Hillel!" Aaron's voice cracked with rage. "A peasant. Wearing rope sandals and ragged homespun, and dirty. He argued with Hillel. And Hillel listened to him as if what he was saying had some meaning to it. A peasant, speaking with a thick Galilean accent. It was shameful."

Joseph shook his head. "No need to be angered, Aaron. Hillel is known for his kindness. He felt sorry for the boy, no doubt. Everyone knows that Galilee is the most backward and ignorant part of all Israel."

"You don't understand, Father. It went on and on. Other teachers, even Shammai, came over to join in. One after another. And they all talked with this dirt-stained peasant, letting him question them and questioning him, and talking with one another about what he had said."

Joseph was intrigued. "What was he saying? What could have interested them so?"

Aaron stood up to pace angrily in front of his father. "I don't remember. It made me so mad I didn't pay attention. I wanted to learn what Hillel was saying, not listen to some peasant rambling on and on. I bore it as long as I could, and then I left."

"You made your farewell to the teachers, of course."

"They didn't care, so I didn't bother. How could they give all their attention to someone like that? And ignore me? I'm one of the best students in the academy. Everyone says so."

"I know, my son. You make me the proudest father in all Israel. Still, you should have explained somehow. It is owed to your teachers. Tomorrow you will make amends."

Aaron's cheeks were splotched with the red of uncontrollable anger. He glared down into his father's eyes.

Joseph held up his hand, palm outward for peace. "Calm yourself," he said quietly. "Calm yourself. You will be thirteen years old in less than a year. A man. Men do not let emotion master them. It doesn't matter about this boy. The teachers may have been using him to test the students like you, who are nearing manhood. Hillel and Shammai are the wisest of men, and the most subtle.

"Put the Galilean out of your thoughts. He's not important. He'll go back to wherever he came from and never be heard of again."

Joseph stood up. "Come. It's getting late, and I have guests for dinner. You may greet them with me if you will behave like a man and not a quarrelsome child."

Aaron looked down at his feet. "I'm sorry, Father."

Joseph clapped him on the shoulder. "Forget this afternoon. All of it. It's not important." Many years would pass before Joseph learned that he was wrong.

1

THE MAN,
JOSEPH

CHAPTER ONE

JOSEPH AND HIS SON WALKED QUICKLY DOWN THE STONE-paved street to their home. There were sets of wide, shallow steps to offset the steepness of the Western Hill, where the houses of the rich were built so that they might receive cooling winds in the dry season and escape the noise and smells of the poor who lived and worked in the valley that crossed the city.

Inside, Joseph's home was very much like that of any wealthy man in the great cities of the world that surrounded the Mediterranean. The floors were tiled or covered with mosaic patterns, the walls decorated with brightly painted frescoes. An open atrium was in the center, with a columned walkway on its borders from which doors or arched openings led to various rooms. Slaves in sashed linen tunics and soft leather sandals moved quietly and discreetly to serve, even anticipate, the needs of the family and their guests.

When Joseph and Aaron entered the house, they sat on the long bench near the door while slaves washed their feet in basins placed there for that purpose, wiped their sandals free from dust, dried their feet, and retied their sandals. Then father and son walked into the atrium. "Stay here for a while, Aaron. I want to talk to you," Joseph said. To Aaron, it sounded like a command rather than an invitation. He stood stiffly; his anger and rebellious feelings were obvious.

Joseph restrained a sigh. And his own anger. What had become of the good-natured, intelligent boy who used to live in this house with him? In recent months a stranger seemed to have taken his place.

Sarah, Joseph's wife, told him that he shouldn't be surprised. "Remember how you were with your own father, my dearest. You two fought every time you came near one another when you were Aaron's age. He's your son; it's logical he would take after you."

But, although Joseph had deep respect for Sarah's wisdom and loved her with all his heart, he believed she was mistaken on this occasion. What his friend Eleazar said made more sense.

"Urges, Joseph, urges!" he had laughed, hitting the table of the wineshop where he and Joseph had met. "We're not so old yet that we've forgotten how miserably confusing it was when those urges ruled our minds and bodies. The boy wants a woman and doesn't even know that's what he wants."

Joseph looked at his angry, handsome son, and his heart sank. How could he talk about such intimate things when there was a wall of hostility around Aaron? He'd have to begin with a different subject and try to gain the boy's confidence that way.

"As you know, Aaron, I will leave tomorrow and not return until summer's end. During that time you will be the man of the family. Also during that time the new government will take control. I am going to tell you about the workings of Roman rule so that you will be able to manage anything that might arise. Sit. Here, by my side. This will take some time."

Aaron obeyed, but with a mutinous air that made it hard for Joseph to maintain his calm.

Disbelief replaced disrespect in his eyes as he listened to his father's description of the policy that governed the lives of the Romans.

"They call it patrons and clients," Joseph explained. "A powerful man—like a senator, they're the most powerful except for the Imperial Family—he gets up in the morning, gets dressed, and then goes to the anteroom in his house. There are already people there—men—anywhere from ten to perhaps as many as forty or fifty. The senator gestures to one of them, and the man comes forward, greets the senator, pays his compliments, then gives him a gift. Maybe a poem he wrote about the senator's wisdom, or his distinguished family or some such. Or it might be a jar of wine, or oil. Or a length of white wool for a toga. Or even a gold armlet with jewels in it. The senator thanks him and wishes him a good morning and success in all his endeavors.

"Then he gestures to another man, and the same thing happens. Then another, and another, and so on until the senator decides to stop. At that moment he may invite one or more of his clients to have breakfast with him. The others wait in the anteroom. Then, when the senator goes out, always to the place in the center of the city that they call the Forum, all his clients walk along with him, hoping he'll speak to them or permit them to walk beside him instead of trailing along behind."

"But, Father, why would they do such a thing?"

"Because the senator has power. He can help a man get an appointment as ruler of a province, like this Coponius who is Procurator of Judea now, or persuade the Senate not to exile him for a crime he's accused of, or influence another senator to agree to the marriage of his daughter to the client's son. There are as many reasons as there are men."

"So they bribe the senator."

"They don't call it that. They call it a gift as a mark of respect."

"So then the senator does what they want."

"Sometimes. Not always. Not even often."

"That's awful. How can a man call himself a man if he does that kind of undignified thing?"

"Because that's the way things are done. By everybody. The senator is their patron. But the Emperor, or someone in his family, may be the senator's patron. And some of the senator's clients may be patrons themselves, for men even less powerful than they are."

"How do you know who is which?"

"If you live in Rome, it's what you learn because you have to know. Also, it's their favorite thing to talk about because the number of his clients and who they are is the measure of a man's power. And power is the only thing that matters in Rome. Men get it, they lose it—there is never any sure stability."

Aaron made a face of disgust.

"Hear this well, Aaron. A man must bend himself to the way things are, or he will be broken."

"I won't do it. Never. I'll never do it. Why should I? I live in Jerusalem."

"Where there is now a Roman Procurator. He has the power of life and death over every Jew in Judea. I have, I'm glad to say, a patron who's more powerful than Coponius or his patron."

Joseph put a hand on Aaron's shoulder. "These are the not-so-pleasing things about becoming a man, son. It's time for you to understand the way the world works. If you don't know these things, you're like the lamb lost from the flock, with wolves drawing nearer by the minute."

He could still feel denial in Aaron's tightened muscles. He struck the boy's shoulder lightly with the back of his hand. "Now, life's not all that bad, really. Granted, there are Romans. But there are also cucumbers, and they are much more gratifying."

"Cucumbers?" Aaron looked thoroughly confused.

Joseph smiled inwardly. The word had come to him from out of the blue. But it was perfect. This was going to be much easier than he'd feared.

He smiled openly now. "That was my secret name for my manhood when I first became a man." He touched his groin fleetingly with an index finger. "It may have happened to you already, that your body demonstrates a will of its own."

He had Aaron's full attention now. "You mean that my thing will get bigger and stand up?"

So it had begun already. Eleazar was right. "Yes," Joseph said in a matter-of-fact tone without a hint of laughter. "It will. And will feel very strange to you, because you haven't told it to. It's like having a separate creature that's part of your body but with an independent life."

He smiled at his son. "You get used to it quite quickly, because once it starts, it happens all the time. Always when it can cause you the most embarrassment. I remember one time, I was talking to my grandmother—about some weeding she wanted me to do in her garden, of all ordinary things that a person could be talking about. Then, all of a sudden, for no reason, I had an erection. It felt to me as if my tunic must have pushed out halfway across the room. I wanted to die from shame."

Aaron's eyes were wide. "What happened?"

Joseph laughed softly. It was, after all the years, a cherished moment. "Rebekkah took no notice. Perhaps she truly did not notice, I'll never know for certain. She has always been a great and wonderful lady.

"At any rate, I did the weeding. And I found a name for my independent appendage. Cucumber."

"Father!"

Joseph continued. "There was a big patch of cucumbers in the garden. One of them was enormous, exactly like my body had felt. I picked it and took it to my room. That night when it happened again, I measured myself against the cucumber. It was more than twice as big as I was. It made me feel much better."

"Tell me about other times."

"You mean, times when cucumber made me feel like a

fool? There were dozens of times, maybe hundreds, but that's the one I remember best."

"Cucumber." Aaron started to laugh.

Joseph joined him, laughing even more loudly. It was a rare, special closeness that he had not experienced with his son for a long time. Perhaps ever.

He wished it could be prolonged, but the lengthening shadows in the atrium were a warning that his guests would be arriving soon, and he needed to bathe and dress.

Joseph stood up. He longed to embrace his son, his only child, but he knew that would ruin the moment. So he said, "I'm off to the bath." The best he could do was to smile when he said it.

The Roman-style bath was in the lower level of Joseph's house. While Jerusalem had all the other facilities of a major city—a theater for music and drama, an amphitheater for athletic contests and gladiator matches, a hippodrome for chariot races—it did not have even one of the bath complexes that were common in the other cities of the Empire. Romans, Greeks, all the other nations, regarded nudity as something natural, unremarkable. Jewish law, however, condemned it. Joseph, as did most other men of his class, had a small version of the baths in his home.

He lowered himself into the deep tiled square that held the hot water with a small groan of pleasure, still thinking about Aaron. Already a man in the physical sense. That was good to know; Joseph told himself he'd have to start thinking about a suitable wife for his son. As soon as he got back in the autumn.

It was too bad that Aaron had no sisters. Too bad, also, that the boy refused to accompany him to the family farms at Arimathea, where there were girl cousins and all the girls in the village. Aaron probably would be tongue-tied if he had to talk to a girl. His life was filled with men—tutors at home and teachers at the academy. He spent very little time with his mother, because she was no scholar and he'd been an avid student since his first exposure to studies when he was only five years old.

Joseph was proud of Aaron's scholarly abilities and somewhat awed by them. Also—though he tried not to be—a bit contemptuous. He had been a doer, not a thinker, himself, by the time he was Aaron's age.

Stop that! Joseph told himself. You have to accept your fair share of blame. You've never taken him to Rome, although you always intended to. Nor any other big city. Alexandria is the world center for scholars, Aaron would probably be thrilled to see it.

Next year would be a good time for it, the year he enters manhood officially. There was no city in the world as certain to make a man enjoy being a man. Joseph was smiling at his memories of Alexandria when he left the hot bath and walked to the next room for the cold bath.

The shocking stimulation of it energized him, and he abandoned reverie for more urgent thoughts. He had many business decisions to make.

What gift should he present to the Procurator Coponius? He'd met the man at the reception held when Coponius arrived in Jerusalem just before Passover, but there was such a crowd that Joseph had only had time to note the Procurator's youth and nervous arrogance. The gift had to be expensive and flattering. For a young Roman pretending to be a man of the world, that meant something Greek. Romans would never admit it, but secretly they all yearned to be as civilized as the Greeks, who had, after all, created what the world regarded as civilization. Why else would all the upper classes speak Greek instead of Latin? Latin was for business and politics—contracts, wills, leases, proclamations by the Emperor.

Yes, a small, extremely valuable Greek statue would be perfect. Joseph smiled as he left the bath and toweled himself dry. He had just the thing in the strongroom of his business offices in Caesarea: an antique bust of a young man. As a devout Jew, he would never keep such a thing in his home; the Law of Moses forbade graven images. As a businessman he could use it to win the favor of a Gentile governor.

Coponius was back in Caesarea now; the Roman headquarters was there. By the time Joseph went there, in about a month, the young Roman would have become bored and lonely. The first rush of petitioners and their bribes would be long since done. Enter a man with no favor to beg and a gift more precious than anything the Procurator owned—Coponius would practically embrace him.

Joseph's smile broadened. I can tell him about the pleasures available in Caesarea, too, things he'd never be able to learn by himself. It's my magical place, still, just as it was when I was a boy and could only dream about the wonder of it. When it was as young as I was.

So young . . .

11

HIS
FAMILY

CHAPTER TWO

JOSEPH WAS EXTREMELY YOUNG WHEN HE BEGAN WANDERing away from the farm at Arimathea.

Even though he knew he'd be severely punished, he often slipped away through the fields and followed any path he came across, no matter where it led. He always managed to return before dark, and accepted his father's lectures with stiff silence. He hated his father. On occasion, his stubbornness goaded his father to the point of hitting him, and Joseph was glad because the blows helped justify his hatred.

When he was just past his ninth birthday, his wandering took him all the way to Joppa. From the top of the hill that cradled the ancient city, Joseph sighted and scented the sea for the first time, and when he ran down through the crooked alleys and streets, the intoxicating smell grew even stronger and more compelling.

The harborside docks were a teeming organized chaos. The boy was pushed and shoved, even knocked down by men carrying bales on their shoulders. Joseph did not hear their shouts or feel their fists. He was entranced by the beauty and mystery of the ship anchored offshore. He saw the final cargo ferries leave its side, and then a great square of red and blue striped sail climbed quickly up its mast, filling with the wind as it rose.

And the vision moved away.

Joseph watched until he could see it no more. Then he ran back to the farm, changed now into the boy who would become the man he was meant to be.

He pestered the Greek tutor to read again the verses from Homer that had bored and annoyed him in the past, to teach him all the words, all the rules of grammar and syntax and meter. He wanted to read for himself about the voyages of Ulysses. In time he copied the scrolls completely, so that he had his own, and could possess, somehow, the life of a seafarer.

As usual, he confided in no one but his special friend Sarah. Her eyes shone with shared excitement when he told her about the ship and its great sail and how it came alive when filled by the wind. The smell of the sea—he could not find words to describe it. She touched his arm with sympathy when he tried.

When the family went to Jerusalem for the religious festivals, Joseph wandered through the crowds at the Temple and in the marketplaces, asking everyone who would listen to him if they had ever been on a ship, or a sea voyage.

There were a few successes, men who had taken trips on coastal vessels that traveled from Joppa to Gaza, which was a major trading center because of the caravans that brought the exotic treasures of the East to the great marketplace there. None of the men had anything good to say about their experiences. They had lived, eaten, slept on a deck crowded with other traders like themselves, and the motion had made them sick.

And then at last Joseph met a Syrian, one of the hundreds of curious visitors to Jerusalem who came to see the famous Temple. The man was a sailor on the kind of ship the trading men had told him about.

"What's a Jewish boy like you doing asking about ships?" the sailor asked. His friendly smile took the sting out of what he told Joseph. Jews weren't seafarers; they never had been in all the years they lived in a country that bordered the sea.

He repeated much the same description of sea travel that Joseph had heard before. And then his heartiness disappeared. His eyes did not look at Joseph when he continued to speak. They were looking at something visible only within his mind.

"What you need to find, boy, is a Phoenician. They're the ones who know ships and the sea. Always have, for as far back as man has been. They have no fear of the monsters in it or the storms that make it into mountains of rushing waves. They are the lions of the sea, kings of the waters. No coast-in-view sailing for them, they sail out into the heart of the waters where no one else dares to go.

"Their black ships are bigger and faster and grander than anything you'll ever see, they're like something the sea god created to make companions for himself."

Joseph tugged on the man's sleeve. "I've got to see them. Where are they?"

The sailor's attention returned to the boy. He laughed, tousled Joseph's thick hair. "Not in Joppa, boy, I promise you that. Maybe in King Herod's new harbor at Caesarea. It's elegant enough to hold 'em—the black ships of the Phoenicians."

Now Joseph's longings had a name, and a place. He had only to get there.

"I bought you a gift in Jerusalem," his grandmother said when they were back at the farm. Joseph stammered his thanks. Gifts were rare and special in the simple, frugal life they lived.

"I want a promise as your thanks," Rebekkah said. "After you read it—it is a book—promise you will come talk with me about it."

Joseph promised, but he was very puzzled. Until he read the book. It was a pagan story, a Greek myth about a hero named Jason and his fantastic exploits while sailing his ship, by name, *Argo*.

"You know my secret," Joseph said to her. "How did you learn it? Have you told my father?"

"Calm yourself, Joseph. Don't rant at me. I demand respect."

He knelt to lay his head on Rebekkah's knee. She was the only one in the family whom he did respect. He loved his mother—at least he thought he did—but she was so devoted to his father that Joseph was unable to feel any admiration or respect for her.

His grandmother stroked his head.

"Enough. Get up and sit beside me. I know your secret now. I only suspected when you suddenly developed such a thirst for scholarship. I had to find out what another story about adventure on the sea would mean to you."

"I have to go to sea, Grandmother," Joseph confessed. "I can't be a farmer when I become a man, it would destroy me. I'd be nothing."

Rebekkah grabbed his chin and held it so that his eyes were opposite hers. Her grasp wasn't gentle, nor were her eyes. "Like your father. Is that what you mean, Joseph?"

He wanted to look away, but he couldn't. And then he wouldn't. Anger made him defiant. "Yes! That's what I mean. He's a coward, afraid of his own shadow. He lets anyone and everyone tell him what to do, and he just goes along with them, like he was a whipped beast. When we go to Jerusalem, he never says a word if somebody else takes the best place to stand or sit or walk or eat. They just push him aside. At the Temple, he's always sold the lambs with the least meat for our Passover meal, and even when we take a lamb with us from the farm, he's always one of the last to make the sacrifice, waiting all day outside the gates to the sanctuary while other men go in ahead of him. I'm shamed by him. We were a great family, he tells us. Were. Why doesn't he make us a great family again?"

"King Herod killed his father and took away all he had,

Joseph. You know that. But we are still a great family; we no longer have the riches we once had, but true aristocracy does not rely on possessions. It lies in the centuries of blood descent, and we are the children of Zadok himself, the High Priest of King Solomon's time, when Israel was the holiest and mightiest of nations."

Joseph wrenched himself from his grandmother's hold. He looked down, hiding tears.

"You are an aristocrat, Grandmother. But my father is not. He's a weakling."

"Oh, my dear boy, listen to me. Listen well. Your father deserves your understanding. You've heard the bare bones of the story, but you don't know the whole of it. There was, when your father was young, a council called the Sanhedrin. They were the keepers of the Law, the judges of Israel. The King himself was under their guidance and rule. They were the great men of the land, the aristocracy. His father, my husband Aaron, was one of them, known for his wisdom.

"Herod became king by warring, not by inheritance. He knew he wasn't a genuine king, not even a real Jew, only an Idumean, one of the tribe that had been made to convert to our ways and our laws. Because of that he feared the Sanhedrin, because they judged him unfit.

"And so he warred against them, too, even though they were not warriors. His soldiers went out with no warning and took away the chief men of the Sanhedrin, forty-five of them, and they killed them. When your father's father was taken, he ran after him, attacking the men who held Aaron in their grip. The soldiers knocked your father to the ground, and they slew his father before his eyes. The blood of your grandfather leapt from his heart and throat and fell into your father's eyes and screaming mouth. He was mute and blind for many weeks after.

"You will see death in your lifetime, perhaps even murder. I wish it weren't so, but the world is like that. However, never will you know what it is to choke to near drowning on the blood of one you love. Nor will you suffer the torment of believing that you should have somehow saved him from death, that you failed to be the man you should have been.

"Your father is not a coward, Joseph, he is a brave man who was defeated and who blames himself still for the defeat."

Joseph tried to understand; he tried to feel pity for his father, but he still condemned him. "You weren't defeated, Grandmother, and Grandfather was your husband."

Rebekkah held back a sound of sorrow. "But, you see, Joseph, I still had my children. Their father wasn't there to be strong for them, so I had to be. When you are a man and a father, you will learn what it means to have children. Their needs give you strength you didn't know you possessed." She leaned forward and kissed his head.

"Leave me now," she said. "I want to be alone for a while. Don't worry, my dearest boy, I will keep your secret. And if the sea calls to you so loudly, I will even find joy in your going when the time comes."

Joseph left her, walking as softly as he could. He was horrified by the vivid picture his grandmother had shown him, but he was still too young to comprehend the full meaning of it. What he was thinking was how extraordinary she was.

He had known the story of his grandfather's death for years. Herod had announced that the forty-five victims were traitors and that therefore the ruler—Herod himself—was entitled to confiscate all they owned. Rebekkah and her children were turned out of their home in Jerusalem with nothing left to them but their bundles of clothing. Their servants were taken to the slave market, their house locked and guarded by Herod's soldiers until he arranged to sell it and everything in it. The same was true for their summer villa at Jericho, and their property at Arimathea.

Rebekkah took the children to the house of an uncle, brother of her long dead mother. She buried her husband and mourned for him, ashes on her head and black garments on her body. For the seven days required by the Law, she sat on the floor in her uncle's house, weeping until she had no more tears, then burning with hatred for Herod and his killers, then—because it was necessary—putting all emotions aside so she could think what to do.

On the eighth day, she dressed and groomed herself to look like the great lady she was, and she wrote a letter to a woman named Mariamne. They had been childhood friends. Mariamne was now—a very recent development— married to King Herod, and he loved her, it was said, to the point of folly.

Rebekkah took her letter to the home of Mariamne's parents, knowing that she'd be remembered there. It was only four days later that a message was sent from the King.

Due to the generous heart of King Herod and his noble concern for the well-being and prosperity of all his subjects, the widow of the traitor Aaron had been granted the lands, justly given to the state and its King according to the laws of Israel, known as the farms and fields and vineyards and village of Arimathea.

Rebekkah located the widows of the other executed Sanhedrin judges. Some of them had no family protection and they were given homes at the farms. Some of the "homes" were no more than corners of the barns, but in them fourteen families found safety. Rebekkah provided comfort and food while they recovered from their grief. In time, all of them left, except Sarah's family, but no one ever forgot what Rebekkah had done.

It was not surprising that Joseph admired his grandmother more than anyone else in his young world. He loved her, also, as did everyone who knew her.

When he ran away the following year, the year of his twelfth birthday, he left her a letter, using one of the wax tablets from the schoolroom.

He told Sarah goodbye in person, asking her to wait for him to return and then to marry him.

"Of course," she said.

*   *   *

That night Joseph crept out of the farmhouse when the moon neared its full height in the sky. He would use its light for walking and would be far from Arimathea before anyone in the house knew he was gone. His brothers hadn't even stirred in their bed when he climbed through the window of the room they all shared. He had a leather pouch of coins hanging from a cord around his neck. He'd been saving every quadrans he earned for two years, in anticipation of this moment. Now, at last, he was truly on his way. To the sea, to Caesarea, and the black ships of the Phoenicians.

At cockcrow, he'd already passed through the area outside Joppa and found the Roman road that led to his goal.

By midday Joseph was wishing he had left his handsome new wool cloak at home and worn his old one of limp, patched linen. He folded the sleeves back as high as they would go.

When darkness fell, he knew he'd been right in the first place. The day's heat was gone in an instant, replaced by the cold of a springtime night. He waited in an olive grove for the moon to rise and light his way. The warm cloak wrapped closely around him felt very good. The soft earth beneath him and the tree trunk at his back felt even better . . .

He woke up when his shoulders slid from the support of the olive tree and hit the ground. How long had he been sleeping? He hadn't meant to sleep at all. No, it wasn't too bad. The leaves of the trees were silvery. The moon was still high. Joseph licked dew from the grass and then rose and stretched the stiffness out of his body.

He found that walking was much easier than by day, when carts and animals hurried along the road and he had to step off the pavement often onto the uneven margins. Now Joseph and the moon had the great Roman road all to themselves. His paces became long and springy, and he started to whistle.

No! Stop! Someone in Joppa had told him sailors

thought it bad luck to whistle. He was going to become a sailor, and he'd better start acting like one.

Joseph's feet were blistered and bleeding the following afternoon when he ran on limping legs through the great gate in the city wall just as it was being closed. The smell of the sea drew him, and when he saw the great harbor in the last of the day's light he forgot his pain and his exhaustion.

Caesarea was a magical white city on blue waters. Brilliant, innovative planning and engineering had created a harbor where there was none. Not by some efforts of earthmoving, making a bay in the straight coastline. No. The coastline held the city. White marble walls thirty feet high held the harbor. They'd been built, with broad stone jetties within them, out into the sea. To contain and calm a great expanse of its waters; to protect the ships moored within them from storms and wind.

Elegant white marble arcades lined the walls, along the jetties. Deep spaces behind their arches held storerooms, workshops, ships' supplies, dormitories for seamen. Broad walkways beneath and beside the arcades extended three hundred and eighty feet into the sea and, connected at right angles to the south jetty, fifteen hundred feet across the water toward the north jetty. It ended at the enormous sheltered opening from harbor to sea and the giant lighthouse that directed shipping to it.

A white marble temple dedicated to the Emperor Caesar Augustus rose in the center of the city's waterfront, a long, stone-paved quay. Its soaring, fifty-foot white columns reflected in the harbor's blue Mediterranean waters. The rest of the city was equally magnificent. King Herod's white marble palace was immense, mansions graced nearby straight streets lined with palm trees. Even smaller houses, taverns, shops, and stables were faced with white marble.

*   *   *

Other white marble buildings contained customs offices, warehouses, shipping agencies, fire and police companies—everything needed for shipping and for harbor maintenance. All of the buildings were beautiful. All of them were mirrored in blue water.

None of them interested young Joseph. He was under the spell of the harbor.

Oh, yes! This was where he belonged.

There were torches and lamp-lit rooms behind windows and open doorways all along the quay. People laughed and shouted and somewhere someone beat a drum. Cymbals clashed. But the boy was too tired to go look. He found a patch of darkness near the wall of a big building, curled up on the ground, sighed one happy sigh, and all the noise was gone, silenced by sleep.

CHAPTER THREE

"BOY!" SOMETHING WAS PRODDING HIM IN THE SIDE. JOSEPH opened his eyes to see another pair of eyes close to his. The face drew back, its mouth grinned, then laughed. The prodder was a boy, no bigger or older than he was.

The stranger squatted beside him. "You'd better move," he said. "The watchmen are cracking the heads of people like you along the quay. What's your name? Mine's Ashibal."

"Joseph." His throat was clogged with sleep and thirst, and the word sounded strangled. "Joseph," he said more clearly as he sat up. "Thanks for saving me from a cracked head."

"Come along with me. I know where you can get something to drink. You sound dry as the desert."

Joseph nodded. He was. He scrambled up, and the pain in his feet woke him fully. He looked at once toward the harbor. The water was flat and colorless in the pre-dawn air, but the sight filled him with the energy that success brings with it. He was here, where he was meant to be. He caught sight of the other boy far in front of him and ran to catch up.

Ashibal led the way into a wineshop. It had obviously

been open all night, and men were sprawling drunkenly all over its benches. Pools of cheap wine and vomit mixed together on the floor, fouling the air. Ashibal picked his way over the messes to the counter. A large dirty man stood yawning behind it. "A cup of your best Cyprian," the boy said.

The counterman's chuckle was a growl. "You think you're the King, do you? The only thing from Cyprus you'll find in here is a sailor. Want to get one to piss a cupful for you?"

Ashibal shrugged. "Doesn't hurt to ask," he said with a smile. "What've you got that's not too nasty?"

The big man didn't answer. He lifted a jug and poured some wine into a clay cup that had a dried crust of sediment inside its rim. Quickly he put his hand, palm down, over the cup. "Show me a sestertius," he said.

"Pay the man, Joseph," Ashibal said cheerfully.

Joseph backed away. "That's too much." A sesterius was the equivalent of sixteen of his precious, hoarded quadrans. He could buy three or four loaves of bread with that much money. All of a sudden his stomach growled, and he remembered he was hungry.

"Come on, Ashibal," he said, and he hurried out into the clean, sea-washed air.

The boy came after him. "They're all robbers on the seafront," he remarked, "but it was worth a try. Sometimes, after the night has passed, a wineshop will sell their dregs for only a couple of quadrans. Let's try the others."

"What I really want is some milk," Joseph confessed. He wanted to appear as worldly to Ashibal as the other boy appeared to him, but his empty stomach was more important at this moment than his pride.

"Of course. You should have said. I know a food shop. We can break fast."

The shop was only an alcove in a building in an alley that led away from the quay. Its shutters banged open at daylight, and the smell of freshly baked bread poured out.

Joseph pulled his bag of money up from its hiding place. He'd give the whole bag right now if he had to, he thought. He'd never been so hungry and thirsty in his life.

In fact, a few of his coins fed him—and Ashibal—very well. When they were satiated, Joseph bought another loaf of bread to carry away. He was determined not to be stuck at a place run by a robber when it came time to eat again.

"Let's go back to the harbor," he suggested. He was longing to see the ships in full light.

Ashibal was agreeable.

He was also knowledgeable. Not one of the sixteen ships in the harbor was Phoenician, he informed Joseph.

"But these are big ships, and three of them are black."

"Anybody can paint any color they like. But these are all coastal vessels, not seagoing. It's still early in the season for setting out to sea."

Joseph looked at the other boy as if Ashibal were a magician. "You know so much," he said.

Ashibal grinned. "Seems like so much to you, Joseph, because you're so dumb. What are you doing here anyhow, when you don't know anything about ships?"

Joseph felt no insult. Ashibal was right. "I'm going to learn," he said, "I'm going to find some kind of work on a Phoenician ship and learn all the things they know." He waited for the other boy to make fun of him, but Ashibal didn't laugh.

"A good plan," he said. "That's why I'm here, too. But you'll never find work on a Phoenician ship, Joseph, or any other kind of ship." Ashibal touched the fringes on Joseph's mantle. "You're Jewish, aren't you?"

"Yes. What difference does that make?"

"Nobody gives work to Jews except other Jews because of that day that Jews don't work."

Joseph's jaw dropped. He had not considered the Sabbath, it hadn't crossed his mind. The Sabbath was such a natural part of his life that he'd never even wondered if perhaps other people might not observe it.

"I didn't think of that," he breathed, more to himself than to Ashibal. "I am extremely dumb."

"I don't mind. I like you. We can still be friends. I'm Phoenician myself."

"Really?" Ashibal was becoming more magical every moment.

With Joseph's admiring eyes and encouraging nods for fuel, Ashibal talked . . . bragged . . . confided . . . stated . . . informed . . . for hours.

He was Phoenician, but not from Tyre or Sidon or any other port city. Not every Phoenician became a sailor. "There aren't that many ships in the world." No, his father was a farmer, and his father's father before him and so on. Ashibal was the youngest of eight sons, and there'd be no inheritance for him. "My father was going to sell me for a slave the way he did three of my brothers, but my mother said no. I'm her baby, being the youngest, you see." So she went to see a cousin, who went to see an uncle, whose son was married to a woman whose stepfather had a nephew who knew a man who was second-in-command on a Phoenician black ship.

"I've got a letter to him sewed up inside the border edge of my cloak. The ships don't allow just any young Phoenician to walk up and say he wants to serve on board."

And they certainly didn't accept anyone who wasn't Phoenician, so Joseph was out of luck even if he hadn't been Jewish.

And so dumb. He was ten kinds of fool to wear his money around his neck. Anybody would know at a glance what the cord led to. He should have his money sewn into a belt, like Ashibal's. He patted himself at the waist, loosened his sash, and allowed Joseph to feel the thickness beneath his tunic. "This is my mother's dowry money," he announced proudly. "She made my father lend it to me because I'm her favorite.

"Well, of course I'll get paid for my work on the ship. And I'll repay my mother. But there's never any way to

know when a ship will arrive in port, and in the meantime I
have to buy food and pay for my bed in the sailors' hostel.
I've already been here four days, that's how I know the city
so well. I get up early, come down to see if my ship has
come in yet, and then I've got all day to go exploring." Did
Joseph know that Caesarea had a big Roman bath complex,
with trainers for the athletic competitions that anyone could
enter? And a Hippodrome. From inside it, the seats looked
like they climbed up to the sky. There wouldn't be any
chariot races for weeks, though, and Ashibal expected to be
gone long before then.

But there was an arena near the Hippodrome, and tomorrow there were going to be fights! Boxing, and animals—
an African lion was going to fight fifty wolves. Why didn't
they go? If Ashibal's ship hadn't arrived by then.

Joseph was more than willing to put his life in his new
friend's hands. The Phoenician was so cheerful, so entertaining, so forceful. Joseph promised himself that he
would learn to be more like Ashibal. Being angry and restless and gloomy was not pleasing, had never been pleasing. He wished—with all his heart—to be like the other
boy. In a way, he wished to be him, not simply like him.

They had eaten Joseph's bread already, and they were
hungry again, so they returned to the food shop for a large
bowl of lentil stew and more bread.

Afterward they walked through the city, admiring its
wonders, loitering to watch the men who were building an
impressively large house and shouting impressively large
curses at one another. Many of them were new to the two
boys; they practiced using them against one another while
they walked back to the harbor to see if Ashibal's ship had
arrived.

When they passed by the wineshop again, it was
crowded and noisy. "The drunks must have waked up,"
said Joseph. "Wonder if the floor was washed." He felt
quite manly, a person knowledgeable about what went on

in wineshops. With an extreme air of casualness, he said, "That dirty counterman sure is a son of a whore."

Ashibal snickered. "Sure is," he agreed. "He's—" A thin man in a stained tunic and short, torn mantle staggered out of the wineshop and into Ashibal.

"—droppings of a bitch dog in heat," the boy said with an explosive poof of air.

The drunk grabbed his arm. "What'd you say, you little bastard?"

"Nothing. Nothing to you, I was talking to my friend."

"He was," Joseph said. "Let him go." He took hold of the man's elbow, to pull him away from Ashibal. The man's other elbow slammed into Joseph's throat and sent waves of pain through his entire head and body. He bent over, choking and coughing. His hands reached out, blindly seeking contact.

"Insult me, will you, prick?" the drunk screamed at Ashibal. He slapped the boy's face backhanded, again and again while Ashibal howled, trying to kick, trying to hit back.

Attracted by the entertainment, seven or eight more men came out onto the quay. Joseph couldn't make sense out of what was said or done, but suddenly there was a general melee, and he was being hit, hitting, being kicked, kicking. He heard Ashibal shouting, men shouting, himself shouting, felt his throat on fire with the agony his shouting caused him. Then his head seemed to explode and everything was gone except darkness, streaked with deeper darkness.

". . . Joseph, wake up." Ashibal's voice echoed painfully through his head. Joseph groaned. He tried to open his eyes, but one of them didn't seem to be working. Ashibal shook his shoulder. It hurt. Everything in his whole body hurt.

"Stop," he managed to say. His throat hurt.

He looked through his good eye at Ashibal's familiar

wide grin. It was missing a tooth. "I guess you got your head cracked after all," the boy said.

Joseph tried to laugh, but he hurt too much. He felt with his fingers. His nose was a mess. All his teeth were still there but his lip was swollen. He smiled as best he could.

"Come on. I'll help you get up," said his friend. "Easy. I think I've got a broke arm or something."

"I can manage." Joseph got to his knees, then, slowly, to his feet. It wasn't as bad as he expected.

"Is everything going round and round?"

"A little, not too much."

"Then you better lean on me. My good side's all right. It's day's end. We'd better get to the hostel before it gets dark—Ooooh."

"What?"

"I think maybe my foot's broke, too, or my ankle. I'll have to lean on you."

Joseph realized that they were in an alley beside the wineshop. "How far to the hostel?"

"Not far." It was the reply Joseph had hoped for. He put an arm across Ashibal's back, a hand under the injured arm and along the boy's side. "I've got you. Let's go. Which way?"

"Stay in the alley to the next street, then to the left. Ow!"

"We'll make it. Hop on your good leg."

Their progress was zig-zag, and very slow. But before they reached the alley's end, they managed to find the spirit and the strength to laugh at their own clumsiness.

At the corner of the street a man saw them. "Here, now, boys, what's happened to you two? You're a pretty pair of messes. I'm glad I missed whatever brawl you were in." Joseph peered up at a white smile in the center of a thick dark beard. The man had a band of bright blue linen wrapped in a sort of turban headcovering.

"Your head's bleeding, boy," he said. "Here. Take this." His fingers pulled the end of the cloth free and expertly unwound it. "Mop yourself up. You look like a jinn come to give nightmares. I'll take care of your friend."

Joseph felt Ashibal's weight being moved and his own hand filled with linen. "Thank you," he croaked. He raised the cloth to his head. The wetness he found terrified him.

"Thank you," Ashibal said. "You're a lot steadier to lean on than he is."

"Where are you boys—Hold on, what's this?"

Joseph looked at their rescuer again. The man's voice sounded different.

"I never knew anybody to wear two belts," it said, "with one inside his tunic, not unless the inside one was filled with money."

Joseph saw Ashibal fall to the ground and the man's hand draw a flashing something from his own belt. "Stop—" He dropped the linen from his hand, lunging.

But during the few seconds it took for him to realize what was happening, it was over. He fell to his knees beside his friend, staring after the man running away into the gathering dark.

"Ashibal—" Joseph looked down. The Phoenician boy's grin was bright, except for the dark space that announced the missing tooth. Blood was bubbling from the long cut that sliced his chest and waist.

"Help us!" Joseph shouted. He gathered his friend in his arms and raised him to rest against his own body. Ashibal was heavy. "Help!" Joseph shouted again. He realized that he was crying, and he was ashamed, but he couldn't stop.

Somehow he knew, without conscious understanding, that the heavy limpness in his arms meant that Ashibal was dead.

He wouldn't admit it. He knelt for hours, crying, rocking back and forward, cradling the lifeless boy in his arms.

Patrolling guards from the Roman garrison found him. They were rough, but kind. By torchlight, they moved Ashibal's body from Joseph's arms, pulled him to his feet and—one guard holding him steady—questioned him.

The guard holding the torch splashed light over the area. Joseph saw the glisten of Ashibal's spilt blood on the pavement. "There's no knife," said the torch holder. "The boy's telling the truth."

"Have you any clothes?" another asked Joseph.

He shook his head. Pain made bright rockets inside it.

"You're a lot bloodier than your friend. His is all over you. Here. His mantle's hardly even spotted. Take yours off and put his on. Wrap it around you, and your tunic won't show. Come on. We'll take you to the hostel. There's a bath there and you can clean yourself up."

It wasn't until the next morning that Joseph was able to think, to remember. I will not weep, he vowed to himself. I will not. I will not.

Someone had washed his tunic. When he dressed, he discovered that Ashibal's cloak had a stiff edge that wasn't dried blood.

Joseph paid for the night's bed and the washing of his tunic. He asked how to get to the food shop near the quay.

I will join the Phoenician ship. I will be Phoenician, not Jew. I will be Ashibal, with a letter to the captain.

CHAPTER FOUR

THE BLACK SHIP *ISIS* DID NOT COME INTO CAESAREA'S HAR-
bor until five days later. By then Joseph's hoard of coins
was nearly gone. But his head was better, and his bruises
had faded to a dull yellow-green.

He also knew every street and alley and corner in the
city. He had found the small Jewish neighborhood in the
northernmost corner, and his immediate urge was to tell
someone who he was and be welcomed into the community
where he belonged.

But . . .

Joseph hurried back to harborside and sat on the wide
stone mole that reached out into the sea. He had to choose,
and he had to think as clearly and deeply as he could before
he made his choice. Was he going to oppose the Law? The
Law was the ruling force of all Jewish life. From infancy
he'd been taught that the Law of God, given to the Jews,
was the most important thing in a man's life. Until he came
to Caesarea, until he met Ashibal, he'd never known that
there were people who knew nothing about the Law and its
vital importance. Yes, he'd heard stories about King Herod
and his transgressions. It was said that he'd murdered his
own wife and that he listened to Gentile advisors. Here in

Caesarea Joseph had seen with his own eyes the tremendous columned marble temple where the Emperor of Rome was worshiped as a god. That temple, like all the rest of Caesarea, had been built by King Herod.

But I don't want to be a king, Joseph told himself. All I want is to go to sea. Would God really mind so very much if I didn't rest on the Sabbath?

He fingered the cloth of Ashibal's cloak, listening to the thrilling crackle of the letter sewn into it.

I'm already breaking the Law. This mantle has no fringes. Does God pay attention to a little thing like that?

His heart and all his childhood teachings told him yes. And Joseph was old enough to understand that fringes and the observance of the Sabbath mattered most as symbols of man's obedience to God, manifest symbols to remind a man and to demonstrate to the world that the Jews were God's people, and reverent.

But . . . the sea.

I'll still be a Jew. I'll still love God and fear Him. Nobody will know it, that's all.

I have to go to sea.

The captain of the *Isis* was a tall, muscular, proud man. His eyes scanned the letter again, looked Joseph up and down again. He was clearly irritated.

"Very well," he said at last. "We'll find some way to make you useful. But I tell you this—" he looked back at the letter—"Ashibal, if you do not work hard and obey all orders without question, you'll be sent back to where you came from."

"I'll do everything you say," Joseph promised eagerly.

"Sir," said the captain. "You will address all the officers of this ship as 'sir.'"

"Yes, sir."

"Your pay will be one sestertius a day, and you'll get it at the end of the voyage, if you have done good work."

"Yes, sir." It sounded like a fortune to Joseph. He had

hoped only that he'd be allowed to work. To be paid for it exceeded all his dreams.

"Go down that ladder to the galley. The cook will be glad enough to have a small helper like you. There's little space down there."

"Yes, sir."

"Don't stand here wasting my time, Boy, go."

Joseph scampered.

The cook slapped him on the side of the head as soon as he entered the galley. "Just a reminder who's in charge here," the cook said.

"Yes, sir," Joseph mumbled. The slap had fallen directly on his half-healed scalp wound, and the pain was breathtaking. But was worth it. He was on the ship, on the sea. Even though he could smell only burning olive oil, not the blue waters of the harbor.

For the next five months, Joseph was able to look at almost nothing of the sea. He was on deck only at night, to sleep on a straw mat that he rolled up and stowed with all the sailors' mats in a long sarcophagus-like wooden box.

By day he was in the galley, scouring pots and bowls and cups or following the cook's orders to chop, or peel, or mash, or grind, or stir, or serve up the food for the seamen. He also carried food to the oarsmen, retrieved their bowls, cleaned and stacked them in a basket.

He collected and emptied and returned the big jars used for the rowers' piss and shit. Joseph also learned the ship's vocabulary.

He felt pity for the men, chained to their benches and their oars, until the commander of the roofed-over rowing deck educated him. "All criminals," he said casually. "They had the choice of ten years at the oars or being sold into slavery for life. Murderers, most of them. They wouldn't bring much of a price in the slave market. Who wants a slave that might kill you in your sleep?"

Joseph remembered Ashibal and wished with a white heat that his murderer would be chained to an oar. After that, he never looked at the rowers, simply handed them their bowls and cleaned up their slop. The few whip marks on their backs gave him pleasure.

The great ship sailed from Caesarea to Alexandria, then to Cartagena, Marseilles, Putedia, and finally to Sidon, the chief port of Phoenicia. In port, Joseph unloaded and loaded cargo, in bales, in boxes, in sacks, in goatskins, in amphorae of all sizes.

He could look out at the sea from the gangplank to the dock, but there was little time to do so.

The harbor entrance of Alexandria did, at least, offer the astounding immense lighthouse. Even with his back bent under oppressive weight, Joseph could see the huge wonder. But the city, the famous city, was out of sight behind the warehouse where he carried his load. And, back aboard, he had to go directly to the galley below deck.

Working on a ship was very different from what he'd dreamed. He never got to help raise or lower or reef sail. He had no opportunity to talk to the steerer, who manipulated the two long oars at the stern. He never could look ahead at approaching land or the open, unmarked sea.

Still, there was the motion of ship on the sea beneath his feet by day. And at night, in the few seconds before he plummeted into sleep, there was the heady smell of water on wind. Joseph never regretted for an instant the choice he'd made. He was where he was meant to be. He'd had considerable strength for a boy his size when he began the voyage. By the time it was completed, he had grown an inch in height and had muscles like iron.

"You've done well, Boy," the captain said when he counted out the end-of-voyage payment. "You can come back next season. Report in Sidon at the middle of May. Do you agree, Boy?"

"Yes, sir." Joseph was elated. He found the cook and told him the news.

"I guess I won't complain to the captain," the cook said.

He cuffed Joseph on the side of the head. "Just don't forget who gives the orders."

He was the closest thing to a friend that Joseph had on the ship.

There was a small coastal vessel in Sidon harbor that gave Joseph passage to Joppa in return for his taking the place of its cook, who was sick.

Near the end of October Joseph walked into the village of Arimathea. He had to visit every house, because everyone had believed he was dead and wanted to see and touch him before they'd be convinced otherwise.

At the farmhouse, Joseph went at once to find his father. He gave to him the thirty-five silver denarius coins he'd earned.

"You know I'll have to beat you for running away like that," his father said.

"Yes, sir," said Joseph. But he had hoped for something more than that. He did know he'd be punished. But his father could have asked where he'd been, what he'd done. His earnings, too. They were substantial, and the family was far from rich. They'd gotten their land back, but not their fortune.

Joseph kept his disappointment to himself. His father was still speaking.

"You missed the wheat harvest and also the grape harvest and wine making. We needed you for the work. Others had to overwork themselves, because they were doing a share that should have been yours."

Joseph hung his head. "I know," he said.

"What you did to other men can be forgotten in time. But you were not here to make pilgrimages for Shavuot and Succoth, as the Law requires. Perhaps the most grievous sin you committed is that you were missing on the Day of Atonement!" Joseph's father's voice had risen to a mighty roar. "If there was one single Jew in all Israel who was heavy with sins that needed atonement, that was you. And you chose not to ask God for forgiveness."

Joseph knelt in supplication. "But I did, Father. I fasted, and I prayed to God to forgive my sins. I didn't turn my back, I was just unable to be in Jerusalem."

"What? You prayed! Who are you that God should listen to your prayers? That is the blasphemy of blasphemies. The High Priest—only the High Priest—speaks to the Almighty. And only on the Day of Atonement. Bend your back, Joseph. As your father it is my duty to whip you until you repent."

Joseph leaned forward until his forehead touched the floor. He was willing to take his punishment; he had expected it. But in his heart, he could find no true repentance. He was glad he'd gone to sea, and he intended to do it again.

After the beating Joseph's father lifted him to his feet. "Now you will go to the Temple and make a sacrifice of confession. Then a priest will pray that your sins may be forgiven."

"Yes, sir. I will leave tomorrow."

"You will leave at once. You will not see your mother or grandmother or brothers until you are free of the taint of guilt."

"Yes, sir." For an instant Joseph thought with glee that his father hadn't mentioned Sarah. Then he had to admit to himself that he was only hair-splitting, accepting the words and deliberately not understanding the meaning behind them.

He was not yet thirteen, the age when his world would consider him a man, but the five months on the *Isis* had been a period of rapid growth for him. Not so much in the inch taller, as in the acceptance of responsibility for his actions and his decisions. Joseph had gone in search of a dream and had attained reality. He found it good. He intended to make it better.

"Joseph—"

"Yes, Father?"

"Take a donkey and some supplies. The road to Jerusalem is long."

"Why did he have to be good to me at the last minute?" Joseph grumbled aloud. "It's just like him. I was thinking he was strong, and he turned soft."

The donkey flicked its ears. It was beginning to rain.

"He even gave me back my earnings. 'To buy a worthy sacrifice,' he said. I didn't wash out slop jars for all those months so I could spend it on a bullock. A sheep would be plenty for my sins."

But when Joseph approached the mighty Temple, his rebellious youthful heart was struck with the awesome mystery of Almighty God, and he felt the enormity of his selfish concentration on going against God's law in order to pursue his own desires.

Joseph cleaned himself in the ritual bath building near the south wall, then climbed the many steps to the great gate that led into the Temple enclosure. Inside the Court of the Gentiles, he found a Levite, one of the Temple guardians.

"I am looking for a sacrificial animal to buy. I wish to atone for my sins."

The tall, bearded Levite in his richly decorated robes looked down at the solemn expression on the boy's face. He did Joseph the honor of taking him seriously, in spite of his youth. "All the animals and doves for sale here are clean and worthy of sacrifice," he said, gesturing to the area under the colonnade where tethered lambs and kids were standing or sleeping near to cages holding white doves.

"No," Joseph said. "I want to buy a bullock."

The Levite smiled. "Your sins cannot be as great as that, my boy. Only the transgressions of the High Priest himself demand such a big sacrifice. The requirement for a king is a ram. You should take a kid, or a lamb."

"Are you sure?"

"I have studied and trained for thirty years. I am sure."

"I thank you," said Joseph. He was truly grateful. Now he knew what to do.

Men in the Court of the Israelites raised their brows and looked questions at one another when Joseph strode through the Nicanor Gate carrying two bleating lambs, one under each arm. He approached the balustrade that marked the limit of the court. On the other side of it he could see the great stone altar and beyond, the entrance to the Sanctuary and the twice-curtained mystery of the Holy of Holies, where God was present.

His voice was unsteady when, following the instructions of a Levite, he placed his hand on the head of one lamb and said, "I offer this sacrifice humbly begging the Lord to forgive my sins. I have not observed the Sabbath, or made it known that I am a Jew and am proud to be a servant of the Lord."

The Levite took the animal and passed it to one of the white-garbed priests. With a consecrated knife, he cut the throat of the lamb. A second priest caught the blood in a gold cup. And while the blood was splashed onto the corners of the altar, the first priest was expertly skinning and sectioning the carcass. The flesh would be burned to ashes in the flame atop the altar, totally consumed so that its smoke, mixed with incense, would rise to heaven as a token of Joseph's past deeds being consumed in worship and forgiven.

While the sacrifice was being made, a priest sent up chanted prayers to accompany the smoke of the burnt offering. When it was over, a choir sang a psalm of praise to the mercy and forgiveness of the Lord.

Joseph felt his heart lighten. It was freed of its burden of guilt.

He begged the invisible Power for courage, then set forward the second lamb and placed his hand on its head. His voice was strong and clear this time.

"I offer this sacrifice humbly begging the Lord to forgive my intention to sin. Next year, I will repeat the sins I have confessed here today."

CHAPTER FIVE

IN EARLY MARCH JOSEPH REACHED MANHOOD. HE WAS THIR-
teen. His father took him to the Temple, in accordance with
tradition, to be recognized as a member of Jewish manhood
and to receive instruction and counseling from a priest
about the responsibilities and the honor that accompanied
his new status.

Joseph's behavior and emotions were all that they should
be. Except for his intractable determination to return to the
Phoenicians in late April. The family stayed in tents on a hill
outside Jerusalem, to celebrate Passover several days later. It
was a happy time for all the family.

Until, after the seven-day festival was done, Joseph told
them about his intentions.

"Father shouted, and Mother wept, and Amos said he
hated me for making Mother cry and he didn't want to be
my brother anymore. Even the baby Caleb cried at me.
Then Father gave me a whipping." Joseph looked at his little friend Sarah, expecting sympathetic cooings.

"What did you think was going to happen, Joseph? Why
didn't you do like you did last year?"

He glowered at her. "You're only a child, and a girl, too.

I'm a man now, Sarah, and men don't sneak off. They announce that they're leaving."

"Pooh! It only means you'll get a whipping twice instead of once. Makes no sense." She poked Joseph in the ribs. "Stop looking like a thundercloud. Tell me the best part. What did Rebekkah say?"

"Grandmother?" Joseph began to laugh. "She always surprises me. She didn't say anything to Father. But she told Mother, 'It's not your fault, Helena. The boy has my blood.'"

"Poor Helena," Sarah said.

"You'll never guess what Grandmother gave me. Can you keep a secret, Sarah?"

"You know I can."

"Well, Rebekkah called me to her room, and she gave me a plain wool mantle, dark blue. With no fringes on it. 'As long as you're set on going,' she said, 'I can't see the sense of you cutting the fringes off the good cloak that you got for your birthday.'"

Sarah sighed. "You are the lucky one, Joseph. Our grandmothers are cousins, but yours got all the fun for that whole family. I wish I had Rebekkah's blood in my veins."

"I think you do. You needn't worry." He decided that he'd bring Sarah a present from his next voyage. She and his grandmother were the only people who seemed to understand that he had to have the sea.

In the summers that followed, the conflict within the family changed very little. Joseph did fashion a kind of shortcut. He went to Jerusalem to make his sacrifices in the Temple before he came home to Arimathea.

At sea, Joseph's life changed every year. After that first summer aboard the *Isis,* he knew enough to experiment with carefully tested variations in his work. He still did everything he was ordered to do, and he did it well. But without the fanatic zeal of the year before. The cooking pots were scoured clean, but not polished. Ingredients were chopped but not so fine. And the oarsmen were given a little less time to eat their food before Joseph gathered up the bowls.

As a result, he had small bits of time to spend on deck. He watched men adjusting sail, he talked often to the steersman about how the two long tiller-oars worked, and he even dared to ask the navigator how one learned to read the sun and stars in order to know where the ship was and where it was going.

Joseph had been such an excellent worker the year before that his wages were now doubled. But for him, the real improvement in the job came from the stolen minutes on deck. This was his dream come true—looking from the bow of the ship out and across the sea, with no land in sight, only the shifting colors of the water, and the changing shapes and sizes of the waves, and the perpetually intoxicating smells and bite of the salt wind on his lips, in his nostrils, in the mouth he opened wide to receive it.

He wrongly believed that the captain was unaware of his moments on deck. But one day he was sent for, and he knew he'd been found out.

Joseph was prepared to abase himself, promise never to leave belowdeck again. However, the captain was not angry. He didn't say as much, but in fact Joseph—who was still known only as "Boy"—reminded the captain of himself when he first went to sea.

"There's something coming up that you shouldn't miss, Boy," he said. "That shoreline up ahead is two countries, Spain and Africa. Those great rock crags are called the Pillars of Hercules. Since time began, men believed that beyond them was the end of the world. If you sailed between them, you would soon fall off into nothingness. Or the underworld. Or into the sky. There are hundreds of stories.

"So we Phoenicians did sail through, to find what was there. For hundreds of years, no one dared follow us.

"You're about to see why. There is a fierce ocean out there, and its currents battle the currents of the Mediterranean in that small opening. These are the waters that reach for ships, try to crush them. This is what real seamanship is about. Find a line and lash yourself to the mast of the foresail. You're about to become a sailor."

The ship rolled and plunged and was rocked by waves crashing onto her decks. Joseph shouted with excitement. At times he looked at walls of spume-streaked water higher than the top of the sails, at others he stared down from the peak of steep, churning waves into dark shadows that could have been the gates to annihilation.

And then suddenly it was over. They were on calm waters again, with a lucent blue sky above.

He heard the captain's laughter and felt the ropes loosen around his body. "Sir—" he gasped. He was overcome with emotion.

"I know, Boy, I know. Now, get down to the galley. The men have earned a good meal."

Joseph started toward the ladder that led below. All of a sudden he stopped, turned.

"Sir, the waters feel different. The crests seem farther apart. Is that so?"

"That is so, Boy. We are on the ocean now, not the sea. You may have become a sailor."

When Joseph reported for work in Sidon the next summer, he learned that the captain of the *Isis* had been given a bigger ship.

This ship, the *Hikane,* was a bireme. It had a longer, wider deck and a bigger, deeper hull to carry more cargo. Also two banks of oarsmen, one above the other, for a total of a hundred men and forty oars.

The galley was little larger than that on the *Isis*. Space was valuable for cargo. However, with more crew and more oarsmen, the cook had to supply more food. Joseph was no longer the do-the-dirty-work-boy, he was assistant to the cook, with a boy—older than he—to take orders from him. His pay was doubled again. Now he would earn a denarius a day, almost as much as a seaman on deck.

He had ten times as many minutes to use for learning, but the crew of the *Hikane* were less flattered by his curiosity than the men on the smaller *Isis*. For the first time every moment at sea was not the precious treasure it had been before.

The route was infinitely less exciting. No Pillars of Hercules, no exciting ports in lands that were still near-wildness, like Gaul. The *Hikane* loaded grain in Alexandria and transported it to Puteoli, to feed Rome. There were two round trips and the season was over.

Again Joseph saw no more of Alexandria than the lighthouse and the docks. It made him furious. On a ship as huge as the bireme, he thought the cook's assistant shouldn't have to double as a loader and unloader of cargo.

On the voyage from Puteoli to the *Hikane*'s home port at Sidon, Joseph asked permission to speak to the captain.

"Sir, I have a request."

"What is it, Boy?"

"Sir, I am grateful to the bottom of my heart for your many kindnesses to me—"

"But you want to transfer to a different ship, am I right?"

"Sir, I don't want to seem . . ."

"Be quiet, Boy. Don't you think I know the difference between transporting cargo and true sailing? If I were your age, I'd feel the same."

"Oh, thank you, sir."

"How old are you exactly, Boy? I can't remember."

"Sixteen years, sir." Joseph lied. He was fourteen.

"And what's your name?"

"Ashibal, sir," he lied again.

"I'll do what I can for you, Ashibal."

The *Thetis* was a ship very much like the *Isis*. Joseph's spirits soared when he saw her. He had already been told that on his new assignment he would be cook, not assistant cook, and he'd worried that the *Thetis* might be a small coastal vessel. Even Phoenicians, he knew now, had vessels very different from their famous black ships.

He found the galley, checked equipment and supplies, then went in search of the captain, to report in.

Hiram was one of the great names in Phoenician history. Tyre, the great city in the days of Phoenicia's empire, had been ruled by the legendary wisdom of King Hiram. This Hiram, ruler of the ship *Thetis,* was a squat, bellicose man with a patch that covered an empty eye socket. He'd had it gouged out in a tavern brawl a dozen years before.

"What is your name, Cook?" he said. His foul breath reeked of stale wine and digestive troubles.

"Ashibal, sir," said Joseph respectfully. He'd learned that men with bad stomachs usually had bad tempers.

"I'll call you 'Cook.' You can go."

Joseph went at once. He intended to keep as far away from this captain as he could.

It was his misfortune that Hiram sought him out after every meal to complain about his ingredients or preparation or seasoning or all three.

Every time it happened, Joseph reminded himself that the *Thetis'* first port of call was Cadiz, the city on the other side of the Pillars of Hercules. He was willing to tolerate a mountain of insults in exchange for a repetition of the excitement of sailing between the Pillars.

By ill chance, the excitement was delayed for more than a week by one of the rare summer storms in the Mediterranean. The *Thetis* had to ride it out in open seas many miles from the passage. When the skies finally cleared, the great sail had to be patched. High winds had ripped three great vents in it. Low spirits affected everyone, especially Hiram. Joseph amused and calmed himself by envisioning the extreme pleasure available to him by poisoning the captain's wine. How could one of the black ships have been cursed with such a commander?

He got the answer at the straits that ran between the Pillars. Hiram was a genius of a sailor. The storm had left the seas running high and tumultuous. Even the most seasoned seamen regarded the white-breaking steep waves with fear.

But Hiram took the ship through as if he were sailing a toy boat on a quiet pool.

"He knows the seas better than Poseidon can," said the sailmaster to Joseph.

Joseph prepared a cup of Cyprian wine flavored with honey and presented it to the captain. It was the only way he could express his gratitude for a demonstration of ship-management he'd never forget.

They sailed into Cadiz harbor with the soon-setting sun lighting their red sail into a beacon of triumph.

Years later Joseph remembered that beacon vividly. In his mind it came to be a kind of omen, a portent of the astounding good fortune that was waiting for him at that very moment.

CHAPTER SIX

AT CADIZ, AS IN MOST HARBORS, A SMALL HEAVY OPEN BOAT
manned by strong oarsmen came out to meet the *Thetis* and
tow it in for tying up to the dock.

But this time, a man was standing in the towboat's bow.
When it neared the *Thetis,* he shouted to the men on deck.
"Be quick. Throw me down a rope ladder. I have to see
your captain."

Joseph heard the loud argument between Hiram and the
stranger. He had been about to climb up from the galley
when it began, above his head, on deck.

"I tell you, Hiram, you have to give him to me. Our
cook's arm was broken in the beating my ship took when
we were caught in the straits by the storm. By the gods,
man, look at the sky. I've got to sail within the next few
minutes."

"You can have my cook's boy, but not the cook. I've finally got one who doesn't set fire inside my belly with his
food, and I won't give him up."

"Hiram," the stranger bellowed, "I am going to the secret
islands. My voyage matters more than yours, and my needs
come first. Call up that cook and tell him to come with
me."

"Secret islands." What could that mean? Joseph was bursting with questions. Wherever and whatever they were, he wanted to go there. "Call me, Hiram," he muttered, "or I promise to give you a fire in your belly that you'll never forget."

"COOK!"

Joseph reached the deck in less than a second.

The towboat carried the stranger-captain and Joseph to a second black ship waiting at the harbor's mouth, held in place by backing oars. The captain didn't speak to him until they were aboard, sail was lifted, and water was hissing along the sides of the bow. Joseph watched everything with fascinated attention. This ship was very different from the other black ships he'd seen. The deck was not solid. In the center of it a long wide opening exposed the rowers on their benches. This seemed like an additional cruelty to Joseph. The Mediterranean sun would burn the poor devils' skin until they were like roasted meat.

It was none of his business. He looked eagerly around him while there was still a last little bit of light. Their course seemed to be set to take them directly into the endless reach of the rapidly darkening ocean. He observed that the captain was a small man, not much taller than he, with a head of thick white curls, almost like a sheep.

When at last he came close to Joseph, his hair was what made him visible. About them all was darkness.

"We'll light lanterns soon," said the voice in the darkness. Its tone was much more agreeable than when Joseph had heard it shouting at Hiram.

"I suppose you know about my cook's accident," he said. "Everyone in Cadiz must have heard me." He chuckled, and Joseph relaxed.

It was a mistake. The captain's next words were sharp, rapid, and cold. "You shouldn't be here. The men on my crew are carefully chosen, with special qualifications beyond their seamanship, which is the best of any men in

Phoenicia. If you don't measure up, you will be quietly and quickly killed. Do you understand?"

Joseph did not understand at all. But he said "Yes, sir," as crisply as he could.

"I am Captain Leontes. What is your name?"

"Ashibal, sir, but usually they just call me 'Cook.'"

"Sensible. This ship is the *Halcyon,* Cook, and you'll find some things are different on her. The oarsmen are Phoenicians—seamen, not prisoners. Their food will be given to them in double portions, because they labor harder than we do. That is one of the things you will tell to no one. There will be others. In sum, you will see nothing, hear nothing, and relate nothing about this voyage whatsoever. Are you a drunk, Cook?"

"No, sir."

"Keep it that way."

A man mounted the ladder from below, holding a lantern. It was not the usual kind, with thin oiled parchment sides that allowed maximum light. This one was made of copper, long since turned green, with horizontal slits shaded by hoods. It lit only a small area directly beneath it.

"Take the lantern and find your way to the galley, Cook. We'll want a hot meal as soon as you can prepare one."

Joseph looked around quickly before he descended. Everywhere was darkness. The wind in his face smelled of salt and immense distances. Beneath him the deck was slanted, evidence that they were turning in some unseen, unknown direction.

This was going to be the most exciting voyage ever. A voyage to the unknown.

"May Astarte be merciful!" Captain Leontes' second-in-command stared at Joseph in disbelief. "You're naught but a boy. How old are you, Cook?"

Joseph pretended to be insulted. "It's not of my choosing that I did not grow as high as a tree. I am twenty." Would he get away with it? He had added five years to his life.

He did. The huge man roared with laughter. "On this ship, no one comments on a man's height, Cook. The captain wouldn't like it. I am Hannibal—and I don't like jokes about elephants."

It wasn't the first time Joseph felt grateful for the hours he'd spent listening to Ashibal's bragging about Phoenicia's past greatness. Hannibal, he knew, was that empire's most famous general, the man who had nearly defeated the Romans after he took his army, and its warrior elephants, over the impossible barrier of the Alps.

Joseph laughed at Hannibal's jokes about jokes. "Have you orders for me, sir?"

"No, but now that I smell that bread cooking, I'll take some when it's done. I come bringing good tidings. The oarsmen say you did something outstanding to the barley stew."

Joseph could feel a blush of pleasure color his cheeks. Oh, why hadn't God granted him the gift of a beard like Hannibal's? His face produced nothing more than a scattering of thin hairs, which he shaved off.

The Phoenician rowers, Joseph had discovered that morning, had a system of upright supports and striped linen awning that protected them from the sun without cutting them off from the sea breezes. They had all been very good to him when he carried their food to them. He was glad it had pleased them.

"I boiled it with sea water," he said. "I couldn't find the salt block in the stores. Maybe some dead fishes added flavor."

Hannibal laughed again. "I won't tell them. Keep your mysteries, Cook. You'll fit in fine with the crew."

And Joseph did fit in well. The men were all older than he, seamen with many years of experience. But they were the best, and they knew it, so they were able to be generous. Also, they sensed, though no one spoke of it, that he loved the sea and the adventure of the great ocean as much as they did. It made him one of them. And, he was the best cook they'd ever had.

Joseph kept his place. He was deferential to all the men, without being obsequious. He got in no one's way when he was on deck. And he asked no questions.

Although he was on fire with curiosity. Why had they been out of sight of land ever since they left Cadiz? And why was the scrub water so warm when he hauled it up from the sea in a bucket?

After eleven days of sailing, the rhythm of activity on shipboard altered dramatically. There was no more shouting, and at night all the lanterns were like the slitted copper one that had lit Joseph's way to the galley that first night. Most dramatic of all, the oars were in use now from first light until deep dark. Furthermore, shaped covers of heavy linen were put on them. There was no noise of splashing water when they made their arc.

And a general air of alert watching permeated the entire ship. Joseph discovered that sometimes he was holding his breath, listening—he didn't know for what—until his chest hurt.

Four days later the cry came. But it was a whisper not a cry, carried from man to man in a relay. "Land, ho!"

At once all sails were lowered, and the pace of the rowing increased.

Hannibal found Joseph on deck. "Quick," he said softly, near Joseph's ear, "go below and put out the cook fire. No smoke must show."

Joseph hurried. The stew would continue to cook itself, he hoped. He covered the pot with its lid and the blanket he used when sleeping on deck. Then he crept silently back to the deck, holding his breath.

He couldn't see land anywhere.

A thin warm rain began falling. Joseph looked up in surprise. There had been hardly a cloud in the sky throughout the entire voyage. Now there was nothing overhead but a low layer of soft gray.

Leontes hurried along the deck to the steering station in the stern. Joseph could see him speaking urgently to Hannibal and the tillerman. Hannibal shook his head vigorously. Drops of water flew from his dark thick beard. He grinned at Leontes and pointed straight ahead.

Joseph stared in the direction Hannibal indicated. Nothing.

What seemed like hours passed.

Joseph's eyes were burning, and his whole body cramped. Nothing. And still nothing.

When it appeared through the curtain of rain, he did not see it at first. It was only a darker gray unsubstantiality within the gray misty moisture that surrounded the ship.

And then it was there. A lone towering mountain, dark and desolate. Joseph couldn't make out how high it was; clouds shrouded its peak.

Leontes rushed to the side of the rowers' pit and waved his arms. The oars slowed.

Before them the mountain grew more distinct. With a soft hiss, Joseph realized that it was not a mountain at all, only a big hill, and that they were less than a half mile away from it.

What was this cloud-crowned bit of earth doing in the immensity of the great ocean? And by what magic had the *Halcyon* found it? Joseph had learned a little bit of navigation lore from his questioning on the ships of earlier years. He knew that steering was done by the ship's location in relation to known landmarks, and the position of the sun and stars overhead. He didn't know how they were used, what to look for. Yes, the lighthouse at Alexandria. It could be seen from miles away. And the mountains of Sicily had a different arrangement from the mountains of Crete. But a hill in the vast emptiness they had traversed for so many days. The hairs on the back of Joseph's neck stiffened. He felt a chill on his spine. It had to be magic.

The oars carried the *Halcyon* ever closer. Soon Joseph could see a wide collar of pale sand rimming the hill. Low waves curled onto it, retreated, returned. They made a soft whispering noise, the only sound to be heard. He realized that the oars were still. The whole universe seemed frozen, except for the quiet little waves lapping at the hull. He felt incapable of movement, under a spell, enchanted.

Then there were footsteps, and he was freed. Joseph shook his head. What nonsense. Magic. Everyone knew that what people called magic was only trickery played on fools who wanted to believe it. Rebekkah had told him that when he was only a boy.

He saw that a small boat was being lowered from the stern. And that the two anchor lines were stretched taut. How could he not have noticed the lowering of the anchors? It must have been done very quietly, just as the boat was being lowered now. He was glad that the rope ladder rasped audibly against the ship's hull when Leontes and Hannibal climbed down into the boat.

Hannibal rowed them ashore, then pulled the boat up onto the beach. Leontes stepped out, then the two men lifted several sacks out and dropped them on the sands.

Joseph whispered to the nearest sailor. "What happens now?"

The sailor shrugged. "We wait. And eat, if you'll bother to remember why you're here."

Joseph remembered Hannibal's visit to the galley that morning. He looked toward the beach. Yes, the big man was taking bread and wine from one of the sacks.

Usually the sailors came to the galley, where Joseph handed them their filled wooden bowls and cups and a quarter loaf of bread. After that he carried food to the oarsmen. This day was different.

The steersman gave the orders. Joseph handed up the bowls and cups in the baskets where they were stored. Sailors leaned down from the deck and took them from his

raised arms. The amphorae of wine followed. Then Joseph
staggered up the ladder with the pots of stew, cradled in his
blanket.

Everyone was on deck. The oarsmen were sprawled or
standing, stretching. There was the appearance of a celebration, but none of the visibly happy men was making any
sound. Even their laughter was silent.

Joseph stepped carefully among them, holding the stew.
They dipped their bowls into the pot and filled them.
"Bread?" someone asked quietly.

"No oven," Joseph whispered in reply. The news traveled through the crowd quickly, but there were no signs of
disappointment. The amphorae, he observed, had been
passed around before he arrived with the stew.

He lowered his buckets over the side to draw up water
for washing the bowls and cups. He wasn't interested in
food, although in general he had a big appetite. His curiosity was more demanding than his stomach.

The rain had stopped. Tendrils of mist floated across the
deck. By the time the bowls and cups were back in their
baskets and stowed in the galley, the mist had thickened to
a pale cloak. When Joseph came back up on deck, the crew
were all rolled in their night blankets and ready for sleep on
the deck.

How could anyone sleep? Joseph felt like shaking the
man nearest to him and demanding an answer. Didn't they
want to know what Leontes and Hannibal were doing on
that mysterious hill? They'd vanished from the beach earlier, when everyone was eating. Joseph was angry that he'd
been careless, had not watched them leave. He sat hunched
in his stew-spotted blanket and tried to see through the
mist. After a while he could hear snores, and smiled.
Maybe the oar covers should have been moved to the
sailors' heads.

He pulled the blanket more closely about him and continued to stare.

What was that? Joseph rubbed his eyes. Maybe he was

seeing things. No. No, it was definitely there. Somewhere, not too very far away, there was light. It was diffused by the mist, no more than a glow, but it was there.

Joseph did not think at all. He shed the blanket and tunic and ran to the ship's rail.

I've never learned to swim. It can't be very hard. Dogs and sheep and goats do it. He climbed over the rail and jumped.

The thick mist muffled the sound when his body hit the water.

CHAPTER SEVEN

JOSEPH NEARLY DROWNED; HE VOMITED GREAT QUANTITIES of sea water when he finally floundered onto the beach, then choked and coughed and gasped for breath for a long time.

The summers on the ships had made him cocky. Steady advancement, increasing competence and confidence convinced him that he could do anything.

But he couldn't swim, and the cockiness had washed away. He sat on the beach, shivering, and examined his predicament.

He couldn't get back to the ship in the captain's boat, because he'd have no way to return it to the beach.

And he couldn't swim to the ship because he knew now that he didn't know how to swim. A lucky current must have pushed him to the beach before he drowned.

He'd have to wait. The captain and Hannibal would find him when they returned for the boat. He couldn't imagine what the punishment would be. Did Leontes really kill people if they gave away his secret? Would he do the same to someone who was only trying to discover what it was?

Joseph refused to believe that. But his mind told him it was possible.

The wind was stronger now, and colder. Joseph was thoroughly miserable. He could see the gooseflesh on his bare body.

The moon was out. The mist was gone.

And he could see clearly a sandy path that led up the hill.

Why not? If he was going to die for his folly, he might as well indulge it to its limit.

And it should be warmer in the shelter of the trees.

The sandy path ended, but the animals that used it had made a narrow route through the thick vegetation that grew beneath the trees. In time Joseph came out onto a rock-strewn plateau on the top of the hill.

The view was astonishing. On three sides the sea was streaked by moonlight on white wave caps. On the fourth, very near, there was land across a wide channel of water. Not another island like the one he was on. Trees on hills and in valleys for as far as he could see.

He stretched out on his stomach and inched forward. Below he could see the source of the tempting light. Hannibal and Leontes were drinking wine beside a tremendous bonfire. As he watched, Hannibal added a piece of wood. Driftwood, Joseph guessed. A tree limb would have too much sap in it to blaze that brightly.

At that moment, he knew how he was going to get back to the ship.

Joseph turned over onto his back and looked at the stars. They were beautiful, but he didn't think about that. He was wondering how Hannibal read their message, how they told him where to direct the ship's course.

The light was growing stronger. Not silver now, but gray. Daybreak was near. He'd better hurry down and make his try for the ship.

Joseph rolled over, got to his knees. And saw, by the growing light, that a wide beach of sand connected the island to the mainland.

There was movement on it, near the mainland. People were coming.

He backed away as fast as he could and plunged with dangerous haste down the narrow rocky path. On his way, he grabbed up a fallen tree limb, and when he reached the water, he waded in before he could change his mind, willing it to float and support his flailings until he reached the *Halcyon*.

The rising sun was waking the crew. "Where are you coming from?" one asked Joseph when he climbed the rope ladder at the stern.

"Went to take a piss over the side when I was half asleep and fell in," Joseph said. "Almost drowned." He ran to get his clothes and begin preparing breakfast.

He wished he hadn't mentioned sleep. Now that was what he wanted more than anything in the world.

Not true. What he wanted—needed—more than anything was exactly what he had. He was safe on board.

When he went to the Temple at the end of this voyage, he would make a sacrifice of thanks as well as the sacrifice of atonement.

"When's the captain returning?" Joseph asked the sailmaster. It was now past midday.

"When he decides to," was the answer.

Joseph wished he could sleep, but that wouldn't be normal behavior for him and he didn't want to call attention to himself. He returned to the galley to invent something he could prepare without a fire.

When he heard hushed hurried movement over his head, he climbed to the deck. He almost cheered when he saw Hannibal on the beach. His arms were held high, and each hand held the horns of a dead goat. Roast. And stew.

The meat was dropped into the boat. Leontes added the sacks, now limp, and stepped in. Hannibal pushed the boat into the water. And while the captain rowed back to the *Halcyon*, Joseph witnessed an act of strength that took his breath away.

A sailor threw a coil of rope toward Hannibal. With elegant precision it turned in a circular motion, unwinding as it flew, to drop a final length at his feet. He picked it up, put it across his shoulder, and walked up the path toward the trees. On board, the sailor played out more rope as needed.

When Hannibal carried the rope around a thick tree and back halfway to the beach, he signaled with a wave, and the sailor secured his end of the rope to the proud prow of the ship.

And Hannibal pulled the *Halcyon* to shore, using only the fulcrum of the tree trunk and his massive strength.

The tide must be higher than I thought, Joseph said to himself, or we couldn't get there. But that did not in any way lessen what the big Phoenician had done.

The oarsmen had been pegging together planks removed from beneath their benches. Now they extended the gangplank to the beach. One by one the crew crossed it to shore.

"Should I go, sir?" Joseph asked Leontes.

"No. They know what to do. You go down the ladder and bring up the meal. That's your responsibility."

Joseph had a thought, rejected it, then could not resist the chance. "Would it be all right if I went over to those woods? I might find some herbs or berries for seasoning the meat."

"Good idea. We'll deserve a feast."

Joseph hoped the plants he chose weren't poisonous. None of them were known to him. He'd try tasting small quantities later. In the meantime, he'd seen what he wanted to see from the brow of the hill.

There was no sign whatsoever of the people from the mainland who had sent him running. But on the beach below there were dozens of baskets—at least he thought they were baskets—filled with something heavy. He knew that because each sailor lifted and carried only one along the beach that circled the island, back to the ship.

And the island was an island again. The causeway was

gone, buried by the tide. He'd learned the secret that the Phoenicians were so careful to protect.

"What's that?" Joseph pointed to the box beside the rower's bench. There were special niches for the boxes between the openings for the oars.

"Don't get excited, Cook. It looks like silver, but it's only tin. You can't spend it."

The man who shared the oar contradicted him. "What do you think your sesterces are made of, fool? Bronze, that's what. And you make it with tin and copper mixed together. Old Augustus Caesar would be in a fine mess if we didn't go get his tin for him. Then he would have to use silver. Or some of that gold they say he's got rooms full of in his palace in Rome."

Joseph eased away, to serve the men on the next bench.

"When's that kid going to be ready, Cook?"

"When the captain says I can light the fire."

"Row faster, men. I've got a taste for something a man can chew, not just swallow."

Joseph believed that the mystery and deception were over when Leontes authorized normal cooking and ordinary noisiness again. But there were two surprises still to come.

The ship did not put in at Cadiz. But as it passed the harbor opening, the *Halcyon* transformed itself. Again the planks were taken from beneath the benches. But this time they were assembled into decking that covered the rowers' open pit. Awnings and their supports disappeared into storage compartments built on the undersides of the benches. And from the storage compartments the oarsmen removed chains and manacles. They put them on before the ship entered Puteoli, the harbor for Rome's cargo.

Also, the *Halcyon*'s crew did not have to offload the heavy baskets. A troop of Roman soldiers, wearing dramatic uniforms, took possession of the tin and carried it to waiting carts with tall closed sides.

"Praetorian Guard," said a workman on the deck. He spit into the water. "Think a lot of themselves, they do. Emperor's special pets."

The *Halcyon* reached Sidon more than a month before the end of the sailing season. Joseph was surprised that no further voyage was to be made. He was doubly surprised when Leontes paid him. The wages were three times what he'd earned before for a full season.

"I don't have to tell you again what I told you in the beginning, do I, Ashibal?"

"I don't know what you're talking about, sir. There was nothing unusual about taking wine to Cadiz and bringing that wine of theirs back to Rome."

"The men like your food, Cook. Are you interested in signing on next year?"

"Yes, sir. With all my heart."

Joseph was glad he had an extra month before he'd be expected at Arimathea. He had a great deal to learn before next year, and the knowledge wasn't available at the farm.

CHAPTER EIGHT

JOSEPH ARRIVED IN ARIMATHEA DURING THE OLIVE HARVEST, as he had for each of the years he'd been at sea. He stood quietly while Joshua tried yet another time to impress upon him the magnitude of his sins. This year, though, Joshua did not whip him. At fifteen, Joseph was too old to be beaten.

And there was something else, something unspoken, that made his father regard Joseph differently. This son had become a stranger, someone he did not know.

A stranger, and a man. Not by some arbitrary traditional reckoning by age. This Joseph was no longer a rebellious youth. A steadfast determination burned in his eyes. He was a man, with a man's assurance that he knew his place and purpose in the world. Joshua felt respect for this stranger, mingled with sorrow that his son was lost to him.

"You're different this year, Joseph." Sarah said the words with a puzzled little frown between her eyes. The question was implicit.

Joseph told her almost everything that had happened. He felt obliged to hold back the secret destination of the Phoenicians, not because of any doubts about Sarah's guarding his secrets. No, he felt bound by honor to the

men of the *Halcyon*. He had become one of that highly select group.

"My voyage this summer was the most exciting one of
all," was the way he summed up the experience.

"It taught me a lot. Sarah, I know now what I'm going
to do with my life. It's going to be wonderful. I want you
to share it. It's time now for our betrothal." He offered her
a gold-decorated leather case. "This is your betrothal present. I was told it once was worn by Cleopatra of Egypt.
I'm going to make you my queen and treat you like royalty—Sarah, don't giggle like that. I'm serious."

Sarah kissed him quickly on his cheek. "I know you
are," she said. But she continued to giggle. "You're talking
such foolishness, and you sound like a father, not my
friend. Telling me what you've decided I should do and be.
Don't be silly, Joseph. I'm only twelve years old. I can't
be your wife, much less your Cleopatra. What's in the
box? An asp to sting myself with? I know the story."

Joseph knocked the box to the ground and grabbed her
small hands. "I love you, Sarah. I thought you felt like I
do, that we belong together."

Her smile was sweet. "Of course I do. I've always
known that, Joseph."

"And you love me, too?"

"You know I do. I always have, and I guess I always
will."

"That's the only thing that matters."

"Of course it is. Why didn't you say that to start with,
instead of all that Cleopatra nonsense?"

He released her hands and awkwardly put his arms
around her. Sarah wriggled closer along the bench and
snuggled her head against his chest. "How nice," she murmured. "Joseph, will you teach me how to kiss?"

He devoted himself to his future wife's education for
well over an hour. Because he honestly loved Sarah with
all his heart, he did not think for even an instant about how
he'd learned what he was teaching her. In Alexandria,

where he had purchased the necklace of flowers carved from lapis lazuli that was her betrothal present.

Joseph found a ship in Sidon that let him work as a deckhand for passage directly to Alexandria. He saluted the lighthouse as the ship entered harbor. "At last I'm going to see something besides you," he said under his breath. His heart was racing with excitement.

"First time in this harbor?" asked the grizzled sailor next to him.

Joseph nodded. He didn't consider it a lie. He'd never been off the dock, or had two minutes' time to look around and stare the way he was doing now.

"It looks so big," he gasped.

"Biggest city in the world except for Rome," said the sailor. "Three hundred thousand people, can you credit it?"

Joseph admitted that he couldn't. The number was just too big. Ten times as much as Jerusalem, which was the biggest city he knew.

His companion took pleasure in displaying his familiarity with the famous city. He pointed to the tremendous buildings ahead of them.

"That's the famous library," the sailor said. "It's nothing for the likes of us, but there's a good story goes with it. Old Julius Caesar, he set fire to it, and the whole city ran back and forth with pots of water dipped from the harbor to put it out. Must have been a sight."

"Must have been," Joseph agreed. Now he had his goal in view. He was thankful for every one of those long-ago Alexandrians and their pots.

After docking and unloading, Joseph was free to go. Into the fabled city. The street that led up from the harbor was the widest he'd ever seen and the most elegant. It was bordered with tall columns that supported a tiled roof which provided shade and protection to masses of people wearing finery that surpassed anything Joseph had ever seen, even the ceremonial robes of the High Priest in the Temple.

But he had a purpose, and it was not going to get accomplished if he spent all his time gawking. He approached the least impressive man he could find and asked him for help. "Excuse me, sir, will you tell me how to get to that place with the library and the people who teach everything?"

"The Mouseion is on that street, there, to your left."

Joseph tried to thank him, but the man was gone, lost in the dazzling colors of the crowd.

So be it. If the Alexandrians were going to be abrupt and unfriendly, he'd be the same. He made his way, pushing through the crowds, and walked with brisk determination to the huge stone building that dominated the street.

"I want to be educated," Joseph said to the imposing dark-haired man who was doorkeeper at the Mouseion.

"A laudable desire," said the doorkeeper. "How do you intend to satisfy it?"

Joseph had no time to waste on conversation, and he didn't like being made fun of. "Where do they teach about stars?"

"At the observatory. Where else would it be?"

"Where is that?"

"What do you mean precisely by 'that'? Where is 'else' or where is 'the observatory'?"

Joseph refused to lose his temper. "Where is the observatory?"

The man gestured gracefully to his left.

Joseph sensibly turned and went back onto the great avenue by which he'd come from the harbor. He entered the nearest shop, a treasure house of silks that glowed like precious jewels. Once he'd convinced the shopkeeper that nothing would tempt him to spend any money, the man's directions to the observatory were succinct and easy to follow.

There was a doorkeeper at the observatory also. Joseph

braced himself for battle. But words held no interest for this guardian of knowledge. "Go to that door," he said pointing, "and ask for help."

An elderly man looked up from a scroll covered with strange symbols. He quickly ascertained the depths of Joseph's ignorance; it made him appear sad. "One of the junior scholars may be willing to assist you," he sighed. "What is your name?"

"Ashi—" Joseph stopped. "My name is Joseph of Arimathea, and I am a Jew," he announced.

The "junior scholar" was a man older than Joseph's father. He was, luckily for Joseph, passionately in love with the mystery of the skies and the meanings of the changes that could be seen in the movements of the celestial bodies. For him, navigation was a lesser, but still worthwhile, application of the little bit of knowledge men had accumulated over the centuries.

"You understand, Joseph of Arimathea, that the majority of our work will have to be done during the hours of darkness. You can learn the travels of the sun in only a few days."

"I will study both day and night, sir. I have a great need to learn."

Those were the perfect sentiments to win Theocrates' favor. He asked Joseph a dozen down-to-earth questions about his experience, his health, his habits, his living arrangements, his prior education. Then he organized his life for him. He led Joseph to a small room that was crowded with tables and even more crowded with young men bent over open scrolls on those tables, disputing loudly about what they read there. Theocrates thumped his cane on the marble floor to gain their attention. "Micah," he ordered, "come with me."

"Here is your mentor," he said to Joseph. To the slender man who joined them he said, "Micah, this is Joseph. He's also a Jew. Find him a place to live and eat, take him to the baths, and attach him to your night walkers. I will see you both when the ceiling is scheduled to open."

Micah smiled at Joseph. "Come on." He led the way through a maze of corridors to an exit onto a narrow street that carried almost no traffic. "There's a quiet wineshop along here. It's in a garden, and you can hear yourself think. I hope you're rich, because I'm broke."

Joseph was on the verge of discovering civilized life brought to its fullest fruition. Alexandria had been, for centuries, concentrated on developing the pleasures of the senses, exploring them, refining them, elaborating them to create an apex of sophistication unknown in the world's history before or since the time that he had the good fortune to arrive there in search of knowledge.

The garden was walled, the walls covered with vines trained into elegant arabesques which framed pedestals holding marble nudes, male and female, single or paired in subtly erotic matings.

Thin blown glass goblets held the wine that tasted like no wine Joseph had ever encountered. He felt tiny explosions of warmth in his throat and in his head when he swallowed.

"Sip, my star-struck friend, don't guzzle. You'll be able to prolong the pleasure that way." Micah lounged comfortably in his silk-cushioned marble chair. Joseph tried to imitate him. He felt as graceless as an ox mired in mud.

"You feel like a great lumpy fool, don't you?" Micah's tone was sympathetic with no underlay of laughter or of malice. "I brought you here on purpose, Joseph, to make you feel like that— No, wait! Don't get angry. This is Alexandria. This is the way people live here, and it's a natural expression of the way they think. By which I mean that there is nothing natural about it. Everything is controlled and manipulated and complicated to near perfection. Some Alexandrians carry things beyond perfection, and that can become very strange indeed. But you won't run into that, I promise you.

"I'm not suggesting that you should become like us, Joseph. I'm just trying to show you the way we are. Don't waste your energies on disapproval or criticism or defiance. Just fit in enough so that you won't be conspicuous and therefore ridiculed or mistreated. If you can do that, you'll be able to concentrate on accomplishing what you came to Alexandria to do, because you'll be left alone to do it."

Joseph thought about Micah's words. They made sense, at least he thought they did. And since he had no one else to help him, he'd have to accept them.

"What do I have to do?"

Late in the afternoon Micah took Joseph to the marble mansion of his aunt Sapphorah. Joseph had been bathed, massaged, shaved, barbered, manicured, and scented at the great bath complex. He was wearing sandals of red-dyed leather that was as supple and soft to the touch as his yellow linen tunic, green leather belt, and red and yellow striped linen mantle with elaborately wrought blue tassels at the corners. He looked and smelled like a Jew of Alexandria.

"I feel like a donkey pretending to be a horse," he complained to Micah.

He repeated Joseph's words to Sapphorah, and she immediately threw her arms around Joseph and kissed him on both cheeks. "I love you, Joseph of Arimathea. You are exactly what has been lacking in this house, a direct, honest man. Of course you'll live here while you do your studies."

"She means you're different, and my aunt is always searching for novelty," Micah told Joseph later. "But she has a genuinely warm heart, a superb cook, and she won't expect you to visit her bed. You'll do fine here."

"I need to learn about the stars, Micah, not fancy food and wine."

"And so you will. A group of us meet every day in front

of the Great Synagogue just when the sun is beginning to set. We walk together to the Mouseion, go our separate ways inside the academy, and meet again after four turns of the sand glass to walk back to our neighborhood. No city's streets are safe at night."

"I know."

In later years, his time in Alexandria became to Joseph more like a dream he'd once dreamed than some weeks he'd lived through. He remembered it with fondness and disbelief. But during the days that he was actually there, every minute had a vivid, stimulating actuality that made him more aware of everything he was seeing, tasting, feeling, thinking than he had ever experienced in his life.

From the first night at the observatory, he was fascinated by astronomy. All the times he had looked at the sky and not known what he was seeing! The orderliness of it. The rising and setting of the sun, the moon, certain of the stars. The waxing and waning moon. The movements in the sky. They could be observed, expected, predicted.

Alexandria's great scholarly center had been founded over three centuries earlier. For all those years men had studied the sky and recorded what they had seen. The enormous library had thousands of scrolls, each filled with hundreds of observations. Other countries' records were there, too, careful copies of the works of Babylonian, Greek, even Chinese astronomers.

Joseph's reverence for the wonders contained in the library caught the eye of one of the hundreds of men who worked there. Joseph never even learned his name, but he was more indebted to him than to anyone, even Micah. The shy, retiring little man introduced Joseph to the beauty and wealth of maps. He'd never known such a thing existed, and he studied them until his eyes felt on fire. To see Jerusalem, Caesarea, the small river that ran near Arimathea—there, on parchment in the library in Alexandria! All the ports he'd visited, plus names he'd heard but known nothing about. They were all there, on one scroll, or two, or five.

He even found what had to be the secret destination of the *Halcyon*'s voyage. Not the single hill, of course, nor the land or larger island that he'd seen connected to it. But from Cadiz, north, north, north, there were lands ten, twenty, thirty times the size of all Israel. He could understand now the muffled oars, the oven smoke shut off, the command for silence. The ship must have passed near to a promontory of Gaul that was clearly outlined on a map. With the way sound carried over water, carelessness could easily have brought discovery, perhaps even attack from the Roman soldiers who occupied Gaul.

He spent entire days in the library, not leaving to get food or even to relieve himself until a thundering headache told him he needed to fill his stomach and empty his bladder.

"Joseph, my friend, you're becoming a veritable scholar," Micah said, only half teasing. "You'd better move to Alexandria for good. A lifetime is barely long enough to see every scroll in the library."

The remark made Joseph remember the passing days and the reason he had come. He'd learned enough to be able to read the Phoenicians' route if he studied the skies on the next voyage. And he'd learned where his country—and he—fit in relation to the rest of the world. He could not afford to spend time learning other things simply for the pleasure of learning them. He had a purpose, and he must stick to it.

"No more library and no more observatory," he told Micah. "I've got one more thing I have to learn, and it's not taught at the Mouseion."

"You intrigue me, Joseph, what is it?"

"I want to learn to swim."

Micah literally fell off his marble chair, bent double with laughter.

When he regained his composure, and the wineglass

he'd broken was replaced and filled, he held out his hands to clasp Joseph's. "My friend, I will never forget you. You've given me more surprises in twelve days than most men find in a lifetime. I am grateful to you."

Joseph was embarrassed. "I am grateful to you, too, Micah," he said, and it was true. "But I'll be a lot more grateful if you find me a teacher for swimming." That was true, too.

"Easily done." Micah leaned back in his chair again and picked up his glass. "Tomorrow is the Sabbath. Instead of going directly to my aunt's gigantic dinner, come with me to a men's group I belong to. We always meet after synagogue to criticize the sermon and talk. It fortifies us against the excesses of family life waiting at home. Don't worry, you won't delay Sapphorah's dinner. My uncle is one of the group, and he always has things timed to perfection."

Joseph had met few people in the Jewish community. He'd been in Alexandria for only one Sabbath, and that had been spent in Sapphorah's company for the most part. She loved to hear every detail he could remember about Jerusalem, especially the Temple. "I dream of making a Passover pilgrimage," she said many times. "But I'm afraid it will never happen. Always there's a sick child or my father or a cousin's marriage or some other family need that comes first."

When Micah took him to the meeting of men, Joseph knew the instant he entered the door that he was in the midst of the world he intended to belong to someday. It wasn't the rich clothing of the men, or the heavy jeweled belts and bracelets some of them wore. It was the certainty they had, the sense of power that they projected. They were the way Rebekkah had described his grandfather to him. They were what he wanted to be: relaxed, contented, confident, and in control of their lives.

Alexandria's Jewish community had no connection whatsoever with the Jews that had been slaves in Pharaoh's Egypt. Or, rather, they had only the connection that all Jews had and celebrated in the Holy Festival of Passover. Moses, giver of God's law, had led those Jews out of Egypt back in the days of antiquity.

These Jews had come to Alexandria by choice, because of the beauty and learning and wealth to be found there. Some were descendants of the dispersion—the Diaspora—of Jews nearly six centuries earlier, when the infamous King Nebuchadnezzer of Babylonia captured Israel and took its people captive and scattered them throughout his empire. Most had been in Alexandria, by choice, for hundreds of years, emigrating from all other lands.

They were respected and protected, even privileged by the laws of the country. Native Egyptians were less important. Only Greek and Roman citizens more so. They had more power over their own lives than did the Jews in Jerusalem and Judea.

Joseph listened to them and talked to them with growing astonishment. It was almost a problem to believe that they were really Jews. They were oppressed by no one, and Judea had been under the heel of oppression for Joseph's entire lifetime, and his father's, and his grandfather's life had been brutally ended by the violence of King Herod.

He mentioned that, in response to questions about his family. "Oh, Herod," said his questioner, "that lunatic. Yes, he's certainly a blot on the history of us Jews. But, after all, he's really an Idumean, isn't he? Not our blood at all. And we have to admit that he's given work to a lot of the poor with that incessant building of his. How many cities is it now? Sebaste, Jericho, Caesarea, and those forts and palaces, too. We can be glad he had the time to rebuild the Temple. I've seen it, and it's magnificent."

"Yes, it is," said Joseph quietly. He wanted to shout: "But he killed my grandfather and robbed my family. All the marble and gold in the world cannot erase his crimes."

It was time he got away from Alexandria, Joseph decided at that moment. As soon as he learned to swim.

Micah led the way, past the library and to the edge of the harbor. The great lighthouse towered on its island on the other side. Joseph cast an expert eye on the ships anchored there. All Roman, and all riding high, their holds empty. He assumed they were in the harbor to be loaded with grain from Egypt's bounteous stores in warehouses throughout the delta of the Nile. He wished their crews luck. The sailing season was ending; they'd have storms to brave throughout their long journey to Puteoli.

"You're not paying attention, Joseph."

"I'm sorry, Micah. What did I miss?"

"I said you're a very lucky man. There's a deep pool that holds harbor water just within the walls of the old Royal Palace. The Roman Governor isn't there, he seldom is. One of his slaves will be your swimming instructor. I'll introduce you to the keeper of the gate beside the harbor. It's all arranged. Be sure to tip him handsomely every time you come."

Looking at the water made Joseph feel again all the terrors of drowning. He was scared. "How many lessons does it take, to learn?"

Micah shrugged. "Who knows? I was taught when I was very small, and I don't remember anything about it. Don't worry. You have a very fine instructor."

There was a strange smothered laughter in Micah's eyes. If he's got somebody in there with a whip in his hand, I'll beat Micah black and blue, Joseph thought.

"Septimus, this is the gentleman who has come to swim in the pool," Micah said. A coin left his hand for Septimus', with a brief flash of silver.

The gatekeeper bowed. "Please enter," he said to Joseph.

"Micah! Aren't you coming with me?"

He was already walking away. "Why should I?" he

called back over his shoulder. "I already know how to
swim."

A wide roofed colonnade surrounded the unroofed pool,
with couches and tables and palm trees in decorated pots
scattered throughout. A young woman got up from one of
the couches. "Hello, you are Joseph, are you not? My
name is Nefert, and I will teach you to swim."

A woman. Joseph didn't know what to say, or do. How
could Micah have arranged for him to make a fool of himself in front of a woman? No wonder he was laughing inside.

"You'll find it very easy, really," the woman said. "See.
Watch me." She loosened her tunic at the shoulders and
stepped out of the cloth puddled around her feet. Then she
walked to the edge of the pool, raised her arms, and dove
into the water, making hardly a splash.

Her full breasts had lifted when she raised her arms.
Joseph was stunned. He'd never seen a naked woman, only
tiny girl children, and he had often fantasized about the
breasts underneath the clothing of women on the street,
even in the synagogue. He wanted to touch them. They
looked more exciting and soft and touchable than he'd
ever imagined.

Shame, he told himself. His hands tried to hide his erection.

Nefert's head broke through the water's surface. Her
arms stretched out on each side of her, hands moving
slowly. She smiled. White teeth between impossibly red
lips. Her skin was a pale golden brown, and gold circlets
held the dozens of looped tiny dark braids of her hair.
Joseph stared. He couldn't speak. Kohl rimmed her dark
eyes in a thick black line, and her eyelids were painted
bright green. Beneath the pool's surface he could see her
breasts moving, floating, their nipples as red as her lips.

"You can't learn to swim if you stay up there," she said.
"Take your things off, sit on the edge, then just slide into
the water. I'll be here to catch you."

His feet would not move, and he could not speak.

"I understand," Nefert said. She placed her hands on the pool's rim and with an easy motion splashed up from the water and seated herself, then swung her legs over and stood.

"Dear young Joseph," she murmured. She walked gracefully to him and put her wet hands on his body. Through his clothing her fingers cupped his testicles, and her thumbs stroked his penis. Joseph cried out. "Slide off that cloak," Nefert ordered. Joseph obeyed. She removed her hands, and he cried again. But she'd loosened his belt by now and pulled up the tunic. Her hands slid inside his loincloth. They were cool against his skin. Joseph moaned, knowing ecstasy. She held him while he ejaculated in strong, thrusting explosions of sperm inside the cloth.

"Magnificent," Nefert crooned. "You're like an elephant. I can hardly wait to feel you inside me. Let's go to a couch and make love, my sweet manly Joseph."

She guided his stumbling walk, removed his loincloth and slid her hands over his thighs and abdomen, pressing him backward until he fell into the cushioned platform. He tried to sit up, but Nefert shook her head and whispered, "No, lie back." Droplets of water fell from her hair onto his chest when she moved her head.

"Give me your hands," she said, but she lifted them for him, holding his wrists. Then she bent over him, dropping a breast into each hand. "Ah, lovely," she said. "Don't squeeze too hard, my elephant. More like this." She caressed his scrotum, then his rising penis. Joseph could feel her nipples stiffen against his palms. Then her knees on either side of his thighs. And then her hands guiding his penis into a warm, close softness that made him cry out again.

"You are wonderful," said Nefert. She put her hands under his and moved them on her breasts while her body moved against the length of his. Then quickly she sat up, and his hands were empty and cold, but his groin was sending heat and unbearable pleasure throughout his whole being from the moving, twisting, tightening, loosening pressures on his manhood inside the mystery that is woman.

His hands grabbed Nefert's buttocks and he tried to push deeper into her by pulling her down into him. Again he came, and again, and again, until he was trembling in every limb and gasping for air.

"Ah, my darling boy," Nefert whispered. She kissed his eyelids and the corners of his mouth. "I am very, very happy that you wanted to learn to swim."

She brought him honeycakes and honeyed wine and grapes as full and heavy as her breasts. Joseph begged her to make love again, and they did. But now he pressed her onto the couch and he put his hands on her breasts and he guided himself into her hot dampness. He tried to move slowly, to prolong the unnameable sensations that pulsated with increasing strength through his body, but he soon lost all thought and all control. He pounded himself into her faster and faster and then spent himself into her with a screaming primitive frenzy.

"Did I hurt you? I must have hurt you—" Joseph was distraught with fear and guilt.

Nefert kissed his lips, a gentle, forgiving caress. "What I want—"

"Tell me, please, just tell me. I'll do anything."

"I want to go for a nice slow swim. Come with me, my Joseph."

He would have done anything she asked. And so he did. She held him, whispering into his ear, telling him to notice how the water was caressing his skin, to feel the joyous freedom of his arms and legs floating in the embrace of the water. And it was true.

They left the pool, made love again, and then she taught him to move his legs in a strong, frog-like action while floating on his back. Joseph was triumphant when he propelled himself across the wide pool. "Now do the length of it, my Joseph, and see if it tires you so that you have no power to make love to me."

He was successful at both.

"It is growing late," Nefert whispered. "Will you leave me now and return tomorrow?"

"No! No, I don't want to leave you. Not ever."

"Then I will light some lamps and we will have wine and honeycakes and we will swim together."

Throughout the night the lessons and lovemaking went on. Joseph had learned to swim underwater without fear by the time the rising sun transformed the pool into a rose-colored mirage.

"It is finished," Nefert said.

Joseph reached for her. "No, no, never."

She caught his hands in hers. "You have given me great joy, Joseph. Now I am going to make you a gift of nearly equal value. Come along with me to the eastern colonnade. Don't speak. Just sit beside me with your hands in mine.

"Look at me, dear one, look closely at my face and at my body. Watch, while the sun's rays reach longer and grow more truthful. Look, Joseph, look at the colored paints that make me beautiful and cover the marks of the years I have lived."

Joseph tried to turn his head away, but Nefert dropped his hands and held hers firmly on each side of his jaw, forcing him to face the tired eyes and pulpy sagging breasts that he couldn't bear to see.

"Good," Nefert said softly when the expression in his eyes told her she had succeeded. "Take this last lesson away with you, Joseph of Arimathea. You told yourself that you loved me, that we were making love. What you felt came to you from this . . . and this." She touched his genitals and hers. "That is pleasure, my elephant, not love. Every woman and every man is able to find pleasure. If you find love, that is a gift of the gods. I wish you that blessing.

"Now I will leave you. You have become a fine, fearless swimmer."

At home in Arimathea, Joseph looked at Sarah and knew he loved her. He told her all about the library at Alexandria, the excitement of maps and of stars. He did not tell her he had learned to swim.

CHAPTER NINE

BOTH JOSEPH'S AND SARAH'S FAMILIES WERE ANGRY ABOUT the betrothal. Things had not been done properly. According to tradition, a man's father selected his bride. Joseph's family loved Sarah; everyone who knew her loved Sarah. It was quite possible that—in time—Sarah might have been the bride Joshua would have chosen for his eldest son. But certainly not now, when she had not yet reached womanhood and Joseph was still a foot-loose wanderer who was away from the farm during the very months when there was the most work to be done. Also, no matter when the proper time arrived for arranging his son's marriage, it was Joshua's responsibility. And privilege.

Sarah's grandmother, Esther, understood Joshua's anger. She agreed loudly with his desire to honor tradition. But privately, she was both surprised and pleased. There would be a bride-price, paid by Joshua, and Esther could hardly wait to get her hands on the money. It had been more than twenty years since she'd had any.

Esther's husband, like Rebekkah's, had been executed by King Herod, and his property confiscated. She had never stopped feeling bitter and sorry for herself. Rebekkah was a distant cousin, so she had accepted the offer of refuge at

Arimathea as something that was her right, not as an act of generosity.

Esther's only child, a daughter, had spent as little time at home as possible. Rebekkah's house and Rebekkah's children welcomed her, and the coldness at home drove her to them. Esther regarded her child as a burden and was glad to be rid of her.

An even greater burden was Sarah, her daughter's daughter, who was sent to live with her grandmother when her parents both died in an epidemic of a virulent fever.

So, Joseph was welcome to Sarah. Esther would be delighted to get her out of the house after the betrothal year. Let Rebekkah bear the load of being her grandmother.

"Are you happy, then, little Sarah?"

"Oh, yes, Rebekkah. I'm sorry everyone's so angry."

"I'm not angry, dear child. I'm extremely glad for Joseph. You are just what he needs; you will steady him. I love him and rejoice in his good fortune. I only hope that the marriage will be fortunate for you, too. He is ambitious, you know."

"Yes, I know."

"He'll never be content with a farmer's life and the small world that encompasses it."

"I've known that for a very long time. But this is where he comes when the adventuring is done. He'll always need it. I look ahead and picture the laughter in his eyes when he returns to me and the new baby I'll give him every year. It can be born in late summer so he'll never have to see me when my belly's at its biggest."

"Come and kiss me, child. You make me feel as happy as Joseph."

Ever since the sea had called Joseph away for the summer months, he had worked twice as hard as any man at Arimathea during the winter and early spring, when he was at home.

This year was no different. He helped harvest the olives and press the oil from them; he sowed the barley and wheat seed, covering two ploughed fields alone in the time it took two men to seed one. It was winter, the rainy season, and like the others he lost all memory of what dry clothes were. But he was warmed by happiness and heated by the dangerous plan he had for the summer to come. He never noticed fatigue or discomfort.

As always the Feast of Lights that was celebrated on the shortest days of the year gave a cheering reason to celebrate in the middle of the months of slogging through the wet fields to do the sowing. Every family lit an oil lamp just as darkness was beginning and set it on the street in front of the house. Joseph walked Sarah down to the village to see the happy flickering on every one of the eight nights of the festival. On the way back to her house they stopped where an almond tree provided shelter, and he added more lessons in kissing. Now that they were betrothed, it was acceptable, even expected.

The rains lessened in February. Often there would be a whole day of sunshine. The planted fields showed tender green color, and the almond tree they'd named "the lesson tree" seemed to burst into bloom almost overnight.

It was near time for the Purim Festival. Everyone counted off the days, and the joking began about the headaches waiting for all the men. No one knew the origin of the rule—Purim was, after all, a religious festival—but it was an absolute requirement that each and every man drink wine until he was slightly—or not so slightly—drunk. The village square was where the celebration was held, and it lasted most of the day and much of the night. Joseph's father, Joshua, made sure that the community well in the center of the square was covered over by mid-afternoon. Music and dancing and jokes were the chief parts of Purim, and there was always the possibility that a dutifully drunk group of men would think it a great joke to dump one of their friends down for a taste of water instead of wine.

Joseph lifted Sarah in his arms so that he could feel her small body close to his and threatened to drop her in the well before the cover went on. He loved the way she squealed and pretended to struggle. It felt so exciting. He wished they were already married.

And now the days became more crowded. Ever increasing sunlight gave the barley its exuberant spurt of growth and then more hours in the day to work in the fields. The sun was warm on Joseph's back when he bent over to cut the grain and tie it into small bundles. Amos, his younger brother, followed him to gather the bundles into sheaves. His other brother, Caleb, was still too little to be helpful. In the adjoining fields village families were doing the same thing, and there was a lot of shouting, and competition, and capering in the furrows when brief light rains gave respite from the hot, cramping work.

Like all the other men, Joseph was stiff and aching at the end of the day. But the harvest was rich, and it was springtime. He called for Sarah every evening, and they took a walk, hand in hand, to their special tree. "I'm going to make your life more wonderful than you can possibly imagine," Joseph promised.

Then Sarah kissed him and said, "It already is."

The threshing floor wasn't a floor at all. It was a large circular area of bare earth, pounded by decades of use into a surface as hard as marble.

Everyone turned out for the days of threshing. The men working in shifts spread the barley and then drove mules dragging the heavy studded board behind them over the grain. This separated the heads of grain from their stalks.

The women took turns bringing milk and watered wine for the men to drink. Threshing was dusty work.

Winnowing was even dustier, but it was always exciting. Forkfuls of the crushed grain tossed up in the air separated, with the heavy heads falling to the ground and the lighter chaff blowing away in swirls. The children loved to run through, dodging the chaff, falling, sneezing, and laughing.

A good harvest—and the year of Joseph's betrothal was a very good one—was always cause for celebration. After the women sifted the barley grain and poured it into storage jars, everyone gathered to sing psalms of thanksgiving while God's share, the one-in-ten tithe, was set aside for Temple officials to collect.

There were no songs when King Herod's tax of one-third the harvest was stored in the barn for collection by his tax officers.

Two of the most important religious festivals came in spring. Joshua was insistent that his sons accompany him to Jerusalem and the Temple for Passover and Shavuot. And so the arguments began again.

"Of course I'll go to Passover, Father. I want to take Sarah this year, it won't be any problem because Mother and Rebekkah will be going, as usual.

"But I will be at sea before Shavuot comes. Please, do we have to have this fight every year? Can't we at least have a happy time together at Passover?"

Joshua's anger made the small group of Joseph's family and a half dozen villagers quiet and gloomy for the first day's walking. But on the second day, they began to meet other groups of Passover pilgrims, who were singing and joyful. Then, even Joshua changed. He was coming closer to the house of God with every step he took, and for a deeply religious man like Joshua, this could only be a jubilant occasion. With him he had the required symbolic stalks of barley, carefully selected and set aside for sacrifice to God in His Temple.

And his oldest son, his firstborn, was carrying across his shoulders a lamb from the flock at Arimathea. It would be blessed by a priest and its blood scattered on God's holy altar, as He had ordered in His Law.

And then they would roast it and feast upon it, his family

and representatives from his village, together repeating their dedication and thanks to the Almighty.

Joshua threw back his head, and his strong, beautiful voice joined in the songs.

"I've never seen so many people or heard such a noise in all my life," gasped Sarah. This was her first visit to Jerusalem.

"Don't let go of my hand, not even for a second, or the crowds will carry you away. I've heard that Jerusalem has more than ten thousand people, but at Passover, it's ten times that."

Sarah held his hand even more tightly. "There can't be enough air for that many people to breathe, Joseph."

"Don't worry, there is. And after the feast, some people start to leave. I'll take you to see everything next week. There's a whole street of spice shops. The smell is wonderful."

"That'll be a nice change. These people and lambs are smelly the other way. You've been here so often, Joseph, you must know every single street. Plus all those other places you've told me about. Was Alexandria as crowded as this?"

Joseph was silent for a moment, remembering. Then he lifted Sarah's hand and kissed it. "No," he said, "Alexandria was very different."

He tried to use his shoulders and torso to protect Sarah from the pushing and shoving. And he thought of the open, empty sea and its clean brisk winds.

This year was going to be the most important voyage of all.

Joseph spent two days in Sidon before he went in search of the *Halcyon*. Would Leontes want him again this year, or would the former cook be back? His broken arm must have healed long ago. *I have to make that voyage.* The urgent message repeated in his head, like the incessant stridencies of summer locusts. He was obsessed by it, and frightened, and eager to learn his fate, all conflicting and all simultaneous. He had gathered much information about Sidon over the years. He knew the ancient port's streets and shops and hostels. Where to go, what areas to avoid, what goods and pleasures offered themselves to all who had money, no matter what manner of desires and appetites they might have.

He went to the best, and most expensive, of the brothels. The owner refused to let him enter at first. "No poor sailors here, and no boys."

Joseph put a gold aureus in the man's hand. "I want an Egyptian woman with golden skin and red lips."

She had gilded nipples and blue eyelids and offered Joseph delights undreamed of by ordinary men. But he rejected them. He needed release, not stimulation. The winter months had been a torment of self-denial. Every time Sarah kissed him or pressed herself close to him, his body had demanded more. His love for her kept him in check, but memories of Alexandria were almost overpowering. He thanked God that the farm work was constant and so exhausting.

Joseph's gold coin bought him three hours. Seven orgasms. The gilded prostitute patted his sweaty buttocks before she left him. "You're quite the young stallion, sailor. Don't waste your money on a place like this or a woman like me. A few coins to a street whore will give you all you need. They'll open their legs standing up against an alley wall.

"You have a turn of the glass to get dressed and go." She upended an ivory-framed glass ball, and sand began to spill from its full into its empty half.

Joseph buried his face in one of the silken pillows strewn on the wide bed and wept. His needs shamed him.

But when he walked out the brightly painted door of the brothel, he was immediately aware of the smell of the sea in the air. His steps were unsteady but his heart was light. His mind was focused on the fulfillment of all the planning and preparation he'd done. Leontes would have to take him as cook. Joseph had even practiced the art of using seasonings to bring variety and flavor to the sailors' customary steady diet of barley and lentil stew. A woman in the village at Arimathea was famous for her genius at the cookpots, and she'd enjoyed the amusement of teaching him.

He had small linen sacks of dried herbs and ground spices in the bundle of clothes he carried. Also a small roll of papyrus with tiny copies of maps of the heavens and the coastline of Gaul.

He was ravenously hungry. Stomach hunger, not the disturbing hungers of the flesh. He walked quickly to a food shop and gorged himself on bread and milk and barley stew with chunks of goat meat.

At the sailors' hostel that night, he feasted on exaggerated stories of storms survived and the exotica offered in various ports. Sailors' talk. It was good to be back in the world he had chosen. "There were four Nubians in a Cadiz wineshop," he said as his offering. "They thought because I was not a giant that it would be easy to rob me. They never thought that for a short man it was easier to reach their groins with a kick or a butt of the head . . ." He'd heard the story from the sailmaster on the bireme two years before, and now he took it as his own. That was the way with stories. No one cared how truthful they were, so long as they were crammed with action and laughter.

"So, Ashibal, how was your winter?" Hannibal asked.

"The usual. My father's farm, me as slave, and a libation to Astarte to celebrate the hour when I could leave the slavery there for slavery in the galley." I'm becoming quite accomplished as a liar, Joseph thought. He grinned at the big Phoenician. He was so happy his heart felt ready to burst. He was Leontes' choice for cook on the *Halcyon*.

Soon he discovered that he'd crossed a barrier he hadn't even known was there. He was fully accepted now as one of the "hand picked" crew. The men had been pleasant to him the year before, so he hadn't been aware that they regarded him with the suspicion that applied to all outsiders. Now they talked openly about everything, including their private lives. When Joseph told them that he was newly betrothed, the advice he received ranged from locking his wife up during the sailing months to how to quiet a colicky baby. The youngest men on the ship were at least seven years older than Joseph. He was collectively adopted as a younger brother.

For the first time in his life Joseph had friends. There'd been no boys close to his age when he was growing up in Arimathea. He'd known the real Ashibal only two days and Micah only a few weeks. Friends were a revelation to him. They took the loneliness out of life.

At times Joseph thought of abandoning the plan he'd made. In some fashion he couldn't identify, it seemed disloyal to his friends. But he held to it. It was too important to abandon.

On deck at night he woke at intervals to study the stars, memorizing their positions and relationships to one another.

When they anchored at the tin island and Hannibal and Leontes went ashore, Joseph noted in his head the changes in the tide level on the beach throughout the hours until darkness fell.

It was time now to act.

He made a tight bundle of his tunic and loincloth, tied it with his belt, and tucked it in a corner near the steering box.

Silently, every nerve raw, he descended the ladder into the sea and swam ashore, his legs making the frog-like kicks he had learned in Alexandria and practiced—in secret, in air—all winter.

It was easy to walk quietly to the other side of the island

and to crouch in the shadow of the hill, listening to Leontes and Hannibal.

They were having a friendly dispute about the supposed superiority of the wine made on Cyprus. Joseph squatted in concealment for hours, growing cramped and dangerously sleepy. Their quiet voices were soporific.

"Are you sure they can see the signal fire? It's cloudy tonight."

The words woke Joseph at once.

"They always have," Leontes said placidly. "The causeway is forming and then they'll come. You can depend on it."

Hannibal's voice was like a growl. "I wish we could depend on how much tin they'd bring. That one year—you remember—they only had seven baskets."

"Even so, we cleared a profit, didn't we? And there was that other year when there was so much we had to risk hiding it under covers on deck when we ran out of room to stow it. These creatures are barbarians, Hannibal, not businessmen. I can't deal with them in any normal way. They bring whatever they decide to bring, and I have nothing to say about it. If I made any trouble, they might stop coming at all."

"I wish we knew where they get it. We could find a way to get more."

"We'll never know. The secret route has been followed for centuries and it's always been the same. That's the only way they've ever done business. They'd never let us set foot on their land. They're barbarians, but they're not fools. They keep their secrets to themselves."

Joseph's questions were finding answers. He'd been right to eavesdrop. It was obvious that the ship's crew were kept in ignorance about the causeway and the men who brought the gray metal. "What do we do?" he'd asked the year before when Leontes and Hannibal left the ship. "We wait," was the answer. This year it had been the same.

He looked anxiously at the sky. Clouds were still obscuring the moon. If they parted and he was seen, it would probably mean death for him.

"At last." Hannibal's deep voice made Joseph start. He all but fell. His legs were numb from stiffness.

In the distance there were tiny dots of light. Carefully and slowly Joseph extended one leg, flexed knee and ankle and toes. Sharp needles stabbed him. He did the same with the other leg. The lights were larger now. He had to be able to run if the barbarians' torches made him visible.

I want to see, he thought with desperation. I need to. I need to hear what Leontes says. I have to know everything: What manner of men these barbarians are. What language they use. What price Phoenicians pay for their tin.

Maybe I can hide in the vegetation on the hill. It comes almost down to the beach. No one will think to look up there. He moved, inches at a time, while the dots of flame moved forward on the causeway. Soon he could hear a heavy dull noise of turning wheels. Then he moved faster. Certainly Leontes and Hannibal would be looking forward now, not behind them.

There were thick bushes. Their leaves were stiff and rustled harshly when Joseph touched them. Too loud. His hands moved hurriedly, groping for something quieter. He pulled his prostrate body along by digging his elbows into the sandy earth.

A tree. The trunk was thick, he could hide behind it. Blessed be the name of God, there was a clump of tall ferns beside the tree. Joseph crept into concealment. The wheel sound was loud now. He lifted his head, parted the feather-like fronds, and looked out.

What manner of abomination was this? Joseph released the fern, let it hide his view. He was terrified. These were not men, not even barbarians, but some kind of frightful beasts. The leaping smoky torchlight had shown it clearly. They had hides that were blue.

They were making some kind of noises, noises that were almost like weird music.

He couldn't bear not knowing. He parted the fern again.

If these were animals, they were animals that walked upright, like men. And, like men, they hid their nakedness with some kind of covering wrapped at their waists. Blue. What manner of creature had blue skin?

Why not? The skin of Nubians was black, of Egyptians brown, of Greeks white. Why shouldn't there be a nation of blue men? Joseph stared in fascination. The noises he'd heard must be their language. It had a strange beauty to it.

Leontes. Where was he? Did he know this speech music?

Joseph almost groaned. Of course. The retreating tide that made the causeway had also widened the beach. Leontes and Hannibal were there, but too distant for him to hear what they were saying. Or for him to see clearly the blue face of the man they were talking to. He was wearing a long pale robe with a deep hood. He must be the chieftain of the blue nation.

The blue men were lifting baskets of tin from the carts Joseph had heard and stacking them on the sand.

I must get back to the ship, he thought. When the blue men take their empty carts onto the causeway I'll have to get away because Leontes will come to order the gangplank as soon as there is light enough.

So close. I was so close to learning all. Why didn't I remember that the beach would have grown? Joseph's hands made fists of angry frustration.

CHAPTER TEN

AND IF YOU HAD THOUGHT ABOUT THE BEACH GROWING, what would you have been able to do about it, clever Joseph of Arimathea? Stroll over and ask Hannibal if they had any wine left to offer you? Joseph lifted a heavy basket onto his shoulder and followed the sailor ahead of him on the trudge to the ship. This year he, too, was allowed to be one of the loading crew.

He was still angry about his failure to discover all the answers he'd sought. Nonetheless he felt more admiration for the Phoenicians than ever, and he'd always admired them. It was nothing short of genius to select a site for delivery of the tin that changed with the tide. The land was only a distant line of cliffs and trees now. No one would believe that there was a road to it, hidden by the tides. Genius.

But whose genius? Joseph laughed aloud. The Phoenicians hadn't chosen this beach. Their genius discovered the route to it, back in the days of their empire. But it must have been the blue men who knew of the causeway and made the rules about delivering the tin. The secret that the Phoenicians guarded so zealously ended here. The greater secret was over there, protected by the barbarians. Only they knew the source of the metal. Did their laughter sound like music, too, like their speech? They must have laughed many times at the mighty black ships' captains.

"What's funny, Ashibal?"

Joseph turned his head to answer the friend who was behind him. "I was remembering all the times I complained about the weight of my stew pots. I thank the gods we don't eat what's in this basket."

The rain began when the last group of seamen were carrying their loads up the gangplank.

"Another cold meal," said Hannibal in disgust. "Day has hardly begun. I hoped we'd sail far enough to light the ovens before the end of it."

Joseph looked down at the deck, afraid Hannibal might see the shine of jubilation in his eyes. "I'll go to the hill and look for more herbs. If there are mustard plants, the food will seem hot enough."

Hannibal looked up at the heavy clouds. "Take your time and find them. There'll be no travel today, or maybe even tomorrow."

The craggy mainland was barely visible through the rain. It was clear enough to swim toward, however. Joseph tied his belt high on a tree limb to mark the spot where he left his tunic and sandals. He'd have to swim back to the same place, dress quickly, and return to the ship before he was missed. He made a low, flat dive into the water.

He was shocked by the pull of tidal currents; for a moment they pulled him down beneath the surface, and he panicked. Then he kicked, the strongest kicks he knew how to do. And—just in time—his head broke water and he could breathe.

Where was he? He could swim out into the ocean and never know his mistake. Quiet, now, he told himself. Think what you're doing. He tossed the wet hair off his forehead.

There! A flutter of red. It was his belt. He needed to turn to his right, then he'd be aimed at the mainland. It looked about a hundred miles away. Could he do it?

He had to.

And so he would.

Joseph could not tell where they came from, but within seconds after he staggered onto a coarse-grained small beach, six of the blue barbarians had surrounded and subdued him. They were talking rapidly in their strange language. It sounded less musical now, more agitated. They pushed him up an incline and tied him to a tall rock that stood alone. He tested the strength of his bonds. They were made of wide strips of leather. When he tried to strain against them, they were hard as iron. Two passed across his chest and arms, flattening him against the rock. Another held his legs just above the knee.

Two of his capturers were arguing. One brandished a wide-bladed sword; the other waved his arms rapidly in front of the warrior's face. Joseph hoped that the latter was trying to keep the warrior from killing him. He also hoped his savior would succeed.

Where were the remaining four? They had disappeared as mysteriously as they had sprung up. He was too frightened to care. The arm-waving man was much shorter and slighter than the blue swordsman.

Pebbles showered down, some striking Joseph, most of them hitting the stone behind him. They heralded the arrival of a large group, all silent, all staring at him with obvious hatred. Even their eyes were blue!

If only he could live to tell the tale of blue men with blue eyes to his friends. They'd call him a liar, of course. But then they'd laugh and fill his cup with more of the wine they blamed for making him believe in such impossibilities.

Joseph closed his eyes. He did not cry. Despair was too deep for tears.

When he opened them he saw the chieftain in the long deep-hooded robe. It was pale and seemed to gleam as if lit from within. He was a thousand times more frightening than the man with the sword. Joseph felt as if ice had filled his veins.

"You should have not come here, Phoenician," said the chieftain. In flawless Greek.

"Oh, sir, I know that now—I mean no harm—sir, I give you my oath—I'll say nothing—I'm a peaceful fellow—sir, I'll do anything—anything—everything you say—" Joseph was babbling, close to tears, almost laughing, half-crazed with relief.

"I have questions," said the robed chieftain. "You will give me the truth. I will know when you do not, and then you will be killed."

"I will not lie."

He did not. Joseph told the chief everything he wanted to know. It included his years on the ships, his name, and the fact that he was a Jew pretending to be a Phoenician.

"Why did you swim from the island?"

"To find where the tin comes from. It is very valuable or the Phoenicians would not take such precautions to keep the route a secret."

"And if you found the tin, what then, Joseph the Jew of Arimathea? Were you going to steal some and sell it?"

"Certainly not!"

"And why is that?"

"I intended to make a fortune, sir, not a pouchful of money. I intended to become a trader myself, like the Phoenicians. That's why I studied the stars, so I could learn the route."

"Did you not realize that they would stop you? It is not difficult to kill a man or sink a ship."

Joseph had forgotten he was a prisoner. He was totally absorbed in the neat perfection of the plan that he'd made, that drove all his actions and promised everything he wanted. He strained toward the hooded interrogator with enthusiasm. He'd never had an opportunity to talk about his plan until now.

"You don't understand," he said eagerly. "The Phoenicians need never know. They'll take their tin and sell it to the Romans, as they always do. But I'll sell mine in Israel, to the King there. He mints his own coins for his own country and they are all bronze. The Romans don't permit any silver or gold moneys except those minted in Rome.

"The way it is now, Herod buys tin from the Romans after they have bought it from the Phoenicians. If I sell my tin to him direct, he can pay me what the emperor of Rome pays the Phoenicians. It's a very high price. But it must be less than Augustus makes him pay."

"Do you know the amount?"

"No, sir."

"Do you know this King of Israel?"

"No, sir."

"And yet you risked your life to find the tin, in anticipation of selling it."

"I can't sell what I don't have."

The chieftain smiled. "It amazes me that you have at least that infinitesimal recognition of reality."

Joseph looked directly into the deep blue eyes opposite. "I believe that I can transform my hopes into reality if I work hard enough and am faithful to the Laws of God."

"Ah, yes, the One God of the Jews. That is a subject that interests me. I would like to question you about that. But there is no time."

Joseph sagged against the leather bindings. "They're going to kill me?"

"The Dumnoni will do as I command. You'll be freed to return to your ship." The chieftain called out in the barbarians' music-speech and the sword-bearing man slashed the leather ties.

"The tide bore you a long distance, but you have luck," said the hooded man. "It has turned now, to carry you back. You will relate nothing of what you did or what you saw."

"I wouldn't dare!" Joseph blurted. "Leontes would flog me, then feed me to the fishes."

His luck stayed with him. When he looked at the stony hillside behind the pillar where he'd been tied, Joseph saw the distinctive sharp yellow bloom of a mustard plant.

"May I take some of this?" he asked.

"If you conceal its origin," said the chieftain. "Go."

"Can I come back when it's possible?"

"To buy the tin?"

"Yes, and to learn the language. You may not be here to translate."

"Or to save your life. I will instruct Gawethin to make you welcome and to find you an instructor. . . . He is the man with the sword. He's chieftain of this people." The hooded man saw Joseph's confusion. "I am a priest," he said.

"When you come, call to Gawethin across the waters. Cry out the word 'Sennen.' It is the name of the plant you have taken; it will identify you."

"Whew!" Hannibal exclaimed. "This cold mush makes my eyes run tears, Ashibal."

"Makes your belly feel hot, though, doesn't it?"

CHAPTER ELEVEN

WHEN THE *HALCYON* WAS WITHIN A DAY'S SAILING OF HER home port, Sidon, Joseph went to Leontes. "Sir, I've decided not to sail with you next season."

The captain looked long and hard into Joseph's eyes. Does he know what I did? Joseph's heart thudded so heavily he was afraid Leontes must hear it. Does he suspect?

"You find the work too hard, Ashibal?"

"No, sir. I like the work. But I'm to marry next month and I don't know how Sarah—my wife, I mean—will feel about me being gone almost half of the year."

"She knows you are a sailor, does she not?"

"Yes, sir. That is, she knows I've been a sailor. Up to now."

Leontes shook his head. "You'll soon learn, Ashibal, that there's not a woman ever born who can replace the sea in a man's heart. But I suppose you'll have to find that out on your own. Come back to us when you do, but I can't guarantee your galley to you. I'll be using the cook I had before. He wasn't happy not to be back for this season. He misses the *Halcyon*."

"I will, too, sir." Joseph was already sure of that. Especially he'd miss his friends.

They teased "the groom" without letup until the ship was tied up and the voyage officially finished. The mockery was good-natured, but it was very specific, with concentration on the randiness of youth and the pleasures of the marital bed. Joseph hated it when they succeeded in making him blush. The men loved it.

Everyone insisted on a celebration for the forthcoming event. They filled one of Sidon's waterfront taverns. "Keep the wine coming until everyone's passed out," Hannibal roared. "Leontes will pay." The crew's cheers were loud enough to drive out the few non-*Halcyon* drinkers in the tavern. In the kitchen, the lamb that had given its blood in grateful sacrifice to Poseidon was spitted and put to roast on the fire.

The men did, indeed, become very drunk, Joseph included. But no one passed out. Because of the secrecy of *Halcyon*'s trading all of them had long ago developed self-discipline that was now automatic.

Perhaps it was because Joseph had had so many fewer years with the *Halcyon* or, more likely, because this last voyage had been his first experience with camaraderie and being part of a group—for whatever reason he broke down and blubbered through uncontrollable tears when he was presented with a marriage gift. "I ... I don't ... know ... how to ... thank ... thank ... thank you." Everyone had put a denarius from his pay into one of the food bowls from Joseph's galley. He held it to his heart and looked over the rim of it with streaming red-rimmed eyes. "I love you all," he cried.

"None of that, Ashibal. That's the kind of thing that gives sailors a bad name. Save it for the wife!" shouted the sailmaster.

Joseph contributed a tenth of his gift to the Temple as a thanks offering. And he made his usual sacrifices. But instead of going at once to Arimathea, he went to the old seaport towns of Joppa, Jamnia, Azotus, Paralius, and

Ascalon. This last, Ascalon, was a tiny state within a state, an independent principality within the territory of Judea. King Herod had given it to his sister Salome, to live in. If she retained his favor, she would inherit it when he died. She already called herself "Queen."

"So she'd have someplace else to rule and get out of his palace," a wizened ex-sailor told Joseph. "She's a tyrant makes Herod look like a lamb."

In fact Ascalon was nothing more than an enormous estate with a small town beside a small harbor. But every square foot of it was immaculately kept, from the magnificence of the Queen's palace gardens down to the marble-fronted public latrine at the port. The only discordant element was a small, battered, half-sunk ship at the most distant spot on the waterfront.

"What's that mess?" Joseph asked his companion.

The old man spat on the ground. "Salome's spice box, we call it. Two years ago a storm caught it at sea. Winds drove it here, near to foundering. Salome claimed it when she heard about the cargo. It was carrying Indian spices worth five fortunes."

"Why didn't the owners save it? Looks like it could be repaired."

"Why bother? They'd lost the cargo, and all their money was spent on that. And the Queen said they'd have to buy it back from her, not just fix it and sail it away. Two Egyptians it was that owned it. The curses they laid on her would have shriveled up a natural woman, but nobody ever mistook Salome for one of them."

Joseph climbed over every above-water inch of the wreck, then dove underwater a hundred or more times to look at the rest and feel with his hands along the hull.

A repairable wreck was exactly what he was hoping to find. He'd already discovered at the other ports that his savings weren't enough to buy a ship, even a very small one.

"How much will she sell it for?" he asked the old man.

"More than it's worth, you can be sure of that, but what the numbers are, I don't know. You interested?"

Joseph said that he was, but only if the price was right. The old man spit again and made lengthy comments on the folly of youth. But in the end he told Joseph what he wanted to know.

"You'll have to talk to a fancied-up fellow named Polythemus. He's Salome's man for business dealings. Hope you can talk Greek. There's hardly more than a dozen of us local people here anymore. It's been a pleasure to hear a mouthful of honest Aramaic from you."

"Sarah, I was planning a beautiful surprise for your wedding gift, but it didn't work out the way I meant it to. What it is, is a ship, a wreck that I'll have to work on all winter. But next year I'll introduce you to the sea. We'll spend the summer sailing the coast and trading."

"Hello to you, too, Joseph. I'm happy to see you, too."

He laughed and grabbed her in a hug. "I love you, Sarah. I've missed you. Let's get married."

"After the oil is pressed and stored away," Joseph's father said, "we will have the wedding."

"It shall be as you say, Father," Joseph agreed, in the old-fashioned, traditional words Joshua preferred.

It was, after all, very near the end of the olive harvest. Sarah would be his wife in only a few weeks.

Rebekkah led Joseph out into her vegetable garden to talk to him. As always the growing beds were weedless and the path swept smooth and clean. Joseph looked around, smiling. "You never really needed to pay me to do garden work for you, did you?"

"'Needed,' no. But I was glad to have you do it. I've always hated weeding. I did not ask you to come out here for a talk about vegetables, Joseph. I am going to tell you about women, and about women and men together."

"Grandmother!" He was shocked.

"Don't gawk at me, boy. Where do you think your father and his brothers and sisters came from? Not hens' eggs, I assure you.

"Now, Joseph, I know you've had women. No, don't waste your breath and my time denying it. You always were a good boy, though, and you're a good man now, so I assume you've never had a virgin. And that is a very different thing altogether." Rebekkah put her hand on Joseph's arm.

"Look at the ground if you want to. I know this is embarrassing for you, having your grandmother talk to you about intimate matters. Your father is supposed to, and I'm sure he will try, but he is only a man. He has no way of knowing what a woman needs and wants. You listen to me, listen carefully, and remember every word."

She told him about maidenheads, about the pain it was certain to inflict on Sarah and on him when their marriage was consummated. Then she talked about tenderness, about embraces that expressed love and not just lust. She described a woman's monthly bleeding, the inconveniences of wearing and washing linen pads, the possibility of cramps, of oversensitive emotions that might accompany the period.

Last, and most astonishing to Joseph, Rebekkah informed him that a woman's body could experience the climactic release that a man's did. Sometimes it could be even greater, she said, and Joseph looked up, staring at her. Rebekkah smiled.

"Women are surprised by that, too," she said. "Some never learn that it's so. Because their husbands don't know that they must play their part to make it happen.

"Some women can tell a man what they want, but Sarah is a shy girl, not the kind of girl I was. Fortunately you two have always talked a lot, opened your minds to one another. If you tell her you want to know what pleases her most, she will learn that you are sincere, and she will tell you. You must do the same for her. She knows nothing about a man's body. This cannot be done in a day or a week or a month. But it is the most important and most precious gift you will ever give her."

His grandmother kissed Joseph on both cheeks. "I love you both and I believe that you will have a life together that gives you bountiful happiness. Now I will tell you one more thing and then leave you here to recover from your shock. There is a cottage on the corner where the road from Arimathea meets the Joppa road. Go there the day before your wedding and take ten sesterces with you. An excellent clean whore lives in the cottage. When you marry, you won't have the problem of injuring Sarah because of pent-up desires."

The wedding of Sarah to Joseph was the most festive and most elaborate that anyone in Arimathea's village had ever seen, including the marriage of his father, Joshua, and his mother, Helena. The entire village participated, as well as all the families in the houses on the farm that Rebekkah had given to friends so long ago. The children of those houses had moved away many years before, but all of them returned for this occasion, to show their own children the place of their parents' childhood. All this was an honor to Rebekkah, but it was also a traditional country festivity, unavailable in the cities that had drawn the young away.

Joshua's sister Abigail came with her husband and children from their tiny house in Bethany. The sons of his dead brother brought their families from Sebaste and Perea. Helena's two brothers, their wives, and their children came from Hebron, the village where she'd been born. Every room in Joseph's house and in Sarah's was crowded with mats and cushions for people to sleep on. The larger houses in the village also sheltered guests.

On the day of the wedding Sarah and Joseph fasted, according to custom. He had to leave the house for a long walk. The aromatic preparation of the foods for the wedding feast was too tempting, and he must not eat until after he and Sarah were man and wife.

When he returned from his walk he saw a group of laughing men erecting the wedding tent in a corner of the courtyard. It was a tiny room, really, made of heavy hempen material colored in stripes of blue, red, yellow, brown, purple, and green. The marriage would be consummated there. Joseph turned away and ran.

He wondered if the day was as endless for Sarah as it was for him. Probably not. She probably liked having masses of people around, wishing her happiness, giving her sly sideways glances, wearing knowing lascivious smirks. He was more nervous than he'd ever been, even when the blue men were all around him and he thought he had only minutes to live.

The blue men. He hadn't told Sarah yet about the blue men. All he'd been able to think about and talk about was the ship in Ascalon. She would love to hear about people whose skin was blue. She would laugh and refuse to believe him. Then, after he convinced her he was telling the truth, she'd laugh even more. Blue people with blue eyes. Why, they might even have blue donkeys and blue sheep.

Joseph could hardly wait to tell Sarah. He loved her laughter.

Finally, the sun was setting. It was time. "You know what you have to do," Joseph said to his brothers.

"We do," said Amos, who was eleven. "Do you?" He started laughing. Caleb was only four. He didn't know what was funny, but he joined in. Joseph looked at his father.

"Do they have to be part of this?"

Joshua smiled. "There'll be others, Joseph. In the crowd you won't even notice your unmannerly brothers. Come along. They're waiting for you outside."

Helena placed a wreath of flowers on Joseph's head. "I'm proud of my handsome son," she said when she kissed him. He was wearing, for the first time at home, the elegant silk tunic and mantle that he'd bought in Alexandria.

The men and boys of Arimathea were in the courtyard, twenty of them holding blazing torches, another twenty carrying musical instruments—small harps, cymbals, flutes and double flutes, even a trumpet and drums. They were all smiling, eager to begin making music.

Joshua and a Temple priest who'd come from Jerusalem led the procession. Joseph was in the center, besieged with wishes for his future happiness shouted by the other men. They fell silent when the procession reached the door of Sarah's house.

Joseph stepped forward through the aisle made for him by the men. He knocked on the door.

The windows of the house were filled with the faces of women and girls, and flames from the small oil lamps they were swinging in string cradles. Their smothered giggles were perfectly audible.

Joseph knocked again and the door opened. Beyond it he could see dozens of the lamps' lights and women's smiles. Then, whispering and nudging one another, the women made room for Sarah's grandmother Esther. She walked to the door. "Who is he that knocks?" she said.

"It is the bridegroom," said Joseph. The ancient ritual had to be done exactly right. He'd been practicing for weeks. "I wish to see my future wife."

Esther stepped aside and he saw Sarah walking toward him. She was wearing a tunic of linen the color of a summer sky, tied at the waist with rose-colored silken rope. Her mantle was white, embroidered with wreaths of roses and twining vines laden with flowers the shade of the necklace of carved lapis lazuli around her throat. A veil of sheer pink linen gauze covered her face to her chin.

According to tradition, Joseph was to lift the veil and cry out in joy at the beauty of his bride. His fingers trembled when he touched the weightless pale gauze. He raised it. Sarah's eyes met his. They spoke of love. She smiled.

Joseph's shout of joy was not for tradition, nor for the crowds of men and women who were watching and listening. It was a cry of triumph; he held in Sarah's eyes and in his heart the ultimate happiness, for today and for all days to come.

Behind him the men were echoing his shout. Behind Sarah, the women were throwing petals from the late roses in Rebekkah's garden. Esther lifted the veil from Sarah's head, revealing a wreath of roses on her shining hair, loosed from its braids and falling like dark silk down her back to below her waist.

The music began.

The crowd returned in procession to Joseph's house. Bespangled with torchlight and tiny dancing lamp flames, it was celebration made manifest, with music and singing, shouting and capering. In the center Joseph and Sarah walked hand in hand, barely conscious of the crowd around them. They did not speak. There was no need.

The priest heard their vows, Joseph slid a silver ring onto Sarah's finger, two witnesses signed the marriage contract, and the feast could begin.

Long tables filled the courtyard; cloths in stripes and bright solid colors covered them; they were laden with bowls and trays and trenchers overflowing with roasted meats and birds, stews of lentils and onions, cucumbers, olives, fishes in brine, fruits in honey, fruits in wine, breads and cheeses and cakes in abundance, plus jugs of wine in groups of three at three places on each table, and jugs of milk in pairs at the places between the wines.

There were benches, there were rugs on the earth for sitting, there were lamps on the table and in the windows and hanging from the branches of trees throughout the orchard outside the open courtyard gate.

Everyone ate and drank, danced and sang, clapped along with the cymbals, celebrating the joys of youth and marriage and generations to come. Joshua stood on a bench and made a toast to the bride and groom. The music grew louder, and the clapping, while Joseph led Sarah to the wedding tent.

"Are you frightened?" he whispered.

"Only a little," she replied in a shaky small voice.

"Let's practice kissing some more," said Joseph. Sarah's timorousness made him feel strong and much older than his sixteen years.

Both of them cried out when he entered her. The sound was lost in the noise of revelry outside the tent.

Joseph was trembling, as was Sarah. He withdrew from her and held her close. "I love you, my wife."

"Say that again, Joseph. I love the sound of the words."

"I love you."

"Not that, the rest of what you said."

"My wife," said Joseph, "my beloved little sparrow, my wife."

The celebration continued for three more days. Sarah and Joseph danced and sang and feasted together with all the guests.

When, on the fourth day, the villagers returned to their homes and the routines of their lives, and the visitors said their farewells and departed, the quiet was like a benediction. It had been a very successful wedding.

The new couple had a room of their own in the house with Rebekkah, Joseph's parents, and his brothers. Their wreaths of roses were hung over their bed to dry and be saved. Sarah folded more rose petals into her wedding clothes and put them away in the carved chest that was their wedding gift from the village carpenter. She wore her necklace.

"It's so beautiful," she told Joseph, "and so blue. I'm going to make believe you got it for me from the blue men." He'd told her the story four times or more. She loved to hear it. Both of them loved having the secret together. Every time the word "blue" was uttered by anyone, their eyes would meet in shared secret laughter.

A week later Joseph left for Ascalon, to work on his ship. The walk there took two days. He'd work for three or four days, then walk back to Arimathea to help with the planting and to be with Sarah. After a few days, he'd leave to go back to the work on the ship.

"You're wearing yourself out, Joseph," Sarah scolded. "This is just foolishness. Go. Finish repairing the ship. And then come for me. You can sail to Joppa. I like a short walk much better than a long one."

"Are you sure you don't mind?"

"Joseph! I mind it much more when you're here and jumping out of your skin to be there."

"I'll miss you."

"I'll miss you. Patch up the what-you-call-it very fast."

"The hull, Sarah. You'll have to learn these things—" He saw that she was teasing him.

"Wicked woman."

"Let's go to bed early tonight. You'll have to be up at dawn to start off for Ascalon."

Rebekkah's advice had proved invaluable. Sarah and Joseph's married life was a never-ending, always improving, delight to them both.

CHAPTER TWELVE

IT WAS SARAH WHO ASKED THE VILLAGE CARPENTER TO carve "a brave, bold eagle" for Joseph's ship. She gave it to him when he came for her late in May.

"It's hard to tell it's an eagle," she said apologetically. "It might be a chicken with a funny beak. But Simon was so proud to be making it for you I couldn't tell him anything except that I thought it beautiful."

"And so do I." He kissed her emphatically. They stayed in their room the rest of the day, and retired early that night.

In the morning Joseph admired his gift again. "You'll see for yourself, this is exactly right for the ship, Sarah. It looks like it's not really a ship. I had to patch the damage with whatever I could find. The sail is about fourteen different pieces of linen sewed together. But all the lines are new, best hempen rope. And the steering oars are new, too, made of Lebanon cedar." A look of apprehension clouded his face. "I think it's safe, but maybe you'd better not come along until I've tried it out some more."

"Don't be silly. I've never even seen the sea, much less been on it. I can hardly wait."

*　　*　　*

She clapped in admiration when Elijah and Johannes and Joseph succeeded in mounting the eagle on the prow of what was now the *Eagle*.

Elijah was the old man Joseph had met in Ascalon and Johannes was his grandson. Both of them, Joseph told Sarah, were working for no pay, only for the promise of a share in any profit Joseph might make. "Elijah used to be a steersman—about four hundred years ago, to look at him— and he's so happy to have a deck under his feet again he doesn't care if there's any money made or not."

Sarah nodded. "That's fine. But you'd better find some for Johannes. He could squash you between two fingers if you made him unhappy." The grandson was a mountain of a man, with such a mass of dark curly hair and beard that his face could hardly be seen at all. Sarah wanted to know if he ever smiled. Joseph said he'd never seen one. "But he laughed for almost an hour when I let the mast fall on me." Sarah asked no more questions.

They had built a tent-like arrangement on deck for Sarah to sleep, dress, and undress in. Its tops and sides were patchwork linen, like the big sail. She declared it greatly preferable to whatever palace Queen Salome might inhabit.

The *Eagle* was a small craft. It used a single sail only, had no oarsmen, nor room for any. The space below deck was the hold, for cargo and nothing else. There was no need for a galley. They would stop every night and tie up, then go ashore to find supplies for a meal.

They'd barely left the harbor at Joppa when Sarah clapped her hands over her mouth. To no avail. She vomited everything inside her, then continued dry retching for more than one hour.

Joseph held her head, bathed her forehead and temples with a damp cloth, offered her sips of honeyed water in a spoon. They made her sicker.

"Turning green," Johannes observed.

"Head back to port," Joseph ordered.

*   *   *

"I was mortified, once I got over wishing I was dead," Sarah told Rebekkah after Joseph took her back to Arimathea in a cart. "We tried it two more times, and it was just the same, maybe even worse."

"Did you ever think it might be—"

"Of course. A baby was the first thing I thought of. But my bleeding started just when the cart was turning off the Joppa road. Right when it was due.

"No, I was seasick. Before I even saw much of the sea. I suppose it's just as well. Joseph needs to have all his mind on what he's doing, not on taking care of his wife.

"But I did think it would be so exciting." Sarah began to weep.

Joseph and his motley crew, in their motley ship, succeeded beyond his wildest hopes. Micah and his after-synagogue group in Alexandria helped him locate small sellers of spices, merchants largely ignored by major traders. He was able to fill nearly half the lockers in the hold with pepper, he even managed to get a large jar of precious myrrh. The other lockers he packed with less-than-top-grade silks in bright colors.

Then the *Eagle* went from small port to small port. In each, Joseph went to the alleys and marketplaces, talking to shopkeepers, offering small quantities of his luxury goods for sale or in exchange for large amounts of the goods they were selling. The lockers in the hold began to fill with more diverse trade goods. At each port, Joseph had more to offer.

In Gaza he was able to obtain turquoise-studded bronze armlets from a caravan that had just arrived from Persia. He paid for them with pepper. In Ascalon he sold the armlets to Queen Salome's man of business for gold coins with the Queen's profile on them. Azotus . . . Jamnia . . . Joppa . . . Sozusa . . . Crocodilon . . . Dor . . . Bucolon . . . Sycaminum . . . Achzib . . . Ptolemais . . . Berytus . . . The weeks passed by, some with good results, some a total disappointment. The *Eagle* reached Tripolis late in September.

Joseph returned from the marketplace with a heavy pouch of coins, and a daring proposal. "The season's all but over. Still, for men like us who are willing to take a chance, the seas are still open. What do you say to this: We'll hug the coast on up to Antioch, sell everything we have left for money only. Then we sail to Cyprus and buy wine. It's considered the best, and we can triple our costs when we sell it in Caesarea."

"'Antioch and Caesarea'? Joseph, we've kept away from the big ports; that was the whole idea."

"But now we're ready for them. Most traders are heading for home ports now, closing down until next summer's season. If we can pay no heed to people laughing at the *Eagle*, we can sail in just as any big trading galley would. What do you say? We'll have the wind at our backs from Antioch down."

Elijah scratched his jaw. "It's open sea Antioch to Cyprus, and a long stretch of open sea Cyprus to Caesarea. Do you know navigating good enough for that?"

"Of course I do, you old coward. Didn't I learn from the best in Alexandria?"

Johannes cleared his throat. "How much is 'triple our costs' when it gets to a man's fist?"

"I don't know exactly," Joseph admitted. "At a guess, I'd say over four hundred denarius for each of us."

Johannes walked across the deck to the mast and began to hoist the sail. "What are you waiting for, Grandfather? Set those oars to take us to Antioch."

A sudden gale blew the *Eagle* off course after she was out of sight of Salamis harbor, where they had loaded the hold full of wine, then added another forty amphorae on deck, lashed to the steering box. The only thing Joseph could do was reef the sail to one-third and pray that the wind wouldn't rip that to shreds and leave them totally helpless. As it was, they had to go wherever the storm took them, hoping not to founder in their overloaded condition.

Two days of calamitous winds and raging seas left them still storm-tossed in the huge waves, but safe. Joseph had no idea where they were.

Beneath cloud-covered skies, he was now learning the truth of what he'd been told. The season was limited to the summer months, but not because the balmy weather was so agreeable. Autumn and winter brought storms, storms meant clouds, and a man could not see the stars or the sun for navigation.

It was three more days—without food—before the clouds dissipated. "To port, Elijah," Joseph shouted. "We've had a lifetime's share of good fortune. Tomorrow we should spot the coast, and we'll be no more than two days south of Caesarea. Take the seal off one of those high-priced wine jars, Johannes. We deserve a drink of the best."

As it turned out, the profit on the wine amounted to over five hundred denarii for each of them.

Johannes grumbled that they should not have opened that jar.

Elijah said that he hoped Joseph wouldn't take offense, but he was too old for any more of that kind of excitement. He thought he'd take his new fortune and his grandson and head back home. On foot.

Joseph stayed in Caesarea for an additional two weeks. He was looking for a larger ship. Five hundred and thirty-four denarii was a great deal of money.

Joseph expected his father's anger. It was a regular part of homecoming. But when the women in the house raged at him—"Where have you been? We thought you were dead!"—he became angry in response.

"I believed at least you'd be glad to see me," he said to Sarah. Her slim body was stiff in his arms and she turned her head away from his kiss. "What's the matter with you? Don't you have any confidence in me? I had important things to do in Caesarea. And then I had to go through the pouring rain to Jerusalem to make my sacrifices in the Temple." He pulled away from her and turned his back.

He ground his teeth, slammed a fist against the wall. Inside, he was shouting: Don't you care that I made a fortune even with a ship that made everyone who looked at it laugh? A man has the right to a welcoming smile and a kiss and some interest in what he's doing for his family, doesn't he? I had work to do, necessary work. And I had my duty to God. I can't live my life the way other people want me to live it. I have to do what I know has to be done.

He was cold and wet and hungry and exhausted and his own wife didn't care. His whole family. Had anyone even offered a basin of water for him to wash his feet? That was a courtesy offered to everyone who entered a house, even a wandering stranger. How dare they treat him worse than a vagrant beggar, when he was doing so much for them?

Sarah had begun to weep. Joseph turned on her. "Stop feeling sorry for yourself!" he shouted. She threw herself across their bed, muffling her sobbing in its cushions.

Ah, but he loved her so much.

He sat beside her, lifted her shoulders and held her close against his chest. Her arms reached behind him, across his back, and she turned, raised her tearstained face. "I missed you so much," she whispered.

"Me, too," Joseph said.

She did not move away from his kiss.

They made love with the urgent hunger that had been building over the months of separation, and then they slept, still holding each other close.

When they woke, it was not yet day. "I'm starving," Joseph whispered in her ear.

Sarah squirmed, rubbing against him. "You'd better not breathe in my ear like that. It makes me feel very—you know."

"I know," he whispered in her ear, "and I want the same

thing. But I need food to get the strength for it. Can you find some bread and milk?"

The next day Joseph and his father had their confrontation. There was no shouting, no indication of emotion on either side. Joshua lectured his son in a manner weighted with a sense of duty and dulled by hopelessness.

Joseph stood, although he hadn't asked leave to do so, and he paced back and forth as he spoke. His heavy footsteps were like drumbeats of emphasis. "I am not, as you say, totally concentrated on myself and my concerns. I have a purpose, Father, and it is everyone's concern or should be. Our family was one of the most respected in all Israel before King Herod destroyed us. I intend to get it all back—the houses, the slaves, the horses, and most of all the respect. I will do it, no matter how hard I have to work, or how long. I am going to be the man my grandfather was and give the family the position he gave it."

He did not add, "that you failed to do," but the accusation was there. Joshua stood and walked away from his eldest son.

Sarah must have talked to Joseph's mother and grandmother. They treated him as if the unpleasantness of his homecoming had never happened.

Joseph walked down to the village to see everyone and to praise the carpenter for the majesty of the carved eagle. "It rode high and proud over the waves," he boasted, "even when a storm found us and beat down on us out in the center of the sea."

"Tell about it. Did you spy any sea monsters? Were the waves truly like mountains?" A few, and then a group, and then the majority of the villagers filled the space in and outside the carpenter's shop, fascinated by Joseph's dramatic adventures. He enjoyed himself a great deal.

Even more so when, later, he told a less exaggerated version of the story to Sarah and Rebekkah. "Oh, if only I didn't get seasick," Sarah moaned. "I wish I could have been there."

"Be grateful that you weren't," Rebekkah said firmly. "Let the men go off and risk their necks. Women have more sense."

It took very little time for Joseph to settle happily into the soothing rhythms and routines of farm life. He worked at planting the fields alongside the other men in the rain, shared meals with his family in the big farmhouse kitchen, shared the marriage bed with his beloved Sarah at night, shared the life and the faith of the villagers at the synagogue on the Sabbath. "It's good to be home," he said frequently.

Sarah seemed to glow with happiness, and that made him happy, too. But one morning he was suddenly wakened by the sound of her crying.

"Sarah?" He sat up. "What's the matter?" He put his arms around her. "Are you ill?"

"No!" She pushed him away. "I'm so nothing wrong that I can hardly bear it."

He tried to embrace her again. "I don't understand. Tell me, my little sparrow, come here, you're getting chilled to the bone."

"Oh, Joseph," Sarah wailed, "my bleeding has started. I'm not going to have a baby."

Joseph had not really thought about Sarah having a baby. Not actually, not at any particular time. He'd assumed, of course, that they'd have children. Married people always did. But a baby, a son? He'd be a father. The idea gave him a feeling of pride as strong as any emotion he'd ever known. For an instant he almost wept with her that the baby had not yet begun to grow inside her.

He understood why she was in such despair. But . . . .

"There's no need to be so miserable," he said. "I understand, but I know you're wrong to be unhappy. There will be many, many babies, as many as you want. This one time doesn't matter."

"How do you know so much?"

"It makes sense, that's all. If babies were made every time a man and wife made love together, there would be so many people that the world couldn't hold them all, isn't that so?"

He heard a choked giggle. "There'd be no room left for trees," Sarah said.

"Or grain fields, and where would we get our bread?"

"Or grapevines, so there'd be no wine."

"Or beds, for a sleepy man to take his rest. Come and sleep, my wife. We'll make a baby as soon as your bleeding's done."

Joseph held Sarah until she was asleep. His eyes were closed, too, but sleep wouldn't come. How was she going to react when he told her that he'd be leaving again in a few weeks instead of waiting until the sailing season began?

It was the eighth, the final day of the Feast of Lights. "The street looks as if stars had come down from the sky, doesn't it?" Sarah said. "I love this festival." She put her hand into Joseph's. "How soon will you be leaving?"

He stared blindly at the lamp-lit village. How did she know?

She nudged him with her elbow. "Come on, Joseph, don't be so silly. When you're about to go off on your adventures, you vibrate like a harp string. It's a wonder you don't make music when I touch you. How soon?"

"After Sabbath."

"Four days. Are you going to tell the family?"

"I thought . . . at Sabbath dinner . . ."

Sarah laughed. "What a coward you are sometimes, my fearless sea captain. When will you return?"

"It depends on how well my plans work. I'm not being cowardly, Sarah, I truly don't know. Maybe at Passover. Maybe not until the end of the sailing season."

"Hmmmm. If it's end of the season, let's see . . ." She counted on her fingers and his. "That's time enough for you to be a father. You'd better bring me a very special gift in return for my gift to you."

"Sarah! Are you sure? How do you know?" Joseph tried to look in her eyes, but the lights from the festival lamps weren't bright enough to let him see.

"I don't know. But it's possible. And I hope."

He kissed the top of her head. "I'll hope, too. And bring a hundred gifts."

"Don't exaggerate, Joseph. I'll probably only give you one baby."

Coming home to a son was very much on Joseph's mind as he made his way along the wide, straight Roman road that followed the coastline all the way to Alexandria. He expected the trip would last at least a month. The distance was more than three hundred miles. Why did anyone ever use a road, even a Roman road, when a voyage by sea was so much faster and easier? Because sailors were afraid of the winter storms and clouds, he thought scornfully. He wouldn't be. He had proved that already. But his ship—his beautiful new *Eagle*—was moored in safety in Caesarea harbor, and there were no crewmen with guts enough to set to sea with him.

So he walked. And he caught rides with carts carrying goods from one town to another. And he stopped before the early darkness brought numbing cold, and bought food and a place to sleep in a farmer's kitchen or stable.

When he reached Ascalon, he asked one of the harbor watchmen about Elijah and Johannes. The man bent close to answer. "Everyone is wondering what caravan they robbed. Rich as kings they are. They've got a villa near the hot springs and a slave to cook for them and rub them down after the dip in the springs."

"Where are these springs?"

Joseph spent two days and two nights with his erstwhile

partners. Sitting in the steaming, bubbling water with Elijah, he agreed that they'd done very well for themselves.

"Wait until it's time for your massage, Joseph. Abitha's got good strong hands. But don't lay yours on her. She's Johannes'. He's already got her with child."

"I won't so much as smile at her," promised Joseph. He wasn't interested in other women anymore, now that he was a married man.

He did smile, nonetheless, when he thanked the big slave girl for the bowl of excellent fish stew and the very fine bread and cheese. Johannes had done well indeed.

No, said Elijah, they weren't at all interested in another voyage with Joseph. Yes, he would be willing to explain how a steersman worked the two tiller-oars.

"But you need to learn by doing," he shouted for the fiftieth time when Joseph was on his way back to the road. "Crazy gambler like you, Joseph, is likely to drive a ship right onto the rocks because he didn't take time to learn."

The trip to Alexandria took weeks longer than Joseph had planned. Finally, he reached the eastern edge of the Nile delta, the massive swampy area where the river divided into a dozen or more shifting waterways that released Nile currents into the Mediterranean. Joseph had never seen the delta region before. Nor the varieties of water craft its inhabitants used for transport and fishing.

He managed, through persuasion, payment, and pleading, to try out all types of vessels that could be propelled by one man, one sail, and one short steering oar. It was possible that he had discovered the solution to a problem he'd been struggling with for more than a year. It was essential that he return to the land of the blue men and learn their language and their ways.

That would call for weeks with them; he had no way of knowing how many. And he could not consider leaving a ship and crew to wait while he was with the blue nation. The Phoenicians had figured it out long ago, obviously.

The ship's crew never saw the blue men, or the causeway to their land at low tide. So none of them could give away the secret to the source of the valuable cargo. A captainless crew would not wait many days before one or more men did exactly what Joseph had done. They would uncover the secret.

If, however, a man could sail a vessel alone, without a crew, to the hill island, or better, around it at high tide . . .

Joseph was courageous, and dangerously overconfident of his sailing skills, but he had legitimate respect for the sea and its unpredictable storms. He'd never heard of any man braving the sea alone, not even in legend. The ocean—it was unthinkable.

Yet, he could not stop wondering.

He presented himself at the door of his friend Micah's house in mid-February.

"Joseph of Arimathea! A happy surprise. Come in, come in. I'll send for water to bathe your feet. How do you happen to be in Alexandria in winter? No, wait. Let me order some wine and cakes. I am overwhelmed with delight."

Joseph sat on the stool near the foot basin. He was delighted, too. He had thought so often of his elegant, funny, Alexandrian friend. "Why need you ask, Micah?" he said, keeping his expression sober. "I swam from Israel. The lessons you arranged for me made me a champion."

"You specialize in the breaststroke, no doubt," Micah riposted without a second's pause.

The two young men grinned at each other.

"Welcome, my friend."

"I am happy to be here, my friend."

The tempo of life in Alexandria was seductively languorous. Joseph had to remind himself many times every day that he had come here to do business, not to indulge in the luxuries and pleasures that waited at every corner and behind every door.

"But we are doing business," said Micah. "You are deciding which glassware you want to buy and sell."

They were in the wine garden, the place where they met almost every afternoon. Joseph had learned, by now, how to feel comfortable in the cushioned marble chairs. He laughed at his friend. Micah had a gift for making even the most serious issues become amusing.

"Yes, I need to select glassware. But it is not really necessary to fill each goblet with wine, Micah."

"How wrong you are, Joseph. Just imagine the damage to your reputation if you sold glassware that soured the wine poured into it. Drink, businessman, and make certain.

"This one, for example." The handsome young Alexandrian lifted a goblet made of yellow-gold blown glass. "It allows you almost to taste the warm sunlight that brought the grapes to full perfection before they were pressed. Drink yours and agree that I'm right."

Joseph tasted the honeyed wine, but he did not empty the glass. He was two years older now than when he was last in Alexandria. Eighteen, a married man, and soon to be a father. He could not be like Micah, who had no responsibilities.

"Why don't you marry, Micah? Has no girl caught your heart?"

"Joseph, my friend, stop sounding like my father. You can talk like that to the son you've told me about, but I beg you to spare me. I'm only twenty years old. Let me enjoy my youth. I'll marry a beautiful young virgin when I'm thirty or thereabouts and need the inspiration of her childish innocence to restore my vigor. For now, there's no lack of energy in my loins. Would you like to accompany me to a dinner tonight? The host is a rich old Greek who gets sleepy from overeating, and his wife is a pretty little creature—not too young—whose appetites are in no way satisfied by the delicacies of the menu. She would be happy to entertain you in her private chambers later. Or, come to think of it, both of us."

"Micah!"

"I was teasing you, my sober, head-of-household friend . . . Perhaps." Micah's eyes glinted with mischief. "Am I to assume that you're not interested in accompanying me to dinner?"

Joseph was interested, but determined not to admit it. "I am meeting with Reuben ben Ezra," he said, naming one of the most important men he'd met in Micah's after-synagogue group.

The young Alexandrian raised his eyebrows and whistled. "You're a bigger business success than you told me, Joseph."

"It's kindness, not business, that made him agree to see me. I need to learn about the ways of King Herod."

Micah laughed. He raised a glass of wine. "I salute you, Joseph. Imagine, I believed I'd shocked you by mentioning the little Greek wife. Herod's palaces, from all accountings, make Alexandria's amusements seem pale and timid."

That wasn't what Joseph wanted to hear at all. He was fervently hoping to find a way to reach the shrewd businessman-ruler. His idea had seemed faultlessly simple when he explained it to the priest of the blue men. He'd sell tin to Herod for much less than Herod was paying when he purchased it from the Roman Emperor. The King should be overjoyed.

Or the King might torture him until he revealed his source for the metal. Joseph of Arimathea was nothing like the all-powerful ruler of the Roman Empire.

Joseph desperately needed to know what manner of man Herod really was. He'd been told since birth about Herod's cruelty and injustice. His own grandfather's death was proof of it. The Jewish people groaned under the burden of his tax-collecting policies.

The man he was meeting tonight was the only voice he'd ever heard to speak good about Israel's king. Herod's grandiose building projects gave work at good wages to thousands of Jewish laborers, he'd said. Joseph had seen the truth of that for himself. In the great marble city of Caesarea, where the sounds of construction were never ending. And at the Temple itself, where the perimeter colonnades and buildings were not yet completed.

Of course, Reuben ben Ezra had also called King Herod a lunatic, a maniac.

Joseph dreaded what he might learn that evening. At the same time, he wished the hours until his meeting with Reuben wouldn't drag so.

CHAPTER THIRTEEN

"LET ME BE SURE THAT I UNDERSTAND YOU, JOSEPH."
Reuben was not laughing at him, at least Joseph didn't
think so, although when he had listened to his own words
stating his problem, he had sounded like a fool to his own
ears.

The older man touched the fingers of his left hand with
the index finger of the right. "One: You know the source of
a commodity that Herod has need of. Two: You will not
identify either the commodity or the source of it. Three:
You intend to voyage to this unnamed source and acquire
an unspecified quantity of this unnamed commodity. Four:
You further intend to sell this commodity, needed by
Herod, yourself, alone, to the man who already has access
to it through other, more costly, purveyors. Five: Herod has
no power over these purveyors, but you worry that he
might remove your head from your body if you attempt to
maintain the secrecy of your source and prevent his taking
control of the supply of this commodity on his own.

"Is that a reasonable summation?"

Joseph, nodded, ashamed.

"I see no insuperable problems," said Reuben.

"You don't?"

"No. You are a seafaring merchant, therefore one can assume that access to this commodity is by sea. Herod has no navy, and if he began to build one, the Emperor Augustus would not be pleased. Navies imply expansion of powers. Herod already has more power than Augustus generally grants to his provincial rulers, for reasons that date back to long before you were born. Augustus is Herod's patron, an enviable situation for Herod. He is unlikely to relinquish that because of curiosity about your secrets."

And now Reuben laughed. "I can't say that I myself would not be bolder. Your secrecy is enticing, and I lease the services of many ships in my trading activities."

Joseph stared at him, alarmed.

Reuben smiled. "I won't do it, young Joseph. I do not waste money that could be earning me money in ways that I already know. Have I answered your questions to your satisfaction?"

"Oh, yes. I'm very grateful, Reuben ben Ezra. If I can continue to impose on your generosity, I do have one more question."

Reuben knew what it was without Joseph's asking. "There are several avenues to Herod," he said. "One is through his close advisor, the only man he trusts absolutely. His name is Nicolaus, a brilliant man with tremendous charm. Do you have any connections in Damascus?"

Joseph shook his head. "Pity," said Reuben, "that is Nicolaus' family home. Are you well read in the philosophy of Aristotle? No? Too bad. That is Nicolaus' passion, probably his only passion, from what one hears.

"Well, then, next there is Ptolemy—an Egyptian, of course—he manages all Herod's finances. Rent collecting, taxes, his enormous holdings in other countries, like his vineyards and copper mines in Cyprus."

Joseph was paying close attention.

"Unfortunately Ptolemy privately considers himself much more important than Herod. He has retinues of petty officials who see to it that he is never disturbed. You would need to spend a lot of time and money bribing your way up the chain of power before you reached Ptolemy himself.

"Third and last, there is Salome, Herod's sister. She can, it seems, make him do anything she chooses. But she is a strange, difficult woman. She constantly involves herself in the plotting that surrounds Herod like flies on carrion. He gave her the use of an estate and built a magnificent palace there to keep her away from his court as much as possible. One of her close friends is the wife of Augustus himself, therefore Herod needs to keep her content."

"I've seen the palace," said Joseph. "It wasn't bristling with guards."

"Almost certainly Salome wasn't there. She's in Rome for the most part."

Even so, Herod's sister sounded to Joseph like his best chance. He thanked Reuben effusively and presented him with a bottle of wine and two golden glass goblets from the wine garden. "Micah swears he can taste the sunlight on the grapes when he uses these," he explained.

"Micah should become a poet; his father can afford it, and it would be more convincing than his claim to be studying at the observatory. He's a charming rascal. With an excellent refined palate, too. I thank you, Joseph, for this wine, which is certain to be more delicious than any I know of.

"By the way," Reuben added. "If you do manage to get close to Herod, this is precisely the sort of gift you should submit. A gift is essential, I'm sure you know that, and Herod receives such a quantity that it takes something unusual to gain his attention."

"Aristotle?" Micah repeated. "Why would you want to know about Aristotle, Joseph?"

"I hoped you'd know everything already. I went to the Library, but there is a roomful of scrolls. I don't have time to read all that."

"Ah, Joseph, men don't 'read' Aristotle's works, they

spend their lives studying every word, and all the words others have written about his words. What you're asking is impossible."

"Even for you?" Joseph smiled.

Micah sipped his wine and thought. "It's irresistible!" he said finally. "I'll find some way to get you want you want. The philosophy of Aristotle in thirty words or less. The mere thought of such a thing will shake the walls of the Mouseion. You are a true scoundrel, Joseph."

"And you are my master. How long will you need?"

"I have no idea."

"Quickly is best. I'll be occupied for some time buying trade goods and finding a crew for my new ship, but I must be on my way shortly after Passover."

Alexandria's Jews celebrated the Passover festival with a piety equal to what Joseph knew from Jerusalem. But it seemed strange and foreign to him. The paschal lamb was not sacrificed at the Temple. Instead, a priest of the Temple who lived most of the year in Alexandria killed and bled the lambs in the large shop of a Jewish butcher, for sale to families for their feasts. Joseph also wondered—but said nothing—why a group of wealthy Jews in Egypt would feel so fervently religious about the celebration of God's freeing Jews in Egypt to go to the land that was to become Israel. These Jews had all come back from there to Egypt.

What also seemed strange was the attitude of the sailors he'd found after days of talking to the seamen near the harbor who were looking for work as soon as the season started.

"Share profits instead of pay?" Most of them rejected the idea at once, sure that it was some kind of trick.

Most of the ones who reacted favorably had a look about them that made Joseph fear they'd cut his throat and take cargo and ship for themselves.

He was close to abandoning the idea that had worked so

well with Elijah and Johannes when he heard about a
Macedonian ship that had sunk thirty miles west, on the
African coast. The six brothers who owned it had reached
Alexandria only a few days earlier. They were penniless,
but they refused to take work that would separate them
from one another.

As soon as Joseph got them sober, he had his crew.

He bought passage to Caesarea for all of them, and himself, on a small galley that was due to sail the next day.

"I'm entrusting you with the papers for the goods I have
in a warehouse," he told Micah. "I'll be back when I can, in
my new *Eagle*."

"I wish you fair winds, Joseph, but not the fastest. I'm
still working on your Aristotle problem."

Joseph's walk to the harbor took him through the Street
of the Perfumers. He still had some money left; passage for
his new crew and himself to Caesarea had cost much less
than he expected. Not a good omen about the quality of the
ship, but there was no point in worrying about that. All the
galley had to do was get him and the Macedonians to Caesarea and the *Eagle*. The luxury goods he had in storage
were certain to make him a fortune.

Especially if he added more perfume. It took up so little
cargo space, and the profit was enormous. Joseph turned
into the next dealer's door.

He bought the best the man had, after lengthy bargaining, and he was quite pleased with his success. But his
pleasure was short-lived. It was the perfumer's practice
to have small boys scented from head to toe, then offered
to important buyers of his wares as week-long playthings
for whatever unusual practices they chose to indulge in.
He brought one from a back room and presented him to
Joseph with a wink and a foul, suggestive leer. Joseph
hid his angry disgust. He looked into the silent child's
eyes, filled with ancient knowledge of evil. "What is your
price for this perfume?" he asked. "Also, what's carrying
it."

The merchant was delighted to offer an excellent bargain of a price. The boy was not beautiful anymore, he was growing too old. Even though he was small for his age, he was not as appealing as he had been in earlier years. Joseph did not take time to haggle, he simply paid the man and got away from him and his shop.

"What is your name?" he asked the boy when they walked away from the Street of the Perfumers.

"My name is Antiochus, Master, unless you prefer a different one."

"Do you prefer a different one? How do you think of yourself?"

The boy's eyes narrowed. What did his customer want from him? "I do not understand," he said humbly.

"Do you have a mother? A father? What name were you given at birth?"

"Antiochus. So I was told by my first owner. He bought me from my father."

"Then Antiochus is what I will call you. I'm going to take you to a ship now, boy, and give you a bowl of salt. I want you to rub that smell out of your skin and your hair. Then I'll think of what to do with you. It won't be what men have done with you before. Probably you'll scour cooking pots in the galley."

Antiochus seized Joseph's hand and kissed it. "I will make them cleaner than new, I swear by the goddess Isis."

Joseph winced. How could he have been so impetuous as to spend money he couldn't afford to buy a heathen sodomite?

The Macedonians looked meaningfully at one another when this additional passenger was introduced.

The galley's captain accepted the new scullery worker with excessive cooperativeness. Joseph didn't care at all for the way he looked at the boy.

"Never mind," he told the captain. "I'll keep him with me."

The captain's smile and wink were even more offensive than the Macedonians' raised eyebrows.

The winds were anything but fair. The galley pitched and wallowed and took on so much water that passengers had to help man the unwieldy hoist for bailing bilgewater. It was a choice of bail or sink. The voyage seemed interminable; it was mid-May when they finally reached Caesarea. The season was well under way.

The Macedonians threatened mutiny when Joseph told them that he was going to see his family and would return after eight days.

"In that case, I won't go," Joseph agreed. "I want to get things underway even more than you do. I did want to get rid of the little boy. But if you'd rather sail with him aboard . . ."

Joseph and the boy Antiochus left within the hour to go to Arimathea.

Fortunately, Rebekkah asked no questions. She was completely focused on the terrified eyes and trembling of the child. And Sarah said that what Joseph had done was wonderful.

Joseph returned to Caesarea in only five days, not eight.

He was eager to set sail. The new *Eagle* was still unknown; he wanted to find out how she handled. She was, to his eye, a creature of incomparable beauty. Nearly sixty feet in length, with a seventeen-foot beam, cargo space for almost a hundred tons, this was a real ship, capable of fulfilling all his boyhood dreams.

And so she did. Joseph spent all but a few silver coins from his store of funds to buy food for two weeks and a thousand small jars of Jericho's world-famous balm. This voyage would have only the finest luxury items for trade. The *Eagle* was large enough and handsome enough to be admitted to even the greatest harbors.

The balm sold at once to traders in Alexandria. Micah gave Joseph a small papyrus with three lines of Greek writing that he promised was all of Aristotle in summary. Joseph particularly liked the statement that, in science, theory must follow fact. Then, with the hold full of rare and expensive luxuries, the *Eagle* put to sea.

"We sail direct to Puteoli," Joseph said to the brothers. "The Romans have a taste for luxury and the money to pay for it."

Also, he needed to find out how much Augustus paid the Phoenicians for tin.

In Puteoli, factors bid against one another for the luxuries Joseph had to offer; the Macedonians regarded him with respect that bordered on worship. He used some of the *Eagle*'s profits to buy the information he wanted about tin prices, some more to purchase enough amphorae of Italy's cheapest wines to fill the hold.

"'Luxury goods,' I see," Philip, the eldest brother, said sardonically. He was disappointed in his hero.

"The Cypriots buy it to add to their wines," Joseph told him, "then sell their famous vintage back to Romans who drink too much to taste what they're swallowing. We'll buy Cypriot wines, too. But we'll taste them first."

The brothers did not even notice the two days Joseph was away on the island of Cyprus. He went inland to see the copper mines that belonged to King Herod and to learn about the smelting, the making of bronze, the pouring and molding of coins.

Yes, it would be easy to deliver the tin direct to Cyprus.

When the time came.

In Caesarea, it was simple to get the top price the best Cypriot wines commanded.

Joseph was careful to find a safe, quiet place to count out the shares. As agreed, he took one half and gave the other half to Philip, to divide among his brothers and himself.

"Next season?" Joseph asked.

The 'ayes' nearly deafened him. He would have liked to stay and celebrate with the brothers, but he wanted much more to get home to Arimathea and see his family. He had kept back two jars of balm. Just in case. Sarah could use one for really good perfume, and the other for any scrapes or bruises that the baby might get. Surely there would be a baby.

He rented a cart and horses to take him to the Joppa road intersection. From there it was only a two-hour walk to Sarah. And his child.

"We must have tried too hard. I wore you out. You're nothing but skin over bones. I should have—"

Sarah put her fingers over Joseph's lips. "Hush, hush, my love. God will send us our baby when the time is right. You mustn't think about it, and neither will I. I'll pay more attention to eating as I should, and you do what you must before the blue men forget you."

As always, Joseph had told her everything, even the madness he'd been trying to forget, the idea of sailing alone to the land the tin came from. "You can do it, if you believe you must," Sarah said. "There is nothing that you can't do."

Except give you a child, thought Joseph bitterly. But he kept the words unspoken.

He looked in on the boy Antiochus and was astounded by the change in him. He was in the schoolroom, engrossed in a mathematical problem. Joseph's grandmother told him that the boy's intelligence and ability to learn were phenomenal.

Rebekkah had put herself in charge of the boy. It had taken several months for Antiochus to begin to trust her. After that it took almost no time at all for him to begin to love her.

She was not an indulgent, outwardly affectionate woman. Rebekkah did not go in for effusive kisses and compliments. What she did offer freely was freedom for a child—or an older person—to find its own way. If the effort was worthy and the way was good, Rebekkah complimented the striver. Congratulations from Rebekkah were more prized than thousands of kisses from other people because her standards were as high for others as they were for herself.

When Antiochus had learned to respect her, Rebekkah offered him a way to earn her respect for him. "There is a tutor in the house, as you know, for my grandsons. You may join the lessons. I rely on you, Antiochus, not to make Amos and Caleb feel stupid. You and I both know that you are more intelligent than they are."

The Macedonians were eagerly awaiting Joseph's arrival in Caesarea. They had already taken the *Eagle* from her winter roost in one of the harbor's off-season shelters. Her red painted sides were gleaming, her deck freshly sanded and oiled. On the prow the Arimathea eagle had a sparkling gilt beak and a shiny black body. Joseph's heavy spirits suddenly soared.

They made a short run south to Gaza to meet the caravans from the East that brought most of the goods they had bought in Alexandria the previous year. There was less variety, but prices were much lower without the profits that Alexandria's traders would have added on.

From there they sailed north again, to Tyre for the dye available at no other place, the dye that created the majestic purple color symbolizing wealth and power.

"Now to Puteoli," Joseph told the brothers. "Then Cartagena."

He needed to test his memory of the stars and how to follow them.

They made port at Caesarea in early September. The season had not yet ended, Joseph said, as if he had not intended things to be exactly this way. Why not take on a good cargo of balm and finish the voyage in Alexandria this year with even greater profit? Agreement was instant. Alexandria offered much better off-season interests than Caesarea, especially for a seaman with money.

Joseph bid the Macedonians farewell after the profits were divided. He had, he told them, friends to visit, then he'd find a coastal trader for his voyage home. "Next year?" he asked. The reply came at once.

He prayed that the reunion would take place. He did not see Micah, or any of his other friends. But he did leave a package at the observatory, with Micah's mentor Theocrates, for delivery two weeks hence. It contained most of his enormous earnings from the voyage, plus the owner's papers for the *Eagle*. A note instructed his friend to sell the *Eagle* and send the proceeds, together with the gold, to Sarah if Joseph himself did not collect the packet within a year.

Joseph hurried from the observatory and into a shabby Egyptian workman's street where he would not risk seeing anyone he knew.

Only Sarah was aware of what he intended now. Even he did not know if it was possible.

He had bought a small sailing craft before he left on the *Eagle*. It was waiting for him in a fisherman's hut in the Delta.

Joseph had considered going to the Library's map collection to learn, if possible, how long his voyage might be—in weeks or in miles. He decided against it, because he didn't want to discover it was impossible.

In theory it was not. He could hug the coast of Africa until it terminated at the Pillars of Hercules. Once through, he had only to turn north and follow the coastlines of Spain and Gaul. Then a short distance surely, to the hill and the tidal road to the land of the blue men. Food and rest would be available at any coastal village, and his small boat could easily be guided to land or anchor very close to land.

Just because he'd never heard of such a voyage, there was no reason to believe it had never been done. There were many, many things he'd never heard of. Like Aristotle. Joseph tried to smile at himself.

He couldn't manage it until he was actually in his little

boat and passing the outer limits of Alexandria's harbors. He waved a farewell salute to the towering great lighthouse.

No matter how foolhardy a man might be, his spirit had to leap when meeting the unknown. There was no greater adventure than that.

CHAPTER FOURTEEN

JOSEPH HAD NEVER SAILED IN A SMALL BOAT BY HIMSELF. The trial rides he'd made in the Nile delta craft had been interesting because of their oddity. The boats' owners, hopeful for a sale, had kept the movement slow and steady. Now he experienced the thrill of sudden racing speed when the sail caught the wind, of water surging over the bow when a wave was met head-on, of near capsizing when wind and waves shifted to broadside. He heard himself shouting with excitement and shouting in fear. It was only then, when no shouts echoed his, that he realized how truly alone he was.

It took him less than a half day to master the handling of the steering gear and the lines that increased or lessened the size of the sail. Several weeks had to pass before he became accustomed to being solitary.

He did, of course, see and talk to others. When he put in to shore for supplies, the inhabitants of the shoreside village or farm were always eager to talk, to ask questions, to give advice and warnings. When he found darkness near, he headed toward land at once, whether there were signs of habitation or not. Often he woke to find curious faces leaning over him to see what kind of intruder he might be. Only twice did he have to threaten strangers with the sword and knife he kept close beside him in the cloak he wrapped around him at night. For the most part, the curious were also friendly and offered to share the food they carried with them. Joseph did notice the signals they made to one another. Touching the temple with a wiggling finger, or the forehead, above wildly rolling eyes. Obviously they thought he was insane. Sometimes—more often than he liked—he wondered if they were right.

He made tiny notches on the side of the steering oar to mark the days. Days that were growing shorter before quick darkness fell, bringing sudden sharp cold.

More than a dozen times he saw, at a distance, the kinds of ships he was accustomed to. They looked very big and safe.

On the forty-second day he felt the pull of a strong current drawing him toward the open sea. He lowered the sail to one-half and attempted to control the boat. The Pillars must be near, those giants of jagged rock on which the biggest ships could be dashed to pieces. Waves grew higher, broke over bow and sides. Joseph grabbed the leather pail and bailed water with his left arm while his right hand and arm fought the shuddering, jumping steering oar. To his left, too near, loomed a rock face; then, within moments, to his right and directly ahead was another, higher, with great waves breaking high upon its wall.

He shouted into the roar of the waves, "Forgive me, Sarah!"

Beneath him the boat rushed, climbing, climbing, and he fell over onto his back in the swimming bilge, staring through salt-clogged eyes into the pitiless gold of the sun.

He felt a sudden lurch, then a terrifying absence of contact with the watery world, then a crashing, slamming into the sea, then an unearthly gentle calm rocking.

Bilgewater washed his face. The stink of it was real, disgusting. Joseph scrabbled to his knees, looked about him, disbelieving. The churning currents inside the Pillars had spat his little craft out and away from their turbulence. He was through the passage. But he was about to sink. The little boat was nearly full of water. He cupped his hands and threw pitifully small amounts back into the sea. No time to search for the pail. No time to look for damage or losses. His hands and arms and will to live must save him.

Darkness found him exhausted, bailing with increasingly slow, heavy measurements. He never knew when he dropped, unconscious, in the night's dark, and the cold, stinking bilgewater.

Daylight on his eyelids commanded wakefulness. Joseph's body ached all over. His arms seemed to weigh a thousand pounds. But he was afloat. And he was hungry. He must be alive.

He pulled himself up onto the thwart by the steering box. The oar was still there! It moved slowly, like a fish's tail, from side to side in the current that carried the boat.

Where?

There was no land in sight.

Joseph squinted up into the sky. All he had to do was watch the sun's movement; then he'd know his direction. But the sun was behind clouds. The entire sky was bright and glaring. The thick white clouds seemed, all of them, to be alight.

Until they broke up enough for him to read the sun, there was much for him to do. He made his way to the copper locker he'd had fitted inside the bow. Its closure was intact. Joseph opened it and removed the fishing net. Next to it was bread and cheese, both half-covered with mold. His hunger was great, but it must be put aside. He threw the small net over the side and wrapped its cord around his ankle. While he waited and hoped to feel the weight that would mean a catch, he concentrated on getting the water out of the boat. Those brilliant white clouds might darken, then rain. He needed to get rid of as much water as he could before more was added.

He surveyed the inside hull as he bailed. His sword, in its scabbard, was still in its holder. The knife, too. The water jar had lost its cover. It would have to be emptied, and the rain might be welcome when it came. The bailing pail was gone, as he'd supposed. But he'd come through almost intact. His shoulders weren't broken, they just felt that way.

His ankle signaled weight. When Joseph pulled in the net, it held two fish. They had both scales and fins and were, therefore, acceptable to the Law.

The larger one he slashed, letting its blood drain through his hands as a sacrifice of thanksgiving to God for his life. He'd make formal sacrifices at the Temple when he returned to Jerusalem. But he did not want to wait to give thanks.

The second fish he killed and put into the locker. He would cook it when he went ashore. As soon as he had a reading of where shore might be. For now, he was in God's hands.

He was adrift and in pain, but he felt an unaccustomed calm. The bread and cheese tasted better than any elaborate feast he had eaten in Alexandria.

The sun set in a blaze visible through the clouds, and Joseph learned that he was heading north-northeast. He could feel the strong current carrying him. In darkness and under a cloud-covered sky, there was no purpose in looking ahead for danger. Joseph lay his head on his aching arms and slept. The air was calm and gently warm.

In the days and nights that followed, Joseph tried again and again to steer toward the coast of Spain. Once he thought he saw it in the distance, but a sudden rain squall blew up and obliterated the sighting. From time to time the night sky was bright and close above, and he greeted the stars by name, with jubilant cries. He was on course. A steady wind filled the sail by day, and augmented by the current, his boat was carried at a speed much greater than he could sense.

Rain provided him with water. When the last crumbs of bread and cheese were gone, he caught fish and ate them raw.

Joseph could feel his growing weakness; his attempts to make shore were more and more difficult. The wind and the current were stronger than he.

He notched the days diligently on the oar. They ended so swiftly now that he had to carve by feel because darkness caught him so soon.

He began to fear death. He knew that wiser men than he scoffed at the old tales of sailing off the edge of the world into nothingness. But it felt as if that was exactly what he was doing. The current that held him in its power would rush to the edge and fall, like the mountain streams he'd seen in the rainy months. They had fallen into rocky pools. If that was his fate, so be it. Just let it come, and be over.

There was land ahead! He must be dreaming, creating what he wanted by the strength of his wanting.

Joseph shook his fist at the thin pinkness overhead. Rise up, sun, grow strong, give me light so I can see.

It began to rain. A squall, not a shower.

Joseph hurried to shorten sail and began bailing. He must not sink now, not when he was so near land, and safety, and food. He would not allow it. His weakened body found strength, and he fought the downpour like a mighty warrior for a time he could not measure.

Then, as quickly as it had come, the rain was gone. The rain-whipped sea was dotted with gleaming whitecaps and blinding sun sparkled light.

The land was close. And he knew its contours.

This was the place where the galley fire had to be out, the oars muffled, and all voices stilled. This was Gaul, and the blue men's land was no more than a day's sailing distant.

That day would come, but not yet. For now, Joseph needed food and rest. He had to be strong for his arrival in the blue nation. He strained against the steering oar, and the boat began to turn.

The rainwater was heavy inside the hull, the progress sluggish, the oar an enemy. But the headland was growing larger by the minute, its remembered outline clearer.

A line of light—no, a line of sand, a beach. Joseph fought the oar.

And won. Curling waves wrapped the boat and carried it with alternate halts and rushings onto the whiteness just when it was beginning to gray. Joseph lowered the wet sail and heaved the anchor overboard into the shallow water. The weight of it pulled him in on top of it, and he crawled slowly up onto the wet sands. His face was wet, too, with weak, grateful tears. The land felt as if it were moving beneath him, like the boat. Joseph stretched out his aching arms and dug his fingers into the sand.

Before the day was done, he was asleep, so deeply exhausted that he didn't hear the footsteps or the voices that came later to the place where he slept.

The smell of food brought Joseph back to life. He held the bowl of steaming broth to his mouth and swallowed hungrily. Then the bowl was taken away, and bread put into his hands. After eating half of the loaf, he began to be aware of his surroundings.

He was warm, wrapped in a heavy wool cloak or blanket. He was sitting on a large smooth stone. He could see a low fire, in the center of a circle of stone, and a large iron pot in the center of the fire. It smelled as if more broth was cooking.

"Welcome to the world, Sennen," said a man's voice, speaking Greek. Joseph turned his head and saw the white-robed priest who saved him from the blue men two and a half years ago.

"Thank you for saving my life . . . again," Joseph responded.

The priest shook his head. "Corrections, Sennen. You

would not have died on the beach. After resting, you would have found food and water. I did not save your life. Nor am I the priest you met in the land of the Dumnoni. I am one of his brothers in the priesthood. All of us learned of your visit, and your name, from him. I have sent word to him that you are here.

"Your full belly is making you drowsy. Lie down now and sleep. When you wake, you will eat again, with meat as well as its broth. Then we will talk some more."

The priest was right. As he spoke, his deep musical voice filled Joseph's mind, and Joseph did as he was bid.

He woke to sunlight and renewed hunger, and saw that he was in a high-ceilinged cave. "You will eat now," said the priest. "I will eat with you." He dipped bowls into the pot and lifted them out, dripping broth and smelling like rich lamb stew. From the stone niche near the fire, he took wooden spoons and a thick loaf of bread. Then he sat near Joseph to share the meal.

"They call me Gulval," he said.

"My thanks to you, Gulval," Joseph spoke quickly. Then he began to eat.

The priest was not so hurried. He found time to feed Joseph information with his stew. Joseph learned that he was in the corner of Gaul controlled by a tribe called the Veneti. They were related to the Dumnoni by blood, by tradition, and by language.

"While you regain your strength, Sennen, I will begin to teach you their words. When you arrive in the tin lands, you will be able to say at least a few phrases of friendship. Lhuyd, the priest you met there, will have prepared the people for your arrival. All will go well. If you are a man of honor."

Two days later the priest led him to a stone-walled enclosure on top of a cliff overlooking the sea. Joseph was going to meet a council of men of the Veneti. He had memorized the words he was going to say, but he forgot them in his shock when he saw the men. They were taller than he, but that did not surprise him. He'd stopped growing when he reached two inches above five feet, and most men were taller than he was. Most men, however, did not have thick hair and mustaches in many shades of yellow or red. Joseph had to force himself to stop staring and to remember his speech.

"Greetings. I am called Sennen. I am a friend."

The Veneti were openly amused by his pronunciation. They laughed, repeating some of the words.

But the long spears they carried stayed loosely held in relaxed hands.

Joseph smiled. And relaxed, too.

What a very strange corner of the world this is, he thought. Sun- and fire-colored hair on these men, and blue skins on their cousins. Sarah would be fascinated when he told her about them. Joseph imagined that he could hear her laughter along with the deep laughter of the big tribesmen, and he missed her suddenly with a pain that made him gasp.

"Are you ill, Sennen?" the priest asked.

"No, no, not at all," Joseph replied quickly. This meeting was too important for him to let his private life intrude. He resumed his staring at the Veneti. It was allowable, he supposed; they were all staring at him.

He had never seen anything like the way they were clothed. Brightly colored wool in stripes or patterns like tiny boxes covered their legs, each leg with a separate covering, a sort of loose tube, that ended inside an ankle-high boot made of what looked like the hide of a goat. The same wool also covered their lower bodies, in one piece from which the leg-covering descended. A short tunic, in a different color or pattern, covered their chests. Some of the men wore woolen cloaks that covered their tunics and strange lower clothing to halfway down their legs. Magnificently wrought bronze brooches held the cloaks closed at the shoulder. Intricately incised bronze also circled the upper arms of the men who wore no cloaks. Joseph's trader's eye recognized them as works of a jeweler's art.

But he was here to make friends, not to bargain for luxury trade goods. He repeated the phrases the priest had taught him.

The tall, fair-headed men clustered around him, saying their names and proclaiming their friendship.

One offered Joseph a ram's horn cup filled with some beverage. Joseph expected some kind of wine, but this was very different. Sweet, like honey, and yet sharply bitter. He drained the vessel, to indicate his pleasure at the gift.

Then, with no warning, his knees gave way under him.

The laughter was louder than ever.

A copper-haired giant of a man caught Joseph under his arms before his body hit the ground. He lifted him and enveloped him in a crushing embrace. "Mead," he roared.

"Mead," Joseph repeated. He thought it must be the man's name.

Gulval the priest extricated Joseph from the fellowship of his new friend. "Sit here by the wall, and do not drink any more. When you feel able to walk, we will say goodbye. You have done well, Sennen."

Three days later, other men of the Veneti transported Joseph to the land of the blue men. Their boats were as amazing as their clothing. They were shaped like deep bowls and were covered by leather. The sails were made of leather, too. Only the long oars they used bore any resemblance to anything Joseph knew.

He held desperately to the rim of the bowl, as he thought of it, when the boat raced, circling, through a riptide between the shore cliff and a small nearby island. Then it rode the regular ocean waves with an exciting, yet oddly comfortable movement. He didn't understand what the big men were doing with sail or oars, but he recognized that they were superlative seamen. He wished he knew how to tell them that. But he could only smile and nod and wave his arms in gestures toward them, the boat, and the sea and shout "Good!" It was inadequate, but they seemed to like it.

"Good" and "not good" were two of the words he'd been taught. "Hungry" and "thirst" were two more. The most important, Gulval kept insisting, was "friend."

Joseph pointed at the hill-island of the tin-traders, shouting "good" and "friend."

"Itkis," said one of the Veneti. "Itkis," said Joseph. He would ask the tin-land priest what the word meant.

More than two dozen men were on the sand opposite the hill to greet Joseph and his companions. They wore the same kind of clothing, had long hair both dark and fair, and beat on bronze shields with swords made of iron to create a din louder than their shouting. The men in the bowl boat shouted back, and Joseph feared that a battle was about to begin. He looked everywhere for the white-robed priest, but couldn't find him. And Gulval had not come along.

Men waded into the water, grabbed the sides of the boat and began to haul it on shore. Joseph saw then that they were smiling, and so were his companions.

Where was the priest?

Where were the blue men?

What was going to happen to him?

"Friend," he said. "Friend, friend, friend, friend, friend."

"Friend," answered one of the beach men. "Gawethin. Friend. Sennen."

Joseph looked in the man's face, recognizing it. He'd seen it before, as close to his as it was now. But then it had not been smiling. And it had been blue. This was the chieftain that the priest had told him to call for when he returned—if he returned.

"Gawethin," Joseph sighed. He felt too shaken to speak.

"They stain their bodies with a dye made from plants," explained Nancledra, "when they expect enemies. The men

who come to trade for tin are Romans, and Romans ɑ͏ ͏ ͏ɛ͏ᴎ͏i͏-
emies. The blue skin, they believe, will frighten them."

Nancledra was a young man, probably close to Joseph's
nineteen years. He had arrived, breathless, not long after
the Veneti and Dumnoni cousins stopped embracing and
shouting.

"I apologize for being late," he told Joseph. "I missed my
way. This is my first visit to the land of the Dumnoni. I was
sent to be your interpreter and instructor."

He was, Joseph learned later, in training for the priesthood, but not yet accepted into the brotherhood.

Joseph discovered at once that Nancledra spoke the
tongues of both tribes easily, as well as fluent Greek.

After they became friends, Joseph asked him how many
languages he knew. The answer was twenty-seven. Aramaic? Yes, of course. Would Joseph prefer they use that?

They developed their own bizarre dialect, that included
Greek, Aramaic, snippets of Latin, and all the new words
that Joseph was learning. This native language was called
"Brythenic" and the land of its speakers "Belerion."

"That sounds like singing," said Joseph. "Belerion."

"So does the language. All you have to do is master the
tune."

Joseph buckled his knees and staggered a few steps. It
was his own wordless language for "I cannot manage to do
what you want me to do, or what I want to do." It had been
born when the Veneti reported to their cousins Joseph's introduction to mead. He'd been in the group, and recognized
the word "mead" and the imitation of his collapse. He then
acted it out himself and was rewarded with roaring laughter, in which he joined. He didn't know it at the time, but it
was the single smartest thing he could possibly have done.
The Celts admired a man who could laugh at himself. It
proved he was not afraid of life in all its variety.

Joseph stayed with the Dumnoni for more than two
months. He learned to wear trousers and found them much
more sensible than anything he'd ever known. He saw the

streams from which the tin was collected, and observed the process used for melting it and forming it into ingots shaped like an H. He lived in one of the round stone-walled houses they had made into shelters of extraordinary comfort. He learned to gauge his capacity for mead before his knees actually buckled, and his genuine, freely and frequently expressed admiration made the Dumnoni accept him as not a Roman.

He was never able to explain, even with Nancledra translating, what a Jew was. But they didn't condemn him for his peculiarities, such as not eating the roasted herb-stuffed pig that was their favorite feast. They introduced him to the milk and the meat of the short-horn cattle they raised. He promised that when he came again, he would introduce them to wine and olives from his country.

"Are you certain," he asked Nancledra, "that the Romans call these people 'barbarians'? They are more civilized than the Egyptians and Macedonians I have met."

"The Romans call all non-Romans 'barbarians.' Including the Jews."

Joseph had not known that. It made him extremely angry.

Spring showed itself early in Belerion. The rocky hillsides were bright with flowering plants when the festival of lambing time arrived at the start of February. It was time to return home.

The Dumnoni ferried Joseph in one of the leather boats, which he now knew were called coracles. They were met by Veneti, celebrated the meeting, and then Joseph was taken through thick forest to a wide river and his small Egyptian boat. He had with him an ingot of tin, a good-sized collection of Belerion's exquisite jewelry, and a carved bone amulet. Nancledra had instructed him about his route. When, after many days, the river neared a mass of snow-topped mountains, he was to stop at a village with two trees standing sentinel at its stone-stepped landing place.

A priest would find him there, and his boat would be pulled on a sledge to another river that led into the Mediterranean.

Joseph embarked with enthusiasm for this new adventure. Before four days were gone, he discovered that winter in Gaul was the most miserable experience of his life.

But he would reach Alexandria well before the season began. Then he could begin the big adventure. The tin would be his whenever he wanted it. All he needed to do was find a way to collect it without the Phoenicians knowing and get to King Herod and convince him to buy it.

Compared with sailing alone to the land of the blue men who were not really blue, those next challenges seemed easily manageable.

CHAPTER FIFTEEN

THE RIVER WHICH WOULD BECOME KNOWN IN TIME AS THE Rhone was still another astonishment for Joseph. He had seen the Nile, but only at its marshy delta, where its tributaries were narrow and shallow with siltage. This great Gaulish river was a magnificent wide waterway of racing currents and constantly changing countryside along its banks. The Gauls had warned him about the Roman camps, small walled cities really, that he would encounter. Whenever he neared one, Joseph had to wait for nightfall and let the river carry his boat past the lights and sounds of the Roman legions in their winter quarters.

Cold, anxious, huddled in his Belerion woolen clothing, Joseph heard and saw the signs of camaraderie and comfort, and felt terribly alone. His life among the Dumnoni had been rich with fellowship, and he missed that. Except for his second year on board the Phoenician tin ship, he'd never been part of a group, on equal terms. At Arimathea, he was at odds with his father, much older than his brothers, and always set apart from the villagers because he was a member of the owner's family and would be the owner himself someday. In visits to Alexandria, the hospitality was expansive, but he was an outsider.

Among the Dumnoni, the laughter at his constant mistakes was in some way warmer than the polished welcome of the Alexandrians.

Joseph never thought of turning back to Belerion. He was feverishly eager to return home to Sarah, to the *Eagle,* to the tiny empire of success that he envisioned. Still, he thought frequently of the people he'd left behind. But he would be going back every year for tin. If he could do all that needed to be done to make it feasible . . . No, not if. When.

The Rhone rushed into the Mediterranean west of Marseilles, and now Joseph knew where he was. With the prevailing winds behind him, he crossed to Sardinia, then to Sicily, Crete, and, at last, five weeks later, past the great lighthouse and into Alexandria's busy harbor.

His wool trousers, tunic, and robe were safely out of sight in his bow locker. Joseph wore a thick linen tunic and coarse wool mantle that he'd bought in Sardinia. His mind and his heart still brimmed over with thrilling memories of his remarkable adventure. But to maintain the secrecy of the source of the tin, he couldn't tell anyone about anything. Not until he got home to Sarah.

He tied the little boat to the stern of the *Eagle,* went to the baths, the barber, the silk goods street market. Then he could present himself at the home of his friend Micah, to retrieve the packet left for safekeeping and to practice the tale he'd invented that would account for his long, unexplained absence.

"She was a great woman, considerably older, and knowledgeable about things even you have never heard of, my friend, and she wanted to carry me away to her island in the Aegean. How could I say no? She promised that her husband would not come to their palace and discover me there, but I didn't dare rely completely on her certainty. Therefore I left my valuables in your care, so that if Sarah became a widow, she'd be taken care of."

Micah's eyes gleamed with mischief. "And my family

keeps insisting that I marry. How long were you wed, Joseph, before the allure of this fascinating Greek goddess turned your head? Three years, wasn't it? I would have succumbed after three months, I'm sure."

Silently Joseph begged Sarah's forgiveness for his lie.

Curiously, the very things that Joseph expected to be most difficult turned out to be the easiest.

By the time the Macedonian brothers arrived to ready the *Eagle* for her voyage, Joseph had already filled her hold. He enumerated the list of luxury trade goods to Philip and his brothers, watching their eyes widen with greed as they imagined the profits they would share.

"Do you believe you could make the voyage without me?" Joseph asked them, then immediately added, "Naturally I'll add another man to fill my place in the crew. But the man I have in mind is elderly, so he'll do little muscle work. He'll just keep records of sales and prices so that when we settle up at the end of the season, everything will be orderly."

Philip frowned. "You can't mean to give this old man your half, Joseph?"

"Of course not. I own the ship and the cargo. I paid for them. I will still collect half the profit. You six will become seven, and divide up accordingly. But there are more and better goods this year. The profit will be greater for each, even though it's a seventh share instead of a sixth. Do you agree?" He held his breath.

The Macedonians agreed.

That evening Joseph went to the home of a Jewish trader in Alexandria whose son had taken over the family's business. Both father and son were overjoyed for the father to become Joseph's watchdog on the *Eagle*.

"I will accompany you as far as Ascalon," Joseph informed the crew. "Then I'll make my own way up the coast in the small boat we'll tow to Ascalon. By that time I'll know that you don't need me as captain, and Philip can take over."

In Ascalon Joseph walked boldly up to the palace of King Herod's sister Salome. He was dressed in his most elaborate Alexandrian silks. "I bring a gift for the Queen," he said, in a haughty manner, to the keeper of the gate.

Four uniformed servants later, Joseph was escorted to a pavilion beside a large artificial lake. Salome was there with her women servants and her favorite eunuch. He was not amusing her as he was supposed to do. She had either heard all his gossip and stories before, or they bored her.

An unexpected gift in the hands of a wealthy stranger sounded intriguing. Perhaps even entertaining.

Joseph walked across the cool floor of colored marbles and knelt in homage. He was thankful that respect for the Queen was traditionally demonstrated by downcast eyes until the supplicant was invited to speak. It was easier to speak the lie he had practiced if he could avoid seeing the heavily painted wrinkled face and the bony, thin body of the woman in front of him. "I beg you to do me the honor of looking at this small token of my devotion to the legendary beauty and grace of the Queen Salome," he said. On his outstretched palms was a handsome and valuable ivory coffer. He'd had it made in Alexandria, in a deliberately simple style, decorated only by an inset small gold keyhole with a delicate gold key inside it.

Salome took it, turned the key, lifted the lid. The brutal beauty of the bronze bracelet that lay within the box took her breath away. She was a woman in her fifties, and she had known every luxury that the civilized world had to offer.

But she had never before seen anything remotely like the interlocking sinuous bronze linkages or the mysterious, spiraling incised designs upon them. The bracelet was savage and delicate simultaneously.

"A magician must have created this!" she exclaimed.

Joseph smiled and was silent.

Salome demanded to know where it came from. Joseph looked up.

"My lady, that is a mystery; it embellishes the beauty."

She commanded that he tell her, but Joseph said quietly that he had been obliged to guarantee secrecy to the bracelet's maker before he was permitted to buy it.

"Who are you? A sorcerer?"

"I am Joseph of Arimathea, my lady, a seaman and a trader, and an admirer of rare objects. All Israel knows that the Queen Salome has the most exquisitely refined judgment about the world's treasures. I felt it appropriate that she be the recipient of my discovery."

Salome admired the dull reddish gleam on her arm. Then she looked intently at the elegant young man kneeling before her. She began to laugh. "You have amused me with your honeyed rhetoric, Joseph of Arimathea, and I am grateful. I am also pleased by your gift. What is the price for the bracelet and the entertainment?"

"For you, my lady, a trifle. For me, I'm beginning to think, two permanently damaged knees." He grinned, mocking his own daring.

Salome laughed boisterously. "Get up, then, you bold silken urchin, and sit on this bench by my couch."

Joseph was suddenly terrified that his outrageous story to Micah might be on the verge of coming true. He sat at a careful distance.

"Do not flatter yourself," said Salome bluntly. "You are amusing, Joseph of Arimathea, but no beauty. I prefer large, manly men. Now name me your price. If it isn't too outrageous I will buy your mysterious ornament."

"I want an introduction to your brother, the King. I have a business offer I wish to make to him."

"About the bracelet? Can you get more? Do you need money or an army to capture them?"

"Nothing so grand, my lady. I want to buy copper from his Cyprus mines at a favorable price."

Salome made a sound of disgust. "How very tedious you

traders are. I hoped for something interesting out of you. Very well. I'll put my seal on a letter to Herod. Go now and tell one of my scribes what you want him to write. You have disappointed me."

Joseph managed to appear saddened by his dismissal. But inside he was elated. *You have made me very happy, you disagreeable, ugly old woman*, he thought. *If you only knew that my Sarah will have a half dozen bracelets more handsome than yours. Plus brooches and a diadem for her head.*

Reaching King Herod and talking with him was a thousand times easier than flattering and fawning over Salome. The King was in his new palace at Caesarea, Joseph learned from the Queen's scribe.

After tying up the little boat in the harbor, Joseph carried the copper locker from the bow to one of the shipping offices on the harbor front and paid the required fee to leave it in safekeeping. He needed only a few things from it, and he could carry them under his arm.

The Roman baths Herod built in his marble port city were smaller but more luxurious than those in Alexandria. Joseph enjoyed them even more, because he was back in Judea now and close to home. And Sarah.

He wore plain-colored, good-quality linen to see the King, not silk. This Herod had murdered his grandfather. Joseph would do business with him, so that he could restore to his family all that the murderer had stolen from them. But he would not bend his knee, nor would he garb himself like a courtier. He would look like and speak like what he was, a Jew who feared the God of his people and not the puppet king given a throne by the Romans.

Salome's letter gained him access to an inner hall, but he had to wait there with other men who wanted to have audience with the King. Joseph contained his anger and irritation. He sat quietly, watching the mosaic craftsmen who were working on a nearby wall. The intricacy of their art and the slowly emerging scene of gardens they were creating was absorbing.

After a long while, an armed, uniformed guard stopped
in front of Joseph. "What is that you're holding?" he
barked.

Joseph's expression was mild, his voice the same. "It is
for the King," he said. He offered the plain cedar box to the
guard, who lifted off the top, looked inside, closed it again,
and returned it to Joseph.

"Follow me," he ordered.

Joseph obeyed.

The heavy sweetness of burning incense filled the
columned reception hall. Guards stood at attention in front
of the columns. Herod sat on a damask-cushioned thronelike chair that was in the center of a platform at the far end
of the hall. The jewel colors of intricately woven Persian
rugs covered both platform and the canopy suspended
above it.

Joseph walked behind the guard, keeping pace with him.
When they neared the King, the guard stepped to one side.

"My sister's letter gives your name, Joseph of Arimathea, but does not specify the favor you beg," said
Herod. He was wearing a toga, like a Roman, and a golden
laurel wreath on his dyed black short curly hair. His dark
eyes were as hard as obsidian.

"I do not beg, King Herod," said Joseph, "I offer." He
held up the box to the man seated so high above him.

Herod took it and removed the lid. When he looked inside, he frowned. "What does this mean?" The box had
three compartments. The center was filled with the bronze
coins of Israel, with Herod's name upon them. To their left
there was a bag of copper, to the right a tin ingot.

"Phoenician traders sell tin to the Emperor Augustus for
the price of eight sesterces a pound," Joseph said clearly.
"Rome sells it to you for twelve sesterces, in Rome. The
cost of shipment to your mines and mint on Cyprus is, on
average, two quadrans per pound. I will undertake to de-

liver tin directly to Cyprus at a cost of ten sesterces a pound."

Herod leaned forward. He considered Joseph's youth, his plain clothing. Then he looked again into the box of metals.

"Do the Phoenicians know what you are doing?"

"No, and they must not learn."

"Nor Augustus," said the King.

CHAPTER SIXTEEN

SARAH WAS FASCINATED BY EVERY DETAIL OF JOSEPH'S ACcount of the men who were not really blue. She especially enjoyed seeing him in his trousers. Most of all—although she did not say it—she was joyful that he was safe and alive and home again.

Her grandmother had died while Joseph was away. Although the old woman had not once demonstrated any affection for her, Sarah found herself missing Esther. As soon as Joseph was home, though, everything was all right.

He had brought back for her one of the garments worn by the women of Belerion. The long-sleeved, green and yellow checked gown was bound about the waist with a belt of the beautiful Celtic bronze work. She looked tiny in its voluminous folds. Joseph found it enchanting.

They put on their strange clothing only for the fun of it. The dry season and its heavy heat had already begun. Also, it was necessary to maintain the secrecy about the homeland of the tin.

"We should have our own house, Sarah, not just a room. This whispering when we want to parade around and laugh as loudly as we like is not good."

"But, Joseph—"

"I have enough money, more than enough. After the *Eagle*'s trading is done, there will be more than you can imagine. We can take your grandmother's place. You grew up there; wouldn't you like to have it for your own?"

"Not really. My memories of the years with Esther aren't something I treasure."

"All the more the reason to wipe them away by making the house ours. We'll fill it with happy days to remember for the rest of our lives." He was full of energy, and ideas about adding a larger courtyard, with additional rooms, and using mosaics for floors or walls, or both.

Sarah envisioned the long months of loneliness when he was away, but she manufactured enthusiasm to match his. It seemed to mean so much to Joseph.

However, she dug her heels in about another of his ideas. She would not wear the many pieces of jewelry he had bought her. "My lapis necklace is all I'll ever want or need, Joseph. These bracelets and brooches are beautiful, but they are too dramatic, too bold for me. I love it when we dress up in the clothes; they are our secret silliness. The jewelry is something completely different. Give it to your mother and grandmother. You never bring gifts for them."

Rebekkah was impressed when Joseph offered her a choice of any piece she wanted. "I assume Sarah prompted this exceedingly welcome show of affection," she said with a mischievous and yet loving smile.

Joseph admitted it was so. He knew better than to try deceiving his grandmother. "Do you like them?"

Rebekkah didn't answer for a moment. She was trying the bracelets on, first one, then another, moving one to the other arm, then adding a third one, piling all three together, moving one to above the elbow. All the while, her face was set in total concentration on what she was doing, Joseph forgotten.

Then she looked at him. "Magnificent," she said. "When I was young, I cared very much, perhaps too much, about how I looked, how I compared with my friends. Of course we lived in the city then, and society was important to me. How I would love to be eighteen again, with things as they were. Ten minutes, fifteen perhaps, would be sufficient. Every other woman in Jerusalem would take to her sickbed from jealousy when I appeared wearing these. I've never seen anything like them."

At that instant Joseph could almost see the Rebekkah of those days. She was still a beautiful woman if one looked beyond her gray hair and wrinkles. But when she was experimenting with combinations and placements of the bracelets, one did not have to disregard the signs of her age. They vanished, and the beautiful, youthful Rebekkah took their place.

Joseph seized her hands and kissed them. "I'm going to make it up to you, Grandmother. The house in Jerusalem, the jewels, the silk robes, the slaves, the sedan chairs and bearers, the villa in Jericho—I'll give all of them back to you."

"Dearest boy." Rebekkah put her cheek next to his. "Look forward, not back. What's gone is gone; let it be."

She looked into the bronzes again. There was a pair of small brooches, worn, Joseph knew, pinned on the two sides of a woman's hair when it was coiled on the back of her head in a pattern similar to the intertwined coils of bronze in the brooches. "Give one of these to your mother," she said. "It will please her very much. Then I will convince Sarah that she should wear the other one; that will please Helena even more. She loves your wife more than you know, Joseph."

He thanked his grandmother for her help. He would never have known how to select anything for his mother, because he scarcely knew her. As long as he could remember, almost, he had been battling with his father, and his mother always supported her husband's position. That separated her from her eldest son.

His younger brothers were virtually strangers to Joseph as well. Every time he returned from a trip, it seemed to him that they had grown beyond recognition. Amos was fourteen now, Caleb nine. Rebekkah's protégé Antiochus was maybe nine, or eight, or even seven. And while Caleb and the boy slave looked up to him, literally and figuratively, Amos now gave orders about farm work to all the men, including Joseph.

"And the worse of it," Joseph admitted to Sarah, "is that he's taller than I am and still growing."

"Give him that satisfaction, my love. He'll never be the man you are, not even the man you were when you were his age."

Joseph kissed his wife, the true anchor in his life.

Neither of them talked about the baby that still did not take life in Sarah's womb, month after month, as the summer went by. Their own house was completed before the big harvest began in August. They gave a party for the whole family, and the village, when the harvest ended and they were moved.

Privately Joseph had an undefined, superstitious notion that having their own house would remove the impediment to conception, but it did not turn out to be true.

And he had to leave now. "Not for long," he promised Sarah. "I'll be home again for the winter. You do understand, little sparrow?"

"You know I do. Besides, while you're away, I'll be able to change all the furniture in our house to where I want it to be."

Joseph pretended to be angry, so that Sarah could coax him to kiss and make up, and then they went to bed although it was the middle of the day.

Perhaps when I come back there will be a son growing inside her, Joseph thought as he walked along the road to Joppa. He refused to remember how many times he had had the identical thoughts at the identical place on this road.

His destination was a new one: Tyre, the legendary city of the ancient Phoenician kings. He had visited the port briefly in the *Eagle*, to buy the royal purple dye. But now he was prepared to stay in the city itself, to visit its wineshops and street markets, to gossip and listen and fabricate tales until he found out if his hopes were true. It was said that the Phoenicians of Tyre were jealous of the men of Sidon, because Sidon now had supremacy over them in the eyes of the world, a reputation for better seamanship to match the better, bigger harbor in Sidon.

Joseph only had to mention the name Sidon on his first evening in Tyre, and he was offered a fight he'd never forget . . . a quick death by hanging . . . immediate castration . . . a visit to the sea god with an anchor chained to his foot.

He had come to the right place to find an experienced crew that would not spill the news of his competition with Leontes for the tin trade.

"Sarah! Sarah, it was as if the Almighty Himself had prepared the path for me!"

"Shh, Joseph, don't blaspheme."

"No, no, I'm not blaspheming, I'm shouting thanksgiving for the goodness shown to me. Do you know who will be steersman, who will help me with the navigation? Milcar, the son of the Hannibal who is second to Leontes on the *Halcyon*, the Phoenician tin ship! You should have been there when we talked, you would have laughed till you burst. I had all I could do to keep from laughing myself.

"It's clear that Milcar knows where his father's voyages take him. No one is supposed to know, that's the first thing a crewman has to agree to. But a father cannot keep such news from a son, I suppose, not year after year—" Joseph realized he was treading dangerous ground. Sarah had not welcomed him home with an announcement about a baby.

He hurriedly resumed his account of the successes in Tyre, hoping he'd be quick enough for his mistake not to be noticed.

Milcar had leapt at the opportunity Joseph offered with the shared profits plan. He must know how valuable the secret tin cargo was. What he also knew, which was invaluable to Joseph, was the history and quality of almost all the seamen waiting in Tyre for the start of the season, when crews would be hired.

"I have a crew, including rowers, who are eager for the adventure nearly as much as for the money they'll earn. The chance to outdo a Sidon ship and crew doubles their energies and excitement."

He made a laughing, guilty face. "Mine, too, if I have to speak heart's truth," he whispered into Sarah's ear. "My truer heart's truth is that I love you, my sparrow." Sarah put her hands on his ears and held his head while she turned hers to kiss him.

"As I do you, my heart's truth," she said.

She asked about the ships later, after love, and after late dinner in the courtyard beneath the stars.

"You mentioned a galley, Joseph. Does that mean the *Eagle* has finished its usefulness?"

"Not at all. It won't be the *Eagle* anymore; I'll move the Arimathea eagle to the bow of the galley, and it will be named the *Eagle*. The *Eagle* of today will also be named. I'm going to call her the *Sparrow*. For you, my love. She'll continue as now, with the Macedonians. Philip can act in my place, while I go to Belerion for tin on the new *Eagle*. Only a galley can handle the currents there past the headland of Gaul. Rowers are absolutely necessary."

"And what bird will you adopt for your ship after this galley you're buying now?" Sarah thought she was making a joke.

She did not begin to comprehend the magnitude of the fortune that resided in the lightweight, unassuming, gray metal called tin. Bronze could not be created without it, and there were hundreds of millions of bronze coins needed— for paying wages, for buying bread, for concealing taxes not paid, for bribing tax collectors not to notice, for renting transport, houses, a woman's body for an hour, a vineyard

for generation after generation. Bronze table legs, topped
with marble, were in demand for fashionable houses, also
bronze portrait busts of the men who owned them. Bronze
bowls, cups, braziers, cooking vessels, hairpins, bottles for
perfume, pots for perfumed creams—the uses for the metal
were beyond numbering.

Joseph and the *Eagle* took wine, and raisins, and olives
packed in oil, and in brine, to Belerion, as he had promised
his friends there. They returned with the *Eagle*'s hold packed
with eighty tons of tin ingots.

"I'll wager the *Halcyon* gets only one of those small
shipments that anger Leontes so much," Milcar said cheerfully.

"You'll have to guard the secret," Joseph warned anxiously.

"Do not be concerned about that, Joseph of Arimathea. It
adds to my enjoyment that my father believes I'm transporting grain and find it tedious!"

That first tin voyage was made the year of Joseph's
twentieth birthday.

When he reached twenty-two, he owned another galley
as well, called the *Heron,* plus the *Sparrow,* with Philip the
Macedonian and two of his brothers in command of a small
crew, and a sister ship to the *Sparrow,* called the *Ibis,* commanded by the remaining three Macedonian brothers. Tin
was an extremely profitable business. But not the only one.
The second galley and the two smaller ships were in use
from May to October, carrying cargo for others, at high
rates, plus buying and selling small-sized, extravagantly
priced luxury goods. Agents in all the ports of the Mediterranean were delighted to add Joseph's fleet to the others
they represented.

He had bought, also, the big old-fashioned house in
Jerusalem that had once belonged to the family. Rebekkah
said regretfully that she was getting too old for the city's
steep, stepped streets, she preferred to remain in the familiar comfort of the farm.

Her response was more gracious than the angry outburst of Joshua. "So my sea captain son is distributing largesse to the father whose words he has been deaf to for all these years? Am I supposed to be grateful for the opportunity to live in the rooms where I witnessed the murder of my own father? May God forgive you, Joseph, for your father will not."

Helena did not argue with her husband; she never did. But she did remind him that his sister Abigail lived in a small house with many children and that Abigail's husband could conduct his wool-weaving business in Jerusalem just as he did in Bethany, perhaps even better.

Sarah added the pleasant thought that now, when they made the Passover pilgrimage, they would have a house to stay in, rather than a tent.

Later, when they were alone together, she tried to comfort Joseph. "Your intentions were generous, my dear, and pure. People will realize that in time. You must understand that their responses come from their own love for the farm, not from a lack of love for you."

Joseph nodded, tried to look understanding. Sarah had, of course, been the first to hear about the Jerusalem house. She was also the first to say she did not want to move into it.

"I have always lived in the country, my Joseph. It is my world. I'd have no friends in Jerusalem and no likelihood of making any. Especially not among the people you know there. I would be terrified to dine with King Herod's wives the way you dined last week with him and his sons." She touched Joseph's arm, tugged at his sleeve. "Tell me again about the palace and the dinner. Did you really have a roast peacock with all its tail feathers stuck back in and spread out in a fan?"

"All its feathers, not just the tail. As I said, Sarah, when it was brought in I was afraid we were going to have to eat a live bird. It looked so real."

"Eyeballs, too?"

"Even the tongue. Herod pulled that out, dipped it in some kind of sauce and gobbled it right down."

Sarah pretended to be retching. Joseph knew she was laughing. It helped make things better. Although it still disappointed him that no one, not even Sarah, wanted to share the fruits of his success.

CHAPTER SEVENTEEN

His partnership with King Herod in the tin-copper enterprise was profitable beyond Joseph's wildest hopes. However, there was a heavy, unexpected price to pay. Not long after he returned to Arimathea, Joseph received another invitation. Invitations from the King were, in fact, commands.

The first dinner, the one Joseph laughed about with Sarah, had been exciting. Joseph had approached Herod's palace in Jerusalem with eager anticipation. He'd never expected such an honor. Business, yes; profits were always welcome, even to a king, and the source of them was unimportant. But to meet socially, to dine at the King's table, with the King's family! That was the kind of eminence his grandfather had enjoyed.

With a different king, of course, one of the Maccabees, true Jewish royalty. Joseph would never forget, he told himself, that Herod's hands were stained with the blood of his own father's father, his beloved grandmother's husband.

But he could not help but wonder if his grandfather hadn't been somewhat older when he began to dine in palaces. He was so overwhelmed by the invitation that he even forgot to think about the effect the King's interest in him might have on his business prospects.

The opulence of the palace had exceeded anything Joseph knew, even among the fabulously wealthy families in Alexandria. Floors and walls were marble, of many colors, in many designs. Marble columns surrounded an enormous courtyard that was planted with trees and sweet-flowering shrubs. In its center a marble fountain tumbled perfumed water, a thing unheard of in Jerusalem, where water supplies were so scanty that peddlers sold it in the dry season for a price more costly than wine.

The dining room was hung with silken tapestries depicting gardens, the couches covered with cloth of gold. The low table for each group of three couches was made of silver; the plates and bowls and cups were gold, with jewels decorating their rims. Jewel-colored striped silks covered the cushions on which the diners leaned. The corners of the cushions dangled tassels of plaited gold threads on which precious amber beads were strung. Lanterns of colored glass hung above the tables, burning frankincense-scented oil to produce jewel-colored light.

There were ten tables and thirty couches for the sixty men who were dining. Herod, wearing royal Tyrian purple silk and a gold crown with amethysts, shared his couch with a beautiful young boy, who smiled brilliantly at the King and held the golden cup to Herod's lips when he drank.

Joseph wondered if this was Herod's favorite son. Rumor said that he had well over a dozen—not surprising, for a man with ten wives—and that they were perpetually in and out of favor with their father. Joseph's fellow diner was a visitor from Syria. Joseph would have liked to ask the man to identify the princes for him, but the Syrian did not even introduce himself. He spoke not at all, concentrating totally on eating and drinking everything that was offered.

Joseph concentrated on not drinking too much and on presenting the appearance of a man who was enjoying himself. He did, in fact, enjoy the music that was performed throughout the meal. The performers were excellent, and the noise meant that he need not try to talk to the guests on the other two couches of his group.

The meal lasted for almost five hours. King Herod left after two. Other men left without ceremony during the following hours. Some of them returned, others did not. Joseph would have liked to empty his bladder also, but he did not know where to do so, or whom to ask for directions, so he bore the discomfort. When slaves cleared the tables and presented golden bowls of water for hand washing, he walked away from his snoring couch partner and the dining room without looking behind him. He could pee as soon as he reached the streets beyond the palace.

When the second invitation to dine with the King arrived at the farm in Arimathea, Joseph asked the officer who delivered it if it was possible for the man to say that Joseph had been away, had not received it. The man did not even smile when he said that it was not possible. "My men and I are to escort you to the palace at Sebaste."

"Sebaste? That's in Samaria. I'm a Jew, Officer. We do not go into that heathen territory."

"Sebaste," the man repeated. "Our chariots are waiting in your village."

Sebaste was only about thirty miles from Arimathea, about the same distance as Jerusalem, and Joseph did not really concern himself much with the heretical reputation Samaritans held among the Jews of Judea. He had come to know and to like too many people from too many other lands to waste time thinking about varieties of religious belief. He had his own, for himself. That was sufficient for any concern about religion that he might have.

The trip was interesting. He had never seen Sebaste, or

its surrounding countryside. Most of Herod's kingdom was unknown territory to him.

He stood in a chariot beside the officer, whose name, he learned, was Lysimachus, who drove the two fine horses expertly and swiftly. Joseph commented on his skill with genuine admiration and envy, and Lysimachus' military stiffness relaxed. For the remaining miles he was quite willing to talk, even to answer questions.

He was Thracian, he said, and had been a professional soldier all his life. A little more than ten years earlier he had been among the bodyguards of Queen Cleopatra, but after her death he'd been hired, with many of the guard, by King Herod.

Oh, yes, indeed. The Queen had been as beautiful as people said. Lysimachus missed her every day of his life. Just seeing her walk by was enough to make a man feel more like a man.

King Herod? Joseph had to understand that Lysimachus couldn't make any remarks about the King. Or his family.

"You can tell me about the palace, though, can't you, Lysimachus? I've only been invited by King Herod once before. In Jerusalem, that was. I didn't know where to go to relieve myself, and I got a pain in my gut that nearly killed me."

The Thracian roared with laughter, then he promised to escort Joseph to the King by way of a latrine so that he'd be able to find it again.

Sebaste, he told Joseph, was not just a palace built by King Herod. He had built the whole city, over the ruins of the previous capitol, and named it after the Roman Emperor. Augustus in Greek was Sebaste. It was handsome enough—the King was a great builder—but it wasn't Lysimachus' favorite.

Masada, that was the palace he admired most. Joseph would really have to see that one. The "hanging palace" people called it. Carved right out of the huge rock that stood up in the desert, the palace was really three, one above another, with steps connecting them. A man felt like an eagle up there.

Others? Well, Joseph knew the one in Jerusalem, so he must know Herodium and Jericho, they were both so close. No? Maybe he'd get to visit them later. Mostly Jericho was the King's favorite, but it was starting to sound as if he might shift to Caesarea when the building noises in the city finally ceased. It shouldn't be long now.

There were other palaces, too, mostly part of the border protection fortresses, but King Herod hadn't lived in one of them for at least the last ten years. "And I would know," Lysimachus said proudly. "My troops go everywhere with him. We are the elite. Don't make the mistake of thinking every uniform you see in Sebaste is one of us. The headquarters of the King's army is based there, but that's not the same thing at all."

Joseph felt a chill run through his body. What was he really getting into? Escorted by guards to a place populated by an army . . . Was he a guest or a prisoner? Maybe the Thracian's affability was just a ruse to make him feel at ease, to put him off guard. For years he'd heard stories about King Herod's lightning-hot attacks of rage. People said he had murdered his first wife, and her father, and her brother. Servants who displeased him might vanish and never be heard of again. Joseph thought of his own grandfather, and he shivered.

"Gets a little colder up here in the hills," said the Thracian officer. A stiff wind was blowing now, bringing rain with it.

"Winter's on its way," Joseph managed to say. His mouth was dry, and his tongue felt as big as a loaf of bread. His palms were wet where his hands held the prow of the chariot, but the rain was not the cause. Mercifully, Lysimachus had to pay close attention to his driving on the steep, wet road, and there was no more conversation.

Until he said, "Sebaste. We've made good time."

The high stone wall around the city looked dark and foreboding in the gray wetness of the driving rain. Joseph was silently talking to himself, telling his heart to be brave and his body to hold itself straight and proud. He noticed nothing about the city they were driving through, except that there were a great many uniformed men on the rainy streets.

He looked over his shoulder. Five chariots were following, each with two guards in it.

Lysimachus pulled the horses to a stop, and Joseph fought to keep his balance. His knees were weak. "Follow me," said the guard, and he jumped easily from the chariot. "This is the palace."

Joseph got down and stumbled to catch up with Lysimachus' long strides. The palace's rich fittings were only a blur to him. He had to force himself to pay attention when the officer gestured with his thumb to a tall door studded with copper flower-shapes, each centered by a green stone. "Latrine," Lysimachus said, out of the corner of his mouth.

That has to be a good omen, thought Joseph. A prisoner wouldn't be offered any comforts. His breathing became easier.

The Thracian stopped suddenly. Joseph nearly ran into him. He smelled patchouli, the expensive blend of perfumes that came from India, and he stepped to one side so that he could see the man beyond Lysimachus. His appearance was a direct contradiction to his odor. He was a burly man, not young, but as well muscled as a gladiator. His tunic and cloak were of plain brownish wool, and he wore boots of brown leather. The only thing about him that accorded with the patchouli was the multitude of jeweled rings he wore, two or even three on each finger.

He gestured Lysimachus aside. "Greetings to you, Joseph of Arimathea. King Herod awaits you. I am Ptolemy, his minister of finance. I know your tin trade well. Come with me."

At no time had the voice of Ptolemy been anything other than harsh, and no sign of warmth or humanity had appeared in his eyes. Joseph lifted his chin higher than he normally carried it. If he was, in truth, walking to his death, he would meet it with arrogance, not the abject fear he was feeling.

Both were pushed aside by astonishment when Joseph entered an overwarm small room where Herod was seated at a large table opposite a thin, silver-haired man. The King stood up when he saw Joseph and walked toward him quickly, his arms open and outstretched for an embrace. "My young sea captain. At last!" He kissed Joseph on both cheeks. "I need your advice. We are all old men here. Come take a chair beside Nicolaus."

Relief raced through every vein in Joseph's body, and his bowels turned to water. "S-s-sire," he stammered. "If I could visit the latrine first?" He could not afford to wait for the King's permission, but turned and fled to the turquoise-flowered door.

Herod and his two advisors were laughing when Joseph rejoined them. He wondered if they were laughing at him, but he didn't care. While he'd been emptying his fear into the bowl of the marble latrine, he'd thought about the shame of making a fool of himself, the folly of being afraid for his life. He had come to the conclusion that his worries were not foolish; he had been right to fear the fatal whimsicality of King Herod, and he'd better watch his step.

As the hours passed, however, it became very difficult to remember his own warning. Of all the tales he had heard about King Herod, not one had depicted him as a man of great charm. But this was the case. He was working on plans for a great festival to celebrate the completion of Caesarea, and his delight, even his pride, was as direct and joyful as that of a child who had made his first treehouse with some boards across two branches.

"You're the sailor, Joseph, what do you think we could

do about hanging lanterns on the ships' masts . . . pennons on the arches of the moles . . . coloring the flame of the lighthouse . . . staging a regatta . . . stringing ropes of flowers from ship to ship . . . floating bowls of burning incense . . . creating a mock battle between pirates . . . covering the quay with silk rugs . . ."

The King honestly wanted to know what Joseph thought of his ideas and what ideas Joseph had to improve or add to the spectacle. In a very short time, Joseph became totally engrossed. When a slave entered and announced that dinner was waiting, he hated to leave the drawings and sketches of Caesarea that covered the table.

"Excellent!" roared Herod. "A little wine will renew the creative spirit. Isn't that what your philosophers say, Nicolaus?"

The tall man smiled. He had been mostly silent all day. "Most certainly dreams are more vivid after wine puts a man to sleep, my lord," he said.

Herod thumbed his nose at his closest advisor. "You're almost as dispiriting as Ptolemy," he complained with a laugh. "I could hear the abacus clicking in his head from across the room, adding up the costs of the celebration."

Then the King put his arm across Joseph's shoulders. "Lucky for me that young Joseph is here. He hasn't fallen into the stultification that comes with the stiffening joints of age."

The room where dinner was served was only a little larger than the one they'd been in before. This one, however, had walls covered with painted scenes, not pinned up drawings of Caesarea's harbor. The scenes were elegant, brightly colored depictions of copulation between men and women, men and men, men and animals, and variations on the theme of sexual gratification that Joseph could never have imagined were possible.

"Stop scowling, my good Ptolemy, and share my

couch," said Herod. "I've ordered a meal that will please your skinflint heart."

Joseph suppressed his sigh of relief. Even in a room such as this one, he was sure that the dour finance minister would not be a physical plaything for the King, like the boy at dinner in Jerusalem. He washed his hands in the scented water offered by one slave and dried them on the towel given him by another. When the bowls of lentils and roasted lamb shanks were put in front of him, he discovered that he was ravenously hungry.

"A salute," King Herod proclaimed when the wine was poured. "To me!" He laughed, and drained the golden goblet. A slave refilled it immediately.

The onset of drunkenness mellowed Herod. He happily saluted his "friends at table" and thanked them for their loyalty. "That includes you, Joseph of Arimathea. You could have named a higher price for your tin, and I would have had to pay it. Or you could have cheated in your reckonings, but Ptolemy has gone over each one and he tells me you are that mythical beast—an honest man."

After many more refills, he became maudlin. "You have only one wife, Joseph, and no children, I know. You don't realize how fortunate you are. My wives and their parents are constantly after me, telling horrible stories about the other ones. They all hate each other. And my children hate me. Especially my sons. They want to kill me so they can inherit my riches. Three times my food tasters have died of poison, and I've never known who put it there."

He sprawled across the edge of his couch to seize Joseph's arm. "You don't want me dead, do you, young Joseph?"

"No, I don't, King Herod." Joseph was embarrassed, for himself and for the King.

Herod squeezed his arm painfully. "Why not? Don't try to tell me you love me."

"I love the profits from our trading, sir."

Herod released him and fell back into his couch, laughing and sobbing. "He's truthful," he moaned to Ptolemy. "Why do I have no sons like him?"

Nicolaus rose gracefully and walked slowly to Herod's couch. "My king," he said quietly, "I am an old man and I want to sleep. Will you grant me that favor?"

Herod stared up at him. Tears were spilling from his reddened eyes. "Go, then," he snarled. "Don't give thought to what I want—my friends sharing my simple meal."

Nicolaus knelt beside him. "No man leaves the table before the King does. I will stay and deny my aches."

Herod turned to his friend, rested his head against Nicolaus' thin shoulder. "Nothing but bones," he grumbled. "Help me, Nicolaus."

Joseph dropped his gaze to his plateful of sugared dates and soft cheese. He didn't feel he could watch the shambling exit of the King of Israel.

When the door closed, Ptolemy told him to finish his dessert.

Before it was done, Nicolaus returned. "I would have conversation with Joseph of Arimathea," he told Ptolemy. "We will go to my studio and then I will show him where he will sleep." He gestured, and Joseph followed him.

"Good night to you, Ptolemy," he said.

"And to you," replied Ptolemy, with a nod.

The studio of Nicolaus was really a library. Its walls were divided shelves, with scrolls in each of the squares.

"It looks like Alexandria!" Joseph exclaimed.

"I pretend that I'm in a corner of the great Library," Nicolaus admitted, "but I know the truth. Every day of my life I miss the wealth of the Mouseion."

"Can't you go there for a visit? I'll be happy to give

you passage; my ships always make at least one call at Alexandria."

Nicolaus thanked him, but declined. He could not leave Herod. "He would allow it if I asked, but I will not ask. He depends on me. Joseph of Arimathea, I know a great deal about you, therefore I am confident that you will not repeat anything that I tell you here tonight. Nor will you tell anyone about the King's demeanor when he feels safe with his friends."

Joseph nodded agreement. Nicolaus then proceeded to tell him things that he would not have believed from any-one else. King Herod really was in danger. His fears that his sons might kill him had firm foundation. Other people also wanted to kill him. Far more than Herod knew. Nicolaus was in charge of the King's widespread network of spies and informers. He kept many reports from the King's eyes, dealt with many conspiracies himself.

"Herod is not an evil man at heart. Rash, often, but his family is like a swarm of buzzing, biting insects. They give him no peace. And no love. In all the world I believe that I am the only one who loves him. Not in any carnal fashion. I am like the brother that his blood brother should be, but he is a conspirator and a potential fratri-cide. Poor Herod. I am all he has, though I believe I have successfully kept that knowledge from him.

"Now, Joseph, I am going to suggest something to you. You may refuse if you like." What Nicolaus recom-mended was that Joseph leave at first light for Caesarea. Otherwise, Herod would try to make him part of his royal entourage. "He took a great liking to you. It's his habit to have instant, excessive likes and dislikes."

But the problem with Herod's friendships was that when, inevitably, the friend disappointed him in some way, real or imagined, the King felt betrayed. What he might do then, no one could predict.

Joseph thought back to his desperate minutes in the latrine. "I came to the same conclusion, Nicolaus. But I don't see how I can leave without giving insult."

Nicolaus had an answer. Joseph would leave in a hurry for Caesarea to initiate a surprise for the King. "You can organize a sort of water-borne parade, led by King Herod. His family, dignitaries from other countries. You can have barges built to carry all of them. And naturally Herod's will be the largest, the most lavishly decorated. Other barges can be filled with musicians. I will arrange the composition of special songs."

"It will be the highlight of the festival," Joseph said with admiration.

"Yes, of course. But Herod must believe that it was your idea and that you couldn't wait to begin working on it."

"Thank you, Nicolaus. You are generous to give up the credit for your brilliance."

"It will make Herod happy for a little while. That's my reward. You agree, then?"

"With all my heart. I won't bother to sleep."

"That's excessive. A slave will wake you with breakfast. Fresh clothing is in your room. Come, I'll show you where you are sleeping and how to get to where your chariot will be."

Before Nicolaus left Joseph's sleeping room, he paused. "I have a question," he said, "if you're willing to answer."

"I can't tell until I know the question."

"Why don't you hate Herod? Almost all Jews do. And you have special cause, in the death of your grandfather."

Joseph had to think for a few minutes. "I don't do much hating," he said. "I'd rather use that time and energy for something that'll give me pleasure." He grinned. "And a profit, if possible."

Then he frowned. "My father does enough hating for the whole family. I don't want to end up like him."

He grinned again. "Also, King Herod is good company when he's sober. I enjoyed the planning for the festival."

"Did you pity him? Later?"

"Not really. I don't doubt what you tell me, Nicolaus. But it's hard for an ordinary man to feel sorry for a king. Especially when the king feels sorry for himself."

CHAPTER EIGHTEEN

NICOLAUS HAD AGREED TO SEND WORD TO SARAH ABOUT Joseph's delay in returning to Arimathea. Remembering his own worries about Herod's intentions toward him, Joseph could easily imagine his wife's concern when day after day went by without news of him.

In Caesarea, his inquiries about building the elaborate barges for the parade were met with both enthusiasm and gratitude. Now that the construction work on the city was almost finished, craftsmen of all kinds were sunk in gloom. Many of them had been employed there for the whole decade since the work had begun.

"I was still young when I started," groaned a foreman of the street-paving gang, "and therefore believed my good fortune would last my lifetime. Now I have a wife and four children and only twenty-six yards of street remaining to be done. I'll take any kind of work I can find."

Stone carriers, carpenters, tile-setters, metalsmiths, pipe-fitters—all told the same story.

Joseph did the job he had come to Caesarea to do. But his mind was busy with other possibilities, too. In Belerion, the tin production was far from organized. Each man could, if he wished, scoop up metal-specked sand from any of the many streams that carried it down from the hills, then wash away the sand in a kind of basket-sieve held in the fast-running water of the stream and collect the bits of tin, to take to the smelting house when he had gathered enough. Or not, if farming or sociability seemed more inviting to him.

Would the Celts accept any kind of organization? Would they allow outsiders to set it up, then supervise it? There was only one way to find out. Joseph had to ask them.

He also had to identify the workmen here in Caesarea who would be willing to leave their homes and go to an unknown land, with an unknown language and customs.

It was probably a ridiculous idea. But he couldn't get it out of his mind.

On the Sabbath he went to the synagogue in the small Jewish quarter of the Gentile city. He asked to speak, and he told the people that he might possibly—but only possibly—have an offer to make later in the year.

"It would mean leaving Israel, traveling far away over the sea, building a new community and new lives for yourselves. Like the Jews did in Cappadocia and Armenia and Cilicia. But you would have work for as long as you wanted it, with more money than you ever earned here."

Excited questions bombarded him from all sides.

"I cannot answer you now," said Joseph. "Until I learn if the work is there, I must remain silent about details. I will return sometime in August with definite information. I tell you this now only because no one can make this kind of decision without ample time to consider it."

A man stood on the bench by the wall to get Joseph's attention. "My brother is a farm laborer in Syria, nearby. Could he join us?"

Joseph spread his arms wide to demonstrate his own confusion. "There is nothing definite yet. You must understand that. No man should give up work that he knows, for uncertain possibilities in the future. But of course you can talk to anyone you want to. As long as he is a Jew. I do not concern myself with work for Gentiles."

"I'm afraid I was too hasty," Joseph told Sarah when he was back at home. "It's probably an insane idea."

"It's a wonderful idea," she argued. "Just think of them when they learn that there's no scorching summer heat and drought in Belerion. I remember all you've told me about the greenness there when our lands are all brown and dry."

"But suppose the Dumnoni refuse?"

"Then the Caesarea workers are no worse off than they are now. When will you go to Belerion?"

"As soon as I can. The festival in Caesarea is to be held immediately after Passover. It will last for a week, maybe ten days. Then I'll sail. I've already told Milcar to prepare everything. I'll have time to talk to the Celts, load and deliver the tin to Cyprus, and return to Caesarea in August. If there will be an immigration, I'll still have enough time to carry the people to Belerion before the season for sailing is closed."

He didn't have to tell Sarah the rest of it. She told him. "You'll stay with them for the winter, to work out all arrangements and help them learn the ways there."

"It most likely won't happen at all."

"If it does, I will go with you."

"Sarah! You don't want to leave Arimathea for Jerusalem. You can't really want to go thousands of miles and stay many months in a foreign land."

"Wait and see, Joseph. You don't know me as well as you think you do. I've wanted to see Belerion ever since the first time you told me about it. Of course I'll be miserably seasick for weeks and weeks until we get there, but so be it. Perhaps it will make me look blue, instead of green, like before. Then I'll fit right in."

She laughed, and kissed him. "Now tell me all about the palace of King Herod. Did you have to eat peacock for breakfast?"

After he described the time in Sebaste, Sarah became solemn. "He always goes to Jerusalem for holy festivals. He'll want you to be in his palace all the time at Passover."

"No, he won't. I've already sent full reports about the Caesarea parade to Nicolaus, for Herod. He only wanted me to make plans for the celebration."

"I hope you're right. We already have to be very, very careful. Abigail and her family are moving to the house you bought in Jerusalem this winter. Rebekkah is working on your father now so that we can all celebrate Passover there together. It's still a sensitive subject."

Sarah had, for once, underestimated things. When Joseph entered his father's house to see his family, he was met at the door by his grandmother. Rebekkah looked old, and Joseph immediately worried about her health. "Are you—" She put her fingers over his mouth to silence him.

"Shhh," Rebekkah whispered. "Go back to your house. I'll be over later."

But she hadn't silenced Joseph in time. Joshua came storming into the front room. "Out!" he shouted. "I know you not. The foul stink of Herod is all around you. Leave my house and leave my lands. No matter how highly you estimate yourself, you are not master here. I expel you, and all mention of you. Go! Now!"

Rebekkah's eyes streamed with tears, and her throat was clogged when she spoke. But her words were clear and her voice strong. "Joshua," she said. "You are my most beloved son. I despair to cause you hurt. You must not send your son away. You are too harsh, and you judge him wrongly."

Joshua was shaking with rage. He raised his fists in the air like clubs. "Don't force me to throw you out," he yelled at Joseph.

Rebekkah placed herself between them. "Don't force me, Joshua, to talk of the past's pain. But remember to whom Arimathea was restored. It is mine, and I beg Joseph to stay."

Joshua's cry of despair was like a great wild animal's caught in a trap. He fell to the floor, unconscious.

CHAPTER NINETEEN

REBEKKAH SAT ON A CHAIR, HER BACK STRAIGHT, HER HEAD held high. Her grandchildren sat on the floor, all of them looking up at her. All except Joseph. His face was hidden in his hands, hanging low between his slumped shoulders.

"My son, your father, is paralyzed on his left side," she said. "His mouth can make sounds but not words. His hearing is clear. On his right side, his hand has a powerful grip and his eye has good vision.

"Your mother is with him, the boy Antiochus at her side. He will act as body servant to your father, for bathing him and disposing of his wastes. Your mother will feed him.

"Your father may live for many years, there is reason to be hopeful. He's only forty-two years old.

"These are the things you need to know. Have you any questions?"

"Can we go to him?" asked Caleb. He was blinking to hide his tears. Big for his age, at ten he thought he should act more like a man than a boy.

His grandmother reached forward and brushed his thick untidy hair from his forehead. "Soon, Caleb," she said. "He will want to see you. But you must wait for a day or two while he learns to understand what has happened to him.

He's a proud man and would not want you to see him weak."

Amos, who was seventeen, wanted to know if his wedding should be canceled.

Rebekkah smiled slightly. "You will go to Rachel's house tomorrow and tell her and her family about your father's misfortune. But there's no reason to alter the wedding plans. We will all pray that your father will be present to celebrate with us."

She looked at Sarah, whose arm was across Joseph's shoulders, and shook her head. Sarah removed her arm. "Joseph," said Rebekkah.

"It's all my fault," he moaned.

"Be a man!" said his grandmother sharply. "Sit up and look at me."

Joseph obeyed. Sarah bit her lip when she saw the desperate pain and guilt in his eyes. Rebekkah did not react.

"I have told you all your life, Joseph, that the past is past. You cannot change it. The only thing a man or a woman has is the future. There may be little of that, there may be much. It is the arena for action. Perhaps even for change, if that is what you desire."

"Yes!" cried Joseph. "I want things to be better between me and my father."

"You know very little about the way the Temple is run," his grandmother said.

Why was she talking about such a thing when his father might die with hatred in his heart for his eldest son? Joseph started to interrupt her, but Rebekkah lifted one single finger. He concentrated on listening.

"There are more than seven thousand priests," she said. Again, Joseph felt the impulse to argue. He'd been to the Temple many times, and he was certain there was not room enough for such a number.

But Rebekkah—as she'd done many times before—was answering his questions and doubts before he could voice them. The priesthood was divided into twenty-four clans scattered throughout Israel, and other lands as well. They rotated in service at the Temple, for a week at a time. For the other weeks of the year, they lived regular lives with their families and friends in the towns or villages or cities where they'd made their homes.

"I know this," said Rebekkah, answering another unspoken question, "from the time when your grandfather was alive and served on the Sanhedrin. Many of the Chief Priests were our friends, and quite a number of the lesser priests. One of these, Nebuzah by name, lives in Thamna, only an hour or so from here on foot. With a donkey, the time will be even shorter. Go bring him here, Joseph. He was a very young priest, a protégé of your grandfather's. He'll be no more than fifty years old.

"The heart of the discord between you and your father rests in your nonobservance of the Holy Days when you are on your voyages. And on your disobedience, against the commandment that you honor your father. Nebuzah will make peace between you and ease your father's mind."

"How? What can he say? Or do?"

"He is a priest of the Holy Temple. He has the power to explain and interpret the Law. Your father knows that."

Sarah spoke for the first time. Anxiety made her gentle voice shrill, unlike its usual soft tones. "Will the priest do it?"

Joseph's grandmother looked at Sarah, not at her grandson. "He will," she said with certainly. "He thought I didn't know it, but he was desperately in love with me, in a sweet, boyish way. I was his first love."

When Sarah and Joseph walked over from his father's house to their own, his steps were slow and heavy. "Did you see your brothers' faces when Rebekkah said that the young priest was in love with her?" Sarah giggled. "Amos blushed as red as a radish, and Caleb's eyes nearly rolled out of his head from staring at her."

But Joseph had no laughter in him.

The following day he left at first light to go to Thamna in search of the priest Nebuzah. Sarah knew that they had returned together—Caleb ran over to tell her—but she did not see Joseph until he came home after dark.

He looked exhausted, but peaceful. She held out her arms to him, and they embraced silently for a long time.

Then he held her face in his hands and kissed her, gently. "I am all right," he said, "and my father looks much stronger. I have promised to take him to Jerusalem for Yom Kippur. We will be together at the Temple on the Day of Atonement."

"But Joseph, that's near the end of the sailing season. How can you take the men of Caesarea to Belerion if you have to be in Jerusalem?"

"I don't know that the Dumnoni will allow them to come," he reminded her. Then he smiled—the broad, reckless grin that was almost his signature. "And if they will allow it, I won't mention to my passengers that we'll probably run into a storm or two on the way there."

Sarah grabbed her stomach with one hand, her throat with the other. "What a happy prospect," she said. "I will quite definitely turn blue."

"So you are determined to come with me?"

"Even if I have to stow away."

At Hanukkah, Joshua felt well enough to go to village to see the lamp-lit street and attend Sabbath ceremonies at the synagogue. Joseph and Amos carried him on a litter that Helena had decorated with large tassels, while the women and Caleb lighted the path with torches held high.

They did the same thing for the carefree festival of Purim, three months later, when winter's heavy, cold rains had stopped, and fresh young green was on the trees and fields.

Passover was now only a month away, with the celebrations in Caesarea to follow immediately after. Joseph had bought a chariot and horses for faster travel. For months he had been going weekly to Caesarea to check on the progress of the barge-building for the water parade of King Herod and his court. Everything must be ready in time.

He was threatening one of the gilders with two black eyes, and several broken limbs, when a great commotion of trumpets and drums on a nearby street announced the arrival of the King himself in the city he had built.

Joseph considered leaving town immediately, then rejected the temptation. Herod would certainly learn about it and be offended. Instead, he shouted one final ultimatum at the gilder and hurried to the baths to be shaved and cleaned and perfumed. Then he presented himself at Herod's palace to report on the parade preparations.

The guards at the entrance refused admittance. Joseph demanded to speak to their superior. "I know him," he said angrily, "and he knows me. He will be more than happy to discipline you for your arrogant stupidity."

After Joseph spent about eight minutes in furious pacing from one end of the columned porch to the other, an officer in full dress uniform came out through the tall bronze palace doors. His bronze armor bore the same design as the great doors: a wreath of laurel leaves surrounding a cornucopia that spilled forth fruits of all kinds. Superimposed on the symbol of plenty was the name Herod I, written in Greek.

Despite his irritation—for the officer was a stranger, not Lysimachus, his escort to Sebaste—Joseph began to laugh. He knew the decorative device on the bronze doors and armor very well. It was the same self-admiring design that was stamped on the bronze coins that Herod minted. The soldier, and the palace, were putting Joseph's tin to good use.

His laughter disconcerted the officer, and he slapped his hand quickly around the hilt of his sword. "Are you amused, small stranger?"

Joseph refused to be insulted. It was too dangerous. Also, the plentitude of bronze had delivered a useful message to him. He was a man who did business with King Herod. He was not the friend of the King and had no legitimate right to expect King Herod to receive him at his, Joseph's, convenience. He had been about to commit an egregious impertinence for which he might have had to pay a fearful, unknown price.

"I was hoping to see the noble Lysimachus," he said mildly. "I would have asked him to tell the Minister Nicolaus that Joseph of Arimathea is ready to report on the work he instructed me to supervise for the celebration. Perhaps tomorrow I will have better luck."

He turned and walked—not too hastily—down the steps to the wide avenue in front of the palace. Only when he reached the nearest street and turned into it, out of sight of the guards, did he allow himself the release of shaking in every limb.

Nicolaus' servant found him at home. His master, he said, was eager to meet with Joseph, and begged him to come to his studio in the palace.

Joseph managed to keep a straight face when the guards strained to open the enormously heavy doors. He was careful not to look into their eyes; they still made him feel uneasy.

Nicolaus was taking scrolls from open leather cases on the floor and placing them carefully in squared shelves on the walls. "I hate moving from one accursed palace to the next," he grumbled. "Forgive my distemper, please, Joseph, and find a chair if you can. Don't move any scrolls, though. I'm sorting things out. My imbecile slaves simply filled up the cases without any order whatsoever."

"Perhaps tomorrow would be a better time to meet," Joseph offered.

"On the contrary. I'm sure you'll have good news for me, and I thirst for some. Every day I hear about some new disaster associated with this celebration. The only thing missing so far is an earthquake. I assume it is waiting until all the notables are here, with their families and retinues."

Joseph perched on a small decorative pillar that did not yet have its bowl of flowers on it. "Tell me your troubles," he said, "it will prevent them giving you dyspepsia."

"Tell me your successes," Nicolaus countered. "That will be even stronger medicine, and considerably less bitter."

The reports from Joseph did not take much time to deliver. The barges for the parade were nearly completed. "I feel much improved," Nicolaus said. "Let us go into the garden and celebrate with one of the palace's finest bottles of wine."

"I'd like that very much. We can talk about Alexandria. I always take wine with a friend in a garden behind a tavern there."

"Is it the one on the Street of the Pearl Merchants?"

"Why, yes. Do you know it?"

"It was my initiation into elegance as a shabby scholarship student."

Joseph grinned. "It was mine as an over-dressed semi-literate." Nicolaus smiled.

"It delights me to know that it is still there," he said. "Come. We will make believe that the pretty little lighthouse in this harbor is really the great Pharos of Alexandria. If we drink enough, we might even believe it is so."

To Joseph's relief, Nicolaus said it wasn't necessary that he pay his respects to King Herod, and they ate a quantity of bread and cheese with the wine, so it was easy for him to decline Nicolaus' perfunctory invitation to stay for dinner. They agreed to meet the following week for a tour of the shelters that housed the barges, and then Joseph was free to go to the hostel where he had engaged a pair of rooms for the months of preparation time and for the celebration itself. He had initially planned to bring Sarah and his brothers and his grandmother, if she wanted to come, to view the multitude of entertainments.

Now, since his father's illness had changed everything, he would probably have to come alone. But at least he had his own place to stay. He would have hated to be forced to share Nicolaus' quarters in the palace, as he'd been invited to do. The number of guests was, according to Herod's Chief Minister, growing every hour. "Disasters," Nicolaus called them.

He was outspokenly impressed by the nearly finished barges when Joseph took him on their scheduled tour. "The King will be stunned," he said. "They are more magnificent than we dared dream of, Joseph. I'll arrange for him to be toured around tomorrow and to hand out bonuses to the craftsmen. You will warn them to be washed, won't you, and to see to it that the floors are clean so that his robes' hems not be soiled? I'll send word to you about the time you should come to the palace to meet the group you'll be leading."

"Group?" Joseph echoed apprehensively.

"I'm afraid so. The earliest disasters have already begun arriving."

To become a disaster for me, Joseph thought.

As it turned out, the anticipated disaster was a fabulous triumph. King Herod was as rapturous about the barges as Nicolaus had predicted, and was even more hugely gratified by the loud declarations of admiration and envy expressed by his guests, who were ambassadors from the neighboring kingdoms of Nabatea, Armenia, and Parthia.

The boatbuilders, wood carvers, painters, and gilders were surprised and more than satisfied with the King's golden largesse.

To Joseph, Herod was pleased to present what he believed to be the most coveted prize of all. "You have exceeded my already high estimation of you, Joseph of Arimathea," he announced in front of everyone. "I am giving you your own room in my Jerusalem palace for the week of the upcoming Passover festival, when I will be in residence there. I will consider you an honored guest."

Joseph bowed deeply. "I am overwhelmed, sire," he said.

It was the purest truth. He was overwhelmed with misery. This year would be the first time Passover would be celebrated in the house that had once belonged to his family. His Aunt Abigail had moved in with her husband, children, and stepchildren months ago. His grandmother would have the bedroom that had been hers when she lived there more than twenty-five years earlier. And, if he had the strength, Joseph's father had consented to be carried in a sedan chair to Jerusalem to be with his sister's family and his own for the Passover dinner.

The King of Israel's "generosity" had just ruined everything.

CHAPTER TWENTY

THAT PASSOVER WEEK IN JERUSALEM TURNED OUT TO BE ONE of the busiest, most demanding, and most rewarding weeks of Joseph's life, in spite of his concern about the Caesarea festival that would follow it.

He was not lodged, as he had feared, in King Herod's great fortified palace on the top of the Western Hill. Instead, he was in a smaller palace that Herod had also built. It was lower on the hill, and was used to house the King's children and their families and slaves. The atmosphere within was one of vicious animosities and quarrels. No one paid any attention to Joseph or even noticed if he was there or not.

Therefore, he was able to spend most of his time away. He used his room for sleeping and took none of his meals with the Herodians. Still, Joseph made a point of learning who was who, and the connections between them. King Herod was in his sixties; when he died, one of his sons—not necessarily the eldest—would become ruler, and Joseph would have to know the man who became his partner in the enterprise of tin and copper and bronze.

The chief steward was his best source of information. He tried to mask it, but his dislike of Herod's sons was

great. There were seven, from five of Herod's ten wives.
Each had wives and children. The palace was not in any
way a peaceful haven.

Joseph's own family's house, not so very far from
Herod's lesser palace, was a haven, but hardly peaceful.
Rebekkah had managed things so that only she and Sarah
came with Joseph from Arimathea. They were plunged instantly into the noisy, happy family of Joseph's aunt, the
much younger sister of his father.

Abigail had married a widower with seven children;
during their twelve years together she had given Matthew
three more offspring. The house teemed with boys and
girls from the age of five all the way up to men and
women of twenty or more years.

Joseph's aunt was a warm, comfortable, disorganized
woman who poured undemanding, indiscriminate love
over everyone around her. At twenty-eight she was only
six years older than Joseph, but she welcomed him and
Sarah as if they were two additions to her brood of children.

Rebekkah claimed to have the impression that she had
somehow fallen into the midst of a herd of wild animals.
But she told Abigail, and also Joseph, that her heart rejoiced to see the old house so full of life.

Joseph felt the same way. The furnishings were not elegant, but the house was richly blessed with happiness. He
could never say it, and he tried not to think it; if he and
Sarah had been able to, they would have had the same constant noises of squabbling and laughter and tears and running and dancing and singing from their own houseful of
children.

He dared not even ask Sarah if it was painful to her to
have so many children around. She found a rare quiet moment during their second day there to tell him that it made
her both sorrowful and happy, but with the happiness ten
times greater than the sorrow. As always, she had known
what he was thinking.

They went out into the streets together for at least an hour almost every day. The yearly tens of thousands of Jews who had come from their homes for the great festival made the narrow streets of the old city feel almost like the inside of Abigail's house, Sarah laughed.

The Western Hill, where Abigail's house was overshadowed by the newer, grander houses higher up, did not have the same packed streets. The Passover pilgrims did not venture into the territory of the rich and powerful upper class.

In those streets Joseph had his first insider's view of the exercise of influence. Every day, men who were complete strangers to him managed to intersect his path to Herod's smaller palace or from the palace to Abigail's house.

They had learned, somehow, that King Herod had taken a fancy to the young shipowner, that he had even put him in the smaller palace, as if he were some sort of adopted son.

Men introduced themselves to Joseph, invited him to come to their houses for a glass of wine or a meal, offered him business opportunities, asked if they could use his ships to transport crops they grew or goods they produced, hinted that they would be interested in investing in his shipping enterprises, mentioned that if he ever happened to be in need of a loan . . .

He was pleasant to all of them, said nothing definite to their suggestions, came to understand that he could have anything he wanted from men who needed the goodwill of the King.

At first the thought repelled him. But then he tried to put himself in the place of these men. They hated Herod, but they were legitimately afraid of him. Currying favor with one of Herod's favorites was simply sensible business practice, a kind of insurance.

And if he could figure out a way to manipulate, to use the reputation of influence that had settled on his name, he might accomplish many things, once he identified his own goals in his mind.

That would have to wait, however. For now, his priorities were clear. He had to get through the week of Passover, then the week of festivities in Caesarea, and then he could sail to Belerion and learn whether a group of Jews would be allowed to settle there.

In the meantime, he was fascinated by the different Jerusalem of the Western Hill, the place of wealth and power that he had never seen in all the years that he had come with his family for Passover pilgrimage.

It felt good to walk the wide, straight, uncrowded streets past the walls of the mansions and to know that he belonged there, that he had made a success of his business through his own efforts, that he, too, owned a house on the hill, the house that his family had occupied for generations before he was even born.

There was a huge marketplace, the agora, in front of King Herod's great palace. Beneath its columned arcade, the most exotic and expensive products of the known world were for sale. Joseph recognized many of them as former cargoes on his ships. He learned about the ones that were unfamiliar to him, with an eye to trading in them in the future.

All in all, the week in Jerusalem was both pleasurable and useful.

Caesarea's festival gave Joseph his first real taste of what the Roman world was like. The seaport for Rome at Puteoli was not notably different from any other seaport, and he'd never had time to visit any nearby city. But Herod had built a Roman city in the land of the Jews, and now Joseph saw what that really meant. He had invitations to all the festival events, and he attended them all.

He saw the thrilling chariot races in the Hippodrome, found himself on his feet cheering with the rest of the spectators, felt the excitement when two of the drivers succeeded in leaving the rest behind and raced at speeds he'd never dreamed of, their whips cracking across the backs of the four matched horses that pulled the tiny high-wheeled chariots. The winners crossed the finish barely inches ahead of the other team, and Joseph shared the bitter dismay of the woman next to him who had screamed encouragement to the loser throughout the race.

Yes, the woman next to him. The stepped tiers of seats were filled with men and women, a circumstance that was shocking to someone with old-fashioned views, like Joseph. He had never questioned the traditions he'd been reared to. Women did not attend dinner parties, or mingle in any way with men who were not in their own family. The only exceptions were at synagogue or village events, and then they were escorted by a husband, father, or brother. Essentially a woman's place was in her home, taking care of her house and her family.

Evidently that was not true of Gentile women. Joseph saw them at the races, also at the theater, where the acrobatic dancers made his heart pound with their dangerous leaps and tumbles, and towers of man on man on man to a dizzying height.

There were even women at the arena, eagerly watching the contests between animals, between men, and between men and animals. He was fascinated by the animals. He'd never before seen tigers or elephants or monkeys. When they were killed, he was more horrified than when they killed men, or when men killed men. He'd seen men killed, but to watch the brutal slaughter of the beasts upset him more. They were ignorant, innocent victims, Joseph thought. And the tigers especially were so beautiful that it was a crime to let them die.

The contests were too many, the deaths too senseless, the blood too red, too much of it. He could not understand why any of the spectators regarded the senseless, inhuman waste of life as entertainment. The thought sickened him.

He said as much to Nicolaus when they met to check on final arrangements for the parade of barges.

"When I was younger, I would have agreed with you whole-heartedly," said Nicolaus. "But after decades of watching the games, I have become deadened to emotion about what I'm seeing. And, I suggest, that is the most sickening thing of all."

King Herod decided, on the day before the parade of barges, that he wanted to see them in their finished state, after they'd been lowered into the water. Joseph was just about to eat his breakfast when he received the message to meet with the King and his party at once on the quay.

His thoughts were far from charitable while he was running through the streets to do the King's bidding. They became more and more mutinous as he walked along at Herod's side, surrounded by bodyguards, listening to the King's criticisms. This barge could have used more gilding, that one had too few cushions for the passengers, the color blue on the sides of the next one was incompatible with the green-shaded blue of the harbor's water.

I put in hundreds of hours of work and worry, Joseph was thinking, without anyone mentioning anything about payment of any kind. Unless you count the nightmare of being in the small palace in Jerusalem with your disagreeable sons and their unpleasant wives as some kind of valuable reward beyond price.

"And where do you berth your ships, Joseph?" Herod asked. "I'd like to see the galleys that bring my tin."

When the King looked over the small fleet that was Joseph's great pride, he nodded his approval. But then a frown creased his mottled forehead. "Very Spartan," he said. "I suppose that's admirable. However, I want you to build one that offers more comfort. You know what I mean. A cabin or two or three with good beds, and some couches on deck with protection from the sun and wind. I may want to ask you to carry my embassies or some of my children across the sea one of these days. Who knows, I may even take a trip myself."

Joseph bit the soft interior of his mouth until he could taste his own blood's salt. He hooded his eyes and bowed. He could be fed to the tigers if he spoke what was in his mind. "I am honored," he lied in a mumble of pain.

Why had he deluded himself into thinking that King Herod's patronage would do good things for him? The old man was causing him nothing but trouble, and now outrageous expense.

"You will join us at the banquet after the parade, Joseph of Arimathea. Everyone will want to applaud your barges."

Joseph managed to speak the expected expressions of delight and gratitude.

He held tight to the thought that in only a few days he would be on the ungilded, uncushioned deck of the *Eagle,* heading away from this marble-columned Gentile city into the clean air and waters of the sea that he loved.

Later that day, when he was scouring the shops on the Street of the Silk Merchants for more cushions, Herod's financial minister, Ptolemy, came up behind him and coughed to get his attention. "The King has instructed me to arrange for funds to be put at your disposal for construction of a galley of sixty oars," he said with his customary stiff air of disapproval. "The treasury here in Caesarea will be notified at once. This is a letter which will identify you to the official in charge there." Ptolemy held out a scroll to Joseph, then turned and left as soon as Joseph took it.

The owner of the shop immediately doubled the price of the cushions, but Joseph didn't bother to haggle. He was too busy thinking about the new galley.

The following morning was gray with clouds, but they cleared before the hour designated for the parade of barges. Joseph squinted up at the sky, enjoying the petty triumph of the blue overhead that matched perfectly the blue on the barge that Herod had criticized. Already Milcar was talking to the best boatbuilder in Caesarea about the new galley. Joseph took his place in the wooden viewing stands that had been built on the quay for spectators of the parade. All he had to do now was watch. Getting the musicians and the notables into their places on the barges, and getting the barges into line and underway, were on Nicolaus' list of disasters.

Joseph intended to enjoy himself, and he did. No one in the stand knew who he was, and he could listen to the cries of admiration without wondering about the truth of them.

He allowed himself to believe in the sincerity of the applause at the banquet, too. The King had him stand to receive it, then called Joseph to his side. "I have a small gift for you, my young Joseph," said Herod. "It is an inadequate token of my appreciation for all you have done to make the celebration of Caesarea a success. Even more, it is an expression of my personal esteem and affection."

The two hundred guests applauded even more loudly. Joseph opened the box Herod gave him. It was the same box that had held the tin and copper coins that he had presented to the King three years ago. Now it contained coins again, but they were of gold, not bronze. And in the center section of the box there was a heavy, curiously wrought gold ring. The band ended in swivel hooks that held a large ruby shaped as a scarab. It reversed, and on the back was an exquisitely carved intaglio galley with a billowing sail and a minute, exact, Arimathea eagle on its tall curved prow.

"Your seal, Joseph of Arimathea," said Herod in a low voice, for Joseph's ears only. "It will give any letters from you immediate attention and will give you instant entry to all my palaces and fortresses, whether I am in residence or not. Use it as you will, for yourself and any who may be with you. I have complete trust in you."

For that moment Joseph could understand how Nicolaus had grown to love his tyrannical, mercurial king. He knelt beside Herod, without falsity or irony, to demonstrate his gratitude and allegiance.

It was many hours later before he remembered that this King Herod had coldly ordered the stabbing of his grandfather and the confiscation of all his property.

Joseph decided not to try to understand. It confused him too much.

CHAPTER TWENTY-ONE

THE VOYAGE TO BELERION HAD ALL THE DRAMA AND EXCITEMENT that Milcar and the crew had come to expect and savor. As before, the *Eagle* was heavily laden with wine, olives, oil, and balm of Gilead. The stated plan for the season, if anyone asked, was to trade at the ports of Cartagena and either Cadiz or Marseilles, depending on weather, and to finish at Cyprus, for the fine wine that sold so well in Tyre and Caesarea. It was rare that anyone asked. Everyone in the world of sailing knew that it was impossible to predict the success of sales in any given port, or the availability of new cargo at a favorable price. The unpredictability was a major factor in the never-ending adventure that created the siren call of the sea.

The *Eagle* left Caesarea in the rose-gold light of early morning and set a course for the coast of Spain. But not Cartagena. Joseph watched sky and sea and wind, and they made the perilous passage through the Pillars of Hercules just as the sun was about to dip below the horizon. Then, in silence, the bright striped sail was quickly lowered, and a black one raised in its place. All black against the darkness of night, the *Eagle* headed west by northwest to pass Cadiz unseen and to find the strong, fast current and prevailing winds that Joseph had come to know on his single-handed journey four years before.

Lookouts both day and night scanned the waters in all directions, in case the Phoenicians might have altered their customary schedule and appear. It had not happened on the two earlier voyages, but a seaman learns very quickly that he can never be completely certain about anything. Especially if he has ventured onto the vastness of the ocean.

When the mysterious hill-island called Itkis was sighted, the crew cheered. The *Eagle* had no fear of the Veneti tribe on Gaul's promontory. They were allies of the Dumnoni of Belerion and would assume the watch for the Phoenicians now. A signal fire, or its signal smoke, would warn the *Eagle* while it was anchored at Itkis. This, too, had not occurred, but had to be taken seriously. Joseph did not know what Leontes and the crew of the *Halcyon* might do if they learned about the *Eagle*'s tin trading; he hoped he would never have to learn.

The Dumnoni chieftain Gawethin and Joseph, or Sennen as the Celts named him, had created a pattern for these trips that made the *Eagle*'s arrival a gala occasion for everyone.

As soon as the tide receded and the road of sand appeared, the Celts ran toward the beach of Itkis with the barrows of ingots. The men of the *Eagle* met them halfway, and helped pull the carts. They had already brought the cargo from the ship to the beach. With excited incomprehension of what the others were saying, both groups greeted each other with enthusiastic goodwill. Then some carried the ingots and loaded them into the *Eagle*'s hold while others filled the carts as soon as they were emptied with the gift food and drink from Israel. After the carts were filled, they raced, laughing together, to get to the mainland before the tide returned.

Joseph and Gawethin exchanged news of events in their personal lives and in the very different worlds they inhabited while the merry cargo shifting was taking place. Also

Gawethin gave Joseph the information about tonnage, and Joseph paid for the tin.

When all the work was done, it was time to go to the village of the Dumnoni for the feast of the drunkards. The name had been coined on the first voyage. Celts drinking the unfamiliar wine had taken in too much, while the men from the *Eagle* discovered the sneaky potency of the mead offered by their hosts. Everyone had an excessively good time, and a tradition was born.

"Gawethin," Joseph said after their news was exchanged, "I have need of a priest to explain the meaning of my words. I have special talk to make with you."

"This is good special talk, Sennen?"

"I believe yes. It is my hope that you believe yes also."

"You want hastiness?"

"Is needed."

"We go to my house. Priest is in village."

As always, the priest was not one of the ones Joseph had met before. This year he was a gray-bearded man named Mulfra. When Joseph began to explain, in Greek, his thoughts of bringing over a colony of Jews, Mulfra stopped him. This was a matter of grave seriousness, he said. He had to send for others of his brotherhood to listen.

"Then we will have the feast of the drunkards now and talk when they arrive," Joseph said cheerfully. The outright refusal he'd feared had not been said. That was cause for celebration.

"Feast?" asked Gawethin hopefully, in his own language.

"Feast!" Joseph agreed, using the same word.

The priest Mulfra left them to their revels.

When three days passed, and Mulfra had not returned, Joseph called the crew of the *Eagle* together. They had the right to an explanation. In previous years, they had left Belerion the second day following the feast, when their heads had had time to clear.

He told them about the Jews in Caesarea and his plan. "Move to the back of beyond, never to return? Why would a man do such a thing?" asked the sailmaster.

"For a better life" was Joseph's only reply.

The men of the *Eagle* were Phoenicians from Tyre. Their city was near enough to Israel for them to have been taught in childhood that the Jews were a strange, God-possessed nation that no normal man could conceivably understand. They heard Joseph's words and shrugged. What Jews did never made sense. This had nothing to do with them.

But the delay did. The ship from Sidon was en route to the tin by now. "How long will you wait for these priests?" Milcar asked Joseph.

"We cannot stay past three more days," he replied. "If they have not arrived by the day after tomorrow, we will sail."

Three hours later a coracle landed on the beach of the mainland. Four white-robed priests stepped out of it. One lifted a golden horn to his lips and sounded a long, sweet, high note.

The Dumnoni began to talk among themselves, agitated and excited. Gawethin walked rapidly toward the sound's origin. After a moment of hesitation, Joseph followed him.

When the priests were in view, Gawethin prostrated himself on the ground. Joseph stared at the four men. One of them, the eldest, was wearing a heavy chain of gold across his chest. A beautiful small sickle made of gold hung from it.

Joseph bowed deeply. This must be the High Priest of the religion of the Celts.

"We are known by the name 'Druid,'" said the priest Gulval, who had saved Joseph from near death in Gaul. "You have the extraordinary privilege to tell your plan to our High Priest, Zennor."

"I am grateful," Joseph said sincerely.

"This is Borlase," Gulval continued, touching the sleeve

of a younger man, "and this is Mulfra, whom you have met." Joseph bowed to them all.

They went into Gawethin's house to talk.

Joseph outlined his idea. "I believe it will produce good results for all," he said in conclusion. "The Dumnoni will have their choice of working fewer hours for as much as they now earn or of earning more money for the number of hours that they are presently working. I know that you are all men of wide knowledge. You understand, I am sure, the increased productivity that organization of effort creates."

"You said 'all,' Sennen. What good does your plan offer your people?"

Joseph explained the burden of taxation by both Herod and the Romans. Also the loss of available work now that the city of Caesarea had been completed. The chief value, he said, was that these Jews would know safety for their families and for the worship of their God.

"Ah, yes," Gulval said eagerly. "I have always regretted that there was not enough time for you to inform me about this One God of the Jews. Instruct us, please, Sennen."

Joseph talked for almost an hour, and answered questions for an additional two and a half.

"Are you sure that these Jews would not worship our gods?" asked the High Priest. He had asked the same question several times.

"I am sure. That is an essential condition. They must have the freedom to build their own house of worship, to observe their Sabbath, and to hold themselves apart, with no intermarrying. It is the way of the Jews."

The High Priest spoke to his brethren. "We must discuss these matters. You will leave us now, Sennen."

Joseph left the house and went to the village's well. His mouth was dry and his head ached. He had no idea what the priests might decide.

The afternoon of the next day he was told that he might return with no more than ten Jewish men. All of them must have wives. Any sexual violation of a woman of the Dumnoni would be punished by death. If she had consented to the copulation, or invited it, she would also be put to death.

"What about children?" Joseph asked.

There must be children, he was told. A Druid priest would be their teacher, he would teach them the language of the Dumnoni, and the children would teach their parents.

For the first time Joseph felt total conviction that his plan would be a success. His heart pounded with eagerness to tell Sarah.

On the voyage from Belerion, the *Eagle* missed being discovered by Leontes in the *Halcyon* by a stroke of luck and its black sail. Joseph's crew saw the lanterns on the *Halcyon*'s deck, and the steersman immediately turned the *Eagle* away, into the darkness. The sounds of voices singing and a flute's accompaniment could be heard, even after the *Halcyon*'s lights were no longer visible.

"Poseidon will deserve a special sacrifice for this," Milcar said quietly.

Joseph agreed with the captain of the ship. But in his own heart and mind he was thanking his God, the One God of the Jews.

He'd been thinking about his God quite a lot in recent days. Also about his father, Joshua. The priest who came to Arimathea had managed to build a slender bridge between father and son, founded on Joseph's fervent admissions of guilt for his past neglect of the Holy Days observances and his solemn promise to take Joshua on the Day of Atonement to the Temple, where Joseph could publicly repent and seek God's forgiveness.

Now Joseph determined to do more. Three Holy Days came in quick succession during the month of Tishri. The Day of Atonement was the second of them. If Joshua's strength was sufficient, Joseph vowed, he would take his father to Jerusalem for the celebration of Rosh Hashanah, then the promised Day of Atonement ten days later, and remain an additional five days until the Feast of Succoth, the most carefree and joyous of all the festivals.

If Joshua was strong enough. Joseph couldn't stop thinking how young his father was. Only forty-two years old, and half-paralyzed. Only twenty years from now, I'll be forty-two, he thought again and again. It is not a very long time, twenty years. I used to believe it was practically forever, but now I know how quickly years pass. Only twenty more voyages to buy tin. Only twenty more homecomings to Sarah.

I want more than that. And I'm certain my father did, too. I'll carry him to the Temple in my arms if it will bring him some peace and happiness.

. . . But first I have to talk to the men of Caesarea, find out how serious they are about emigrating, select the ten families, redo the cargo space to give accommodations for the voyage, talk to Milcar and the crew, tell them what's going to happen . . .

It wasn't easy for a man of action to concentrate for long on things of the spirit. Life kept getting in the way.

The tiny synagogue of Caesarea was a riot of shouts and cheers. Joseph was tempted just to say it was all a mistake and make a hasty, ignominious exit. How could there be so many men who wanted to go somewhere—anywhere—for a life of steady work, no matter how backbreaking it might be.

He could take only ten.

His mind raced. Then he raised both arms. "Quiet," he shouted. "Let me speak."

He told them that there would be a long sea voyage to the place he could not name for them. And that they would never be allowed to return to Israel, because the place had to remain a secret.

A thick swarm of men who had been shouting and cheering looked at one another, at Joseph, at exile. And they were silent.

"Go, now," Joseph ordered. "Talk to your wives, your

families. Come back tomorrow if you still believe you want to go."

After they left, he turned to the leader of the synagogue, who stood beside him.

"I've done this badly," said Joseph.

"You'll be lucky if you don't get stabbed in your bed tonight," said the rabbi. He was as disgusted with the withdrawn hope as the men of his congregation were. "What is the unnamed, unknown place you painted as the Garden of Eden? Maybe you're really looking for galley slaves, to use in your ships or sell to the Romans."

It took hours for Joseph to convince him that he wanted the best for Caesarea's men, that he honestly believed his offer was a good thing, in spite of the mystery and restrictions that surrounded it.

Then he had to talk for many more minutes before the synagogue's leader agreed to help.

"I'll even give you a corner of my house to sleep in tonight," the rabbi said. There was laughter in his eyes. "You'll be safe there. Except from my son, maybe. He is one of the men who believed your pretty picture. I'll try to convince him that his mother would not want bloodshed in her house."

The rabbi's house was two rooms on a courtyard, where a goat was grazing near to a clay oven in which his wife and daughter were baking bread.

On one side of the courtyard another building held a fireless forge.

Joseph was depressed and tired. He'd had a long, hard time convincing the men of the *Eagle* to undertake a second voyage to Belerion, especially in the months after the sailing season ended. Then the scene in the synagogue.

But when he saw the cold ashes of the forge, his fatigue was washed away. Could it possibly be? Was the rabbi one of the out-of-work men of Caesarea, too?

No. It would be too huge a coincidence, practically a

miracle. And Joseph didn't believe in miracles. Hard work was what he believed in.

Nevertheless, strange things did happen. Many had intruded into his own life, for no logical reason. And it was possible. He knew that the leaders of the synagogues were not priests; they were usually working men who became leaders because of their piety and their knowledge of the Torah.

While he was sitting on the floor with the rabbi and his sons, eating the bread and thick vegetable stew served to the men by the rabbi's wife and daughters, Joseph looked at the family and their clean, scantily furnished house, and he decided to risk everything.

"Rabbi," he began.

"Isaac," said the rabbi. "We're no longer in synagogue, Joseph of Arimathea."

"Isaac," Joseph repeated. He smiled. "Your family's names?"

David was the stony-faced son, Jacob the young one; Rachel was the rabbi's wife, Esther and Miriam their daughters.

"Would you and your family like to hear a story, Isaac?"

It took a long time to tell about the boy who worked as a cook's helper, then a cook, then discovered a secret from his hiding place atop a mysterious fern-softened hill that rose from the sea.

Rachel and her daughters brought their meal to eat, sitting on the floor near their men and listening to the strange, beautiful tale of a strange, beautiful land where flowers covered hillsides and sparkling streams frothed over and between rounded gray stones.

Joseph grew increasingly hoarse. Little Miriam brought him a cup of water.

He told about the dull shine of metal in the streams, and the men who collected it, wearing strange garments, speaking a strange tongue that sounded like music.

Beside him, Joseph felt the silent strong alertness of Isaac and his sons.

He spoke of blue eyes like pieces of summer sky and of women and girls with long braids as golden as the sun.

Then he described a man, dark of hair and eyes, from a foreign land, who talked with the white-robed priests of the blue-eyed people about bringing men with eyes as dark as his to live beside the people of the golden hair and eyes like the sky.

The dark people would come as families, and would build homes for themselves and a place to worship the God they brought with them. The men would show the blue-eyed men how to find the metal's home places above the streams that carried bits of the gray metal from its original mass. They would help, instruct, create a design for the gathering of the metal, direct the activity of the blue-eyed men.

While their children learned the strange language in a school, to pass to their parents, and learned the games of the blue-eyed children while teaching them their own. And their wives discovered the wonders of the unknown herbs and fruits of the land and drew milk from the teats of the strange animals that ate the rich grasses on the hilltops beside sheep and goats like those of other hilltops in other lands already known to them.

Joseph was finished.

"Esther," said the rabbi's wife. "Bring a cup of milk for Joseph, with a spoonful of honey in it. His throat is raw."

Joseph and Isaac climbed the stairs to the roof and sat under the bright stars with a skin of wine and two cups, talking until the stars faded and the wind from the sea made their tired bodies chill. Then they wrapped themselves in blankets to sleep for an hour before the sun rose.

Joseph felt boneless, completely relaxed in body and in mind. The decisions had all been made. Isaac would choose the families to go to the unknown place. He knew everyone; his selections would create bad feelings, no doubt, but his authority as leader of the synagogue would forestall trouble.

"David's marriage will have to take place sooner than I had intended," Isaac had said. "I haven't told him about it yet, but the terms of the contract are all agreed upon. The bride's father is an old friend. We have always intended that our children would wed. That will leave only eight others to choose."

"Do they know one another—David and his bride?"

"No. My friend lives in Galilee. It will be a good match, though. Sarah is a girl of firm resolve, and David needs to learn that he cannot always have things his own way."

"Sarah? That's my wife's name. She will go with me for the half year that I'll stay with the ten families. It will ease the way. I know the leader of the people, and I am known by their High Priest."

"Your wife will be with us? I almost begin to believe that this transfer will take place."

"Have everyone and everything ready three days after the Feast of Booths. We will set sail on the fourth day."

As Joseph's eyes closed, he imagined taking Sarah's hand and walking on the soft sands of Belerion's beaches, away from all the dreams of his business and his ambitions. He slept with his mouth curved in a smile.

CHAPTER TWENTY-TWO

Joshua had made remarkable progress during the months of Joseph's absence. He could speak, although only Helena understood everything he tried to say. He fed himself with his good hand, and his appetite was improving with every day that passed.

He could not walk, but when he rested his good arm on Amos' strong shoulder, he managed to part hop, part shuffle from his bed to a cushioned armchair that the Arimathea carpenter had made for him.

Sarah told Joseph how pleased everyone was with Joshua's recovery. When Joseph visited his father, however, he could see only the twisted face and body, and he wanted to weep aloud. But he kept his shocked grief inside.

"Would you be willing to stay in Jerusalem for a longer time than we'd planned, Father?" he said with forced cheerfulness.

"Ssst," Sarah hissed. "Lower your voice. Your father's hearing is perfectly all right."

Joshua tried to laugh. His mouth grimaced, and a thick rattling noise emerged.

Joseph dropped to his knees and buried his face in the blanket across Joshua's lap. He sobbed broken words of sorrow and apology. His father pushed him away. Joshua's good arm was as powerful as ever, perhaps even stronger.

Rebekkah led her grandson away. She let him pace back and forth in her room and watched with interest when he hit his forehead against the wall beside the window.

"A useful response to misfortune," she said. "Stop being a fool, Joseph, and pour us some wine. You know where my so-called secret supply is kept."

When he gave her the goblet, he managed to make it obvious that he hadn't poured any for himself.

Rebekkah made an exasperated clicking noise with her tongue. "Listen carefully," she said. "I know that you had a fine tutor for your study of Greek. I trust that you have not forgotten the word 'hubris.' You are not responsible for your father's attack. You are not God."

Joseph's eyes widened. "You don't blame me?"

"You are not flawless, my Joseph. I know most of your faults, although you are here so infrequently that there are probably some that I'm unaware of. But your father's condition is not of your making. Therefore you must stop blubbering like a child and distressing your wife.

"And your grandmother." She lifted her face for his kiss.

"Now go to Sarah and let an old woman enjoy her self-indulgence. Tomorrow we will make plans for Jerusalem. I do hope Abigail hasn't had another child since our last visit."

The family traveled to Jerusalem in wooden carts, pulled by donkeys. Joshua's cart was heavily padded, and his cushioned armchair was securely attached to its side; a long couch with many cushions filled the other half of the space.

Joseph had won his argument with his mother, thanks to Rebekkah's influence. There were two male slaves, riding alongside Joshua's cart. They were Egyptians, trained in Alexandria's famous center of medicine to care for the feeble or crippled.

"I don't know where Abigail is going to put them," Sarah had commented.

"We have the tents," Joseph reminded her. "And Abigail's garden is large." Two cartloads of baggage followed the little caravan. They were driven by slaves, also. Their responsibility was to provide comfortable quarters for the family if the trip proved too arduous to complete in one day. They would also carry one end of the litter for Joshua's transport to the Temple. His medical attendants would take the other end.

Joseph had tried to foresee all needs and all possible problems.

He had, he soon learned, overlooked one very big one. There was a scroll of papyrus waiting for him at Abigail's. The seal on it was the wreathed cornucopia of King Herod.

It notified Joseph that guards would accompany him and his father whenever they left the house of his aunt. Four guards would push aside anyone on the streets they took, six more would hold the people back while Joseph's father, carried in one of the palace's sedan chairs by four additional guards, was transported to his destination.

"How could he have known?" Sarah asked.

"He has an army of spies and tale bearers," Joseph said in a low voice. "Don't let Joshua hear of this. When anyone asks, say it's an invitation to the palace. I'm going there now to put a stop to this."

"Nicolaus, I hold you responsible. You're in charge of the information gathering. You should have kept word of my father's condition from the King."

"You don't understand Jerusalem, Joseph. Your aunt tells a friend, that friend tells another, the slave of one tells his lover, who is a slave at the palace. And so on, ad infinitum. The King's barber is the man who actually told him about your family's misfortune."

Joseph slumped. Without his anger, he felt weak. "Tell

me you can cancel the orders, Nicolaus. Please. This is important."

"You know I cannot. Herod gave the orders; only he can rescind them."

"Then I need to see him."

"Not the way you look now, Joseph. Get bathed and shaved and freshly clothed. Then come back. Smiling. Happy to see your king. Grateful for his kindness. You know what you have to do."

Joseph did know, and he did do it, although bile was bitter in his throat.

Herod greeted him with delight. "How proceeds our new galley?" he wanted to know.

"Well, sire, it has been taken to Tyre, on a barge, for the cedar walls of the cabins to be fitted. At least that's what I was told. I will be able to see it when I return to Caesarea."

"What other appointments have been ordered?" Herod was interested in every detail.

A long time passed before Joseph could bring up the subject of the papyrus in his sash. The King was puzzled, then hurt, then offended by Joseph's refusal to accept his arrangements.

"I am not pleased by ingratitude, Joseph of Arimathea!"

"King Herod, you do not know my father's heart." In desperation, Joseph blurted out the real reason. "His father was executed by your orders. He witnessed the death, and he will never accept anything that is in any way associated with you."

Herod pursed his lips, frowning, searching his memory. "Who was his father?"

"He was one of the Sanhedrin. When you became king."

Herod was still frowning. "But that was nearly thirty years ago, Joseph. I can't recall every little detail of a time so far in the past. I'm sorry your grandfather had to die. And that your father has such a want of understanding."

His brow cleared. "At least all this nonsense is due to a sick man's foolishness and not to any difficulties between you and me. I will cancel the orders if my attempts to show my friendship will create discord in your household."

"I am most grateful, King Herod."

"Come dine with me after the New Year. Nicolaus will let you know the day."

"I shall be most honored."

The King turned to one of the councilors beside the throne.

Joseph left as quietly as he could.

Belerion, he said to himself. Soon I'll be far away from the friendship of the King of Israel.

The piercing, stirring sound of the shofar seemed to be splitting his heart. Joseph put his hands over the heavy beating he could feel in his chest. The horns sounded again, and yet again, their notes twisted into unmatchable resonance by the turning of the horns of the rams, the horns that gave the call to remembrance. Remembrance of one's sins, of one's God.

Attention, the horns demanded, attention to your failings, attention to your soul's need for God. Attention. A new year begins with the music of the shofar. A new beginning. Attention. Bring to the new year a newly cleansed heart, open to the will and the word of God.

Joseph felt that it was so. Beneath his palms, his beating heart was like life itself, given by God, belonging to God. He experienced renewal, became a boy again, before the world and its battles and rewards took precedence over this shattering, emotional response to the mystery of the Almighty and His Temple.

I should have been hearing the shofar and not the music of the wind in the sails, he thought, and the sweet pain of repentance filled his heart, healing the cleft slashed by the shofar's sound. He looked for his father and found him nearby, supported by Amos. Joshua's eyes were closed, tears seeping from beneath his lids. Joseph wanted to go to him. But he might be pushed away. He contented himself with praying to the Almighty, sending his pulsing heart's message toward the hidden home of God, beyond the incense-clouded altar, behind the tapestry hangings woven with the map of the heavens, the map he had learned to follow and to entrust with his very life. Give peace to Joshua, he prayed, grant him a whole heart within his half-lost body.

"You are very quiet," Sarah murmured near Joseph's ear. "Try to join in, my love. This is a feast of celebration, a welcome to the new year."

The whole family was together, in the home they'd regained, sharing the traditional ritual of Rosh Hashanah. A single large bowl of honey rested on a table in the center of the room, with Joshua in his chair beside it. One by one, men and women and children, each approached the table, broke off a piece of bread from the piled loaves and dipped it into the honey. Then, with laughter on all sides, each raised it and ate it, trying to capture the heavy golden drops of honey before they could fall.

It was a symbolic appreciation of the sweetness of new beginnings in a new year.

I should be as happy as they are, Joseph thought. Why do I feel the rapture of this morning at the Temple slipping away?

"Now I feel the happiness you wanted me to feel at the honey bowl," Joseph told Sarah. The note from Nicolaus contained no mention of dining at Herod's palace. It was, instead, an apology. The king was suffering from a congestion of the chest and would have no guests for a while.

Ten days later Joseph stood by his father's side. This was the Day of Atonement, Yom Kippur, and they were together at God's Temple, as the priest Nebuzah had ordered them to be.

In front of them the High Priest, wearing the sacred vestments reserved for this holiest of Holy Days, led forward two goats. Two of his chief priests held them still while the High Priest cast lots, ivory plaques with symbols carved in them, to receive the Almighty's decision about the sacrifice of the animals. He indicated one of the goats, and it was led off to an inner part of the Court of the Priests.

Other than the clicking sound of the goat's hooves on the floor, there was complete silence everywhere. Hooves sounded again when a young bull was led in by a priest.

"I have sinned against God," the High Priest sang. "I sacrifice this bull as an offering for my sins and the sins of all priests." He walked to the block of sacrifice, where he selected a knife and slashed the throat of the bull. He caught blood in a golden bowl, then set it down.

After he cleansed his hands in the enormous circular laver, he lifted a golden censer and began to ascend the steps that led to the Holy of Holies, the hidden inner room that held the presence of God.

Joseph could hear drawn-in breaths of fear. The High Priest pulled on the outer curtain and stepped behind it, in front of the inner curtain that covered the doors to the sacred enclosure.

Soon the smell of burning incense became strong, and smoke from the sacrifice eddied from between the curtains.

The High Priest followed, and the long-held breaths were released in a collective sigh.

God had accepted the first sacrifice.

The High Priest raised the golden bowl of sacrificial blood, then returned to the Holy of Holies.

For a second time God accepted sacrifice, and the High Priest emerged again.

Now he sacrificed the goat and captured its blood.

For the third and last time he entered the Holy inner room, carrying the sacrifice.

When he returned, Joseph heard men sobbing their thanks that all sacrifices had been acceptable to God.

He looked at Joshua. They had begun the ritual fast at

sundown of the previous day, and he was worried about his father's endurance.

But Joshua was steady. He leaned on two stout canes, having rejected Joseph's offer of support.

Click-click, click-click. The second goat was returned. The High Priest laid his hands on its head and chanted the ritual confessions for all the people, thus transferring their sins into the magically selected scapegoat.

A different priest took the scapegoat's tether and led it on the path made by the celebrants through their midst.

Levites played solemn music while the silent men waited inside the Temple. Everyone knew what was supposed to be happening. The priest was leading the scapegoat into the desert.

Twelve miles away, it would be pushed from a steep cliff into a deep, jagged ravine, carrying the sins of the people to extinction.

After relayed signals reached the High Priest, he announced the atonement of their sins. And then he pronounced the blessing:

"The Lord bless thee and keep thee;
The Lord make his face to shine upon thee,
and be gracious unto thee;
The Lord lift up His countenance upon thee,
and give thee peace."

The music swelled in a joyful crescendo, and Levite choirs began to sing.

The Jews of the world had been cleansed of sin.

"Don't expect too much." Sarah had told Joseph several times that it made no sense to assume that his father would forgive him just because God had done so. "It's been over ten years since you ran away to sea, Joseph. Your father has collected a lot of anger, and time magnifies things."

But, Joseph discovered, he had expected some clear

manifestation of change, some look or gesture or nod from Joshua directed toward him.

When the sun went down, the Yom Kippur fast was ended. Abigail outdid herself. There were huge bowls and platters and pitchers of food and wine, plus a basket of breads in front of each diner. As was customary, the men were served first. There was considerable easygoing laxity in Abigail's home. All the boy children were allowed to share the meal with their elders. Caleb, who was only ten years old, felt quite manly to be at Joseph's side. He was exceedingly proud of his older brother's exciting life. "When do you sail next, Joseph?" he asked in what he believed was an offhanded, worldly manner. "Will it be Alexandria again?" Joseph had promised to take Caleb there someday, but "someday" hadn't arrived.

"Not this time, Caleb. But I haven't forgotten," Joseph said. He was very fond of this eager little stranger who was his brother.

"I've been offered an interesting-sounding land investment in Spain. I'm taking Sarah to see it. We will leave after Succoth." It was the story he and Sarah had decided to tell.

Caleb's chubby face clouded, then returned to its usual bright happy expression. "Maybe you'll bring something special back for Amos' wedding gift. What do they have in Spain that's special?"

Joseph had intended to wait until the festivals were over, but he was forced to break the news now. "We won't be back in time for the wedding." He looked at Amos. "I'm sorry."

"I'm not surprised," Amos mumbled. He would not meet Joseph's eyes, but fixed his concentration on choosing an olive from a bowl.

Joseph's heart felt heavy; he wished Sarah were with him. They had talked a great deal about Amos' wedding. "He won't know whether you're there or not," Sarah insisted. "Do you remember our wedding? All the music and dancing and feasting, and all those faces, all laughing and talking. While all the time the marriage tent was the only thing that I could really think about. It was the same for you, Joseph, I know it. And it will be the same for Amos."

She was right. Joseph was sure of that. But he couldn't say that to Amos. Especially not in front of all the children. And his father.

"I'm sorry," Joseph said again.

"It doesn't matter, Joseph," Amos replied, and this time he looked directly at his older brother's face.

"It does matter," Joshua said. He was sitting in his armchair with his own table full of food. The others were on the floor, half-reclining on straw mats, sharing food from a low platform in the center. Joshua seemed very far above them.

"You are wrong about that, my son," he said in his slow, difficult, blurred speech. "It matters very greatly. But you are also right. It is no surprise.

"Help me to my bed, Amos. My hunger has left me."

Joseph unclenched the fists his hands had made of themselves. "I am starving," he said loudly, "and the feast is a true feast. Matthew, will you push that beautiful cheese closer to me? I've been longing to dig into it. Your wife is gifted at feast-making."

The next day Amos took his father back to Arimathea. Joshua said he had had his fill of Jerusalem.

"I'm glad he's going." Sarah stamped her foot. "Now the rest of us can enjoy ourselves. It is a shame, though, that Helena had to go with him. She's been looking forward to Succoth so much."

Joseph caught her to him and held her tight. "Such a fierce little sparrow," he said. There was a catch in his throat. "You always make everything all right. I love you."

*   *   *

The festival of Succoth was also known as the "Feast of Booths," "Feast of Tents," "Feast of Tabernacles." Farmers usually called it simply "Ingathering."

It celebrated the year's final harvest and the short breathing spell before work began again with preparation and plowing of the fields.

The booths . . . tents . . . tabernacles were small temporary shelters that people built in the gardens or on the roofs of their houses or—if they were making pilgrimage for this most joyous of all the festivals—on the hills and in the valleys surrounding Jerusalem.

Matthew and his sons had already gathered most of the materials for the booths. Tall smooth branches made the corners, with thinner ones bracing two sides and laid in spaced rows across the top. They waited on roof and in garden. When the festival began, a week after Yom Kippur, the tops would be covered with fresh green boughs of myrtle and willow and palm fronds.

The huts were replicas of the ones farmers made every year close to their grape vines. They were shelters for the man who guarded the ripe fruit from thieves and marauders day and night until the harvest was completed.

And it was. Completed. The grapes had become raisins and wine, both safely stored away. It was time to celebrate. The men of the house would dedicate the booths with hearty appreciation of the new vintage, and the boys would have their first taste of manhood. All males older than five slept in the booths at night. Caleb was so excited he could hardly wait.

"Let's go buy things, my rich, successful husband," Sarah said in the morning. Joshua had left the day before, and there were still three days before the beginning of the festival.

"Anything you want, my love, and several of them. We'll go to the agora."

No, Sarah wanted to go down into the narrow, crooked streets of the lower city, the part she called the real

Jerusalem. "I want to find playthings for the children. The ones in Belerion and the ones who'll go with us. And 'several' won't do. I want lots and lots, as many as the *Eagle* has room to carry. Sweets, too. I want our arrival to be a celebration that everyone will remember as a happy, happy time."

Hours later they returned, laughing, to Abigail's house, laden with huge soft woven baskets that bulged into globes stuffed with whistles, tops, balls, tiny lambs, donkeys on wheeled platforms with linen pullcords, and sacks of honeyed dried figs.

"Now we'll find out what the favorites are," said Sarah. "These we'll give to Abigail's children and see which ones they like the most. Then, tomorrow, we'll go buy more of them."

"Thank you for not buying any cymbals," Abigail shouted over the cacophony of whistles and shouts of joyous discovery.

Sarah clapped her hands. "Of course! We need cymbals, and real flutes, not just whistles, and little harps. I always wanted to learn to play the harp when I was a child."

Joseph groaned dramatically. "What we need are strong-backed bearers to carry Sarah's beneficence." He'd had difficulty inventing an explanation for the toys until he thought of the children of his ships' crews. Of course, Sarah had agreed. They'd buy playthings for them, too.

There was barely enough time during the days before the start of Succoth to buy and carry all the things Sarah had decided were necessary. Every day the crowded ancient streets became more thronged, and a short distance took a long time, plus sharp elbows on occasion.

There were as many Jews in town from outlying regions as there had been for the Passover festival. Perhaps more. Succoth was so joyful that many chose it for their once-a-year or once-in-a-lifetime pilgrimage to Jerusalem. Even before the festival began, Joseph and Sarah came across impromptu parades, lines and groups of people singing and dancing and waving the tall switches of braided greenery known as "lulabs."

Sarah held tight to Joseph's arm. "If it's like this now, what will it be when the feast really begins? I've never been to Succoth."

"Better," Joseph promised. "And louder," he shouted. "I don't remember much, I was very young the time I was here, but the noise made a strong impression on me. Little boys like making as much noise as they can."

"Big boys, too, I think. You don't have to shout quite so loud."

The festival exceeded anything she could have imagined. There were smiling, laughing, happy people everywhere she looked. Music, too. Best of all was Joseph's joy when he answered a shout from a stranger in the crowd. Sarah couldn't hear what they were saying to each other, but she could see the affectionate embrace. Joseph and the stranger made their way through the jubilant throng to her side.

"Sarah, this is my friend Micah from Alexandria that I've talked about so much."

Micah knelt with flawless gracefulness before Sarah. "Not as much as he talked about you," he said. "Now I understand why he was a faithful husband in Alexandria in spite of my best efforts to corrupt him. I'm honored to know you, Sarah."

"And I, you, Micah. Are you able to come with us for a glass of wine? Joseph owes you a river of it after your hospitality in Alexandria."

"I'd like nothing more. I've discovered a little place over by the City Hall that's quite extraordinary . . ."

Joseph poked him in the back. "Get up, you reprobate, and stop charming my wife." He held out a hand to Sarah. "Come along. We might as well let Micah show off. Trust him to find the most elegant establishment in Jerusalem." Joseph was beaming with delight.

*   *   *

Sarah felt delightfully indecent to be sitting in a public wine garden, even though there were many other women there who were clearly not indecent at all.

She sipped her generously watered wine and listened happily to the bantering conversation of the men. Joseph was enjoying himself hugely. She liked Micah very much for the pleasure he was giving Joseph. Even more for his obvious affection for him.

". . . so I chose Succoth," Micah was saying. "I hadn't made a pilgrimage to the Temple since I was a child, a thousand years ago, and this promised to be the most entertaining. I had to show that I wasn't a total godless wastrel. You see, my friend, the dreaded moment has arrived. I am going to be married, and I have to become a respectable, adult man."

He looked from the corner of his eyes at Sarah. "I begin to believe I might even learn to like being a husband," he told her. Sarah felt her face turning pink.

"Who is the brave young lady?" Joseph demanded to know.

"As courageous as she is beautiful," Micah replied, "and she looks like Cleopatra, say those who knew the tragic Queen. Not a 'young lady,' however, for which I am extremely grateful. She is a widow of obscene wealth with three children who are old enough to live in a separate house with their tutors and servants." Micah dropped his languid, sophisticated drawl. "I am totally besotted with her. She is called Julia, and the sound is like music to my ears."

Sarah kissed his cheek. "I'm happy for you, and for your Julia, Micah."

"I echo Sarah," Joseph said. "But I am surprised there wasn't at least an earthquake when you decided to mend your ways."

Micah pantomimed horror. "I never said that!"

*   *   *

"Your friend is very sweet, Joseph," Sarah declared when they were walking up to Abigail's. "I'm glad you'll be able to celebrate with him tonight."

"We'll have a good time. Whenever Micah is around, the celebration becomes more festive." Part of the Succoth festival was the mighty singing and dancing and wine drinking by men in the Temple's Court of Women. Levites played music all night from the steps of the Nicanor Gate. Rich and poor, artisan and scholar, merchant and shepherd—all were equal. They carried swinging lighted lamps in their hands, formed processions that twisted, dancing and singing, through the throng, then dissolved into other patterns of joyfulness. At daybreak a fanfare of music saluted the dawn and proclaimed the conclusion of the celebration.

"Go to the booth in the morning and cover Joseph's ears with cushions to close out the noise of the household. Lay a cloth over his eyes against the light."

Sarah was with Rebekkah, enjoying the private time with the older woman she loved so deeply. "I appreciate your advice," she said with a tiny chuckle. "What cure do you have for when Joseph wakes up?"

"Be as far away as you can manage. We will go shopping, with Caleb as our mighty male protector. The boy's ankles and wrists are inches out of his cloak, and it will soon be getting colder. An excellent excuse to go to the weaveries. By happy accident they happen to be near the rose gardens and their perfumes."

"I'll enjoy that. You know, we will be leaving the following day. We have to set sail as soon as possible, and we can't stay for the whole week of the festival." Sarah's eyes filled with tears. "I'll miss you terribly, Rebekkah."

Rebekkah embraced her. "I'll miss you, Sarah. And Joseph, of course, too, but especially you. There will be little lighthearted spirit at the farm when you go."

"What about the boy Antiochus? You told me that he's quick at learning and at laughing, too."

"A not-so-small surprise for Joseph is in the works. I've been up to my old bad habits and conspiring with the young. Now that there are the trained slaves to care for Joshua, Antiochus has run away, with my aid and blessing. He'll be waiting for you at Caesarea."

"Joseph will be furious."

"He'll get over it." Rebekkah smiled. "You can see to that."

CHAPTER TWENTY-THREE

AS SOON AS THEY PASSED THROUGH THE GATE INTO THE streets of Caesarea, Sarah started looking for the boy Antiochus. She saw the clean, white, breathtaking beauty of Herod's city, but not the impudent bright face of the boy.

When they reached the harbor, she exclaimed about its magnificence again and again. "That's exactly what I felt when I saw it for the first time," Joseph agreed. "And I feel it anew each time I return. It is so perfect, I have even wondered if I dreamed it, if it is unreal." He smiled into Sarah's eyes.

"But we both know that I don't have enough imagination to invent all this, so I have to believe that it's really here."

Sarah returned his smile. But she was wondering where a gangly, determined and clever boy would be.

He was not on the ship, and none of the crew had seen anyone like her description, so she asked them not to mention her questions to Joseph. He'd become worried, probably, and go to Arimathea to make sure Antiochus was safe. There was no time for that.

Also, Sarah knew the boy much better than Joseph did. She was certain he was all right. He knew the dangers of the world only too well; he would have avoided them.

Probably he had changed his mind when he realized how angry Joseph would be. He would not risk the wrath of his hero. No doubt he had stayed at the farm, or had started out, then turned back.

Sarah was glad. She didn't want Joseph to turn against Antiochus.

But she was disappointed, too. It would have been fun to have Rebekkah's lively young protégé with them in Belerion. He'd probably learn the language and everything about the place and the names and histories of every single person there—all within three days. He had already mastered Greek, Latin, Aramaic, and Arabic in the schoolroom.

Well, he wasn't in Caesarea, and that was that. She could concentrate on enjoying herself and the adventure that would begin so soon.

Joseph rushed from one necessary piece of business to the next, with Sarah in tow. For the first time she fully realized how demanding his business life was. And why it excited him so. His activities ranged from the minutia of examining the clay amphorae of olive oil stowed on the *Eagle,* looking for cracks that would permit unseen leakage, to the major decisions—made in an instant—about the next year's routes and cargoes for his three other ships. The *Eagle* would be sailing to Belerion, of course, for tin and to bring Joseph and Sarah home.

He talked at length with the men who were building the luxury galley and went over every inch of the work already done. Then he let Sarah select the silks and linens for covering cushions and couches. She could happily have spent hours doing it. The colors and textures and designs were more varied and more luxurious than anything she'd ever seen. But she could feel the energy surging from Joseph, the effort he had to make to keep himself from pressuring her to hurry. So she mimicked what she had seen him doing. "That one," she said briskly, "and that trim for the edges. Then three of the blues—no, the one beneath the one you're holding—and that deep copper color, two cushions in that . . ."

Privately she promised herself a whole day at the cloth merchants when they returned. Just touching.

She went alone to the house of Rabbi Isaac and introduced herself to the family. His son's marriage was going to take place the day before sailing, and she would meet the other families there.

Isaac's wife Rachel took Sarah aside and confided a special secret wish. "My only sorrow is that I have to leave my pomegranate tree," she whispered. "I planted the seed the day we moved into this house, and I think of it almost like another child. Could I take a small jar of cuttings, do you think? Will there be water enough to keep them living? Will there be room enough for them? Will they take root in this new land?"

Sarah had already seen the arrangements on the *Eagle*. Rolled up mats and blankets that could be spread on the curved bottom of the cargo hold for sleeping, the same for the deck. Every possible space was filled with food and drink for the voyage, and the sanitary facilities were nothing more than a curtained-off area at the back of the rowing deck.

There isn't room for a pomegranate seed, never mind cuttings, she thought, and who can say what the climate in Belerion will be like? But she assured Rachel that the cuttings would survive the voyage and would thrive in the garden of her home there.

Why not be optimistic? Sarah said to herself. These settlers are the bravest people I've ever heard of, and they have a terrifying journey ahead of them.

So do I, for that matter. If the mixture I got from the herb woman doesn't work, I don't know what I'll do . . . I'll just have to be optimistic.

She looked at the men setting up the wedding tent, next to the pomegranate tree in the garden. I'm going to have Joseph for six whole months, Sarah thought. Her smile was so beautiful that people turned to look at her on the street, but she didn't notice. She was remembering everything

Joseph had told her about Belerion. The land of the blue men, she still called it to herself.

Joseph had arranged more comfortable accommodations for his wife than the ones for the settlers. Behind the steering box a snug tent now stood, firmly bolted to the deck, with side flaps for privacy and protection from the cold winds and possible rains.

"I have a wonderful idea," Sarah told Joseph. "Instead of that drab hostel, let's spend these last two nights on the *Eagle*."

"But, Sarah, even in harbor the ship will still have some motion to it."

"How dense you can be sometimes, Joseph of Arimathea! I saw the tent for tomorrow's wedding at the rabbi's house. Don't you understand? It made me feel like a bride again."

"The seasick bride," Joseph said, teasing her. "It's a delectable idea if you promise not to turn green."

"Joseph!"

He put his arms around her, tight. "I feel like a groom," he said into Sarah's ear. "Let's go to the *Eagle* now."

The wedding of David ben Isaac to his Sarah was both joyful and tearful. There were goodbyes to be said alongside the congratulations.

Joseph and Sarah slipped away as soon as they could. There was much to be done to ready the *Eagle* still, and they wanted their final night of privacy together to be unhurried and rich with love.

It was also gladdened with laughter. "I am quite certain that there is a herd of wheeled sheep massing for an assault on my spine," Joseph mentioned at a crucial moment. The playthings were stowed in the corners of the tent. There was no room for them in the hold.

Antiochus appeared on the fourth day out. He showed up at Joseph's elbow, with a bowl of warm water, a towel, and shaving supplies. "Good morning, Master," he said. "A beautiful day, a calm sea, and a following wind. Everything is perfect. Are you ready for your shave?"

When Joseph recovered from his shock, he scolded the boy, raving and threatening terrible things. The Caesarea Jews, who were sitting fearfully on deck, were too frightened to take in the beauty of the skies and waters, and considered the movement of the ship a proof that the sea was anything but calm. Their fears were doubled by Joseph's fury, and mothers gathered their children closely around them.

But eventually Joseph began to laugh. Then he tousled Antiochus' thick curly hair. "You scamp," he said fondly, "I think I should put you to work in the galley again. That's what I had to do when I ran away to sea at your age."

"If I might remind you, Master, I break kitchen objects. I'm much more skillful with a razor."

"We'll go to the tent, then. Sarah will be glad to see you, I suppose."

"I've already seen her, and she is. She gave me your shaving things."

The voyage was smoother than Joseph and the crew had dared hope. Nonetheless, many of the people from Caesarea were sick most of the time, and all of them were frightened. Small screams and large moans were constant, and friction among the overcrowded grew every day.

Sarah was not seasick; the herb mix she'd brought with her was successful. Unfortunately, it also gave her an unremitting ache in every bone in her body. She moved slowly, stiffly, and as seldom as possible. Often she had to lean on Antiochus.

"Not a happy ship," Milcar commented to Joseph. "But it does mean that the oarsmen are willing to exert themselves beyond anything they've ever done before. I don't know if you planned it this way, Joseph, but you have brilliantly succeeded in making all of us anticipate the return voyage with joy, even knowing that the seas and skies are certain to be stormy." The Phoenician captain's deep-chested laughter made even Sarah feel better. Antiochus tried to imitate it. He was trying to learn how to be a ship's captain. Oarsman or crewman wasn't good enough for him, he said. He preferred to aim high. Joseph tried to swat him, but the boy skittered easily out of reach. His sea legs were better than even the most experienced sailor's.

Joseph dug into the stacked, lashed baskets of toys, causing a collapse that covered the deck area of the tent. "It doesn't matter," he said when he saw Sarah's consternation. "We are nearly there. See—look to your right, far over. That's smoke rising to make that cloud. It's the cliffs of Gaul, and the Veneti are signaling to the Dumnoni. Come to the bow, my love, and watch how the hill called Itkis will suddenly be there, ahead of us." He held up the shiny toy trumpet he'd found. "I will signal success to our poor, miserable passengers."

He stepped between the huddled, unhappy families that crowded the deck in daylight hours and stood by the curved prow with the Arimathea eagle. Sarah followed, slowly, and settled into the protection of his left arm.

The biting wind made her eyes water. She wiped them on her sleeve and strained to see.

Then Joseph blew hard into the little trumpet, making dissonant inadequate noises that were, even though pitifully weak, filled with the excitement he was feeling. Antiochus ran forward to join them.

And, all of a sudden, the hill was there. It was green. The scent of earth and of growing things filled the wind and surrounded the people like a blessing and a promise.

Isaac stood, his arms raised to heaven and began to sing a psalm of thanksgiving, called "A Joyful Noise."

"O come, let us sing to the Lord
Let us make a joyful noise
to the rock of our salvation!

Let us come into His presence
with thanksgiving;
Let us make a joyful noise
to Him with songs of praise!
For the Lord is a Great God,
and a great King above all gods.
In His hands are the depths
of the earth;
the heights of the mountains
are His also.
The sea is His, for He made it,
and the dry land,
which His hands have formed.
O come, let us worship
and bow down,
let us kneel before the
Lord, our Maker!
For He is our God,
and we are the
people of His pasture,
and the sheep of His hand."

They knelt, all the men and women and children. They
were pale and drawn and trembling. Tears covered their up-
lifted faces, as they looked at this unknown land, and
smelled its richness, and praised their God for His mercy.

Sarah knelt, too, and Joseph beside her. He took her
small hand in his hand and held it tight.

Antiochus stood behind them. His eager, curious gaze
was scanning the wonders ahead.

The tide was still high enough for the oarsman to bring
the *Eagle* close to the seaward beach of the great hill. The
loud rattle of the anchor chain sent a burst of white seabirds
up into the sky to circle overhead. When the gangplank was
laid, Antiochus was the first to race down onto the sands.
He began leaping, turning cartwheels, collapsing with cries

of surprise onto the white beach. The older boy travelers were right behind him, scampering and stumbling. They were discovering the disconcerting phenomenon of sea travel: When the movement of the deck is left behind, the land attained feels as if it is moving, and the legs become unsteady on the firm earth beneath them.

Joseph stood at the top of the gangplank. He warned each passenger to expect the sensation, and he reminded them all of the word he had taught them, in the language of the Dumnoni:

"Friend."

The men and women were laughing giddily. At the antics of the boys, from relief that the voyage was over, because of the fear of the unknown that they feared to express aloud. While they moved restlessly, gathering the few goods they'd been permitted to bring along, Antiochus ran back up the gangplank.

"Please forgive me," he said to Joseph. "I lost my head. What shall I do to be useful?"

"Keep those boys in sight. Their parents have enough to worry about without thinking they've lost a son."

Antiochus looked at the crowd on deck. The ten families from Caesarea had eighteen children among them, and eight of them were under five years old. "Why don't I make those five come back and help their mothers?" Antiochus gestured toward the capering boys on the beach.

"Good idea. If you can manage it."

In less than a half hour all the families were on the beach, with their possessions. Sarah was there, too, as excited as they were. She waved eagerly at Joseph, urging him to join them.

"Round up the crew, Milcar," Joseph told his ship's captain. "Tell them to bring the wine. I'm sure the mead is ready and waiting."

"I think you'd better go without us, Joseph. The tide has

turned, and we'll have to row out to a deeper anchorage. I want the men to get the *Eagle* cleaned and ready to load the cargo, too. We don't have time to waste on jollity and hangovers when we have the season of storms at our shoulders."

As if to reinforce the Phoenician's statement, a thin misty rain began to fall.

"Give me two men to carry the wine. Our passengers will have need of it. After the wine is in the village, the men can return with a sheep. You'll want to make your sacrifice of arrival."

"Tell them to bring two. I'll want to make another one when we sail, to ask the gods' protection."

"Done. I'll join Sarah and the others now. Send the wine bearers after me."

A thousand questions met him on the beach. "We have only a short way still to go," Joseph said, not answering. "There will be time aplenty for your questions after we reach the village of the Celts. Remember the word you have learned. It's the only one you need to say."

He smiled, pointed to himself and repeated the word, in the language of Belerion. "Friend."

"Friend," the families chorused.

"Very good. Now follow me." Joseph took Sarah's hand and began the long walk to the opposite side of Itkis. He walked slowly so that the families could match his pace. He wished that the rain would stop. This wasn't the best way to encourage the settlers.

When the straggling, stumbling men and women and children were past the island hill's halfway point, the mainland came into view. And the showers moved on. The cliffs, their rushing streams, trees, flowers, all were softened by the thin mist left behind by the rain. The Caesarea travelers began to point and to talk excitedly.

Joseph felt a great deal better. "Come on," he called to them. "We have a way to walk yet."

Sarah squeezed his hand. "You told me, Joseph, but it's

even greener and more beautiful than you said. I'm so happy I want to run and dance."

"We will, my love. Every day. Ten times a day, if you want. But we've got to get there first. Let's keep walking."

At first Joseph didn't notice the change in the voices behind him. Not until he heard a woman cry out in the ancient, thin, high sound of grief and mourning.

He turned to hasten back and learn what had happened. A fall? A child lost? What could it be? Everything was working well; they had nearly completed the long half-circuit of Itkis. The mainland was near.

Suddenly he remembered. What a fool he was. He'd forgotten to tell them about the causeway and the tide. To the worn-out, anxious Jews it must look as though they'd have to swim a half mile to Belerion.

Just before he reached David and his bride, who led the group of families, Joseph heard another cry, a shout of jubilation.

"Hosanna!"

It was the voice of Rabbi Isaac. He was pointing. "Hosanna!" he shouted again.

Joseph stopped running. He knew everything would be all right now. The fast-ebbing tide was performing its marvel. Joseph turned back toward Sarah. He had promised her that they would be together for her first viewing of the sand bridge's appearance from beneath the waves.

They were all shouting now, the voyagers from Judea. And running. Up to the place Joseph stood with Sarah and past it, to the rapidly widening path of shimmering wet sand.

People knelt to touch it; some knelt to thank the Lord. They thought they were witnessing a miracle.

Sarah pulled on Joseph's arm. "Look," she said. "Oh, Joseph, look."

His eyes followed the direction of her gaze. Above the

land of Belerion, out of the soft colorless mist, a rainbow was taking form.

"The Lord's blessing is on this unknown place," cried Isaac. "See His covenant of the radiant arch in the heavens! Come, my brethren, let us enter with a song of praise on our lips." His strong voice was vibrant with reverent joy as he sang. The others joined in.

And they walked between the waters of the sea to the green hills that were to be their new home.

CHAPTER TWENTY-FOUR

"ISAAC, THAT WAS NOT THE PARTING OF THE RED SEA," Joseph said. Patiently, he hoped. The rabbi was wearing his patience thin. "There was no miracle. The tide has exposed that path and then later covered it, time after time, day after day, for as long as men have been here to see it."

Isaac refused to agree with him. He smiled. And patted Joseph's arm. "Once more only I will tell you, Joseph. No man—not you and not me and not the headman of this village—can know that the Lord God did not plan, when He created the world, to make a way between the waters so that when we came, we would feel His care for us. And see His hand in all his works."

Isaac's patience was boundless, like his faith. Joseph surrendered.

But when the long day was done, and he was alone with Sarah, he went over the whole thing again. "I couldn't make the rabbi see reason," Joseph complained, "so I gave up."

Sarah's laughter was rich with love. "My poor businessman Joseph. You can't accept anything you can't understand." She kissed the frown from his forehead.

"Myself, I like seeing the Lord's hand at work in things

that I don't understand. It comforts me. Like the strangeness of the language and Antiochus. Who would ever have
thought that the people in the land of his birth would share
the blood of the people in Belerion? Galatia is so very far
from here.

"And yet, when he heard them speaking, he knew so
much of what they were saying. They were the words of his
early years, before he was sold into slavery."

She nestled closer to Joseph, and now her forehead was
wrinkled. "What I cannot bear is that the word you taught
him was a word he didn't know at all. 'Friend.' He had
never heard that before. I hate the pain he grew up with."

Joseph smoothed away the wrinkles with his thumbs.
Then his fingers pushed through her thick unbound hair to
cup her head and bring her mouth to meet his. "We can
shut out the world, my sparrow. While we are together. I
love you."

"And I, you, my love." Her arms closed behind his
shoulders.

The months that followed—a full half year—were like a
continuous idyll of happiness and love and beauty for them.
Sarah and Joseph would remember it for the rest of their
lives by their secret name for it: "The Magic Time."

They were together more than ever before, even in
their childhood. Both were busy, sometimes together,
more often separately, but even so, there were opportunities for long walks, exploring the beauties of Belerion,
watching the majestic power of the sea waves crashing
with jets of foam and roaring sound at the base of
windswept cliffs, discovering colonies of tiny flowers
and shrubs in protected pockets, even on the shortest,
coldest, days.

And when darkness fell, they had their private sanctuary,
a round stone hut, built for them by the Dumnoni. There
they could exchange stories of their experiences when they

were apart, and share the ever-growing love of their hearts
and bodies.

There was a big stone hut, ten times bigger than Joseph's
and Sarah's, where the Dumnoni were accustomed to shelter their horses and oxen and cattle in winter. The building
had been scoured clean, whitewashed inside and out, and
rethatched by the villagers. When the *Eagle* arrived, its passengers were given the shelter to live in until their own
homes were built.

It was there—on the very day of their arrival—that
Joseph poured wine for all of the men and women, Celts
and Jews, and Sarah gave out playthings to all the children.

The yelling, laughing, games, and the din of toy trumpets
and cymbals and whistles made all the adults cover their
ears, in a communication that needed no language. The
children had no use for words at that moment. They were
too busy throwing balls or making noise.

After a while, flaxen-haired women brought in massive
quantities of food and drink—mead, milk, water flavored
with herbs. They gestured to the stacks of straw-filled mat-
tresses along the walls, made gestures of eating, yawning
then closing the eyes in sleep.

The tired travelers showed their thanks by clasping their
hands together and bowing to their benefactors, with smiles
and nods and the word "friend."

"Friend" repeated the Celtic women. Then they gathered
their men and their children and left the Jews to feast and to
rest.

Joseph was delighted when he saw Nancledra, the young
man who was studying to be a priest, his interpreter from
the first visit he'd made to Belerion. He greeted Nancledra
with a grin and the salutation the young Celt had taught
him.

"Sennen!" Nancledra's smile was as wide as Joseph's,
and he corrected Joseph's pronunciation just as he'd done

dozens of times before. It pleased Joseph to remember, and to hear again the name the Dumnoni had given him. "Mustard."

He switched to Greek; he wanted to talk. Was Nancledra going to stay in the village and translate for the passengers from the *Eagle*?

Yes was the answer. And no. Nancledra was to be in charge of the school for the Jewish children. He had four students for the priesthood as assistants. They would serve as day-to-day interpreters.

"Our weeks together took place four years ago, Sennen," he said. "I have progressed in my studies in that time. I have passed the tests, and I am a Bard now."

"I congratulate you, my friend. And I am very happy to see you again. My wife is with me; I want you to meet her."

Nancledra was eager to do so, he said. But he had to be at the school; he was on his way to the building now. Sennen could be helpful to him by telling his countrymen where their children should go. Themselves, too, if they wished, and their wives.

Joseph went to the big round building at once. The interpreters were already there. Also Gawethin, the chief of the Dumnoni, and his wife. The enterprise was under way.

During the winter months the mild climate made it easy to work outside. The men from Caesarea, with willing, experienced help from the men of the village, built stone-walled houses of their own.

They were different from the circle huts of the Celts. The influence of Caesarea was very apparent to Joseph. The houses were oval, not round, with a wall enclosing house, workshop, and stable around a courtyard. Each family had one, larger or smaller according to individual needs, and the houses lined a paved street. It was a village of its own, and in the center was a special building, smaller than the others and lacking a courtyard, but the product of the most careful attention of all the craftsmen.

As part of the celebration of the Feast of Lights in December, the Jewish colony dedicated their synagogue.

"I can be sure now that my crazy idea is going to work," Joseph said to Sarah. "Soon the fields will be ready to plow, and the Dumnoni have already started telling and showing the settlers where they will have land, plus what to plant and how to plant it. Many of the crops are the same as those of Judea. Barley, wheat, lentils, peas—everyone knows them.

"The language learning is going well—Antiochus is in on every single thing that's gone on, and he's better than the best of the interpreters."

"The children are inventing their own mixture of all the languages," Sarah added. "It confuses poor Nancledra no end, but he manages very well. He really cares for them."

"And for you," Joseph teased. It was true, and he was glad about it. Sarah went often to the school. After language lessons Nancledra was teaching her to play the harp.

Not one of the Jerusalem toys; he had given her one of the beautiful lyre-like instruments that the Druid Bards used for making their complex, ethereal music.

It was a difficult instrument, and the music was more so. But Joseph didn't mind the dissonances and interminable repetitions of short phrases in Sarah's hours of practice in their house. She'd said when they were buying the toys that she had wanted all her life to learn to play. Joseph wanted her to have everything she had ever longed for.

Perhaps—in some small way—the harp might make up for her sorrow that she had not yet conceived a child, not even in this magic time together.

However, there were still four months of intimacy in this special land before the *Eagle* returned to take them away. There was every reason to hope.

They didn't talk about it. Neither wanted to cause the

other pain. About everything else in their minds and hearts, they could be totally open to each other, and they were. It added to the oneness that made the magic.

Gawethin was the Dumnoni chief, and he regarded Sennen as the chief of the Jews, no matter how often Joseph tried to correct him. In mid-January he sought a meeting to talk about tin. Antiochus begged to be the interpreter, and the two men indulged him. "Provided," Joseph said sternly, "that you do not interrupt, make suggestions, or tell us when you consider our decisions to be wrong."

Gawethin hid his smile. So did Joseph. The Galatian boy had become a favorite of everyone's.

"My people have always taken the tin from the streams," Gawethin began, "regarding it as a gift from the goddesses of the earth and the waters. Your people, if I understand what you said last year, will be looking for other ways to gather the metal. I am concerned that disharmony between our peoples might result."

They agreed that any disagreements or misunderstandings would be a terrible thing. In the short time the Jews had been in Belerion, a remarkable synthesis had occurred. Men worked together on the buildings, women exchanged the age-old stories of childbirth, methods of cooking, secrets of soothing cranky children, and husbands.

Caesarea's women had seized upon many of the practices of the women of Belerion. They dressed in the brightly colored, patterned, woven wool and linen dresses, because they were both prettier and more comfortable than the tunics and cloaks they'd always worn. They wore their hair plaited, too, like the Celts. And they had begun to collect some few pieces of the beautiful bronze jewelry that Belerion's women adorned themselves with in such profusion.

The women of the Dumnoni were generous with possessions and advice. In their society women were fully equal in importance and power to the men, and they urged the Jewish women to demand the same from their men.

Wisely, the women from Caesarea replied that nothing could be hurried. But they liked what they saw and heard. They kept their men in contented ignorance.

The male Jews were in general much more conservative than their wives and daughters and sisters. Most of them refused to adopt the Celts' trousers. But they did buy the Belerion wool for their cloaks. Jerusalem was famous for the woolen textiles produced there, but they were much thinner and less durable than the thick plaids and sturdy tweeds of Belerion.

So far, everything was proceeding more easily and more successfully than Joseph had dared hope. He listened closely to Gawethin's words. He didn't want things to turn sour.

"We Celts believe that water is sacred and that stone—because it is the oldest thing we know—must be honored and reverenced. If this tin search and gathering will change the waters and stones, it may be an offense to our gods. I am not wise enough to know about these things. Therefore, I have sent word to the Druids. They are our wise men, our keepers of the law, and our interpreters of the wishes of the gods. They will tell us what to do. Until the priests arrive, I must have your guarantee that nothing will be done with regard to the tin."

Joseph gave his promise.

"I hope these Druids won't be too long in coming," he said to Sarah. "I want a new and better method to be in operation before I leave."

She poured mead into a cup and passed it to him. "I'm sure they won't be long," she said. "They communicate by signal fires from the hilltops; that's much faster than a messenger."

Joseph drank deep. He smiled when he felt his knees weaken a bit. "Nancledra tells you much more than he ever told me when I was with him every day. He made me think everything about the Druids was a secret."

"He hadn't passed his tests yet when you were here before. Maybe he didn't know anything himself. And I believe there's still a lot he doesn't know."

Sarah told Joseph the little she had learned from Nancledra. The best, brightest, bravest of the Celts often aspired to become Druids, because it was the wisest, most respected caste in their society. Not only on the island that included Belerion, but throughout many countries in the Roman Empire.

The studies began when the aspirants were very young. They were both boys and girls, and the rigorous training was the same for all of them. For twelve years, every day of the year, they studied all the languages of the world and its history. They also learned music, the performance and creation of it, and astronomy. Everything was memorized. There were no scrolls to remind anyone of forgotten facts.

Many students withdrew. Some could not meet the demands of the teachers and were dismissed. Those who persevered and were successful went on to learn the sagas that recounted the long history of the Druids and the stories of their gods. Then they were permitted to learn the laws by which Druids governed and judged all the Celts of all the lands.

Nancledra had passed the tests of his knowledge only the summer before. Now he would study medicine. Druids were famous for their medicines, created from the 365 herbs they had long ago identified, classified, and ascertained which, or which blending of them, was best for various illnesses and conditions.

If Nancledra learned all that—plus how to repair damages and fractures and how to perform surgery—in the three years of instruction that would be given him, then he would be eligible to attempt the three-year program that followed.

Those years were devoted to reading omens and foretelling the future from them. Plus the performance of Druid magic.

"Nancledra couldn't, or wouldn't, tell me what kind of thing he meant by 'magic,'" Sarah said with a shrug. "And I'm sure he was telling the truth when he said that if he learned all that he was taught and never lost a single piece of what he learned in all those years, then he would be allowed to continue his instruction into the highest rank, the Druid priest. He doesn't know what that instruction might be, or what the final tests for initiation are. He does know it's all very frightening. He turned white as sea foam when he was talking about it.

"Right now Nancledra is a Bard. That means he has completed those twelve years and passed whatever the tests are." Sarah smiled. "It also means he's a very good music teacher. I'm very lucky to know him."

She refilled Joseph's cup. "Now you know as much as I do. It isn't much. Nancledra was pleased to tell me he had learned history and music and languages and law, but he didn't tell me any details of what he'd learned. It's clearly much more than how to play the harp."

Joseph swirled the mead in his cup. "You do realize that you're getting me drunk, Sarah."

"Not drunk, my love, just relaxed and interested in making love."

Joseph set the cup on the floor and opened his arms to his wife. "I don't have to drink mead for that. Come, let's go to bed."

Sarah agreed with enthusiasm. And when they were joined together in their own magic of love, she was able to forget her guilt about the one careful omission in her report on the Druids: Nancledra was going to get her some of their medicine to cure barrenness and give her a child.

Many miles away a Druid called Dinasa was measuring precise amounts of ground, powdered herbs and dropping them in a particular sequence into a bronze cup that held water from a sacred well. Dinasa was a Druid priestess, a woman of astonishing fair beauty, thirty-one years old.

She sang secret incantations as she brewed the mixture.

This was not the medicine for Sarah that she was making. That was finished, in powdered form, and sealed in a container carved from the wood of a rowan tree.

The liquid mixture was ready now. Dinasa seated herself in a grassy glade that was bathed in moonlight. She sang to the stars, and the moon, and the shining waters of a nearby pool, and then she drained the cup. In moments, the trance of prophecy stiffened her strong, graceful body and turned her eyes into gleaming blankness.

While she saw, in her mind, the love between Sarah and Joseph, her pale skin seemed to take on the radiance of the skies above her. She saw visions of their future, experienced the joys and pains, raptures and agonies. Before the visions were completed, Dinasa cried aloud and fell, senseless, onto the ground. Her mind and spirit could sustain no more.

When she recovered from the trance, she was too weak to move. She lay still for hours, until the rising sun warmed her and strengthened her. Then she made her way to the five Druids who waited nearby.

"The signal to Nancledra must say that the future did not reveal itself," she told them. "He is not yet one of us, and he cannot know the mysteries that came to me. He must be content with the potion I will take to the woman."

CHAPTER TWENTY-FIVE

IT WAS ONLY FOUR DAYS AFTER JOSEPH'S MEETING WITH Gawethin that three Druids arrived. All the Dumnoni were excited when they walked down from the crag above the village. The Jews were apprehensive and confused. These were not translators who were students of some pagan lore. These were the priests of that paganism. And one of them was a woman.

The day before had been the Sabbath. After the readings and the sermon and the psalms, Joseph had addressed the people. He told them about his meeting with the Dumnoni chief and the reason Gawethin had given for a delay in doing anything about the tin.

"Priests of the Celtic gods will determine what can and cannot be done. I know what your feelings must be about these pagans, but we will all have to be respectful of them. Remember: They do not worship idols, they worship the creations of the One God. Sun, moon, water, stone, trees—the Lord God made them all.

"The Celts are not enemies; you have already seen that. Their gods and their priests must not be reviled, or the Celts will become enemies."

"How was that?" Joseph asked Rabbi Isaac later.

"Not bad. I will go myself as representative of our people to meet these Druids. That will prevent confrontation."

"Thank you, Rabbi."

"Pray for all of us."

The possibilities that worried Joseph most turned out to be nonexistent. He and Gawethin climbed with the two male Druids along the course of each tin-speckled stream to its source in the granite hills. Joseph knew everything would be all right when the Druids needed no consultation to declare that it would be no violation of the ancient rock to widen the fissure from which the stream issued.

He asked them then about the tin, and they actually laughed. If men wanted more of it to be carried down by the waters, of course they could hack or gouge it from its heavy, visible concentrations—if they were so eager that they preferred to make the arduous climb instead of waiting for the generosity of the waters to bring it to them. Obviously the priest did not believe in unnecessary effort. Except, Joseph thought to himself, the effort of memorizing something that could easily be preserved in written form.

"Some other person might have carried away the manuscript you wished to read," commented the elder Druid. Joseph lost his footing and nearly fell. He had often teased Sarah about reading his mind, but he had never considered the possibility that a stranger might do so.

His manner was respectful and absolutely forthright when he described the system of sluices and woven reed sieves he wanted to install in the streams.

That did require consultation.

And then many questions. Would the path the waters had chosen be changed? Would the movement of the waters be delayed? Accelerated? What were the dangers of fouling the purity of the waters? The Druids had to repeat the questions at each of the streams, and at various places in each of the courses of descent.

While the men were in the hills, the Druid priestess Dinasa was with Sarah inside the circle hut that was home for her and Joseph. Dinasa spoke Aramaic perfectly and adjusted her accent to match Sarah's as they were talking. She asked Sarah about the history of her attempts to have a baby. The questions were so intimate that Sarah was embarrassed. But she wanted a baby so desperately that she answered them with all the details that the priestess demanded.

When the ordeal was completed, Dinasa smiled for the first time. Sarah was shocked by the difference in the Druid's appearance. Why, she was really lovely. And friendly, not intimidating at all.

"You've been wholly truthful, despite the difficulty it gave you," said Dinasa. Her voice was warm with approval. "You couldn't know this, Sarah, but for Druids, truth is the essence of good, the ultimate goal of our seeking for knowledge. I am grateful for the privilege of knowing you."

Sarah shook her head. "Thank you, but you should know that lots of times I'm not truthful at all. My husband doesn't know I asked Nancledra to get me the medicine."

"Would he object?"

"I don't know. I was afraid to ask him if he approved because he might say no."

Dinasa made no comment on the Celtic woman's very different view on the rights of a husband to control his wife's actions. A small smile quivered on her lips at the idea that her own husband might even consider such an absurdity.

"Sarah, what will happen next will be even more difficult for you than my questions," she said. "I am going to examine your birth canal and womb with my hand. I will give you a medical concentrate of herbs to drink, to relax the contractions that might limit access. While it is taking effect, I'll wash my hands and arms, and you will remove your clothing."

Dinasa was correct. The physical examination was a hundred—a thousand—times more upsetting than the questioning.

But when it was over, Dinasa said, "There is no reason why you cannot have a child." And Sarah felt such happiness that the examination began to feel like a blessing. Her smile was radiant while she listened to Dinasa's instructions about the herbal medicine.

Then the priestess said, "Your husband's seed may be the cause of your childlessness, of course. Some men have very weak seed."

That was worse than Sarah's worst nightmares. She refused to believe it. Still, a tiny doubt had been planted.

That night, when they made love, Sarah embraced Joseph with more tenderness than passion. What the Druid had said could not possibly be true, but if there was even a chance of such a thing, she wanted to comfort him.

Joseph had become very good at understanding the language of the Celts, though he still had much trouble speaking it. But now Gawethin was so overcome with excitement that Joseph couldn't make sense of what the Dumnoni chief was trying to tell him.

"Antiochus," Joseph shouted. "Come here. I need you."

When the boy heard what Gawethin was saying, he got so excited himself that his translation was hard to comprehend. Finally Joseph made sense of it: On February 1, ten days hence, the Celts would be celebrating their yearly festival called Imbolc, the lambing. And the triad of Druids were going to remain in the village until then, to perform the special rites that only Druids could perform. Belerion was so distant and so isolated from the other regions of Albion, the great island on which they lived, that the Dumnoni always celebrated without the rites. Gawethin had never in his life had the opportunity to witness them. Indeed, there was only one man in the village who'd ever been so privileged. He had seen them in Gaul, when he was but a boy. And now he was a very old man.

"That sounds very exciting, Gawethin," said Joseph. "I'll tell my countrymen, and learn how many will be there."

"No, Sennen! No! No!" Joseph had no difficulty understanding what Gawethin was saying now. "Outsiders are forbidden at Druid rituals. They can be punished by death."

Joseph promised that they would all stay in the village, in their houses if necessary. He thought about the warnings in the Temple's Court of the Gentiles. It promised death to any non-Jew who entered the sacred precincts beyond the Beautiful Gate that opened to the Court of Women.

Rabbi Isaac was telling the Druid called Pelynt about that warning at the same time that Joseph thought of it.

"Therefore, you need have no concern about any intrusion by any of us. We understand that priestly rites cannot be witnessed by the curious."

They were in Gawethin's circle hut. The chief and his family had moved out, so the priests could stay there. Isaac had presented himself there, as formal representative of the Jews, expecting a formal exchange of greetings, perhaps, not much more. Instead, he was enjoying himself immensely, with a cup of excellent wine in his hand, instead of the potent, sour-tasting mead, and an interesting companion who had a never-ending supply of fascinating stories and a lot of intriguing information.

The wine was a good example. Pelynt told Isaac that it wouldn't be difficult at all to obtain regularly delivered supplies. There was a steady trade between Gaul and the part of Albion to the east of Belerion. "We sell Gaul woolens and metals and horses—you won't see them here in Belerion, but we breed horses, and ponies, that are the envy of the rest of the world—and we buy from them wines and goods brought from the ends of the earth, like spices. You will discover that peddlers show up with all manner of foreign things when the days become longer and less chill."

The Druid also gave Isaac an amazing view of the society of the Celts. They were still widespread, living in many lands. But at one time they had covered territories that extended all the way around much of the Mediterranean Sea. Four hundred years before, Celtic warriors had conquered Rome and had been bribed to retreat. "We say now that we should have destroyed totally the small city-state that was Rome at that time. Most of Roman growth to an Empire consisted of conquering and subjugating Celtic tribes. The Romans are the world's doom."

Isaac was wholehearted in his agreement. It was because of Roman oppression and taxation, through their puppet king, that he and his fellow Jews had left the land of their fathers to come to Belerion.

Pelynt was intrigued by Isaac's account of the Law of Moses. He had heard of the invisible One God of the Jews; most educated men knew about the extraordinary concept and the Jews' adamant adherence to it, in far-flung places as well as in their homeland, and against powerful pressures, even if the result was death.

"Do I understand you correctly, Rabbi? As a nation and a people you are ruled by religious law alone?"

"In our hearts and in our homes, yes. But our oppressors inflict their laws on us as well."

"Setting aside the Romans, do you have, in your Law, rules to cover every possible occasion?"

Isaac nodded with solemn pride. Then a wide white smile gleamed within his thick dark beard. "Your stories have both entertained and instructed me mightily," he said. "Now I give one of our stories in return.

"We have a tradition of examining our Law so closely that men of learning can debate the fullest meaning or the deepest meaning of even one word for hours, or weeks, or their whole lifetimes. At the present time two of our notable teachers of the Law are men named Shammai and Hillel. Frequently they differ about the meaning they find.

"Now . . . it is said that a Gentile one day went to the Temple, to the place where students gathered around these teachers. 'I will convert to Judaism,' he said to Shammai, 'if you can teach me the Law during the period that I can stand on one leg.' Shammai was insulted by the man's blasphemous frivolity; he hit him with his staff and drove him away."

Isaac smiled at his attentive Druid companion. Pelynt was nodding his head in silent agreement.

"So then," said the rabbi, "the Gentile went to Hillel. He took one foot in his hand and made the same challenge, standing on one leg. Hillel answered him at once. 'What is hateful to you, do not do it unto your neighbor,' he said. 'That is the whole of the Torah, the five books of the Law. All else is commentary.'" Isaac chuckled mightily, rocking back and forth with delight at the wit of Hillel and the consternation that he imagined for the impious Gentile.

Pelynt laughed with him. "I should very much like to know your Hillel. I have several Shammai as acquaintances." He lifted the wine pitcher and filled Isaac's cup and his own. "Let us salute him, Hillel."

Later, when Isaac had returned to his house and the other Druids had joined Pelynt in Gawethin's circle hut, Pelynt reported on the investigation he'd made.

"We do not have to kill these newcomers. They are no threat."

The Celts' celebration of spring called "the lambing" was over. So was the Jews' celebration of Passover. The tin extraction, and collection, and smelting, and shaping was in full, efficient operation, with impressive production. It was the month of April, and Belerion was a land of sweet, gentle air perfumed by the flowers that carpeted the hills and by the tang of salt from the sea.

Sarah had never known such beauty.

Or such happiness. Joseph's work was done, and he could be with her all the hours of the day and the night. Until the *Eagle* came for them in May, at least.

She knew piercing sorrow, too. The planned six-month stay was nearing its end, and there was no baby, even though she had faithfully taken the herbal medicine daily.

Also, she could feel Joseph's growing restlessness, even though he was as yet unaware of it himself. When he accomplished what he had set out to do, he needed to discover some new challenge. Sarah knew that, had always known that.

Even so, she could not stop herself from trying to change things. Or, at least, postpone the inevitable.

One day, when white seabirds seemed to be playing high-spirited, singing, salute-to-spring games among the small, scudding, fluffy white clouds, Sarah carried her harp along on the walk she and Joseph were taking. She had, she told him, a special place to show him, and a song to go with it.

"Can there be a place we haven't already visited together? Have you been keeping secrets from me, my sparrow?"

"Stop teasing, Joseph. This is something Nancledra showed me. And a song he taught me, so that I could sing it in this place. He did it so that I could make a gift of it to you."

They didn't have far to go. When they got there, Joseph saw immediately what Sarah meant. They were in a narrow cove below the high rocky cliff that rose abruptly from the small area of sand to tower darkly against the blue, blue sky.

But the stark rock he knew was no longer dark and forbidding. Spring warmth and misty showers had brought it to luxurious life. Graceful gentle-green ferns sprung from even the tiniest crevice to clothe it in delicate new life and beauty.

"Sarah . . ."

"I know. Sit beside me on the sands, my love, and I'll sing you the music of the gift." Her fingers were sure and loving as she drew sounds from the harp that were as fragile and lovely as the shimmering green above their heads. Her voice was gentle, too; its tones held the sweetness of her nature, her love for him, even spring itself.

She was wearing Celtic dress, a thin woolen gown of blue with thin green and white bands woven in squares across the front, in stripes along the wide sleeves. Her dark hair hung down her back in braids that brushed the sands. Colored woolen yarn was plaited with her hair to create twisting brightness.

She was part of the moment, the place, the music, the magic of Belerion, like the song she sang.

> "From the cliffe they fell,
> the words.
> From the winds they were spun,
> the strings that shaped the music,
> From the stars she came,
> the goddess of the song.
>
> The cave it was her habitation.
> Her couch was made of ferns.
> The night sky was her birthplace.
> Her father was the sun.
>
> White birds bore her on their wings
> to her fern-filled home.
> Their beaks pulled softest down from their breasts
> to weave her robes.
> They fed her with their music.
> And named her in their songs. Lhuysa of the ferncliffe,
> daughter of the stars."

When Sarah completed the song, Joseph took the harp from her hands and laid it aside. Then he folded his arms around her and held her close, in loving quiet, for a long minute.

After, he put his finger beneath her chin to tilt upward so that he could kiss her. "The most wonderful gift ever, my heart, I thank—Sarah! Why are you crying?"

She turned her face into his shoulder again. "Forgive me," she whispered. Joseph could barely hear the words.

"For what? For giving me this magical gift, the magic time of these months? I am grateful beyond my ability to find words magic enough to tell you how I feel . . . Sarah, don't. Don't cry. It breaks my heart. Tell me what sorrows you."

Sarah moved away from him, wiped her eyes with the heels of her hands. "I spoiled everything. I'm sorry, Joseph. I believed I could be stronger."

He didn't understand. He knew only that his Sarah was unhappy. "What can I do?" he asked, begged.

"You can't do anything, and neither can I. That's not what I'm crying about. Not yet, anyhow. No, I'm being foolish, Joseph, inventing foolish, impossible dreams."

Joseph caught her hands and kissed the tears on them, then the tears on her face. "Tell me, tell me the dreams, Sparrow. Maybe I can make them come true, if you'll only tell me."

Sarah smiled tremulously, through her tears. "You might try, my love, but it's not possible. I was just imagining that this magic we've known might last, stay exactly this way, that we might remain in Belerion for the time we have left before you send me away."

"But I will never send you away! You are my life, Sarah."

"You don't remember the Law, Joseph. Isaac's wife told me about it, and I asked him, and it's true. The Law says that a man must divorce his wife if she is barren for ten years. We have been married for more than seven.

"And I no longer have hope for a baby."

CHAPTER TWENTY-SIX

THE *EAGLE* WAS CARRYING GIFTS AND LETTERS FOR BELERI-on's Jews from their families and friends in Caesarea. Also the foods and wines of home. Isaac and Rachel hosted a celebration in their courtyard, beside the pomegranate tree, grown from a cutting to a healthy two-foot-tall plant.

Joseph and Sarah attended, embraced everyone—men, women, children, babies—and said their goodbyes.

The morning after, they made their farewells to their friends among the Celts. Sarah took Antiochus aside for a talk. "You can stay here," she told the boy, "and Joseph will not think badly of you. These are people of your blood. You're so very, very smart and able, Antiochus; you shouldn't throw it away. You could study, like Nancledra did, you could become a Druid, be honored by everyone. Back in Judea you're a foreigner, and a slave. Why won't you stay? I want you to be happy."

"Joseph gave me happiness when he rescued me from my degraded life; you and everyone at Arimathea gave me happiness when you gave me a home and a family to care for. I am going back." He was adamant, as he had been for all the weeks before when Sarah and Joseph, separately and together, had urged him to accept a new life.

There had been moments when Antiochus had been tempted to stay. His blood was Celtic. Even though he'd been cruelly cast out from his birthplace, some deep, dim memory responded to the musical meter of the language, and he knew that these golden-haired people were his kinsmen of blood and spirit.

And to study, to become a Druid . . . His brains had never truly been tested; the tutor at Arimathea had admitted that Antiochus had long since learned everything that the farmhouse classroom could offer. Could he meet the high demands of the Druids' educational system? It was a tantalizing challenge.

In February, at the Imbolc festival, Antiochus had crept unseen into the wooded area where the rites were being performed. He knew he was risking dreadful punishment, but in him, curiosity and an adventurous nature were stronger by far than fear.

He peered from his hiding place, fascinated, and saw wonders.

As dusk was spreading through the clearing in the wood, the three Druid priests chanted incantations, words Antiochus did not recognize, while the Bard Nancledra drew unearthly, entrancing melodies from his lyre's strings. The Dumnoni villagers became excited, then frenzied, then calm. Their calmness was more frightening to Antiochus than their frenzy had been.

It was almost dark when the Druids folded back a jointed metal rectangle in the center of the clearing. The night was suddenly darker. A bed of yellow-red-orange glowing hot coals had been revealed.

The music began again. One by one the Druids walked slowly across the length of the fiery rectangle, their long white robes—colored by flickering red reflections—held up to expose their bared feet.

The Dumnoni cried out in ecstatic amazement. Then the priest beckoned to Gawethin.

Even at a distance Antiochus could feel the chief's terror.

He held his breath when Gawethin approached the red path of burning. The Druids chanted. Gawethin removed his boots. Chanting and music grew softer, more compelling, and Gawethin stepped onto the coals. He emitted a cry. Not of pain, but of celebration. His red-lit face was transfigured with exaltation when he emulated the priests' slow walk across the coals. After it was done, he looked at the unblemished soles of his feet and shouted his triumph to his villagers. "I, Gawethin, have passed the trial by fire!"

Antiochus felt a surge of longing to test himself, to run to the center and walk the coals. He had to grasp the thorny branch of a nearby bush to keep control of his compelling desire.

The villagers had no need to control themselves. Fully a third of them—men and women—bared their feet and ran to the glowing redness. They did not walk the path of coals, they danced, turning with upraised arms in an ecstasy of celebration.

The lyre sounded strong chords, and the dancers returned to the edge of the clearing. Then there was silence.

Two of the priests then brought forward a villager named Mulvirn. Mulvirn had been an unsolved puzzle to Antiochus all winter long. There was nothing especially distinguished in his appearance or his nature or his skills. At least nothing that Antiochus could identify. He was a stocky blond man, no longer young, with slightly bowed legs and an air of absentminded concentration on things unseen and unspoken. Yet all the villagers treated him with even greater respect and admiration than they bestowed on their chief, Gawethin.

Perhaps, thought Antiochus, Mulvirn was related to the Druids who were escorting him and that was why he was treated so well. He was glad to have found an answer to the puzzle.

He watched intently. Was Mulvirn going to walk across the coals? The music was different now. So was the chanting, by the third Druid.

What was this? All three priests were bowing to Mulvirn. So were all the villagers.

The third priest continued to chant as he straightened up, then lifted his arms to shoulder height and spread them wide. His robe's deep sleeves were like giant wings. Mulvirn knelt in front of him and looked up.

It seemd to Antiochus as if the great wings then embraced Mulvirn's head and shoulders in a rapid swooping motion that contained a glittering flash of light. Long moments later, Antiochus comprehended that the two Druid escorts were keeping Mulvirn from falling over. His throat was an open, spurting red slash; his life's blood was pumping out onto the earth and the hem of his executioner's robe.

Punishment? For what? If Mulvirn was a criminal, why had everyone bowed to him? Been so respectful for so many months?

The third Druid raised his arms again; Antiochus understood the words he chanted.

"The Earth has accepted our brother's willing sacrifice. The harvest will be rich and abundant."

Music began again, music of joyous celebration, and the pair of priests raised Mulvirn's dead body up to carry it on their shoulders in solemn procession.

Antiochus never knew where it was taken. He was stealing away, crawling through the dark wood, on hands and knees, so frightened that he had no strength to stand up.

He knew he must never tell what he had witnessed. And he knew he did not want to remain in Belerion.

The tin had been loaded, the tide had turned. Sarah and Antiochus hurried across the sands to the great hill-island and the *Eagle*. "Don't look back," Antiochus said to Sarah. "Don't look back."

Milcar had baskets full of correspondence for Joseph on the *Eagle*. Also hours of talking to tell the news of Israel to Sarah and Joseph. And Antiochus. The boy convinced them that he was old enough to listen. As close as he could guess, he was thirteen now, or soon would be. A man.

The news was not good. King Herod had massed his army and attacked the Arabs of Nabatea, the country that bordered Israel on the east and the south. Milcar didn't know the outcome, or even the magnitude, of the conflict. By the time they arrived in Israel, the whole country might be at war.

"That might mean confiscation, or even destruction of your ships, Joseph. I sent them all to sea, to trade, without waiting for you to reach Caesarea and give them instructions. It wasn't what you had ordered, but I thought it best to get them away from possible trouble."

"Good man," Joseph said to his ship's captain and friend. "Now tell me about the King's fancy galley."

Milcar rolled his eyes. "It's finished, except for choosing a crew. I've never seen a ship like that in my life." Joseph asked eager questions and laughed mightily while Milcar gave details of the ship's excessive, voluptuous opulence.

Sarah smiled, but she couldn't match Joseph's high spirits. She knew why he was so cheerful, and she thought he was mistaken.

"Isaac doesn't know anything," Joseph had pronounced after talking to him about the divorce. "He's only a Pharisee and a rabbi. I'll talk to priests of the Temple. They are Sadducees, and so am I and all my family. The Temple is the only true authority on the Law. These Pharisees and their synagogues came into being only in the time of our grandfathers' grandfathers. We Sadducees have led the people since the days of King Solomon." Joseph refused to believe what he wanted to disbelieve. He could not accept the idea of divorce or discuss anything to do with it.

So Sarah concentrated on the dramatic positive aspect of her life at that time. The medicine to improve fertility had the unexpected bonus of curing her seasickness. She could, and did, take pleasure in the great blue expanses of sea and sky and the hypnotic curls of white foam created by the pointed, eagle-topped bow of the ship.

And if the Druid medicine was so effective against one misery, perhaps it would be equally magical for the other. There was still time . . .

Joseph ordered Milcar to sail directly to Caesarea, where Sarah and Antiochus would disembark. "I, too," Joseph said. "I have a small personal matter to attend to, as well as escorting Sarah to Arimathea. Take the *Eagle* to Cyprus, do our business there, and then meet me in Caesarea."

"And if there is war?"

"We will know by the approaches to the coast. If local shipping is active, that indicates normality."

Sarah changed from her comfortable Celtic dress to an appropriate linen tunic and cloak for arrival in Israel. But she did not return to her pre-Belerion way of dressing her hair. She kept it in plaits, wound around her head and fastened with elaborately patterned, long bronze pins, like a Celtic woman's. The look of it was very becoming, and she knew it, and she was not going to give it up.

She had pins for Helena and Rebekkah, too, as gifts. Perhaps they could, together, transform the farm into a slightly Celtic world, as far as costume was concerned. Her cloak and tunic felt cumbersome and clumsy to her now.

Sarah longed to see Rebekkah. The old woman's face-facts view of life was what she had great need of when the facts awaiting her were so frightening. I am going to be strong, realistic, without any self-pity, exactly like Rebekkah, Sarah promised herself.

But then she passed through the village with Joseph, accepting the welcome of the people whom she cared for so deeply, and she remembered that after only a few years she would no longer have a place here.

And she saw the trysting tree where she and Joseph had met to whisper their love and learn to kiss.

And she entered the house that was the shelter of her marriage.

Sarah ran to the nearby house of Joseph's family, found Rebekkah in her garden, and without a word of greeting threw her arms around the neck of Joseph's grandmother and burst into a torment of wailing and sobs.

Rebekkah held her, silently, until Sarah had no tears and no strength left. "Come into my room," the older woman said then. "You must rest before you see the others."

Deep in the shadowed corners of the garden Antiochus stood, like a statue, not knowing what was wrong or how he might help.

Joseph had not witnessed Sarah's breakdown. After they left the village, he got out of the cart, telling Antiochus to drive it to the farmhouse. "I will return soon," Joseph said, without explanation.

He walked across fields and vineyards to the road that led to the house of the priest Nebuzah, the man who had used the Law to bring at least a modicum of peace between him and his father.

It was after sundown when Joseph returned to the farm. Dark roads were dangerous, but he was too excited to be careful. He had to take the news to Sarah right away. Nebuzah had given the answer to their problem.

His house was dark, lampless. Joseph was enraged. He wasn't ready to see his family, especially not his father, and that must be where Sarah had gone. His good news would have to wait, and he was bursting with it. But it was his and Sarah's, nothing to do with anyone else.

For a few minutes he tried to tell himself that it would be all right if he simply went inside and went to sleep. He was tired enough, and he'd be much more agreeable company for the others after some rest.

No. Better to get it over with. And Sarah might be worrying about his safety. Joseph forced his steps to be brisk and quick, and he went to the house of his youth.

"Joseph! Welcome home!" The room was full of people.

Sarah hurried to his side and tucked her hand in the bend of his elbow. "When I arrived, your mother sent word to Amos *and his bride Rachel* that we were home, so they came over." The emphasis was not so heavy that anyone else would notice it, and it saved Joseph from making a terrible mistake. "I've been teasing them awfully. I told them that we brought a special wedding gift from *Spain*, but I wouldn't bring it out until you were here, too."

Sarah led him to a man and woman, identified them as Rachel's parents, visiting from Galilee. Joseph murmured all the proper welcomes, expressions of joy about Rachel as his new sister, regrets at missing the wedding, hopes that their visit would be lengthy and would give them pleasure . . .

Helena, his mother, rescued him with an embrace and a demand that he speak to his father and grandmother.

"And brother!" Caleb added. Joseph's laugh was unforced, for the first time since he'd arrived.

So was his admiration for the handsome copper bowl Sarah produced as the gift for Amos and Rachel. Joseph was certain he'd never seen it before, but he didn't say so. Nor did he mention his recognition of the distinctively Celtic beauty of the swirling lines incised into the metal around the large green stones imbedded as a decoration on the bowl's sides.

"I was stunned by the Spanish craftsmen, too," Sarah was saying demurely. Joseph wanted to pick her up in his arms and spin around until she squealed, just the way he had done when they were children and he was particularly delighted by her antics.

The evening was not as long as it seemed to be, by Joseph's reckoning. Rebekkah kissed his cheeks. Joshua grunted a sound that might have been a welcome. Helena sat beside her husband after her initial greeting and rescue.

Rachel's parents were pleasant people, their daughter a charming girl who obviously adored Amos and was adored in return.

But to Joseph the evening felt longer than a year. Ten years. A hundred. He had good news to tell Sarah.

As soon as they were in their own house, with the door closed behind them, Joseph took Sarah in his arms and hugged her until she gasped for air. Then he held her more gently, while he kissed her cheeks, eyes, lips, nose, chin, hairpins.

Sarah giggled. "You're a madman. What's going on?"

Joseph planted a loud smacking parody of a kiss on her forehead. "That's for being a perfect wife. I would never have remembered Amos' wife, or even that he had married."

Another noisy kiss. "And that is for remaining my perfect wife forever and ever. I went to the priest in Thamna, and he found a way for us to stay married. No divorce, my love. I knew the Rabbi Isaac must be wrong."

"Oh, Joseph," Sarah hugged him fiercely. "Oh, I'm so happy." She laid her head on his chest, her face more light-filled than the flame of the oil lamp on the table.

It dimmed, bit by bit, as he enthusiastically reported what the priest had said. The meaning of the Law about required divorce really had to do with the survival, even increase, of the Jewish peoples. A man must father future generations.

But there was no law against polygamy. Witness Herod's ten wives. True, the ordinary man rarely had more than one wife. But it was allowable.

Therefore, the only thing necessary was that Joseph take a second wife and father a child before ten years of his marriage with Sarah was finished. In that case, no divorce would be required, even though she was barren.

Sarah could feel her limbs grow cold. And her body. This is death, she thought, how curious it is to be dead without dying first. I should be jealous. Angry. Hurt. But I feel only cold. Dead. My life has ended. Why is he still talking? The dead do not hear.

"Of course the mother of the child—whoever she may be—will have to be from an honorable family. And I'll have to give her a house and servants, so that the child will have the right kind of care.

"But you will be my wife, my only true wife. For all time. I cannot lose you, my love. I'll do anything to prevent that."

Joseph suddenly noticed Sarah's stillness, and silence. He put his hand on her shoulders and moved her away so that he could look into her face.

"Sarah. What is it? Did I not explain it clearly? We will not have to divorce. Doesn't that make you happy?"

"Yes," the voice of the numb, cold woman said. "That's perfect." She backed away from the touch of his hands. "I am very tired. I am going to sleep now."

Sarah slept for more than sixteen hours. If she dreamt, the dreaming did not make her body toss and turn. She lay motionless and pale, her shallow breathing not disturbing the lightweight linen coverlet.

When she woke, her eyes opened, but she did not stir.

Not until she heard the warm love for her in Rebekkah's voice. "My grandson is a man, and it is generally accepted as a fact that men are fools." Joseph's grandmother put her hand on Sarah's cold arm, lending it warmth.

"For my sake," said Rebekkah, "I hope you will choose the foolishness rather than the divorce. I do not want to lose you."

Sarah's hand found Rebekkah's and closed around it. "I cannot bear it."

"Of course you can. We can endure whatever we must endure. In a while—a little while, really—you will recognize that this is the best that he can do in circumstances that allow no good choice. Like me, Joseph does not want to lose you."

"I do not want to talk to him about this. He is happy, and I cannot look at his face."

"Naturally. I encouraged him to go to Caesarea and his ships."

Sarah sat bolt upright. "And he did? Just like that? His miserable business affairs meant more to them than me? I'll kill him!"

Rebekkah laughed. "You're getting better. Good. Now let's find something to eat."

CHAPTER TWENTY-SEVEN

JOSEPH WAS ONE OF SEVERAL HUNDRED OF CAESAREA'S prominent men invited to the celebration of King Herod's victorious foray into Nabatea. The palace was decorated with thick swags of laurel leaves, the symbol of triumph, and troupes of musicians moved from one reception area to another, sounding the trumpets' battle signal for attack.

Herod was expansive, laughing, boasting. He wore purple and gold silk robes, and a jeweled crown, plus bracelets studded with jewels on his arms above and below the elbow.

He abandoned a group of sycophants and their praises when he saw Joseph. "My ship builder!" he shouted. "When do I see the completed galley?"

"Whenever you choose," Joseph replied. "I will value your guidance on the final details."

"At once!" Herod boomed. "Tomorrow at first light. Quick decisions and rapid action are the ingredients for success. I have just demonstrated that. Ask the Nabateans! Hah! Their scurvy prime minister will tell you. Ask Syllaeus!" Herod's laughter was louder than the blare of his trumpets.

* * *

The galley was unlike any ship that the harbor of Caesarea had ever sheltered. It was not painted black, like Joseph's other ships. It was vermilion, with carved gilded leaves surrounding the openings for the oars. They were painted the color of precious Persian turquoise and decorated with painted scrolls of vermilion. The deck was wood, but painted to look like mosaic tiles that portrayed the fantastic creatures of Ulysses' voyage. On the afterdeck, pavilions of striped silk hung with gold fringe and tassels shaded gilt couches cushioned in jewel-toned silks.

Below deck there were six cabins, each with an inner wall of sandalwood carved to look like flowering vines growing through trelliswork. Persian carpets softened the decking of the cabins, and the fittings included wide divans in gilt frames studded with turquoises. Vermilion and gold striped silk gauze tented the divans, pulled back at the corners by ropes made of strands of gold that threaded pearls and nephrite beads.

"It is spectacularly excessive," Joseph had said when he saw it. "The King should be well pleased."

His prediction was accurate. Herod sat on every couch and every divan, one after another, testing for softness, smiling with satisfaction.

He even tested the narrow tiered sleeping arrangements in the cabins designated for the servants of the passengers. Only the lowest ones, but Joseph assured him that the upper ones were equal in comfort.

When he saw the bath and latrine for the cabins, he pronounced the rose-veined green marble from which they were carved even more handsome than what he had in his palace.

"But where are the towels?" he asked. "And the jars and vials for perfumes and oils? You must have fine linens, Joseph, and gold containers."

Joseph thanked Herod for calling the oversight to his attention and promised to correct it as soon as humanly possible.

The King roared with laughter. "Bring them out from wherever you hid them, Joseph. You've given me the pleasure of finding fault, now you can stop pretending to be a fool, and taking me for one at the same time. I don't hold your excellence against you."

Nicolaus was, of course, accompanying his ruler. He smiled and winked at Joseph. The morning was as successful as the two of them had plotted to make it.

Skilled palace slaves served wine and honeycakes and dates stuffed with almonds on the upper deck while Herod, Nicolaus, and Joseph gave the silken couches their first true trial.

Then slaves brought silver bowls of warmed water for them to cleanse their sticky fingers, and handed them scented towels for drying them.

Herod declared the visit a total success. "Now I will have to decide on a destination for a voyage," he said, in great good humor. "Perhaps a tour of the mines on Cyprus that brought you to me, my good Joseph. You would enjoy it, I am sure. The women of Cyprus are almost as exquisite as the wines."

The King got to his feet. "See to the planning, Nicolaus. Now we must return to the burdens that await us at the palace. Ptolemy should have an accounting of the payments from Nabatea. The couriers should have arrived by now."

Nicolaus thanked Joseph while Herod was entering his sedan chair. "You have added to Herod's happiness, and therefore to mine. It gladdens my heart to see him so pleased with his world. It's been a long time since that was so."

"An obscenity," Milcar labeled the royal galley. "You'll have to keep it out of sight or we will all be the butts of humor throughout the world of seafaring."

"It will be towed back to its shelter this afternoon. I brought it out today for the King's inspection."

Milcar hawked and spat. "I'll wager he liked the floating

bordello. It's Herod's style; only he gets new wives while honest men get new whores."

Joseph did not wince outwardly, but he felt as if Milcar had kicked him. To take a second wife was certain to be seen as an outburst of unrestrained sexual appetite on his part. An insult that he couldn't even take offense at, because he'd rather people thought the worst of him than have them know about Sarah's condition. If he heard her name in any man's mouth in such an intimate context, he'd have to kill the profaner.

"Let's move the men along a little faster, then open a jar of the cargo, Milcar. Entertaining a king leaves a humble businessman with a bad taste in his mouth."

The *Eagle* had arrived from Cyprus no more than an hour after Joseph bid farewell to Nicolaus and the King. Now Joseph wanted to get the Cypriot wine into the warehouse and the moneys from the tin sale divided. The crew could take some time with their families before the *Eagle* set sail again. It was still early in the season, so there would assuredly be another sailing.

When Joseph got back from Jerusalem. He had to make sacrifice of thanksgiving for the success of the Belerion settlement. And he needed to ask the priests' advice about finding . . . he couldn't think of her as a wife . . . the mother of his child.

As Milcar and Joseph were watching a glorious red and gold sunset, sitting on the edge of the quay, with their feet dangling, like children, a half-empty amphora rested between them, balancing in a coil of rope.

"I still say Alexandria," Milcar was insisting. "Part of the Cyprus cargo of wine could be sold there, and the silks and spices are a guaranteed high-profit return load."

"But if we go to Pireus, we'll have the winds at our back for the return. And Greek wine is so filthy, the Cyprus cargo will bring double the price it gets in Egypt."

The argument was heated, but not angry. They were enjoying themselves and neither really cared that much about where they went. It was sailing that mattered, the sea and the wind and freedom from the land and the problems it housed.

Suddenly Nicolaus hurried across the quay to see Joseph. He was alone, without a bodyguard, and he looked distraught.

"I need to talk with you. Can you come? At once. It's an emergency."

The crisis was caused by the victory that Herod was so proud of. The Emperor Augustus was very angry about it. It was a firm, fervent Roman policy that subject states' rulers could not extend themselves beyond their own borders. Specifically, any relations of any kind between two separate countries were forbidden, other than quasi-social visits by diplomats to celebrations like the festivities that had marked the completion of Caesarea. Military action was absolutely out of the question.

"The King received a message from the Emperor by courier today," Nicolaus told Joseph. "It arrived while we were enjoying ourselves on the new galley. Augustus has been Herod's protector for decades; now things have changed. 'Heretofore,' the Emperor wrote, 'I have treated you like a friend. Henceforth, you will be considered a subject, like any other.' It is a disaster of the greatest magnitude."

Joseph was impressed by the change in Nicolaus, even a bit disturbed. The scholarly older man had always been so easy-going and relaxed. This Nicolaus was distraught, and he looked ten years older than he had that morning.

The situation was serious for the King; Joseph could under-stand that. But what did it have to do with him? Yes, he sold Herod tin, but he'd only seen the King—as a person—a few times in his life. He could hardly be considered a close associ-ate. Herod had been generous to him, shown him favor, even if it was something unwanted, like the room in the small palace in Jerusalem. But that hardly made Joseph an intimate, or an advisor, like Nicolaus.

"Why do you tell me these things?" he asked Nicolaus.

"I'm not part of the palace. I'm only a sailor, not anyone who deals in power or policies."

Nicolaus took a deep breath. It calmed him somewhat. "You're right, Joseph. Of course. I'm so shaken that it's made me indiscreet, and that is the greatest folly and the greatest wrong an advisor to a throne can commit. It is curious how a man as young as you can create so much confidence in your abilities and judgment.

"I've gone too far, but it's done. I can rely on you to keep this information confidential, can't I?"

Joseph nodded. "It has nothing to do with me."

"The reaction to it will involve you. The floating bordello—oh, yes, I've heard what the seamen of Caesarea call it—is going to be put to use. We are going to Rome."

"You and King Herod?"

"No. You and I. And possibly someone else, not the King."

"But, Nicolaus, I haven't even hired a crew. And I need to take care of a hundred other things as well."

"We do not have to sail tomorrow. It may be no sooner than next week, though I can't give you my word on that. Ah, Joseph, there are so many threads in this web."

They had been walking rapidly toward Herod's palace, speaking in low voices and in Greek. Now the palace was in sight, and the people there were not the uneducated dockworkers and street vendors who had been the only other pedestrians on their route.

"We'll have wine in my garden. This will be a friendly, unimportant hour spent talking about further refinement of the galley's fittings, do I make myself clear?" Nicolaus dropped his voice even more, to a near whisper. "The garden offers no hiding place for a listener."

Joseph entered into the playacting with no trouble. But his apprehensiveness was doubling by the minute.

Syllaeus, the prime minister of Nabatea, was the crux of the problem, Nicolaus confided when he and Joseph were safely alone. "Five or six years ago, the King's sister Salome decided she was in love with him. So ridiculous, Joseph! She was well over forty years old, several times widowed or divorced, and acting like a girl desperate to lose her virginity. Syllaeus began to sigh and write poetry—stolen from the classic poets, I've no doubt—and woo her like a lovesick boy. This was his opportunity to become part of the royal family, instead of the employee of a doddering old Arab king. Obodas has been senile for a decade."

Nicolaus's face was a picture of distaste. "So Salome went to her brother the King and told him she wanted to marry Syllaeus. Of course Herod forbade it. Salome became hysterical, and we lived amid a constant storm of scenes and threats and denunciations and vows that she'd kill herself. It was even worse than the chaos of the children's perpetual battles and plotting against one another."

Suddenly Nicolaus chuckled. Joseph nearly jumped from his skin in surprise. "Herod is a crafty old fox," said Nicolaus. "He knew what Syllaeus was up to, of course. Not only where Salome was concerned. He knew that Syllaeus was a 'swordsman' of phenomenal energy and notoriety. Every female in Nabatea was at risk if he was within grabbing distance. So Herod had a message delivered to Syllaeus, saying that he could marry Salome—if he had himself circumcised and became a Jew.

"The thought of a knife touching his famous phallus terrified Syllaeus, and he broke off all contact with Salome. She blamed Herod, of course. But not one hundredth as much as she blamed Syllaeus. There are some things a woman is incapable of understanding." Nicolaus was holding his own legs close together, Joseph noticed. Herod's advisor was a Gentile.

Joseph was incredulous. He remembered Herod's sister. She was the frightening woman at Ascalon, the one he'd taken the Belerion bracelet to, so long ago. She was old. The idea of her in love like a girl was disgusting.

"So King Herod lost his friendship with the Emperor of

the Romans to save his sister's hurt pride, is that what you're saying, Nicolaus?"

"What nonsense. Of course not. Herod attacked Nabatea to frighten Obodas, who had borrowed money from Herod and didn't repay it. Syllaeus persuaded him to withhold payment because he resented Herod's interference in the affair with Salome."

"It must have been a great deal of money if it was worth more than the friendship of Augustus Caesar."

Nicolaus made an eloquent gesture of despair, hitting his forehead with his fists.

"You'll injure yourself! Stop!" Joseph cried.

"I'm trying to knock what I know into a new arrangement. Maybe the missing piece is in there someplace. Herod is sure that the Roman governor of Syria encouraged him to attack. That's the equivalent of Augustus giving the order, because the Roman legions in Syria are the threat we always have at our backs. I can't figure out what went wrong."

"Syllaeus?"

"That's the most logical answer. Maybe he managed to bribe the Roman governor. Using the money owed to Herod, no doubt. I simply do not know, and it's driving me mad."

Nicolaus shrugged. "What I do know is that Syllaeus has already gone to Rome. He complained to the Emperor, and the no-longer-friends letter to Herod was the result. He must have lied as eloquently as Homer. The attack on Nabatea was hardly more than a skirmish. Fewer than a hundred Arabs were killed.

"However, Syllaeus has done serious damage to Herod. It's up to me to discredit him and restore the King to the Emperor's favor. That's why we must go to Rome. With Salome. She'll be happy to hurt Syllaeus any way she can. The King has already sent his fastest messengers to her. She has a palace in the south, a sort of miniature kingdom of her own that Herod gave her a long time ago to get her away from his own palace where she made his life miserable after he executed her husband."

"Nicolaus, please stop. Now. I am beginning to believe that I should never have left the farm. I am not wordly enough to listen to all this talk about kings and emperors and queens and prime ministers without thinking that I am imagining things, or you are making sport of me. This casual in-family execution is just too much for credibility."

Nicolaus shrugged again. "I'll stop. Someday, though, you will have to learn the rest of it. You did leave the farm, Joseph of Arimathea, and there is no going back. You are involved with the very small number of people who control a very large part of the world. How old are you, Joseph? My informers tell me you're twenty-three; is that true? Yes? Well, start broadening your mind and your horizon, my friend, because I predict that before you're thirty you will be a familiar figure at every center of power."

Joseph felt ambition burn hot in his belly. Then he squashed it. "That can't happen, Nicolaus. I am a short, barely educated Jew from a village no one's ever heard of. I know my limitations."

"So you say, and so you believe. But life is a capricious adventure. I was a too-tall, too-thin, too-solemn boy in a poor family of weavers in Damascus. I made my way to Alexandria because all the writings of Aristotle could be found in the library there. Scholars noticed me and taught me, and I found work tutoring slower learners so that I could earn money to buy bread.

"One day, with no warning, I was informed that I was to be tutor to the children of Queen Cleopatra and Mark Antony. There was no question of saying 'No, I thank you, but no'— Joseph, why are you laughing?"

"I cannot help it, Nicolaus. Just think of the names that have been mentioned here in this pleasant, out-of-the-way garden. Herod . . . Augustus . . . the King of Nabatea . . . and now the forever famous Antony and Cleopatra. You must see the comic quality of all this."

Nicolaus' smile was wry. "I see it. But heed my words, Joseph. Don't laugh so much that you forget caution. The masks of comedy and tragedy hang side by side in every theater."

He poured the last of the wine into Joseph's cup. "I must return to the King's chambers now. Finish this and be on your way to find a superbly trained crew for the bordello. I loathe sea travel; I'm terrified of every wave and every cloud in the sky. I'll send word about our departure as soon as I know it. Be ready before five days have passed."

Joseph stared down into the ruby-colored liquid for several minutes. Then he began to laugh. What he'd been hearing was too absurd to think about anymore. He set down the cup of excellent wine, and left the garden and the palace of King Herod.

He had many things to do.

CHAPTER TWENTY-EIGHT

JOSEPH NAMED THE VOLUPTUOUS GALLEY THE *PHOENIX*. THE fable of the phoenix was older than the fabulous tales of Homer or even the myths of classical Greece. Supposedly it was the most gloriously plumaged bird in all the world, it lived for five hundred years, then died in a spontaneous tower of fire, only to be reborn from its own ashes.

Joseph told Nicolaus the phoenix might convey the happy message that this inaugural voyage would result in Herod's return to the Emperor's good graces. But his real reason for choosing the fabulous bird as the galley's figurehead and name was its excessive gaudiness. An Egyptian jeweler in Caesarea was overjoyed to work day and night and hire a dozen helpers in order to transform an ordinary carved wooden rooster that Joseph brought him into a comb-less, gold-covered, jewel-studded bird with emerald eyes, centered in a burst of flames made of red-gold rays bordered by rubies.

The phoenix cost almost as much as the galley *Phoenix*, but Joseph wasn't concerned. After all, Herod was paying all the costs, and he would probably like the figurehead better than anything else about the ship.

It certainly caught the eye. When he returned from his

hasty trip to Jerusalem, Joseph saw a thick crowd of people on the quay, with guards from Herod's palace watching them from the distance of a sword's length.

"What's going on?" he asked a rope-mender who was squatting nearby.

"They're looking at the King's bird, trying to figure a way to get away with it without getting their heads sliced in half."

Joseph knew then that the jeweler had finished his work in time. That was good news.

And he had managed to do what needed doing in Jerusalem, too.

Incense and a sheep—two sacrifices he had made to thank the Almighty for the safe voyages to and from Belerion.

Ten lambs he'd given as burnt offerings for the ten families of Jews there.

And a bullock, the mightiest of sacrifices, in gratitude for the preservation of his marriage.

Afterward he talked with one of the Chief Priests about the problem of finding a woman to marry who would certainly be fertile. And in time to prevent the divorce. The priest promised to identify several candidates for him when he returned from Rome.

Joseph felt he could begin to relax now. It remained only to write to Sarah and tell her he was taking Nicolaus to Rome, but not why.

Then to get a good night's sleep. And in the morning he had to find a courier to take the letter to Arimathea, hire a cart and donkeys, and hurry back to Caesarea before the five days were over.

Now all those things were done. Only the most difficult and uncertain task remained. He had to persuade the men of the *Eagle* to act as crew on the *Phoenix* . . .

"It will be a normal voyage to Puteoli. The passengers are bringing their servants with them. You have only to handle the galley. They might get in our way sometimes, but so did the human cargo to Belerion, and you know it created no serious problems."

"They'll try to give us orders," the sailmaster grumbled.

"I give you my promise. I won't allow that."

"The ship is untried. Who knows how it will handle without making a trial run? Marble latrines and baths aren't normal ballast, Joseph. And those cabins—all that space with nothing in it but some whorehouse furnishings. The first real blow might capsize us before we know what's happening." The steersman was the speaker. He was not complaining; fear was in his voice, and he was a man who never showed fear, not even in the currents of the Pillars of Hercules, where hundreds of ships had met their end.

Joseph had no easy answer. He said so. "The builder of the galley is the best of Caesarea; the outfitter—including the marble fancies—is the best in all Phoenicia. Both of them guarantee that the ship is little different from any normal galley. If they are right, we will learn the differences and make adjustments. If they are very wrong, we may lose the ship and our lives. But that is possible every time we leave harbor, no matter what ship we're in. Isn't that what really calls a man to the sea?"

Joseph grinned. "At least we're getting our hire in advance. There's no profit to be gained from selling the cargo, so we're being paid for transport only. And you men all know what an hour in a luxury bordello costs. Multiply that by the number of hours it will take to sail to Italy and return. That will give you an idea of the cost I quoted to Herod's money man. The gold will be delivered today. You'll be rich men tonight.

"Unless you spend it all in the Academy of Terpsichore."

The artistic name of the opulent bordello near the quay always brought laughter. This time was no different.

Joseph breathed a sigh of relief.

Milcar dispelled the good mood. "I will not sail with you," he told Joseph, away from the laughing men. "I have my pride, and I will not be captain of a gold-trimmed travesty of an honest ship.

"I'll meet you here for the *Eagle*'s next sailing, Joseph. I'm not turning my back on you, only on that obscenity."

Nothing Joseph could say or do would change the big man's mind.

And so it was Joseph who gave the orders to haul in the decorated oars after the *Phoenix* passed through the opening in Caesarea's harbor wall two days later. "Get the honest ones from beneath the benches," he shouted, "and put them to work, men. We're going to Italy."

Milcar's defection meant that Joseph was constantly occupied with a captain's duties. He was, in fact, glad that it was so. Queen Salome made him feel as uncomfortable and threatened as she had at their previous meeting, and Joseph was happy not to have time to accept her invitations to dine, or to watch the sunset from the deck pavilion with her.

Nicolaus suggested that Joseph find a way to accept at least some of the offers. "She is not coming along only to seek revenge on Syllaeus. Augustus is too shrewd to be influenced by a woman who was spurned by a lover. What matters is that Salome has spent many months in Rome, over the years. She is a close friend to Livia, the wife of the Emperor, and it is said that he is often influenced by his wife.

"Salome can arrange for you to meet Caesar, Joseph, if you become friendly with her."

Joseph shook his head. "I'm not ready to try and learn the footing at the Emperor's court. I'm sure I would stumble."

The *Phoenix* reached Puteoli in early September. The waters of the harbor were flat and oily-looking from the weight of the late summer heat and humidity. But the glittering figurehead and luxuriant silk pavilion brought all the port's businessmen and sailors rushing to the docks.

Four of King Herod's bodyguards had accompanied his sister and his councillor. They left the *Phoenix* as soon as she was tied up, to stand guard against any kind of trouble. Joseph and his crew enjoyed watching the armored and armed guards while they struggled to steady themselves on the stone paving.

Nicolaus waited until a Roman centurion pushed through the crowd to speak to the guards. Then he left the ship and talked briefly with the officer. He learned that the Emperor was still in his summer villa on the Bay of Naples and would return to the city after the heat lifted.

Nicolaus stepped back onto the *Phoenix* where Joseph awaited him. "Events may move more quickly than I predicted," said Nicolaus. "Depending, of course, on the Emperor's mood. But I don't have to make the journey to Rome, and that saves a great deal of trouble and time. The centurion will send word to the villa announcing Salome's arrival. I'll accompany her, find out how things stand, and let you know how long I'll probably be staying."

"You know, Nicolaus, that the best sailing season is already behind us. We must have the *Phoenix* on the way back by five weeks from now, and even that is dangerously late. She's not your ordinary galley."

Herod's advisor lost his habitual patience. "You have told me that approximately seventy-four times, Joseph. And now for the seventy-fifth I tell you that if the Syllaeus matter looks thorny, I will pass the winter months in Rome and you can return for me next year.

"For the moment, the legionnaires will stand guard over the ship, and the harbormaster will make arrangements for moving the galley to shelter. You and your men can enjoy the questionable pleasures of Puteoli."

Joseph smiled. "They can. I am going to see Rome. I'll return four weeks from today for your instructions, if you think that schedule will suit."

Nicolaus agreed. His mind was on other, more important, matters, and he was glad to be rid of the *Phoenix*, its captain, and the dangers of its fragile-seeming walls as his only protection from the powerful waves of the sea.

What a coward, Joseph thought, laughing inside. He's been as pale as milk with terror the whole voyage, and it was as smooth as silk.

The harbormaster was still hovering nearby. Joseph asked him how to find Puteoli's Jewish neighborhood and set off briskly to follow his directions.

One of the many advantages of being a Jew was the certainty of welcome by other Jews wherever in the world they might be settled.

CHAPTER TWENTY-NINE

How can people breathe here? Is this what they call living? Joseph walked very slowly along the narrow, crooked street. He felt like running as fast he could back to the river.

On both sides of the street brick buildings rose four, five, six stories high, with no space between them. To Joseph they looked as if they were leaning against one another to keep from falling. They seemed to be leaning toward the buildings opposite them, too, on the other side of the shadowy street. He half expected bricks to fall on his head at any instant.

But none of the people seemed to notice or care. The tiny street was noisy with voices, laughter, shouting, the wails of little children. People were shopping. Every building was a series of tiny stores at street level. They were nothing more than indentations, not even rooms, with a table or shelf across the opening from the street. All manner of things were for sale. Bread; clay pots and bowls and cups; the carcasses of birds hanging from hooks, of rabbits the same, of slabs of meat; silver mirrors and hair ornaments; cloth; sandals; hot soups and stews; fish of all sizes; spices; wine; copper and iron cauldrons; flowers; charcoal; oil and oil lamps; dried beans and fruits; fresh pomegranates and figs.

If he didn't look up, and if he closed his ears, he could almost imagine that he was in the lower city of Jerusalem. There was the same merriment here, the same swarming activity.

But always overhead the mountainous windowed walls threatened and shut out the sky. And the language was foreign. He could understand maybe one word in twelve. It was Latin, but spoken with a rhythm and intonation that made it incomprehensible.

The tall buildings captured the smells, too. All the shop smells—fish, meat, bread, rotting carcasses—and the city smells of urine, burnt rancid oil, decay, rats, feces, sweat, dirty garments and hair and bodies. Jerusalem's streets produced odors, too, but they rose into the sky, and the dry air from the nearby desert dispensed them.

Rome was completely different. How could anyone stand it?

"Do you need help, stranger?" The voice came from somewhere near Joseph's knees. And it was speaking Greek. Joseph looked down into a grimy face with bright wide eyes and a snaggletoothed grin. "I am Marcus Appricus," said the child.

"And I am called Joseph. I am trying to find a man." Joseph looked at the scrap of vellum in his hand. "He is named Rufinius Archon."

The boy Marcus laughed. "Archon is a title, not a name. You must be looking for the synagogue. I will lead you to it if you will buy me a pot of wine."

"Willingly."

The boy lifted two sticks from the street and pushed himself upright, back against the door post of a wineshop. He was so nimble and practiced that Joseph didn't realize what Marcus was doing until he had done it.

"I'm a cripple, but I can show you the way," said the boy. "First, you buy me wine."

"How do I know you'll earn it? I'll give you a coin after I find this man."

"How do I know you'll give me the coin? You need guidance more than you need coins, Joseph the stranger. Buy my wine and let's get going."

The boy was right. Joseph could easily afford to take the chance. He took a denarius out of the purse sewn into his belt and put it on the counter. The man behind the counter half-opened his closed eyes, whisked it away, then resumed his nap.

Marcus winked at Joseph. "My father. He'll always wake at the sound of silver. This way." He set off at an astonishing speed, holding the sticks under his armpits. His left leg dragged beside him. It was as thin as the stick that was its substitute.

Joseph moved quickly to catch up with the boy. Cripples were an everyday part of life. At the gates to every city, on the steps of every temple, even under the colonnades of the Temple itself. They begged, pointed to twisted or missing limbs, plucked at the cloaks of passersby, pleading, whining, accusing, blessing the almsgiver. Joseph had never seen a cripple who ignored his affliction and allowed others to forget it. He felt tremendous admiration for his young guide.

Marcus stopped beside a fountain in the center of a widened area where another narrower street intersected with the one he and Joseph had walked. He laid the right-side stick against the fountain's rim and dipped his hand into the basin of water to drink.

Suddenly Joseph realized that he was thirsty, too.

When the two of them were finished, the boy pointed to the narrower street on the left. "Take that. It ends at the door to the synagogue."

"My thanks, Marcus." Joseph held out another denarius to the boy.

Marcus palmed it in an instant. "You already paid me. Did you forget?"

"No. This is for the water. I was thirsty."

Marcus grinned his urchin's grin. "I like you, too, Joseph stranger. Next time you get lost, I'll let you hire me again." He took up his stick and was gone before Joseph could speak.

The synagogue occupied half of the street-level space in one of the tall brick apartment buildings. It was not locked, but it was empty. Joseph sat on a bench that rested against the wall to the right of the door and waited. The peacefulness of the solitude was welcome after the noisy crowded streets. His eyes closed and in his mind he repeated one of the psalms of thanksgiving. He had many things to be grateful for.

Not the least of them was that he didn't have to live in Rome . . .

A quiet voice and a light touch on his shoulder woke him. "Welcome," said the man.

That evening Joseph heard a great deal about Rome. The man who discovered him in the synagogue was not the Archon Rufinius, the name Joseph had been given by the Jews in Puteoli. This was an older man named Juda. A presbytic, Juda explained, that was his title. It meant "elder" and honored his years of devotion, no more, whereas an Archon was an elected official who was in charge of the synagogue's business affairs. Lease of the premises, payment of the rents, recording and banking the offerings and gifts of the synagogue's members, and more.

Juda apologized that he could not take Joseph to Rufinius. The Archon was at his villa in the hills outside the city. Everyone who could manage it left Rome in the heat of the summer.

But many Romans—most Romans really—could not afford to vacation. Juda took Joseph to his home, where his wife served refreshments in the building's courtyard, and he met more than thirty of the synagogue members who had not left the city. All of them were eager to learn about Jerusalem from Joseph and to tell him about the wonders of Rome.

For Joseph's comfort they spoke Greek, lapsing into Latin only when the Greek word was too elusive. As the evening passed, Joseph added many words and even phrases to his vocabulary. When they talked about the great capital that was their home, there was no Greek equivalent for many Roman objects or customs.

It seemed that he had seen nothing of the city yet. The barge that had brought him up the Tiber from the sea had let him off at the closest point to the neighborhood he wanted, but the Transtiber could hardly be called Rome at all. The city was on the other side of the river.

And what a city! Joseph listened attentively, with growing incredulity. He did not like what he was learning.

The tall buildings that he'd seen were called insulae, islands, a sort of joke because each one housed enough people to populate one. The lower two floors might contain large apartments with large rooms and exceedingly large rents. But as one climbed upward, each floor had less expensive places to rent, because the apartments were so much smaller, with so many of them crammed into the space. And the top floor generally had only rooms, not apartments, with a family—or even two—living in each room.

They did collapse from time to time, from the weight of humanity on floors that couldn't support it.

More often they were destroyed by fire. The apartments had no kitchens, so people had to eat cold food or go to food shops. Also there was no heat in cold weather. As a result, many tenants used braziers or clay ovens fueled by charcoal. Accidents were inevitable.

Even so, Rome's citizens would never consider living anywhere else. The city provided them with weekly rations of grain or bread and fish or meat and enough money to buy a few extras or—even better—to gamble on sporting events or games they played in the taverns.

And more than one third of the days in the year were holidays. Working was not the perpetual drudgery in Rome that it was in other places in the Empire.

A good example was the Ludi Septemtilis, the festival that celebrated the end of summer and the resumption of constant activity in the Senate and the law courts and all the government offices. Everyone would return from holiday after summer was done. But in Rome, they would not have to settle down right away. The Ludi, the games, lasted for fifteen days, and during that time the Senate and the courts and factories and businesses were closed so that citizens could enjoy the theater and parades and the contests and combats in the Forum and the races in the two Circuses. The races most of all. They went on all day, twenty-four of them in all, each day.

The government made sure that Rome's citizens had good lives.

To Joseph it sounded totally unacceptable. Living on handouts, instead of earning your way. And spending weeks of every year going to amusements instead of to work.

He thought he'd probably spend a day seeing the sights, the famous Forum and the pagan monuments, and then head back to Puteoli.

On the other hand, he really had enjoyed the chariot races in Caesarea. Perhaps he would take in just one or two—not twenty-four—before he left. He had come a long way to get here, and he certainly didn't intend ever to return.

Roman life wasn't the life that gave him satisfaction. He liked to win, not to be rewarded for doing nothing.

The next morning Juda led Joseph through the bewildering maze of streets and alleys to the river. "You will have no difficulty finding the boat island," said the old man, "there are no others in the Tiber. I will be waiting to meet you there when the sun begins to sink."

Joseph thanked him and walked onto the tall arched bridge that led to the strange mid-river construction. One end of it did look like the tall curved prow of a ship. But this was made of stone, not wood, and behind it was a huge travertine temple surrounded by porticos, with tremendous stone columns.

"Stop blocking the way!" An angry voice and a rough shove assaulted Joseph from the rear. He turned angrily to face his enemy. The knife tucked in his belt was under his fingers and already loosened in its scabbard.

Then he saw the man who had pushed him. He was one of four carrying an uncovered litter. The woman on the litter was young, fair-haired, and so pale that the thin blue veins on her forehead and throat looked garishly bright. Her eyes were closed. Tears seeped from the corners of them. Her breathing was shallow and slow and horribly loud. Joseph backed away even more. He did not want to see such an unhappy, wasteful death of so much loveliness.

The deep intricate carving on the mock prow made sense to him now. The serpent was the symbol of Aesculapius, the Greek god of healing. The building must be a temple to him.

When Joseph crossed the island, he saw the accuracy of his suppositions. Under the portico, people of all ages, colors, shapes were waiting to enter the temple and supplicate the god for a cure to whatever afflicted them.

Joseph thought for a moment of his father. At least Joshua had his home and his family around him, not a mass of strangers in some pagan temple. What fools these idolaters were, searching for help from some statue, a graven image carved by an ordinary man. When the all-powerful One God sent illness to one of his creatures, the one stricken knew that it was a righteous punishment and he prayed for forgiveness but did not delude himself that im-

provement or cure could be found by travel to a strange island in a muddy Italian river.

Joseph had the intolerant arrogance of youth and robust
health. Also, it was more comfortable to despise foolishness than to think about the pitiful wretches in the porti-
coes. He hurried to the bridge on the other side of the
island. The city was over there. Its noises would overcome
the unforgettable sound of the dying woman's breathing.

Straight ahead of him was a crowded street, with people,
animals, litters, making it an exciting blur of shifting colors
in front of a high building made of arches between
columns, tier upon tier, in mammoth curves that fashioned
its circular shape. To the left of it were gardens, colorful
with plants and populace.

And above all the movement and color, beyond the massive round of stone and marble, a great white temple
seemed to reign over Rome.

Joseph ran to the end of the short bridge and into the
city. Everything is so huge, he thought. It looks the way the
capital city of an empire should look.

He was spotted as a foreigner instantly, and two brightly
painted prostitutes came from separate directions to practice their skills of allurement, leading to robbery. Joseph
had gone no more than four paces from the bridge when
one woman had his left arm in her grasp and the other was
pulling his right hand around her waist.

The two whores hissed and cursed at each other while
Joseph tried to shake them off. He knew that his belt
needed protection from them. It held his purse and his
knife. But the women had him pinioned. He couldn't believe their strength. And they were moving, twisting,
pulling, pushing, in constant shifting pressures on every
part of his body.

Like every seaman on every ship on every sea, Joseph
had been accosted in every port he'd entered. Cutpurses

haunted docks, usually cooperating with well-practiced prostitutes. He'd been warned when he was only a boy, by older seamen And he had never, ever, been caught off guard.

Until now. He felt like the world's biggest fool.

Then the woman on his left began to scream. Not the curses she had been spouting; this was a scream of pain.

Followed in under a second by a howling on his right.

And he was free.

Joseph gaped at the thin small man who had his hands buried in the women's hair, twisting it and practically yanking it out of their scalps. They were bent over from agonizing pain, shaking their heads slowly from side to side, trying to free themselves from his iron grip.

The muscles on his sinewy thin arms looked like thick mounds of rock. The veins on them were like ropes. He shook the whores and laughed at their yowls of pain. His teeth were tiny, and very white in contrast to his sunbrowned skin. That skin was smooth, gleaming with oil on his neck, face, and head. He was totally bald.

He released the women and, with fierce sharp speed, kicked each of them in the rear and sent them sprawling.

"Stranger," he said to Joseph, "I believe you owe me a cup of wine." He laughed again, looked at the women, corrected himself. "Make that two cups."

His name, he said, was Achilles, but his heels never gave him any trouble. He was an actor, an Athenian by birth, but with no one place he could call home because he was part of a company that traveled from theater to theater, festival to festival, all over the Mediterranean world. "I also do juggling, acrobatics, wrestling, and mime. Whatever is called for."

Achilles and his fellow actors had come to Rome for the Ludi. They had done so for many years and many Ludi. There were five a year.

He appointed himself Joseph's guide. "You wouldn't last an hour on your own" was his friendly assessment.

And he gave Joseph a day of unparalleled laughter and misinformation. In the Roman Forum, Achilles pointed out the small circular Temple of Vesta, goddess of the hearth and home. "It's shaped like that to represent the hole between a woman's legs, because that"—he gestured to a long, low building nearby—"is where the priestesses of Vesta live. They're called the Vestal Virgins, and they service the Emperor and the generals of the Army."

He nodded significantly at the triumphal arch immediately in front of them. "To commemorate Augustus' valor. You can imagine what kind and where."

On every side temples in white marble, with gilded and brightly colored decorations, seemed to be competing for attention. Achilles rattled off their identifications, with scurrilous commentary.

"That huge thing is the Castor and Pollux Temple. You should know them, they're supposed to be the patrons of sailors. Twins and giants. That's why the temple had to be giant sized. It's one of the best places in the city to find those notables, the senators. They accept bribes in one half of the temple and lose the money in dice games in the other half.

"Opposite is more money action. Those tables and the fat men behind them are for money changing. Sometimes, if I'm very bored, I stand nearby and bite the gold and silver coins to test them for the unfortunate victims of the changers." Achilles' tiny teeth flashed when he laughed. "I enjoy bending them and spitting them out. The changers pay me to go away.

"We won't bother them today, it's not amusing enough to waste time. Too bad the politicians haven't returned yet. They climb up on this"—Achilles patted a high broad platform—"and make speeches about the excellence of themselves. The one who succeeds in being heard by anyone more than two steps away has a temple built in his name and paid for by the fines that the city collects from drovers who allow their donkeys to bray."

Achilles nodded his gleaming head toward a smaller, lower building with only a six-columned porch. "That drab edifice is the Curia, where the senators usually meet. It was put just far enough from the dice games and bribes in Castor and Pollux to give Rome's noble leaders a touch of exercise. Usually their slaves carry them everywhere, but to get to the bribes they hustle through the crowds on their own aristocratic feet."

Joseph looked at the crowds. It wouldn't be easy to get through them for any reason. Food sellers, wine sellers, water sellers, sellers of souvenir models of the monumental buildings, many soldiers in pairs and threesomes, many more prostitutes shouting invitations or insults to the soldiers, groups of young men, clustered families buying honeycakes for tired children, curtained litters carried by slaves wearing tunics in colors that matched the paint on the litters, boys running, reckless of the danger to the people around them, solitary men reading poetry aloud to the few people who pretended to listen, orators on the steps of all the temples preaching passionately to no one at all.

Joseph had no trouble telling which were Romans and which were foreigners, like him. The outsiders' eyes stared up at the monumental columns of the great temples in wonderment at their size. Taller than the tallest trees, they seemed almost to be holding up the skies as well as the roofs of the temples.

The real Romans were dwarfed by the scale of their city's structures, but they were obviously unaware of their own insignificance. They used the temples, the Forum, the city, with a casual familiarity that made Rome their own.

Joseph admired their spirit without envying them the life that gave birth to it. He did not believe that that life—without room to breathe, in rooms that might tumble you into a tomb of broken bricks on a crowded noisy street—was a fair trade for the privilege of being a citizen of the world's biggest city, the heart of the Empire.

"You chose a good time for your sight-seeing," Achilles told Joseph. "The city's almost empty. When people return from the country, the Forum can get quite crowded."

Joseph laughed. Achilles expected it, he'd decided, and the laughter felt good.

"I didn't expect it to be so small," Joseph commented. It was true. The court of the Gentiles at the Temple was a bigger area than this center of the Empire. He was rather disappointed. All the buildings crowded so close to one another created an impression of a kind of disorder, even carelessness. It was like what had happened in the galley, when Queen Salome had insisted on filling every inch of space in her cabin with something—tables and stools brought from other cabins, braziers for sweet incense burning, large cauldrons of water for bathing her feet ten times an hour. Similarly, some building, or statue, or arch, or obelisk had been tucked in wherever there was an open piece of paving in the Forum.

"Cluttered," Achilles agreed, though Joseph hadn't said precisely that. "That's why Julius Caesar added another one and Augustus yet another. They're over there, behind the Curia. We can go there, of course, but I propose something to eat first."

"Are the other forums the same as this one?"

"Not at all." Achilles pinched his nose between finger and thumb. "Much more imperial. The Julian one has a single temple, to Venus, with reasonable imitations of Greek statues arranged in front of it. Mainly it is the upper class shopping area. The two long sides are porticoed, with rows of shops full of imported luxuries.

"Augustus built himself an outdoor throne room. All classic and grand. He allows ambassadors to bring gifts and money to him there. Occasionally hosts a banquet or gives a speech.

"The old, messy, first Forum is the real one. You can

hear the heartbeat of the Empire in the melodious lying calls of the vendors."

Joseph looked alarmed. "We're not going to feed our-selves from their baskets, I hope. I had no breakfast and I'd like a proper meal."

Achilles made a moue of regret. "I would take you up on the Palatine—that tree-covered hill—to share a nibble with my dear friend the Emperor, but unfortunately he's out of the city. I'm afraid we'll have to settle for a tavern I use that's near the theater.

"The food is excellent and ample, the wine copious and not bad. The only drawback is that it is usually filled with actors."

Joseph said that sounded like perfection to him. "If all actors are like you, Achilles, it will be the most enjoyable meal of my whole life."

"There are few that match my beauty," Achilles replied, "but they're an amusing lot."

As, indeed, they were. And Joseph was a perfect audi-ence for their stories. His laughter and admiration were to-tally genuine.

He heard about adventures in performance, in theaters, in the cities where the theaters were located. Achilles and his friends knew Caesarea well, Jerusalem, too. Better than Joseph did, in fact.

He enjoyed himself so much that he emptied his purse on the table where they sat. "Allow me, if you will do me the honor, to pay for the food and drink we have all had today."

"That's too much silver, Joseph," said the corpulent actor who was sitting beside him.

"Then take more refreshment. Now, or later. I must go now."

The troupe of actors applauded Joseph's exit.

With the exception of Achilles. "I intended to relieve you of that burdensome weight of silver without your noticing, Joseph," he said dolefully.

Joseph laughed. "I thought you might," he said with a grin. "My friend."

Juda was waiting near the island end of the bridge. Joseph could see him when he left the tavern. It was close to the cityside end of the bridge.

"A good day?" Juda asked.

"Very good."

"The Archon Rufinius has returned to the city and hopes that you will be his guest at his home, Joseph. I expected you to accept, so I did so on your behalf. Is that all right?"

"Of course," Joseph said. He was sure that the bed he slept in the night before was Juda's. The old man's two rooms on the fourth floor of his insula were very small.

Juda patted Joseph's shoulder in an avuncular way. "Excellent," he said. "I will take you to Rufinius' house now. I have brought with me the pouch of gold you asked me to safeguard for you."

CHAPTER THIRTY

JOSEPH PUSHED ASIDE THE CURTAINS THAT CLOSED THE ENTRANCE to the bedroom and walked into the peristyle. He stopped there, in the shade, and looked at the charming scene in the garden court just ahead.

A woman was combing the thick auburn hair of the young girl who was seated on a bench beside the fountain. The sun made rainbows in the fountain's spray and lit fires in the girl's hair.

"Forgive me for intruding," Joseph said. "May I pass through to the door? I am going into the city."

The girl turned to look at him, and he caught his breath. She was wearing a yellow linen tunic, the color of the flowers in the clay pots that sat on the rim of the fountain, and she was eating a pomegranate. The juices had stained her full lips deep pink.

"Go right ahead," she said. "I'm just drying my hair." She turned her head again, to let the woman continue combing. The movement caused the tunic to slide from her shoulders on the left side, where Joseph stood. She pulled it up again, using two fingers of the hand that held the pomegranate. Some of its juice fell onto her soft neck.

"You're going to stain your tunic, Miss Deborah," scolded the woman.

"I'll be careful, Meneptah," the girl promised. "Don't be cross."

She's still a child, Joseph thought, trying not to anger her nursemaid. But when her clothing was disarrayed, he had seen the demi-globe that was the top of her breast, and the sunlight reached through the pale linen to outline a woman's body.

He made himself walk through the garden without trying to talk to her. But he wanted to hear her sweet voice again. It was artless, not yet aware of its power to stir a man. As he was stirred. From the corner of his eye he saw her bare soft feet with their tiny clear pink nails.

The Archon Rufinius was a successful man. His villa outside Rome had extensive olive orchards, and he did a good, steady business selling the three grades of oil pressed from the olives. He was a man in his mid-fifties, and he was not extravagant, so he had amassed a fortune large enough to buy his house on the Aventine Hill, and to leave the insula apartment in the Transtiber neighborhood behind.

He had droned on and on, telling Joseph every detail, at dinner the night before.

Now Joseph stood on the street outside the back door of the house and looked down at the Tiber and across it to the clamorous streets that were home to the poor.

He had to respect Rufinius for what he had accomplished. After all, wasn't he, Joseph, doing much the same thing, making his way in the world and building a fortune?

But—olive oil? Where was the adventure in that? Rufinius was altogether too much like Joseph's father, Joshua. At dinner when Joseph told him about his day in Rome, the Archon had frowned and deplored the thought that he had associated himself with actors and admired pagan temples.

Was the girl in the garden Rufinius' granddaughter?

Or—grotesque thought—his wife? The Archon had said that the mother of his children, his honored wife, had died several years earlier. Old men did marry young girls. The idea was disgusting. Joseph rejected it with hot anger. Then turned his anger against himself.

What is wrong with you, Joseph of Arimathea? He did not like his response to the scene in the garden. Maybe he needed to visit a good brothel instead of the baths and barber, his destination this morning.

But who could he ask about clean brothels? Rufinius? Joseph smiled at the thought and felt better. No, he'd get himself and his clothing cleaned up, and then he'd take a look at the famous Circus Maximus. That way he'd be able to leave the next day for Caesarea. It would hardly make a big difference in his life to miss seeing the actual races. It was a small price to pay for getting away from the self-satisfied, critical Archon.

And the pomegranate girl. He could just imagine himself peering between the curtains of the bedroom in hopes of seeing her again. Disgusting!

The baths and a stiff massage after made Joseph feel more like himself. The barber had a superlative touch with the razor, and the cloth cleaners turned over to him a tunic and cloak that looked even better than new.

Joseph went to the shops Achilles had told him about, in the Forum of Julius Caesar. It was a good idea to learn what imported luxuries were popular in Rome. What about the Belerion jewelry? Would that be good? He was always interested in possible expansion of business. And he could buy presents for Sarah and his mother and his grandmother.

The Circus Maximus was at the base of the Aventine Hill. He could see that on the way back to Rufinius' house and a final tedious dinner.

Joseph was trying hard not to feel intimidated by Rome, not to be too impressed. But the immensity of the oval racetrack and the miles of tiered marble seats were grand beyond imagination.

The entire population of Jerusalem would fill only a small segment of the seating. Now Joseph understood, truly comprehended, the size of Rome. And he was impressed.

Rufinius had the numbers instantly available. The population of Jerusalem, he said, was slightly above thirty thousand people. The Circus Maximus seated slightly fewer than a quarter of a million spectators.

Then he paused, to give Joseph the opportunity to comment on his wealth of knowledge. Joseph obliged.

Yes, the Archon said, the precision of numbers had always pleased him. And a good memory was one of his blessings from God. That was, no doubt, the reason he was elected Archon time after time. The members of the synagogue knew that he would keep all the business affairs in precise order.

Even his patron relied on his memory, Rufinius said. His small smile was the essence of smugness.

Joseph was wondering how many more minutes he'd have to listen politely to this disagreeable old man before dinner would be announced. What or who was a patron? he inquired idly. Let the man boast. He was providing food and a bed and this was the last evening Joseph would have to suffer the boredom.

However, what Rufinius explained to him about the system of patron and clients did not bore him at all. It outraged him. The indignity, the sycophancy, the perpetual anxiety that the clients must know. Joseph could hardly hide his feeling of revulsion for men who could tolerate such degradation.

". . . King Herod," Rufinius was saying.

Joseph nearly cried out. "But that's business, not lickspittle self-abasement."

"Yes," the Archon continued, "his generosity has been extraordinary. Last year he gave us a gold menorah. We have never regretted naming our handsome place of worship the Synagogue of the Herodienses."

Joseph felt a malicious urge to say that he'd tell Herod how pleased Rufinius and his friends were—the next time he dined at Herod's palace.

But he held his tongue. All he'd told the men he met was that he was a shipowner/trader on his first visit to Rome.

Rufinius' doorkeeper entered the living room to announce the arrival of Aurelius Hermias. Maybe we'll eat now, Joseph thought. He hadn't known Rufinius was expecting a guest. His mood was not optimistic. Any man who would accept dinner at the Archon's house was likely to be as unpleasant as he.

Aurelius Hermias proved him wrong. He was considerably younger than the Archon and a hundred times more interesting. He owned one of the shops Joseph had visited in the Forum Caesareum that afternoon, a treasure trove of Persian rugs and slippers and intricately wrought brass ornaments. Joseph took his place in the dining room filled with pleasant anticipation of the conversation to come.

They did not, of course, begin talking business at once. Hermias asked the usual question: How did Joseph like Rome?

With complete sincerity Joseph replied that he found it amazing.

To his surprise Hermias laughed heartily. "A diplomat and a skillful rhetorician," he said to Rufinius. "You did not praise this man sufficiently when you told me about him."

The Archon bristled.

And Joseph grinned at Hermias.

After that, they got along very well together. Hermias, Joseph discovered, was the head of the synagogue's Gerusia, the council of elders that formed policy and judged disputes between members. "I flatter myself that I still have some years to live before I feel like an elder," Hermias joked. "In fact, I was awarded the honor because my family is Sadducee."

"As is mine," the Archon said peevishly.

"And mine," Joseph offered. "My grandfather was a member of the Sanhedrin before King Herod took away its powers. And my grandfather's head."

He said it lightheartedly, intending to match Hermias' mood.

But religion and the oppression of Judaism were not issues to be taken lightly by Jews, a small group in the midst of the center of imperial power.

Joseph regretted his flippancy almost at once. The Archon launched into a description of the constant scrutiny he was obliged to maintain over the warehouse that distributed the dole to the citizens of Rome. Julius Caesar, and now Augustus Caesar, made special regulations for the Jews. Their distribution schedule was adjusted to respect the Sabbath. But the administrators at the depots changed frequently. Every time a new man was appointed, he had to confront him, inform him of the rule, and often obtain the backing of a higher official.

"And you do an admirable job, Rufinius." Hermias interrupted the Archon expertly, and changed the subject without giving offense. "How many guests do you think I should invite to the celebration of my son's coming of age? All the men of the Gerusia? Of the congregation?"

Rufinius quoted the exact numbers of each at once, then the cost of food and wine for each group if Hermias bought wisely.

Joseph carefully avoided meeting Hermias' eye. He was afraid he might laugh.

"How blessed you are, Hermias, to have such happiness to anticipate. One son who is becoming a man, and four more to follow him in turn. My dear wife gave me nine children, all of them girls. I cannot understand what sins I am guilty of, to be punished in such a manner. Her sisters gave their husbands five strong sons to be proud of."

"For shame, Rufinius. Your girls are a credit to you, all of them. And they have given you many grandsons."

"But their duty is to their husbands, not their father. Who will take care of me in my last years? I have only Deborah left, and when she weds I will be alone."

The table held a bowl of figs and pomegranates. Joseph had a flashing memory of the red drop of pomegranate juice on the white skin of the girl in the garden. Deborah.

"Archon," he said, "I wish to marry your daughter."

CHAPTER THIRTY-ONE

REBEKKAH AND SARAH WERE ON THEIR KNEES IN Rebekkah's garden, pulling the weeds that Antiochus had overlooked. The recently turned soil was moist and pungently alive. The first rains had come, and the air was sweet.

"I rejoice more every year when the dry season finally ends," Rebekkah said. "The sirocco makes my old bones brittle."

Sarah laughed. "'Old bones' indeed. My knees crack much louder than yours when we kneel down."

"I have given serious thought to whipping Antiochus," Rebekkah said. "Slaves are supposed to do everything they're ordered to do, and I'm sure he left more weeds than he pulled. Joseph used to prepare the garden for planting without a single weed in it, when he was a boy."

"What do you think she'll be like, Rebekkah?"

"Who?"

"You know who. The new wife."

"She'll have wide hips and a good supply of milk. That's all that matters. You know what Abigail told us last week when she visited. Joseph has the Temple priests looking for her. They're trying to find a widow with children, so they know she's fertile. Not more than ten years older than Joseph, or she might be coming near the end of her child-bearing years."

Joseph's grandmother looked lovingly at Sarah. "You know full well that she will mean nothing to him, Sarah, but you refuse to accept that knowledge. You are too sensible to keep brooding this way. Life must be taken as it is sent to us, and this breeding is the only way to prevent divorce."

"I keep seeing them together, and it drives me mad."

"You are a fool. Stop it. You're not a foolish woman. You are my grandson's wife, and he loves you. He will spill his seed in this woman with no more feeling than if he was mounting a ewe. Or a whore. You must know that much about men. They relieve themselves. Only rarely do they make love."

Sarah sat back on her heels. "I never allowed myself to think about that. Do you believe that he has used prostitutes?"

"Certainly. He is a sailor for half every year, and seaports have more brothels than wineshops, I've been told."

"Who told you?"

"Not Joseph, if that's what you were thinking. It was a slave, a hairdresser, that we owned in the fancy Jerusalem years. She had worked in a brothel, a very exclusive one."

"Was she a hairdresser there or . . . the other thing?"

"I never asked her. She made me look very beautiful."

"You still do, Rebekkah."

"You lie prettily, my dear. I will happily listen to as many as you care to tell me. But you must not lie to yourself. Hard facts have to be faced. When Joseph returns, he will take a second wife, and he will get a child on her. He will buy a house somewhere, and furnishings, and treat her with respect and generosity, because she will deserve it. He will also spend time there, because he will love the child; it is his nature.

"But you will remain his wife, his only wife, in his heart.

I am as sure of that as I am that the sun will set today and rise tomorrow."

"I believe you, Rebekkah. And I will learn to accept the facts." Sarah tore the weeds she was holding into ragged pieces. "I just hope that she will be very ugly."

"Hideous would be even better," Rebekkah said. "Abigail and I agreed that dark hairs on her upper lip would please us."

CHAPTER THIRTY-TWO

"I WISH TO MARRY YOUR DAUGHTER." JOSEPH STARED wildly at the space in front of him as if he might see the words written on the air or carved into it.

He couldn't have said that. Not possibly.

And yet he knew that those words had leapt out of his mouth. And that they were there, in the air of the room.

"Out of the question!" The Archon Rufinius did not quite shout at Joseph, but his refusal was sharp and loud.

Joseph swallowed. His relief was dizzying; he had difficulty breathing.

Aurelius Hermias made an attempt to pour oil on troubled waters. "Come now, Rufinius, there's no need to speak so harshly. You do not want to let Deborah go, that's understandable, but you do not have to bite this young man's head off."

Rufinius mumbled something incomprehensible. Hermias made him repeat it. "It was the suddenness. I wasn't expecting . . ."

He looked at Joseph. "I ask your pardon for my rudeness," he said. His dignity was admirable.

Joseph hastened to reply. He was somewhat incoherent himself, speaking too quickly, muddling Latin and Greek words in hopeless syntax. Rufinius obviously could make no sense of what he was saying.

Joseph took a deep, steadying breath, then spoke. "There is no need for you to apologize, Archon. I was at fault. I ask your pardon for my impetuous, improper words. And I withdraw what I said."

Hermias raised his wine goblet. "There, all settled, no damage done. Let's have a drink." He looked at Joseph, vivid curiosity in his eyes.

Joseph looked away. He wanted desperately to get away from the mess he'd made and the awkwardness that was its residue.

But the only thing he could do was to lift his goblet and drain it.

It was empty. Ridiculous. A dreadful bubble of laughter tried to escape his throat, and he choked, then coughed in spasms of agonized airlessness. Hermias leaned toward him and pounded him on the back.

At last he was able to gasp, get some air into his lungs, croak "Sorry."

"Perhaps some water?" Hermias was solicitous.

Joseph nodded.

Rufinius clapped his hands to summon a servant.

Hermias was also merciful. While Joseph was gulping the cup of water, he said that Rome often tired visitors more than they realized, fascinated as they always were by the city's wonders. "Your young guest should probably make this an abbreviated evening, go to bed early and have a long restorative rest. Don't you agree, Archon?"

Rufinius was glad to say yes.

Joseph was sleeping, but restless. When Deborah's fingers were laid across his lips, he woke instantly and fully. "Ssssh," she whispered, "don't make any sound."

She was holding a tiny lamp, with a low unsteady flame. The flickering light was reflected by the widened pupils of her dark eyes. Her face was only a blurred paleness in the darkness.

Her whispering was urgent and frightened. "I heard. I listened at a crack in the door. I heard you talk about the theater . . . and the circus . . . and me. Oh, please, make my father say yes. I'm never allowed to go anywhere. Make him let me marry you, and take me with you."

Her childishness made Joseph feel as if his twenty-four years were two hundred and forty. Could it be possible that she would marry a man simply because she wanted to see a play, or horse races? Could she be that ignorant? Know nothing about what marriage really meant?

He sat up in the bed, taking her hand to remove it from his mouth. Then he put his lips close to her ear. Her hair smelled of some flower essence in water, and her quick, nervous breaths smelled like milk.

Joseph's whisper was even quieter than hers. "You must go back to your room. Never come to a man's room, Deborah."

She began to cry.

"Hush, hush," Joseph whispered. "Go. Go to bed."

"But I want to go with you. You said you would marry me." She crawled up on his bed, and the lamp wobbled dangerously in her hand, spilling oil. Joseph hurriedly extinguished the flame before it could set fire to the bedclothes. He felt her warmth in the dark, her trembling sobbing. "Don't send me away," he heard her breathe into his ear. Her arms were extended, her hands fumbled to find him, brushing his chest, his shoulders, his neck.

Joseph's reaction was involuntary and uncontrollable. He felt himself hardening, and his groin became acutely sensitive to the linen coverlet across his lower body.

"No." He was no longer whispering. "Go away, Deborah." He pushed his hands in the direction of her warmth and felt her softness against his palms. "No," he insisted, but his fingers were stroking her, tracing the shape of her breasts, touching the soft neck where the red juice had fallen.

Then he gained control. His hand moved down to her waist, caught it firmly on each side and lifted her down from the high-legged bed. "Go away. Now. I mean it."

"You mean it?"

"Yes. Go away."

"You'll make Father let me marry you?"

"Just go away. Anything you want, if you'll go. Go away, Deborah."

The curtains rustled, and she was gone. Except for the scent of her. And the spilled oil. And the unsatisfied, demanding heat in Joseph's loins. Many hours went by before he slept.

He was nervous about leaving the bedroom in the morning. Surely someone must have heard, must know that Deborah had been in his room, that his hands had— He must not remember that. He had to say his thank-you and his farewell and leave at once.

The doorkeeper was waiting in the peristyle. "A man to see you, sir. He is in the hall with the master."

Who could it be? For an instant Joseph wondered if bald Achilles was scandalizing the Archon, then realized that it must certainly be Juda, or one of the men he'd met at Juda's courtyard festivities. Good. He needed to thank him, too, and say goodbye.

"Nicolaus!" Shock and delight made Joseph stumble over the threshold to the wide reception area near the main entrance to the house. He righted himself and hurried to embrace his friend. He could read in Nicolaus' face that all had gone well with his reconciliation efforts for Herod.

He remembered belatedly that some basic courtesies were required. "Archon Rufinius, may I present my friend Nicolaus of Damascus?"

"I introduced myself, Joseph, and the Archon has been a most gracious host. While you slept the morning away, I might add, you indolent scoundrel. Hurry now. You'll have to find a very quick barber. We have an appointment that you cannot miss. Don't worry, I've already told the Archon that I'm stealing you from him."

Nicolaus grinned broadly. "We will return, you can count on it. I am most eager to meet the lady."

Rufinius cleared his throat. "I spent many hours of the night thinking about my hasty emotional outburst, Joseph, and I realized that I was completely in the wrong. While he awaited you, I told your noble friend about the betrothal between you and my Deborah."

Joseph felt as if he'd been kicked in the stomach. So Rufinius knew about last night. Perhaps he'd even seen Deborah entering or leaving his room. I am trapped, Joseph moaned silently. No, I did it to myself.

In fact Rufinius knew nothing about his daughter's midnight wandering. What he did know, because Nicolaus had told him, was that Augustus Caesar, Emperor of Rome, had invited Joseph to come to his house on the Palatine Hill.

No one that Rufinius had ever known, or even met, had ever set foot inside the private quarters of the Emperor. He did not even know anyone who knew anyone who had done so.

And this Joseph of Arimathea was going to meet the Emperor. In person. At his home. The visitor from Jerusalem was an extremely important, powerful man. Rufinius wanted to have the close alliance with him that marriage to Deborah would guarantee.

He could barely contain himself. What a thing to tell everyone at synagogue.

"There's nothing to worry about," Nicolaus assured Joseph. "The laws of Rome do not allow polygamy. You already have a wife in Israel; therefore, you cannot become the husband of a Roman citizen."

Joseph had told Nicolaus everything about his predicament. He'd also blamed Nicolaus for making it worse. "If you hadn't told Rufinius that I was going to meet Augustus . . ."

"But I did, and you are, and I tell you that Rome will not allow the marriage. So put that out of your mind and be grateful for the imperial opportunity."

"Nicolaus, I don't dare do such a thing. The Caesar, the head of the whole Roman Empire. I can't do it. Look at me. I need better robes, some decent shoes. I look like a Transtiber fishmonger."

The worldly-wise Nicolaus smiled. It was reassuring, he said, to see that Joseph was a normal human being. There had been times when he'd wondered if there was anything in the whole world that could frighten him. "Augustus will approve of everything that you think might be wrong. He believes in simplicity, deplores ostentation. You'll see."

Joseph did see, but he could hardly believe what he was seeing. Augustus' home on the Palatine Hill was not much bigger, or much grander, than Joshua's farmhouse at Arimathea. Only the richly uniformed guards and sleekly groomed slaves gave the impression of a royal residence. Even the secondary, smaller palace that Herod had built in Jerusalem was ten times more luxurious than the living quarters of the Roman Emperor.

Augustus himself was in a garden beside the house, inspecting the yellowed leaves of a fig tree, talking seriously with two men who were obviously gardeners, even though they were more richly clothed than the Emperor.

Nicolaus and Joseph stood quietly near the garden's entrance arbor, waiting to be noticed. As soon as Augustus saw them, he waved the gardeners away, with a final order about additional manuring, and started toward them.

Joseph could not help it, he stared at the most powerful man in the world. The Emperor showed little resemblance to the beautiful youthful portrait of him on the golden coins that Joseph had in his purse. He was more than slightly overweight, and his hair was thinning to such a degree that the freckles on his scalp were clearly visible. He wore a homespun coarse linen tunic belted with a rope that was beginning to fray at the ends.

Nicolaus stooped and peered closely at an insect on the earth in a garden bed when Augustus had nearly reached them. "Princeps," he said, "this strange species of fly might be worth studying. I've never seen one exactly like it. This is Joseph of Arimathea, the young Jewish ship captain I told you about."

Joseph wondered if he should kneel to the Emperor, but if he was supposed to, there was no time for it. Augustus put two hands on Joseph's shoulders and smiled down at him. "Welcome to my house," he said, "and to Rome. Nicolaus tells me it's your first time here." He patted Joseph twice, then lifted his hands from Joseph's shoulders and clapped twice.

He smiled at Joseph again. "I thought I might order some barley water, but if you'd prefer wine . . . ?"

"I prefer barley water, Princeps." That was the title Nicolaus had used, so Joseph had to assume it was correct. He wanted to be very, very, very correct. Looking up into the Emperor's smiling face, Joseph could see that the small light brown eyes above the smile were not smiling at all. There was no anger in them, no hostility, no emotion of any kind. They were measuring, assessing, gathering data before making any judgment on the unknown man they saw.

Joseph felt a thread of cold climb inside his spine, and he knew, without knowing how he knew, that he was in the presence of an intelligence beyond normal reckoning and the possessor of unlimited power who was at all times unafraid to use it.

Two slaves came running. They bowed to the Emperor, awaiting orders. "Nicolaus? Wine or barley water?" said Augustus.

"Water, if I may."

"A pitcher of barley water and something to go with it," Augustus said to the bent heads. He smiled again, looking at Joseph. "I hope you enjoy your refreshments. I'm afraid I must go, work to do. But Nicolaus knows about the little problem you can solve for me. He'll tell you all about it."

He squeezed Joseph's arm briefly. "I will be indebted to you if you're able to help me, Joseph of Arimathea."

Augustus's clasp on his arm had been as strong as iron, but Joseph wasn't alarmed. The Emperor's smile had been in his eyes, too, this time.

Joseph couldn't imagine any way he could possibly solve a "little problem" for Augustus Caesar, but he would be willing to do anything whatsoever that might be asked of him.

He had fallen completely under the spell of the mysterious, unique charm that bound many thousands of men, and women, to the Emperor of Rome.

"Help me up, please, Joseph. I've gotten as crumpled as a broken stick." Nicolaus' voice was warm with endearing laughter. His young friend looked like a lovestruck boy.

Joseph hauled Nicolaus upright. "Why are you so interested in flies? Do you think they're harming the figs?"

Nicolaus stretched his long arms and legs, one by one. "I know only one thing about flies, Joseph. They are pests. But whenever Augustus Caesar is standing, I find some reason to be near the floor or the ground. He's very sensitive about his height, and I'm so tall it bothers him."

"But he's quite tall, Nicolaus. I had to look up a good way to meet his eyes."

Nicolaus decided to wait awhile before telling Joseph about the sandals that Augustus wore, with the two-inch-thick soles that made him taller. Why should he deflate Joseph's hero worship? Particularly when it seemed that the Emperor had decided to like Joseph, and not only because he was considerably shorter.

The barley water and "something to go with it" turned out to be a small feast, with wine as well as water, breads, cheeses, cold meats and fowl, and an assortment of fruits and sweet cakes. Both men ate heartily, at a table and chairs in a shaded corner of the garden.

Nicolaus described the success of his mission. While he was waiting for admission to the Emperor's presence, an unexpected new arrival had appeared with a retinue of a hundred slaves bearing gifts of every description, from caged tigers to golden, jewel-studded coffers of precious myrrh. He was Aretas, the new king of Nabatea. While Syllaeus was at Augustus' court denouncing King Herod, and Nicolaus was on his way to defend him, old King Obodas had died, and Aretas had seized the chance to proclaim himself King.

Such a presumptuous act was a much more serious breach of Roman law than Herod's misguided military adventure, and Augustus' anger was diverted. But Aretas was accompanied by lavish evidence of his loyalty to Rome's ruler. And also—to Nicolaus' great delight—he was eloquent in his lengthy, colorful denunciation of Syllaeus' duplicity, dishonesty, dis—everything else that would damage his reputation.

Queen Salome, meanwhile, was doing a magnificent job of blackening Syllaeus' character and repeating treacherous things she claimed—and invented—he had said about Rome's rulers.

"By the time we finished, King Herod's crime began to look like a boyish prank when compared to the iniquities of Syllaeus," Nicolaus concluded.

"What will happen to him? More important, what service can I do for the Emperor?"

"He's in prison now. I suppose he'll be executed. And, my poor Joseph, I'm afraid you will need five times the wisdom of your legendary King Solomon to provide what Augustus wants from you. Salome, you see, was wearing a bracelet that her friend the Empress admired exceedingly. According to Salome, you gave it to her. Livia will make her uxorious husband's life miserable until he acquires one for her. Or, even better, two, so that she can outshine Salome."

Joseph was bitterly disappointed; he'd hoped for some

act of valor, some defiance of danger, something dramatic for his fulfillment of Augustus' unidentified request.

"I gave my grandmother three of them, and they're all more beautiful than the one I used to bribe Salome for my introduction to King Herod."

"Oh yes, I remember that. I didn't know how you'd managed it. Well, if your grandmother will part with the bracelets, there'll be no problem. The Emperor will send orders for couriers to bring them to Rome with the same speed they carry more customary dispatches, like declarations of war or similar less important matters. But we'll need all of them, you know. Augustus can give two to Livia, and after she's had her fun crowing over Salome, he can give the remaining one to her. Women—!" Nicolaus' imprecation had all the exasperated, frustrated, energetic despair that a survivor of Cleopatra's court was entitled to.

They walked slowly down the Palatine Hill, enjoying the views of Rome. "Will you do me a favor, please, Nicolaus?" Joseph asked.

"If I can, with minimal effort. And if you will do one for me. I offered King Aretas a cabin on your galley for our return to Caesarea. Salome is going to visit Livia for the winter."

Joseph smiled. He'd be glad to transport the new King of Nabatea. Especially if he was also rid of Queen Salome. "With or without tigers?" he joked.

"Without, you'll be sad to hear. And I told him no more than twenty of his hulking attendants. Thank you, Joseph. What can I do for you?"

"Get me out of that house. I'll sleep in a tree if I have to, but I cannot spend another night there."

"Simple. You can have the floor in my room at the Emperor's house. It's almost certainly more comfortable than the bed. And we'll leave at first light tomorrow, whether it pleases Aretas or not. We don't want to get caught by the

Ludi festival. I have to take the good news to Herod as soon as I can."

Joseph agreed, with all his heart. He wished they didn't have to wait for dawn. "Walk back with me, let me break the no-wedding news, and then you impress Rufinius again," he said. "Afterwards, I'll buy you the best wine in Rome to celebrate my escape. Freedom!" He did a silly hop-skip-jump dance in the very center of the Roman Forum.

Rufinius had brought together the head of the synagogue, Archisynagogos Gadias, and Hermias, the head of the Gerusia, who'd been at dinner the day before, also Juda, the presbytic who'd been Joseph's first host; and another elder named Martius. They were at his house to witness the betrothal ceremony. And to witness Joseph's agreement to the ketubah, the contract that outlined the specific terms of the bride's dowry, the wedding-price paid by the groom, the financial compensation due to the wife if separation or divorce occurred, and any other special monetary commitments.

The Archon had composed it and written it on the best vellum, in neat, even letters that always won him compliments from the synagogue members when he presented any documents associated with the business responsibilities that were the concern of the Archon.

Joseph was appalled. He was a decent man, and he regretted the embarrassment he was about to cause Rufinius. But it had to be done. He told him, before witnesses, why the wedding could not take place.

Three hours later the Archon dipped a freshly sharpened pen into an inkpot and gave it to Joseph for him to use, to sign the ketubah.

Moments later Deborah entered the room with her nurse. Her auburn hair was curled and arranged on top of her head with ivory hairpins carved in the shapes of flowers. She wore a tunic of pale green silk, tied twice, in Roman style, by gold-colored ribbons around her small waist and below her firm, full breasts. The hem of the tunic was embroidered with flowers, in gold thread, and the sandals on her small feet were a delicate webbing of gold cord.

Her cheeks were flushed, her lips looked as if she had been eating pomegranates, and she was perfumed with the scent of spring.

She looked directly at Joseph and smiled a beguiling shy smile that dimpled the corners of her mouth. "I'm so happy!" she said.

The Archon took his daughter's hand, and the hand of Joseph that had signed the contract, and placed them together atop his palm. He pronounced his blessing in a solemn voice, and the betrothal was done. Deborah's nurse led her away, Nicolaus said diplomatic goodbyes for Joseph, and they departed.

According to Jewish law, Joseph was effectively the husband of Rufinius' daughter. Roman law, the Archisynagogos had said decisively, was of no importance in the eyes of God.

Nonetheless, the wedding would take place in Jerusalem, where there was no question of the legality of a polygamous union. Rufinius would be there, naturally. He had wanted, all his life, to make a pilgrimage to the Holy City. His new son would transport him, together with Deborah and her nurse, in one of his fine ships.

That was all spelled out in the ketubah. Together with the requirement that Joseph provide a house and servants for his wife as well as a thousand shekels in her name to be kept in the Temple treasury, plus the normal expenses of housekeeping, clothing, and miscellaneous needs.

Deborah's dowry consisted of two hundred gold aureii, held in her name by her father, for safekeeping.

"I tried to help, Joseph, but I was outsmarted at every turn," Nicolaus moaned. "I'm truly sorry." He refilled their wine goblets.

"Still," he said after a long drink, "she is a delectable little creature. You aren't exactly to be pitied, you must agree. A virgin is always a prize."

Joseph drained his goblet. He was resigned to the mistake he'd made, and he had nothing to say. Also his thoughts weren't anything he wanted to speak aloud. Not about a girl he had pledged—in writing—to honor and to marry. This marriage was about children, not sex. He had to remember that. It was no cause for pride that he was already regretting the months that would pass before the marriage was consummated. Green silk had covered, but not disguised, the body of his bride.

CHAPTER THIRTY-THREE

"YOU WERE SUPPOSED TO FATHER A CHILD, JOSEPH, NOT marry one!" Sarah grabbed the nearest thing to hand and threw it at his head. By unhappy chance it was the lyre she'd been given by the Bard Nancledra, a prized possession. Its strings jangled horribly when it struck the wall, a sound of anger and desperation. Then it fell to the floor, and its frame cracked with a noise like a thunderbolt. Sarah burst into tears. "Get out of here," she sobbed and screamed simultaneously. "I don't want to see your face in my house. Or in my bed."

Joseph took his troubles to his grandmother. Together with the request that she give back the bracelets he had given to her.

Rebekkah laughed gently. "Forgive me, my Joseph. I do not find your plight amusing. Life is comic, not the lives of people we love. Take the bracelets; you can get me new ones.

"And I do believe you should leave Arimathea for now. You have an obligation to build or buy a house in Jerusalem. That will keep you busy for a while, then we'll see if you can come home. Take Antiochus with you. He can carry messages back and forth, and he'll be useful to you in other ways, too.

"Oh—Joseph, it would not be a good plan to stay with your Aunt Abigail."

Joseph was pleased to have Antiochus' company. Even though his family were all disapproving, at least the boy still admired him and wanted to be with him.

"Boy." That no longer described Antiochus, Joseph reminded himself. The frightened, suspicious boy of Alexandria's Street of the Perfumers was now an educated, competent man.

Who deserved the opportunity to make his own way in the world. On the road from Arimathea to Jerusalem, Joseph told Antiochus what he was thinking, and made him a generous offer.

"With your intelligence—especially your genius for mathematics—the world is open to you, Antiochus.

"You can be a teacher, or I will lend you the money to start a business," Joseph said. "You have only to decide what you want to do with your life. I will give you your freedom."

"I know what I want."

"Good. What?"

"I like being your servant and I want to be your friend. Take me with you wherever you go."

Joseph realized within a few days that he did not really know Jerusalem at all. The Temple, the wine and food shop Micah had discovered, Abigail's house, and the two palaces of King Herod were the extent of his familiarity. Even in the exciting small streets of shops in the lower city, he had never really looked at the faces of the men who owned the shops, or at the men and women and children in the streets. They had been only components of a crowd.

Now he paid attention to what he was seeing. And he felt a growing pride in his people and their city. He had been told from his earliest childhood that he was singularly blessed to have been born a Jew, one of the people of God, privileged possessors of His Holy Law. It was so ingrained that he had never questioned it, or examined it. Walking Jerusalem's steep streets, exploring the alleys and neighborhoods, the meaning of living according to the Law was brought home to him at every turn. Jews were governed by morality, not by a government. Yes, shopkeepers haggled over prices, trying to extract the highest prices possible. But they also gave some of their goods to the hungry, if they were sellers of food, and some of their earnings to the blind or crippled beggars, if they dealt in other sorts of wares.

People jostled one another in the marketplaces, trying to get the best and freshest foodstuffs first. But they made room for the old or infirm, who had no strength to jostle.

A child who had lost his mother was reason for all the buying and selling and shouting and shoving to stop, while he was comforted by some people and others searched until the frantic mother was located and reunited with her child. Joseph remembered the Alexandrian sellers of luxuries who provided prostituted children for good customers, and he knew that the ancient dirty alleys of Jerusalem's lower city were more to be admired than the magnificent marble colonnades of Egypt's beautiful seaport.

Inevitably he compared the seven hills of Rome with the two hills that held Jerusalem. The houses of Jerusalem's poor were tiny and often shabby. They straggled down the sides of the Western Hill in such close proximity to one another that there was no order, no street longer than fifty yards before it ended at a wall or in a cramped courtyard that served houses surrounding it. But each house, even the smallest, had a flat roof where people could eat, sleep, talk to neighbors on nearby rooftops. Above them were the skies and the stars, not the weight of floor upon floor of apartments. A poor man in Jerusalem was still a man, not an animal trapped in a cage with dozens of his kind.

And a man earned his way. The Roman dole offended Joseph even more than the degrading system of patronage. He delighted in the symbols that many workmen wore as a badge of their professions. Dyers tied a bright colored bit of cloth to their arms; carpenters tucked a chip of wood behind one ear; tailors wore cloaks with a large needle carved from bone driven through the cloth over their breasts.

He had to admit, even to himself, that the handsome Hippodrome that Herod had built was distinctly inferior to the Circus Maximus, and the theater could have been lost in the vastness of the Theater of Marcellus. He remembered the scornful views of Achilles, and he couldn't argue with them. He remembered the actors' quick wit and bawdy humor, too, and he winced when he realized that even if Achilles and his company did come to Jerusalem's theater, he wouldn't be able to spend a raucous, carefree afternoon with them in a tavern. In Jerusalem he was not simply Joseph the shipowner. He was Joseph of Arimathea, with his family's dignity to uphold.

Uphold and increase. Joseph's ambition was by no means satisfied. He was in Jerusalem to buy or build a house; therefore he spent only part of his time learning the streets and admiring the people in the lower city. He respected them, but didn't want to live like them. He didn't even want to live like the Emperor. He had tasted luxury, and he liked it very much.

He had found a small house to rent in the market area, a low hill that occupied a corner between the Antonia Fortress and the city's wall. It was above the lower city in altitude and in prestige. Successful merchants had their homes here as well as their warehouses, and the streets were both wider and cleaner.

But it was only a temporary roosting place. He wanted a house in the upper city, on the Western Hill, where the ordinary houses were mansions and the best ones were palaces, including those of the High Priest of the Temple and King Herod.

And he had no idea where to begin. "The house that was once my grandfather's was easy," he complained to Antiochus. "I just walked up to the door, asked to see the master of the house, and offered to buy it at any price he cared to name.

"But when I tried the same thing at a handsome mansion near the agora, the owner's doorkeeper told me that his master wouldn't even talk to me."

"Leave everything to me," said the boy. "Slaves always talk to slaves. I can find out anything you want to know."

Joseph didn't doubt him for an instant. Antiochus, he was starting to think, had no limits to his abilities. It was he who had searched out the craftsman who made the harps for the Temple musicians. And Antiochus had persuaded the man to break his own rigid rule against dealing with anyone outside the Temple establishment.

The boy had taken the harp to Arimathea, too, as Joseph's gift to Sarah.

And, he promised it was true, he had almost persuaded her to let Joseph come home. "Not quite," he admitted, "but almost. She cried like a baby and held the harp close to her heart. And when I mentioned your coming home she didn't say no immediately. She waited for nearly a full half minute."

Joseph tried to find comfort in Antiochus' report, but a half minute didn't sound like a very long wait to him. He missed Sarah every time he saw something or thought of something new. For as long as he could remember, she had been the one person he could talk to about what he was thinking and feeling, all the private things that he kept to himself. He had missed her many times on his voyages and adventures, but always before, he'd been able to save up the things he wanted to tell her, knowing that the time would come when they'd be together, when he'd talk, and she'd ask questions or laugh or tease him out of any slips into self-importance.

Never, ever, had she shut him out. He felt lonely and abandoned. Also a little bit afraid. And a wisp of anger. He didn't really believe he deserved to be punished for what had happened in Rome. Did he? He'd thought about it so much—too much, probably—that he didn't know what to think anymore, except that he was sick to death of thinking about it.

Joseph was on the verge of going to Arimathea and breaking down the door of his house if necessary. Then Antiochus brought him news of success.

"A wonderful house, Joseph, just finished, with the best and latest styles, and you can get it, if you act fast, for practically nothing . . . relatively speaking, you understand.

"It was done for a gigantically successful man in Corinth who'd decided to spend his final years close to God. The final came sooner than he planned, though. His business partner murdered him and ran off with all the money he'd accumulated. So the builder needs money to pay all the costs. Quick. Or the stonecutters are likely to murder him."

"Where is it?"

"Not far from the agora. The builder's there now, hoping that I wasn't spinning a tale and that I'll bring you to meet him."

"It's a very special mansion," said the builder. His face was shiny with nervous sweat. "You'll think you're in Rome, not Jerusalem, when you go inside."

He didn't realize that it was the wrong thing to say to Joseph.

Some years later, after they'd become friends, Joseph told him, "If you hadn't mentioned Rome, I'd have paid at least ten thousand more. The minute I walked through the door I knew I had found exactly what I wanted."

The house was, in some respects, not unlike the home of Rufinius, Deborah's father. It had a peristyle around a garden, with a fountain in the center. The builder proudly showed the ingenious arrangement of catch basins for the wet season, which made the fountain possible in water-poor Jerusalem.

Joseph was more impressed by the doors to the rooms

that were entered from the peristyle. They were made of solid wood, with secure latches.

He remembered Deborah more often than he meant to, or wanted to.

Sarah should be, and was, the only woman who mattered.

Joseph had almost decided to go to Arimathea with the excuse that he wanted to be there for the Feast of Lights celebration—hoping for the best—when King Herod came to Jerusalem, as he did for all the Holy Day observances. He heard about Joseph's house, and within hours, Joseph found himself besieged by dozens of artisans and merchants of every conceivable fitting and object that a house could possibly use.

Plus unpredictable, unannounced visits by the King himself. Herod had decided to give his "favorite sailor" the furnishings for his new home. Selected by Herod.

The only positive aspect to the nerve-wracking experience was Nicolaus. There was time amidst the chaos for several short meetings with the man who had become the closest friend Joseph had.

Excepting Sarah.

The first words Nicolaus spoke to Joseph in privacy were an apology for his inability to extricate Joseph from the betrothal.

Joseph's first words were "You haven't told the King I'm getting married, I hope."

Nicolaus reassured him. "I'll let that wait until the last minute. You can make your plans without Herod's energetic assistance."

At other times Nicolaus told Joseph the news, both good and bad, from the imperial house. The Ludi had been very successful, with the high point being the dedication of an Altar to Peace that Augustus had built near the Tiber. But shortly afterward, the Emperor's courier service had brought the alarming word that Livia's younger son, Drusus, had been severely injured in the army camp in Germany. Her other son, Tiberius, had ridden, by night and by day, to his brother's side. He had returned to Rome, escorting Drusus' bier, for the state funeral, the grandest spectacle since the days of Julius Caesar.

Augustus was even more profoundly grieved than his wife. He had loved his stepson, people said, more than the boy's own mother.

"I tell Herod over and over again that the death of Drusus is the reason Augustus has ceased sending the informal, friendly messages he used to write. But my king cannot believe it. He's convinced that the Emperor will never restore him to the position he once occupied in Augustus' affections.

"The worry is constant with him, and it's having an ugly effect that disturbs me. I am very grateful to you and your new house, Joseph. This is the first happiness he's shown since the Nabatean mistake so many months ago."

Joseph said he was glad, and he meant it. There were times when he actually rather liked Herod; and if it made Nicolaus' life easier, then Herod's pleasure in transforming Joseph's house was a good thing.

Still, he was glad that the Feast of Lights lasted no longer than eight days, and that it was nearly over.

Then he would definitely go to Arimathea. No matter what.

"I miss you so much that I don't know what to do, Sarah. It's tearing me to pieces."

He'd found her alone in their house, playing the haunting Celtic song on the harp he'd sent by Antiochus. Joseph knelt, at a respectful distance, before he spoke.

Sarah's fingers silenced the music when she saw him. After he made his plea, she looked at him for a time that seemed to Joseph to last forever.

Then she smiled. "I don't want to throw this one at you. It took an age to get it tuned. Stand up, Joseph, you'll get cramps in your legs." She placed the harp on the floor.

"Come and kiss me," Sarah whispered while she spread her arms wide to welcome him. "I've missed you, too."

Sarah had a series of "insists."

She did not want to hear Joseph mention that "child's" name. Ever.

She did not want to know anything about the wedding. Nothing. Not the date. Not the place. Not how he felt about it or anything to do with it.

She would not allow the "child" to set foot in the village or on the farm, no matter what his father, or Helena, or even Rebekkah might say.

She would continue to visit Abigail anytime she wanted to, for as long as she pleased. Joseph would have to see to it that the "child" never went to Abigail's house during the time that she, Sarah, was in Jerusalem.

And when Joseph came to Arimathea, he would go to Joshua's house before he came home, and at Joshua's he would take off the clothes he arrived in, bathe—head to toe—and put on country clothes that Rebekkah would keep there for him.

With no hesitation Joseph agreed to every condition.

"And," said Sarah, "if you ever talk in your sleep, Joseph of Arimathea, I promise you solemnly that I will suffocate you with a cushion."

CHAPTER THIRTY-FOUR

JOSEPH TRIED TO CONVINCE HIMSELF THAT EVERYTHING WAS just the way it always had been at Arimathea and with Sarah.

But nothing was really the same, no matter how hard everyone tried to pretend otherwise.

After several weeks he found himself becoming restless and irritable. It was actually a relief when Sarah sent him away again. It happened after Sabbath dinner at Joshua's house. The whole family was there, and Amos proudly told them that his wife Rachel was pregnant. Rachel turned pink when the chorus of congratulations rose. Sarah became deathly pale, even while she was loudly joining the chorus.

"I am truly happy for Rachel and Amos," she told Joseph when they were alone in their house, "but this is hard for me. I can't not notice, we're all here together. And I don't believe I can keep on being 'dear Sarah, she's so brave about her troubles' when someone else is having the Arimathea baby that I should have, plus your betrothal, coming both at the same time. Go away, my love. I'll see you at Abigail's for Passover. Go on."

*   *   *

Like most of Judea's businessmen, Joseph kept his money in the Temple treasury for safekeeping. When the tin trade began, his profits had been so great that he bought the house where Abigail lived now and still had money left over. Since then three years had gone by. Three loads of tin. Three seasons of trading by the Macedonian brothers, using his second galley and the two smaller ships, and sharing the profits with Joseph.

When he bought the Jerusalem mansion, he was certain that he had accumulated enough money to pay for it, and he went to the Temple in calm confidence. He discovered that he could comfortably afford the very high price—and ten more exactly like it if he so chose. The fortune he was so proud of was alarmingly greater than he'd supposed. He was not the good businessman he thought he was, or he would have known.

As soon as he left Arimathea, he set himself to work correcting his mistakes. Caesarea was his first goal. He inspected his ships, then sold the two small ones and bought two galleys to replace them. Now he had four seagoing ships capable of handling large cargoes. And, if needed, he would have four galley crews, including oarsmen, so that if King Herod wanted to use the bordello galley, it would be one quarter of Joseph's best men taken away, not one half.

He went to Milcar in Tyre, to make peace with him after the hullabaloo about Herod's galley. And to get his help in finding men to fill out the crews for the bigger ships.

Joseph was back in the world of ships and sea. His element. He felt whole again, healed, able to do what he did best, away from kings and emperors and cities and silks.

He dashed to Jerusalem for Passover. When he told Sarah his most exciting news—Milcar's son Barca was going to join the crew of the *Eagle*—he didn't understand why that made her even more happy than he was.

"Because you're my Joseph again, and I love you," she said. Her words mystified him, but her kiss was like coming home again, for him.

And then it was time to go to Belerion. As soon as the new galleys and reorganized crews were in place and working well. And the special cargo for Belerion's Jews was selected and loaded. And Antiochus was found in his hiding place in the hold.

At last everything was ready. The *Eagle* passed through Caesarea's entrance, into the current. Her sail was raised. It bellied with wind, and the oars were pulled in.

Life is wonderful, Joseph thought.

Rebekkah was, she said, "charmed by the new bracelets, Joseph, and the necklace. What did you say it was called? 'Torque,' is that it? I shall call it wrinkle-hider. Or is that what 'torque' means in Celtic?" His grandmother smiled at the expression on his face. "Come, now, my Joseph. Did you believe for a minute that I swallowed your ridiculous story about looking at land in Spain? It took no more than time to sneeze for me to extract the truth from Antiochus.

"Oh, yes, Sarah knows that I know. She's glad of it. It allows her to tell me all the fascinating stories about the months you two spent there. My real complaint is that I can't go myself. Don't worry, I won't ask you to take me. I'm not prepared to learn a new language, and I don't want to leave my garden. I have a new boy from the village working for me, and he's even better than you were."

"She's known for ages," Sarah confirmed. "You know Rebekkah; no one can keep secrets from her."

Sarah was delighted with the hairpins Joseph had for her. She had lost one of hers. And the dress Nancledra had sent her was, she declared, the most beautiful garment any woman, including even Cleopatra, ever owned. It was made of the finest Belerion wool, combed as fine as silk, and woven into a light weight that could be worn on all but the hottest summer days.

"Although it's almost too lovely to wear. Look at the color, Joseph, the blue of a night sky. And the embroidery is stars, mingled with green ferns. It's the song he taught me."

"With you as the goddess," Joseph added. And he meant every word.

"A blue goddess, you'll observe," Sarah giggled. Her favorite of all the things he'd brought back from Belerion was the story Rabbi Isaac had told him. When the Phoenician ship came, as it still did every year, the Dumnoni still stained their skins blue and had spears stuck in the sand of their beach as a palisade. The color was to frighten enemies, and the Phoenicians had never become friends.

"I'll admit it now, Joseph. I was really disappointed that not a single one of them had blue skin. I feel much better knowing that they didn't dye themselves because they like us."

She kissed him quickly. "Be on your way now, my love. I know you have to make another voyage this season. To Rome. Don't worry. I'm fine."

"I'm not," Joseph complained. "Nicolaus came to me as soon as we docked in Caesarea. King Herod wants me to bring his sister Salome back."

"Isn't she the nasty one?"

"A demon."

Sarah clapped her hands. "How delicious. The child will be thoroughly miserable. I hope she gets seasick, too. Have a *wonderful* voyage, my love."

Barca didn't share his father's prejudice against "floating bordellos" and he wanted to spend every moment at sea that he could, so he took on the menial jobs that Antiochus had done on the *Eagle*. Milcar's son was a strong, handsome fifteen-year-old with blue-black curls and brilliant black eyes. Thanks solely to him, the voyage of the *Phoenix* was a resounding success.

Salome had been anything but gracious when Joseph told her about the other passengers.

"A petty official at a synagogue and his daughter! You

have no right to expect me to tolerate companions like that."

Joseph had stiffened his back. "The young woman and I will be married when we arrive in Judea, my lady, and her father is entitled to every dignity that I am able to bestow."

Livia was privately pleased to see this spunky little man stand up to her ill-tempered friend. Salome sometimes behaved as if she, not Livia, was the Empress. Livia did not find that amusing.

Such was the origin of the wedding gift that Joseph and his bride received from Caesar Augustus. Joseph was officially made a Roman citizen; the decree was rolled, sealed with the Emperor's seal, and enclosed in a tubular container made of gold with silver portrait profiles of Augustus and Livia at its center.

Rufinius exhausted himself scurrying from one friend to another to display it. But his fatigue was unimportant. Salome, and all those accompanying her, traveled to Puteoli in silk-cushioned-and-curtained wheeled carts pulled by horses from the stables of the Praetorian Guard and escorted by a mounted cohort of the famous Twelfth Legion.

Rufinius was too awed to notice his fatigue.

Deborah was so thrilled to be leaving home at last that she would not have cared if she had had to walk barefoot the whole way.

And Joseph was in a daze. He had forgotten how breathtakingly beautiful the girl was. Also, what effect she'd had on him the first instant he saw her. When he went to Rufinius' house to announce his arrival in Rome, Deborah ran to meet him, and the impact of her unconsciously sensual beauty literally staggered him. Ever since that moment he'd been in a condition of barely controlled sexual arousal; it dimmed his awareness of anything except his desire to make her his wife.

Once on board the *Phoenix*, the seaman Joseph pushed aside his carnal appetites. The sea was his deepest love. And the voyage was virtual perfection.

Salome took Barca to her cabin and her bed as soon as she set eyes on him. And he was able to offer all the indiscriminate sexual gluttony of youth. The Queen of the invented tiny state of Ascalon was a thoroughly gratified woman, and it made her agreeable and gracious to everyone around her.

Deborah was her enthusiastic adorer. She had never dreamed that she would find herself in the company of nobility. Royalty was beyond imagination. She saw little of the Queen. Salome spent the major part of the day and the night in various configurations of copulation with the eager young Phoenician. But she did come on deck to lounge in the silken pavilion and enjoy the sea breezes from time to time. When she was there, sipping wine and eating delicacies prepared by her own cook, she liked to have Deborah around. To worship her.

While poor Rufinius remained in his cabin, miserably seasick. And out of Joseph's way.

The prevailing Mediterranean winds were strong and steady. The *Phoenix* reached Caesarea with excellent speed, on October 4.

Joseph and Deborah married, in the gardens of the Jerusalem mansion, on October 10, or, by Judaic reckoning, 27 Tishri.

The guests included many of the businessmen Joseph had met while the house was being furnished by King Herod. Their wives accompanied them, anxious to see the mansion, its owner, the friend of the King, and the Roman woman who'd been fortunate enough to win his affections.

Joseph's family was represented by his aunt, her husband, and their horde of children. Also his grandmother, his mother, his two brothers, and the wife and child of the elder one.

King Herod's regrets that he could not attend were expressed by Nicolaus of Damascus, who also presented the King's gifts. A necklace of Indian pearls for the bride. And a tray, ewer, and twelve goblets of gold, decorated with Persian turquoises for the groom.

Nicolaus also kept a sharp eye on the servants and the elaborate array of food and drink. Joseph had made a shrewd bargain with his friend. "If I'm going to save you from your terror of the sea by bringing Salome from Italy by myself, Nicolaus, you can find me all the slaves needed to make that house run even more smoothly than your king's palaces. I'll be glad to pay whatever price I must.

"I want the best, remember, and they must be Gentiles. We Jews don't enslave ourselves."

City weddings were not the communal events that were the custom in country villages. There was no tent in full view of all the guests where the marriage was consummated while everyone drank, danced, joked, and speculated openly about the likelihood of conception on the wedding day in the wedding tent.

City weddings permitted the couple the privacy of a bedroom with a closed door. Joseph and Deborah were applauded when he took her hand and led her to the bridal chamber.

He was nervous. He wanted to make her first experience of sex as easy and unfrightening as possible. But his hunger to possess her was urgent, perhaps uncontrollable. And they had never been alone together before, never kissed, never known tenderness.

"Do you know what we're going to do with each other, Deborah?" He was afraid of her ignorance.

"Oh, yes," she said brightly. "Meneptah, my nurse, told me. You take off your clothes, and I take mine off, too. Then you stuff some stick thing on your body inside me. It doesn't take long, she said."

Joseph groaned inwardly. It could be worse, he told himself. "Take off your clothes, now," he said hoarsely. He was frantic to see her breasts and hold them in his hands.

Joseph pulled his tunic over his head and tore off the loin-cloth beneath it.

She was unutterably beautiful. Joseph put his hands on her breasts, his lips on hers. He was on fire.

Deborah was passive. She didn't respond to his kiss, or his caresses. But she didn't seem to be frightened or offended.

"Open your legs," Joseph begged. His hands stroked her soft stomach and thighs, then spread her to receive him.

She screamed when he took her virginity, and her hands pushed his chest and his belly. Joseph rolled away. "Meneptah didn't tell me it would hurt," Deborah wept. "I don't like being married."

Joseph was thankful for the thick, solid, tightly closed door.

It wasn't difficult to make Deborah happy, Joseph discovered. She had been so protected by Rufinius from what he considered the corruption of the world that the simple act of leaving the house was exciting to her. "Take me out, please, Joseph," she asked on the first morning of their marriage.

"Where would you like to go?" He would have taken her to the moon if she wanted to go there and it was in his power to give it to her. Her heartbroken weeping had echoed in his ears all night, even though she was sleeping peacefully. Joseph was determined to change that echo. Deborah must like being married; he could not bear the idea of her unhappiness.

"Out. I want to go out. Anywhere at all, just out."

He smiled at her fervor. She was adorable, her soft cheeks pink, her wide eyes eager and pleading. "Then out we will go," he said.

The house fronted one of the chief streets of the upper city. It was interrupted by wide shallow steps at close-set intervals to provide an easy descent to the viaduct that crossed above the lower city to the Temple. Almost the first thing

Deborah saw that morning was its awesome gold roof glittering in the sun.

"Oh, look!" she cried. "It's wearing a crown. Does a king live there?"

"Deborah, the Almighty God lives there."

Her smile dimmed. "Like synagogue," she said in a flat tone. "The only place I ever got to go was synagogue. I've heard enough about God to last me the rest of my life. Let's go the other way." She turned her back on the Temple, the glory of Jerusalem and the reason for its existence.

Joseph reminded himself that she was very young. She didn't realize what she was saying. He'd sacrifice some doves later, in her name, to ask the Lord's forgiveness. She was as innocent as a dove, herself.

The street climbed a short way, and the agora was directly on their left. Deborah clapped her hands. "Is that a forum, Joseph? I've never been to the Forum."

"There's no forum in Jerusalem. You might like this even better, though. This is the agora, and it's full of pretty things to buy. It would make me happy to buy you something. A special present for the first day of our marriage."

"Oh, I'd love that. Thank you, Joseph." Her smile is brighter than the sun, Joseph thought dotingly. Her auburn hair glowed richly through the thin rose-colored silk stola that covered her head and shoulders. Her skin was whiter than milk. He felt as if he could look at her forever.

But he'd promised her a present. He made his eyes move away from his bride's beauty. "Come this way, Deborah. I know where we might find a brooch for pinning your stola to your tunic."

She was enraptured by the jewels in the shop, had to try on every single ring, brooch, bracelet, earring.

Joseph knew the jeweler, a Syrian called Miletus. He was famous for his elevated tastes, and prices to match. "My bride will select a brooch today, Miletus," Joseph said with a smile. "Only a brooch, but judging from her interest, I'm sure more selections will follow."

Miletus' dark eyes laughed with Joseph's. He'd been mentally adding up at least a half dozen sales, and they both knew it.

"As a salute to your happiness, I'll make a very special price for the brooch, Joseph. In the future, we will have to discuss such things."

Deborah was holding a silver mirror in one hand; the other held a brooch of twisted gold to her shoulder. Its waterfall of faceted rose quartz drops scintillated when she moved it a half inch higher. "This one," she said. "Don't you think this one, Joseph?"

"The lady shows exquisite discernment," Miletus crooned happily, and Joseph knew that Deborah had selected one of the most expensive pieces.

"Shall I pin it on for you?" he asked.

"Oh, no. I know how it goes," she answered.

"I'll return," Joseph told Miletus; the jeweler nodded agreement. No need to talk money in front of a beautiful young bride.

The agora contained nearly fifty shops. Deborah exclaimed over everything in every one of them. "I just love pretty things," she told Joseph artlessly.

They spent the morning shopping. When Joseph suggested they go home to eat, Deborah's animated face clouded. "Do we have to? There are still so many things and places to see."

Joseph laughed. "And purchases to unload." He was carrying more than a dozen packages. "I'll have to buy you a special slave whose only duty is to carry your shopping."

Deborah looked at him; her mouth was slightly open in astonishment. "Could I? Could I really have a slave of my own?"

"Dear child, the house is full of slaves of your own."

"Do you mean it, Joseph? That I can tell them what to do, and they'll do it? Meneptah is my slave, but she's always been the one who told me what to do."

"That part of your life is over, Deborah. You're a married woman now, with your own household. You need never do what a nursemaid tells you to do, never again."

Her heavily lashed eyes closed in ecstasy. "Oh, Joseph," Deborah sighed. "I just love being married."

Joseph's mother, Helena, came from the living room to the hall when she heard them come in. After greetings were exchanged, she said, "I didn't think you'd mind if your father and I came over from Abigail's for a visit."

Joseph's eyebrows rose in surprise. His father? Wanted to visit him? "I am very pleased, Mother. I'll order some refreshment."

"Rufinius has done that already. He and your father are in the living room."

"We'll join you in a few minutes." Joseph and Deborah were seated on the bench inside the door, for their foot washing. Joseph waved off the kneeling slave who was about to dry his feet and put his sandals back on after dusting them off. "Never mind," he told the man. "I prefer doing this myself."

Deborah clearly preferred the reverse. She was smiling happily at her own feet, while someone else washed and dried them. "No," she said, "I don't want to wear those sandals again. Go get me another pair." There was a quaver of tentativeness in her voice. When the slave stood and began to hurry to her bedroom, she looked at Joseph with a giggle of delight. "I did it," she said. "I did just what you said. And it worked."

Joseph's life had delivered many surprises, but, for him, nothing had ever been as amazing as the scene that met his eyes when he entered his living room.

Joshua, his father, and Rufinius, Deborah's father, were seated in two throne-like chairs, close together, and conversing with animation. Clearly they were in agreement about whatever they were discussing. While one spoke, the other nodded in vigorous affirmation. Then the roles were reversed.

"Mother?" Joseph looked to Helena.

"For more than an hour," she replied. "I don't know how, but Rufinius understands your father's stricken speech better than I do. And Rufinius' Roman accent doesn't cause any difficulty at all for your father, whereas I have to ask him to repeat everything he says to me."

Rufinius pounded on the arm of his chair with his fist. Joshua did the same, albeit with less force. And the two of them nodded at each other.

"What can they be talking about?"

Helena tried not to smile, but the corners of her mouth twitched upward. "Everything that's wrong about the world. They particularly like the decline in obedience to the Law—for a topic, that is."

Joseph gaped. "Where did those thrones come from? I've never seen them before."

"You didn't exactly devote your attentions to outfitting your house yourself, I'm told," his mother said. "Rufinius saw them in a room that has a wall covered with niches holding scrolls. The servants brought them to the living room."

Joseph began to laugh quietly.

"What's funny?" Deborah wanted to know.

"Everything."

"I don't understand, but it doesn't matter. Can we go out now?"

Helena mimicked the pounding on the chair and the agitated nodding. "They keep it up even when their meals are brought to them. Poor Joseph, if you could have seen his face when he finally understood that Joshua was telling him he was going to stay for a prolonged visit!

"I was quite unneeded. Joshua's medical caretakers moved in with him. So I came on home."

Rebekkah was still chuckling at Helena's description of

the two men. "Personally, I like the part about the thrones the best. Abigail's gossip must have been absolutely true. King Herod really did do all the outfitting of Joseph's house. Who else would have extra thrones lying around unused?"

"Poor Joseph," Sarah said. There was not a trace of compassion in her words.

The three women looked at one another. They burst into laughter simultaneously.

Helena bit her lip. "I'm dreadful. I shouldn't joke about my husband and my son."

"Nonsense!" Rebekkah said. "You have been a dutiful, obedient wife for over twenty-five years, Helena. Joshua's my son, and I have always been grateful to Almighty God that He sent you to us, because you are Joshua's greatest blessing. And a blessing to me as well. Nothing will ever convince me that you cannot laugh at someone and love them no less for having laughed. I most sincerely hope that you have had some fun at my expense from time to time."

Helena's mouth twitched. "I do remember when you bought that wig—you know, when you first started going gray. Joshua put it on one night after you were asleep, and stood up very straight, the way you do when you're angry, and repeated the lecture you'd just given us about something. I've forgotten—ages ago—what the lecture was, but I remember he had it word-for-word accurate. And in that wig! We laughed ourselves silly."

Sarah felt her eyes sting with tears. She had never dreamed that Helena and Joshua could have once been young and silly together. The thought of it made her heart ache with tenderness. Helena had always been a kind but distant figure to her. If only she had known.

She blinked back the tears, ran to her mother-in-law, and hugged her. "I love you," she blurted. "And high time, too." The tears spilled over and she wiped them away with the back of her wrist. "Now, let's please make fun of Joseph. I need it quite a lot."

Rebekkah believed firmly that bad news was best faced head on, and as soon as possible. She had returned to Arimathea on the day after the wedding, with Amos and his family, Caleb, and Antiochus. Then she took a jar of her special store of wine to Sarah's house.

"We are going to drink a little more than we should while I tell you about Joseph's house, and about his bride. Whether you like it or not, Sarah, you're going to hear me." She poured two large cups brim full.

"Take this," she said to Sarah, forcing the cup into her hand. "Drink. You may cry, scream, break the cup, lie on the floor, and kick in a tantrum. I'm here, and I won't mind.

"Her name is Deborah, and she is the most beautiful girl I've ever seen in my long life. Her hair is red, her lips are red, her skin is flawless, and her body is like the descriptions of Venus . . ."

Helena was as frank as Rebekkah had been. "Joseph is ludicrous, Sarah, but not in a way that you're likely to laugh at. He doesn't know his own house, or even the names of the very, very superior slaves who are in charge of it. He's like a visitor there. He looks confused.

"He is confused. He dances attendance on his child bride, and she thanks him prettily, then gives him his next order. He is her slave, and the indulgent father that one can tell she never had. I was there for only one day, to get Joshua settled in, and she had him take her shopping morning and afternoon.

"At dinner she got him to promise that he would take her to the theater, to the races, to see Herod's palace. And she told him to arrange at least two receptions every week so that she could meet people and begin a busy social life. We were halfway through the meal when she mentioned that she had ordered some slaves to move her things into a bed-chamber that she had chosen. He could come there, she said, to do what husbands do, but she wanted the bed all to herself for sleeping.

"Sarah, Joseph did not even seem annoyed. He asked her whether she'd prefer to go to the races first and then the theater, or the other way round. I was appalled."

Helena looked anxiously at Sarah. "I'm sorry, my dear."

"One day is not a long time," Rebekkah commented.

"Don't baby me," Sarah said. "It's better knowing. I would have imagined something much worse. I did imagine a hundred things a hundred times worse." Her chin was very firm.

"Have dinner with us," Rebekkah urged.

"No, thank you. I'm a little tired." She kissed them both, with a strong hug for Helena, then left.

Back at home, Sarah stirred her dosage of herb medicine into some soft cheese then sat by a window to enjoy the sweet freshness of the air in this season of the first rains. It was misty, a bit like the air in Belerion. The magic time.

She pushed away romance and self-pity. Why am I still taking this medicine? she asked herself. It didn't work. She thought about the outrageous thing the Druid priestess had told her. Weak seed? Suppose Joseph's new wife— No, Deborah. Don't be afraid of a name, Sarah. Suppose Deborah doesn't have a child. Then will he have to divorce me? And, after ten years, divorce her?

With scalding honesty Sarah admitted to herself that she would prefer to be divorced than to have Joseph's beautiful wife give him a beautiful son.

CHAPTER THIRTY-FIVE

THE SITUATION IN JOSEPH'S NEW HOUSE IN JERUSALEM WAS not as dire as Helena's description of it, because Antiochus was there, and he was deeply devoted to Joseph. Even when he was being foolish. Within a few days Antiochus had learned every detail about everything that went on in the house. He was a slave, accepted by the household slaves, included in their gossip, aware of their amused scorn of their master. He knew that they were cheating on the household accounts, and selling valuable small ornaments that Joseph didn't know he owned, and eating better food than they prepared and served to Joseph's family and guests. Antiochus listened, remembered, and bided his time. When Joseph came to his senses he'd talk with him about the changes that had to be made. He was sure Joseph would come to his senses someday.

Joseph genuinely enjoyed the social life that Deborah had asked him to build. People always interested him, even when he didn't like them. Also, almost everyone in Jerusalem had information about something, no matter how trivial, that he was glad to learn.

And it was a never-ending pleasure to see Deborah's excitement and happiness. Also, he had the ignoble gratification of recognizing admiration for his beautiful wife and envy for him in the eyes of all the men at the entertainments.

The most immediately useful thing he learned from men talking among themselves in a group was that Deborah's view of marriage was widespread, regarded as normal. Wives submitted to the sexual act; they did not participate.

Joseph had believed that if he was very gentle and patient, she would begin to love love and to want it. What he heard told him that such an outcome was not to be hoped for. He was unusually lucky because she permitted him to look at her nude body by lamplight and to move his hands and lips along the curves of her waist and breasts and high-arched little feet.

Joseph's mind filled at unguarded moments with memories of Sarah in his arms, in his bed, hungry for him. He shut the memories out; it would be the most despicable of all things if he brought her into his life with another woman.

The practical things he learned were extremely useful for his future. Because King Herod openly favored Joseph, the men he was meeting assumed that Joseph knew all about power: where it lay, how to gain it, use it, protect oneself against it, trade in its reality, possibilities, reputed degrees.

He had the long-held habit of silence. Joseph confided nothing about himself or his business. He was fascinated to learn that most men interpreted silence to mean what they wanted or feared it to mean.

The single most important thing he learned was the value of information. He had discovered that inadvertently, but he'd never thought about it before. Now he was brought to the realization that information had to be sought, frequently bought, and always, at all times, mistrusted, even when it was being used and traded.

Before long Joseph added dinners to the entertainments

at the Roman-styled mansion. Jerusalem's dinner parties, unlike those in Rome, were still limited to male guests. The conversations about male concerns could be begun right away and proceed, uninterrupted by social attentions to women, for as long as the participants chose.

Deborah pouted when he hosted the first dinner, complained when he accepted an invitation to another. But then she found out that women had their equivalent pastimes. Mid-morning refreshments or light meals. Shopping excursions with slaves to substitute for masculine family members. Visits to a friend's house to talk about other friends.

It took surprisingly few weeks for Deborah and Joseph to become a sought-after couple in Jerusalem's upper city society, with a life very much like the lives of everyone they knew.

Except that he went to her room on every night that she did not have her bleeding and became despondent when her menses began. Because she was not with child, not because it meant that he could not lie with her.

He still pampered her and took pleasure in her childlike glee when he gave her a present. And his heart stopped for an instant when he looked at her beauty. But her bed was for impregnation, not for love.

After more than two months of energetic accord, Joshua and Rufinius happened upon an issue on which they disagreed. Joshua banged his stick on the floor to summon his attendants and Rufinius stalked away, into the unused library, where he took down a scroll and carried it to the rain-streaked window for examination.

Joseph could go to Arimathea now. His father had decided to go home.

He returned after only three days at the farm. The family welcomed him, but somehow made it known that the problems of Amos' son's teething were more vitally important than the descriptions of the people Joseph was meeting in Jerusalem. And Sarah was bleeding. She said.

Rufinius is going to drive me to murder, Joseph thought. He tried to walk quietly, but the old man's hearing was unimpaired by age, and he called to Joseph from the living room every time he heard his step. Then Joseph had to hear one of the tirades that Joshua had relished, that set Joseph's teeth on edge.

Deborah was no help. She had gotten away from her father's lectures when she married, she said, and she was never going to listen to another one. Never. The only person in the house who could tolerate Rufinius was Deborah's old nurse, Meneptah. Joseph shamelessly bribed her to distract the old man in the mornings so that he could get out of the house. And he was willing to accept invitations from almost anyone to avoid dining with his father-in-law.

When he came in one afternoon and found Rufinius waiting for him by the foot basins, his heart sank. "Don't stop! Don't take off your sandals! You're wanted at the palace of King Herod." Rufinius was smiling, a rare occurrence.

Joseph turned and left at once, before the old man could suggest that he go along. He'd seen Rufinius' cloak on the bench.

Nicolaus was in the palace's immense garden. He hurried to meet Joseph when the escort guard brought him to the entrance. At the sight of his face, Joseph's happy greeting died in his throat.

"My friend." Nicolaus was abrupt. "Can you take me to Italy right away in one of your ships? Not the bordello. The fastest one you have."

Joseph spread his hands, palms up to gesture at the low gray skies. "There is no sailing in the rainy season, Nicolaus. I thought you knew that."

Herod's councillor looked up, then down, dejected. "I hoped— If any man could do it, it would be you."

"I cannot risk the lives of my crew, even if a ship were ready to sail. What is it, Nicolaus? Is there something else I can do to help you?"

"No." Nicolaus smiled. "It's nothing. Only a letter from Herod to Augustus. I thought you'd be glad to go with me to see the Emperor."

Joseph knew that his friend was lying to him, he believed for the first time. He didn't know what to do. He couldn't accuse Nicolaus of the lie. Nor could he ask what was in the letter. Nicolaus was the King's confidential advisor. Joseph did the only thing available to him. He touched Nicolaus briefly on the arm. "I am deeply sorry," he said.

Nicolaus clasped Joseph's shoulder. "I believe you. Don't concern yourself. I'll send it by the Roman courier service. It's slower by road, but weather doesn't halt it."

Joseph searched for something, no matter how inadequate, to offset Nicolaus' bleak spirits. "Can you dine with me? We will be thoroughly Roman and include my beautiful wife. Deborah will wear her prettiest tunic."

"Thank you, Joseph, but I cannot. I must get back to the King. We're at Masada. The rain doesn't weigh so heavily in the desert. Come, I'll walk you out."

Joseph didn't try anything further. It was patent that his friend wanted to be rid of him. Nicolaus' long legs were taking fast strides.

As the guards swung open the door, Nicolaus stopped Joseph for a minute. "I thank you, Joseph." His smile had no merriment in it, but it was genuine. "I thank you three times. One, for coming. Two, for understanding. And three, for not letting it be known that I was in Jerusalem or what I said to you."

"Come back soon. For dinner."

"Tell Deborah to wear green. I'll be back in the spring."

*   *   *

The agora was busy and crowded, as usual, in spite of the rain. Joseph was greeted by many. He knew they wondered what he was doing in the vicinity of Herod's palace. He laughed and joked about his wife's power over him. "She sent me to buy her some perfumed oil for her bath, and I could not say no." Everyone knew, he was sure, that he gave Deborah everything she set her heart on.

The owner of the perfume shop was there, talking to the man who ran it for him. "Joseph of Arimathea," he boomed. "The price of everything just doubled."

Joseph laughed. He liked Eleazar more than any of the businessmen he'd met. The importer was from Alexandria originally; he knew Joseph's friend Micah and shared Joseph's fondness for him.

"What delusion made you believe I'd buy that dung-scented rancid oil you call perfume, Eleazar?" The bantering was always fun. Eleazer had typical Alexandrian quick wit.

"Not a delusion, my friend, it was a vision. You were kissing a camel and longing for a memento of the romance."

When the perfume was bought and the transaction celebrated with a cup of wine, Joseph rose to leave. "Don't say farewell just yet, Joseph. I'll walk a way with you. The stink in here makes me long for a bath of rain." Eleazar donned his cloak.

"What did you discover?" he asked once they had left the marketplace.

"What do you mean?"

"Come now, Joseph. You were seen going into Herod's palace. What did your informant tell you about the arrests?"

Joseph felt the chill of the rain on his neck. Was Nicolaus in danger? Was that why he had lied?

"I don't know anything, Eleazar, I give you my word. Who's going to be arrested?"

Eleazar stared into Joseph's face. "By all the stars, I believe you really don't know. Herod has arrested his sons Alexander and Aristobulus. What were you after, if not news of that?"

Joseph thought quickly. "I wanted to make sure of an invitation to the masquerade at Purim. Deborah will not speak to me for months if I fail to arrange it."

"Hmph! Sometimes I despair of you, Joseph. You have access to Herod's palace and have not bought yourself any informers from within. I have seven. They told me about the arrest, but they have no details, they claim, not even for the pouch full of gold I offered."

Joseph told Rufinius and Deborah a similar story about his visit to the palace. She was thrilled. "I'll visit Miriam and her sisters right away. They'll know what people wear to costume parties."

Joseph told her that she must go as the Queen of Sheba, or Cleopatra, even though they were less beautiful than she.

He hoped Herod would follow his usual practice of coming to Jerusalem for festivals. If not, there would be no costume party. Next day he made an offering at the Temple to ask God's protection for Nicolaus.

"Antiochus, I've hardly seen you. I need your special talents. Find out for me, please, what manner of costumes people wear for the Purim masquerade parties at King Herod's palace. My invitation was just delivered. Can you do that?"

The look Antiochus gave Joseph could have withered a strong tree.

Joseph laughed. He'd missed the young Galatian's impertinence.

"I need to know where to get them, too, or how to set about having them made. The time is short." He looked at Antiochus for the first time in months. "What has happened to you? You've grown a foot. You'll need new clothes; that tunic is much too small."

"It's been so for weeks. You just haven't noticed."

"I've been busy."

"Too busy for your family at the farms. For your real wife."

Joseph's temper erupted, a thing that almost never occurred. "How dare you?" he shouted, and he raised a hand to hit his slave.

Antiochus cowered for an instant in an automatic reaction. Then he stood straight.

Joseph was horrified. "How could I? I don't understand. Can you forgive me?"

Antiochus' voice was much older than his years. "I forgive. And I understand. I am your friend, Joseph. You can depend on it."

He grinned at the man who owned him. "It's said that there's some special kind of costume cap that signifies a fool. Maybe I can find you one."

Joseph grinned in turn. "Maybe I should have struck you after all. Go on, rascal, and do what I told you to do."

Before he was out the door, Joseph called out: "Antiochus?"

He turned. "Sarah is strong, and she loves you, Joseph, even though she suffers."

He had known all along what Joseph needed to hear and was afraid to ask.

Purim was the celebration of the delivery of the Jews from massacre hundreds of years before, as told in the Book of Esther.

On the day preceding the festival, a solemn fast was required. That was the only solemnity connected with Purim. The festival itself was an all-day-and-into-the-night celebration of the beginning of spring, when the land burst forth with flowers and the blossoms of the almond tree perfumed the air. In Jerusalem it was much more elaborate than in villages like Arimathea.

People of all ages thronged the streets, many in costume, many more blowing cheap horns, rattling noisemakers, shouting and singing and dancing.

At Herod's palace the garden was filled with flowers, and lamps hung from every tree limb, ready to be lit when darkness fell. The palace was in fact two palaces, one at each end of the huge garden. Both were decorated with garlands and wreaths and bouquets. In each, the immense dining hall held a banquet table loaded with delicacies of every kind and dozens of smaller tables with couches for nine guests, both male and female. King Herod patterned his entertaining on the styles of Rome. Musicians provided sweet melodies in the banquet halls, more lively ones for dancing in the garden and in the great marble-walled reception rooms.

It was a traditional Purim requirement that every male celebrant take enough wine to become pleasantly drunk but not sick.

Rufinius followed the dictates of tradition in all things. Joseph laughed until he wept at the cranky old man's antics. He danced, blew noisemaking ribboned tubes into the ears of anyone close to him, and returned again and again to the fountains that flowed with wine.

Deborah enjoyed herself even more than her father. She wore a tunic made of cloth of gold, a mask of green silk embroidered with gold thread, and her hair was caught in a gold net scattered with emeralds. She was surrounded by admirers, followed by men who begged her to unmask, bowed to by King Herod himself, who took an emerald ring from his finger and placed it on her thumb.

There was one serious interlude for Joseph amid the celebrations. Nicolaus took him into an empty room for a brief talk. The news about the princes was true, he told Joseph. They had been arrested and were being held under guard in the palace at Herodium.

If only they could have left Salome in Rome, he groaned. She had come back to her brother's court, not her own palace, and she'd spent every minute of her time at her favorite pastime, fomenting discord and suspicion. And she had succeeded in convincing Herod that his sons were plotting to kill him. Their friends and servants had affirmed it, under torture.

"The letter to Augustus asked him to judge what punishment is due Alexander and Aristobulus. Herod doesn't want to act again without imperial authority, not like in Nabatea."

"What does Augustus say?"

"No reply as yet. There hasn't been time. But I fear the worst. My king is going mad, Joseph. He has a burning in his bowels some days of such insupportable pain that he swears he will kill himself."

"Are you in danger, Nicolaus?"

"No, my friend. As you know, I am the only man Herod trusts. But I must warn you. Stay away from us. It's the only safety any normal person can know. We go to Jericho tomorrow and will return for Passover. By then, Augustus will have replied."

Deborah had made a new friend at the masquerade. She was giddy about it. "Her name is Roxana, and she's sixteen and not even betrothed yet. Joseph! She's a princess! The King is her father. And she wants to be my friend."

Joseph tensed. "Where does she live?"

"With her mother, in the palace. But only for a while. Then they'll be in Jericho. She told me all about it, and it sounds so wonderful, Joseph. Can we have a house there, too?"

"No," Joseph said.

"No?" Deborah echoed. He had never said no to her before. "Why not? I want one."

"Because it is inconvenient for my business." She'd have to accept that answer. He could not say that he wanted to keep as far away from Herod as he could.

Deborah didn't waste time pouting. She was invited to the palace to see her new friend.

Passover was less than a month away. Rufinius spent most of his day now at the Temple, preparing his heart for this holiest of festivals. He was determined to extract every possible moment of piety from the holy place and holy day. Most members of his synagogue in Rome had never been to Jerusalem and would never be able to go. Rufinius intended to be generous, to tell them every detail about what they had missed.

Joseph went daily to the Temple also. He sacrificed incense or lambs and asked God to protect those he loved. Nicolaus had frightened him terribly. And all the family from Arimathea would be in the city, at Abigail's. Very near the palace of King Herod.

Deborah's friendship with Roxana worried him, too. His young wife was in Herod's palace altogether too often. He ordered her to stop going there. Such was his right as a husband. She giggled and told him not to be silly. Roxana and her mother were moving that very day to the smaller palace, she said. So she would get to see the inside of another palace. Deborah considered that very exciting.

"Does Roxana know that her father the King has arrested two of her brothers?"

"Oh, she doesn't care, Joseph. They're so much older, they already have wives and children. They're not real brothers anyhow. Her mother isn't their mother. King Herod has so many children that Roxana couldn't really remember for certain which brothers these were."

Joseph remembered the pandemonium of the smaller palace when he stayed there. What Roxana said was true. The palace had more than fifty bedrooms for the children of the King. He decided not to make an issue of Roxana as friend to Deborah. It was more than likely that Herod did not even know this girl existed. The King's attention was centered on sons, not daughters. Sons could inherit the kingdom.

He and Rufinius were at the Temple on Passover Eve,

waiting with hundreds of others for their turn to sacrifice their paschal lamb. As always, the bleating of the lambs drowned out the music of the Levites, and the atmosphere of body smells, animal smells, burning blood plus thick clouds of incense was suffocating. Rufinius was loving it, but Joseph just wanted to get the sacrifice over with. Passover had always been a joyous time for him. The family had all been together, a happy thing that Joshua's stern piety could not diminish.

But this year Joseph would preside at the ceremonial dinner of lamb, unleavened bread, and bitter herbs. Deborah and Rufinius would share it.

While Sarah and Rebekkah and the others were dining at Abigail's. Lucky Antiochus—he'd be at Abigail's, not at the mansion. Rufinius would never countenance a Gentile slave at dinner, but in Abigail's noisy, loving household Antiochus was another member of the family.

The Temple Guards marched into the Court of the Jews to move the crowds back.

"The King is coming." The word raced through the crowds. Joseph heard muted grumbling. Herod was not popular at the best of times. Now, when all Israel knew about his sons' imprisonment, the family-loving Jewish men were making their disapproval heard.

But not too loudly. In addition to the Temple Guards, everyone knew that Herod's own army was in Jerusalem to guard the King. Because most of the army's men were Gentiles, they could not accompany Herod into the inner regions of the Temple, but it was probable that they were massed nearby in the Court of the Gentiles.

The High Priest himself held the cup for the blood of the lamb for the King. Herod's hand was unsteady, and he had to make five cuts before the lamb was dead.

Joseph was not far away. He could see Herod's lined face below his rich crown. The King's lips were pale and compressed. He was in pain.

Was it because of his sons? Joseph wondered. Or because of the burning pain in his bowels that Nicolaus had spoken of? He realized he'd never know the truth of it. He could see, however, a greater truth. King Herod was old, and he was going to die.

CHAPTER THIRTY-SIX

JOSEPH AND MILCAR WERE EXAMINING THE *EAGLE*; EVERY inch of her had to be perfectly sound, to meet the stresses of ocean currents and waves. Milcar rubbed the mast. His tanned, seamed, sailor's face was bright with anticipation. Like Joseph, he always was excited by the adventure of outsailing and outwitting the Phoenicians on the voyage to Belerion. Envy was sour in Joseph's mouth. He could not go this year.

He had to get Deborah pregnant.

She had to give birth before autumn of next year.

Or he would have to divorce Sarah.

"What is that?" Milcar shaded his eyes to look toward a sudden commotion. Joseph turned from the harbor to look also. The great city square beyond the quay was filling with running, shouting people, coming from every street that entered it, from the quay itself. The men on ships' decks were leaping ashore, the offices and warehouses were emptying. Everyone wanted to see what was happening. Joseph and Milcar followed them.

"Up here, we'll see better." Milcar raced from the quay up the steps of the monumental temple to Augustus Caesar. Joseph darted through the swarm to follow Milcar. On the columned temple platform, they'd be able to see above the heads of the confused masses in the square.

At first he couldn't figure out what was happening. An uneven ring of soldiers was facing outward, their spears pointed, but he couldn't see what was inside the circle, what the soldiers were protecting.

The jabbing spears created a path for the beleagured party within the ring, and for Joseph's eyes. He saw more uniformed men, more spears, unsheathed swords. And Alexander and Aristobulus, Herod's sons, standing in a cart. Heavy chains circled their wrists, arms, waists, ankles. Their tunics were torn and dirty, their faces swollen by bruises. Joseph was near enough to see the fear beneath the bruises, in their eyes.

He'd met the two only a few times, and he'd not liked them at all. They were overbearing, arrogant, contemptuous of their father's young partner in the metal trades. But their debasement now gave him no gratification. Perhaps they had indeed plotted against Herod, as the King believed. Perhaps they merited prison, even execution. But public humiliation—no man should have to suffer that. People in the square were throwing rocks, shards of pottery, clods of donkey droppings at the princes.

He turned his head from the spectacle. When the troops succeeding in moving the cart onward, toward Herod's palace, the crowded temple platform emptied, with Joseph one of the men streaming down the steps. He found Milcar back on the quay. Neither of them referred to what they'd just seen.

"I'm planning to send Barca on the *Heron*," he told the *Eagle*'s captain. "She'll be going direct to Puteoli, to carry Rufinius back to Rome. He's an aggravation, but less exhausting than Queen Salome was for your son."

Joseph's attempt to lighten the mood fell flat. He and Milcar continued their examination of the ship. When they heard another outbreak of noise, they did not follow

the men who were running from the quay. They had no
desire to see more of what they'd already witnessed.

They shared a meal in a seafront tavern after the sun
set. Two men there told them what they'd missed. Hundreds of soldiers had left their permanent encampment
outside the city and come to the plaza in front of Herod's
palace for a demonstration to protest his treatment of the
princes. Aristobulus and Alexander were popular with
the mercenary troops—who could say why?

Messages must have been sent, because more troops—
three times the number of protesters—swarmed into the
city, fully armed. They arrested the demonstrators and
were holding them captive in the amphitheater.

Tomorrow was going to be plenty interesting, said the
two men. They wouldn't miss it for anything.

After they finished their stew, Milcar suggested they
walk back to the *Eagle*. Joseph agreed. "We'll go to the
hostel and get whatever crewmen are there. Tonight we'll
sleep on board, and at sunup row her out into the harbor,
away from the dock. Judging by our two table companions, every rat in the sewers will be roaming the streets tomorrow. I don't want any coming on board."

The wild frenzy in the square could be heard clearly
by the men on the *Eagle*'s deck. The noise lasted for
hours, until military bugles cut through the roaring and
ended it.

The next morning the demonstrators were marched
under guard into the center of the square, passing
through the hordes of curious by means of a corridor
formed by soldiers wielding bared swords.

Additional soldiers made a wall inside the four sides
of the square. Then, from the temple steps, an officer
loudly proclaimed the King's decree: The mob was ordered to beat the three hundred demonstrators to death.
Clubs and rocks were piled at the corners of the square
and at the foot of the white marble stairs that climbed to

the majestic gleaming purity of the white marble Temple of Augustus.

"What happened?" Joseph asked Nicolaus when he saw him next, some months later.

Augustus, in reply to Herod's letter, had ordered the King not to act on his own, or to attempt to shift responsibility to his Emperor. He was to convene a court of one hundred and fifty prominent men in the Roman province of Syria. The King could present evidence of the princes' treachery. The court would determine what, if any, punishment was due.

"They voted death," Nicholaus said. "Aristobulus and Alexander were strangled, in Sebaste, after they'd been displayed in other cities as a warning not to engage in plots against the King."

"The Syrians did that? Who chose the hundred and fifty?"

Nicolaus' shoulders sagged. "Herod," he said.

CHAPTER THIRTY-SEVEN

SARAH WAS WEARING A WIDE STRAW HAT FOR SHELTER FROM the sun, spreading the early ripened grapes on mats to dry into raisins. Rebekkah fanned herself with a handled straw paddle, sitting nearby in the wide-leaved shade of a fig tree. The dry season was on the land, with three months still to come before the first rains.

Joseph rode into the gentle scene on a donkey, shouting Sarah's name. He slid off the animal's back and ran to her, oblivious to the neatly arranged grapes that he was trampling. "Sarah!" He picked her up and spun around. "Deborah is with child!" The hat got in the way when he tried to kiss her, so Joseph tore it off her head and threw it aside. Sarah was trying to speak, but he paid no attention. He was kissing her face, her head, her eyelids, her mouth's corners, her chin. "No divorce," he said, then pulled her close to his sweaty chest and held her tight. "No divorce, Sparrow. I'm the happiest man in the world."

Rebekkah was grateful for her tears. In the few seconds before the dry heat evaporated them, they cooled her cheeks a bit. After Sarah and Joseph ran off toward their house, she stood up, caught the donkey, and led it to shade and water.

Isn't it fortunate, she thought, that I don't particularly like raisins. Her smile was serene; her eyes were misted.

Sarah and Joseph made love in the dimness of their shuttered bedroom, murmuring endearments, relishing the salty taste of each other's sweaty skin, exulting in recapturing the rapture both had been hungering for. Afterward, still breathing rapidly, they sprawled, separated, in the heavy heat, trying to cool off. Their fingertips touched. Neither could let the other go completely.

"I thought I'd hate her giving you the child I couldn't have," Sarah said dreamily. "Now it doesn't seem to matter. Later I'll start hating."

"The child's unimportant, you know that. The only thing that matters is that we needn't divorce."

Sarah frowned. "That sounds so heartless, Joseph. No child is unimportant. Aren't you filled with pride? You're going to be a father."

"I don't care about that. I care about you. I've missed you so."

Sarah's smile was private, not for him to see. She was sure he'd care very much indeed, once his child was real. But for now she was gladdened by his words.

Nonetheless, she sent him back to Jerusalem the next morning. "Deborah must be taken care of, Joseph. If she's not already frightened, she soon will be. She's hardly more than a child herself."

Sarah felt triumphant. She had said "Deborah" without even one tiny pang. Before, the mere thought of the name had made her cry.

"Oh, Joseph, I'm so scared. I told my friends about the baby, and everybody who's had one told me all about it. It hurts, Joseph, it hurts a lot to have a baby."

She looked little more than a baby herself. Her cheeks were tearstained, and her tumbled hair was slipping from the ribbon that held it up off her neck and shoulders.

Joseph patted her hand. "We'll find some ways to stop your fretting," he said. "Would you like to go to the sea? There's always a breeze off the water."

"I'd rather go to Jericho. Roxana told me there are pools of water, nice and cool. You sit in them and slaves bring you fruit juice and little cakes."

Herod might be in Jericho.

"Beside the sea it's even cooler. You remember Queen Salome. She has her palace by the sea, at Ascalon."

"Does she? She'd know much better than Roxana. Let's go to the sea."

Joseph had no trouble finding a house in Caesarea. Or the workmen to dig and mosaic a pool in the center of the enclosed garden. He shuddered internally whenever Herod's name was mentioned, but he continued to love the city Herod had built of white marble. The long miles of Herod's aqueduct brought fresh cool water to every house, in quantities ample for fountains and pools.

Deborah clapped her hands when she saw the pool. "Can I invite Roxana to visit? She'll be so jealous. I don't have to share my pool with a lot of brothers and sisters and cousins."

Joseph wasn't sure that any connection with Herod was safe. But he agreed. Six months was a long time to keep Deborah happy until the baby was born.

Antiochus had a request, too. "The house in Jerusalem was already staffed and running when I came there. But this one, I want to be in charge."

When Joseph protested that he was too young, Antiochus pointed out that Joseph was master. If he told his slaves to obey Antiochus, they'd have to comply with the order. The impish boy who'd nearly disappeared was reborn for a moment in Antiochus' laughing eyes. "I will tell them that I'm your bastard half brother, by a slave girl, and that's why I'm given preference."

The suggestion that Joshua could ever have done such a thing made Joseph gasp. Then he began to chuckle. "If you have to spin a story like that, make me your father. The early manhood that implies will make them respect me so much they might even steal a little less."

Antiochus blinked.

"Of course they steal," Joseph said. "It's the way of the world we live in. You thought I didn't know? I don't know how much. If you can lessen it, well and good. But don't stop it altogether, or they'll feel deprived of their rights and start spitting in the soup."

He put his hands on Antiochus' shoulders. "What I do not want is that any of them sell information about my activities or what goes on inside my house. That, too, is the way of the world. If you discover that, take the guilty man or woman to the slave market at once and sell him. Or her. To a trader from another place. I'll give you a scroll of authority so you can do whatever is necessary or important even when I'm away."

"Would you trust me so much, Joseph?"

Joseph was not smiling when he answered. "So much, and more. To any limits."

Antiochus abruptly turned his back. "I'm a grown man," he said in a clogged voice. "It's ridiculous for my eyes to water like this."

"You must have gotten some dust in them."

"I suppose that's it."

Later that day Antiochus found Joseph again. "I forgot to mention it earlier, but I had a second request. A suggestion, really. Why don't you bring Caleb to stay for a visit? He's close to Deborah's age, and he'll be company for her. Also, he's been growing more and more restless these last few years. Amos is a good farm manager, but he's very impatient with Caleb. Rebekkah is worried that he might run away, like you. Joshua couldn't live through that again, he's weaker every year."

"I'll feel like an old man in a houseful of children," Joseph said. But he did as Antiochus suggested.

And his joking remark proved more accurate than was comfortable. He was approaching the age of twenty-six. Antiochus was sixteen, Deborah fifteen, Caleb thirteen. Roxana's arrival added another sixteen-year-old.

With Caleb as self-important male escort, the young women took full advantage of Caesarea's summer entertainments. They saw the pantomimes at the theater, the weekly races at the Hippodrome, and the jugglers, animal shows, acrobats, dancers who performed in the city square or on the wide quays. Joseph forbade their attending the four-day gladiatorial combats in the arena that were the specialty of Caesarea's summer, and Deborah pouted for a full hour. But then Roxana reminded her that two new shops had opened in the arcade on the square, and everything returned to normal.

Joseph had his time to himself for the most part, and he used it to good advantage. He was on hand when a shipbuilder's client was unable to pay for the galley he had ordered because of financial reverses. Joseph bought it for a good price. When the *Eagle* reached port in September, he and Milcar transferred the Arimathea eagle to the prow of the new ship, and Milcar sacrificed a hundred doves on her afterdeck for good fortune.

As the rest of his fleet came in, one by one, Joseph was able to reckon how very good indeed was fortune. He set up an exclusive contract with the most successful cargo agent in Caesarea. In the future Stratos would use his renowned abilities for Joseph's fleet alone, and make certain that no ship ever left Caesarea or returned there without a full load.

Joseph limited himself to one trip to Arimathea, when he went to take Caleb back. He stayed for only a few days. But those days brightened his weeks and months for the remainder of the season. And every Sabbath he gave thanks in the synagogue for God's manifold blessings.

*　　*　　*

They returned to Jerusalem in early October when the first rains had cooled the air. The trip was slow because Deborah was in a litter this time. She was over six months pregnant, visibly so, and it made her miserable. She complained of backache, which alarmed Joseph, and of boredom, which irritated him.

Antiochus went ahead with half of the slaves to prepare the Jerusalem house. The other eight, including the cook and Meneptah, traveled with Joseph's party. In midafternoon the tents had to be unloaded and set up, the cooking vessels and ovens and utensils arranged in a separate tent, distant enough from the others so that the smell of cooking would not bother Deborah.

Joseph had rented guards from among King Herod's mercenaries, and those men set up a perimeter of watchfulness against the brigands who were a danger on all roads. There were twenty of the guards so that they could sleep in shifts, leaving more than enough in full alertness. Normally half that number would have been considered adequate. But this was not a normal situation. Deborah must have no worries, no disturbances, no distress. Now that Joseph could see that she was with child, he would do anything to protect her. The baby must be healthy, must have a normal birth, a strong body. So that he would not be required to divorce Sarah.

In the morning everything had to be repacked, and then they could set off again. Slowly.

It took nine days to reach Jerusalem. By the time they arrived, the Succoth festival was over, so Joseph and the guards escorted Roxana to her mother at King Herod's Jericho palaces.

Joseph had never visited the famous old town, with its springs and verdant landscape. He had a deep dislike for it, learned from his father. Herod's palace was built over the foundations of the family's summer season house, confiscated at the time of his grandfather's murder.

Those old animosities no longer troubled Joseph; his success had erased any sense of deprivation. But the presence of the King did disturb him. Joseph knew it was not possible, but he imagined that he could still see bloodstains on the paving stones of the square in Caesarea.

He approached the palace with trepidation. Roxana ran ahead, without saying goodbye.

Joseph showed his ring to the door guards. "I would like to pay my respects to King Herod and to the councillor Nicolaus." Door guards delivered him to a pair of the King's bodyguards. They took away the knife he always wore in his belt, then escorted him to one of the gardens.

Herod was seated in a chair beside a pond, with a small fishing net across his knees. A guard held a sunshade over his bare head.

"Come and help me catch our dinner, Joseph of Arimathea," Herod called. His voice was strong.

Joseph approached him, and bowed.

"No formality in gardens, Joseph. Sit here on this stool beside me. I'll cast the net, and you haul it in." He threw the weighted circle with an expert touch, handed Joseph its cords. "They tell me that you entertained one of my children for many months. I am indebted to you. What do you require in return?"

Joseph was surprised and insulted. "Nothing, King Herod. I did not invite Roxana with any idea of payment."

Herod chuckled, which turned into a cough. When he could breathe again, he smiled at Joseph. "I had forgotten your stiff neck," he said. His smile was like a death's head grin. He was a very sick man. Pity overcame Joseph's apprehensions.

"Roxana was a blessing to my house," he said with a slight smile. "I have a young wife, you may remember, and your daughter was a much better companion for her than I could have been."

Herod coughed again. "Don't amuse an old man too much, Joseph. You have my full sympathy. I'm familiar with the tedious company of young wives . . . Watch out, the water's moving. Haul in the net. Quick!"

Joseph acted at once. But the fish escaped capture. Herod sighed.

"So be it," he said. "You may leave me now."

The guards escorted Joseph to Nicolaus. Joseph's friend looked better than when he'd seen him last. More rested.

Things were reasonably quiet, he told Joseph. Doctors had made up a potion to reduce Herod's pain.

"He's changed his will again. His eldest son Antipater is now his heir, and many of the tiresome duties of hearing petitions and such are being taken over by the prince. They were draining Herod's strength, so this is a good thing."

"But?" There'd been something in Nicolaus' tone.

"The usual. Salome. She tells Herod that Antipater is eager for him to die, which is probably true. And she taunts him about their brother. Pheroras fell in love with a slave girl and married her against Herod's orders. Salome stops unwitting slave girls in Herod's presence and asks them if they're related to the King."

"Why don't you find her a handsome boy with hot blood? I told you about Barca. Salome gave no trouble on the voyage from Italy."

Nicolaus said he'd try it. He was willing to try anything. Was Barca available?

Joseph shook his head. "He's discovered there's plenty of young flesh eager to accommodate him. Salome couldn't possibly compete now."

They agreed it was a pity. Then Joseph had to go. He didn't like to leave Deborah alone these days.

The baby came in the middle of the night in early February, when the almond trees in the garden were in full sweet bloom.

A boy child, wrinkled and red, with a strong cry. The midwives washed him, wrapped strips of linen tight around his torso and legs to make them grow straight, then took him to Joseph.

"His name will be Aaron," Joseph said. It was the name of his grandfather and of the first High Priest of the Israelites, the brother of Moses. Joseph was ambitious for his son.

In accordance with the Law, Aaron was circumcised eight days after his birth. And after forty days Joseph took Deborah and their son to the Temple, where Joseph sacrificed a sheep and put five shekels into one of the shofar-shaped golden receptacles for gifts to the Temple treasury, to redeem a firstborn son.

At the house they welcomed family and hundreds of guests to a lavish reception to celebrate Aaron's birth. He was sound asleep at the breast of his wet nurse in the suite of quiet rooms designated as the nursery. Deborah was uncomfortable. Her strapped breasts were still tender because lactation had not yet completely stopped. But she was glad to be slim and beautiful again and the center of attention.

Also, she could happily anticipate the future. After the birth she wept telling Joseph how much it had hurt. "I don't want to do that again."

"You don't have to, Deborah. You have given me what I wanted most in the whole world, and you can have anything you want, including no more children."

"Really?"

"Really, dear child."

"And I won't have to let you come to my room?"

"I will not come to your room."

Deborah smiled through her weeping. "A wet nurse, too. All my friends had wet nurses."

"You shall have a wet nurse."

"I don't think I'm going to mind being a mother, then. Thank you, Joseph."

Another satisfied participant in the celebration was Joshua. He had seen his firstborn son's firstborn son.

Helena and Rebekkah were satisifed, too. They knew how ecstatic Sarah was that divorce had been averted.

In the farmhouse that was hers and Joseph's home she was singing the Celtic star song as a lullaby to the baby she loved because he had given her husband back to her.

Joshua died only a few months after Aaron's birth. Joseph learned of it only when the family came to Jerusalem for Passover.

"Why didn't you send word to me?" he cried. "I would have come at once. I didn't know he was sick, not that sick."

His mother's shadowed eyes gave evidence of her grief, but she was composed, serene. "My son, you had given him what he needed to make his life complete. He was ready for it to end. There was no sickness. He simply did not wake one morning. He was gone."

According to the Law, Joseph was now owner of the farms and fields and village at Arimathea. When his family returned, he accompanied them.

Before doing anything else, he went to Joshua's tomb. It was a natural cave in the rock of the low hills near the vineyards. A large stone covered the opening, whitewashed to signify a recent burial. According to custom, when Joshua's body had decomposed, its dry bones would be placed in an ossuary, a stone box with simple carving that gave his name and the date of his death. The ossuary would join the containers that held the bones of his ancestors on a natural outcropping of rock that made a shelf in the tomb.

Joseph placed his hands on the whitewashed stone and said goodbye to his father. Then he went to the village that now belonged to him.

It was much like thousands of other small communities throughout the countryside. In the center was an earthen square, a widened area of the narrow road that ran through it. A well in the middle of the square provided water for the villagers, and a meeting place for sociability among the village women when they went to draw water. The little synagogue stood on one side, shaded by trees.

Small houses and shops lined the road, each with one or two rooms, built of blocks of baked clay with a flat roof reached by ladder or exterior steps and an earthen courtyard where a shed housed a goat or two for milk and a chicken roost. A clay oven sat to one side of the courtyard for baking bread, and for some houses a fig tree provided welcome summer shade in one corner. The roof, with built-up edges for safety when small children played there, was the living and sleeping area in the dry season, when stars and moon created a ceiling of beauty and celestial light.

There were seventeen families in Arimathea village. Most of the men were laborers in the fields and vineyards; there were also a carpenter, a blacksmith, and a potter. Every man, woman, and child knew Joseph and was known by him. They made him welcome.

He visited each house and each shop, listening, talking, sharing memories, accepting condolences for his father's death, offering his own sympathy for deaths that had occurred in the families of the villagers.

He learned details of the lives of his people. Their worries, their hopes, their joys, and their sorrows. They were his responsibility now.

When the visits were finished, Joseph walked up the path to the big farmhouse that had been his father's, where his grandmother lived, and his mother. On his head was the woven straw hat that he had bought from the open stall on the village square. It was identical to the one he had worn as a little boy, except in size. It was good to be home. The city and its problems seemed far away.

Now for the hard part. His brothers were waiting to talk with him.

According to the Law, the eldest son inherited twice what younger sons received. According to tradition, the eldest bought the shares of his brothers so that the land could remain undivided.

Amos knew the Law and the traditions, but he was unhappy about the unusual conditions in their family. "I have been running everything since Father was stricken, because I was the eldest son at Arimathea. I worked for two, our father and myself. I don't see why I should do that for you, Joseph, because you happened to be born first. You've never really worked the land. I'd prefer to take my quarter of the land for myself and farm it for myself, not you."

"I can understand your feelings, Amos, but not your thinking. Which quarter will you take? The wheat fields? Then you'll have no wine and no oil and no barley. Let me make a proposal first. I use a system in my shipping business that I learned from our grandmother." Caleb and Amos looked at each other, eyebrows raised. Joseph chuckled.

"Yes, you heard correctly," he said. "Rebekkah taught me how to run my business successfully. When I was a child, I worked in her garden. Not that I wanted to, mind you, I was told to, and I did not do the digging and weeding and water-hauling with good grace. Not until the wisest of women sat me down and talked sense to me. 'It is my land and the seeds are my seeds,' she said. 'The labor is yours. Therefore, we will each take half the produce, or the coins earned by selling it in the village. You will discover, my dear, that if you put in more effort you will end up with more vegetables and more coins for your share.'

"As she generally is, Rebekkah was right. I tell my ships' men the same principle, and we divide the trading profits half and half. The results are remarkable. My ships sail on time, with a full crew who follow orders with no slacking. Because it is to their advantage."

The same, Joseph suggested, would work as well at Arimathea. On the lowest level, where the men of the village worked for day wages, assigning them their own fields and areas of the orchard and vineyards would provide the same pride and incentive that worked so well on the galleys. It would also give them larger incomes.

"The other half, the half that on the ships is mine, should,

I believe, be yours, my brothers. I do not work on the farm, I work at sea. Therefore, half the money made at sea is, I believe, rightfully mine. Not so at Arimathea.

"I will pay you well for your shares. You could buy yourselves other farms. But they would be smaller, and this has always been your home. I believe it a good idea to use that money, and the earnings from Arimathea, to buy land for your sons to own someday. Meanwhile you will be in control of the lands here, just as if you owned them. Although in fact you'll be preserving them for my son's inheritance many years from now."

Joseph continued to explain his plan. He said nothing about what Caleb had talked about at Caesarea, his resentment that Amos ordered him about. "I believe that Caleb should have control of the olives and the vineyards and, you, Amos, the fields and the fruit orchards. That will give each of you some weeks without daily labor, and clear definition of which revenues are yours."

Caleb was so overjoyed at the prospect of being in control instead of under Amos' thumb that he agreed at once to Joseph's plan.

Amos was less hasty. What Joseph was saying was different from what he was accustomed to, and it took hours of questioning and arguing before he could understand it. Finally, however, he could see the great advantage to him. And that made him suspicious. "How can you be certain that I will not cheat you, Joseph, will not work poorly or show bad judgment?"

Joseph smiled. "Because you have already formed your habits, Amos. You like to see the land produce its best. You are the finest of farmers."

In the end, his brothers agreed to allow him to make them wealthy men. By their own efforts. Joseph considered it a good day's work.

And now he could go home to Sarah. To boast about his cleverness.

She complimented him excessively. "You're laughing at me, Sparrow. What's so amusing?"

"As always, my love, it's you. Yes, you did well for Amos and Caleb. But you did better for Joseph. You cannot help being a businessman. Aaron will inherit the finest farm in the Plains of Sharon, without your having to do so much as pick one single grape."

He tried to hide his annoyance. Sarah made it vanish by talking about how fortunate Aaron was to have such a remarkable father. Whom she loved with all her heart.

That night he lay with Sarah, and there was no world other than the universe of happiness within their love. Afterward he held her in his arms and breathed in the clean sweet scent of her hair tumbled across his shoulder and throat.

"You know, Sparrow, I think perhaps I might come home to Arimathea to live," he murmured drowsily, speaking in Aramaic, like a country man. "I sat on the roof of a village house, drinking wine from a cup of clay shaped by the village potter, and the cool breeze of day's ending was strong with the sweet smell of grapes from the vineyard and I saw that the farmer was richer with his mud-bricked two rooms than King Herod was with all his great palaces."

He felt Sarah's warm body shaking with laughter. "Oh, Joseph, I do love you so. You would make the worst farmer of all time. You cannot live slowly and without new and different challenges every hour."

A moment's anger woke him. Then he realized that of course she was absolutely correct. He began to chuckle. His eyelids grew heavy again. "You know me too well," he said, his voice rich with pleasure that it was so.

"Go to sleep, farmer. The cockcrow will call you to your fields in a very few hours." Sarah turned over, freeing his arm from the weight of her, and pulled the woolen coverlet up. Nights were still quite chilly.

She said nothing to Joseph about what distressed her. But

when he left to go to his ships and the sea, Sarah discussed it with Rebekkah and Helena.

He showed no true love for Aaron. He'd said nothing about how the baby looked, what he weighed, what he did that won the heart.

"Men are like that," Rebekkah told her. "Infants don't interest them."

Helena agreed. "Babies are their mothers'. Boys belong to their fathers."

Sarah accepted their knowledge. Also, she admitted, in a shameful way she was happy that Joseph had so little interest in his child by another woman. Still, she felt sorry for Aaron.

Helena kissed her. "You are soft-hearted, and I love you for it, Sarah, but you're wrong. Joseph's life was perpetually happy until his father began to take an interest in him. From then on, he was always miserable, or angry, or both. Mothers adore. Fathers discipline."

None of the women at Arimathea had any way of knowing that Deborah intended to leave Aaron with his wet nurse and Meneptah in Jerusalem. She was going to the house in Caesarea as soon as the days were warmer. And she was sure that Joseph's ship had sailed.

When he returned from Belerion and learned what Deborah had done, Joseph was enraged. She was no longer a child, he shouted, she was a mother, with adult responsibilities.

Deborah responded with her own rage. In spite of her orders, the slave Antiochus had accompanied her and the household to Caesarea and he never, ever, let her go out alone, but went everywhere with her.

After he had calmed down, Joseph was able to hear what Antiochus had to tell him: In essence he had two children and must arrange that both of them be cared for.

It was not, in truth, all that difficult. He hired a former Roman slave who had earned his freedom after serving twenty years as servant to a legate, commander of a Roman legion. Aulus was a fearless, toughened veteran, who had learned Latin, Greek, and polished manners from his owner. He was in his late thirties, and had a wife of twenty-two, also a freed slave. Drusilla had been the personal body slave to the legate's wife. Aulus had bought her and freed her and married her, all on the same day. They'd been lovers for ten years.

They were Deborah's protection and companions when she wanted to go out. Drusilla also became her advisor about cosmetics, skin care, and complex arrangements of her hair. These were engrossingly interesting to Deborah, and she regarded her guardians as a wonderful gift.

For Aaron, Antiochus found a Syrian slave, a woman whose own child had been taken from her and sold. Joseph's tiny son, only seven months old, became the recipient of the boundless love and devotion that should have belonged to Glaphyra's own little boy.

Joseph's life was, in most ways, quite satisfying. In Jerusalem he had his business friends, also an increasing range of business knowledge and investments. He was a sought-after guest, a host whose rare invitations were highly prized. For receptions and other large social events he was the fortunate husband of the most beautiful woman present.

Privately, he was the happy husband of the wife he adored and saw often during frequent trips to Arimathea.

Thus the autumn and winter months passed. Joseph relaxed into a kind of complacency. The new arrangements on the farms were beginning to settle into a productive routine; the fields were showing the prospect of a rich harvest. His informants in King Herod's household reported that Antipater was shouldering even greater responsibilities and handling them with skill. That promised a smooth transfer of power when the old king died.

Joseph was actually pleased when he received a letter from Herod, even though it meant he would have to miss his cherished voyage to Belerion. "My highly valued son Antipater will be acting as ambassador to Caesar Augustus," the letter read. "I ask you to take him to Rome in comfort aboard your special ship."

Joseph sent a response immediately, by fast messenger. In it he expressed his feelings of gratitude for the honor of the King's request, and gladly agreed to fulfill it.

What luck, he thought. I'll have lots of time to get to know the next King of Israel.

As soon as the King's enormous retinue was in residence at the palaces for the Passover festival, Joseph garbed himself in fine, sober-colored silks and went to see Herod and to meet his son.

He met some others, too. "This is Berenice," Herod said. He gestured to the attractive, slightly plump, elegantly dressed woman on his left. "She and her children will be traveling with you, along with Antipater."

Is this another one of Herod's wives? Joseph wondered. He expressed delight, aloud, while his mind was racing through all the names he'd heard through the years.

He also stole glances at Herod's face. It was thinner, and more deeply lined. Pain had marked dark depressions around his eyes.

Nicolaus came forward to rescue Joseph. With the King's permission, he said, he would take Joseph to his study to discuss the arrangements for the voyage.

When they were alone, Nicolaus offered Joseph several pieces of advice and information. "Antipater," he said, "is already beginning to consider himself King of Israel. It's going to his head. Treat him with more deference than Herod has ever needed.

"But do not neglect Berenice. She is potentially of much greater importance to you than Antipater. Her husband was the prince Aristobulus, whom Herod executed. He and Alexander were wonderful boys. Lively and attractive and naturally engaging. They grew up in the household of Augustus, and he was extremely fond of them. Lucky for you, he didn't see them after they returned to Israel and became the disagreeable men you met. The Emperor remembers the boys. Therefore he'll welcome Berenice with warmth and affection.

"Which she'll deserve. She's a warm and affectionate woman herself. I'm sure she will like you, Joseph. You have the gift of friendship. Cultivate Berenice, it will be a pleasure for you. More important, it will be a direct route into the household and the affection of Augustus.

"True, Antipater is necessary for your position in Israel. But Israel is only one small part of the Roman Empire. Berenice can make you important in a wider world."

Nicolaus was entertained by the expression on Joseph's face. "Don't worry, my friend, Berenice is no Salome. Your virtue is safe."

CHAPTER THIRTY-EIGHT

IT WAS INESCAPABLE FACT: THE VOYAGE TO ITALY WAS going to require another galley, too. The *Phoenix* could not possibly hold all the baggage that Berenice intended to take. Cart after cart was drawn onto the quay by teams of horses.

Joseph went to the palace, his anger simmering. Nicolaus had worked out arrangements with him, but this had not been part of them.

"Women!" Nicolaus said. "How could I have known Berenice would have so much to move to Rome? I didn't realize how crammed the rooms were in the part of the palace where she lived with Aristobulus."

"I had already booked cargo for that galley. What's supposed to become of it? I stand to lose my reputation as well as the fees."

"Ptolemy will make up your losses, Joseph. And pay the same fees again for transporting Berenice's goods. I can't do better than that."

Joseph wasn't satisfied, but he had to accept the terms. He calculated rapidly. The doubled charter fees added up to nearly the cost of a galley. If he could find one, with a crew ready, he could buy it and meet his obligations for the cargo to Alexandria. Then pick up another one there, which would offset the wages of the crew. He'd break even, and he would have a sixth ship for his fleet. It was worth a try.

"I'll have to delay departure for a week," he said. "No negotiating that."

Nicolaus shrugged. "It will probably take that long, or longer, for Berenice to gather every moveable object."

The few galleys available were a sorry bunch. But the mysterious, instant spread of information had alerted their owners. Joseph had to pay far more than it was worth for the least sorry of the lot.

The ship's crew was as second-rate as their vessel. "Now we'll see what your boy can do," Joseph said to Milcar. He made Barca captain of the ship.

By the time the *Phoenix* sailed, Joseph had developed a thoroughly hostile attitude toward Berenice.

Before an hour at sea had passed, he adored her.

She arrived on the quay with her tutors, nursemaids, servants, cooks, her three pet dogs and four pet children. Dogs and children were outfitted with little body harnesses and leashes. She was wearing a plain linen tunic, loosely sashed, and a scarf around her head. "Greetings to you, Joseph of Arimathea," she said. "I won't be able to keep the small animals out of sight, but I promise you they'll be kept under control. Now—where are my cabins?"

Antipater's attendants were his personal slaves, his barber, his bath attendant, and twenty bodyguards. "Show the servants where to go," he ordered Joseph. Then he settled himself on a couch in the afterdeck pavilion. He was dressed in red silk, bordered with gold. The oldest of Herod's many children was a thick-set man in his early forties. His hair, like his father's, was dyed raven black.

It promised to seem a very long voyage.

In fact it was so enjoyable that Joseph hardly noticed the days passing. All because of Berenice.

As soon as they cleared the harbor and entered the sea, she appeared, carrying two baskets of food and drink. She walked easily on the tilting deck, giving fruit to each of the seamen and to Joseph.

"Don't argue," she told him merrily. "You know it will go bad if we don't eat it quickly. It was going to waste in the palace kitchen.

"I trust you won't object to what I've done, Joseph. I had the servants remove all the fancy silk bedcoverings and spread some blankets I brought with me. There's no point in ruining all the elegance you worked so hard to create, and the dogs would have it in shreds in no time at all.

"Antipater! Make room for me, will you?" She put the baskets on the deck and sat on the edge of the couch nearest his.

"I've brought you some of that wonderful honeyed wine from Alexandria, and I intend to keep you just a tiny bit drunk all the time. I don't know how else you can possibly bear having my children around. They are so noisy when they're excited and happy, and even noisier when they're upset and howling.

"Let's turn this trip into a sort of floating Purim; don't you agree that's sensible?"

Antipater was very conscious of his position and dignity. "I have weighty matters that concern me, Berenice. I shall be too deep in thought to be aware of your children."

Berenice regarded him with sincere pity. "You poor dear," she said, "you simply have no idea." She patted him on his red-silk-covered arm. Berenice was probably twenty years younger than her dead husband's half brother, but she gave the impression that he might well be another of her children who needed comforting.

"All right," she called loudly. "Let them out of their cage." In less than a half minute, the deck was a jumble of running dogs and children, each pulling a slave behind, at the other end of a leash. Squeals and shrieks, yipping and high-pitched laughter jangled the air.

Without calling attention to the act, Berenice hefted a large wine jug and filled a heavy-bottomed cup for Antipater. She ate ripe figs with obvious pleasure and watched her pets having a good time. She looked perfectly comfortable.

After a little while her children and dogs ran to her and begged for a fig. Some climbed onto the couch beside her; one dog and one child got into her lap; another dog lifted its leg and wet her ankle. "Poor darling, you're overexcited, aren't you?" Berenice crooned. She dampened the end of a linen towel in a pitcher of milk then wiped her ankle and foot.

"Be little birds," she said; the two youngest children turned their faces up to her, mouths open, and she popped a dripping half fig into them. The two older ones already had figs in their hands. Berenice threw bits of cake to the dogs.

Antipater stood up. He gathered the folds of his magnificent cloak about him and walked away without a word, to go to his cabin. Berenice watched his exit with sympathetic eyes.

"Now, children," she said after he was gone. "Sit crosslegged like tailors on the deck here, and you may have one cup of milk and one honeycake. Only one. You mustn't ruin your appetite for dinner.

"Walk the dogs a bit, please," she asked their holders. "They can have this milk when the children finish theirs.

"Look at the sail against the blue of the sky, children, isn't it beautiful? You are going to love the sea and the way the ship sometimes feels like swinging in a hammock. Do you want Mother to tell you about the first time she ever went on the water?" Berenice poured milk into four bowls as she was speaking.

"Yes!" the children yelped. She held one bowl up.

"'Yes!' what?"

"Yes, please, Mother." The bowls were given to reaching small hands.

"It was a very small boat." Honeycakes joined the bowls. "But I was a very small girl, smaller than Herodias." The smallest child giggled. "So it seemed very large to me . . ."

The story meandered on and on. When it was done, the little girl called Herodias was asleep in Berenice's lap, and the other three children were cradled against her sides, held fast by her sheltering arms.

Joseph looked at them, and he realized who it was that Berenice made him think of. It was his Aunt Abigail. Berenice had the identical gift. Love and comfortableness flowed from her onto everyone around her.

Later Joseph got the children's names and the dogs' names straightened out. Aristobulus, named for his father, was eight. Herod Agrippa, named for his grandfather, was five. The little girls, both plump replicas of their mother, were Miriam, four, and Herodias, three. The dogs were Fluffy, Boots, and Wags, all from the same litter, and all approximately two years old.

As the days went by, Joseph became particularly fond of Herod Agrippa. The sturdy little boy had bright eyes and a quick, bright mind. He was fascinated by the ship and everything Joseph told him or showed him about sailing.

Joseph imagined his own son in four or five more years. He'd be just as bright and lively as Herod Agrippa. Perhaps more so. No, not perhaps. Probably. Certainly, even.

Berenice shared another trait with Abigail. People talked to her. Not mere polite exchanges. They talked about themselves, their hopes, their disappointments. She was genuinely interested. And so understanding.

The sailmaster told her about his wife's sweet singing

voice and how sometimes he fancied he could hear it in the wind.

The steersman told her about his son, a potter, and the magic his fingers wrought in spinning clay. He even brought to her the carefully wrapped packet that had been an object of curiosity to his fellow crew members for years. For Berenice he opened it to show her an elegant small ewer, with ram's horn handles.

Even Joseph, who never talked about himself, mentioned his fantasy of Aaron in Herod Agrippa's place, on the deck of the ship and excited about sailing.

And Antipater—who resisted joining Berenice on deck for weeks—ended up recounting the history of the bitter years after King Herod sent him and his mother into exile. When the Emperor Augustus put Herod on the throne, he had discarded his first wife and son, to take a new wife, of royal blood.

Berenice reminded Antipater that his father was very young then. "Much younger than you are now, Antipater. You must have made mistakes when you were young, too, isn't that so? And remember this, too. When he was older, he brought you back. And now . . ."

She didn't have to finish the sentence. Antipater smoothed his windblown hair, readying it for a crown.

Joseph accompanied Berenice to Rome, at her request. He was glad to do so, for many reasons. Primarily, he had to admit, he wished to see Augustus again. And to be seen by him, in company with someone who knew the imperial family well and was well known by them.

Loved, too, Joseph was sure. No one could know Berenice and not feel a warm affection for her. He certainly did, and that was his second reason for going with her. He would honestly miss the combination of comfort and chaos that she and her "animals" created.

He had noticed, too, the way Berenice invited confidences. If he could develop a continuing friendship with

her, he might learn many, many things from her that
would be useful.

In addition to the very real pleasure of being with
Berenice, the trip to Rome kept him close to Antipater. He
hadn't exactly warmed up to the older man, even after Antipater relaxed. But the next King of Israel was important
to cultivate. When Antipater became King, Joseph would
be glad to have spent so many weeks with him within the
confines of the galley.

And finally, when he was in Rome he'd go see
Rufinius. Naturally he'd sent him a message about the
birth of Aaron. But there had been no reply. That was
probably due to the nature of things. Unless one had access to the couriers who bore messages for the Empire's
business—which Joseph did not have—the only way to
send a letter was to entrust it to a traveler going to the
place where the recipient lived. The news about Aaron had
left Jerusalem with a shipowner headed for Tyre, who
gave it to the captain of a vessel bound for Italy, where he
would find someone going to Rome.

The letter must have reached Rufinius. It had left
Jerusalem more than a year ago. Still, Joseph owed it to
Aaron's grandfather to tell him how well and strong and
handsome his grandson was growing.

"Dead? How? When?" Joseph couldn't believe it.
Rufinius was old, yes, but he was tough as old leather.

"I'm sorry I shocked you, Joseph." The speaker was
Deborah's eldest sister, Rufinia. "I was sure Deborah must
have gotten the letter I sent; it was so long ago. One of the
synagogue members was making Passover pilgrimage last
year, and I gave it to him. I'm sure he told me he'd delivered it."

Joseph had to accept Rufinia's words. Also a serving of
nasty date and almond cake; she made it herself, she
bragged.

Walking back to the Palatine Joseph shrugged off any

thought of collecting Deborah's dowry now. He was hardly surprised.

At Augustus' house he found the Emperor on his knees in the garden, playing a game of knuckle bones with Aristobulus and Herod Agrippa. He was happy to join them. He rather fancied his skills at knuckle bones.

Herod Agrippa beat them all.

"I used to play this game with your father," said Augustus. "He always beat me, too."

After the children were collected by their frantic tutor, the Emperor looked at Joseph. "I will always sorrow for Aristobulus and Alexander. How is King Herod, Joseph?"

"Very ill, with great pain. No one can say how much time he has left."

Caesar Augustus sighed. "Time passes more quickly every year. He was still a boy when I knew him first. So was I, for that matter." The Emperor put some extra spring in his knees and got quickly to his feet. "I could enjoy a cup of barley water," he said. "How about you, Joseph of Arimathea?"

Joseph stood, too. Close to Augustus. "I would like that very much, Princeps."

He had seen the Emperor's thick-soled sandals this time and understood. He'd been sensitive about his own short stature all his life. For his hero Augustus Caesar he was happy to stand up and be looked down on. There were times when power was irrelevant. A man wanted to be tall. Joseph knew all about that.

He left Rome with genuine regret. The few days in the domestic, informal atmosphere of Augustus' inner family circle had been very special.

At the ten-mile marker on the Appian Way, Joseph dug his heels into the side of his hired horse. It was still quite early in the season, and he had seven weeks before he was to meet Antipater for the *Phoenix*'s return to Caesarea. He could sail the good galley that had carried Berenice's things, find trade in at least three ports in Greece, before the weather began to change.

He'd have time later to think about Rome and the Emperor and his privileged time in Augustus' house. He didn't know whether it was smart—or safe—to think of Caesar Augustus as a man and not an Emperor. Surely rulers must be different from ordinary men.

CHAPTER THIRTY-NINE

JUST WHEN JOSEPH WAS STARING AT THE BEAUTY OF THE Parthenon, Salome was warning her brother Herod about Antipater's secret plan to poison him and assume the kingship, according to Herod's will. The will was the cause of Antipater's embassy to Rome. Its provisions had to be approved by the Emperor.

Herod dismissed Salome with harsh words about her never-ending attempts to turn him against his sons. He did not tell her about the nightmares that were disturbing his uneasy, drugged sleep. In the dream Aristobulus stood over him, a bared sword at his throat, intent on retribution.

Salome continued to torment Herod about Pheroras' wife, the former slave, and Herod raged at her. But then, suddenly, Pheroras died. The slave girl probably killed him, Salome said viciously. It had to be investigated, so Nicolaus sent secret police to Pheroras' palace in Perea. They questioned Pheroras' servants under torture, seeking any incrimination of his wife. What they learned was much worse. When they reported to Nicolaus, he was staggered.

Salome had been right. There was a plot to poison Herod. Pheroras' and Antipater's plot. Herod's brother was to have done it while Antipater was in Rome, so that no suspicion could fall on Herod's son. The poison itself was in a vial in Pheroras' private chamber.

And it was Nicolaus' job to tell the King. Stricken already in body, the information struck Herod now in the wishful sentiments he had developed toward his eldest son.

Before Nicolaus' eyes, Herod the dying man became, again, Herod the King of Israel. "See to it," he commanded his councillor, "that not a word of this reaches Antipater in Rome. Let him continue to believe that he will return to the surprising news that his father is dead and he is the King."

In September the *Phoenix* left Puteoli with one passenger only. Antipater's mission in Rome must have been successful, Joseph thought. Herod's son was in high spirits.

Of course it might be something simpler. Maybe Antipater was simply glad that the pandemonium of Berenice's pets was not part of the return journey.

A cohort of the King's army was on the quay in Caesarea when the *Phoenix* entered the harbor. Antipater positioned himself in the prow, one hand resting on the jeweled bird, his red and gold cloak billowing in the steady wind.

When the galley docked, Antipater walked regally to the head of the gangplank. He received the officer's salute, then asked what news the officer had for him. The reply was that he was under arrest.

Joseph and his crew stared, thunderstruck, as Antipater was bound and led away.

While, on the coast of Syria, north of Sidon, a Roman courier was bent over the back of his mount, urging speed. He was carrying dispatches from King Herod to Caesar Augustus. Including a new will for the Emperor's approval.

Back in Jerusalem again, Joseph confronted Deborah with the news of her father's death. Oh, yes, she said blithely, she knew all about that.

"Why didn't you say anything, Deborah? Why didn't you tell me?"

"What was the point of it, Joseph? He didn't leave me anything. I just forgot about it."

As soon as Joseph had seen his son, who was sleeping, and heard Antiochus' report that all was well in the household, he left for Arimathea.

Everything there was even better than well. Amos and Rachel had a new child, Susannah. Their son David, now three, was entranced by his tiny baby sister. Caleb's store of filled wine jars was, he claimed proudly, nearly a quarter more than any previous vintage.

And in his own house, Sarah was waiting for him with open arms. She found his account of Augustus' built-up sandal soles touching, teased him about his fondness for Berenice, said that she had missed him more than ever and that it was overdue for them to make love.

More than ever before, Joseph hated it when time came for his return to Jerusalem.

Joseph's friend Eleazar knew the sad history of Pheroras' and Antipater's plot that Joseph had missed. However, Joseph was able to add the dramatic moment of the arrest to the story.

Eleazar was impressed. "Poor fool," he said. "Expecting to be escorted with all honors to a waiting throne, and instead he was led to Herod's prepared trial. The governor of Syria was with Herod to hear the evidence. Antipater's in prison somewhere; he'll be executed as soon as the Emperor's agreement arrives."

"In the rainy season? It'll take months."

The two free, healthy friends went to the wineshop near City Hall to toast the good fortune of their distance from the family of King Herod.

Joseph thought grimly that he'd wasted a lot of time getting on good terms with the expected next King of Israel.

But then he thought of Berenice and her children and her dogs. Without question, the voyage had been a good one.

Who was going to be king when Herod died? Eleazar and Joseph speculated for hours. The sons still living were all quite young. Too young, they thought.

"Listen to us," Eleazar said with mock mournfulness. "We've turned into two old graybeards. How old are you, Joseph?"

"Twenty-seven."

"And how old were you when you bought your first ship?"

Joseph grinned. "Sixteen. If you could call that wreck a ship."

"There you are, you see. I was fifteen when I started in business with my two brothers. We're in no position to say that Herod's sons are too young to start in the ruling business. Whoever gets the throne will have Herod's army, his advisors, all the routines in place. It hardly matters which one is named."

Joseph thought of the pain-wrecked old man who was King of Israel. "I hope it will be soon."

"So do we all. We wait, there's nothing else to do. At least things are quiet. Everyone is waiting."

Not everyone. On street corners in the lower city, at city gates, at the Temple gates, on the steps, in the Courts of the Temple itself, fervent men were preaching, shouting, proclaiming that Herod's burning pain was the punishment of God for his sins, for his betrayal of Judaism and the Jewish people to the godless powers of Rome.

Some of these preachers were followers of two Pharisee scholars who taught at one of Jerusalem's academies for study of the Law. Mattathias ben Margalit and Judah ben Zippori were very different from the famous older teachers, Hillel and Shammai. These younger teachers were more radical in their beliefs. They talked eloquently about a new doctrine, the belief in eternal life after death, with everlasting reward or punishment depending on the righteousness or sinfulness of the individual soul.

The righteous man, they told their zealous students, could not stand by and watch the defilement of the Law that Herod's rule had brought. They must cry out against it, no matter the consequences, even death. Martyrdom in the service of God was a guarantee of eternal bliss.

Early one morning in March these teachers directed their students' attention to what they said was Herod's most outrageous defamation. Decades before, when he had built the Temple, Herod had erected a graven image above the great gate in the Court of the Gentiles. It was an immense gilded eagle with outstretched wings.

"Destroy it!" urged the teachers. "Smash the abomination." They led their pupils, dozens of them. In the crowded streets of the lower city people screamed and made way for them when they saw the flash of sunlight reflected from the axes in the hands of some of the students.

They pushed people aside on the wide steps that mounted to the Temple platform. Inside the court of the Gentiles there were the usual groups of worshipers, sightseers, animal sellers, animal buyers, people changing money, people meeting friends, scholars debating, rabbis lecturing, young men questioning them. The young zealots poured in, shouting, and swarmed around the base of the gate, pointing at the giant gold eagle above it.

While people gaped, three of them climbed onto the backs and shoulders of their fellows, then scrambled up the high stone walls to the top. Others handed up ropes, and still others climbed up to join them, carrying axes. They lowered six of their number by rope to hang suspended in front of the hated eagle.

Throughout the Court of the Gentiles people were pointing at the shocking goings-on, and a mob collected at the gate, drawn by the sounds of the axes hacking at the glittering gold statue. When huge pieces of it began to fall to the pavement below, the mob cheered. And then the students down there swung their axes to smash the fallen wings and head to golden dust. Excitement was so contagious that most of the mob did not notice the advancing phalanx of Temple police. Those who did see them edged away from the tumultuous disturbance, and escaped arrest.

Several hundred, in all, were surrounded by police and herded to Herod's palace. Palace guards pushed them into the soaring column-bordered reception hall, where they cowered before the magnificence of the colored marble walls and floors and furnishings and their own fear of what was to come.

Not so the Pharisee teachers and their eager students. When guards officers demanded to know who was responsible for the outrage, they stepped forward proudly. Guards led them into the presence of the King. He had been clothed in a regal robe of purple silk embroidered with gold and a tall crown studded with huge glowing jewels.

The teachers were not awed. Fired by zeal, they announced that they were not ashamed of their actions. They were proud. It was Herod who should be ashamed, because he had desecrated the Temple when he put the eagle within its precincts.

"You criticize your king? You could be called traitors." Herod's skin was ashen, but fury made his voice loud.

A student ran toward him. Guards grabbed his arms. "Do what you will with me—with us—you cannot frighten us. We will welcome death in defense of our God because it will deliver us to eternal glory and joy."

"Bind them," Herod ordered. "All of them."

That night, when the city lay quiet under bright moonlight, soldiers unbolted a gate in its walls. The prisoners, loaded with chains, were driven through it onto the stony road that led to Jericho.

While the straggling procession stumbled through the night and the morning along the fourteen miles to the luxuriant oasis city, Herod was carried to his palace there in a closed litter.

Soldiers "escorted" the prominent landowners of Jericho to the amphitheater at the city's edge just after midday. The prisoners were already there, in the center of the arena, where the same prominent citizens had often been entertained by fights between gladiators, or wild animals.

On this day the battle was between Herod and a few hundred footsore, dust-covered men of his capital city. It was the duty of Jericho's citizens to pass sentence. There was no question in anyone's mind what that sentence had to be. All of them had been told of the events in Jerusalem.

A delegation of Jericho men, three in number, approached the King after the charge of treason had been made. They were all known to Herod, had known him for many years. They were, to a man, moved by horror and deep sympathy for his condition. They were also quaking inwardly from fear of what a man in Herod's pain-wrecked state might do to anyone who defied him in even the smallest way.

They were courageous men. With calm words and quiet patience they succeeded in persuading him to release the bystanders who'd been caught up in the general arrest and to punish only the students and their teachers.

There was a full moon that night, and the arena's sand looked especially white.

Then red, when two rabbis and forty young followers were burned alive.

Then a shadow moved slowly, slowly across the scene, creating darkness broken only by the flames.

The terrified spectators of the execution covered their heads with their arms in fear. While overhead there occurred a total eclipse of the moon.

Eleazar shook his head solemnly. "I will never, ever, disagree with my wife again. Never. I wanted to go down to our house in Jericho early this year because the days have been so warm. She said no, we always go down after

Shavuot and she likes things to stay the same. If she hadn't been so stubborn—I mean, if she hadn't been right when I was wrong—I would have been one of those men in the amphitheater.

"Burning men alive! Can you imagine their cries, Joseph?" Eleazar shivered. "The old king must have gone completely mad."

"Who knows? His disease is burning him alive. That's enough to drive any man mad." *Why doesn't he die?* Joseph was thinking. *Then Antipater will probably still be King.* In a few weeks it would be time to leave for Belerion, and Joseph didn't want to miss it again this year. But who would be his partner in the tin business after Herod's death? He needed to have a contract with that man, whoever he might be.

Neither Joseph nor Eleazar mentioned the eclipse. They'd heard of it, of course. People were saying that it was a sign from God that miraculous happenings lay in the future, perhaps the end of the world.

But they hadn't seen it. Like most people, they were inside their houses with lamplight or asleep in their beds when it happened. If it happened. Who could believe the story of a man who had just been forced to watch forty-two men burn alive? An experience like that could easily make a man imagine that a cloud across the moon was something else.

CHAPTER FORTY

EVERYTHING WORKED OUT WELL FOR JOSEPH. KING HEROD died only weeks later, and Ptolemy remained, with Nicolaus, as advisor to the new king. Ptolemy readily agreed to renew the bronze partnership; it was extremely profitable.

Antipater would not enjoy the profits, however. He was dead. It was almost as if Herod had kept himself alive by force of will until the letter from Augustus arrived. It authorized Antipater's execution and agreed to the terms of Herod's final will.

His kingdom was divided among three sons. Archelaus, eighteen, was king of Judea, Samaria, and Idumea. His brother Antipas, seventeen, received the provinces of Galilee and Perea. And the rich area east of the Jordan River that was called Trachonitis went to their sixteen-year-old half brother Philip.

The Passover was at hand, and all Jerusalem was unsettled. Many were still seething over the atrocity of the executions at Jericho. Many more were angry that their new king was the son of a Samaritan woman, a people who'd been scorned by Judean Jews for generations. As always, pilgrims would be flooding into the city, adding the potential of thousands more angry men from the cities and towns and villages outside Jerusalem.

Joseph sent word to Arimathea: Do not make pilgrimage this year. He had iron shutters made for the windows of his house and for Abigail's, and he forbade Deborah to go out. She locked herself in her room.

On Passover Eve, he was one of the first to sacrifice the required lamb, and he hurried back home with it. All the Temple courts were crowded, as usual, but the mood was not the usual one of devout celebration. Belligerence filled the air.

He was just in time. Young and inexperienced Archelaus sent a cohort, a troop of 480 soldiers, to maintain peace among the angry crowds at the Temple.

The sight of uniformed oppression enflamed the people, and they stoned the marching men. More than four hundred died; the tribune in command was so badly wounded that he pulled himself up the steps from the Temple court to the Antonia fortress on his torn, bleeding belly.

And Archelaus unloosed the rest of his army. The cavalry attacked the tent villages of pilgrims on the hills around Jerusalem. The infantry moved in close order through all the streets and alleys of the lower city.

Even behind the iron shutters Joseph could hear the screaming and groaning of the massacre. Running sandals and pursuing boots passed his house. Aaron jumped up and down, begging to go out. He believed people were playing games outside, and wanted to join them.

By day's end, nearly three thousand dead were strewn throughout the streets, the valleys, the hills of Jerusalem. The cries of lament filled the night.

The following day, the day that celebrated the deliverance of the Jewish people from slavery centuries before, the air above the city still rang with the sounds of grief. It was forbidden by the Law to bury the dead on a High Holy Day, and the bereaved had to wait until Passover ended at sundown.

Joseph walked to Abigail's to make sure that the family was all right. There were no signs of disturbance in the upper city's wealthy neighborhood, save for the presence of soldiers in the open spaces of the agora and in ranks outside Herod's palace, now the home of Archelaus.

Abigail assured Joseph that all was well, and she declined his offer to let him get an escort and take them all to Arimathea. "Our family was driven out of this house once, by Herod. I will certainly not permit some child of his to do it a second time. The ugly shutters you provided are beautiful protection, Joseph. We need nothing more."

Even so, Joseph used his ring to reach Nicolaus, who used his influence to obtain regular patrols past Abigail's house and a dozen soldiers to serve as escort for Deborah and Aaron and the servants to Caesarea. The gate was opened for them to leave at sunrise.

Antiochus insisted on accompanying Joseph to Arimathea. They left the escorted party at Emmaus and traveled on alone.

The roads were peaceful, the farms and villages beside them quite as usual. So was Arimathea, village and farms. Joseph spoke to all the men, warning them to be on the alert, in case the troubles spread through the countryside.

He also persuaded Sarah to move into the house with Rebekkah and Helena and Caleb. "You'll have to protect our women," he told his brother.

"I will," said Caleb in a firm, manly tone. Joseph believed him. His "little brother" was sixteen now, a big, muscular man.

"We will be perfectly safe," Sarah told Joseph. "Go on to Belerion. I send warm affection to everyone there, and I want you to bring me some more lengths of warm wool. Rachel and Amos' children have worn out the robes I made them, and Rebekkah will be glad of another blanket when winter comes."

"And you, my sparrow, what can I bring you?"

"Yourself. You know that."

*   *   *

Nicolaus had asked for passage to Italy for Archelaus in one of Joseph's ships. The new king had to obtain the Emperor's confirmation of his position. Especially now, after the disastrous beginning of his reign.

Joseph agreed readily. Provided that he need not be aboard as captain of the ship and that the ship need not be the *Phoenix*.

It was probably imprudent not to cultivate the new ruler, but Joseph had had his fill of political prudence. He could not stomach the thought of spending months with the creature who had just massacred thousands on what had always been a joyous day of celebration.

"Welcome aboard," said Milcar from the *Eagle*'s deck. Joseph leapt from the quay.

"Cast off," he ordered. "I need the clean air and spaces of the sea."

Antiochus waved from the quay. He was sad not to be going, too, but Joseph had entrusted him with the safety of his household in Caesarea. Which meant his son. It was a responsibility that Antiochus took very seriously.

Archelaus left his country in the care of the Roman governor of Syria, a man named Publius Quintilius Varus. Varus had been Rome's overseer of Herod's kingdom for years. He expected trouble from a people now under the uneasy control of three young men who had spent most of their youth in Rome, being educated in the languages and histories and styles of Greece and Rome, not those of their own people or even that people's language.

Troubles began at once and were widespread. There were revolts in Galilee and Perea, and in Jerusalem an enormous raging mob drove the legion sent by Varus into Herod's palace, on which they launched repeated unsuccessful attacks.

Varus posted troops in Caesarea to protect it. The seaport was less than three miles from the Syrian border; it could not be permitted to become a base for attacks on Syria.

Then he marched, with two legions, nearly ten thousand hardened professional soldiers, to wipe out rebellion among the Jews.

Galilee was nearest. Varus burned the capital, Sepphoris, sought out the pockets of insurgents and defeated them. Those who were not killed were chained and sent to Syria, to be sold into slavery.

Then he marched to Jerusalem, along the way burning any towns or villages that offered resistance. In Jericho he captured the slave named Simon and his followers, who had burnt Herod's palace there and declared Simon king. They were taken, in chains, to Jerusalem for punishment.

In Jerusalem Varus captured many of the besiegers of the legion in the palace, although many more in the mob had already fled. Those captured joined the prisoners from Jericho.

Varus left one of his legions in Jerusalem to keep peace. The one that he had rescued was put in charge of the captives taken during the march from Galilee, and the legionnaires took revenge for the ignominy of the siege. They lined the four main roads from Jerusalem with crucified figures on both sides of the road. The number of crosses totaled two thousand, and carrion birds darkened the sky.

The country that Herod had ruled was partly in ruins, but it was pacified, and Varus returned to his headquarters in Damascus before the summer was over. The Roman Army was the Empire's strongest and most efficient component.

In Rome Augustus granted conditional approval to Herod's will. He did not grant Archelaus the title of king, however, as Herod had named him. Instead, Archelaus was designated Ethnarch, a prince. Herod's other sons were also titled prince, but of a lower order, Tetrarch. Israel had been divided and devalued.

Joseph learned all these things when he returned to Caesarea. After a hurried visit to Deborah and Aaron, he rushed immediately to Arimathea and found it untouched. The Romans' route went by way of Perea, not the Plains of Sharon.

He spent as much time as he could with the family and the wife he loved, then returned to Caesarea to greet his returning ships and take care of too-long-delayed matters of business and family.

The *Phoenix* was stripped of her finery and stored in a dry building. The sorry substitute galley was sold, its crew divided by Barca into two groups, one to keep, the second to dismiss. With Barca's assistance, and Milcar's proud approval, a new galley was ordered from the builders. "You will fill in the crew," Barca was told, "and you will all become part of the shared profit system."

Milcar hosted the celebration for his son's advancement.

Joseph tried to envision the equivalent, many years away, when he would celebrate the achievements of his own son. It was hard to do. At two and a half, Aaron was a roly-poly, happy, undistinguished, normal child. Joseph found a very few minutes to be quite enough time to spend with his son, before he became bored.

The same, unfortunately, was also true of Deborah. The tragic events of the summer had benefited her personally. She had a new friend, the wife of an officer in the company of Roman troops Varus had posted in Caesarea. Deborah chattered along happily about the new hairstyles her friend had introduced her to, and the ribbons and combs they required, and the high rope walker they'd seen go from one side of the square to the other, way up above their heads.

"Is it always like this?" Joseph asked Antiochus.

"Or worse," Antiochus replied.

"In the future you will stay with me, and go where I go. Find someone to run the household and take your place."

Antiochus grinned. "If I were a proper slave, I'd kiss your feet for your kindness."

"And I'd kick you for doing it. Go and do what I said.

We need to leave before the heavy rains or it will be a highly disagreeable trip to Jerusalem."

Once returned to Jerusalem, Joseph went in search of Nicolaus while the others were getting settled back into the house.

Even before his friend confirmed it, Joseph could see the disorder of Archelaus' rule. It showed itself in the lax postures and almost impertinent demeanor of the guards at the palace.

Nicolaus looked pleased with life. Joseph was astonished, until he learned that his friend had already told Archelaus that he intended to retire when his new employer would allow it.

"I don't think it will be slow in coming, Joseph. This wretched boy is the kind of unfortunate creature who cannot recognize who his friends are. He resents my advice and will be glad to be free of it.

"Then—oh, the inexpressible joy of it—I will go to Alexandria, locate a room near the Library and a decent place to eat and drink, and I will be content for the remainder of my years."

"You will leave a hole in my life, Nicolaus. And in my heart." It was true. Joseph had never fully realized how much he cared for this wise, decent man until he thought of his leaving.

Nicolaus knew Joseph well, infinitely better than Joseph could ever know him. He was moved by Joseph's emotional statement, because it was self-exposing, therefore unlike Joseph. He embraced his younger friend warmly.

"You will have to visit me in Alexandria, Joseph. I have many correspondents there, and one of them wrote recently that he had heard a friend of yours named Micah bemoaning your lengthy absence."

"I'll do it, you can depend on it. That Micah! I'll be interested to see how marriage has changed him."

"When I meet him, I will tell him to expect you soon."

Nicolaus had little to tell about Archelaus. That was precisely the problem, he said, there was no fixed identity in the prince. "He doesn't know what he wants to do, so there's no predicting how he might act. He has already dismissed the High Priest of the Temple in some senseless hope that by so doing the responsibility for the disaster at Passover can be shifted to the Temple from the palace.

"Expect no good from him; he has not the capacity for it. Expect no bad, either. It will happen, but it will be due to his inadequacies rather than any considered villainy. Strengthen any bonds you have made with Caesar. Ultimately the future of Judea is in his hands."

"I'll simply keep out of the Ethnarch's way. That shouldn't be difficult."

Nicolaus smiled. "What an optimist you are, Joseph. But you are, I'm afraid, out of luck. Herod's daughter Roxana is in residence at the palace and has been waiting eagerly for your wife to return to Jerusalem."

Thus it was that the earlier pattern repeated itself in Joseph's life. Many, many social events, and at home many, many visits from Roxana.

He created his own escape. Deborah was happy to have her husband's "estate" to refer to, and she had a repugnance for non-city life. Therefore he could invent problems that needed his attention at Arimathea and go there often.

Always accompanied by Antiochus, who loved the family, in his own way, equally as much as Joseph did.

Joseph had time, and the quiet, and Sarah's encouragement, to think about his life and to design a pattern for it.

"With some happiness in it, Joseph, that comes from something other than your work."

"You are the happiness in my life, Sarah."

She made an impatient clucking noise. "Silly. You always have me, and I always have you. That's our greatest blessing. But everyone should have other happiness, too. I do. I have my good times with everyone here, full of stories and memories and laughter and the good kind of tears. You should have that, too."

And so Joseph told Milcar when the season began that the *Eagle* was to have a new routing and a new schedule. Beginning now they would sail first to Alexandria, where they would stay for a week or more, then on to Belerion and Cyprus, as usual. But now, instead of selling the prized wine from Cyprus in Caesarea, they would take it to Puteoli so that Joseph could see his friend Berenice and her children in the household of Augustus Caesar.

After that, home again, at the end of the season instead of a month earlier.

It worked wonderfully. When, two years later, Deborah told Joseph that she would prefer to live in Caesarea all year, not just for the summer, Joseph's life became even more satisfying.

Aaron stayed in his care, of course, and Joseph was able to choose interesting men for his son's tutors in Greek and Latin and mathematics and geography. They lived in the house, and they provided company for Joseph when he wanted to talk about something other than business.

Two of the men had once been slaves themselves, so they saw nothing untoward in the presence of Antiochus when they were having a meal or a cup of wine with Joseph.

From the tutors Joseph learned that his son was an exceptional student. Antiochus assured him that it was true, not simply what teachers always say to the father of their pupil.

And Joseph polished up his daydreams for his son's future. Aaron would become a priest, yes, but he would eventually rise to become High Priest, the most honored man in the world of the Jewish people.

If only Archelaus would stop appointing High Priests and dismissing them so often. Joseph was determined to make himself known to, and then, in some fashion, useful to, the High Priest, so that when the time came, Aaron would be chosen for service in the Temple. The priests of the Temple were invited to take the honor. No matter how well educated Aaron might become, neither he nor his father could apply for the honor to be granted him.

If only there ever were a lasting High Priest, one worth cultivating. Joseph had never forgotten the effort and time he'd wasted on Antipater.

Time, he was beginning to understand, was the irreplaceable element in a man's life. That made it extremely valuable.

Rebekkah smiled when he mentioned this discovery. "I have thought, from time to time, that the real wisdom within God's Law that a man become a father is that it forces exactly that understanding upon him. Nothing makes you as aware of time passing as the growth of your children."

She laughed, still sounding young. "I didn't really notice that I was an old woman until Amos' David made me a great-grandmother."

Joseph protested: "You will never be old, Rebekkah. I won't allow it."

She touched his cheek with one of her still-graceful fingers. "Don't take my age from me, my Joseph. I cherish it. It makes me value every hour all the more as the supply of them diminishes. When you're young, you're too busy to pay attention to the rich pleasures in everyday food and drink, or to look at the beauty on all sides of us, in everyday light and shadow and earth and sky."

Joseph took his grandmother's hand in his. "I do look, Rebekkah, when I'm at sea. There, I lose my blindness. The space, and the wind, and the stars, and the colors of the rising and setting sun fill a man with wonder. Even if he tries to deny it, it overcomes him."

"It is God," said Rebekkah quietly.

CHAPTER FORTY-ONE

AFTER THIS CONVERSATION WITH REBEKKAH, JOSEPH BE-
came more and more aware of the truth of what she had
said. He marked the years now by the changes in the children he knew.

Not only Aaron. Joseph was fascinated by the growth of
Berenice's children. His favorite, Herod Agrippa, was a
child of insatiable curiosity and exuberant enthusiasms. He
assaulted Joseph every year with glee. He had an endless
supply of questions, and always something that Joseph had
to see, an example of his newest discovery: one year birds'
eggs, another year a pony that he could ride standing on its
back, a third year a stack of small paintings depicting sexual acts so depraved that Joseph felt his face redden with
embarrassment.

That was the year Berenice married again. Her husband
was an aristocrat, formerly a senator, now a legate, commander of one of the legions stationed along the Danube to
maintain Rome's control of its territories in Germany.

"The wedding was a perfectly ordinary occasion," Berer-
nice told Joseph. "So pleasant, after all the gaudiness of the
ceremony when I married Aristobulus. Emilius just took
my hand and muttered something. I suppose he was saying

'I take you for my wife,' or some such. Then he had to go racing off to Germany.

"All very hurried, and terribly discreet. Not my wedding. I mean, all the things that were going on that forced Emilius to be in such a rush." Berenice lowered her voice to a near whisper. The problem was Julia, Augustus' daughter. She was his only child, fathered by him, not adopted, and he doted on her. That was why everyone kept him from hearing the stories that had been circulating about her for at least twenty years.

"Sex," Berenice hissed, her eyebrows high, to indicate what extremes were included in the single word. "But some poor fool from the night watch didn't recognize her and arrested her a few months ago. She was in the Forum, on the steps of the Rostra, inviting any man who happened by to come and 'get some for free'—I think that was the phrase she used. Julia was so furious about being arrested that she actually went to Augustus and demanded that he punish the guard. After that there was no way to keep everything— well, far from everything, but quite a lot—from coming out.

"Augustus went half-mad, mostly from grief, I think. He exiled her to some tiny nowhere island. The thing that bothered him most, poor innocent creature, was the idea that her children would hear all these awful things about their mother. As if they didn't already know. So he packed them off quick as a wink out of Italy. Lucius went to Gaul and Gaius to Germany. As commander of the legions, no less. So my handsome Emilius is legate under the command of this eighteen-year-old boy. Nursemaid is what he really is. Augustus asked him to take care of Gaius.

"The men in his legion aren't exactly thrilled, either. They had been back from Spain for only a few months."

Berenice giggled. "Long enough for a courtship. Dear man, he's rather smitten by my charms. Very shy around women. He was married, ages ago, and I'm told it was disastrous. Wife a social climber and a shrew. After she had the decency to die, he kept away from any possible entanglements.

"You'll have to meet Marcus, his son. He's my new pet. As shy as his father, the dear boy. He's eleven, and is still a bit terrified of the racket that we live in. You know us, Joseph."

"And applaud the racket," he said. Sincerely. At the same time, he could feel a certain sympathy for Marcus. The boy was exceedingly polite when he was presented. Joseph wished he could tell him that there was nothing to worry about. Berenice would wrap her disorganized lovingness around him, and he'd be happier than he'd dreamed was possible.

Berenice had that effect on people. Joseph felt himself relaxing as soon as he'd been with her for five minutes, and he could see the same thing happening to others. Her closest friend was a tall patrician woman, Antonia, a widow, whose son and nephew were Herod Agrippa's closest friends. All three of them gave the impression that Berenice's home was the magic source of happiness in their view.

At Abigail's, in Jerusalem, the same racket and love prevailed. Joseph took Aaron there whenever he could find the time. After Deborah began staying in Caesarea year round, Joseph wanted to take Aaron to Abigail's for the big family Passover feast, but he decided against it for Sarah's sake. She had seen Aaron only once, and she'd told him later that she was torn between love for the child and pain that he was not theirs. That one time had been at Arimathea, when he'd shown his three-year-old son the lands that would someday be his. The visit had been a mistake for everyone. Aaron was afraid of the animals on the farms, and he hid his head in his nurse's lap whenever anyone tried to talk to him.

Rebekkah recommended a long wait before bringing

Aaron there again. "You have a city child there, Joseph. He's a different breed of creature."

As the years passed, Joseph saw, more and more clearly, the truth of his grandmother's observation. Amos' children, three in all, were like the village children. Sun-tanned, barefoot, strong, happy, little country folk. When Caleb married a girl named Hannah, they added three children of their own to Arimathea's population, indistinguishable from all the rest.

While Aaron was becoming increasingly scholarly, and thriving in his particular land of words and pen and ink, instead of sunlight and rain and growing green things. Even during the summer months in Caesarea he preferred to stay indoors rather than play in the pool in the garden or walk along the quay to watch the seabirds feed and fly.

Joseph admitted, with undisguised pride, that his own son was a mystery to him. "I was the worst student in the world, I never paid attention. My tutor used to come close to tears, and the teacher in the village school of the Torah tried and failed to beat the words into my backside when my head didn't hold on to them."

Aaron, in contrast, absorbed the Torah the way dry earth welcomed the first rains of spring. Like all Jewish boys he began the morning school, called "house of the book," when he was five. Because he lived in Jerusalem, he was taken to an actual school. His cousins in Arimathea had their lessons in the synagogue, or beneath a tree nearby. City, town, or village, the lessons were the same. First, the letters of the Hebrew alphabet. Next, individual words. After that, phrases. Then the actual verses of the Torah, the Law. Pupils repeated the teacher's sounds in unison, again and again, memorizing the meaning of the written symbols the teacher was holding up for them to see.

Hebrew was the ancient language, used only in the Temple and the synagogue, where the Law and the psalms and the words of the prophets were offered to the people.

Aaron's rapid grasp of the lessons and his faultless memory made Joseph rejoice. There was no possible doubt. His son was meant to be a priest.

For Joseph of Arimathea, the ten-year reign of King Herod's son Archelaus passed by smoothly, after its chaotic beginning, each year very much the same as the year before, excepting the interesting changes and growth in his child, his brothers' children, and the children of his friends in Jerusalem, Alexandria, Belerion, and Rome. Or, for his friend Eleazar, the growth of his grandchildren.

Joseph led, in effect, three lives. He had his summer life of travel and trade and the never-ending lure of the sea; his winter life was divided between Jerusalem—Abigail's family, his son, his business friends—and Arimathea: his family and his love, his wife, his Sarah.

Deborah was a lovely, talkative stranger whom he saw for a few minutes of the few days he spent in Caesarea. Antiochus was his companion, his friend, his valet, the one person who knew him in all his lives.

Life was good.

As in any life, there were sorrows, some greater than others. Milcar gave up the sea after an accident left him blind in one eye, and Nicolaus was found dead in his room in Alexandria, his gray head resting on an opened scroll of Aristotle's writings. But Barca took his father's place as captain of the *Eagle*. And Micah, who was ageless, introduced Joseph to "another philosopher who you'll never be able to keep up with," a young Jew named Philo, and his brother Alexander, who Joseph could easily understand, because he was the customs official for the trade goods that passed through the fabulous Egyptian seaport.

There were also some changes and developments in the wider circles of Joseph's life. The incompetent Archelaus, Prince of Judea, Samaria, and Idumea, was perpetually short of money to maintain the luxury of his fearful life behind guarded palace doors, safe from the sporadic uprisings and attacks on his troops that always failed. He sold to

Joseph the copper mines he had inherited from his father, Herod, and Joseph was suddenly the owner of the largest supply of bronze in the Eastern Mediterranean. Among the major buyers that dealt with the long-established bronze factory were Herod's other two sons, who minted coins there.

In this way Joseph came to know Herod Antipas, and his rebuilt city of Sepphoris, and his land of Galilee. He also traveled to the court of Herod Philip in the city he had built, named for himself and his patron Augustus. Caesarea Philippi was nothing half as grand as the earlier Caesarea, which was now officially known as Caesarea Maritima, but still called Caesarea. Philip's city was pleasing. Like him, it was handsome, neat, quiet, unpretentious, altogether agreeable.

Not nearly grand enough, in Joseph's opinion, to deserve the name of Augustus. The Emperor continued to be his hero, even though Augustus had aged visibly and suffered from asthma and poor digestion.

He had an official heir now, his stepson Tiberius, a man he had never really liked. Both grandsons, Gaius and Lucius, were dead, one drowned in a shipwreck, the other of wounds received in battle.

Berenice was convinced that the Emperor's dislike for the next Emperor of Rome was what had given him asthma and indigestion. "But don't tell anyone what I said, Joseph. Antonia would never forgive me. Tiberius is the brother of her dead husband Drusus, and you know she's given over her life to being the most devoted widow in the history of the world."

Joseph himself quite liked Tiberius. He'd met him on several of his visits to Berenice. He'd met and liked Emilius, too, Berenice's husband. Evidently the feeling was returned. Emilius agreed to be Joseph's patron.

Yes, the end of Archelaus' ten-year rule found Joseph in very good spirits and very well fixed. The Romans were now in control, which should bring peace. And he had very useful connections to the new Roman regime.

During those ten years, Joseph himself had grown and developed. Grown in wealth and influence. Developed a businessman's skepticism and unconscious, automatic self-interest.

He was a thoroughly Hellenized Jew, multilingual, at ease in the great cities, a cosmopolitan man of his world.

It was fortunate for him that he still spent part of his life at Arimathea. There he became the Joseph of old, the Joseph with a heart.

CHAPTER FORTY-TWO

The year 6 C.E. Date April 9

ARIMATHEA. JOSEPH ROSE BEFORE DAWN, EAGER TO BE ON his way there. Perhaps Aaron would come this time. The day before had been so good between them, once Aaron stopped sulking about the Galilean boy who impressed Hillel and Shammai. The talk in the atrium, laughing together about the cucumber nonsense—that was the way a father and son should be together. Joseph smiled as he remembered it.

Then his smile vanished. He was being foolish. The surest way to destroy that fragile bond was to urge Aaron to go to Arimathea. He wanted to have nothing to do with his family there, not even his grandmother and great-grandmother. He'd made that clear. Antiochus said that it was because Aaron had figured out long ago that Joseph loved Sarah and did not love Deborah, his mother. That was nonsense, in Joseph's opinion.

He shook his head. He wouldn't ruin his mood by trying to think about all the whys and maybes. It was sufficient to take pleasure in the memory of yesterday's shared laughter and in the imminent journey to Arimathea. He'd have almost a month there before the sailing season began, calling him to Caesarea.

His bedroom door opened, and Antiochus came in, holding a lamp. "I didn't knock because the house is still quiet," he said. "It's good that you're already up. Eleazar is here. He says he has news you must hear before you leave for the country."

"Before daylight? It must be serious. Where is he?"

"I put him in the library. His bodyguards stayed in the hall."

"Bodyguards? I'll go at once. He must be in trouble."

"We're all in trouble, Joseph," said his friend. "I got the news in the middle of the night, and it's sure to be all over the city by midday. In Caesarea yesterday Coponius received a dispatch from Rome. My informant had to risk hours of riding through darkness to get word to me right away. There's going to be a census."

Joseph groaned. "Coponius will make a mess of it."

Eleazar shook his head. "He won't have the opportunity. The new governor of Syria, a man named Quirinius will come do it. With five legions of infantry and two cohorts of cavalry. The Romans expect resistance. It must mean that taxes are going up."

"My poor farmers," said Joseph. Men like Eleazar and Joseph could afford to pay higher taxes on the large profits of their businesses. They also knew ways to hide those profits and thus pay only a portion of what Rome demanded. But in the countryside, the tax collections were made by a man of the region, who kept his eye on crops as they grew and knew what Rome's portion would amount to. Rome already claimed a fourth. Also, farmers were required by the Law of Moses to give a tenth of their produce, or the income from it. This tithe went to the Temple. So did the half-shekel Temple Tax that every adult male Jew was expected to contribute.

At least Arimathea's villagers did not have to pay rent for their houses or their land, as most small farmers did. But their half of the produce was not so great that they could easily part with a larger portion of it. Nor could

Joseph's brothers. In addition to paying the same taxes, they bought the seed, the plows, the carts, the oxen—all the things needed to work all the fields.

"The Romans are right," said Joseph. "There will be widespread resistance when the census discovers the fields and vineyards and animals that have come into being since the last census. Local collectors overlook them in exchange for a few coins.

"How could Emperor Augustus be so foolish? This is the worst possible timing. People need to get used to the change. Archelaus wasn't much, but at least he was Jewish. Partly, if you want to quibble about his ancestry. But certainly not a Roman or a Gentile."

Eleazar threw up his hands. "Joseph! Don't you know anything? There's near famine in Rome. Augustus is afraid of what will happen when the grain in the storehouses runs out. The plebs will riot. He needs the added tax money to buy corn for the dole."

Joseph's shoulders had been sagging, as he thought about Arimathea's people. But now they straightened, and he grinned. He slapped Eleazar on the shoulder.

"Think, my friend," he laughed. "Think what this means. The warehouses at Alexandria are bulging with grain, but Rome's ships won't go there until the sailing season begins. With a good wind and my crews' strong backs at the oars, I can have six galleys there in less than a week. Also, news of the famine may not have reached Alexandria yet. How did you hear?"

Eleazar shook his head. "I should cut out my own tongue. The famine is a secret."

"Come on, Eleazar." Joseph's irritation was obvious. "It's bad enough that I have to admit your informants are better and faster than mine. I'm far from pleased with my spies or myself. I don't need you to name names. Just tell me if word will have reached Egypt."

Eleazar couldn't resist a satisfied smirk. He seldom bested Joseph at anything. "My man in Rome managed to get the message to me into the Imperial dispatch pack. The news is as fresh as spring itself."

"Then I'll pay you well for the information. You and I will buy as much of Egypt's stored grain as we can find money for. I'll load my ships, of course, but we don't have to touch the rest of it. As soon as Alexandria learns of the famine, the prices will double, or more. Then we'll sell what we own that's still in the warehouses."

"My friend Joseph, you are a genius. How soon can you sail?"

"I am no genius, Eleazar. If I were, I'd have your Rome informant on my payroll instead of yours. The seas are not really safe until a month from now, so we have time to prepare."

Eleazar started to speak, but Joseph gave him no opportunity. "No, we won't wait for safety, Eleazar. Captains and crews know better than to expect such softness. This is what you and I will do . . ."

While he hurriedly dressed, Joseph told Antiochus what he'd learned from Eleazar, and what his plans were. "I'll have to ask you to stay here, Antiochus, to see to Aaron's safety while I'm away."

"Of course."

"Send messages to the Damascus gate for the hire of carts and drivers and horses. See what we can do about guards for my trip, for the house, and for Arimathea. I'll be there before sundown if all goes well, and I'll tell everyone about the Roman census tomorrow. It's the Sabbath, and they'll all be in the synagogue. Now I have to go to the Temple."

"I'll have the boys out before your return." Every important household had a half dozen or more young slaves who were trained to memorize messages which they hastened through the streets to deliver. Only in rare instances was a written document sent. Papyrus and vellum were extremely expensive.

* * *

The sacred rites of the Temple began every day as dawn broke. Joseph made his way quickly down the stepped streets of the Western Hill and along the viaduct that overpassed the lower city, to one of the Temple gates, just as it was opening.

He greeted the Temple officials without pausing to converse. Then he walked briskly across the Court of the Gentiles and the Court of the Women toward the gigantic copper doors of the Nicanor Gate. The first blush of sunrise was streaking the sky, and the metal glowed red as if the Gate were made of sheets of flame.

Joseph stopped, unexpectedly awestruck. The music of the sacrificial rite that greeted the day seemed to be coming from the glowing firmament itself, not the Temple sanctuary, and the weighty sweet smell of burning incense was mysterious because of its sudden presence in the dawn freshness.

It was a rare event, to be so nearly solitary in the great, still shadowy expanses of the Temple courts. Soon they would be full of people, of animals, of Temple police and priests and Levites, of noise and movement and voices raised, to make themselves heard above myriad other voices. For Jerusalemites, the two outer Temple courts were more commonly used as secular spaces, where one met friends, by arrangement or coincidence, talked, laughed, even did business. It was all too easy to be somehow unaware of the holiness that rested within the sanctuary, invisible and all powerful.

Joseph felt it now. He also felt shame, because he had hurried here for his own purposes, not for worship, which was the purpose of the Temple.

Joseph passed reverently through the shining copper gates into the Court of the Israelites. The music was all around him now, and the smell of incense, mingled with the smoke of burning flesh from the sacrificial lamb being consumed on the mighty stone altar beyond the open gates that led to the Court of the Priests. It was the offering to the Almighty, commanded by the Law of Moses. Joseph stood silent.

After the ceremonies ended, Joseph spoke quietly to one of the priests, a young man named Tarphon. Shortly more than an hour later Joseph returned, accompanied by Eleazar. Tarphon was waiting for them.

Within the Court of the Priests, accessible only to them, there were many treasury chambers. Some held the untold treasures and wealth of the Temple, its gold and silver vessels, incense burners, lavers, candleholders, its vast accumulation of coins, tithes of all income from every Jew in Israel, the annual half-shekels paid by every adult Jew in the entire world, and offerings of precious metals and jewels given by the wealthy in gratitude for God's blessings. In addition, some of the chambers acted as repositories for the treasure of individuals, held for them in safekeeping. Joseph and Eleazar had come to take away a part of their holdings, to purchase the great stores of grain in Alexandria.

"You cannot carry the weight alone," Tarphon observed.

"Men are coming to the Court of the Gentiles to bear it away," Joseph replied. "They should have arrived by now. The guards will help us take the sacks to them, will they not?"

It was customary practice.

Tarphon smiled. "Of course," he said, "but it will take a bit longer than you might expect. I was able to arrange things as you requested."

The leather bags of gold were heavy with sand, added to prevent the distinctive sound of metal against metal.

"And the other request?" Joseph asked, even though he was sure of the answer.

"You may be sure of it," Tarphon said, smiling.

Joseph and Eleazar returned the priest's smile. They had asked that bags of their gold—without sand—be transferred as gifts to the Temple treasury, offerings of thanks to God for the blessing of the Alexandria grain opportunity.

In the Court of the Gentiles, Antiochus and the household slaves he'd selected lifted the sacks onto their shoulders. They carried them to the waiting hired carts. The economy of the Mediterranean world had not yet developed any system of credit or promissory notes. Gold and silver and bronze were the means of buying and selling.

Before sunset that day, Joseph was back in Arimathea with his family. Every part of his plan had worked out—at least so far. Antiochus had hired ex-soldiers to accompany Joseph in the large hired cart. All were trained for battle and equipped with a full range of weaponry. None of them knew what he was carrying in the bags that were piled beside him in the smaller cart.

The synagogue service was the same as usual the next morning. There was a reading from the Torah—the five books of the Law—in Hebrew. Then another villager repeated the words, this time in Aramaic, to ensure that everyone understood the reading. Afterward, a third villager spoke about the segment of Torah, explaining and interpreting its meaning.

On this day the three men were the village potter, who was also the teacher of the small school for boys, followed by one of the farmers, then by the father of the previous speaker-translator.

A psalm of praise was sung by all, and then—according to common practice—any member of the congregation could stand and speak to the group. Joseph got to his feet, and the assembled villagers leaned toward him eagerly, anxious to learn the meaning of the armed men who had accompanied him to Arimathea.

There were agitated exclamations when he told them about the census and its probable consequence, increased taxes. Most of the people there had no memory of the last time a census was taken. Many had not yet been born; others—like Joseph—had been small children, unaware of the meaning of uniformed men from King Herod's army looking over properties and asking questions of all the adults.

"Listen carefully, and believe what I tell you," Joseph said. "Do not try to hide anything from the men who will come. And do not resist them, no matter how rough or insulting they may be. If they steal your fattest lamb or break your jars of wine, make no protest, even though your heart be raging. I know the power of Rome. It is greater than you can imagine. It overcomes any defiance, and the costs are reckoned in your blood and the blood of your children, spilled by the Romans' swords."

Murmurs of anger, of fear, of despair filled the small building that housed the synagogue.

Then a youth leapt to his feet. "Is the power of Rome greater than the power of God? We are taught that the earth and all its creatures and all its fruits belong to Him. To the Almighty, not to idol worshipers from Rome. I say that if there are those who will fight to regain the land of God for the people of God, we should join with them. I am shamed by the cowardly weakness that has ruled us for all our lives. Are we supposed to live like dumb beasts, bound to the plow and whipped until we pull it so that our rulers can take the fruits of our labor? Are we men? We must act like men."

The boy's father grabbed his arm and jerked him down onto the bench beside him. "I beg all here to forgive my son," he cried. "His head is full of dreams, not knowledge."

Arguments in low voices made the air turbulent with anger.

Suddenly all was quiet. Rebekkah was walking slowly to the front of the room. "Enough!" she said sharply. "Each man, and each woman as well, has been granted the gift of life. If there are those who do not value it, they are free to sacrifice it for their beliefs. But they have no right to expect all others to do as they do. Or to offer as sacrifice their neighbors' lives or their children's lives. Keep your own counsel and do not turn one against another.

"I am an old, old woman. But I tell you that I will find

my joy in every day that is granted me before my end comes. Life is a gift more precious than pearls. I know whereof I speak.

"Now go to your homes and eat your Sabbath feast with your family. That is what I am going to do. I am hungry."

She walked to the doors, then on to the square. As the others followed her outside, they saw her raise her face to the sun and sky and smell of growing things from field and vineyard. Rebekkah smiled, and she was, for a moment, as beautiful as a young girl.

"Truly, God is good," she said.

"You are a wonder," Joseph said to his grandmother when he took leave of her the next morning. "Let your mind rest easy about the future. I'll tell the soldiers to keep a special eye on that young hothead in the synagogue yesterday.

"I will come back when I can. We'll drink the harvest's new wine together."

His grandmother laughed. "You can drink your fill, dear Joseph. I will have some of the old wine from my special hoard. It has a much better effect."

The larger cart bought in Jerusalem was left at the farms. Two soldiers marched alongside an even bigger one borrowed from Amos. With high sides and six wheels instead of four, it was designed to transport produce to market. Today it was fully laden with giant clay jars, packed in straw to prevent breakage, containing the poorest grade of olive oil, from the third pressing, suitable only for burning in lamps. Joseph had bought the stored oil from the family farms. After breaking the wax that sealed the jars, he and Sarah had dropped in linen-wrapped gold coins, then applied new seals.

CHAPTER FORTY-THREE

IN CAESAREA, JOSEPH DROVE TO HIS OFFICES NEAR THE PORT. His agent, Stratos, was startled to see him so early in the year. His greeting was joyful.

Joseph looked at him with appreciation and a certain affection. "Stratos, we are about to do the impossible."

Stratos put his arms across his head, as it to protect it from danger. "Not again," he moaned theatrically. Then he looked at Joseph and began to laugh. His round cheeks reddened, and his belly shook. "Why do I suspect that decent rest and food will soon become strangers to me?"

"Because it has already happened. I have a load of very special oil and it must be put in the strong room at once. Give me the keys, and I'll see to it while you send for all the seamen and start at once to ready the ships for sailing."

The Greek had ceased to laugh. "The men are mostly at their homes, Joseph. The season for sailing is not yet really open. Some live as far away as Damascus."

"Then you will have to send very fast heralds to notify them, won't you?"

"I fear the answer, but I have to ask. When do you plan to sail?"

"No later than four days hence."

"It cannot be done."

"And yet, it will. We'll see to it."

Driving through the streets, Joseph had seen that the Roman presence in Caesarea was ubiquitous, so there was no need to guard his house here. After the amphorae of oil were safely locked away in the office's strong room, he paid the soldiers who had moved them from the cart.

"Return the wagon to my brother at Arimathea," he told them, "then make camp outside sight of the village, near the road where it enters and where it leaves. I do not expect trouble, but if it comes, protect my people. I will find you when I return, hear your reports, and pay you for your time there."

Deborah was also surprised when Joseph appeared, but her welcome was less enthusiastic than Stratos' had been. "Don't distress yourself," Joseph told her. "I'll take some food in my room then go directly to bed and sleep. I'll only be here a few days, and my time will be spent at the harbor."

Stratos worked wonders. Joseph's small fleet was manned and loaded and ready to sail in only three days. During that time Joseph found an hour for a visit to Coponius, wearing his most elaborate silk tunic and mantle, bearing the gift of the Greek statue. The young Roman was as impressed and grateful as Joseph had expected.

Joseph missed Antiochus. The Galatian would have learned, somehow, the identity of Eleazar's valuable informant within Coponius' household and probably persuaded him to work for Joseph as well. Stratos had hired three informants, but clearly Eleazar's was better.

It would have to wait. The voyage was more important at this time. Joseph greeted his captains as they arrived and confided the destination and the reason for haste. When all the crews had reported, he supervised the loading of the fragile cargo. It was evenly divided among the six galleys. Thanks to God's mercy he had never lost a ship. Yet, the good weather was still weeks away, and it did not do to be complacent. If storm and sea swallowed one of the galleys, at least only a sixth of the gold would be lost.

The *Eagle* passed Alexandria's great lighthouse seven days later. Joseph saluted it with relief. A powerful squall en route had reminded him of the reasons for the limits sailors had long ago placed on the season's opening.

"Keep watch for the other ships," he told Barca. "I'll go make the business arrangements for the cargo, whole or part." Neither he nor the captain spoke of his worry about the rest of the fleet. It would do no good, and danger was an accepted fact of every sailor's life.

"Joseph of Arimathea! Welcome!" The customs' official, his friend Alexander, embraced him warmly. "Let me pour you a glass of wine, early bird. Then you can tell me what particular worm brings you to Egypt at this time."

"I couldn't wait to learn if your brother's new book was finished," Joseph jested. "You know how much I enjoy his writings."

Alexander roared with laughter. He and Joseph were both frank to admit they didn't understand the philosophical theories that were making Philo of Alexandria a famous name throughout the Roman Empire.

"He'll be happy to put you to sleep talking about it at dinner tonight," said Alexander. "Unfortunately, Micah won't be with us. He's away until next month. Generally you don't honor our city with a visit until much later in the year." Alexander was practically twitching with curiosity.

Joseph smiled. "Very well, my friend. Refill my goblet, and I'll tell you why I'm here."

Alexander was an invaluable ally. Also, he was so delighted by Joseph's audacious venture that he made his "commission" only slightly higher than usual.

"You won't even notice the rise, Joseph," he laughed. "I'll buy your cheap oil for the lamps in the lighthouse."

Within ten days everything was done. All the galleys had reached port safely, unloaded their cargoes of oil, filled their holds with grain, and prepared to sail for Italy. Joseph and Eleazar were the owners of more than a fifth of the grain stored in Alexandria's warehouses. Alexander would sell it for them after news of the famine in Rome sent prices soaring. He'd hold their profits in safekeeping until Joseph returned to claim them. After the Roman census and taxation were completed.

"Congratulations, Joseph," Alexander said when they parted. "All this, and the sailing season has still not yet begun. Your friendship honors me."

Joseph laughed. "Especially when it fattens your purse," he said. "Mine, as well. My heartfelt thanks, Alexander. Tell Philo I have been greatly enlightened by his discourse. I'll see you when circumstances permit."

The voyage from Alexandria to Rome was exceedingly slow. The winds blew consistently out of the north and northwest, creating a kind of wall, for that was the direction to which they were sailing. Ships moved in long, shallow diagonals, making forward progress of about five miles for every sixty they covered. Joseph left Alexandria the third week of May and landed in Italy at the beginning of July.

He'd seen several of Rome's enormous biremes from the *Eagle*'s deck. Many more were on the sea, he knew, but not within view. All were headed for Alexandria to buy grain. Joseph laughed to himself. He felt exceedingly clever.

In truth, the huge profits he was making were not the cause of his pleasure. He—and Eleazar, too—already had enough treasure to last the rest of their lives. What counted, for Joseph, was the adventure of the undertaking, the excitement of braving the winds and seas before good weather began, the thrill of recognizing and seizing an opportunity. Joseph liked to win.

When the *Eagle* entered the great harbor at Puteoli, Joseph grumbled to Barca about the repeated delays in the Emperor's stated intentions to improve the small shallow harbor at Ostia. "There's a hundred miles of road for cargo to be hauled to Rome from here. At Ostia, it could be transferred to barges and taken straight up the Tiber to the capital." Barca agreed. Just as he had done for years, whenever they neared Puteoli. And would continue to do for many more, he was convinced, although he never said so to Joseph.

As soon as the harbormaster learned the nature of the *Eagle*'s cargo he sent runners to the grain dealers in the port city. Soon Joseph was able to enjoy the spectacle of the noisy, frantic bidding of five eager buyers competing for the tons of wheat and barley.

"I'll stand the costs of a well-earned holiday for all the crew while I'm away visiting my friends in Rome," Joseph told Barca. "For you, my fine captain, I suggest the most luxurious establishment on the Bay of Naples. You deserve that, and more."

"And 'more' there will be. Plenty of it. Our half of the profit from this trip will keep me, and the men, smiling for a long time. Added to the Belerion profits, we'll all be able to retire from the sea. Then what will you do, shipowner?"

"I'll greet you as usual in Caesarea at the start of the season next year. By then, your wives and children will have driven you back to the quiet life aboard ship."

"Ha!" Barca said, in denial. But they both knew it was true. "When should we schedule departure for the tin lands?"

Joseph had to think for a moment. Being in Italy at the start of the season instead of after the Belerion voyage changed the customary dates. "I'll have to stay here until the other galleys arrive, to sell their grain," he mused. "Then plan the season's routes with their captains. After that, it's six days' travel to Rome and back, and I'll want some time there. How long?" He shook his head, laughed. "I'll tell you tomorrow, Barca. I'll be able to think more clearly after a good meal and a comfortable bed tonight."

But the next day his instructions to the *Eagle*'s captain were to ready the ship for sailing as soon as the other galleys arrived and unloaded. Joseph had learned that famine in Rome had recently become almost a minor concern when compared with the horrifying new dangers that threatened the entire Empire. Including Judea.

Opposite the boot that was Italy, across the narrow Adriatic Sea, two large provinces were in revolt. Chaos, bloodshed, fighting, looting had spread throughout Dalmatia and Pannonia. Uprisings were common occurrences throughout the Empire. Joseph could attest to that, from his own knowledge of Judea. However, the fabled Roman legions always made haste to the site of the revolt and quelled it, with death for the rebels as the inevitable outcome.

Now the rebels were winning. In Pannonia the fortified camps of four legions had been overrun and destroyed. Villas of wealthy Roman citizens, seaside resort towns with Roman populations—all had been plundered and burned, their inhabitants slaughtered. The invincible power of the Roman Army had been proven only a myth. The rebels were united, and their army comprised over two hundred thousand troops and nearly ten thousand cavalry, all outfitted with arms and equipment captured from Roman troops the rebels had defeated and massacred.

"They are on the march," a weary centurion in a tavern had told Joseph as they drank together. "Augustus has sent all the upper classes from the city to their country estates, and he has conscripted every male old enough to fight. Even slaves and senators." The hardened veteran drained his cup then laughed, a harsh, bitter sound.

"Senators! Can you picture it? The Emperor went himself to their useless assembly in the Curia. 'The barbarian hordes may be in the streets of Rome inside ten days,' he

told them. 'You are all conscripted into the army.' What
does Caesar expect them to do—bore the rebel leaders so
much with their speechifying that they'll surrender to stop
the oratory?"

"Ten days? It that possible?" Joseph was incredulous.

"It hasn't happened yet, and that was two weeks ago. But
if Tiberius doesn't get his legions down from Germany in
time to stop the rebel advance, the passes through the Alps
will be their roads to Italy and Rome. The danger is real.
I'm here now to conscript the locals and herd them to
Macedonia. The legions there are at only quarter strength
and need reserves to replace the men who've gone north in
pursuit of the Dalmatian army. When the world learns that
our legions can be defeated, every other province might try
to repeat what the Dalmatians have done."

Joseph slept little that night. Judea was an "other
province." Undergoing a census.

True, communications were slow, unpredictable, and
often unreliable. But news of the defeat and destruction of
the legions in the Adriatic provinces was so earthshaking
that it would certainly spread throughout the Empire. Even
to Judea's already rebellious populace.

He had to get home as soon as possible. Before those he
loved were harmed by either side—rebels or Romans.

CHAPTER FORTY-FOUR

THERE WERE NO EVIDENT SIGNS OF CONCERN AMONG THE Roman soldiery in Caesarea. Or among the inhabitants. The square was crowded with well-dressed shoppers and brightly clad street entertainers. Shows were playing at the theater and combat at the arena.

Nevertheless, Joseph hired guards for his trip to Arimathea and Jerusalem, and Barca assigned guard duty to the *Eagle*'s oarsmen aboard the docked galley. "I don't know when I'll be able to return," Joseph told Barca, "but if we can sail to Belerion this year, we will."

He did not visit Deborah, but left at once. He was hardly more than on his way when the attack came. Joseph was riding at the side of the leader of the eight guards, a Syrian named Sareptes, and he laughed when Sareptes pulled his sword from its scabbard. It was impossible, he thought, to take as a real threat the dozen shouting boys who were running toward them from the nearby hills.

Then a sharp stone launched from a slingshot hit Sareptes on the side of his brow. Blood erupted in a geyser that spattered Joseph's head and shoulders. His horse whinnied, reared, threw him onto the hard road, ran away.

Stones were striking people and pavement, horses were

snorting in fear, the deep-toned bellows of men's voices were loud in the confused din.

The youthful shouting became thin, shrill screaming, as guards on horseback swept their swords down in arcs or plunges to slaughter the boy bandits.

It was all over in under two minutes. By then Joseph was on his feet; he hurried toward Sareptes.

"Do you need treatment for that wound?" Joseph asked the bloody-faced guard. "We can return to Caesarea."

Sareptes dismounted. "I have salve in my pack, and one of the men knows how to stitch it. I'll see to it while your horse is caught and brought back." He gestured to two of the guards, and they set off along the road at top speed. "First, I'll make sure we've finished here." He motioned to the five remaining guards, and they slid from their mounts to join him. One was holding his right arm bent, supported by his left hand. "You keep the bridles in your good hand," ordered Sareptes. "I'll see to that broken arm in a minute."

The man with the broken arm sat, resting it on his knees and cursing fluently in several languages while Sareptes and the others walked among the crumpled fallen bodies, turning each one over with a booted push to make sure the boy was dead, stabbing down into the throats of any that were still breathing. When they returned to the road, their boots and legs were stained with gouts of blood.

By that time there were other travelers approaching, a group of men driving sheep toward Caesarea. Joseph walked quickly to meet them, his two hands raised, palms outward to demonstrate that he was unarmed.

"What's going on?" asked the youngest shepherd.

"An attack by child-bandits," said Joseph. "Where is the nearest village? I have to arrange for their burials, and if I can learn who they are, I'll send word to their families."

The young shepherd looked frightened. An older man, perhaps his father, stepped forward. "Go see if your brother is one of them," he said. Then he looked at Joseph. His eyes were set deep in a web of wrinkled, pouched skin.

"Any damages to your people?" he asked. There was no emotion in his voice, only a lifeless resignation.

Joseph shook his head. "Nothing of importance," he replied. "I hope the same for your son, shepherd."

"If not this time, or this place, then the next, elsewhere," said the shepherd. "He is infected by the rebellion led by Judas the Galilean.

"The Galilean's own men are more organized, and armed. Also they fight only Romans. But the fever is spreading fast. The young are hot, and ignorant. To them, any man on a horse must be an enemy." He was looking over Joseph's shoulder now. For an instant his eyes held a spark of feeling. Joseph turned, saw the young shepherd coming toward them, shaking his head and smiling. His brother, obviously, was not among the dead.

The older man pointed to a narrow path leading away from the road. "The village is under a half mile away," he said. "I leave you now." He lifted his shepherd's crook high as a signal, and the men who'd remained with the sheep began to give out the special calling sounds that only they and their flocks understood.

Joseph walked to the path and began to follow it. When he returned, four men from the village were with him. They quickly ascertained that the dead boys were not from their village, but they recognized two of them. "We will see to everything," one said to Joseph. "Our thanks for coming to tell us about this."

"Will the families permit me to pay for flute players and mourners?" he asked. "I will regard it as an honor."

The man accepted the coins Joseph offered. He did not insult him by thanking him. Joseph rejoined Sareptes and his men. The broken arm was in a sling, and Sareptes' forehead bore a track of knotted dark threads where his wound had been stitched.

"We make haste to Arimathea," Joseph told them. Sareptes ordered his men to mount and boosted Joseph onto his recovered runaway horse. Before Joseph had a firm grip on his reins, Sareptes was mounted and beside him. They set off at a gallop.

All was peaceful at Arimathea. The census takers had come and gone without incident, and no one at the farm or in the village had ever heard of Judas the Galilean.

Joseph told his family the little he knew about the rebellion and about the uprising in Dalmatia. His brother Amos would tell the villagers whatever he believed they needed to hear.

"Will Rome really fall to the rebel army?" Caleb asked.

"If it does, we will learn of it eventually," Joseph replied. "It may have already happened, but I saw no special activity among the troops in Caesarea. Who can say what might occur? We can only go on with things as they are here, and now. And wait to hear what has taken place."

"This Judas," Amos said angrily. "Why couldn't he do his mischief in Galilee? Why bring trouble to Judea?"

"Because Jerusalem is in Judea, and that is where trouble always centers itself. Even when it doesn't begin there. I will go to the city tomorrow. If I learn anything you should know, I will send word."

That night, with Sarah in his arms, Joseph was able to forget that the world outside their home was in ferment. When he kissed her goodbye the next morning, he felt strong enough to face down any problems that life might fling at him.

He paid the guards posted outside the village with a generous hand. They agreed to remain until he told them they were no longer needed.

"Ready," he told Sareptes, "for Jerusalem."

Antiochus assured him that all was well. Yes, there were groups in the Temple courts and on streets throughout the lower city, raising loud complaints about the census and Roman oppression or speaking in hushed tones about ideas and plans that were probably seditious. It was Jerusalem just as it had been for decades.

Everyone talked of Judas the Galilean, but no one seemed to know much about him. It was said by some that he was a respected rabbi in his homeland. Others claimed that he was the son of an earlier Judas, who had led an uprising in the days of King Herod, and been executed. But Judas was a common name; there must be thousands of men named Judas in Judea, as well as Galilee. The one certainty was that this particular Judas had not yet attacked any Roman forces in Jerusalem. They were clearly ready for him if he did.

A successful rebellion in Dalmatia? No, there'd been no mention of that at all.

At the house, everything had been placid. As usual Aaron spent most of his time at Hillel's academy and with his fellow students at the nearby cookshop. When he was in the house, he was in his room studying or sleeping.

"All in all, Joseph, I see no reason for you to cancel your voyage to Belerion. With your faithful Celtic slave as companion. I have been extremely bored."

"But the census—"

Antiochus laughed. "I showed them through the house, showed them my meticulous, creative, financial business records and your Roman citizenship scroll, with the Emperor's profile relief, signature, and seal. They were exceedingly well behaved." The Galatian smiled. "I forgot to mention that you were in Egypt, making and concealing a gigantic fortune. The adventure was successful, I suppose?"

Joseph had nearly forgotten that triumph. Dangers and discords had pushed it from his mind. "Superbly so," he told Antiochus, grinning. "Details later. I'd better hasten to Eleazar's offices with the good news."

His spirits were high when he returned home after celebrating with his friend. They soared when he found Aaron waiting for him. Perhaps the boy wanted to learn more about cucumbers, Joseph thought happily. Perhaps he had seen a girl he admired . . .

"Father, it is only a little more than six months until my coming of age, until I am acknowledged to be a man," Aaron said. He seemed to feel awkward, and uncertain about what to say next.

Joseph smiled warmly. His suppositions were accurate, he thought. "That is so, my son. It will be one of the most important occasions of your entire life. I have given it much thought. Usually, a priest delivers counsel and admonitions about the Law to a boy before he is admitted to the Court of the Men of Israel to make his first sacrifice as a man. But I intend to have the High Priest himself counsel you. And for your sacrifices, there will be a dozen rams and the purest frankincense.

"Then, the celebration at our house will be a feast finer than any that ever was served in Jerusalem, even in the days of King Solomon." Joseph waited for Aaron's admiring response. But Aaron's young face hardened.

"That is what I want to talk about. I do not want to be counseled by the High Priest," he said. "I prefer to take instruction in the Law from Hillel." Joseph's happy expectations plummeted, and were transformed into anger.

"Fool!" he shouted. "Imbecile! No son of mine would be such an idiot. It's one thing to listen to what those Pharisee teachers say, you can never spend too much time talking about the wisdom of God's words. But we are Sadducees. Our family has always been Sadducee. We take our wisdom from the priests of the Temple, those chosen by God. Not from some lower-class self-appointed so-called 'sages.' You will uphold the dignity and position you have the good fortune to be heir to. You will not lower yourself to the level of some cheese maker in the stinking streets of the lower city."

Aaron stalked off, as angry as his father. Joseph stared at his son's stiff back. Anger was still hot in his veins, but he wished with all his heart that he had kept his temper under control. Now what was he going to do? Would he never find a rapport with his boy?

The next morning he walked rapidly to the Temple without pausing to look at its splendor or to invite the sense of wonder and awe that the sight of it could inspire. Joseph felt no piety today, only anger and resentment. He was looking for Hillel, the man who had taken his son's affections. Joseph made his way thorough the crowds of men and women and animals that thronged the Court of the Gentiles, his ears closed to their exclamations of admiration of this world-famous edifice and to the cries of vendors and arguments about prices of the myriad objects for sale. On most occasions he enjoyed the color and sound and bustle, but he had no time for enjoyment. When he entered the Court of the Women, he spotted Hillel and strode toward him. Joseph's frown and set jaw were clear indications of his mood.

The renowned teacher murmured a few words to the people surrounding him and walked forward to meet Joseph.

"Peace," he said as greeting. Hillel was an ordinary looking man wearing ordinary clothing, a homespun tunic belted with a striped linen sash and a loose mantle of coarse linen in faded brown. His large feet were sandaled in brown leather. He was in his late sixties, but he looked younger. He was muscular and browned by the sun; he worked as a laborer when he was not teaching. His shoulder-length hair was brown, somewhat lighter in color than his long beard. Both showed only a few gray hairs. There was nothing at all remarkable about his appearance.

Until one looked closely at his dark eyes. They gleamed with intelligence, and humor, and—at this moment—compassion. Joseph had the uncomfortable impression that this man knew exactly why Joseph had asked to see him. If he is laughing at me—if, even more insupportable, he is feeling pity—Joseph's thoughts increased his discomfort and resentment. "Peace," Hillel had said. Was he being sardonic?

Joseph gestured toward the Antonia, the fortress that adjoined and overlooked the Temple's great public spaces. Roman soldiers were standing on the towers, looking down. "Does that look peaceful?" he said. "They're waiting for trouble, maybe even hoping for it."

"Is that what you would like to discuss with me, Joseph of Arimathea?"

"No, not that . . ." Joseph couldn't clarify, even to himself, exactly what he wanted to say. The uncertainty was so unlike him that he felt confused.

Hillel touched him lightly on the upper arm. "Let's walk while we speak. I've always found movement of the legs helps. It's so much easier than the movement inside the head."

Joseph fell into step with Hillel. "This Judas the Galilean," said the teacher, "is already a failure." Joseph began to listen intently. What did Hillel know?

"He is a rabbi, a teacher, a servant of the Lord. The same is true of his companion, Zadduk." Hillel sighed. "They believe that the Law given to us Jews is the only law, and that we must refuse to obey the laws of the Romans, even if such refusal costs us our lives. His zeal will cost our people a terrible price. And it will not free Judea from the yoke of Rome." Hillel sighed, more deeply this time. Then, shocking Joseph, he smiled.

"Joseph of Arimathea," he said, "the words of the High Priest Joazar are the correct words for these grievous days. Daily he addresses the people gathered at the Temple and urges them to submit to the census ordered by the Romans. Now, what do you think of Hillel? I am saying that the High Priest, a Sadducee, gives better counsel than these rabbis, who are Pharisees. You are a Sadducee yourself. Do my words delight you, or do they confirm your view that no Pharisee can be trusted because he is a slippery juggler of words who twists them to mean something different from what they plainly say?"

Joseph didn't know what to say. He said as much. "Hillel, I am not like Philo the Alexandrian. I do not have a subtle mind and tongue. What are you telling me?"

Hillel's smiling ceased. His wise dark eyes looked directly into Joseph's. "I am telling you that I am no enemy of yours, not in any way. I would like to have your friendship, but that may not happen. I believe that I am deserving of your trust and that I can earn it. Is my meaning clear, Joseph? This is very important."

Now it was Joseph who smiled. It was impossible to doubt Hillel's sincerity, or to maintain anger and resentment in his presence. "You have my trust, Hillel, and I am honored that you want my friendship. Please allow me to offer it now."

Hillel chuckled. "Wait a bit. First, we shall talk about Aaron."

Joseph braced himself, hoping that Hillel wouldn't notice, knowing that he did.

"Your son honors you," Hillel said, "as our law requires. Yet he is certain that he can never equal your extraordinary successes. For that reason he resents you, Joseph; he is sure that you will always consider him a failure. In his own eyes he will always be one, compared with his father."

"But . . . his scholarship . . . I could never equal that."

"Scholarship does not build mansions of marble, Joseph. Aaron is still young; youth creates confusion and excessive emotions. Was that not the case for you? I remember that it was for me."

Joseph felt drawn to Hillel's warmth. He could almost understand how Aaron must feel. He told the teacher about the confrontation with Aaron over the coming-of-age ceremonies and celebrations.

Hillel listened attentively. "I can understand both attitudes," he said when Joseph finished his account. "I will explain this to Aaron, listen to him, and also remind him that he is not yet a man, regardless of how he thinks of himself. He owes obedience to his father. You may trust me to express myself to him in a more palatable manner."

Joseph laughed with the wise Hillel.

*   *   *

He was still smiling when he left the Temple Mount. He'd had no realization of how much time was passing while he walked and talked with Hillel. He felt better about Aaron, about himself, about the future. That was the effect Hillel had on people.

They had spoken, without animosity, about the long-standing gulf between their two sects, Sadducee and Pharisee.

Sadducees were traditionalists. They accepted the first five books of the Bible, the Torah, as the only truth, the only Law. They claimed descent from Zadok, the High Priest of King Solomon's Temple, and the priests of Jerusalem's Second Temple came from their stock. They rejected the books of the Prophets, forerunners of the Pharisee practice of interpreting and expanding the words of the Lord as written in the Torah. For them life was in the present, a man owed obedience to the Law and would be rewarded by success in his own lifetime. Life after death was contained in the honor of a man's name, passed on to his heirs.

Pharisees were a more recently formed, still developing aspect of Judaism. They respected the Temple and supported it with tithes, the half-shekel annual Temple tax, and sacrifices at its altar. Their main activities, however, were concentrated in the synagogues, the place for common people to meet, learn about the teachings of the Torah and the Prophets, and reaffirm their worship of the One God.

They believed in a Messiah, who would redeem the Jews from suffering and destroy their persecutors, and in resurrection of the dead on a Last Day of Judgment, when the good would be rewarded with eternal life and the sinners thrown into eternal suffering in hell.

For the scholars like Hillel, the chief objective in life was the discovery and teaching of God's truth. He recognized, as did all Pharisees, that the world had changed since the ancient times when the Torah was written for a seminomadic agricultural people. Therefore, the Law had to be searched for its deepest meaning and interpreted to cover the changed conditions and needs of the Jewish people.

Joseph acknowledged the strength of Hillel's position and reasoning. But he didn't see its application or value for him and his son. Sadducee beliefs were proven by his own success. It would be the same for Aaron and his children and his children's children. "And this Messiah talk—that only provides a rallying cry for people like this Judas the Galilean. Furthermore, Hillel, I cannot take seriously the Pharisee invention of angels and devils hovering invisible somewhere in the airs above us."

Hillel looked upward. "I am not altogether certain about them myself, but I cannot say definitely that they do not exist. It is interesting to consider.

"We have our differences in particulars, Joseph, but we are as one in our belief in the Almighty and His word. That's His great gift to us Jews, and we are both grateful for it."

Joseph bowed his head in agreement. "Let us share in a sacrifice of thanksgiving," he suggested. "I will buy two rams."

Hillel shook his head. "I will gladly share the sacrifice and accept your payment for it, Joseph. But I suggest a pair of doves. A better symbol of our new friendship, don't you think?"

Yes, Joseph thought, smiling. Doves had been exactly right. They were the final proof of Hillel's greeting: "Peace."

When Joseph returned from the voyage to the tinlands of the Celts, he found that peace was ruling in his house and his country. Aaron was not joyful about his obligation to celebrate his admission to manhood in the way Joseph wanted, but Hillel had convinced him to be gracious about it, as well as obedient.

Judas the Galilean was no longer talked of. He had escaped to unknown parts when he led an attack on a Roman cohort and more than two thirds of his followers were killed. Small pockets of guerrilla bandits still operated from caves in the Galilean hill country, using his name as their justification.

But bandits had always been a danger in Israel, whether in Galilee, or Samaria, or Judea, or Idumea. Only the name they gave themselves differed over the centuries.

And Dalmatia, Pannonia—they were battle-scarred, but pacified. The Empire was intact. The Pax Romana ruled.

CHAPTER FORTY-FIVE

THE NEWLY APPOINTED HIGH PRIEST PERFORMED THE SACRI-
fices at the Temple when Aaron came of age. He was a
man named Annas, with an ascetic hawklike visage, and
deep-set, burning, dark eyes. He looked exactly the way a
High Priest should look. Joseph was honored that he had
agreed to officiate at the very first sacrifice Aaron made.

Joseph also had reason to hope that Annas would continue
in the position for a long time. The Governor of Syria, acting
for Rome, had made the appointment. That implied stability.

The celebration banquet and reception for Aaron were as
lavish as any ever held in Jerusalem, even in the time of
King Herod. The wines were from Cyprus and Alexandria,
the roast kids were stuffed with olives and almonds, the
lambs with garlic and herbs. There was even peacock, its
plumage replaced after roasting. Joseph wished Sarah were
there to see it; they had laughed together about just such an
extravagance on Herod's table.

Rebekkah promised to tell Sarah about it, and to take the
tail feathers home for her.

Helena embraced her son and grandson warmly. "I wish
your father could have lived to see this day, Joseph. He
would have been so proud."

To Joseph's surprise and Aaron's joy, Deborah had come from Caesarea for the occasion. She looked strikingly beautiful, with her henna-tinted hair wreathed in pearls and her eyes expertly outlined in kohl, like an Egyptian queen. She was nearing thirty, and maturity magnified her charms. She no longer chattered like a girl; on the contrary, she was silent for the most part, occasionally bestowing a radiant smile on someone who reminded her that they were acquainted. Also on Aaron's classmates from the academy of the revered teacher Hillel, who blushed and stammered in confused admiration. Deborah was not displeased.

For a moment only she took Joseph away from the convival hubbub. In a quiet corner of the peristyle she congratulated him on the success of the reception and agreed that Aaron was a son to make a parent proud. Then: "I have a favor to beg," Deborah said.

"If I have the power to grant it, it is yours," said Joseph.

It wasn't anything difficult, Deborah assured him. She simply wanted to see her sisters in Rome. After so many years they would be strangers, and that disturbed her. Could she have passage in one of Joseph's ships?

Of course she could. He would make the arrangements as soon as he arrived in Caesarea, in about two weeks.

"Thank you, Joseph. That makes me very happy."

For a moment she sounded like the girl Deborah again, when she had received a gift. But when Joseph looked at her, he saw an exquisitely gowned and decorated stranger. It was altogether impossible to believe that this was Aaron's mother. He wondered if the boy felt the same way.

No, he had to remember; he could no longer refer to Aaron, or think of him, as a boy. He was a man now.

"Father, I am a man now. I would like to speak to you as a man." Aaron was standing very tall.

Joseph hid his irritation. What a bad time the boy—no, man—had picked to want to talk. Barca would be getting more and more impatient. The usual sailing time had been delayed in order to celebrate Aaron's coming of age. I should be happy he wants to talk to me, Joseph reminded himself.

"I would like to hear what you want to talk about," Joseph said. "Let us sit on the bench in the garden."

". . . No! You don't realize what you're saying."

"But I do, Father. I have given it much thought. I know that you have dreamt of me as a priest, but that is not the way I believe God means for me to travel."

"You've studied God's word since you were five years old, Aaron. You've been the best. At the House of the Book, and later in the more advanced studies. Even at the academy of Hillel. How can you turn your back on God now?"

"I am not. I believe that the priests have turned their backs. Long ago."

Joseph was stunned. "Blasphemy," he gasped.

Aaron stood up to deliver the speech he had memorized, and practiced again and again. He believed in the teachings of the Pharisees, he said, the interpretations of the Law that daily grew more rich in understanding the deeper meanings of God's Law. Joseph's Sadducee belief in only the Torah, as written, was too limited. And his devotion to the Temple and to its priesthood was too old-fashioned. The Temple would always be vitally important, as the center of Jewish spiritual identity. But the synagogue, and the rabbis, were the life of Judaism now, for its growth and enrichment.

The Sadducee world was too rigid, too trapped in tradition. It had not accepted the revelations discovered by the teachers, the rabbis, the Pharisees. "Our world is changing, Father, and you are not willing to change with it. I pity you."

"*You* pity *me*? You're only a child. What do you know about anything? You've spent your life inside classrooms, not in the world."

Aaron sighed. With dramatic exaggeration. "I feared that

this talk would be a failure. You are unable to hear or to understand."

Joseph controlled his anger. "You're right about that, Aaron. I don't understand. What does it mean, what you're telling me? Not the Sadducee–Pharisee descriptions. What does it mean about life, your life? Do you want to be a rabbi instead of a priest, is that it? Or do you want to join one of those communities of religious fanatics, like the Essenes? What do you want?"

Aaron sighed again. "That is typical of the closed mind, labeling men 'fanatics' because they do not live as you do, always thinking about business instead of the glory of God."

Joseph had had as much as he could stand. He could feel his control slipping, his anger growing. "Aaron, I am losing patience. I don't care to be chastised and condescended to by my thirteen-year-old son. I will overlook your disrespect for now. I am leaving, to take care of the business that you disapprove of with such superiority. At the end of the season, when I return, I will expect you to have come to your senses, and we will talk again. Not on the trip to Caesarea. Are you packed and ready to leave?"

"I am not going this year. I will spend the summer studying with the elders."

Joseph lost control. "Good! That will make the trip much more pleasant for me." He stormed into the house, bellowing Antiochus' name.

"The man named Aaron is going to stay here for the summer," he told Antiochus. "Make sure there's a servant or two to take care of him. He doesn't have enough sense to remember to eat or to tie his sandals by himself.

"Come on, come on. Take care of it. We have to get going to Caesarea."

The sea worked its magic, and Joseph put all thoughts of Jerusalem behind him. He didn't think about Aaron at all until he saw his favorite youth, Berenice's Herod Agrippa.

"You look magnificent, Joseph of Arimathea," he cried when he saw Joseph. "It's those paler lines around the eyes, I think. Against a tanned face, they tell you that those eyes have seen far, exotic shores. Why don't you come out with Drusus and me tonight? We're going to drink the taverns dry and find some excitement. The women will fall on their backs the minute they look at you. Drusus and I still have to give them a push."

Berenice pretended to be shocked. "You're a wicked, wicked child. I'll ask Joseph to forgive you. Now run on, I have no time for your foolishness."

There were times, she told Joseph, when she almost regretted being Jewish. Herod Agrippa and his friends really did behave outrageously; it was the accepted, expected thing for Roman youths to racket all over the city after dark. They drank too much, they broke into brothels and did terrible things, they destroyed property, beat up the night patrolmen.

All that ended when a Roman became eighteen, because then he received his toga, became a man, and had to join one of the legions for at least three years of military service. "Twenty miles or more of marching with that sixty-pound pack of equipment sweats the high spirits out of them pretty fast, Emilius says. Marcus, too. He's following in Emilius' footsteps.

"But you know, Joseph, Jews are exempt because they cannot fight on the Sabbath. So Herod Agrippa might never grow up."

Maybe he should marry, Joseph offered.

Berenice threw up her hands. Pity the poor girl. Besides, he was just barely seventeen. She wouldn't worry about it in advance. There were so many more interesting things to think about.

"Marcus is to be married next month. Can you stay for it, Joseph? Emilius would be so pleased. Me, too, of course. Cornelia is the bride's name. She's a dear. Not a beauty, but so very sweet. I think they'll have a wonderful marriage. It's a love match, not the usual thing at all."

Berenice tapped Joseph's arm. "And here's a deep, dark secret for you," she said with glee. "Herodias is also going to wed. You'll never guess who! Herod Philip. She'll be a princess. Just as I was, only old Herod's not around to make her a widow."

"She's so young, isn't she?" Joseph clearly remembered the overweight giggly girl from the previous summer.

"You'll be amazed, Joseph. Herodias has suddenly become a woman."

Berenice was accurate in her prediction. "Amazed" was Joseph's reaction when the beautiful dark-eyed girl walked into the room. Herodias was fourteen now, but her supple recently slender body suggested a sensuality that the pagan goddess Venus would envy.

Considering what her mother had told him about the habits of Rome's rich young men, Joseph thought Berenice must know exactly what she was doing when she betrothed her daughter to Herod Philip. The sooner Herodias was out of sight, far from Rome, the better for her mother's peace of mind.

"Perhaps I'll see you in Philip's city—what's it called? —one day, Joseph. Mothers always have to meddle in their daughters' lives. Sons, too, some mothers think. Antonia will probably come over a bit later. Don't mention the trouble in Dalmatia, please, Joseph. Augustus has sent her boy out there to join Tiberius."

"I won't say a word," Joseph promised. It was an easy one to keep. Except when he was actually in Rome, he gave no thought to the Empire's problems on its borders. They had no effect on him directly.

He was glad to hear that he'd be seeing Antonia at Berenice's house. Antiochus was in the back part of the house, holding the gifts, waiting for Joseph's summons, and milking the servants for information. It was much more graceful to present gifts to Berenice and Antonia at the same time. Not so obvious that he was buying the goodwill of the sister-in-law of the future Roman Emperor.

Deborah might still be in Rome. Joseph wondered if he should make an effort to see her and her sisters.

He convinced himself—easily—that he should not. The season for sea travel was close to its end, so she had probably already returned home, he reasoned, and he should take the *Eagle* home, too.

On arrival in Caesarea, he discovered that Deborah was, indeed, back home. But he was not. The house in Caesarea was no longer his. Deborah had taken possession of it, by the terms in their betrothal contract, when she divorced him in Rome.

"You are a Roman citizen, too, Joseph. You remember the Emperor's wedding gift. So I got a divorce by the laws of Rome. All they require is that I take my dowry and leave you with no intention to return. I've done the leaving. All that's left is for you to return my dowry."

Deborah was as calm as a country pond. Joseph almost admired her. What did it matter that Rufinius had never turned over her dowry to him? It would be considerably less costly in the long run to give her the two hundred aureii than to continue paying her bills.

"It will be returned to you in the morning," said Joseph, with matching calm.

"And of course you keep our child," Deborah said. "That's Roman law, too."

What was he going to tell Aaron? The boy was so proud of his beautiful mother. He had chosen not to go to Caesarea this summer, but another year he might feel differently.

"Sarah, what can I say to the boy?"

"Tell him he'll have to be a man now, not just call himself one." Sarah had gotten furious when Joseph told her about Aaron's confrontation after his coming of age.

"That's part of my troubles. I left him on such bad terms. I was already dreading the next meeting, but now, with the news about the divorce as well . . ."

"All right, Joseph, I'll tell you what I just told you to tell Aaron. Be a man. When you get to Jerusalem, send for him. Begin at once, before another disagreeable scene starts. Just say, 'Aaron, I have something to tell you that will cause you pain. Your mother has decided to have nothing more to do with me and you. The two of us.'

"If he breaks down, you may be able to comfort him. If you cannot, send him to that teacher he admires so much.

"If he doesn't break down, maybe he is a man after all. But send him to that teacher anyhow." Her expression softened. "If only Aaron could have had Rebekkah in his life, the way you did. Now that I think of it, I can feel sorry for the poor boy.

"But not half as sorry as I feel for you, my pitiful dear Joseph. Are you very upset?"

Joseph looked closely at her innocent, questioning eyes. "Why do you ask?"

Sarah poked him in his side. "So that you'll say no. And you know that perfectly well."

Joseph laughed, hugged her close. Sarah had worked her magic again. The world was not gloomy, after all. Not when she could make him laugh. "I love you, Sparrow," he said.

Aaron stood like a soldier at attention while Joseph told him about Deborah. And afterward.

Neither of them ever again mentioned Deborah to the other. Nor did they refer at all to the denouncement Aaron had launched against his father.

In fact, they seldom saw each other. Aaron stayed all day at the academy, then spent the evening hours with fellow students at a food shop nearby. It was a small room with one long bare table and two dozen rough-hewn stools. Students and teachers kept it filled with fervent debate at all hours. The shopkeeper gave them bowls of soup and slabs of barley loaf, which they ate without awareness of doing so.

Joseph returned to his customary habits of talking, drinking, eating with business friends at his house, or theirs, or the elegant wine garden near the City Hall. He hosted a farewell banquet when Eleazar moved back to Alexandria. He invited himself to Abigail's occasionally, went to Arimathea often, occasionally dined simply with Antiochus, talking about possible routes for the next season's sailing.

When Joseph made sacrifices at the Temple, he always bought two lambs, and sacrificed one in Aaron's name. For the Feast of Lights, he went to Arimathea. And when Purim came, he gave a masquerade party there, for the entire village.

The next day Rebekkah sent for him.

He blew one of the toy horns from the party to herald his entrance into her rooms. His grandmother covered her ears with her hands, laughing.

Joseph smiled, bowed, presented the horn to her. Rebekkah lowered her hands and accepted it. The shiny metal glinted when she held it. Her hands were slightly palsied.

But her voice was as it had always been, clear, warm, and ageless. "Sit here by me, my Joseph." She patted the side of her bed where she was sitting, cushions supporting her straight spine.

"Your celebration was fine, but a bit tiring," she explained.

"Would you like a cup of your special wine?"

Rebekkah shook her head. "I would like to talk about what I have been hearing in the synagogue. And to hear you talk. Joseph, what do you know about this doctrine of resurrection?"

"I have heard of it. They say that God will end the world one day, open the tombs and restore the dead to life. For all time."

"Do you believe this doctrine?"

Joseph never lied to Rebekkah. "No," he said, "I do not. But I have great respect for a man named Hillel who does."

"I am not afraid of death, my Joseph."

"Rebekkah—"

"Hush. Listen to me. I am not afraid. But I do not want to die, Joseph. Life is so precious. I do not want it to be over."

"Is there something—?"

"I am not ill. I am old. Very old, Joseph. Seventy-six years is very old. My bones tell me that, and my tiredness. I should be happy to sleep and not wake. But I do not want to. I am not happy to think of it. I want life, not death."

Rebekkah smiled. It was not forced. It was Rebekkah. "I wish I could be convinced by this talk in the synagogue, but I cannot. I wanted to know your thinking."

Joseph could not smile. "I wish I could tell you something different, something you want to hear."

"Joseph! Truth is the only thing I have ever wanted to hear. If I live a hundred years, that will not change."

"I love you, Rebekkah of Arimathea. And I honor you, with all my heart."

His grandmother touched his cheek, with one finger, a touch delicate as an insect's wing. "I will rest now," she said. "Thank you, my Joseph."

He kissed her lined cheek and left her to rest. Joseph would not believe that Rebekkah was going to die. She was too full of life to die.

When he returned from that year's sailing, he brought her a pot of rouge and a vial of strong perfumed oil.

"Adorn yourself," he ordered, "and we will have a feast. Your wine and a strange fruit called carrot that the Romans bring down from Germany."

Rebekkah looked at the handful of orange roots he was brandishing. "Have you eaten of them?"

"Yes. I cannot think why the Romans like them. But they are very costly, so they believe they are very good."

Rebekkah laughed. "Get the wine, and bring Sarah and

Helena. We will paint our faces and enjoy watching you eat. Bring Antiochus, too. He will eat a half."

The next year, while Joseph was at sea, Rebekkah did not wake up from her sleep one morning.

Joseph rocked forward and back, letting the pain wrack his body and heart.

"She did not want to die!" he cried aloud.

Sarah stood beside him until the first anguish diminished somewhat. "Remember the carrots, my love, and how we all laughed," she told him gently. "She would want you to remember her humor as well as her wisdom. Rebekkah is not dead, because we can remember her and love her still.

"Also, she did not know she was going to die when she went to sleep. She just didn't wake, but she could not know that. She is still sleeping."

"She is dead, Sarah."

Sarah kissed him. "You are Rebekkah's own blood. She would applaud your truth."

Rebekkah's death meant that Helena was now the sole occupant of the largest of the Arimathea farmhouses. One weekday was appointed moving day; Joseph and Antiochus helped Amos and Caleb and Helena transfer their furnishings to new quarters. Helena took her things to the small house where Sarah lived, the house Joseph called home, and the fun began. The women provided a constant supply of food, drink, and advice while Amos, as the eldest son living at the farm, moved his family into the big house. Then Caleb, his wife Hannah, and their two sons and daughter, left their cramped cottage for the house that had been quarters for Amos' family.

There was an abundance of laughter, a minimum of mishaps, and the inexhaustible energy of Joseph's many nieces and nephews, who got in everyone's way while trying to be helpful.

As evening approached, Joseph and Sarah walked hand in hand along the paths that linked the family's homes, enjoying the glow of lamplight in the windows and the quiet of the countryside after the noisy, happy day.

"I burned with envy," Joseph admitted to Sarah. "My only son is a stranger to me, and my brothers' sons love their fathers."

Sarah had nothing to say. She had lived with that envy every hour of every day for seventeen years. Mercifully, her capacity to feel it had grown numb in time. Only the pain of her barrenness remained as sharp as it had always been. For nearly a quarter of a century.

Late in the year, Joseph shared the triumphant jubilation of all Judea and Galilee and Perea, when they learned about the disaster that had struck the Roman legions in Germany.

A newly appointed Roman Procurator, Marcus Ambibulus, issued the proclamation. Three Roman legions had been destroyed by a tribal chieftain's forces in the dark forests of that rebellious province. The Jews did not rejoice that fifteen thousand men were dead. It was the fate of their leader, the destruction of his reputation as well as his body, that was the cause of their triumph. For the dead and disgraced Roman was Varus, who, as Governor of Syria, had led his legions through the country, burning and killing, and crucifying two thousand Jews.

For a Roman general, disgrace was worse than death a thousand times over. Varus had received the greatest punishment there could ever be for him.

The following spring, just before Passover, Joseph received the honor that fulfilled his determination to restore his family to the position it had once held.

His house in Jerusalem was bigger, and grander, than the house of his murdered grandfather, where Abigail lived now. But that had not satisfied him.

His fortune was far greater than his grandfather's, but that was not satisfaction enough.

In March the Roman government restored the power and prestige of the ancient institution that Herod had destroyed. The Sanhedrin was reborn. And the High Priest Annas came himself, with a full panoply of Levite escorts, to Joseph's house, to announce that he had been appointed one of the members of the religious court that had, for centuries, been the final place of judgment, the ultimate authority on the Law of the Jewish nation.

He, Joseph of Arimathea, was one of the seventy members of the Sanhedrin.

He had reached his goal, after thirty years of striving. His family's pride was restored.

If only Rebekkah could have lived to know it. Joseph climbed to the roof of his house that night and wept under the stars that had guided him across the vastness of sea and ocean. His heart was swollen with joy and with pain.

Above, the heavens were even wider and more mysterious than the seas. A sharp wind bit his skin with cold.

What could he seek now?

Satisfaction had left him hollow.

CHAPTER FORTY-SIX

"THAT'S WONDERFUL!" SARAH SAID WHEN HE TOLD HER about the Sanhedrin.

"That's absurd" was her comment about his despair.

Joseph was hurt. Sarah always made everything better, not worse. This dismissal of his agonizing emotions was cruel.

"You want me to be sympathetic, my love, don't you? Oh, Joseph, there's nothing heart-wrenching about a man who is too successful. Even when that man is you. No, I don't want you to be miserable, but I will not agree that you have any right to feel sorry for yourself. You've done what you have set out to do? Fine. If it doesn't satisfy you, think of something else to challenge you."

She smiled, a mischievous sparkle in her eye. "Here's a big one. Find a wife for Aaron. It can't be good for a man of sixteen to spend all his time reading about things like King David's passion for Bathsheba and Delilah's dalliance with Samson when he's never even kissed a girl."

Joseph thought for a minute. Then, "Cucumber!" he said. That was a good memory, the afternoon when he and his son had been close.

"Cucumber? You want some cucumber? Are you losing your wits? They won't be ripe until summer."

"No, no, it's just something I remembered."

Sarah was intrigued. "Tell me."

So he did, and she giggled like a girl. "You poor little lamb. Does it still happen?"

Joseph ran his hand across her lap. "Only with encouragement," he said.

"I'll bet you that I can get my clothes off faster than you can."

Antiochus supported Sarah's suggestion about Aaron. "A man has appetites, even if he doesn't know what they are. I, for example, discovered that roast suckling pig was what I had been yearning for. Once I tasted it. Before, I'd wasted years eating lesser delicacies like peacock . . ."

"Be serious."

"I always take pleasure in tormenting you, Joseph. Serious pleasure."

"Stop that. Help me think of a wife for Aaron. I meant to do something years ago, but I gave up. I don't know where to begin."

As always, Antiochus was a treasury of information. He knew the names, ages, and temperaments of every young woman in the upper city, plus the inside story on their families, even to the most distant cousin. Joseph's head was reeling long before the roll call was finished.

"Do you really believe that Aaron will marry a bride I choose for him? He has no high opinion of me, you know that."

"But he's a big healthy man. He has to have urges, like every other man. His overworked mind may disapprove of you, Joseph, but I cannot believe that his body won't overcome his books."

"I hope you're right. I'll get to work on it after the season."

"Coward. Do it now, Joseph. There's a week before Passover. Select the girl. Talk to her father. When the deal is made, tell Aaron—no! I know what you're about to say.

No, do not discuss it with Aaron first. Tell him after all the arrangements are made. All tradition is on your side."

Joseph stumbled across an unexpected supporter of Antiochus' view when he went to Abigail's one afternoon. He mentioned the subject of Aaron's possible marriage very obliquely, without identification.

His caution was a wasted effort.

"Buy your boy a bride," said Abigail firmly. "You can afford it, and it's the only way he'll ever get one. Any girl with any sense would take one look at him and run."

Joseph thought he probably should be insulted on his son's behalf, but he couldn't argue with his aunt's opinion.

"I'll talk to my friend tomorrow and make all the plans. Then you talk to the father the next day, after my friend tells him what he thinks about it."

"What in the world are you talking about, Abigail?"

"My friend Veronica and her daughter Ruth. Veronica's husband Moses is the man who sells salt fish in the marketplace below the steps to the Temple. He's a rabbi, too, with less practical sense than one of his fish. Pay an exceptionally high price for Ruth, Joseph. Moses doesn't even earn enough to put any food in his family's mouths except the fish he didn't sell. And there are eleven children.

"Ruth will be the perfect wife for Aaron. She grew up in a house where religion was more important than bread, so he won't seem as strange to her as he would to a normal girl. And she won't expect much. That's the secret for a good marriage. Don't expect too much. Then, anything you get seems like a great gift."

Joseph was sure that Antiochus' summary had not included the daughter of a fishmonger. But what Abigail said made a lot of sense to him.

"Which is Moses' fish stall?" he asked her. "I'll be there two mornings from now."

That evening he told Antiochus about his decision. "Trust a woman to be smarter than any man living," the Galatian said with a shake of his head. "I was thinking of alliance between two important families. She has her eye on the way marriage works."

Aaron was even more practical than Abigail. "I like fish" was his comment on Joseph's nervous declaration of what he wanted his son to do.

"I told you his body would rule his head," Antiochus said. "I just didn't expect it to be his stomach."

The betrothal ceremony was held in the room that Ruth's family lived in, behind the fish stall. Joseph had sent over a dozen amphorae of wine. Veronica and Ruth had made a big pot of fish stew. The entire neighborhood joined the celebration. Aaron looked thoroughly uncomfortable and uninterested. Ruth was busy ladling stew into bowls. Antiochus worried that Joseph had a fish bone caught in his throat when he began to cough uncontrollably during the celebration. That wasn't true at all. Joseph had swallowed wine the wrong way when Veronica offered him a dish of cucumbers cured in brine.

The Sanhedrin had a chamber inside the Temple with a wide, deep, semi-oval of magnificently carved and painted high-back chairs, one assigned to each member, and an even more elaborate one in the center for Annas, the High Priest, who was also president of the body. At the end of each side stood a table with papyrus, pens, and ink for a recording scribe.

When Joseph was shown the chair that would be his for the rest of his life, he felt the pervasive sense of fulfillment that he had been missing. He made his face impassive and allowed himself only one cursory scan of the other faces in the group. He recognized many, among them Aaron's mentor Hillel; many others were unknown to him.

But not for long, he knew. The strangers would be as interested in him as he was in them. They were, together, the authority of the Law, for its meaning and its observance. The Sanhedrin had its own police force. It could order arrests on civil and criminal charges as well as on the basis of religious wrongdoing.

During the rule of Herod and his son only religious disputes had come under its authority, but now Rome had returned all its powers, save one. It could not order the death penalty. However, imprisonment, forced labor, fines, and severe whippings were all punishments it could decree. Decisions were reached by discussion or debate. A majority of votes was needed, unanimity was greatly preferred.

It met every other week Sabbatheve day. Not all members had to be at all meetings; Joseph's sailing schedule could continue. Special meetings could also be convened for special needs. In exceptional circumstances, it was possible for the High Priest to convene a smaller group to hear witnesses, judge guilt, and impose punishment. Annas, addressing the full conclave, admitted that he did not anticipate or welcome such an event. "I do not want it said that I entertain thieves and prostitutes," he said with a flash of teeth.

The little touch of humor proved relaxing for the tension Joseph was feeling, and he was able to concentrate on the words of the accusers and the accused and the witnesses for both sides in the matters that were brought before the court that day.

He described it all to Antiochus during dinner. "It wasn't that difficult to decide whether a man was guilty or not, but the punishments caused debate every time. Some of the judges would like to put everyone in prison for at least a decade, even if the crime was stealing a cabbage from a stall in the market. Some others seem to consider a fine of one quadrans punishment enough for anything, even rape."

"You tried a rapist?"

"Yes. It was sickening. The girl's father was the accuser, and his shame was heartbreaking."

"What did you judge?"

"Annas was brilliant. The rapist was a man of some means. He fined him enough to provide the girl with a dowry that will make many men willing to overlook the truth that she is not a virgin."

"When do you meet again?"

"Don't look so worried. Yes, I am excited about becoming a judge, but we still leave tomorrow for a short visit to the farm and then on to Caesarea. The season is beginning."

Helena and Sarah were both fascinated to hear about the Sanhedrin and delighted to learn that Aaron was betrothed. Joseph told the anecdote about the cucumbers only to Sarah. "I do wish my mother lived with one of my brothers instead of you," he complained. "I don't feel that I can speak as openly or relax as much as I did when the house was yours and mine alone."

"Selfish, Joseph, and unobservant. Helena's good company for me. And why do you suppose we had dinner at Caleb's? Because Helena will stay there tonight to leave us alone. Tomorrow you get to dine with Amos and his family, then walk me home."

She put her arms around his neck. "Are you going to let so many people go to so much trouble and then do nothing to profit from their considerateness? Kiss me, Judge."

"A judge, Joseph? What good fortune for me." Herod Agrippa was still an incorrigible, charming rascal. "Now if I ever feel an overpowering urge to be a good Jew, I can go visit our famous temple in Jerusalem, and when I get in trouble you'll get me out of it."

Berenice made a show of disapproval. "I will make Joseph promise me that you'll be whipped. I should have done that when you were little. You're a disgrace."

Herod Agrippa swooped upon her, lifted her in his arms, and swung her round and round until Berenice screeched. Then he kissed her loudly and deposited her back onto her couch. "But you love me," he said, "and I adore you.

Admit, my darlingest of mothers, that I am much more amusing than my upstanding, tedious brother."

"Aristobulus is a highly respected advisor to the Emperor."

"Of course he is. Augustus had trouble sleeping, and Aristobulus bores him into refreshing naps."

"Do run on, Herod. Go away. You're exhausting me."

"In a moment, Mater. I have to learn more about being a judge. Tell me, Joseph, if I did return to Judea, could you get me a seat on the Sanhedrin? I'd make a good judge. There's nothing—almost nothing—criminal that I haven't done myself. I understand the criminal mind. I'd know at once if a man was lying or telling the truth."

Beneath the exaggeration and bravado, Joseph sensed, Herod Agrippa was asking a real question. He gave Herod a real answer. "Your grandfather and your uncle are still remembered with ill feeling; I don't believe Jerusalem is ready for you yet, Herod Agrippa."

The handsome young man smiled. "Such a good friend. Thank you, Joseph. In Rome, no one ever speaks honestly. So be it. I fear Jerusalem would bore me to extinction within two days anyhow.

"Now, to make my beloved beautiful mother happy, I'll be off. Drusus is depending on me to help him design the handsomest uniform ever seen on a newly minted officer." Herod clasped Joseph's arm. "You make me proud to be a Jew, Joseph. Come see us more often."

There was no denying it. Herod Agrippa was gifted with an unfairly large quantity of charm. Joseph was sure he should disapprove of a twenty-year-old man who did no work of any kind, had little regard for the laws of any country, and manipulated everyone from the lowliest slave to Caesar himself.

And yet, he always found himself smiling after a meeting with Berenice's outrageous son.

He settled down for his usual comfortable time with

Berenice. And all the gossip that sounded so frivolous but was, in fact, invaluable.

"Augustus had to have another tooth pulled," she began. "He's lost so many that he sounds quite odd when he speaks. Liquid, sort of . . ."

CHAPTER FORTY-SEVEN

ABIGAIL ADMITTED THAT SHE LIKED TELLING OTHER PEOPLE what to do. "You're especially gratifying, Joseph, because you're such an important, powerful man, and you're much more obedient than any of the children ever were."

"I'd be lost without you, Abigail." Joseph wasn't flattering his aunt, he was speaking blunt truth. Left to himself, he would have staged a gala wedding for Aaron, even grander than the celebrations for his coming of age. Abigail made him see that such an event would be inappropriate.

"Joseph! Think! A fish seller's daughter in a gold crown on a silk-bedecked elephant. It would be extremely entertaining, but that's not exactly the kind of progression that Ruth's family would be comfortable in. And if Aaron paid any mind to anything at all, he would disapprove of everything about it. No, you leave everything up to me. We'll observe all traditions, but with the utmost simplicity."

Abigail selected the house for Aaron and his bride, too. Not in the upper city, and not in the congested alleys of the lower city's lowest area. The neighborhood was on the hill, above the Street of the Perfume Makers. It was just slightly disreputable; the rabbis condemned perfume because it was worn by disreputable women. Therefore, the houses were not expensive. Most of Abigail's children and stepchildren lived there. And the air was sweet. "After growing up behind a fish stall, Ruth will probably faint from happiness."

Abigail furnished the house, too. "I simply love spending your money, Joseph." And she arranged with her friend Veronica to provide the couple with a comfortable allowance, but not so much that it would cause comment. It would be called Ruth's dowry, but it would come from Joseph, via Abigail.

"Why can't I just give Aaron some of the fortune he will inherit? Why such deviousness?" Joseph would, in fact, prefer some reason for his son to be grateful.

"Because I enjoy being devious," said Abigail in a tone that closed the conversation.

After Aaron moved to his new home, Joseph tried to persuade Sarah to come live in Jerusalem. He'd never had the luxury of coming home to her every day, he said, not since the earliest days of their marriage. Why shouldn't they live together now? With the scheduled and unscheduled meetings of the Sanhedrin, he could not stay in Arimathea for very long at one time.

"Joseph, I have spent my entire life—forty happy years—in the country. I wear my Belerion dresses, my hair in braids down my back, and everyone thinks I'm somewhat peculiar, but they know and love me, so it doesn't matter. I won't give that up, not even for you."

Forty years! Joseph looked at his beloved Sparrow. She looked exactly the same to him as the girl he'd married. "You don't grow old, Sarah," he said in wonderment.

"You're blinded by love, my love." She'd never tell him about the herbal mixture the Druid priestess had given her. It had not given the promised fertility, but it had made the cramps with her bleeding go away, and her skin was still smooth and supple as a girl's. Magicians, Nancledra had told her. Druids studied magic. Sarah knew it was a pagan, ungodly thing, but she liked to feel and look young. Antiochus got her a fresh supply of the herbs every year. It was their secret.

Joseph had become quite aware of his increasing age. Perhaps it was because he was now a judge, but he was becoming more concerned about appearing dignified. He wore boots instead of sandals, richer tunics, and cloaks in darker colors. He was even toying with the idea of growing a beard.

When he mentioned it to Sarah, she doubled over from laughter. Antiochus was more tactful, but Joseph could see his friend's mouth twitch. "Good thing you're a slave, I can sell you," he said. But he stayed clean shaven.

Until the accident that scarred him.

It was three years after his beard suggestion had caused so much merriment. That year's voyage to Belerion had been both gladdening and a cause for sorrow. The ever-growing colony of Jews he'd transported from Caesarea more than twenty years before had finally persuaded him to bring some of their kinsmen. In Caesarea, anti-Jewish sentiment had been increasing ever since the first Roman Procurator, Coponius. His replacement, three years later, was worse. And the man who followed him, a fat older man named Rufus, had tried to enforce an edict insisting that Jews who owned shops must open them on the Sabbath. Refusal resulted in crippling fines. The shop owners went out of business.

And then one morning when the teacher went to open the synagogue for the lessons of the book, he found the door broken and the room full of pigs.

Rabbi Isaac talked to Gawethin, chief of the Dumnonii. The Celts and Jews had long since developed a harmonious side-by-side way of life. Gawethin asked for a decision by the Druid priests in Albion. In time, they agreed to allow an additional hundred people.

This was the year that Joseph carried them there, with his

usual safeguards that they not know how they reached their destination.

The occasion of their landing should have been one of unrestrained joy. And for the old and new settlers it was, as families found the kinsmen they'd only heard of, and the Caesarea men marveled at the trousers their uncles and great-uncles and cousins were wearing, and the Jewish women of Belerion opened their houses and their arms to welcome the newcomers.

But for Joseph there was only strangeness. Gawethin had died the winter before. The new chieftain was a man he'd never known. The same was true of the Druids who were there to observe while they acted as translators. The villagers were welcoming, as always. But Joseph was more conscious than usual of the shrinking number who'd been their companions when he and Sarah had spent their magic time in the green, gentle land.

"It's very different, Barca," he told the *Eagle*'s captain. "I'm glad your father wasn't here with us."

"I'm sure he is, too, Joseph. He was frightened by the Belerion priests. He could feel strange powers all around them, he said."

"Phoenician nonsense," Joseph said quickly. He did not want talk like that to infect the crew. He was glad when everything was normal on Cyprus, even the annual mystery: A significant number of the wine jars developed leaks on the voyage to Puteoli. It was a staple, much enjoyed joke every year, and as long as the crew was careful not to drink too much, he didn't interfere.

He left the unloading to Barca. This year they were behind normal schedule because of the immigration. And so he and Antiochus did not hear the news until they were well along the road to Rome. They saw the soldiers first. They were stopping all travelers.

"Rebellion?" Antiochus speculated.

"More likely a new tax, for using the road," said Joseph.

It was neither. The soldiers told them that they must ride slowly past the temple in the village a mile ahead. Without noise, even speech between themselves. "It is to show respect," their officer said. "The Emperor's casket is resting within."

"Ah . . . no . . ." Joseph felt his eyes spill tears. Augustus. His hero. The man who had created the Empire. The man who had lost at knucklebones to Berenice's little boys.

The funeral cortege moved only at night because of the heat. Senators carried the casket in relays. Tiberius marched behind it, his tall, strong body held stiffly, his helmet under his arm, the armor of his uniform polished every day to fresh burnish for the night march to come.

Joseph followed at a respectful distance, also on foot. He sent Antiochus ahead with the horses. He preferred to be alone in his grief.

An honor guard met the procession outside the gates to the city. They took the casket to Augustus' home on the Palatine, the simple house that eschewed grandeur.

No one was permitted to follow them. Joseph went to the Forum and joined the crowds waiting inside the Temple of Castor and Pollux. There was a holiday atmosphere that angered him deeply. But at least he was alone among the crowds. He could not face the prospect of talking to anyone, not even Berenice.

The next day all activities surrounding the funeral were in the Senate. Joseph left the throngs massed in front of the building and made his way to the baths. He needed somehow to be clean and looking his best in honor of Augustus. He slept on one of the couches, after wine and a massage.

Before dawn he was on the Palatine, above the way that led to the Forum. As the sun rose, he saw the procession leave the house and descend. A coffin had replaced the casket. It was covered with a cloth of gold and purple, and on the cloth rested a wax effigy of Augustus, youthful, wearing the victory-proclaiming golden armor and leather kilt that had clothed his real body when he celebrated his triumph over Antony and was proclaimed Emperor of Rome. The coffin and its two Caesars lay on a couch of ivory and gold. The red light of dawn made the gold look like copper and the ivory like the petals of a blown rose.

"Farewell, Princeps," whispered Joseph. "I will miss you."

Joseph was to meet Antiochus at Berenice's house on the Esquiline Hill. But the crowds in every street were all pushing toward the river, and he was carried along in spite of all his efforts to get through. From a distance he saw the flames of the funeral pyre rise upward, far higher than the heads of the people surrounding him.

"He stopped having the gladiators," said the man to Joseph's left. "But the old fart's giving us a good show now."

Joseph's fists hit the man in the mouth that had spoken the words.

"You little bastard!" The words were sputtered through blood. Then Joseph felt the first blow, a fist in his stomach, the second, an elbow on his ear.

He fought back, for Augustus, with a ferocity and strength far greater than he'd ever known, until he was grabbed by two of the soldiers posted in the area to keep the crowds under control. They dragged him to the river and threw him into the muddy water.

The shock brought Joseph to his senses. He swam to the island that looked like a ship and crawled up into a tangle of summer-browned bushes. His head was still ringing, and his middle felt as if it were on fire.

His hands hurt. Joseph looked and saw that his knuckles were bleeding. He smiled.

The Jewish Quarter was nearby, just across the bridge. Away from the diminishing flames and the holiday crowds. Joseph got to his feet, pushed his way through the sharp dry twigs and branches to the stone-paved area surrounding the Temple of Healing.

He had not eaten in four days, and he was hurt. He did not see the loose, tilting paving stone, but tripped on its edge and fell sprawling at full length, his head against the lowest marble step of the temple portico. The impact knocked him out. He never felt the sharp fragment of marble enter his chin, just below the right corner of his mouth.

The smell of food woke him, and Joseph blinked at the brightness of the lamp that a hand was holding near his face. Then it moved away, illuminating the features of the man holding it. For a moment Joseph thought it was a Druid. The man was wearing a hooded white cloak.

But the skin was dark, not fair, and when the man spoke Joseph recognized his accent as Egyptian. "Welcome back," he said. "You suffered an accident, and you seem to have been in a fight of some kind, but you are quite healthy. I have brought you a bowl of barley broth. Drink it, but be careful. You had a cut near your mouth that required stitching. Do not stretch it or you will tear the stitches. The bowl has a funnel you can use to pour the broth into your mouth. I will demonstrate. Watch."

"The beard is going to make you look very distinguished, Joseph, but you didn't really have to go to such lengths to justify it."

"Not funny, Antiochus." Joseph's words were slightly garbled. He hadn't yet adjusted to the new contours of his mouth. The scar was thick, like callused flesh. It pushed the corner of his mouth upward in a perpetual misshapen half smile. He had not yet felt like smiling.

Not because of the pain of the wound. It diminished more with every hour that passed, was shifting from pain to a maddening deep itch that scratching could not reach. What had been far more uncomfortable than the deep cut was the solicitous care that he'd suffered in Berenice's busy household. Too many well-wishers, too many delicacies to tempt his appetite, too many voices, words, too much attention. He'd been battered by kindness, for more than two weeks, until he could return to the temple's doctors to have the wound examined and the stitches pulled out.

He was tired of encouragement and good humor. He was angry that his mouth made his words sound so peculiar. Most of all, he was furious that this had happened because of a stupid clumsy fall. He could blame nothing, no one but himself. It was galling to feel like such a fool.

When the *Eagle* was back at sea, land out of sight, Joseph began to feel more like himself. By the time she docked in Caesarea, he was beginning to enjoy feeling the surprisingly soft inch of hair on his chin. And his words were clear when he called out the familiar commands for securing the ship.

"Don't forget to go to the arena, Joseph."

"Antiochus, will you stop playing doctor? I'm sick of it."

"So am I. This is positively the last time. The Egyptian at the Temple of Healing said that you had to go to the doctor at the arena here for a final check on how you're mending. This one will know more about wounds than the one in Rome. Here he sews up gladiators after every fight so that they can fight again. They are valuable creatures, Joseph, worth much more than you. The tickets to the fights make thousands for their owners."

"I hate the arena. It's barbaric."

"Exactly why so many tickets are sold. You don't have to go to the fights, Joseph. You only have to visit the doctor."

Joseph knew the Galatian was right. It was one of Antiochus' most annoying traits. "Very well," he conceded, "but I won't have you hovering. Go open the house and get us some food. I'll be along later." He grinned, lopsided.

When Deborah took possession of the villa in Caesarea,

Antiochus had found a smaller house that was for sale. Joseph bought it at once. He hadn't cared that the house was extremely well designed and had a severe beauty. He was simply too fond of his comforts to settle for a plank in a hostel. Beds were bought and moved in right away, and everything was fine.

Stratos, with ostentatious discretion, did not refer to Joseph's changed appearance. He put records of the other galleys' trading on the table in front of Joseph and waiting for comments. Joseph always spotted his skimming. Some of it he overlooked, but he made Stratos correct just enough so that he was reminded that he wasn't fooling his employer.

But today Joseph allowed everything to pass. He was in a hurry. It was late afternoon, he had to go out of the city to the arena and get back inside the walls before the gates were locked at sundown.

Good! The placards announced combats for the next day. There'd been none today. The doctor should be available at once. Joseph found the small unobtrusive door that led to the behind-the-scenes areas of the arena. It opened with an ugly screech.

Inside, a muscular guard came to meet him. "Public not allowed," he growled.

"I'm looking for the doctor," Joseph said. He indicated the red scar on his chin. "An accident in Rome. They sewed it up at the Temple of Aesculapius, and told me to come to the doctor here to check on it. I'll pay whatever fee, of course." Joseph took a silver denarius out of his belt. "This is to thank you for telling me where to find him."

The guard tested the coin with a bite. When he was satisfied, he pointed to a corridor. It was dimly lit by small lamps in niches.

Joseph hurried off. He lifted the latch on the door nearest the vestibule.

"No!" the guard bellowed. "Not that door."

But the door was already open, and Joseph was staring at the scene it revealed.

At least twenty lamps burned bright. The small, bare room had concrete walls and a concrete floor. The light revealed every ripple, every flaw in the whitewash on the concrete. It also showed every detail of the couple on the tall massage table in the center of the room.

The woman was on her back, her knees near her ears, her ankles crossed behind the neck of the man crouched over her. His body was heavily muscled and shining with oil. The scars on his back, shoulders, thighs, arms were white and corded. He pumped, grunting, thrusting himself into the woman's soft body while she screamed, "More. More. More. More. More." Her head was moving, turning from side to side, and her white throat—as white as the gladiator's scars—vibrated with urgency. Her hands kneaded her full breasts, red-painted finger nails scratching her skin, drawing drops of blood. Her hair gleamed in the light, spilled over the end of the table like a curtain of silken copper and bronze.

"More. More. More." It was Deborah.

Joseph closed the door. "Where is the doctor's door?" he asked. His calm voice reflected the numb shock he was feeling.

"Joseph! What a surprise." Deborah held her red-tipped fingers out toward him, formed into languid, lovely hands. She was wearing a Roman-style gown of red silk, bordered in blue. Blue ribbons were woven into the multiple braids that wrapped her head, and blue-enameled flowers made the bracelets that circled her milky white arms. Her face was exquisitely painted, the eyebrows plucked to form high, graceful arches.

"Thank you for the letter about Aaron's marriage. I keep meaning to send a nice gift, but—" She was really looking at Joseph for the first time. "What do you want?" The lilting charm had left her voice.

"I made a mistake yesterday, Deborah. I opened the wrong door. You and a German slave were—" He couldn't continue.

"Oh, Joseph, say it. You're still such an old woman. Cyrellus was fucking the eyeballs right out of my head. He's the latest craze in Caesarea. Very expensive. I mean *very*. But worth his weight in gold. All my friends agree. The other gladiators weren't nearly as good." She laughed at Joseph's disgusted expression.

"You should see your face. It looks just like mine probably did when you were so diligently working to plant your precious son inside me. So tender you were. So concerned not to hurt me. I didn't know what men were for until Rome really came to Caesarea. You never hurt me, Joseph, after the first time. No wonder I despised it every time you touched me."

Joseph turned. Left. He'd meant to talk harshly to Deborah, demand that she remember that she was Aaron's mother, that she behave in a way that would not shame him. She was a devil. He could only pray that Aaron would never know.

Joseph was no innocent. He'd had many women, experienced ecstacies that they were trained to evoke, strange and unnatural some of them. But pain—inflicted or received— was an abomination. Deborah sickened him.

CHAPTER FORTY-EIGHT

AARON HAD A CHILD, A DAUGHTER. JOSEPH COULDN'T BE-
lieve it. That made him a grandfather.

Worse—much worse—Aaron had a beard, too. It was
thick and glossy and black as night. Joseph stroked the
thinnish, elegantly trimmed hair on his chin and felt inadequate.

But he was genuinely happy to see the pretty baby, even
happier to have been invited to visit Aaron's house. It was
the first such occasion. Joseph was sure that Abigail and
her friend, Ruth's mother, had managed it. Nonetheless,
the invitation had been extended, and here he was. Ruth
and Aaron and Leah. They looked like a family, and their
home looked comfortable, and their neighborhood was obviously a real community of families more or less like
theirs.

"Aaron is teaching now," said Ruth with pride. Then,
quickly, she covered her mouth with her fingers and cast
her eyes downward.

Oh, thought Joseph, so it's that kind of family. The wife
cooks, cleans, has babies, admires her husband, and doesn't
speak unless spoken to. His happiness faded. Clearly Aaron
was even more deeply committed to the self-righteous, law-

of-our-fathers view of Judaism that liked to call itself "orthodox," thereby declaring anyone who differed from it a
second- or third-rate Jew. More than ever Joseph felt sorrow about the death of Hillel several months earlier. Who
would be the voice of reason and compassion now?

Joseph congratulated the parents again, then made his
departure. His son did not urge him to stay longer.

He suddenly saw, in his mind, the unrepentant laughing
face of Herod Agrippa. Berenice's son was all the things a
parent fears. Herod was totally concerned with pleasure, he
lived on the money his mother gave him, never thought of
any kind of work or responsibility, had charm instead of
character, and was, quite possibly, an inveterate liar.

And yet, Joseph felt an affection for him that Aaron did
not inspire. I am, he thought, quite probably an immoral
man and a bad father.

For the moment he decided to assume Herod Agrippa's
attitude: He wouldn't let his failings bother him. Joseph
smoothed the thick silk folds of his cloak and went to the
Temple for the regular meeting of the Sanhedrin. He felt
more comfortable there, with his own kind.

It was, it turned out, a year for new babies. Berenice was
full of excitement about her daughter's daughter. "She must
be a real beauty, Joseph. Herod Philip is really a very good-
looking man, and you know Herodias. They named her Salome. I hope that's not a bad sign. If she turns out like old
King Herod's awful sister, I'll just refuse to have her in my
house. But that would be years and years from now. So I
have lots of presents and a letter to Herodias, begging her
to bring the baby for me to see. You'll take them with you,
please?"

Joseph said he'd be glad to. And he would. His fondness
for Berenice grew every time he saw her, and that covered
many years. Twenty since he had sailed with her and her
"pets" aboard the *Phoenix*.

But that wasn't all the news, Berenice continued gleefully. Her dear Emilius was a grandfather. "Marcus and Cornelia had a little boy. The very same month as Herodius' girl. Wouldn't it be delightful if they married when they get older? After all, Marcus isn't my blood son, even though I love him just as much. So they're not really related. And the baby—Julius is his name, Julius Emilius Flavius, so much name for such a tiny little thing—Julius won't be anti-Jewish or anything nasty like that, not with a Jewish grandmother."

Joseph asked about Berenice's other children. All good news. Aristobulus was working at some kind of administrative job for Tiberius, and Miriam was, Berenice hoped, going to be married soon. She'd been staying with cousins in Chalcis, and there'd been an interesting offer from a big landowner there.

And Herod Agrippa?

"Oh, as hopeless as always, Joseph. Drusus is back now, and they're as irresponsible as they always were. Even though his father arranged for him to be made consul—terribly grand and important—Drusus still prefers to go to one party after another with Herod. Naturally, they get invited absolutely everywhere. People are already whispering about what a handsome emperor Drusus is going to make when Tiberius dies. Every man in every Roman city in the world is trying to get on Drusus' good side. And the ones with daughters! Well, you can just imagine it."

"Matchmaking again?" Berenice's husband laughed, entering the loggia where she and Joseph were sitting.

Joseph stood to greet the retired senator, his patron. Joseph admired and liked the handsome aging aristocrat. Emilius was a man of honor.

The three of them talked comfortably. Emilius brought Joseph up to date on the Empire's military news, his main interest; Joseph was glad to hear that a rebellion in Illyria had been successfully put down. Not that he was personally concerned, but some of his business friends would be grateful for authoritative information.

Not long after, Herod Agrippa arrived, accompanied by Drusus. He is, indeed, handsome, Joseph thought when he was greeting Tiberius' son. Not like his father.

Berenice asked the young men if they were going to have dinner at the house. Joseph was. And a few friends were coming.

Almost in unison Drusus and Herod said that they couldn't.

"A party?" asked Berenice.

"Of course," Herod answered. "It should be . . . memorable. There's a quartet of women dancers who are, by all accounts, triple jointed, maybe quadruple. They do the most extraordinary things with their—"

"Enough." Emilius stopped him. "You're giving your mother more reason to wring her pretty hands and moan about your depravity."

Herod Agrippa smiled at his stepfather and went to kiss his mother. "That's why I invent these tales. In fact, Drusus and I are going to hear that rhetorician read some chapters from Claudius' latest history book."

"I don't believe that for a minute," Berenice said.

Herod made a broad gesture of injured innocence. "There. You see. No matter what I say, you're determined to believe the worst."

Drusus bowed to Emilius, Joseph, and Berenice, said his thank-yous, and prodded Herod. "We have to leave. I've got to stop at my father's place first."

Herod Agrippa was saying goodbye, too, when he suddenly interrupted himself. Joseph should come with them, he said. It never hurt a businessman to get to know the Roman Emperor.

Joseph protested. It was too intrusive. Berenice said that the Palatine was too long a walk. Herod contradicted both of them. Tiberius wasn't at the House of Augustus. When he had a great deal of work to do, he carried it to the house on the Esquiline that had been his home before Augustus died. No one knew about it, and he could be quiet there. As for Joseph's remark, he'd be doing both Drusus and Herod a favor if he came.

"Anything you or I would say in ten words, Tiberius turns it into ten thousand. If he's droning on and on at you, Joseph, we'll be able to make our escape." Herod winked at his mother. "For Claudius' history reading."

Rome's new Emperor was seated behind a table stacked with scrolls. He looked decidedly gloomy.

He accepted the scroll Drusus had brought and added it to a pile. Whether it was true or not, he said he remembered Joseph from their meeting some years ago.

"Sit down," said Tiberius. "I'd like to hear about conditions in Judea. What's the opinion of Valerius Gratus? I had good reports of him, and that's why I made him Procurator. I have always believed that the short-term provincial representatives were handicapped by their few years in the position. In my opinion . . ."

Herod grinned wickedly at Joseph as he and Drusus slipped out the door.

Joseph had heard talk that Tiberius honestly did not want to be Emperor. But Augustus had chosen him, named him Emperor in his will. Tiberius was too conscious of duty to disobey. It might have thrown the Empire into another civil war, like the one that Augustus had fought and won, thus becoming the first Emperor.

Tiberius had the hardened body and determination of the military man. He had been in the army for forty of his fifty-seven years, a successful general for the second half of that time. Now, trying to cope with the administration and politics of his inherited empire, he looked miserably unhappy and out of place.

Joseph could see that the talk he'd heard was true. And also—sadly—that Augustus was truly gone. His heir had none of the enthusiasm, humanity, or genius of the man who'd been Joseph's hero.

Tiberius was hardworking. That was obvious. And conscientious. He asked Joseph questions without number about details of life and attitudes in Jerusalem, Caesarea, the smaller towns, the farming villages. Joseph's replies were honest, but cautiously limited. He began to wonder if he was going to be kept there through the dinner hour. He was hungry, for one thing. And it would cause Berenice great inconvenience, with other guests arriving and no certain knowledge of when Joseph might return.

He was beginning to compose a get-away speech in his mind when Tiberius abruptly pushed a group of scrolls to one side. "I can see that you are a man of deep intelligence, Joseph of Arimathea," he said. "Wait . . . wait . . . There's some blank papyrus here. I'm going to give you a letter to Gratus. He doesn't know whom he can depend on in Judea. I will tell him you should receive every consideration and that he can consult you for decision-making."

Joseph sat very still. What Tiberius was offering was more influence and power than any Jew in Judea could ever hope to attain. He'd apologize to Berenice for the rest of his life, every day if necessary, but he would not leave the Emperor now, not if he talked all night and for the entire month to come.

Tiberius completed the letter. Then, after looking in four places, he found the box that held the wax for his seal. There was, of course, no flame on the small lamp used to melt the wax. The Emperor of Rome looked at it, enraged. Without a word he stood up and left the room.

When he returned, Tiberius was carrying a large burning lamp. He put it on the table, held the stick of wax to the flame, then carefully deposited a large soft gob of it on the bottom of the letter he'd written and pressed his seal ring into it.

Except for the last, every other act could have been, should have been done by some kind of secretary or assistant. Joseph himself was at fault for wanting to be too much in control of many details about his shipping business. But he had enough experience and enough sense to recognize the fault and to turn many, many matters over to others.

And that was a company of six galleys, a warehouse, and a supply of extra sails, oars, paint, and wood for repairs.

This one man was trying to run the Roman Empire, seemingly without any help. Twenty-five-year-old Drusus the party-goer suddenly looked more promising.

Tiberius asked Joseph next about the goods produced for export in Judea and Galilee and the comparison of Caesarea to other ports. Joseph was on sure ground now, and he answered all the questions with authority.

He was halfway through a sentence when his stomach growled as loudly as a dog. Tiberius laughed, and his sharp, short bursts of laughter were so like a dog's barking that Joseph began to laugh, too.

"I forgot the time," said Tiberius. "Go quickly now. I don't want Berenice angry at me."

He did not thank Joseph for his time or his information. Tiberius was not a graceful man.

Joseph did thank the Emperor. Tiberius was already opening a scroll, he noticed, when he closed the door behind him.

The hall was dimly lit. Joseph began to make his way to the house's entrance door. Carefully. So as not to trip. Then he remembered the letter. It was still on the table.

He hurried back the short way he had come, knocked, and opened the door to Tiberius' workroom. The draft blew out the flame of the lamp.

"I am most awfully sorry," Joseph said. He could see only Tiberius' darker bulk in the shadowed room. "I forgot the letter."

"No, no, don't worry. Bring me one of the hall lamps."

After Tiberius relit the large lamp, he gave Joseph his letter and bid him an affable good evening.

Joseph arrived at Berenice's just as dinner was being served. He apologized profusely, but Berenice waved his words away. "I didn't wait, Joseph. We all know Tiberius. He could have kept you all night."

Joseph laughed. He greeted the others and took his place on a couch with a former senator, like Emilius, and Berenice's friend Antonia. "I am not proud of what got me away," he said. "My stomach made a hungry growl that must have been heard all over the city." He washed his hands and dried them, then took some olives from a bowl on the table. Before he put them in his mouth, he completed the story of his misdemeanors. "I had left something on the Emperor's table, so I went back, and when I opened the door the breeze it made blew out the flame. Two disasters, the second worse than the first."

Antonia spit olive pits into her palm. "Not a disaster at all, Joseph, quite the contrary." she said. She deposited the pits carefully on a plate and took some more olives. "My brother-in-law has always been very susceptible to omens and signs. He believes that a lamp flame extinguished by a gust of wind is the greatest sign of good luck that exists. You've made a new friend, Joseph."

CHAPTER FORTY-NINE

WHEN THE *EAGLE* DOCKED IN CAESAREA AT SEASON'S END, Joseph went to Herod's palace, where the newly appointed Procurator Gratus lived and had his offices. Joseph knew he would always think of the lavish marble buildings as "Herod's Palace." Time had allowed Joseph to push aside the memories of Herod's atrocities and remember his kindnesses and his surprising charm. The palace now looked shabby and bleakly military. Soldiers seemed to be standing at attention everywhere.

As Joseph expected, Tiberius' letter won the Procurator's full attention and respect. Joseph stayed a short time then left, pleased with himself. He would be able, certainly, to use his influence to the benefit of himself and many of his friends.

At Arimathea his account of his stomach noises made the whole family laugh. He told the part about the lamp only to Sarah.

"I've decided that I like the beard," she said later. "It tickled at first, but now it's like a soft baby animal. Rub it on my stomach and see if it makes it growl."

The soft rumbles of pleasure deep in her throat were nothing like growling.

*   *   *

Life had settled into a regularity that—now that he was growing older—Joseph found comfortable, largely because of its predictability. He liked the authority and prestige of his position in Jerusalem and, with Tiberius as unofficial patron, in Rome. He loved his time at Arimathea.

There were the inevitable sorrows. Hillel had died early in Joseph's years on the Sanhedrin. Emilius, Berenice's husband, was thrown by a young horse that he was too old to be riding and died instantly of a broken neck. Such losses saddened Joseph.

His mother's death broke his heart. "I never knew her. I always meant to spend time with her, to ask her about herself, to tell her how very much I regretted the disruption and unhappiness I caused her," he told Sarah. "I kept putting it off. I did not know my own mother."

Sarah put her arms around her husband, as if she were his mother and he were a little boy. "She knew you, Joseph. That was enough. I'm sure, truly I am. We talked about you so often in the years we lived together."

Helena's death was a great sadness for Joseph, but there was a greater one connected with it. He had not received the message about her heart attack in time to get to Arimathea before she died, but he was there for her funeral. He tried to help Amos and Caleb and their sons—four in all— move the great rock to cover the entrance to the tomb, but they worked well together and he was only in the way, so he stepped aside.

I stepped aside long, long ago, he realized. I call Arimathea my home, but I do not work the land or truly know the lives and hearts of the people in the village. Or even my own brothers and their families.

He was doubly bereaved. He had lost not only his mother but also his home.

At the next meeting of the Sanhedrin he presented his case. The Law directed that land be passed from father to eldest son, and from him to his eldest son, and so on, throughout the years.

"You all know me as Joseph of Arimathea. In my heart I will remain, until I die, Joseph of Arimathea, because it is the home of my birth and of my heart. But I am not of the land, only owner of it. I ask for a reading of the Law's meaning as well as its words. I have two brothers, good men both, and they have sons who are also good men. Fathers and sons, they plow the land and seed it, tend it and harvest it, and love it for the bounty with which it rewards their labors.

"I also have a son. You know him. He is a teacher, the Rabbi Aaron, leader of the synagogue beside the Pool of Siloam. When he was a boy I carried him to Arimathea, the place of his ancestors. The farm animals frightened him, the trees and vines and fields did not interest him. He is a scholar, and pride in his knowledge gladdens my heart. But his heart is in his scrolls, not in the earth of Arimathea.

"I ask for this: that you judge it lawful for me to make my brothers the rightful owners of the land of their fathers."

The question was an interesting one. The debate lasted for more than an hour, with many questions posed to Joseph and answered by him.

He paid special attention to two men, perhaps the most important on the Sanhedrin. They were Gamaliel, the grandson of Hillel, and Eleazar, son of Annas and now High Priest.

In the end, the vote was forty to thirty. Joseph, of course, could not judge his own case. His fellow judges ruled that he could give the lands to his brothers.

Joseph went, uninvited, to Aaron's house. He discovered there that Aaron's Ruth had recently given birth to a second child, a second daughter. Joseph told Aaron about the ruling of the Sanhedrin. The land would have gone to him, Joseph told his son. He asked Aaron if he was willing to give up his land inheritance in exchange for the value of it in money, which Joseph would give him.

"I will open my own academy," said Aaron. "It will plant the word of God in many minds and give a harvest more pleasing in His eyes."

The next week Joseph bought a tomb cut into rock near to the city wall and the Damascus Gate. There were six tombs, all of them newly carved, in this area. They were large, which meant expensive, and widely separated one from another, which meant extravagant. It was a worthy representation of Joseph's position in Jerusalem. I will be buried here, thought Joseph, and so will Aaron and his wife and his children. We are of Jerusalem. Arimathea will shelter Sarah's bones. She belongs there.

On his next regular visit to Rome, Joseph's slightly complacent sense of his own importance met with a serious shock.

At Puteoli there was a message waiting for him from Berenice: *"Hurry. Terrible trouble."* He left all the business of the *Eagle* in Barca's hands, hired horses, and rode, with Antiochus, day and night, to arrive in Rome just before sundown the following day.

"Joseph!" Berenice threw her arms around him and laid her head on his chest. "Thank the Lord, you're here."

He was at a loss. There was a long-standing affection between him and Berenice, but never to a degree that produced this kind of intimacy. And Joseph did not for an instant think that Berenice's embrace was any indication of some out-of-the-blue physical attraction. He gingerly patted her shoulders, hoping that this was the right thing to do.

"What is it, Berenice? How can I be of help?"

She released Joseph, stepped away, stamped her foot and burst into tears. "I'm so angry," she wailed, "and so frightened, and there's nothing I can do."

Joseph finally managed to get some sense out of her incoherent phrases and sobs. Her message, he learned, had not been overdramatic. There was trouble. And it was terrible.

The Roman Senate had issued a decree that four thousand adult Jewish men were to be deported to Sardinia. Rome's Jewish population was between twenty and thirty thousand, including women, the old, and children. Four thousand men would account for virtually every head of every family with growing children.

Joseph was certain that Berenice must be wrong. "When did this happen?" he asked.

"About a month ago. It hasn't been implemented yet, but any day now, soldiers are likely to descend on the Jewish Quarter and—" Berenice stamped her foot. "It's that miserable man Sejanus, I just know it. But no one will listen to me."

"What does Herod Agrippa say about all this?"

"Herod!" She began to cry again. "What does he know about being a Jew? He doesn't eat forbidden foods, at least he tells me he doesn't, but he refuses to take this seriously. He says the Senate is only a group of men who talk and talk and do nothing."

Joseph's opinion was much the same. The power of Rome resided in the Emperor and the Army, not in those toga-clad men who paraded to the Senate with their host of clients following them, to demonstrate how important they were, or thought they were.

Still, he'd have to find out what the truth was, if only to dispel Berenice's worries. "I'll take care of it," he told his old friend.

"I knew you could, Joseph. I feel better already."

In the morning Joseph walked alone to the river and across the bridge to the Jewish Quarter. Antiochus was collecting information, in his own inimitable fashion, from the senators' households.

When Joseph plunged into the tenement-crowded streets, the disturbing feeling of oppression came over him again, just as it had so many years before. He got lost at once. But this time there was no plucky crippled boy to help him. He asked for directions to the synagogue, tried to follow them, got lost again, at least a half dozen times.

He finally found it, but the door was locked. He had just turned away when he thought he heard voices inside. He knocked on the door, and the sounds stopped.

Yes, there were people inside. Joseph pounded on the door for a long time. Finally it opened. Just a crack. He could see one eye and a sliver of face.

None of the men I knew will still be here, Joseph thought. I could be anybody. The locked door means fear. How can I convince anyone that I want to help?

Because now he was beginning to believe that perhaps Berenice's alarm was warranted.

He made his voice strong and recited the words he'd been taught when he was a child. "Hear, O Israel: the Lord our God, the Lord is One!"

The door opened quickly; his arm was grabbed, and he was pulled inside the synagogue. Behind him the door closed at once. He could hear the bolts as they dropped to hold it locked.

"I am Joseph of Arimathea and Jerusalem, and I have come to help," he said. If I can, he added silently, to himself. His sense of importance and power had been severely diminished.

The synagogue was crowded with men, women, children, all of them praying despairingly, some beating their breasts in rhythm with their plaintive words. Joseph was shown the proclamation that the Romans had nailed up inside the building. The words were simple and harsh. Even with his faulty command of Latin he could read them easily.

On September 20, five days away, all healthy adult male Jews between the ages of twenty and thirty-five were to stand on the street in front of their homes for inspection and collection by a troop of the Roman Army.

Five days!

"Can you stop them?" The man who asked the question

sounded skeptical. Joseph couldn't blame him. He wished he could lie, but it wasn't in his nature, not in serious matters.

"I do not know," he said. "There is a chance, only a chance. I will do my best."

Joseph went to the door, unlocked it, opened it, went out into the tiny square. He had to try to see Tiberius. Would the Emperor remember him? What could Joseph say to him if he did gain audience?

"Master! Master! Master!" A very small boy was chasing him. Joseph stopped.

The child's plump little feet slipped out of the too-big sandals he was wearing. He scooped them up and kept running, barefoot, toward Joseph.

When the child reached him, he looked up into Joseph's face with huge dark eyes. "Master. Are you the Messiah?"

"Of course not. Give me your sandals, you'll bruise your feet on the street."

"You must be the Messiah. My father says He will come soon and destroy the Romans and set us free. And now all the grownups are afraid of the Romans, even my father. But you have come. You must be the Messiah."

Joseph caught the child around the waist. "Hold still, pick up your foot. There. Now the other one. There." Once the sandals were on, he turned the little boy to face him.

"Listen to me. I cannot destroy the Romans. No man can destroy the Romans by himself. It would need many armies. I am just going to talk to a very important man I know. He may be able to change what the Romans are planning to do. Do you understand?"

The child shook his head. "No," he answered.

Joseph turned the small body again, to face the synagogue. "Go back to your father," he said. "Don't lose your sandals."

Antiochus was sitting on the steps of the Temple of Healing, eating some dates. He stood, walked to meet

Joseph, held out a hand, open, three dates on the palm. "Have something to eat," he said. "You look a bit drawn."

Joseph took the dates, then looked down at his sticky hand in surprise. He hadn't really thought about what he was doing. He threw the dates into the bushes. "I have bad news," he said.

"I have worse," said Antiochus placidly. "It doesn't affect my appetite. If you weren't going to eat them, you could have returned them to me."

Joseph had no patience with raillery. "What did you learn?"

A great deal. They walked across the other bridge and along the river while Antiochus talked. There had been a recent scandal. A Roman noblewoman, a convert to Judaism, had given a valuable gift, a golden bowl and some priceless silk dyed purple, to be used in the Temple of Jerusalem. Unfortunately the men—rabbis, she believed—were crooks, and they'd kept the goods, tried to sell them. Yes, they were Jews.

That was the pretext for the expulsion of the Jews. The real reason was represented by the woman, though, not by the crooks. There had been more and more converts in recent years, most of them women, and many of them noble. They were attracted by the morality of Judaism in a Rome that grew increasingly depraved with every day that passed. People attended the festivals of the Roman gods, they frequented the temples, for meetings licit and illicit, not for worship. Their gods no longer had meaning for them.

More important still: The reason behind the reason was the violent anti-Jewish prejudice of the commander of the Praetorian Guard, the permanent military force in the city. He was a man named Sejanus.

"Sejanus!" Joseph broke in on the Galatian's account. "Berenice said something about him. Who is he?"

"He's a smart, hardworking, handsome and ambitious man. The Emperor's administrator, secretary, whatever Tiberius needs. Sejanus reads reports and petitions, tells

Tiberius about the important ones, takes care of ordinary things for him."

"He certainly needs help. I saw that for myself."

"Help is one thing, Joseph. Manipulation is quite another. This Sejanus has made Tiberius totally dependent on him. The Emperor considers him his closest friend."

"Tiberius isn't a man who has friends. That's what everyone says. He was close to his brother, but he died thirty years ago. That was Antonia's husband—you know, Berenice's friend. Even Antonia says that Tiberius is a cold fish. And Drusus, who's his son, dislikes spending time with him. It's not logical that he'd start making friends now."

"Think, Joseph. Imagine you're a lonely man, with no friends and a son who avoids you. You're also buried in work you hate and have no skills for. Tiberius is a soldier, not a politician or a diplomat. Along comes a man—another soldier—who acts as though he likes you, admires you, is willing to neglect his own needs and pleasure to help you, because he cares so much for you. You soon begin to depend on him. After a while you can't get along without him. For work. For companionship. For admiration.

"It's only a small step from that to allowing that man to tell you what you think. You've become his puppet without noticing what was happening."

Joseph nodded. "I can imagine it, but I can't believe it. Tiberius is the Emperor of Rome. He can't be a fool."

"Who can more easily afford to be a fool than an emperor?"

Joseph had no answer to that. "All right, all right. Let's say that everything you've told me is true. But why would this Sejanus hate Jews so much?"

Antiochus showed his empty hands. "There I failed. I couldn't find out. But he is a Jew-hater. Everyone agrees that's so."

"I'll have to think of something, some way to change

Tiberius' mind. Is it true that he can make the Senate withdraw a decree?"

"If they want to keep their privileges, they'll do what he says. That's not the law, but it's the fact."

Apprehension sent a chill down Joseph's spine. He shivered, then shook it off. "I have to try," he said. "I'll go talk to Tiberius. Let's hope he remembers the lamp flame blown out."

It felt strange—and sad—to be walking up the Palatine to Augustus' house. Joseph had to force his shoulders out of their slump.

Two of the Praetorian Guard, the Emperor's bodyguards, stood at the door, one on each side. They moved their javelins to cross it when Joseph approached.

He assumed an air of importance. "Send word to the Emperor that Joseph of Arimathea is here to see him."

It didn't work.

"The Prefect Sejanus decides who is to see the Emperor," said one of the guards. He did not look at Joseph.

"Then I will talk with the Prefect Sejanus," Joseph said. He had to try.

"The Prefect Sejanus is occupied," said the soldier.

The second one did look at Joseph. His expression was wooden, but there was a sneer in his eyes. "Petitioners can wait outside the Prefect's house in the morning. He sees some of them."

Joseph did not show the humiliation but he felt it. He turned and walked away.

"Berenice, I want to ask a favor of Antonia. How do I go about it?"

"Just ask. Don't try to be clever or subtle. She hates that. Her house is close by. I'll walk over there with you."

"Better if you don't, I think. She may say no, and it would be embarrassing for you and for her if you were there."

"Don't be ridiculous, Joseph. Antonia and I have been

friends for too many years to be embarrassed with one another."

"Then let's say it would be embarrassing for me. I prefer to go alone."

"It's about the Jews, isn't it? That rat Sejanus won't let you see Tiberius."

"That's it. I can't think of what else to do, other than ask Antonia if she can help me get past Sejanus."

"Very sensible, Joseph. You go ahead. Follow the road to the right when you leave here. Antonia's is the second villa. You don't need me. She loathes Sejanus."

The guards seemed to wilt under Antonia's imperious look. This was the daughter of Mark Antony and Octavia, the sister of the Emperor—now deified to the god—Augustus.

"The Lady Antonia, what an honor." The officer was extremely good-looking. "What can I do to be useful to you?"

"Get out of the way, Sejanus. I'm taking a friend of his to see my brother-in-law."

The Emperor of Rome was eating one from a pile of small roasted birds on a plate that rested on the table beside his chair. He was dressed in a purple-bordered tunic and sandals.

He took the half-eaten bird from his mouth and stood when he saw Antonia.

"Sit down and finish eating, Tiberius," she said generously. "You remember our friend Joseph who's such a help to you in Jerusalem. He's here to keep you from letting some idiots in the Senate make trouble for you."

Tiberius dropped the bird onto the table. "What are they trying to do this time?" Suspicion was thick in his words.

After that it was easy. Joseph talked briefly about the danger of unrest and rebellion in Jerusalem, perhaps throughout Judea. The Procurator's army could put it down, of course, but the destruction would be costly and the olive harvest, soon to come, would be interrupted, with the loss of the taxes on the fruits and the oil.

"Why are these Jews being sent to Sardinia?" Tiberius asked.

"I'm told the senators intend to use them to destroy the bandits that plague travelers there."

Tiberius threw his big head back, and his barking laughter filled the room. "Jews? Fighting bandits? Better to send a flock of these." He dumped the birds from the plate. "At least they have sharp beaks and know how to peck with them. Jews are soft. They know nothing except how to do no work every seventh day and blame it on their god."

He shouted loudly for Sejanus. "I've just heard a fine joke," he said when the prefect came in. "Send word to whichever idiot in the Senate came up with the idea, that they're to leave the Jews in Rome alone, not ship them off to Sardinia. They'll have to decree that their decree is annulled."

Tiberius continued to laugh. "I thank you, Joseph. I don't often hear anything that makes me laugh. I knew you'd be lucky for me."

"Please tell me," Joseph begged Antonia after they left the Palatine, "what I can possibly do to show my gratitude. Anything, everything, in my power."

Now it was Antonia who laughed. Quietly. "You've more than repaid me, Joseph. Did you see the look on Sejanus' face? He was swelling, like the toad he is. I thought he might even pop his eyes out. It was glorious."

In the synagogue the little boy, now with only one sandal, scandalized the whole congregation when he looked up at Joseph and said, "I knew you were the Messiah."

The feelings about Joseph in the Jewish Quarter were not blasphemous, like the child's innocent mistake. But they did regard Joseph with gratitude that bordered on worship.

He did not let it go to his head. The entire drama had a salutary effect on his view of himself. He was not—without friends and a good deal of luck—powerful and important at all.

The luck stayed with him. On their way to Puteoli he and Antiochus were attacked by brigands armed with clubs and knives. Four of them.

Antiochus was carrying a goatskin bag filled with perfumed oil, a gift from Berenice for delivery to her daughter Herodias. He slashed it open as he threw it at the attackers. Then he and Joseph were able to get away while the brigands' horses were slipping and sliding in the oily puddle.

They reached a post house tavern and turned into its courtyard. When they had left their lathered horses with the ostler, Antiochus spoke quietly to Joseph before they entered the tavern. "Best to say nothing about our little adventure, Joseph. I don't suppose you had time to notice the horses that those men were riding. They had harnesses with the brass emblem of the Praetorian Guard."

CHAPTER FIFTY

IN PUTEOLI JOSEPH'S LUCK WAS STILL HOLDING. HE LEARNED, in talking with the captain of a galley that was loading cargo, that part of the cargo was the same perfumed oil that had saved his life. He bought a duplicate of Berenice's gift for her daughter.

"What a very devoted mother," he commented with a whistle. The oil cost three times as much as any he had ever traded. He did not begrudge a single denarius. Berenice was more precious to him than ever now. She was responsible, in a roundabout way, for the valuable deflation of his self-importance.

After docking in Caesarea, he decided that he'd take Berenice's letters and gift to Herodias himself. It was a considerable distance to Herod Philip's capital at Caesarea Philippi, but this way the letters and oil would reach Herodias more quickly, and also he'd be able to tell Berenice about Herodias and her little girl when next he saw her.

Herodias was, if possible, even more beautiful than she'd been when Joseph had last seen her, six years before. She had an air of majesty, of grandeur, appropriate to the wife of a ruler, even though he be only a prince, and his principality not of major importance.

She begged Joseph to tell every tiny detail that he could remember about her mother, brothers and sister, and Rome. Especially Rome. "I miss it so, Joseph. I've been here for five years, and I'm terribly homesick. Could you take me with you when you go visit my mother next time?"

For Berenice, Joseph said he'd be delighted. He hoped Herodias did not remember the *Phoenix*. He had no intention of putting that ship into the sea ever again.

After visiting Herod Philip, Joseph went to see Herod Antipas, his partner for bronze. Antipas was emulating his father, though on a smaller scale. He was building a city of his own on the sea. It was the small Sea of Galilee, not the Mediterranean. But it was extraordinarily beautiful, with glistening black rock in the nearby hills and fresh white-topped waves on its clear deep waters.

Antipas announced proudly that he was going to name his new capital Tiberias, in honor of the Emperor, and that he had hopes that Tiberius would come to the dedication. His wife's father would be there, of course. He was Aretas, the King of Nabatea. A king and an emperor. That would indeed make the dedication impressive.

Joseph agreed; he hoped his manufactured enthusiasm was convincing. He was feeling very old all of a sudden. Aretas, King of Nabatea. Joseph was remembering his trip to Rome with Nicolaus when Herod—the real Herod—was in trouble with Augustus. Aretas had seized his throne that year. So long ago. Nicolaus dead. So long ago.

I'm only fifty-one, Joseph told himself. If I feel old, it's because I look back too much. I will stop that right now. I'll go home to my Sarah. She always makes me feel young.

"Why, Joseph! You've got some gray in your beard and your hair. It makes you look quite distinguished—what are you laughing about, Joseph?"

Sarah's long braids were black as ink. To Joseph's loving eyes she always looked like the girl he had married—so long ago.

*   *   *

He let Barca make the Belerion voyage on his own the next year so that Herodias could be carried to her mother as soon as the season began. When they arrived in Rome, he thanked God for the decision. Berenice was fatally ill.

No one knew what was killing her, Herod Agrippa told Joseph. The ebullient, joking young man Joseph had known for all those years was gone. This Herod was sober and serious; his worry and grief was deeply etched on his face.

Except when he was with his mother. Then he put on the Herod she loved, and loved to scold. He told her outrageous, invented accounts of carousing and gambling and misbehaving, always with a laughing, teasing refusal to accept any responsibility or shame. Berenice's giggles were weak, and interrupted by coughing, but she was obviously brightened.

Joseph had always liked Herod Agrippa, even though he believed that he should disapprove of him. Now, for the first time he admired and honored Berenice's wayward son.

Herodias did her best. She had none of Herod's liveliness or wit, but she gladdened her mother's heart with stories about elegant receptions she gave and attended, what she wore to them, how she had changed and improved the furnishings of Philip's palace. Her soft-voiced accounts would lull Berenice into tranquil sleep. And then Herodias could run from the room to weep and whimper piteously, clinging to her brother for comfort, even though he had none to give.

Joseph thought he should leave the family alone, but Antonia forbade any such thing. She had taken over the running of her friend's household, even to the degree of preparing Berenice's meals herself and feeding her.

Herod told Joseph why. Antonia's son, her favorite child Germanicus, had died late the year before. He'd been poisoned, everyone was sure, by the Roman governor he was visiting in an eastern province. The governor had killed himself before he could be tried and executed.

"She can't truly believe that your mother has been poisoned."

"No, of course not. But she can do for Mother what she wasn't able to do for Germanicus. It helps her some. Mother knows that, so she lets Antonia fuss over her. They've been close friends for a very long time, Joseph. They love one another."

Antonia seemed much as she'd always been; imperious, organized, emotionless, even cold. Under her control Berenice's household had lost its warm disorder. Everything was clean and neat, meals were ready and served on time, visitors were offered the freshest of fruits and breads and cheeses, with the finest of wines in scrupulously polished silver pitchers. It was a depressing change for all who had relaxed and warmed their spirits in the happy chaos that was Berenice's endearing style.

There were, Joseph saw, many, many people who cared for Berenice as much as he did. Marcus, her stepson, came from his post in one of the army's encampments on the Danube, bringing his wife and five-year-old son. Berenice considered little Julius to be her own grandson and was moved to happy tears when he hugged her too hard and then bounced on her bed, telling her all about his pony and how fast he could make it run.

Marcus scooped up his son and carried him away, and then he, too, allowed his tears to flow. Joseph was astounded. Marcus was in full uniform, the epitome of the hard-bitten Roman officer. For a man like himself, from the acceptably emotional eastern lands, weeping was normal. But not for the disciplined, unsentimental professional military man. It was, perhaps, the ultimate tribute to Berenice. Though there were many others. Tiberius commissioned a poet to read the flowery salute to her beauty that he had written at the Emperor's behest.

And when Antonia's daughter Livilla came, with flowers, she was escorted by her brother Claudius, the historian that Drusus and Herod Agrippa had joked about in the past. Claudius was their age, twenty-five, but he was sadly lacking in their good looks and charm. He had an awkward lurching gait and a stammer that was as embarrassing for the people around him as it was for Claudius himself.

It vanished, however, when he was with Berenice. He sat on a stool beside her bed, holding her hand, and spoke, with clear melodious beauty, the lines of an ode he had written for her. The subject of it was her love for everyone around her and their love for her.

"Thank you, dear Claudius," Berenice said.

He kissed her hand. "Thank you, beloved Berenice."

Herod Agrippa let out a mighty howl of heartbreak, and the household knew that his mother was dead.

"She opened her eyes very wide, she looked surprised, she said 'oh.' And then she was gone," he told them later.

She was cremated on a pyre, as was Roman custom for those the Empire honored. Herod gave the finely wrought silver box containing her remains to Joseph. Berenice had asked him to, he said. She wanted to be buried with his father, in his tomb at Alexandrium, near Jericho.

"Will you come with me, Herod Agrippa?"

No, said Berenice's son. He didn't have any memory of Judea. Rome was the only place he knew. Marcus was the owner of Berenice's house now. He had inherited it from his father, with the provision that she had the right to spend her life there. Now Marcus would be returning to the Danube, with his wife and child. He had told Herod to use the house as long as he liked. Herodias, too. She planned to stay for the autumn and winter, then return to Caesarea Philippi next year.

When Joseph departed, Herod Agrippa was moving through all the rooms and the garden, deliberately making everything untidy. He would be all right.

There were over two months left in the sailing season, Antiochus pointed out. What did Joseph plan to do?

Take Berenice home, of course.

"No," said Antiochus. "She told me you'd want to do

that and made me promise not to permit it. She knew you well, Joseph. 'He'll be brooding and gloomy,' she told me, 'until he's too busy to have time for it. Keep him busy.' What shall we do? Tour Italy? Sail to Spain?"

"I don't know."

"Then I'll give the commands. Take us to Alexandria. Your old friend Micah always rejuvenates you."

It was as Antiochus predicted. Micah was older than Joseph, but he looked much the same, except for gaining a little more weight every year, and he still had the eager hedonism and elegance that made him Micah.

Eleazar took them to the latest, most luxurious gambling palace and encouraged Joseph to discover the pleasures of poverty by losing all his money. He did it often, Eleazar declared, it made him work that much harder to earn it back so that he could lose it again.

Joseph's friend Alexander was with them, too. He could top Eleazar's story, and did. "I gamble with the money I've collected in customs duties for Rome. I have to win. Because if I lose, I don't only lose the money, I lose my head."

Joseph joined in the laughter of the others, but inside he felt a shudder. If Tiberius continued to be influenced by the Jew-hater Sejanus, almost anything might happen.

He and Sarah went together to Jerusalem, to Abigail's, and then to Alexandrium to carry out Berenice's wishes. After the ceremonious delivery of her ashes, Joseph and Sarah visited Jericho. Its rich greens and splashing fountains took Sarah's breath away. It was still the dry season in Judea, the five months of heat and brown desiccated vegetation.

"This is what we'll do," Joseph said. He was pacing with excitement. "I'll buy the land where Herod's palace used to be, clear the ruins, and build a house for us. My grandfather's house once filled that space. We'll spend the summers here together. Barca can manage the Belerion voyage quite as well as I can. He did it this year on his own."

Sarah stopped his pacing to hug him. "I'd love that. Are you sure you could bear to give up the sailing?"

Yes, he was sure. Completely. They would be together.

For hours the two of them climbed over the ruins where Herod's palace had been, planning just where to locate which rooms, the garden, the loggia. They found bits of tile, a broken fountain, roses and a fig tree that had survived.

They spent the night at the fine inn that housed visitors to Jericho in stylish comfort, talking and making plans. The next morning they went over "their house" again, then returned to Abigail's to tell her and Matthew about the special room, with its private garden, that the house would have for them.

Everything was decided. In the months ahead, while Joseph was in Jerusalem, he would arrange to buy the land and clear it. The rainy season would pose no barriers to that. Nor to his finding the best builder and working out the plans for the house.

The house would be built during the summer, while he was at sea. They would live there year round. No matter that it wasn't considered fashionable to live in Jericho except in the summer. What was fashion to people who knew what they wanted?

Joseph and Sarah had disagreed about his going to sea. He wanted to stay at the inn at Jericho and watch the builders.

But Sarah was adamant. On two counts. He had to make a final voyage to Belerion, to tell the Dumnoni chief that Barca had full authorization to take his place. And he had to leave the builders alone, or they would deliberately put in doors that refused to stay locked or pools with irreparable leaks.

* * *

Joseph went to Arimathea more often that winter than he'd ever done before. After the meeting of the Sanhedrin, the next day was the Sabbath, and the day after, the meeting with the builder, to add refinements and choose from the assortment of tiles and paints and marbles.

Then he took the samples to Arimathea, and went over them all again, with Sarah. Back to Jerusalem then, and to the builder, to change anything he'd previously decided, if Sarah had decided differently.

Joseph could hardly wait for summer to come, so that the house could be built.

The builder was eager for summer, too. So that Joseph would go away.

The family came from Arimathea for Passover, as always. All of them had heard more than enough about the Jericho house, so they declined Joseph's invitation to come to Jericho and view the now-clear building site. Everyone stayed an extra day at Abigail's to give Sarah time to go. She and Joseph had a glorious day and night in Jericho, then hurried back to Jerusalem. It was time for her to return to Arimathea with the family. And for Joseph to go to Caesarea, the *Eagle*, and Belerion.

He didn't visit Alexandria that year. Or Rome. He wanted to get home as soon as possible. In Belerion the Jewish community gave a farewell feast, with music and dancing, in his honor. The Dumnoni did the same. Druid Bards sang an epic ballad, "The Man Named Joseph," about his travels over all the years. Many gifts were presented. For him. For Sarah. For the two of them together.

Joseph was deeply moved by both celebrations. "It didn't show, did it, Antiochus, that I was longing to leave?"

The Galatian reassured him. "Only the Druids could tell. They know everything that's inside a man's head."

* * *

Joseph heard the Belerion song when he neared his house at Arimathea. Sarah was playing her harp and singing.

When Joseph walked in, Sarah smiled at him. She continued plucking the harp, but she sang different words. They were Aramaic not Celtic.

"Behold," she sang, "the old man comes, with his gray beard, to his wife Sarah."

She giggled, once. "Welcome home, Abraham."

"Sarah?"

Her smile was tremulous now. "I made up that song to prepare you for the miracle. Oh, Joseph, oh, my own dearest love, I can hardly say the words. I am with child. Joseph, at last, at last, after so many years, it has happened. I'm going to have your baby."

She put the harp aside, and her hands caressed the small mound beneath her dress. "Come, feel me, say hello to your child."

CHAPTER FIFTY-ONE

THEY WERE BOTH GIDDY WITH JOY. WHEN JOSEPH FELT THE
baby move inside Sarah's womb, beneath his fearful, gentle
palms, he cried out, jerked his hands away so quickly that he
fell over onto the floor.

Sarah laughed at him. She'd had months to get accustomed to the wonder, to begin to believe that it was true, to
adjust to the certainty when it came.

Joseph knelt at her feet, felt her belly, waited, waited,
waited. Then the movement again. He began to weep, and
to laugh, and to kiss Sarah's face.

At least an hour had gone by before he thought to shout
for Antiochus and to tell him the news.

The Galatian was a handsome, dignified, worldly man of
forty-some years, but he blushed when Sarah took his
hands and placed them on her belly. When the baby moved,
his jaw dropped, his eyes rounded, and he looked from her
face to Joseph's, to Sarah's again, speechless.

"Dear Antiochus," Sarah said, returning his hands to
him, "you should flop around some. You look like a just-
caught fish." She regarded her husband and his closest
friend with the tender smile of fond superiority that had
curved the lips of mothers-to-be since time immemorial.

* * *

Later, when Joseph was more or less able to think, Sarah told him all the things she'd been thinking. The baby must have been conceived in Jericho when they went there after Passover. So he would be born in January. Here. At Arimathea, where his father had been born. She had already arranged for the midwife from the village and her daughter to come the instant they were told that it was time.

Naturally the baby would grow up in Jericho. They already knew that was the place that wanted him.

They could move there now, Joseph interrupted. The house must be finished. He'd go at once to make sure, get everything ready.

No, Sarah said. "I know that Abraham's Sarah was ninety when she bore Isaac, according to the Torah. But I still don't think that I'm a girl at the age of fifty. I'm being very careful. No travel, no extra excitement. I'm excited enough as things are . . . What do you think about naming the baby Isaac, Joseph? That's what Sarah and Abraham called their son."

How could she be so sure the baby would be a boy? Joseph would love to have a girl, exactly like her mother.

Certainly not. She was going to give him a boy, a wonderful lively, laughing boy, to make up for the misfortune that was Aaron.

"But you must hurry to Jericho right away, Joseph. I want to know every single thing about our house. And I want you to have all the furnishings done so that we can move in as soon as Isaac and I are able to travel."

Joseph was ready to argue. He didn't want to leave her, not even for a minute. Then he caught his breath. "I'll go tomorrow," he said. "I'm going to make the biggest sacrifice and gift of thanksgiving that the Temple has ever received."

"At least a dozen doves," Sarah agreed.

"A hundred sheep. A thousand. And two thousand kids. Plus a hundred pounds of gold. No, two hundred. Four. There's no limit to my thanks to God."

Sarah's lips curved. "Keep enough of your fortune to pay the village carpenter. I've asked him to make a bed for the baby."

Inevitably, they both became calmer with time. Sarah insisted that Joseph go to his meetings of the Sanhedrin until the Festival of Lights. After that she would want him with her.

And, as the weight of the baby increased, he insisted that she bring the midwife's daughter from the village to live in the house with them to prevent Sarah from doing too much.

He forbade her going to see the lights in the village when the Festival came. Sarah was glad to obey. She was *very* big with child, she laughed, and quite black and blue inside, she was sure. "Isaac is going to need discipline. He likes to kick people."

Then the waiting began. Joseph brought the midwife up to join her daughter, even though the two of them, plus the regular cook-housekeeper, and visits from Amos' and Caleb's wives and daughters crowded the little house to overflowing every day.

Joseph and Antiochus put on two cloaks for warmth and sat in the courtyard in the thin rain, drinking more wine than they should, talking about past adventures to keep their minds off the present one, in which they had no role.

At last it started. The midwife came to the door of the house and flapped a towel at them. "Go away. Go to Amos' house. Tell his wife, Rachel, she can come, but you two stay there until you're sent for. You, Joseph, don't you get drunk. Sarah's going to want a sweetmouthed kiss when it's over, not a gust of sour wine smell."

"I'm going crazy," Joseph moaned.

Amos wasn't overly sympathetic. "I was the same way with the first one. But then I got used to it. It always seems longer than it really is."

Darkness came. Joseph could see the lamplit windows of his house in the distance. He imagined terrible screams, even though he knew he was too far away to hear anything.

The sky had just begun to take on the gray lightlessness of predawn when Amos' wife, Rachel, came home. "Sarah is fine," she said immediately. "She's tired. So am I, for that matter. But everything was perfectly normal—"

Joseph was running, Antiochus at his heels.

"You have a beautiful daughter," Rachel shouted at their backs.

In the lamplight Sarah's radiant happiness was like a glow of purest gold. She was holding a tiny, bald, mottled, sleeping creature in her arms.

"Shhh," she whispered. "She just fell asleep. Come and look, Joseph. The tiny fingernails. And toenails. And her ears. And the little nose. And the dimples in her elbows. Isn't she beautiful? She's perfect."

Joseph was afraid to touch such fragile miniature perfection. Sarah teased him. "Coward. Take her hand." Joseph put one finger out, touched the wrinkled palm, and four tiny fingers grasped his own. His eyes met Sarah's; love joined the mother and father and poured from them onto their infant child.

"Enough of that," the midwife scolded. "Do you want her to catch a chill? Let me get her swaddling bands around her, and a blanket." She opened the baby's fingers, lifted her with expert hands from Sarah's embrace and bustled over to the table in the corner where the wide strips of clean, warmed linen were stacked. Wrapped snugly around side-by-side legs, and torso, they would ensure that an infant grow straight-spined, with no bowed knees or twisted feet.

While she wound the bands around the baby's legs and chest, she continued to fuss. "Joseph, go away now. Sarah needs to rest. Sarah, you lie down and go to sleep this minute. You—slave man—what's your name—you draw the curtains over that window. The sun's coming up."

*   *

"Don't take her away," Sarah begged. "I want to hold her."

"And so you will," the midwife said. "After she's washed and has fresh bands. Whew! Come here, little mess." She took the baby and bustled off to the kitchen.

Sarah smiled at Joseph. He took her hand in his, returned her smile. They were isolated from the world, wrapped in happiness.

Both of them were endlessly fascinated by the baby, whether she was sleeping or awake.

"Are you sure you didn't want a boy?" Sarah asked for the fiftieth time.

"I wanted another Sarah, and that's what you gave me," he replied, as he always did. He meant it with all his heart.

Sarah's brow creased. "We haven't even named her. I always called her Isaac before she was born, but I don't think that will do." She giggled at Joseph's expression. Then she became serious. "I'd like to name her Helena. Your mother was very dear to me."

Joseph said he'd like that. "It's a pretty name for a pretty girl."

"Blind man! Beautiful, not pretty."

"Beautiful," said Joseph obediently. "As soon as she grows some hair."

Sarah hit him. He pretended to be injured, although the blow had been barely a touch.

Then the midwife returned, with a fresh, tightly wrapped, howling package. "Someone's hungry."

Sarah held out eager arms. "Open me," she said to Joseph. The midwife turned away. She'd never heard of a man watching a baby nurse. She considered it indecent.

Joseph spread Sarah's gown apart. The tiny, greedy mouth and intense concentration of the baby were astonishing.

Sarah sighed with contentment. "It's wonderful. I feel so important. You know, Joseph, there are all sorts of extra benefits to motherhood. I was always embarrassed that my breasts were so small. But they're nice and big now, thanks to Helena."

The midwife hustled out of the room. She'd never been so shocked in her life. Women talked about such things, yes, but never to their husbands!

Helena was six days old, sucking noisily, and Sarah was smiling at Joseph, sharing the marvel. Then, in a nightmarish instant, he became aware of the seemingly transparent luminous quality of Sarah's skin. He'd seen that before. In Berenice.

Sarah read his eyes. "Yes, my dearest," she said in a calm, loving tone. "I didn't want to tell you. I'm getting weaker every day."

"No!" Joseph cried out.

Helena jerked, her mouth lost Sarah's nipple, and she started to whimper. Sarah guided the tiny mouth back to its food.

"That's a perfect way for you to see what you have to do, Joseph. You cannot let my death make you forget our child. She'll need you. Rachel knows of a wet nurse, but that's only milk. You'll have to give her love from both of us. You'll be father and mother. Promise me, Joseph."

It was the only thing he could do for the woman he loved more than life itself. "I will," he said hoarsely.

"I know you will," Sarah said. "Take the other one, Greedy." She shifted Helena to her other breast. Then she looked at Joseph.

"I'm sorry, my love. I hate to leave you, too. When it hurts terribly, think of this, Joseph. I do. You have given me everything I ever longed for, ever since we were children. See—I'm wearing my necklace. It will go to Helena, who is the best gift of all, the only thing that I lacked. Joseph, I will die happy. If I had lived for a hundred more years—without having a baby—I would have died feeling I had missed the one thing that mattered."

* * *

Sarah lived for another three days. On the final one, she was so weak that Joseph held her in the bend of his left arm while his right arm held Helena to her breast. Sarah's bliss shone through her colorless skin like a flame.

And then, later, by lamplight, her flame faded and was suddenly gone. Her eyes were open, but lifeless. Milk seeped from her breasts.

Joseph choked. He gently closed her eyes, and pulled the coverlet up over the spreading wetness on her gown. Following her earlier request to him, he removed the lapis flowers that circled her white throat. It was the last favor he would ever be able to perform.

He bowed his head, touching his forehead to the bedside, and his shoulders heaved with the sobs he was holding in his throat. He held the blue stone flowers to his lips.

"We'll have to get the wet nurse as soon as dawn lights the path," whispered the midwife's daughter.

"Who's going to tell him that the baby's legs don't move?" said her mother. "At least Sarah never had to know. That's a blessing."

III

HIS
MISSION

CHAPTER FIFTY-TWO

IT WAS ANTIOCHUS WHO TOLD JOSEPH. HE FOUND HIM, BROKEN, on the bench in the courtyard. "Get yourself together, man," Joseph's friend shouted at him. "We've got to find a doctor."

The wet nurse had told Antiochus. Sitting outside in the spring morning with Helena at her breast, she'd startled him when she spoke, because he hadn't noticed her.

"Shame about the baby's legs, don't you think?" said the girl in a friendly way.

When he asked what she meant, she showed him. Helena's swaddling clothes were loose, ready to be changed. Her little legs were perfectly formed, but they hung, useless and limp, over the nurse's arm.

Antiochus grabbed the girl's wrist and hauled her after him while he searched for Joseph. Instinct kept her other arm crooked to cradle the baby at her breast.

"*Joseph.*"

"No doctor, Antiochus. She's dead."

"Joseph, look. It's Sarah's child that needs the doctor. The fool midwife didn't send for one."

Joseph gaped, disbelieving. He lifted one of Helena's legs. It was warm, living. And yet lifeless. His mind worked rapidly. His pain would have to wait. "Caesarea," he said. "The roads are all mud to Jerusalem. We can get horses and a wagon at Joppa for the paved road. Hurry." He looked at the girl who was holding Sarah's child. "Wrap her warmly. Here. Use my cloak, it will cover both of you." He flung the cloak over her shoulders.

The girl pulled herself free of Antiochus' grip. "What are you going on about? I'm not going anywhere."

"Yes you are. My child needs food."

She threw Joseph's cloak on the ground. "So does mine, at home."

"Bring her along, Antiochus. Wrap them well."

The girl backed away. She bent quickly, put Helena on Joseph's cloak. "Leave me alone. Don't you dare put a hand on me. I'm not going to let my son starve while I feed a cripple. Find yourself another nurse. Or a goat." She ran toward the path to the village as if a hundred devils were chasing her.

"Get a goat, Antiochus. I'll carry Helena." Joseph stooped beside his little girl and folded the cloak carefully around her tiny form. She was sleeping, milky bubbles on her lips.

The baby was so small, she seemed to weigh almost nothing. Joseph looked down at the helpless damaged child, and he was more frightened than ever in his entire life. There was nothing he could do. Except find someone to cure whatever was wrong with her. He did not worry about Sarah's funeral. He knew what she would want him to care about.

In Caesarea the almond trees were clouds of blossoms, but Joseph and Antiochus noticed neither their beauty nor the intoxicating scent of spring, early come by the waters of the sea. Antiochus drove the horses mercilessly, and their wagon careened along the streets to the arena. Joseph was holding Helena in his right arm. His left hand held on to the side of the cart. The baby was crying, had been crying for so long that her wails had subsided to a whimper. Almost the same sound was coming from the tethered goat in the rear of the wagon.

There were games going on at the arena. They could hear the shouting and high-pitched screaming of the crowd as they approached. The wagon had not quite stopped when Joseph jumped over the goat and down onto the road. He pushed through the door, as he had done before. The same guard was there, but he was standing this time, in full uniform.

"Here you. Stop!"

Joseph did not slow his pace. He took a small sack of money from his belt and threw it at the man as he passed him. "Doctor," he said and hurried along the corridor.

This time the doctor wasn't alone. Another man stood behind him, looking down at a third man who was stretched out on a table in the center of the room, groaning. His hands were on his belly, just below the waist, red with blood. More blood stained the shiny loops of intestine he was pressing against. A gaping, bleeding wound in his belly had set them free.

"Drink this." The man beside the doctor raised the gladiator's head and held a cup to his lips. "No, all of it. It will deaden the pain while you're being sewn up. Drain the cup."

"Doctor," Joseph said loudly. "I need your help."

"Go away, man. I'm busy."

"Sew him up later. I need you now "

The second man looked at Joseph. His gray eyes narrowed. "What have you got? The noise sounds like a baby."

"It is. It's my little daughter, and there's something wrong with her."

The gray-eyed man laughed. "She's hungry, man. Where's your wife to feed her?"

"My wife died last night."

"Well, your baby won't starve to death before we finish here. Wait outside."

Antiochus came in as the man was speaking. Joseph thrust the cloak-wrapped baby into his arms, then stalked over to the doctor. "I need help now. The gladiator can wait. I'll buy him and cut his throat if I have to, to get him out of the way so you can look at my baby."

"No need for that," the doctor said. "As soon as the drug works, this man will be dead. There was no way to save him."

The second man lifted the gladiator's eyelids, then nodded. He picked up a gong and hammer and sounded a loud summons.

Four men in matching red-bordered blue tunics hurried into the room, picked up the body, and carried it out. Blood made a thin trail behind them.

"Put your baby on the table," the doctor ordered. "We'll have to hurry. The battle against the lions always gives me a lot of sewing to do."

Joseph looked with disgust at the blood-pooled table. "I won't put my baby in that."

"Then you can put her and yourself out in the street."

Antiochus mopped ineffectually at the blood with the sleeve of his coat. Then he lay Helena, wrapped in Joseph's cloak, on the center of the table. When he opened the cloak's folds, the doctor stepped back. "It's an infant. I don't doctor infants."

Helena waved tiny fists and cried. Loudly, again. Her mouth was moving, searching for food.

The gray-eyed man laughed. "She needs a breast, not a doctor. You're wasting our time, there's nothing wrong with her."

"Her legs," said Antiochus.

The mocking laughter suddenly stopped. The doctor's helper put his strong hands on Helena's limp legs. His touch was firm, but gentle. His fingers moved rapidly, feeling the little knees and ankles, the flesh. He drew a fingernail across the sole of one foot. Then the other.

He turned his dark curly head toward the doctor. "No reflexes. There's nothing to be done."

Joseph said, "I will not believe that. Where do I find a better doctor?"

The gray eyes narrowed, chilled. "Don't be a fool, man. You love this baby, do you? Then feed her. Do what you can. You cannot cure where there is no illness."

"What do you mean? 'No illness'?"

A gong sounded from outside the door.

"Get out," ordered the doctor. "They're bringing in an injured man. That's who I'm here to help, not your crippled child."

Joseph threw his arms up. "Not crippled, no. No! You're wrong."

Antiochus wrapped the cloak around Helena. It was bloodstained. "Joseph," he said, "*Joseph*. The man is wrong about her legs but he's right about her hunger. Let's feed her first, then we'll find another doctor."

Joseph swung his head from side to side. "I don't know what to do." His words were quiet. Despairing.

Antiochus walked through the door holding Helena. Joseph started to follow him, but a strong hand closed around his arm. "Come on, man. I'll help you." It was the gray-eyed man. "You're no good to that innocent little creature."

Joseph jerked his arm away. "I handle my own problems."

"The problem isn't yours; it's your child's. Will your pride fill her belly?"

Joseph looked into his gray eyes. "Do you know what to do?" Humility was in his tone.

"I know who does. I'll take you there."

"My name is Homer," said the man with the gray eyes. "Where's your friend?"

Joseph pointed toward the wagon. Antiochus was sitting

on a bench beside it, trying to quiet Helena, rocking her in his arms and making a wordless tune.

"A goat," said Homer. "Maybe you're not as stupid as you seem to be."

The tavern that Homer led them to was nearly empty. It would fill rapidly when the games ended.

The dried-up waspish woman near the door was the owner of the place. Homer walked over to her and whispered in her ear.

She frowned, listening to him. Then she scowled at Joseph and Antiochus. "Where is the goat? Bring it to the back. The baby, too. Where did you leave it?"

Antiochus held out his arms. Helena had fallen asleep again, exhausted by crying. She was hidden in the thick folds of Joseph's cloak.

The sour old woman named Miriam marched over to Antiochus. She opened the folds that hid Helena. "Shhh," she moaned softly. "Such a new one. Poor little thing." Her hands slid under Helena, waking her, and the baby started to cry. "Wet, too," Miriam crooned. "What do these simpleton men know about what a girl's entitled to, eh?"

She glared at Joseph. "And where is the goat? Are you deaf, old man?" Her words had a knife edge. Then became a lullaby as she lifted Helena in her arms. "A little warm wash and a warm blanket and some warm milk will make you a happy girl, you'll see."

She was totally correct. An hour later she was sitting with Helena in her lap, sleepily sucking still at the twisted linen wick Miriam had used to feed her diluted goat's milk. The three men sat on the opposite side of a table, facing her, drinking watered wine. Outside the door people were knocking, demanding entrance. Miriam had closed and bolted it.

They talked for hours. That is, Miriam, Homer, and Antiochus talked. Joseph nodded occasionally, when his agreement was required, and he called on all his self-discipline to force himself to listen to what the others were saying. But he was unable to believe any of it was true: Sarah's death, Helena's helplessness, his ignorance, and—above all the rest—the lifelessness of Sarah's baby's legs.

He heard Miriam guarantee to find a wet nurse.

He heard the details of Homer's profession. He was a trainer for the games. He kept the boxers, gladiators, wrestlers in top condition, with specialized exercise and massage.

He heard Homer argue against leaving a demanding but well-paid post to take care of an infant, like some kind of nursemaid instead of a man working with other men.

He heard him agree, eventually, with an admission that Helena's condition interested him. He'd made only a cursory examination but it felt as if her bones were properly formed and the muscle tissue in place. He could manipulate the legs, keep the muscles from atrophy, help them develop. And try to find out why they were not working.

He heard Antiochus tell the story of Sarah. It did not hurt him to hear her name. His heart was dead.

He nodded when Homer named the amount of his wages.

He nodded when Miriam ordered him to provide his child with a safe, comfortable home and delay racing around after doctors until she was older and not so delicate.

He nodded when Miriam asked him sharply if he loved Helena. He had to. He had promised Sarah.

Dosha was a young, sturdy, blond slave girl, captured from one of the German tribes. She'd been raped by Roman soldiers, the slave master who'd bought her, other slaves in the group that had been sent to Damascus, the slave trader who had bought her there. By one of them she had started a child. When it was born dead, she was wildly gratified, believing that her gods had destroyed a particle of the rapist that had fathered it.

She cared nothing for the baby she was bought to nurse.

It mattered only because its avid mouth relieved the painful pressure of the milk in her big breasts.

Helena was fifteen days old when the strangely assorted group left Caesarea. She rode with Dosha in a curtained, cushioned litter. Homer stopped it many times a day to unbind Helena from her swaddling and move her legs, then massage them.

He rode in a wagon packed with his possessions. Antiochus drove the four donkeys that pulled it.

Joseph rode a horse, amid the six guards, also on horseback, that he'd hired to protect them on the long, slow trip to Jericho.

The villa there had a pool. Homer needed one for Helena's exercises.

Joseph closed out all thoughts of what that house had been built for—the happiness he and Sarah were going to share. He wasn't strong enough to stand the torment those thoughts contained.

Instead he concentrated on the litany of remembered sins: Holy Days without sacrifices, Sabbaths unobserved, failure to honor his father, breaking fast on the Day of Atonement . . . What had happened to Sarah's baby must be a punishment for his sins. Nothing else made sense.

He would spend the rest of his life striving to atone, to obey the Law without failure or excuses for nonobservance.

And he would find a cure for Sarah's child. For Sarah's sake.

CHAPTER FIFTY-THREE

THE HOUSE AT JERICHO WAS PERFECT FOR HOMER'S PUR-poses. "If I had known my new employer was the kind of man who had a full Roman bath complex in his home, I'd have named a much higher wage."

He was speaking to Antiochus. The Galatian said only, "You are caring for the daughter of a very important man," then turned away. He did not like the Greek trainer. Homer, he believed, regarded Helena only as a specimen, not as a child.

He detested Dosha for much the same reason. To her Helena was only a mouth that had to be fed. There was no affection in Dosha's embrace when she held the baby to her breast.

He made allowances for Joseph's coldness. He knew that Joseph was walled in, unable to feel any emotion for fear of the agony that was waiting to overcome him if the walls were lowered.

Antiochus himself showered Helena with love, flooded her with attention and affection whenever he could get to her. Even though Homer's massages and movements of her legs occupied most of the minutes that she was awake, Antiochus always managed a few occasions every day when he could hold her, rock her, talk to her, sing to her. Her wobbling milky smiles broke his heart, because they were so innocent and so vulnerable. He desperately wanted her to remain happy and smiling forever, but he knew that the day had to come when she would discover that her legs had no strength.

Joseph was often away from the house and the lush oasis city in the desert. He walked the winding narrow road that climbed the hills that rose to the heights on which Jerusalem was built, always looking down at the stony path, oblivious to the rapid advance of spring with its bounty of wild flowers and warming sun.

There were the Sanhedrin meetings, and the messages about business, and always the sacrifices and prayers at the Temple. His Jerusalem house was kept fully staffed—Antiochus bought more slaves for the Jericho house—and he stayed there when he was in the city. He didn't give dinners now, or accept invitations for them. He wanted to be left alone behind his walls.

Abigail would not permit it. She marched into his house, waving off the protestations of the door guard, and found Joseph in the showy, never-used library.

"Joseph." He looked up from the open scroll in front of him. His eyes were dull, and he did not greet his aunt. "Joseph," said Abigail in a stern voice. "You have not come to see me, you have not been to Arimathea, you are behaving very badly. It will not do."

"Abigail, I do not want to offend you. But I do not want to see you. Please go away."

"I will not. When there is sorrow, a man needs his family. Joseph, I can understand your grief. I know what Sarah meant to you. I know, also, about the baby's affliction. These are hard blows. But life goes on. You cannot hide from it. There are things you have to do. All the village and many of the family at Arimathea are appalled that you left the way you did. It's shocking that you did not even take part in Sarah's funeral. And you terrified the girl who was nursing the baby. You owe them an apology. They are your people, Joseph."

"No, they are not. Arimathea is nothing to me."

"Joseph!" Abigail stared, as if she were looking at a complete stranger. Anger made her pale. "Your family. Amos. Caleb. Their wives and children. Aaron has a son now, Joseph. Did you know? Do you care?"

"No."

Abigail shuddered. This was monstrous. "You must be possessed by a devil. Isn't there anything you care about?"

"Yes. I care about finding a cure for Sarah's baby."

Abigail walked to Joseph. She slapped his face with all the strength she could summon. "Joseph of Arimathea, that poor baby is *your* child. Not Sarah's alone."

She left him there, sitting where she had found him. The marks of her fingers were red on his cheek. Joseph bent his head to read the scroll. When he was sure that it did not hold the answer for which he was searching, he threw it onto the floor with the others he'd already discarded.

He intended to take Sarah's baby to Alexandria after the Holy Days of spring were past. The best doctors were there. The answer, the cure, must be somewhere in the many thousand scrolls in the great library. All the world's knowledge was contained there.

Until it was time to leave, he would continue to look through the miscellany that Herod's finishers had put into the library in his house. He would leave no possibility unexplored.

He had succeeded at every goal he'd set in his entire life. He was determined to succeed this time, too. Unswerving determination and hard work always overcame challenges, he'd proved that. Now he would prove it again.

On Passover Eve Joseph sacrificed the lamb required by the Law and took it to his house in Jerusalem to be roasted whole. He ate of it the following day, with bitter herbs and unleavened bread, according to the Law. And burned all that he had not eaten, on the next morning, as the Law dictated. For the remainder of the week he forced himself to eat unleavened bread. He did not like the heavy flat rounds of floury dough. In earlier years he'd found it easy enough to avoid bread altogether since the Law forbade leaven. But now he made himself eat the unleavened. He was not going to evade any of God's laws, ever again.

The High Holy Festival of Shavuot was six weeks away. That gave Joseph ample time to go to Caesarea and make sure that the instructions he'd sent by messenger were being carried out to his satisfaction.

They were. The *Phoenix* had been brought from its warehouse and thoroughly cleaned, then checked for soundness of all its planking and decks. "Take away all the silks," Joseph told the ship outfitter. "Replace them with plain linen."

Sarah's child was not going to sea in a bordello.

He had barely time to hire a crew before he had to leave for Jerusalem and the meeting of the Sanhedrin. He ordered them to begin rowing and sailing, short daily trips, to become accustomed to the idiosyncrasies of handling that each ship possessed. "Make them the best crew in the entire Mediterranean," he said to Sidonus, the Phoenician captain he had hired. "Replace any man who is not perfect with one who is. Wages for the final crew will be three times normal."

After the Sanhedrin, he went back to Jericho. In four weeks, he told Antiochus, they would be leaving for Alexandria. "The cure will be there."

He told Homer about the departure, too. "Do not alarm yourself," Joseph added. "There are deep tubs for bathing on board. Tell Antiochus what oils and unguents you will need to supply you for three months."

The time allotted for the voyage wasn't generous, but he was going to be back in Jerusalem for Yom Kippur. It was not a High Holy Day, but it was one of the festivals ordered by the Law. And it was the beginning of a New Year. A better one, please God.

He sacrificed four sheep as well as offering the requisite two loaves of leavened bread for Shavuot.

Dosha was as stolid and silent as usual on the trip to Caesarea and on the ship. Homer let out a low whistle when he saw the luxurious vessel. Helena made a burbling, chirping sound. She was nearly five months old now, with a soft cap of dark tendrils and a repertoire of happy sounds, usually accompanied by soft, enthusiastic clapping hands.

Antiochus observed with a heavy heart that Joseph seemed unaware of his daughter's growth or of the almost singing noises she made. He was trying to teach her the syllables *Ab-ba*, Aramaic for "Father." Perhaps when she learned to say "Father," her father would learn to be one.

He saw the old Arimathea eagle mounted on the prow in place of the jeweled phoenix and decided to view it as a hopeful sign. The *Eagle* had always been the leading ship in Joseph's fleet.

Joseph had sent a letter to Alexander, the Customs Director, and his request was successfully executed by his friend. Alexander was notified as soon as the *Eagle* passed the lighthouse, and he was waiting to meet them at the special mooring Joseph had requested. It was a private area of the harbor formerly reserved for royalty. They would use the *Eagle* as living quarters, Joseph informed his party. Steps led from their mooring up to the former palace of Cleopatra and the great library, the Mouseion.

"My dear friend," Alexander boomed, "I am as always overjoyed to see you, even though the occasion for your visit is such a sad one. Where is the unfortunate little one? Ah, there. What a lovely baby! Oh, my, yes, what an enchanting smile. Don't worry, little one. Your father has brought you to the home of wisdom, where all ills are remedied."

Joseph's unresponsiveness made Alexander look worriedly at Antiochus, who shook his head slightly, confirming Alexander's impression. It was useless to try and evoke the Joseph he knew from this grim man.

"I am grateful to you, Alexander," Joseph said stiffly. "For the mooring and for coming to greet us. Do you have the name of the doctor for me?"

"Four of them, Joseph. World famous they are." Alexander made no effort at jollity, or even friendship. He gave Joseph a sheet of papyrus, then said his goodbyes. His eyes brushed Antiochus'. The Galatian nodded. Yes, he'd come later to tell Alexander all that he could about Joseph.

All of the doctors were fascinated by Helena's condition. They asked Homer numerous questions, moved the little legs themselves, felt the rest of Helena's body, made her tired and fretful.

Each prescribed a different medicine. "To activate the humors" . . . "To fortify the blood" . . . "To stimulate the muscles" . . . "To energize the mind's fluids that control the appendage apparatus."

One made the baby listless; the second made her restless and unable to sleep; the third made her violently ill, with hours of vomiting, until she was ejecting a thin, bloodstreaked fluid.

Antiochus begged Joseph not to insist that she be given the fourth nostrum. Joseph looked at the tortured little girl, and his eyes showed the guilty torment he was feeling. But they hardened. "The last may be the cure. Give her time to recover, then administer it." And he turned away, to return to the library, where he questioned all the scholars there for hours, no matter what field of study they might be pursuing.

Helena rejected Dosha's breast. Homer rubbed her legs with balm, then stroked her back and shoulders with gentle, oiled fingers to soothe her. She looked at him with the puzzled hurt of a small animal beaten by the people it trusted, and he wept. "I am sorry, little one, forgive me, brave little Helena."

At that moment Antiochus began to change his attitude toward the Greek expert in the working of the body. "You love her," he said to Homer.

The handsome younger man looked at Helena. His skillful fingers smoothed the lines of pain from her tiny forehead. "She has broken my heart," Homer said, "and made a home within it for herself. I want her to be well, to have the freedom and happiness of children who can run and play."

When the fourth doctor's medicine, given at half the dosage ordered, put Helena into a cold-skinned coma for hours, Antiochus and Homer had to combine their strengths to hold Joseph down and bind him with rope. He'd sworn to kill the man.

The medical men—the three Joseph consented to see again—made up unguents next, to be massaged into the inert limbs.

When they failed, the doctors advised sacrifice and prayers at the great Temple of Semiramis in the center of Alexandria. "I am a Jew. I do not worship pagan gods," Joseph replied with hatred. They had failed him, and now they were insulting him and his One God, Who was alone able to remove this punishment for his sins.

When Alexander offered a barge to Memphis and the temple of the miracle-working god Imhotep, Joseph shouted abuse at the man who had been his friend.

"Joseph, Joseph," Alexander said soothingly, "remember that I also am a Jew. Imhotep was a man, a man of brilliance that has never been equaled. He lived and died, as men do, thousands of years ago. The Egyptians named him a god, as the Romans named Augustus a god. This is reverence for accomplishment, Joseph, not religion.

"Imhotep was architect, astrologer, physician to the Pharaoh. His feats have become legend. People say that some emanation of him still exits in the sanctuary dedicated to him. What harm can it do to try a visit there? There are mysteries beyond the understanding of men. This is no blasphemy."

Joseph agreed. He had to try. He had been so sure that Alexandria's men of learning would have the answer he sought. Now he had discovered that they were as helpless as he was. He was shattered and confused.

His heart was confused, too. He had seen Helena's hurt, seen her close to death. Because of him. He really understood, for the first time, that he was entrusted with a living creature, capable of pain and emotion.

As the barge moved slowly through the Nile's delta, the countryside stretched away from view on all sides, flat and shimmering with a light that was water reflecting the rays of sun. It was mysteriously beautiful and unworldly. Antiochus began to feel a quivering hopefulness. Perhaps, in a land like this, the spirit of ancient genius might endure through the centuries, to bring about wonders that man could not understand.

The temple to Imhotep was at the ancient city of Memphis. It rested on the bank of the great river, facing, on the opposite bank, the awesome pyramids of ancient Pharaohs.

Petitioners for release from sickness and pain were given thin woven mats and instructed to burn their petitions, together with the special incense sold them by the temple guards, then sleep on their mats on the marble floor of the temple, with their hearts and minds open to receive the visitation of the god.

Joseph brought great quantities of incense, named his petition—the healing of Helena's legs—and took the thin strips of papyrus on which a guard had written in symbols he could not understand.

Helena, in Homer's arms, chortled and made singing sounds to the paintings on the temple's interior walls. She reached out and touched the brightly colored birds and grasses, boats and crocodiles, fish and men portrayed, talking to them in her language that was no language any adult could understand.

"Maybe the paintings know what she was saying to them," Homer said. "I certainly didn't."

The petitioner was supposed to sleep, and dream, and receive an answer to his petition in his dream. But Joseph could not sleep. He stared at the clean, clear, rational yet wonderful geometry of the white stone-clad pyramids. They seemed so near in the pure dry night air, shining in the darkness around them, lit by the great burning stars that seemed so close to the sleeping land and river beneath them.

The mysterious strangeness awakened a hope in him. It grew as he waited for dawn. When red-golden light slowly penetrated the temple's darkness, he stood and walked softly to where Helena was sleeping beside Dosha.

But Helena was awake, her eyes moving from painted bird to painted fish as the light brought their colors to life. She saw Joseph's face, bent over her, and she smiled, holding her arms out to him. He picked her up and carried her to meet the sunrise. Beside the rose and gold reflecting river, he unwrapped her bindings, setting her legs free to move. Helena gurgled and spoke her private words of pleasure.

The sky had changed to gold. It extinguished the golden stars, gave bright clarity to the air, to the mighty pyramids, to the dreadful limpness of Helena's little legs.

Joseph saw the happy, smiling delight on the face of his innocent crippled child, and the thick cold walls that had protected him were torn asunder to admit pain greater than fire. He had not the strength to shout, to release the agony within his heart in brute-like howls. He could only hold the small warm body close to his heart and weep with despair.

The early light made rainbows in the prisms of Joseph's tears. Helena reached for them with fat little fingers, laughing when she felt the moisture. "Ab-ba," she said, "ab-ba-ab-ba-ba-ab-ba-ba."

CHAPTER FIFTY-FOUR

IT WAS SEPTEMBER WHEN THE *Eagle* REACHED CAESAREA. Helena was eight months old, the joy and the heartbreak of Joseph's life. For he was alive again, with all the pain that living brings, as well as all its marvels.

There was just enough time for him to take her home, with the others, to Jericho, and to return by himself to Jerusalem for the Temple ceremonies on the first day of the New Year, with its promise of new beginnings.

He sacrificed each day at the Temple and prayed, readying himself for the Day of Atonement, when his sins, together with those of all other Jews, might be forgiven by God and driven into the desert and destruction in the symbolic reality of the scapegoat.

Helena's affliction, he believed, was the manifestation of God's punishment for his sins. When he had atoned for those sins, when they were forgiven and driven out, he could hope that she would be cured.

The Law required fasting on the day preceding the Day of Atonement. Joseph fasted, on his knees, praying throughout the night and the day.

He held his breath each time the High Priest entered the Holy of Holies to sacrifice, fearful that the Almighty would

words came too quickly, her emotion was too

arely spoken at all during all the months, all the
es." "No." "Baby." "Hungry." "Sleep." Those
were her total vocabulary. And they were al-
n in a dull drone.

voice rose and fell, on and on without stopping.
ere fixed on Antiochus' face. They were hot
ng.

ed at last that she was speaking Celtic. The ac-
fferent, many words were strange to him. But he
out many more. Questions. Who was he? What
be? What was the song? She asked them over
ain.

us took Helena from Dosha. Luckily the baby
satiated. He held her to his shoulder, rubbing
he'd seen Dosha do until the shockingly loud
d.

inued to rub Helena's back, and he talked to
e Celtic he knew, a mixture of Galatia and Bele-

ke too, with fervor. He had to ask her often to
, to repeat what she'd just said.

came upon them, stopping some distance away.
hardly believe what he was seeing. Dosha—ani-
iling, ecstatic.

ng that day Helena was always given music with
gs. Little Celtic songs that, said Dosha, all babies
ntry learned with their mother's milk.
us often played accompaniment, after the harp
. And he often joined Dosha in song.
showed no reaction; she seemed to hear only the
tomach sang: Fill me.

ny season and its cold winds caught Joseph by
very time he went up from Jericho to Jerusalem.
that surrounded Jericho seemed to draw in the

reject the sacrifice and with it his, Joseph's, repentance for
his sins. Three times the High Priest passed behind the curtain and through the door. Three times he came out again,
the sacrifice being acceptable to God. Then he magically
transferred the sins of men, including Joseph, to the sacrificial goat. When the news of its death was received at the
Temple, Joseph cheered, with those around him, until his
throat was raw.

He hurried to Jericho, almost running. Several times he
stumbled on the rocky path and fell, but he didn't care. He
wanted to see for himself the blessings of God's forgiveness, the motion of his baby's legs.

Helena was floating in the heated water of the bath, supported by the ring of inflated lambs' bladders that Homer
had devised for her. She loved to play in the water, splashing, pushing herself in circles with her hands, talking her
special talk to the tiny waves she made with her splashing.
"Abba!" she said when Joseph appeared. She splashed him
a welcome.

He jumped into the pool, making a greater splash that delighted Helena. Under the water he moved her legs, demonstrating what he thought she could do now.

But she could not.

The next Festival was the High Holy Celebration of Succoth, the Feast of Booths, less than a week away. Joseph
gathered palm fronds from the date trees near the villa, and
myrtle from the shrubs that bordered the garden. Willow he
cut from the growth on the steep bank of the wadi, the
stream that ran beside his property.

He carried them all to Jerusalem, with Dosha and Helena, in a cart pulled by a donkey. Antiochus and Homer
walked alongside with him.

Helena was delighted with the booth he and the other
men built in the garden of the Jerusalem house. She pulled
leaves from the myrtle branches and put them in her mouth
until Antiochus noticed what she was doing and took them

away. She could sit alone now, and pushed herself up whenever she was laid on a mat to rest.

After taking part in the Temple celebrations, Joseph went back to his house every day of the week-long Festival, to be with his daughter on these Holy Days and to prepare himself for what he knew he must do.

When Succoth ended, he carried Helena to Abigail's house so that the family could begin to know her. He had sent a message to Aaron, too, but he had not replied. After the visit Joseph took the cart and donkey again and carried his daughter to her birthplace, and the birthplace of her mother and father. Arimathea.

He visited the villagers first. Abigail was right, he saw at once. Everyone was angry and disapproving, because he had not been at Sarah's funeral. But when they saw Helena, his surpassing devotion to her, and the pitiable reality of her condition, their anger became compassion. Joseph was deeply moved by the generosity of these close-to-the-earth people. They knew, without discussion or philosophizing, what truly mattered in life. It was love.

He had the courage now to go up to the farms, to his family, to the house where he had been with Sarah.

Unthinking anger filled his heart when he saw that someone was living in the little house. It's Sarah's, he thought. No one should touch it.

Then his mind cleared. Shelter was for people, not for memories. Amos' sons were grown men now, Caleb's were, too. There was more need for homes where new families could live and grow.

Joseph went to make his peace with all of them. They were not as immediately compassionate as the villagers, but they were as kind and sympathetic as was in their natures.

Rachel, Amos' wife, had kept Sarah's things for him. Joseph nearly broke down when he saw them. There were so few. The betrothal necklace he'd given her so many years ago, her dresses and hairpins from Belerion, her harp.

"You keep them, Rachel. I ___ member her."

"Your daughter should ha___ Joseph. She won't have any m___

Of course Rachel was rig___ thanked her. Then he carried ___ needed to have her with him ___ "Your mother's bones are in th___ hending little girl. "Your gra___ great-grandmother's. You f___ women, Helena. You, too, will ___ way. You may have to be the ___ even consider such a thing nov___ left for us to see."

Helena pulled his beard, laugh___

Antiochus lifted Sarah's ha___ strings. It was hideously out of t___ down. "Forgive me, Helena. I v___ laby your mother played to you ___ forgotten. Let me try to rememb___ sing them now, we'll have the ha___

"It certainly is flattering that y___ so little time with you that I'd be ___ your chirps and smiles for me."

Helena was concentrating total___ Dosha held Helena firmly, whil___ into the distance. It was depress___ that the woman cared nothing fo___ Helena didn't seem to mind. She ___ finished with a look of satisfacti___ face.

Antiochus hummed, then bega___ song. "From the cliffe they fell, t___ was alarming.

Dosha looked at him, her eyes ___

speak. The___
strong.

She had ___
travels. "___
few word___
ways spok___

Now he___
Her eyes ___
with plea___

He real___
cent was ___
could mak___
was his t___
and over ___

Antioc___
was near___
her back ___
burp erup___

He co___
Dosha in___
rion.

She sp___
slow dow___

Josepl___
He coul___
mated, s___

Begin___
her feed___
in her c___

Antio___
was tun___

Hele___
song he___

The ___
surprise___
The de___

rains and warm the winds before they could reach the oasis.
It was balm to Joseph's worries that at least he could give
Helena this much.

As they'd done the year before, Joseph's party left for
Caesarea immediately following Shavuot. The *Eagle* was
ready, and they sailed at once for Puteoli. Joseph had
learned about a doctor in Rome. Aulus Cornelius Celsus
was on his way to becoming the most famous man in the
world. He'd already written eight books about his discoveries and treatments. They were in such demand that a scriptorium with fifty tables had been organized for the sole
purpose of making copies.

CHAPTER FIFTY-FIVE

JOSEPH WOULD NOT BE ABLE TO OBSERVE THE NEW YEAR and the Day of Atonement in the Temple. The voyage to Puteoli would be slow, against the prevailing summer winds. Then, a hundred miles by road to Rome, and how long with the doctor, who could tell?

This was a bitter thing for him. Yes, he knew that Rome's Jews were godly men, that all the Holy Days were celebrated with solemnity and special services in their synagogues. But, as a Sadducee, he had never been able to believe that worship in a synagogue could even begin to equal worship at the Temple. And he was so dedicated to regaining God's favor. He even observed the Sabbath now at sea, something he'd never done in all his regular sailing years. It was a mercy that his captain and crew were Gentiles, or he would have had to risk shipwreck. As it was, he did not labor; even when he saw that the reefing of the great sail needed adjustment, he waited for someone else to observe it and give the orders. It was hard.

Putting his faith in the validity of synagogue worship would be even harder. The synagogue was the world of the Pharisees. However, he would find the faith.

For Joseph had a different, nonreligious faith. Faith in

books. A doctor who wrote books . . . books that other doctors studied. This must be what he'd been searching for. Now Helena would gain the use of her legs. She had devised a shockingly rapid method of locomotion, using her arms and elbows to pull or push the rest of her body across floors, paths, courtyards, any reasonably flat surface. Whenever he saw her scrabble along on her arms and hands, pulling her useless legs behind her, his heart broke again.

Joseph was arranging the hire of vehicles and animals and guards for the long miles from Puteoli to the capital city when a disreputable looking, dirty man edged to his side.

"My crew is filled," he said. Every port had its supply of men like these, usually hopeless drunks, looking for work as a loader or member of the crew.

"Don't say anything," said a quiet voice beside him, "and don't look at me. Joseph, this is Herod Agrippa, and I need your help. Keep on with what you're doing. Meet me later behind the sailmender's shack. I'm going now."

"Thank God you've come!" Herod Agrippa clasped Joseph's hands in his. "I've been hiding in the hills above the harbor, watching for your ship. If you'd not come this year, I don't know what I would have done. You're the only man I can trust."

Laughing, insouciant, impertinent Herod Agrippa was no part of this man. It wasn't the dirt, or the rags, that made the difference. It was the fear. This man was genuinely terrified, frightened for his life.

It was Sejanus, Herod explained. He was gaining more and more power over Tiberius, over Rome, over the Empire.

Tears sprang from Herod's eyes. "Ah, Joseph, he killed Drusus, my oldest, closest friend. Because Drusus was

Tiberius' only son and perhaps he would listen to him. Drusus was trying to warn his father about Sejanus.

"Sejanus is always devious. He seduced Drusus' wife. Livilla is crazy in love with Sejanus. So crazy that she used the poison he gave her to kill Drusus. Slowly, so slowly. He just kept getting weaker and paler every day. There was nothing I could do. Drusus wouldn't believe that his wife would kill him, even when I brought him the eunuch who informed on Livilla, the man who had told me about the poison.

"The eunuch is dead now, too. And I'm next, Joseph. I know it. You've got to smuggle me away. My life isn't safe anymore."

The tale was preposterous, and Herod Agrippa was noted for his tall tales. He was not known as a fool, however. Or a coward. And this man with Joseph now was a cowardly desperate man.

He grabbed the sleeve of Joseph's cloak. "You've got to get me away, Joseph, or I'm a dead man. I managed to get out of Rome, but I left a pile of debts—"

"Don't worry, Herod, I'll pay your debts."

"It's not that. Don't you see? Sejanus will use them as an excuse to arrest me, and then I'll be at his mercy. He knows I know about Drusus. He can't let me go on living."

"Where will you go?"

"The whole Empire is dangerous for me. But my grandfather, King Herod, was a Nabatean. He's admired there, not like in Judea. And the Nabateans are basically nomads. If I can get to relatives there, they can keep me out of sight as long as necessary.

"You could take me to Ascalon. It's so small and even Sejanus can't have guards everywhere. From there I can get to Nabatea."

"All right, Herod Agrippa. But it's going to be tricky. I have to go to Rome, and I don't know how long I'll be there. You'll have to trust my crew. I'll think up some story, they'll say you're one of them. Start right now getting some calluses on your hands. No one with eyes would believe those hands of yours had ever done a day's work. Stay here. I'll be back with my captain, and he'll take over. I've got to go. I hired guards, and they'll wonder where I am."

Joseph really cared for Berenice's son. He'd have to help him. But not if it meant danger to Helena. The trip to Rome was first in his mind.

Like all other traders and shipowners, Joseph had a network of agents, factors, money handlers, warehouse owners, and informants throughout the Empire's major ports and major cities. Fast courier service from Puteoli had requested his business representative to arrange for comfortable living quarters, with servants. The same courier service delivered an order to his information collector to hold himself available for a meeting with Joseph, and to prepare a full report on the physician Celsus.

On the day of arrival, in August, Rome was sweltering under a metallic blue sky and a miasma of unmoving air. The place where Joseph's party would be staying was a large, overpriced luxury apartment in one of the tenements built especially for the wealthy on the Aventine Hill. It was on the second floor, had a balcony with potted trees and—on better days—a breeze from the river. This day there was no breeze, and even in the shade of the trees stifling heat was inescapable. Joseph sat there, brooding, in his tunic, with his feet in a basin of water to cool his blood. No wonder the apartment's owner went away from the city in the summer. He was worrying about whether the famous physician did the same.

When one of the servants announced that he had a visitor, Joseph thought it must be his business representative checking on the acceptability of the apartment. He wasn't prepared for the tall army officer who walked onto the balcony with the swagger of authority.

"Marcus!" Joseph greeted him with surprised pleasure. It

was Berenice's stepson, last seen three years ago at her funeral.

"Joseph of Arimathea?" Marcus looked even more surprised than Joseph had been. "I had no idea it was you." The swagger was gone completely.

Joseph ordered the slave to bring wine. "Come sit down," he urged Marcus. "The shade helps a little. Tell me your news. How's that handsome boy of yours?"

Marcus was visibly upset. He looked almost like the shy young boy Joseph remembered from Berenice's household so many years before. What was he now? Mid-thirties, Joseph supposed, and obviously accustomed to authority, not awkwardness. His uniform proclaimed him a legate, as his father had once been. Why, Joseph wondered, was Marcus here, and what was bothering him?

When they were seated together, sharing the pitcher of wine, Marcus told him. The apartment was owned by the father of his wife, Cornelia. Her parents always spent summers at their country estate.

The manager of the apartment building had hurried to report to Marcus as soon as Joseph and his party took possession. "All he told me," Marcus said, "was that the renter was a Jew. I came to tell you to get out. I had no idea it might be you.

"Joseph"—Marcus leaned toward him urgently—"you should stay away from Rome. You can't know how things are here. The Emperor has a close advisor, a very powerful man, who hates Jews."

"Sejanus." Joseph knew. Marcus was surprised.

"Yes. If you know about him, I'm amazed you came to Rome. He's becoming more dangerous every day. The latest thing is, he gets a man to accuse another man of treason. Just saying something critical is pretext enough for the charge. There's a trial, so called, the accuser brings witnesses, and the accused man is condemned. His properties are confiscated, usually sold. The accuser and the witnesses get part of the proceeds, Sejanus gets the largest part.

reject the sacrifice and with it his, Joseph's, repentance for his sins. Three times the High Priest passed behind the curtain and through the door. Three times he came out again, the sacrifice being acceptable to God. Then he magically transferred the sins of men, including Joseph, to the sacrificial goat. When the news of its death was received at the Temple, Joseph cheered, with those around him, until his throat was raw.

He hurried to Jericho, almost running. Several times he stumbled on the rocky path and fell, but he didn't care. He wanted to see for himself the blessings of God's forgiveness, the motion of his baby's legs.

Helena was floating in the heated water of the bath, supported by the ring of inflated lambs' bladders that Homer had devised for her. She loved to play in the water, splashing, pushing herself in circles with her hands, talking her special talk to the tiny waves she made with her splashing. "Abba!" she said when Joseph appeared. She splashed him a welcome.

He jumped into the pool, making a greater splash that delighted Helena. Under the water he moved her legs, demonstrating what he thought she could do now.

But she could not.

The next Festival was the High Holy Celebration of Succoth, the Feast of Booths, less than a week away. Joseph gathered palm fronds from the date trees near the villa, and myrtle from the shrubs that bordered the garden. Willow he cut from the growth on the steep bank of the wadi, the stream that ran beside his property.

He carried them all to Jerusalem, with Dosha and Helena, in a cart pulled by a donkey. Antiochus and Homer walked alongside with him.

Helena was delighted with the booth he and the other men built in the garden of the Jerusalem house. She pulled leaves from the myrtle branches and put them in her mouth until Antiochus noticed what she was doing and took them away. She could sit alone now, and pushed herself up whenever she was laid on a mat to rest.

After taking part in the Temple celebrations, Joseph went back to his house every day of the week-long Festival, to be with his daughter on these Holy Days and to prepare himself for what he knew he must do.

When Succoth ended, he carried Helena to Abigail's house so that the family could begin to know her. He had sent a message to Aaron, too, but he had not replied. After the visit Joseph took the cart and donkey again and carried his daughter to her birthplace, and the birthplace of her mother and father. Arimathea.

He visited the villagers first. Abigail was right, he saw at once. Everyone was angry and disapproving, because he had not been at Sarah's funeral. But when they saw Helena, his surpassing devotion to her, and the pitiable reality of her condition, their anger became compassion. Joseph was deeply moved by the generosity of these close-to-the-earth people. They knew, without discussion or philosophizing, what truly mattered in life. It was love.

He had the courage now to go up to the farms, to his family, to the house where he had been with Sarah.

Unthinking anger filled his heart when he saw that someone was living in the little house. It's Sarah's, he thought. No one should touch it.

Then his mind cleared. Shelter was for people, not for memories. Amos' sons were grown men now, Caleb's were, too. There was more need for homes where new families could live and grow.

Joseph went to make his peace with all of them. They were not as immediately compassionate as the villagers, but they were as kind and sympathetic as was in their natures.

Rachel, Amos' wife, had kept Sarah's things for him. Joseph nearly broke down when he saw them. There were so few. The betrothal necklace he'd given her so many years ago, her dresses and hairpins from Belerion, her harp.

"You keep them, Rachel. I have no need of them to remember her."

"Your daughter should have them when she's older, Joseph. She won't have any memories."

Of course Rachel was right; Joseph told her so, and thanked her. Then he carried Helena to Sarah's tomb. He needed to have her with him for this hardest moment. "Your mother's bones are in there," he told his uncomprehending little girl. "Your grandmother's, too, and your great-grandmother's. You follow a line of wonderful women, Helena. You, too, will be wonderful, in your own way. You may have to be the bravest of all. But we won't even consider such a thing now. There are lots of doctors left for us to see."

Helena pulled his beard, laughing.

Antiochus lifted Sarah's harp, ran a finger across its strings. It was hideously out of tune. He made a face, put it down. "Forgive me, Helena. I wanted to play you the lullaby your mother played to you before you were born. I'd forgotten. Let me try to remember the words and tune. I'll sing them now, we'll have the harp tuned later.

"It certainly is flattering that you're so interested. I have so little time with you that I'd be glad if you'd do some of your chirps and smiles for me."

Helena was concentrating totally on feeding. As always Dosha held Helena firmly, while she stared impassively into the distance. It was depressing, Antiochus believed, that the woman cared nothing for the child at her breast. Helena didn't seem to mind. She ate hungrily and always finished with a look of satisfaction, almost bliss, on her face.

Antiochus hummed, then began to sing Sarah's Celtic song. "From the cliffe they fell, the words . . ." The result was alarming.

Dosha looked at him, her eyes avid, and she began to

speak. The words came too quickly, her emotion was too strong.

She had barely spoken at all during all the months, all the travels. "Yes." "No." "Baby." "Hungry." "Sleep." Those few words were her total vocabulary. And they were always spoken in a dull drone.

Now her voice rose and fell, on and on without stopping. Her eyes were fixed on Antiochus' face. They were hot with pleading.

He realized at last that she was speaking Celtic. The accent was different, many words were strange to him. But he could make out many more. Questions. Who was he? What was his tribe? What was the song? She asked them over and over again.

Antiochus took Helena from Dosha. Luckily the baby was nearly satiated. He held her to his shoulder, rubbing her back as he'd seen Dosha do until the shockingly loud burp erupted.

He continued to rub Helena's back, and he talked to Dosha in the Celtic he knew, a mixture of Galatia and Belerion.

She spoke too, with fervor. He had to ask her often to slow down, to repeat what she'd just said.

Joseph came upon them, stopping some distance away. He could hardly believe what he was seeing. Dosha—animated, smiling, ecstatic.

Beginning that day Helena was always given music with her feedings. Little Celtic songs that, said Dosha, all babies in her country learned with their mother's milk.

Antiochus often played accompaniment, after the harp was tuned. And he often joined Dosha in song.

Helena showed no reaction; she seemed to hear only the song her stomach sang: Fill me.

The rainy season and its cold winds caught Joseph by surprise every time he went up from Jericho to Jerusalem. The desert that surrounded Jericho seemed to draw in the

rains and warm the winds before they could reach the oasis.
It was balm to Joseph's worries that at least he could give
Helena this much.

As they'd done the year before, Joseph's party left for
Caesarea immediately following Shavuot. The *Eagle* was
ready, and they sailed at once for Puteoli. Joseph had
learned about a doctor in Rome. Aulus Cornelius Celsus
was on his way to becoming the most famous man in the
world. He'd already written eight books about his discoveries and treatments. They were in such demand that a scriptorium with fifty tables had been organized for the sole
purpose of making copies.

CHAPTER FIFTY-FIVE

JOSEPH WOULD NOT BE ABLE TO OBSERVE THE NEW YEAR and the Day of Atonement in the Temple. The voyage to Puteoli would be slow, against the prevailing summer winds. Then, a hundred miles by road to Rome, and how long with the doctor, who could tell?

This was a bitter thing for him. Yes, he knew that Rome's Jews were godly men, that all the Holy Days were celebrated with solemnity and special services in their synagogues. But, as a Sadducee, he had never been able to believe that worship in a synagogue could even begin to equal worship at the Temple. And he was so dedicated to regaining God's favor. He even observed the Sabbath now at sea, something he'd never done in all his regular sailing years. It was a mercy that his captain and crew were Gentiles, or he would have had to risk shipwreck. As it was, he did not labor; even when he saw that the reefing of the great sail needed adjustment, he waited for someone else to observe it and give the orders. It was hard.

Putting his faith in the validity of synagogue worship would be even harder. The synagogue was the world of the Pharisees. However, he would find the faith.

For Joseph had a different, nonreligious faith. Faith in

books. A doctor who wrote books . . . books that other doctors studied. This must be what he'd been searching for. Now Helena would gain the use of her legs. She had devised a shockingly rapid method of locomotion, using her arms and elbows to pull or push the rest of her body across floors, paths, courtyards, any reasonably flat surface. Whenever he saw her scrabble along on her arms and hands, pulling her useless legs behind her, his heart broke again.

Joseph was arranging the hire of vehicles and animals and guards for the long miles from Puteoli to the capital city when a disreputable looking, dirty man edged to his side.

"My crew is filled," he said. Every port had its supply of men like these, usually hopeless drunks, looking for work as a loader or member of the crew.

"Don't say anything," said a quiet voice beside him, "and don't look at me. Joseph, this is Herod Agrippa, and I need your help. Keep on with what you're doing. Meet me later behind the sailmender's shack. I'm going now."

"Thank God you've come!" Herod Agrippa clasped Joseph's hands in his. "I've been hiding in the hills above the harbor, watching for your ship. If you'd not come this year, I don't know what I would have done. You're the only man I can trust."

Laughing, insouciant, impertinent Herod Agrippa was no part of this man. It wasn't the dirt, or the rags, that made the difference. It was the fear. This man was genuinely terrified, frightened for his life.

It was Sejanus, Herod explained. He was gaining more and more power over Tiberius, over Rome, over the Empire.

Tears sprang from Herod's eyes. "Ah, Joseph, he killed Drusus, my oldest, closest friend. Because Drusus was

Tiberius' only son and perhaps he would listen to him. Drusus was trying to warn his father about Sejanus.

"Sejanus is always devious. He seduced Drusus' wife. Livilla is crazy in love with Sejanus. So crazy that she used the poison he gave her to kill Drusus. Slowly, so slowly. He just kept getting weaker and paler every day. There was nothing I could do. Drusus wouldn't believe that his wife would kill him, even when I brought him the eunuch who informed on Livilla, the man who had told me about the poison.

"The eunuch is dead now, too. And I'm next, Joseph. I know it. You've got to smuggle me away. My life isn't safe anymore."

The tale was preposterous, and Herod Agrippa was noted for his tall tales. He was not known as a fool, however. Or a coward. And this man with Joseph now was a cowardly desperate man.

He grabbed the sleeve of Joseph's cloak. "You've got to get me away, Joseph, or I'm a dead man. I managed to get out of Rome, but I left a pile of debts—"

"Don't worry, Herod, I'll pay your debts."

"It's not that. Don't you see? Sejanus will use them as an excuse to arrest me, and then I'll be at his mercy. He knows I know about Drusus. He can't let me go on living."

"Where will you go?"

"The whole Empire is dangerous for me. But my grandfather, King Herod, was a Nabatean. He's admired there, not like in Judea. And the Nabateans are basically nomads. If I can get to relatives there, they can keep me out of sight as long as necessary.

"You could take me to Ascalon. It's so small and even Sejanus can't have guards everywhere. From there I can get to Nabatea."

"All right, Herod Agrippa. But it's going to be tricky. I have to go to Rome, and I don't know how long I'll be there. You'll have to trust my crew. I'll think up some story, they'll say you're one of them. Start right now getting some calluses on your hands. No one with eyes would believe those hands of yours had ever done a day's work. Stay here. I'll be back with my captain, and he'll take over. I've got to go. I hired guards, and they'll wonder where I am."

Joseph really cared for Berenice's son. He'd have to help him. But not if it meant danger to Helena. The trip to Rome was first in his mind.

Like all other traders and shipowners, Joseph had a network of agents, factors, money handlers, warehouse owners, and informants throughout the Empire's major ports and major cities. Fast courier service from Puteoli had requested his business representative to arrange for comfortable living quarters, with servants. The same courier service delivered an order to his information collector to hold himself available for a meeting with Joseph, and to prepare a full report on the physician Celsus.

On the day of arrival, in August, Rome was sweltering under a metallic blue sky and a miasma of unmoving air. The place where Joseph's party would be staying was a large, overpriced luxury apartment in one of the tenements built especially for the wealthy on the Aventine Hill. It was on the second floor, had a balcony with potted trees and—on better days—a breeze from the river. This day there was no breeze, and even in the shade of the trees stifling heat was inescapable. Joseph sat there, brooding, in his tunic, with his feet in a basin of water to cool his blood. No wonder the apartment's owner went away from the city in the summer. He was worrying about whether the famous physician did the same.

When one of the servants announced that he had a visitor, Joseph thought it must be his business representative checking on the acceptability of the apartment. He wasn't prepared for the tall army officer who walked onto the balcony with the swagger of authority.

"Marcus!" Joseph greeted him with surprised pleasure. It

was Berenice's stepson, last seen three years ago at her funeral.

"Joseph of Arimathea?" Marcus looked even more surprised than Joseph had been. "I had no idea it was you." The swagger was gone completely.

Joseph ordered the slave to bring wine. "Come sit down," he urged Marcus. "The shade helps a little. Tell me your news. How's that handsome boy of yours?"

Marcus was visibly upset. He looked almost like the shy young boy Joseph remembered from Berenice's household so many years before. What was he now? Mid-thirties, Joseph supposed, and obviously accustomed to authority, not awkwardness. His uniform proclaimed him a legate, as his father had once been. Why, Joseph wondered, was Marcus here, and what was bothering him?

When they were seated together, sharing the pitcher of wine, Marcus told him. The apartment was owned by the father of his wife, Cornelia. Her parents always spent summers at their country estate.

The manager of the apartment building had hurried to report to Marcus as soon as Joseph and his party took possession. "All he told me," Marcus said, "was that the renter was a Jew. I came to tell you to get out. I had no idea it might be you.

"Joseph"—Marcus leaned toward him urgently—"you should stay away from Rome. You can't know how things are here. The Emperor has a close advisor, a very powerful man, who hates Jews."

"Sejanus." Joseph knew. Marcus was surprised.

"Yes. If you know about him, I'm amazed you came to Rome. He's becoming more dangerous every day. The latest thing is, he gets a man to accuse another man of treason. Just saying something critical is pretext enough for the charge. There's a trial, so called, the accuser brings witnesses, and the accused man is condemned. His properties are confiscated, usually sold. The accuser and the witnesses get part of the proceeds, Sejanus gets the largest part.

"With Sejanus hating Jews the way he does, I was afraid that having a Jew in the apartment would turn his malice toward Cornelia's father. Then, maybe, one of those fabricated accusations."

"You were right to act," said Joseph. "I'll get my man to find me something else at once."

Marcus shook his head. "You will not do anything of the sort. You'll come to us. Cornelia and I are in the house on the Esquiline, the one you know. I brought her home from the camp on the Danube because she's expecting a child. We're overjoyed. Julius is nearly eight, and we'd almost given up hope of another one."

Now Joseph shook his head. "I won't do that. If renting to a Jew would endanger your father-in-law, what would it do to you if you had one as a guest?"

Marcus no longer resembled a boy. "Joseph, I won't accept that, not even from an old family friend like you. Cornelia's father can be as timid as he wants, but I am an officer in the Army of the Empire. Sejanus has the Praetorian Guard under his command, but he has no say with the real soldiers. And even if he did, I would consider it my duty and an honor to defy him. My mother was a Jew."

Marcus put aside his military stiffness to smile. "I always think of Berenice as my mother. She loved me and made me so happy, and I loved her with all my heart. I still do."

Joseph continued to protest. This time on account of his unusual group of companions and the special demands created by Helena's condition. "The racket when she's awake is practically deafening. Dosha's singing, Homer's shouts when Helena gets away from him while he's massaging her legs, the crashes when she scoots under a table and tips it over, Antiochus twanging the harp in his interminable attempts to tune it. I tell you, Marcus, I thought sometimes I'd jump overboard and swim to Puteoli."

Marcus laughed heartily. "You gladden my heart, Joseph. With all of you there, the house will be almost like it was when I was a boy. I will not accept a refusal."

"Cornelia may not share your fondness for chaos."

"She's an army wife. That makes her adaptable."

Marcus' son, Julius, immediately appointed himself Helena's watcher and catcher. He was disappointed when she had a nap or an exercise and massage session with Homer during the hours he was free, after his tutor was finished with him. Julius tried to crawl the way Helena did, but he wasn't half as proficient. He was fascinated by her abilities.

His mother did not in any way share his interest. "I wish they'd go," she told Marcus. "When I see that pitiful little creature it scares me to death about the child I'm carrying."

"It won't be long," he promised. "As soon as this doctor returns to the city, he'll see Joseph's little girl, and that will be that. Either he will have a cure or he won't. There's no in between."

Waiting for the doctor was just as hard for Joseph as it was for Cornelia. He knew by now that he should not let his expectations rise too high. The crash when they weren't met was too agonizing. Nevertheless, as day after day passed, he could feel them mounting again. His information agent had collected nearly a hundred reports praising Celsus' astonishing skills.

When would the man be back? The agent could learn nothing. Celsus' house, with his treatment rooms inside, was locked and empty. Neighbors and everyone who dealt with him—from the sausage maker his cook patronized to the brothel keeper who provided his women—knew only that he had taken his servants to an unnamed vacation spot.

Joseph was finding the chaos that Marcus so enjoyed to be increasingly difficult to bear. He stayed at the house because he was cautious about bringing trouble down on Marcus and his family. As a result he could not enjoy the theater or the never-ending busy-ness of the forums.

He would have attempted to content himself with teaching Helena new words and trying to understand the ones she already knew but couldn't pronounce exactly. She called Dosha "Sha," and Homer "Ho," and Julius "Yus," and herself "Ella." Antiochus was "Och." Joseph alone had a full, accurate name. He was "Abba."

Unfortunately, others took up Helena's free time: Julius and one of Cornelia's maids who had fallen completely under Helena's spell. Chloe was a young Greek slave; her main duties were to brush Cornelia's hair and obey the orders of Cornelia's hairdresser when the elaborate daily ritual of dressing-the-mistress took place. Chloe especially loved Helena, she told Homer, because "the baby has only baby hair, not enough for a thousand plaits and pins."

She helped Homer with Helena's bathing and dressing. On her own she introduced Helena to honeycakes and milk from a cup, not Dosha's breast. Helena made the change in a day. Breasts do not deliver honeycakes.

"Abba, look!" Helena crowed, exhibiting her new skill. Joseph applauded, and kissed her soft, wet, sticky cheek.

That afternoon Antiochus asked Joseph for a quiet talk.

"It's been a joke between us for many years, Joseph, but I am not joking now. I want you to give me my freedom."

Joseph was dumbfounded. "Of course," he said, "you know that. I'll draw up the papers today."

"And a favor, Joseph. Set Dosha free, also. I haven't told her yet, but I am going to take her home, back to her own people. She will never cease missing the life she was taken from."

Joseph thought he understood. Unbelievable though it was, Antiochus, the Galatian Celt, loved Dosha, the German Celt.

Antiochus began to chuckle. "I can read your mind, Joseph, and what you're thinking is laughable. I grant you, the breasts are astonishingly fine. But my interests don't run to the excessive.

"No, I have sympathy for the girl, that's all. In a different way, I'd like to save her, as you saved me. You gave me a home and a life. I can restore her earlier ones to Dosha.

"But it would not be safe for her to travel all that long way alone. So I will accompany her as a free man, because slaves have to be returned to their owners. Marcus has the power to give me safe passage through Roman Army encampments and the knowledge to advise me on the best route to follow.

"I will return, Joseph. You may rely on it. If you have left Italy, I will make my way to Jericho." Antiochus grinned, with the characteristic mischief in his eyes. "I am assuming, naturally, that you will present me with a fat purse along with my documents of manumission.

"When I get back, I may even sell myself back into slavery to you. I'm worth a very great deal of money."

Antiochus and Dosha, freedman and freedwoman, set off on their long journey a week later. Antiochus embraced Helena and Homer, and Joseph, with especial warmth. Dosha was apparently as wooden as always. But she kissed Joseph's hands and said, in Celtic, "May all the gods bless you and your child."

The next day Joseph received the news that Celsus, the physician, was back in his house.

"Maybe the Celts' gods brought him," laughed Homer.

Joseph shuddered at the blasphemy.

CHAPTER FIFTY-SIX

AULUS CORNELIUS CELSUS WAS A SELF-IMPORTANT MAN IN his forties. His toga was immaculately white, and draped with elegant precision. It hid, to perfection, his sunken chest and pot belly. Homer, who could read bodies through any disguise, felt an immediate aversion to the self-indulgent lack of discipline implied by Celsus' physical condition.

Joseph, on the other hand, was impressed by the doctor's air of omniscience and by the scrolls that were his books, lined up neatly on shelves on the wall behind Celsus' head.

"Interesting," said the doctor. "Yes, extremely interesting." He was sitting behind a table on which were arrayed bowls of olives and shelled almonds and dates. He reached elegantly into each bowl in turn with his white fingers, a large gemmed ring on each finger. While he chewed, he looked into space, thinking. When he deposited the pits of the olives and dates, each in a bowl reserved for its disposal, he concentrated fully on the graceful arc of his wrist and fingers.

Helena reached for the foods when she saw them going into his mouth, but she was much too far away to cause any disturbance. She pulled Joseph's beard. "Abba. Ella eat," she suggested.

"Later," he promised her. "Helena will have milk and honeycakes."

She settled comfortably against his chest, satisfied for the moment.

Aulus Cornelius Celsus turned toward a smaller table nearby, where he washed his fingers in a bowl of water scented with rose oil, then dried them on the linen towel that lay next to the bowl.

"I will look at her," he said. "Bring her to the examining room."

An attendant in the room respectfully removed Celsus' toga and rings. Homer was not surprised to see that the doctor's tunic was unbelted and rather full.

"On the table, if you will."

The table was covered by a drape of clean linen. Helena's rosy skin looked very bright and healthy on top of the white expanse.

Celsus' epicurean elegance was laid aside with his toga. Even Homer had to admire the strong competence of his manicured hands as they moved over Helena's body, from the top of her skull to the tips of her pink, useless toes.

"You have done an excellent job of maintaining bone and muscle conditioning," said Celsus briskly. Homer was gratified. Only a true professional could understand the difficulty of his task and the success of his efforts.

The doctor put one hand across Helena's chest and abdomen. With the other he lifted one of her legs, pressing it back toward her chest until she screamed from shock and pain.

Joseph started forward, but Homer restrained him. What Celsus was doing was a legitimate investigation.

The second leg brought a louder scream and a sobbing wail. "Abba, Abba, Abba."

Joseph couldn't bear it. He pushed Homer aside and went to his suffering little girl. Celsus stepped back. "Take her outside until she quiets down," he said. "Then meet me in my office. I know what is needed."

Joseph held Helena close, making hushing sounds.

"Outside," Celsus repeated.

"It is perfectly evident that the connection between the muscles of the body and those of the legs is missing," said Celsus. He was toga-clad again, behind his table. He selected an olive. An almond followed, and a date. When all pits were disposed of, he continued to speak.

"I will operate. Open the body at the site of the missing connection. Depending on what I find, I will attach the muscle to the existing but unconnected piece or I will fashion a connection out of animal tissue. Catgut, most probably." His fingers lifted an olive.

It sounded so logical, so businesslike, that at first Joseph did not quite realize what the doctor was saying. Then he didn't believe what he had heard. "What does that mean? 'Open the body.'"

The almond crunched between Celsus' teeth. He swallowed before he spoke. "Quite simple. I will cut the place where the leg is attached to the hip. Open up the *locus* of difficulty. From the center of the front to the center of the back should provide adequate viewing area."

Homer stood, too enraged to remain quiet. "You're going to cut the child's leg half off so that you can find out whether you're wrong or right?"

Celsus frowned at the Greek's tone of voice. He returned the date he was holding to its bowl. "There is no other way." His manner was one of patient superiority. "I have no doubt about the accuracy of my findings. If—by some inconceivable remote chance—my findings prove incorrect, there will be no harm done. I will close the incision. Except for some scarring, the leg and hip will be as they are now, to a large extent."

Homer stalked to Celsus' table and swept the bowls off it onto the floor. "'A large extent.' Very scientific sounding, you butcher! The child will be in pain for the rest of her life, if she lives through your carving!"

Celsus had backed away, pushing his chair by rapid scrabbling of his feet. He was alarmed, but his confidence was intact. "I rarely lose a surgical specimen. Medication can allay the pain. What is the difficulty here? You bring me a cripple. If I do not succeed, you will have a cripple. You are no worse off. If I succeed, which is far more likely, you will have been part of a major discovery in medicine. I will write of it in my next book."

Homer looked at Joseph. What was he thinking? Why was he so quiet?

Joseph was holding Helena close, stroking her straight little back. "Control yourself, Homer," he said. He stood. "This man hasn't comprehended anything you've said. But he'll understand me.

"Aulus Cornelius Celsus, if you lay a hand on my daughter, I will cut it off and make you eat it. You can put the bones in a bowl."

He strode from the room. "Who'd like a honeycake, Helena? Do you know anybody like that?"

Homer followed him.

When they returned to Marcus' house, Homer gave Helena her favorite warm water-splashing bath and a long, gentle massage. No exercising today. He could still hear her screams when Celsus pushed her legs to her chest.

Chloe helped him dress Helena in her little tunic and diaper-like loincloth. "Cakes," said Helena with confidence.

"Let me," Chloe asked. "Please?" Homer agreed.

He walked to the loggia, where Joseph was standing, looking out over the city.

"What do we do now, Joseph? Will we wait for Antiochus' return?"

Joseph shook his head. "That could be many months. And the sailing season is nearing its end. Tomorrow is the New Year's beginning, according to Jewish calendars. I will attend a synagogue for services, on the following day we will make our preparations and our farewells, and the day after, we will leave for Puteoli." His voice and his posture were heavy with sorrow.

"I am regretful, too," said Homer, "and you have my sympathy."

Joseph straightened his shoulders. "Thank you, friend. Let's put that nightmare behind us. I need to find a gift for Marcus and Cornelia, as thanks for their hospitality. Have you any thoughts?" He glanced at Chloe and Helena, playing clap-hands with each other. "I want to buy a gift for that slave girl, too. She's been good with Helena.

"What is it, Homer? You look pale."

"Joseph—" Homer's words tumbled out in a rush. "Why don't you buy Chloe from Marcus? Without Dosha, we could use a woman to care for Helena. Not that I'm not happy to do so, but maybe a woman would be better for some things. Certainly, when she gets older and a man shouldn't be bathing her and so forth. And you'll save whatever Chloe might cost because you won't need to hire a Greek tutor. Helena will need to speak better Greek than I can teach her, I only know the language of the taverns and—"

Joseph was holding up both hands to stop him. "Wait a minute, Homer. I've never heard you talk so much or so fast. Do you want this girl for yourself? Is that what you're saying?"

"No!" Homer was angry. "Not what you're thinking, Joseph."

Joseph looked at the anger on Homer's classical face, and he smiled a kind, small smile. "Is it like that, then? You love her. Don't be ashamed to admit it, Homer. I loved Helena's mother from the time we were children, and it was the best part of me for all those years. It still is, I believe."

Homer admitted that Joseph was right. But Chloe was still a girl, an innocent. He didn't want to frighten her with his feelings. He thought that, after a few years together, in the same household, she might begin to feel some affection for him, and then—

"Suppose some other man comes along and wins her affections. What then?" Joseph couldn't resist the opportunity to tease the hard-bitten trainer of gladiators.

"I'd drag him to the great doctor Celsus and have his balls cut off."

Joseph burst out laughing. It felt very good.

"Thank the gods, they're gone," Cornelia said with relief.

"It was a profitable bit of hospitality, my dear," Marcus laughed. "You sold that little girl you always said was incompetent for enough money to buy four hairdressers. And those pearls Joseph gave you will make all your friends sick with envy."

"Ha! I suppose you object to the four horses he gave you. No one you know has any half as good."

"I'll miss Ella," Julius said sadly. "She made me laugh."

"The poor little thing is named Helena," his mother corrected. "And you'll have your own baby sister soon, so you'll forget her. Your sister will be perfect, not crippled."

"Suppose it's a brother?"

"He'll be perfect, too. Just like you."

When the Roman soldiers demanded to inspect his cargo, Joseph, for the first time, believed that Herod Agrippa had not exaggerated the danger he was in. Herod had been frantic when Joseph told him that the *Eagle* wouldn't sail until after the Day of Atonement. "I'm going to observe it in the ceremonies at the synagogue here in Puteoli," Joseph told him. "You should do the same."

"Show my face where Sejanus' men might be looking for me? You're mad, Joseph! We should leave at once. I've already been around here for too long. You took your own sweet time in Rome."

"We sail when I say so. If you want to sail with me, you'll have to wait. It's only four more days, Herod Agrippa."

Now Joseph was beginning to understand Herod's panic. These men looked determined. And ruthless. He thought of

Herod, below, on the rowing deck, sitting on one of the benches, pretending to be an oarsman. It wouldn't fool anyone who knew anything about rowing. Herod had managed to blister, then callus his hands. But his shoulders and arms lacked the muscles of a genuine galley oarsman.

Joseph looked at the soldiers. "I have been sailing in and out of this port for more than thirty years, and no one has ever had the insolence to make a demand like that. You will not look at my cargo, and you will leave my ship at once."

One of the men drew his sword partially. Joseph spoke to his superior officer. "Your troops need better discipline, Centurion. I suppose I'll save time by showing you some things." He walked deliberately to the watertight locker where he kept important small cargo and removed the gold-cased papers of citizenship that Augustus Caesar had given him and the letter with Tiberius' seal on it.

He carried them to the centurion, offered him the golden tube. "This was given to me by the Divine Augustus. You see his profile, and that of the Empress Livia. I am a Roman citizen, by his gift. If you have any accusation to make against me, I will use the right conveyed to me in that gift. A citizen of Rome can go direct to the Emperor for judgment."

Joseph waved the letter bearing Tiberius' seal in front of the officer. "I would be glad to tell Tiberius about your effrontery if you force me to do so. However, I don't want to lose the wind and the last of the good weather, so I will let you go. At once."

Two hours later Joseph sent the genuine oarsman below and invited Herod Agrippa to join him on deck.

"We're out of sight of land. I imagine you could use a cup of wine."

"Joseph, I could feel my hair turning white with terror. A cup is laughable. Have someone bring me a full amphora."

The Herod Agrippa Joseph knew was himself again. It was going to be an entertaining voyage.

CHAPTER FIFTY-SEVEN

WHEN THE WINTER RAINS PROVIDED SOME MEASURE OF COOL-
ing, Joseph and Homer took Helena across the desert to the
large community of the reclusive sect known as the Essenes. They had a reputation, some people said, as healers.

There were many groups of Essenes, some in their own
settlements, some in their own neighborhoods within towns
throughout Judea. They avoided contact with anyone outside their brotherhood. As a result, strange stories circu-
lated about them: that they were angels, that they were
devils, that they were magicians, that they were lunatics.

Joseph was leery about having anything to do with such
unknowns. But he had heard enough stories about their
healing abilities to risk the arduous journey.

The landscape was desolate and dangerous. Shifting
sands hid nests of vipers and blurred landmarks. Outcrops
of wind-eroded rock were sere, reddish, jagged. Their goal,
in the distance, was a range of high, cave-pocked cliffs. Beyond it was the mysterious great body of water that some
called the Dead Sea.

Indeed, everything around them looked dead. Joseph had
hired camels and a camel driver who claimed to know the
desert and the route they must follow. Joseph had had little

experience with camels, and he disliked them. It was disquieting to be seated so high above the ground, on the uneven back of a beast that moved with such unfamiliar undulations. He felt as if he were in constant danger of losing his balance and falling to the harsh sand and rocks below. Holding Helena in his arms, his sense of precariousness was even more alarming.

"Isn't this exciting?" Homer said enthusiastically. A trained athlete, he had no difficulty adapting to the camel's movement.

When they neared the base of the cliffs, Joseph was amazed to see fertile irrigated fields. White-garbed men straightened from their labors and looked at the three-camel caravan with silent hostility. One of them walked forward.

"Who are you and what do you want?"

He spoke Aramaic, like any other Judean farmer. Joseph instantly felt relieved. The man was unfriendly, but he looked and sounded like a hardworking, sweaty farmer. Not angel or devil or lunatic.

Joseph explained his presence. "Can your healers help my little girl?" he concluded.

"Leave your camels and follow me," said the Essene. "Leave your companion, also."

He led Joseph along a precipitous, rocky path to an entrance cut through a natural wall of stone at the top of the cliff. It led to an antechamber with a second gate-like opening on its far wall.

Helena was babbling in her own polyglot Celtic-Greek-Aramaic tongue while they climbed, pointing to rocks, bits of vegetation in crevices, some birds that flew by overhead. Once inside the unroofed room, she pointed to the big cistern carved from rock that stood to one side of the entrance. "Bath," she said distinctly and with joy. She loved her splashing sessions in warm water.

The Essene looked at her. There was no smile on his face. "You and the child are tainted with oil," he said. "You must be cleansed before you may enter. Remove your garments."

The unheated water in the cistern was not to Helena's liking. Nor did she care for the vigorous rubbing with pumice stone that the Essene inflicted on her. She made her displeasure clear by her loud wailing.

Joseph understood her reaction. Two Essenes who had joined their guide were submitting him to similar treatment.

When he and Helena were adequately "purified," as their guide said, they were led to a vast, light-filled room with large window openings overlooking the desert. Three men clad in white linen tunics entered, and the guide left.

"We will examine the child," said the eldest of the three. Joseph held Helena more closely against his chest. Her little hands were holding tight to his beard. Joseph was intensely aware of their nudity and the feeling of vulnerability that it produced.

"Little one, we will not hurt you," the elder said to Helena. His voice held no particular quality that Joseph could discern, but Helena released her grip and held out her arms to the Essene.

He and his companions knelt on the clean scrubbed stone floor, with Helena lying on her back in their midst. Joseph could see that their fingers and hands were gentle on his child's body and limbs and head.

The Essenes did not speak to one another, but they must have arrived at unvoiced consensus, because they all stood at the same time. The youngest of the three was now holding Helena.

"Joseph of Arimathea," he said, "we can do nothing for the child today." His manner was extremely cheerful, considering his message. "Do not despair," he went on. "The final battle between good and evil will soon be fought, and the forces of good will be triumphant. On that day, when this corrupt world comes to an end, your daughter will become whole, because she is an innocent and free of sin."

He passed Helena to Joseph. "Bathe her frequently in water and keep her pure until then."

The three left, and the guide reentered the room. Following his gesture, Joseph, holding Helena, was led to the anteroom where their clothing had been left. After they were dressed and on their way down the path, Helena began to talk and sing again. After her bath she had made no sound at all until this moment.

The camels returned them to Jericho, and luxury. Joseph tried, and failed, to convince himself that this life, free of want and care, would be adequate for Helena's happiness. When the season for sailing arrived, he took her, with Homer and Chloe, to Sicily, and the hot springs there that were renowned for relief of bone and muscular diseases. Sogesta . . . Himera . . . Selinus . . . At each there were physicians, confident that the mysterious substances in the spring's water would heal her, then, afterward, amazed that they had not. The tiny island of Lipari was next, in the Tyrrhenian Sea. On each side of it other islands loomed, living islands that were volcanoes, sending dark smoke high to stain the clear blue skies.

Antiochus was in Jericho when Joseph returned. "What a big girl you've got there," was his greeting. "Come to Antiochus, Ella. If you've forgotten me, I'll perish from grief."

Helena regarded him with puzzled curiosity. She was almost three years old now, and had last seen him more than a year before.

Antiochus began to sing one of Dosha's Celtic songs, and Helena's face lit up. She joined in, with gusto.

Joseph was surprised by how much Antiochus' return meant to him. He had longed to have the Galatian's unvoiced sympathy each time hopes for a cure for Helena proved false. Homer cared deeply for his daughter, Joseph was sure. But Antiochus cared for Joseph, too, and his presence would have helped Joseph bear the agony of the failures.

He couldn't voice these things; instead he embraced his friend when the singing ended and said, "I'm glad to see you." Antiochus looked at Joseph's haggard face.

"Not good," he said. The comment did not refer to Joseph's appearance. It was a recognition of all that Joseph had suffered, and was still suffering—no cures.

"Songs, more songs," Helena begged.

"I am yours to command, gracious lady," Antiochus told her, holding out his arms. "We'll talk afterwards," he said quietly to Joseph as he lifted Helena from the cushioned chair in which she was sitting. Her small arms circled his neck. The Galatian's blue eyes moistened with emotion, but his voice was clear and full of laughter when he began to sing a nonsense song about flowers that he had learned, especially for Helena, when he was in Germany.

The two friends had much to tell each other. It was good news for Joseph to learn of Dosha's new home and new happiness with cousins in a village on the Rhine.

Homer's infatuation with Chloe delighted Antiochus when he heard about it, but his laughter was kind. He made no comment when Joseph reported the visit to Rome's famous physician; his eyes expressed his fury, and his compassion for the anguish in Joseph's heart.

"I wish I had been with you," he said about the trek to the Essene community. "I've been curious about them for years." Then he put his warm hand on Joseph's shoulder. His voice was laden with affection when he spoke.

"Hear me out before you reply, Joseph. You know how much I respect your beliefs and your piety. Sometimes I envy you your One God. However, there are some ungodly things that I believe you ought not reject without examination.

"The ship I traveled on from Marseilles made port in Gaza. While I waited there for transport to Jericho, I heard much about a magician who performs miraculous healings."

Joseph could stay quiet no longer. "Magic is for pagans, Antiochus. Your Celtic Druids claim to do magic. It is something filthy, unclean, an abomination to God."

Antiochus took no offense. "Think about it, Joseph. Take your time. If it works . . ."

Joseph refused to listen any longer.

But he couldn't stop thinking about what Antiochus had told him. He sent a man, a Gentile, from Jericho to gather information on the magician in Gaza. He told no one, including Antiochus, what he had done.

The Gentile returned, with reports of all the stories Antiochus had heard and more. He himself had met a man who'd been deaf for years and now could hear, thanks to the Magus, as the magician was called. Also a woman, who had been tormented by a plague of boils. Gone in an instant, at the touch of the Magus. Even he, said the Gentile, had asked about release from the headache that had been ruining his life for months. The Magus had commanded it to depart, and it had vanished.

What the Magus produced was called a "trance." He put people into a kind of waking sleep, and then he could make them do anything. Bark like a dog, lift tremendous weights that two normal men could not budge, speak in languages that they should not know. While entranced, people's minds and bodies were completely under the Magus' power. He could do anything with them, anything he chose. He had even made a crippled man walk again.

It was a measure of Joseph's mounting desperation that he sent Antiochus to Gaza with a fortune in gold aurei and orders to bring the Magus to Jericho, to Helena.

"He had fled Gaza," the crestfallen Galatian told Joseph when he returned. "The authorities there had gotten word from Petra about him and were going to arrest him, but he escaped. It turns out that he has spent time in dozens of places, always with the same result. He has a couple of actors with him who get 'cured,' and when word gets around, he starts receiving requests and offers. He promises a rich sufferer a cure, grabs the payment in advance, and leaves town in haste, at night, with his confederates. I ask your pardon for leading you down this chimerical path, Joseph."

Antiochus sighed. "I tried to find solace in the fact that I got to Gaza too late to make you the rich victim, but it was little comfort. I know the same must be true for you."

Joseph turned away from his friend. He could not say what he was thinking and feeling. He felt betrayed by the man he had trusted, who had given him hope again, only to plunge him into renewed despair. Murderous anger was in his heart.

"Joseph, it's time we thought about Ella," said Antiochus some weeks later.

"Her name is Helena, and I think of nothing else. Who do you think you are, speaking to me like that?"

"I am your friend, Joseph. That is precisely why I speak this way. You are so obsessed with healing your child that you are almost unable to see her as she is."

"A cripple! Do you imagine I don't know that? Don't think of it every day? Don't dream of it every night?"

"Joseph. She is a bright, beautiful, three-year-old girl with an affliction. The affliction is tragic, but you cannot allow her to make it the center of her life, as you have done. Let her be what she is, Joseph. Make some kind of peace with it yourself so that she can be happy.

"She loves music. Find someone to teach her how to play the harp. I do it too badly myself to be a teacher. She needs a little cart or something to ride in. She doesn't like being carried and held all the time. She has a child's normal curiosity. She wants to see the town, the shops, the people, other children.

"And . . . Joseph . . . she prefers to be called Ella. She says it sounds like singing."

Joseph felt wounded. How could Antiochus know more about his own daughter than he did? "She told you all these things?"

Antiochus nodded. "We sing songs, and we talk. I never say to her that she will get well one day, as you do, Joseph." He put his hands on his friend's shoulders.

"She asked me, Joseph, if I thought Abba would become happy if she could just learn to walk. I am sorry to tell you such a painful thing, but it had to be done."

CHAPTER FIFTY-EIGHT

"HELLO. MY NAME IS ELLA, AND MY DONKEY'S NAME IS Clip. Because of the sound his hooves make, you see. 'Clip-clop.' I get to drive him and ride in this bright red cart because my legs don't work."

Helena—now Ella—made herself known to everyone in Jericho. When vacationing visitors came to the oasis city, she introduced herself to them, too.

"I don't like for people to stare and wonder," she told Joseph in the forthright manner that was rich and astonishing maturity in one so young, not yet five.

Ella went anywhere she wanted to go in Jericho. There were few hills, and those were low. Homer always accompanied her, because he knew the limits of her strength and endurance better than she did. But he left her alone, unless she wanted him to join in her conversations with everyone from the tax collector, Zacchaeus, the most august personage in the town, to the slaves who cleaned the fountains and clipped the hedges in the marketplace.

When Homer told her it was time to return to the villa, Ella always obeyed. She had a lifelong habit of obedience when Homer spoke. For several hours of every day he moved the legs she could not control, massaged the mus-

cles, trained her in the development of strength in her upper
body, arms, and shoulders.

He designed a wheeled chair with leg rests for her. Now
any of the slaves could push it when she wanted to go from
one room to another, or to the garden, or the pool.

He also designed a chair that covered a chamber pot. Ella
could move herself from one chair to the other, using her
arms. The arrangement provided a privacy she valued highly.

A series of overhead bars permitted her to get in and out
of the bath and the shallow garden pool where she often
sang to the decorative fish that lived there.

The deeper, heated pool inside was for her exercises.
Homer had taught her to swim. It was her reward for patiently floating in her inflated ring while he moved her legs.

As is so often true of only children surrounded by adults,
Ella was especially sensitive to their unexpressed wants and
needs. "Why don't you tell Chloe that you love her?" she'd
said, in her direct way, to Homer. "She wants you to love
her but she doesn't know that you do."

For the marriage ceremony, Ella made flower wreaths
for Chloe's head and her own. She had clever fingers.

She often used them to comb Joseph's beard. She asked
frequently to have him hold her in his lap and tell her stories about when he was a boy, or when he and her mother
had stayed with the blue men, because she knew how much
her Abba needed to believe that she loved him.

Ella persuaded Joseph to take her to Jerusalem, too. She
loved to be carried in a sedan chair to the Temple for the
morning and evening ceremonies when the Levite musicians and choirs filled the courts with their music.

Abigail fell "totally in love with Ella," as she phrased it
so extravagantly, and Ella loved to hear Abigail's stories
about all the uncles and aunts, cousins and grandparents
that were hers, even if she never knew them.

*   *   *

Antiochus complained—not altogether in jest—that Ella had hardly any time for him. "And I received suitable punishment for my whining," he told Joseph with a rueful, but genuine, laugh. Ella had arranged with her music teacher to add Antiochus to the weekly lessons on playing the harp.

After a few months there was general agreement that the harp was not his instrument. But Antiochus did not escape. He was assigned a set of finger cymbals and became her partner for each tune.

It was good to have the Jerusalem house filled with laughter and music when he was there, because Joseph, as a member of the Sanhedrin, became deeply involved and worried by developments in that council and, soon, in the city.

The wily old High Priest Annas was now the advisor— some said the puppeteer—for his son-in-law Caiaphus, the titular High Priest. Joseph did not like or trust either of them. They were interested in increasing their power and importance, he believed, far more than they were interested in justice.

And mercy seemed to be a concept totally foreign to them. Joseph argued for hours about the just sentence for a Nabatean camel driver who unwittingly broke the law by entering the Court of the Women. Warnings carved in stone were distributed freely in all areas of the Court of the Gentiles, which was open to all people. In Aramaic and in Greek the notices warned that any non-Jew who passed into the inner precincts of the Temple was responsible for the death that would be his punishment.

"The man is an Arab," Joseph proclaimed. "He cannot speak Aramaic or Greek. He cannot read his own language. How much greater, then, must be his inability to read languages that he cannot even understand when spoken?

"Death is too great a punishment for error. Life and death are in the hands of God. How can we, six dozen men, presume to take the life of one of God's creations, even though he be a Gentile?"

There was more debate, more speakers. In the end, the vote was close, but Joseph won.

For his own punishment, Caiaphus made Joseph watch the lesser penalty the court had approved. He saw the hapless camel driver's back torn open by the lashes of the whip when he was flogged.

"You were eloquent, Joseph of Arimathea, but you made a great mistake, I fear." The speaker was a man Joseph knew well, another judge, another Sadducee. "The High Priest has enough trouble trying to control the Pharisees. We Sadducees need to form a unified group, we must support Caiaphus."

Joseph did not agree, but he didn't argue. It was true that more and more Pharisees were becoming members of the Sanhedrin. These new men were not from the school of Hillel, or his grandson Gamaliel. They were insistent on the Law, and on the ever-growing quantity of interpretations of the Law, which meant additional strictness and elaboration. In effect, an increasing number of laws, all in the name of the Law.

"Joseph! My good friend Joseph." Herod Agrippa, in full finery, embraced him on the street near the agora.

"I am overwhelmed," Joseph said frankly. "How do you come to be here? Let's go to my house and have a talk and some refreshment."

Herod was living with his uncle, Herod Antipas, in Tiberias. "The dreariness of the place defies description, Joseph. But it is nothing compared to the desolation of Idumea. My relatives were glad to take me in, to hide me from the wrath of Sejanus. But—more camels than people, Joseph, and their idea of excitement was to have a race, in the desert, to determine who was the owner of the fastest of the filthy creatures. I stood it for nearly a year, I don't know how, and then I simply had to get away.

"So I presented myself at the door of the palace in Tiberias. 'You are the brother-of-sorts of my father, and you managed to keep your head, unlike my poor father. Will you take me in?' I was so piteous that I was nearly moved to tears myself.

"What could Antipas say? There he was, in his brand-new palace with its hundred empty bedrooms.

"But, Joseph!" Herod Agrippa rolled his eyes. "He gave me work to do. Can you imagine? I am some kind of fancy government inspector—of what, I do not know—with a salary! A salary, Joseph. My word is no good in Galilee. I must pay for things. I don't know how I'm going to bear it. I almost kissed Antipas when he said I could accompany him to Jerusalem for Passover next week. He comes every year, to show what a good Jew he is, even though half of Galilee and almost all of Tiberias is Gentile.

"Do come see us, Joseph. We are in my grandfather's old smaller palace. The Roman Procurator stays in the big one when he comes from Caesarea. My other uncle, Philip, is here, too. You remember him; he married my sister Herodias. Too bad she didn't come, I would have had someone to talk to and laugh with. Please take her place, Joseph. Come have dinner with us. Tonight, and every other night."

Joseph was smiling at Herod Agrippa's dramatics. "I'll do much better than that, you reprobate. My friend Antiochus will be here soon. He knows where every unsavory spot in Jerusalem can be found, and what goes on there."

"I always knew you were a true friend, Joseph. No wonder my grandfather liked you so much. I wish I'd known the old terror. Even though he killed my father, at least he did it out of passion. And he had style, everyone admits that, even those who hate him the most. Antipas has neither. His palace is unspeakably dull, and he has all the emotion of a dead fish.

"Ah . . . who is this large handsome fellow? Antiochus,
I hope."

It was, and he took Herod Agrippa off Joseph's hands.
Ella's exercise time would be finished soon. Antiochus
knew that Joseph was planning to take her to Abigail's.

Joseph and Ella went to Abigail's for the Passover
feast, too. All the family from Arimathea were there.
Joseph watched his little girl's enjoyment and thanked
God for His blessings.

Joseph took Ella to the Temple every morning of
Passover Week to hear the music. He concentrated on the
awesome beauty of the sunrise and the music and the
Temple. And on the transported, blissful response Ella always had to the music.

Deliberately he did not look at the porticos that surrounded the Temple area. Roman soldiers stood, closely
spaced, on top of them. The Procurator Valerius Gratus
had begun the offensive display eleven years before, when
he was named the Roman ruler of Judea. True, there had
been no uprisings at Passover, and that was good. But it
was a constant, grating reminder that the Temple, the
heart of Judaism, was dominated by the forces of pagan
Rome.

Gratus was being replaced in a few months. Joseph
wondered if the new Procurator would have the decency
to show more respect for the sensibilities of the people he
was to govern. Reports on the man hadn't arrived yet
from Joseph's information agent in Rome. But they
should be in hand soon. Ships from Puteoli would dock in
Caesarea well before the new Procurator took office.

The new Procurator was named Pontius Pilate, and he
was a protégé and friend of Sejanus.

The news could hardly be more troubling, Joseph
thought. Until he read a second report, with infinitely
worse news. Tiberius had retired to the island of Capri,

where no one could get to him. Except Sejanus, who was now, in effect, the acting Emperor of Rome.

Sejanus the Jew-hater.

Joseph sent Antiochus to find a fast, reliable messenger while he hurriedly wrote a letter to Herod Agrippa. He had no way of guessing what this news would mean to Berenice's son, but it was important that he know it.

Once the messenger was dispatched to Tiberias, Joseph returned to the things he had come to Caesarea to do. Every year at the start of the sailing season he hosted a dinner for the captains of his ships, while Antiochus presided at the bigger, rowdier celebration for the crews.

"I wish you would be with me this year," said Barca, as he did every year.

"I wish with all my heart that it were possible," Joseph replied, as he did every year. And meant it, too, every time. He missed the sea. He loved the smell of it, the colors, changing with every hour, every current. The expanse and the adventure. It was hard to be done with those days. Even though he was only two years shy of sixty, when he looked out at the waters beyond the harbor he felt the same excitement he'd known as a boy when first he saw them.

Yes, he loved it. But he loved Ella more. And she needed him. The sea did not. There always had been, always would be, many thousands just like him, in love with the sea.

There was a great bustle of activity at Herod's palace. What was going on, Joseph asked Stratos, his Caesarea shipping agent.

Stratos was getting older, too. He was so fat he could hardly move. And he wheezed when he talked. "Gratus leaving," he puffed. Stratos used as few words as possible these days. He looked down, over his cascade of chins, unable to meet Joseph's eyes. "Wife going with him," he mumbled. "Deborah."

"Good riddance," said Joseph without emotion. He'd

known for years that Aaron's mother had become the Roman Procurator's mistress. Now there'd be no chance at all that she might enter his life again, or Aaron's. "Good news," he told Stratos.

Antiochus said the same thing when Joseph told him. "Good news."

Then, "but also bad," he said. "This Pilate will be arriving sooner than expected. You'd better get back to Jerusalem. I'll go to Jericho to take care of things there. By the way, I asked Barca to bring two young dogs back from Belerion. Ella will think they're pets and stop hinting for one. I'll train them."

"Good." Joseph and Antiochus had talked about it more than once. The dogs of Albion were known for their loyalty, strength, and ferocity. They would be excellent protection if Ella ever needed it. In previous years they had decided against getting them because of the heartache for Ella that she could not chase them or tumble in play with them. Now, with a Sejanus appointment as ruler of Judea, protection had become more important.

"Maybe I can teach them to pull the cart," Antiochus said. "I can certainly try." As usual, he and Joseph were thinking on the same lines.

Pontius Pilate did not wait for one of the religious festivals to show his intentions. In Roman parlance he "showed the standard." Each Roman legion had its own standard, a tall wooden staff, topped by a golden eagle, with a series of identifying metal plaques beneath. These included, first, the legion's number, with its special, chosen symbol, often a wild animal. Other medallions bore a portrait of the Emperor, or a god, honored a notable victory, the legion's duration of service, and the campaigns in which it had seen action. The standard was a legion's identity, history, and pride. Loss of a standard was a shame beyond reckoning.

For decades any legion entering Jerusalem had carried a special, substitute standard. A numeral identified the legion, and medallions might have names, but there were no representations of men, gods, or animals. Augustus Caesar had wisely avoided a blatant disregard of the Jewish Law forbidding graven images.

Tiberius, influenced by Sejanus, had authorized Pilate to include a portrait of him, the Emperor, on the standards. Pilate ordered several legions to Jerusalem, with specific instructions that they enter the city by night, move into their quarters at the Antonia Fortress, and set up their standards inside.

The Antonia overlooked and abutted the Temple.

In effect, an image—a graven image—of Rome's pagan Emperor was looking directly down on the sanctuary that sheltered the Holy of Holies, the place where God was honored by His High Priest.

Demonstrations began at once in the Temple Courts. The news spread rapidly through the countryside, and more excited and outraged Jews rushed to the Temple.

When they learned that Pilate was at Caesarea, self-appointed leaders organized a march. Thousands of protesters traveled day and night. They mobbed the plaza that surrounded the palace and lay on the pavement, so close to one another that there was no place for man or beast to place a foot. No one could get in, or out.

Pilate gave audience to a delegation of Jews, who detailed the objections to the standards. In Jerusalem. He might do as he pleased in Caesarea, which was Gentile.

He refused to remove them from the holy city.

The protesters stayed where they were around the palace.

After five days Pilate sent word that he would meet them and listen to their message again in the central marketplace.

When the Jews were all moved there, troops of soldiers marched at maximum speed to surround them, three ranks deep. Pilate addressed the crowd from the portico of the Temple of Augustus. "Look around you. See the peril you are in. Go back to your homes immediately, or I will have you sliced to ribbons."

The protesters looked around them, uncertain what to do. Impatient, Pilate shouted the order: "Draw swords!"

The protesters threw themselves on their faces, on the ground. Their leaders raised their heads. "We prefer death to blasphemy," shouted one. Others took up his cry.

Pilate ordered his troops to return to barracks. "The standards will be moved to Caesarea," he bellowed.

The sound of cheering followed him to his newly acquired palace.

CHAPTER FIFTY-NINE

JUBILATION REIGNED IN JERUSALEM. "WE BEAT THE ROmans!" was the shout heard everywhere.

Joseph was highly skeptical. If this Pilate was one of Sejanus' people, he was very likely made on the same model as his patron. Devious, patient, relentless, totally unscrupulous.

He kept his thought to himself. Time would tell, but for now why shouldn't people relish their moment of triumph?

Besides, there was a different epidemic of excitement that he really had to pay attention to. A special meeting of the Sanhedrin had been called, to talk about it.

One of the Pharisee judges described the problem. Simon was an older man, a longtime judge, a man of sincere devotion and humanity. Joseph had great respect for him.

"Word has reached us," said Simon, "of a wild, shaggy beast of a man who calls himself a prophet. He is attracting many followers."

"Another of those messiahs?" another judge asked. "Going to destroy the Romans and make all the Jews rich?"

Simon shook his head. He was smiling slightly. They all knew many instances of would-be messiahs who had come before the Court. Some were simple cases in which men had persuaded people to give them money for their cause. Out and out fraud. The so-called messiahs were flogged, and whatever money they hadn't spent was returned to the people who'd been cheated.

The difficult cases were the few genuinely delusion-gripped ones, usually young and burning with fervid conviction. They had to be handled with care, because they were the ones who might ignite a rebellion, resulting in horrifying loss of life when the Roman authorities stamped it out.

Almost always they could be shown their error when a group of priests read to them from the sacred works, describing what the real messiah would be like: a mighty, heavenly being, accompanied by angels and with powers beyond the reach of any human man.

And if—sadly—they couldn't be made to see reason, then there was always prison. But without the admiration of their followers, these messiahs soon realized that they were only men and went on their way, no longer a problem.

The judge Simon said that this latest phenomenon called himself a prophet, denied being the Messiah. "He says he has come to warn people that the Messiah will soon arrive. To judge between the sinners and the saved. This John is calling on everyone to repent their sins in preparation."

"Repentance is a good thing," said another judge. "Why stop a man who can bring forth a good thing?" There were murmurs of agreement from all sides.

"Because this John is baptizing the sinners. He stands in the River Jordan, they confess their sins to him, and then he immerses them in the river to signify the washing away of the sins."

Caiaphus leaned forward. "Does he forgive their sins? Only the Almighty can forgive sins."

"No. But the sins are washed away, so the people say. I've never heard of such a thing."

No one had. The High Priest could transfer sins to the scapegoat, but that was altogether different. The High Priest was acting with the authority of the Almighty on the Day of Atonement, in the Temple.

"We must investigate this baptizer," said Caiaphus. "Joseph of Arimathea, you are at Jericho, near the Jordan. You will lead a group of judges to observe this man."

What Caiaphus meant, of course, was that Joseph would feed, house, and entertain his fellow judges. He did not object. He did wish that he might have some say in choosing them, but of course he did not. Caiaphus named six, three Sadduccees, including Joseph, and three Pharisees, including the newest, youngest, most rigid judge of law in the entire Sanhedrin.

He was Aaron, Joseph's son.

John the Baptizer was a strong, wild-eyed man wearing a rough camel-hair tunic tied with a leather belt. His hair was unkempt, and his skin burned dark by the sun. "Repent," Joseph heard the Baptizer shouting when the Sanhedrin group neared the river. "Repent, for the kingdom of heaven is at hand!"

Joseph sighed quietly. Another end-of-the-world preacher. Why did they keep showing up, year after year after year? Did no one remember that the end of the world had been proclaimed so many times—and had never come?

The Baptizer saw the judges coming. "Brood of vipers," he shouted at them. Joseph and the others made no response. They were there only to observe.

And, incidentally, to enjoy the hospitality of Joseph's Jericho villa. All except Aaron stayed for three days and nights, ostensibly to re-visit the river, then decide on what their report should be.

Joseph presented their opinion to the next regular meeting of the Sanhedrin. "This John the Baptizer is drawing large crowds, mostly men, from all classes of society. He preaches repentance, and those who have come to him appear to be serious in their confession and repentance. At no time did the Baptizer preach against the Romans or call for rebellion. He promises his followers the imminent arrival of a more powerful leader, but he does not name him or the day he is supposed to come. We conclude that this baptism in the Jordan is appealing to people because of its novelty and drama. But it is not blasphemous or an incitement to riot. There is no need to arrest this man."

Aaron stood. "What of the one who is to come?" he asked loudly. "I believe we should question this Baptizer, find out about this other man, and arrest him. He will be the leader of rebellion."

"We have no cause to arrest the Baptizer and no reason to believe that the one he promises is any more than his own crazed vision," Joseph replied. He hated to argue with Aaron like this; if only Aaron had made his opinion known to their group, as he should have. Joseph was proud that his son was respected enough to be named one of the Sanhedrin at such a young age. But, at the same time, he wished that this particular young man was not his son.

Aaron had, for years, made it quite clear that he wanted to have nothing to do with his father. So be it, thought Joseph. I want the same thing now.

Caiaphus accepted the group's report, with graceful thanks for their efforts. In effect he dismissed Aaron without addressing him directly. Joseph's son sat down. His eyes fixed on his father, full of anger.

After the unsavory episode with Aaron, Joseph had the perfect antidote. He was going to have dinner and sleep at Abigail's, then take her with him to Jericho in the morning. The dry season was particularly hot this year, so she had finally accepted the invitation that he had extended many, many times.

Her house seemed so different, now that it was empty. Matthew, her husband, had been dead for three years now, and all the children were grown, married, living many miles away. Only at Passover did Abigail's still feel like Abigail's to Joseph. She was meant to be surrounded by clamor and affection, disorder and family.

Abigail expressed much the same idea after a bit more than a week of Jericho's cool breezes and splashing fountains. "This is wonderful, Joseph. But I keep wishing I could be at Arimathea. We are so few here."

They were sitting in the shade of a tall, spreading fig tree, watching Ella play with the fishes in the garden pool. She looked up at Abigail. "Yes. I want to go, too. All my cousins are there that were at your house."

Abigail smiled. "You remember Passover, do you, Ella?"

The child nodded. "I had a good time."

"Joseph?" Abigail was smiling still. "You seem to be outnumbered. When are you going to take us to Arimathea?"

He yawned. "Maybe when the first rains cool things off. It's much too hot now."

Abigail was uncharacteristically argumentative. "The roads are better before the rains make them muddy."

Joseph looked at this aunt's familiar placid expression. Her eyes were different. They were pleading.

He had to agree. Abigail had always been the one who gave—love, laughter, sympathy, understanding. She had never asked him for anything.

It took some organizing. Arimathea's crowded family houses had no room for all of them. Abigail, yes. She could have one of the children's beds at any one of the houses, and if the child was still in it, that would suit her fine, too.

But, in order to take Ella along, Homer and Chloe had to go as well. The exercises and massages could not stop. Also, Ella's special chairs must be transported. And her cart. And Clip, to pull it.

Plus tents for them to live in, beds for the tents, and rugs. And . . . and . . . and . . .

"I feel like a nomad," Joseph said to Antiochus. "You're smart not to come along, but I shall probably never forgive you."

"I'll take that chance. I intend to lie under the fig tree and eat each one as it ripens."

The figs were still green when Joseph and the others, except Abigail, returned.

"What happened?" Antiochus asked anxiously.

"I'll tell you later. Go tell the music teacher Ella is back. I have to get everything unloaded."

The vintage had been under way at Arimathea. When Ella saw her young cousins dancing in the great cistern full of grapes, to squeeze out the juice, she seemed to understand fully and for the first time what it meant to have no strength in her legs.

"She's a different child, Antiochus. So quiet. She doesn't complain. She doesn't cry. She doesn't do anything except what she's told to. I can't think of anything that might help. Except, maybe, the music."

The music did help. Greatly. Ella was able to lose herself in the dancing notes she could create on the strings of her harp. When she played the instrument alone, her eyes became dreamy, and from time to time a smile would curve her little lips. No one asked what she was imagining or thinking. It was sufficient that she could find happiness there.

She did most of the things she had done before. She sat in the pool and watched the fish, she swam after her exercises, she took her music lessons, she drove Clip through the streets of Jericho. When the many who knew her called out her name, she stopped and talked politely with them. But she initiated no conversations. Not with strangers, not with the people she knew in Jericho, not with those at home. And she never sang. It was as if something within her, some flame, had been extinguished.

The first rains signaled the end of the summer and the beginning of the New Year.

Also the beginning of the emergence of the real Pontius Pilate.

The coins were the first visible manifestation. Any ruler—whatever his title or his territory or his tenure—minted coins for use in his lands. Old ones were not retired all at once. New ones were simply added, with additional mintings as needed. In Judea there were still some coins in circulation with the marks of King Herod, dead now for thirty years. Others bore the designs of Archelaus, Gratus, and the three short-term procurators before Gratus. In the cities there were also coins from the other principalities, provinces, countries. It was the reason that every major city had its money changers. Roman currency was the only one accepted throughout the Empire.

Pilate's coins did not carry a profile of Tiberius, like the ill-fated legion standard, or another design that was clearly a graven image and therefore a violation of the Law of the Jews. They were far more subtle. They looked innocuous. A ladle and a staff. Only the most worldly, knowledgeable Jew could know that these were used by the Emperor when performing the ritual sacrifice to the gods of Rome.

In Jerusalem there were a number of such men. And in Jerusalem news traveled faster than the fleetest runner.

Pilate was in the city to honor the Holy Days, as was Rome's custom in its territories. He was on a platform under the portico of the palace, a governmental installation called the "tribunal," where he heard formal complaints, petitions, civil law suits, and other governmental matters to do with Jerusalem.

The tribunal overlooked the agora, the immense marketplace of the upper city. It was always crowded, but it became more so as the news spread about the coins.

Pilate showed no sign of worry that a mob was gathering right under his nose. He made a ruling on a dispute between two tax collectors about the line of demarcation between their territories. The first angry shout was accompanied by a hail of the new coins, thrown at Pilate. They fell short. He lifted his hand as a signal.

And then the extent of the overcrowding in the agora showed its real purpose. More shouting and brandished fists and pushing toward the tribunal began to spread throughout the crowd. As they did, men, dressed like the Jews around them, reached inside their cloaks and pulled out heavy clubs with which they began to batter the heads and bodies of the protesters. Soldiers in disguise were spread throughout the entire agora. Their ruthless, bloody work was completed in a very short time. Injured and uninjured Jews ran from the agora, leaving the fallen behind.

Pilate ordered the next petitioner in line beside the tribunal to step forward.

It was the Sejanus style, Joseph and Herod Agrippa agreed. Preparation, then sneak attack.

Herod said perhaps he would stop begging his Uncle Antipas to take him along when he went to Rome in the summer. Herod managed a laugh. "If he can tear himself away from his pathetic little kingdom. Did you know, Joseph, he has told the Galileans to address him as 'King' Herod Antipas? Oh, yes, another reason why he might not leave. He is fascinated by the wild man who's dunking people in the Jordan. I certainly hope Antipas isn't going to turn religious. Things are dreary enough in his palace as it is. I'm delighted that he pretends to be pious for the Holy Days. It gives me a chance to come to Jerusalem, get a change of scene, and see the few civilized people I know in this part of the world.

"You being first on the list, of course, Joseph. Now, where is Antiochus? I like having company on my wineshop sorties."

Joseph visited Abigail often during the eight days between the New Year and the Day of Atonement. She was the chief actor in the special conspiracy he and Antiochus had created. Barca had brought the two dogs from Belerion as Antiochus had requested. A male and a female. The female was going to give birth in about four or five weeks.

For Ella's fifth birthday Joseph hoped to have five puppies as her gift, one for each year.

Abigail would be midwife. It was the least she could do for the poor child, she said. It had been her idea to go to Arimathea.

"Although we both know, Joseph, that the moment would have come, when she understood the real meaning of her affliction. I just wish I hadn't been the instrument for it."

After the Day of Atonement Joseph made the necessary visit to the palace so that he could meet Pontius Pilate. His letter with Tiberius' seal would, he knew, gain him admittance and a welcome.

No matter what his personal opinion or attitude might be, he had to present himself as a friend, even an advisor, to the Roman Procurator. It was a necessary protection for his business enterprises and possibly, at some future time, a way for him to influence Pilate's actions regarding the Jews.

Not his attitude. If he was Sejanus' man, Pilate would surely be a Jew-hater. And his first months in office confirmed the stamp of Sejanus.

Pilate was coldly affable. A sturdy man with thinning hair and a thin nose above thick sensual lips, he had peculiarly pale eyes of yellowish-brown that looked at Joseph's chest, rather than his face, while talking to him.

Joseph was neutrally dignified. He graciously refused the Procurator's offer of a glass of wine, asking if he could receive it when next he was in Caesarea instead.

"I shall look forward to it," said Pilate. He made no attempt to sound sincere.

"I, also," said Joseph. "And may I ask that you convey my warmest greetings to the Emperor in your next dispatch? To his family, too, of course. The Lady Antonia and I have been friends for twenty years or more."

Pilate's eyes found Joseph's then. Joseph regarded him with a bland expression. Then he bowed, said farewell, and departed.

That got your attention, you miserable viper, Joseph exulted. I thought it would. I've seen for myself that Sejanus is no match for Tiberius' sister-in-law.

CHAPTER SIXTY

THERE WERE SIX PUPPIES, NOT FIVE, AND THEY BROUGHT back Ella's laughter and songs. She played with them in a large pen enclosed by willow branches that Chloe wove together with bright ribbons. Ella wanted them to sleep with her at night, but settled for taking them in turn. Chloe showed her how to make woven ribbon collars for them in different colors so they could be identified for rotation.

"And now you will learn to write their names on their collars," Joseph told her. "Your tutor will start your lessons tomorrow."

He was determined that his daughter learn to read and write. Girls weren't generally taught, but books might be her salvation. He remembered the wonders of the *Odyssey* when he was a boy. He lived every one of Ulysses' adventures with him. A chair-bound child could do many things with books and imagination, things that would never be possible for her any other way. The puppies grew—too fast—into young dogs. Ella watched them run, from her chair. But one still slept with her every night. They had learned the rotation themselves. Joseph vetoed every suggestion from Homer to stop them. Then it became apparent that another litter was on its way. "We're going to be overrun," Antiochus laughed, "and I'm going to begin barking instead of speaking." He was in charge of training the dogs.

"And soon the last litter will be old enough to breed," Joseph said helpfully. "It's in the air." Homer had recently made the proud announcement that he and Chloe would become parents in the summer.

Joseph and Antiochus returned from sending the fleet on its way just after the birth of Daphne, Homer and Chloe's child.

"Ella thinks she has a new pet," Homer told them. "She's very annoyed that babies sleep so much."

"And the baby's legs?" It was Joseph's main concern. How would Ella feel when she saw the way a normal baby could move?

Homer squeezed Joseph's arm. "She kissed the baby's feet. 'I'm so glad,' she said. We all know how brave Ella is, Joseph."

Yes, Joseph knew. He only hated the repeated testing of her bravery. He noticed that she was playing the harp more than she had been recently.

He hoped the puppies would come soon.

The sailing season always brought the greatest volume of reports from Joseph's informants. From Rome he heard that Tiberius had not returned from Capri for even one visit to Rome and that Sejanus was gaining arrogance and power every day. Joseph winced. He had another report: Antonia showed no signs of ill health. Joseph relaxed a bit. A third report defied belief, but a fourth confirmed it. Herod Antipas, a dull man in his fifties, had fallen in love! He had been married for thirty years to the daughter of the King of Nabatea, a vital alliance since Nabatea bordered his lands called Perea. But he was talking of divorcing her to marry the woman he'd lost his head over. And his heart to.

What was beyond credulity was the identity of the woman. Herodias! Berenice's daughter. Herod Agrippa's sister. And

Herod Philip's wife. Philip and Antipas were brothers. Half brothers, true, but still, brothers. How could Antipas think of such a thing? Was Herodias supposed to divorce Philip?

Joseph burned the two reports. All mention of such a lunatic rumor had to be destroyed. No one who knew anyone named in the gossip should ever hear of it.

In October five puppies were born, and Jericho's villa filled with joy. Also the King of Nabatea went to Tiberias with a company of soldiers. He returned to his country with his daughter. Someone else had heard the unbelievable story about Antipas. And had believed it.

In November, battered by storms, a ship barely made it safely into Caesarea's harbor. Aboard it were Herod Antipas, his recently wed wife Herodias, and her daughter Salome.

Joseph did not learn about this from Stratos, his Caesarea news source, for six weeks. He heard the news at a meeting of the Sanhedrin, much sooner.

The Baptizer, who had remained a concern for more than a year, was no longer a problem. He was in prison, at Machaerus, the desert fortress built by King Herod, the real King Herod, fifty years or more before, to protect his border with Nabatea.

Herod Antipas had imprisoned the Baptizer because the wild man prophet had stopped warning people to repent in favor of nonstop preaching against the sins of Herod Antipas and—even more—the sins of Herodias. She was an adulteress, he thundered, and—according to the Law of Moses—should be stoned to death. He was now exhorting the thousands who had received baptism at his hands to punish the fallen woman.

The fallen woman's new husband arrested the Baptizer as soon as troops could find him.

Ella was six. She gave Joseph a kiss, and a hug, and a tug on his beard. "Thank you for the six books, Abba. I'll learn to read them, I promise . . . Don't make that worried face, I really am happy to get them." Ella smiled. "I was worried that you might give me six baby camels or something. Really, truly, Abba, you have to stop worrying all the time about me. I'm a big girl now. I'm not going to forget my legs because of presents. I have to remember them, so I can figure out the best way to manage without them." She patted his dampened cheek.

"I'm not going to worry about you worrying, Abba. So stop it."

That spring Daphne made Homer ridiculously nervous by beginning her first reckless experiments with walking. Ella watched, curious to see how long it took to learn such a skill. She also concentrated seriously on her lessons in reading and writing.

Joseph was relieved and glad to see Herod Agrippa when he entered his Jerusalem house during Passover week. He admitted it to the younger man. "I should be ashamed of myself, Herod, but I'm as avid for gossip as an old woman. What happened to your uncle, and why did your sister agree to marry him? They must both have known it would be a scandal."

Herod Agrippa's gesture said, dramatically, that he was still incredulous. "Antipas, of all people, Joseph! I cannot believe the evidence of my own eyes. The man is like a rutting goat. He practically pants with passion every time Herodias enters a room. I was sure he was a eunuch by nature, but I was grotesquely wrong. It's embarrassing to be at dinner with them. His hand is on her bottom or her neck or trying to lift her skirt the whole time. I have to admit I watch every move. He's so wonderfully inept you would swear he's never been near a woman in his life.

"Herodias, of course, threw Philip over for Antipas because she was bored. She's been bored for years in that back-of-nowhere capital of Philip's. I think he was relieved by the whole thing. Now he'll be free of her nagging about how homesick she was, for Rome.

"Antipas is just as boring, and Tiberias won't entertain her for long. But she's got a husband now who'll do and give her anything she wants. I wouldn't be surprised to see them both in Rome within a year. Antipas can let me collect all the taxes and send him as much as he wants."

"Keeping a respectable share for yourself, I don't doubt."

"Joseph! You underrate my talents. I'll keep twice as much as I send my uncle. Maybe I'll spend some of it on my astonishing little niece. That's the most exquisitely comic part of the entire drama. Herodias is desperate to get Salome betrothed and out of sight before the goat notices that she's suddenly becoming a hundred times more attractive than her mother. I would bed her in a minute, but I don't want to get stuck in Galilee with a wife and children. I want to get rid of Sejanus and go back where I belong—the street of brothels in the Subura district, right behind Augustus' elegant forum."

Joseph was doing numerical calculations in his head. Herodias must be thirty-five or -six now. He'd always think of her as the chubby, giggly little three-year-old on the *Phoenix*. Herod was close to forty, and still thinking and talking like a naughty boy. What would Berenice have thought of her children if she had lived to see the mess they'd made of their lives? It was sad.

At least Herod was amusing. Joseph had a definite revulsion toward what Herodias had become. He had intended to visit Antipas sometime soon, about the bronze factory and their partnership. It was long past time for replacement of some equipment.

But—not the way things are now, he decided. The metal can wait.

"Abba, can we take a trip after the dry season?" Ella's eyes were bright with excitement. "I've been reading in one of the books you gave me. It's all about the sea."

"Did I give you the *Odyssey*? You're not old enough for that."

"I never heard of that. This is a story about a fish that could sing beautiful songs that made all the stars come down from the sky to listen. You and Antiochus go to the sea all the time. Will you take me next time? I promise to be very good. Antiochus told me that when I was very small you took me. But I don't remember it."

"I'll think about it."

"And you'll decide no. Please, Abba. I've already asked Antiochus, and he said yes."

How can I say no? Joseph thought. She may have gotten a love for the sea from my blood.

"Then I'll have to say yes, too, I suppose," Joseph said. Ella's smile was reward enough in advance for all the baggage they'd have to carry.

Chloe was unhappy about leaving Daphne behind. "If we can go on the road with chairs and carts and dogs and a donkey, what will it matter to have another little girl, too? Or, why can't I stay here with her? Ella can dress and undress herself and do her own hair. She mostly makes me stand back instead of helping her."

"You are going because it is your duty to go. The slave woman will do all that needs to be done for our child. Joseph didn't buy you from that Roman woman to take care of Daphne. He paid a great deal to have an attendant for his daughter."

"He pays you a great deal to attend his daughter, too. Why can't you spend all that money you've saved to buy my freedom, and then I can do what I want."

Homer adored his wife, but at this moment he wanted to throttle her. His voice was weighted with ostentatious patience as he tried to explain that if Chloe had no recognizable position in the household, he would have to set up a home for them elsewhere. In a resort town like Jericho, that kind of neighborhood simply did not exist. His savings were impressive, but they were not a fortune. "Only a man like Joseph with a fortune too great to count could afford to live the way we do here."

Chloe was still unhappy. "I wish he did not have so much

money. Then he wouldn't be able to hire so many carts and drivers and animals to carry his precious daughter and all her furniture and pets and servants wherever she has a whim to go. There must be many, many crippled children in the world without fathers who have fortunes. They manage to live, doing the best they can. Ella should do the same."

Homer put his hand over Chloe's lips. "Don't say such things. Haven't you seen Ella's eyes when she watches Daphne's first steps? Ella doesn't talk about it, but her pain is greater than any we've ever known or could imagine. Suppose it was Daphne whose legs were useless? Would you say the same thing about her?"

Chloe stopped his mouth with her hand. They looked at each other for a long moment, each muting the other's voice before worse could be said. Then Homer took Chloe in his arms and held her close while she cried bitter, remorseful tears.

Neither of them knew that Ella was close by and had heard everything they'd said. Her own two hands were held tight over her own mouth so that no one could hear the racking of agonized despair that shook her young body.

The next day she asked Joseph if Daphne was a slave, too. "Antiochus told me that when a slave has a baby, it belongs to the slave's owner."

"But Chloe isn't a slave, Ella. I bought her freedom, not her services. I pay Homer one sum for the work both of them do because he's her husband and husbands always control any money that belongs to their wives."

Ella wondered if Homer knew that Chloe was a freedwoman. She thought she'd better not ask him about it. If she did, he might guess that she had heard them talking.

"Abba, I'd prefer it if Chloe didn't come to the sea with us. She makes such a fuss over brushing my hair and braiding it. I'd much rather do it myself."

"You need her to help dress you, Ella."

"I do not! I'm over six and a half years old, and I always

dress and undress myself. All she does is hand me things or take things away. Anybody can do that, even you."

"Are you sure?"

"Sure as anything. I like to do things for myself."

Joseph was dubious, but Ella was vehement. He let her have her own way.

Carts filled the courtyard of the villa. Donkeys stood nearby, ready to be hitched to carts. Slaves with loaded arms moved in a steady stream from the house. Dogs barked.

Herod Agrippa pushed his way through the organized confusion, his outstretched hands clearing a route. He was stumbling, and covered with dust.

"Joseph!" he croaked. "Joseph! Joseph!"

Herod Agrippa was lying on a couch, weak with exhaustion, trembling with fear and horror. Joseph put a calming hand on his shoulders when the shaking became violent, or Herod's voice veered near breakdown into hysteria.

His story was truly horrifying.

For months King Aretas had been sending small bands of armed Arab horsemen across the border, from his kingdom of Nabatea into the rocky heights and desert lowlands of Antipas' small principality of Perea. They did little damage, making quick, testing raids on the small, scattered communities. Antipas sent formal written protests to his former father-in-law, considering the raids as only outbursts of temper.

But when Aretas began massing an army, Antipas acted at once. He sent two legions to reinforce the border fortress of Machaerus. The balance of his troops, he decided, he would lead himself, in a show of strength, to intimidate Aretas and to reassure the nervous townspeople and landowners in the border area. It was vital that he seem unimpressed by Aretas' raids and unafraid of his army. So Antipas took along his family, chief councilors, musicians, cooks, and twenty camel loads of imported wines and delicacies. He invited the important men of the border area to a great banquet in the luxurious private section of the fortress.

The caravan was cause for wonder on its eight-day-long-trip. Antipas intended it to cow Aretas with its wealth and magnificence. Queen Herodias rode with him in a large shaded litter borne by eighteen Nubian slaves wearing wide gold necklaces, armbands, and ankle bracelets.

Much of the route followed the banks of the Jordan River, where there were several ugly incidents. Small groups of people threw rocks at the litter, from a distance, and shouted insults at the royal couple, especially Herodias. "Adulteress" was the most frequently used, "whore" the second.

The banquet was, of course, for men only. Antipas lounged on his silk-clad couch at the center of the table, urging his guests to eat more, drink more, enjoy themselves. Musicians played, acrobats and jugglers performed. The final—and most enthusiastically greeted—performers were dancers, women in gauze-like silk Arabian costumes, including transparent veils over their faces. It was a finely calculated insult to the Arab king of Nabatea, and Antipas' guests roared with approval. The fast-paced erotic dance was heightened in its blood-racing stimulation by the insistent, ever louder pulse of beating drums.

Then, in an instant, they stopped. Their reverberations echoed, thrown back by the hewn stone walls of the great chamber. The dancers fell supine on the floor. The guests— and Antipas—were startled. They looked at one another, confused.

A single flute began to play. And a lone dancer moved slowly into the area in front of the table. It was Salome, Herodias' fourteen-year-old daughter. She had the innocence of childhood, the still-undiscovered sensuality of a woman, and a soft-firm, newly developed, voluptuous virgin body that shone alluringly through the floating silks.

Salome did not dance as well as the women who had preceded her. She was unskilled and therefore a thousand times more exciting because of her youth and innocence.

When she finished dancing, there was the silence that signified more than even the most deafening applause. She ran quickly to kneel beside Antipas' couch. "Was it all right?" she whispered. "Mother said you'd like me." Her eyes were huge and dark, and her long unbound hair clung to her glowing skin, dampened by the efforts of her dancing. Antipas lifted a soaked tendril from her forehead and stretched it across and down her head and behind her ear.

"She has asked me if her dancing was acceptable," he said to his guests.

Their loud approval had a wildness in it, and Salome trembled. "You were superb, dear child," said Antipas. His beringed hand caressed her smooth, quivering throat. "I will reward you. Name anything, and it is yours, even unto half my kingdom."

His guests applauded Antipas' extravagant language and grandiloquent offer.

Salome looked toward the door in the corner of the room. It was open, a few inches only. Herodias, standing behind it, gestured to her daughter. Salome jumped up and ran to her mother.

Herod Agrippa sat up and caught hold of Joseph's cloak with gripping, desperate hands. "The door swung wide," he said, "and Herodias was there, Joseph, in all her jewels and a tall golden crown. She walked out to face Antipas, and she spoke.

"'The head of the man John who baptized in the Jordan, that is what my daughter wants. Is it not so, Salome? The man who reviled your mother, you want him killed, to avenge her!' Her fingers tightened on Salome's arm, and Salome nodded.

"Then Herodias stared at Antipas. 'Before your guests you offered Salome anything, even the half of your kingdom. Do you deny it, Herod Antipas?' He shook his head.

"My sister laughed at him, Joseph. The sound of it will not leave my ears. She mocked her husband, asked him if the head of a prisoner in the dungeon below them was more valuable than half of his kingdom.

"I couldn't believe what was happening. Salome began to weep. Herodias shook her. 'Tell your king, your new father, that this is your wish, Salome. The severed head of the Baptizer, brought here to the banquet hall, on a large plate for the dinner's final course. Tell him.'

"'This is my wish,' Salome said.

"Joseph, I had to get away from there, from what was happening. But my limbs would not move, would not carry me. I believe the others were the same.

"Herodias ordered the musicians to play. She spat at Antipas' bodyguards, who were standing behind the couch. 'Obey your master. Order them, Antipas. *Order them.*'"

Herod Agrippa's voice was shaking, like his body. "Antipas gave the order. The music played and played. Then the instruments gave a noise of dying, and the guards walked in. They bore a wooden plank. The grisly horror was at its center, on a great golden platter. The hair streamed over the sides, of platter and of plank. It dripped hot blood onto the marble floor.

"On all sides of me men were sick, were gasping, were scrambling to their feet to run from the monstrous deed. I, too. Somehow I managed to flee, in their midst. Behind my back there was a sound. The laughter of Herodias.

"My sister, Joseph, that I loved from childhood. How will I live with that sound?"

"How did you get here, Herod Agrippa?" Joseph deliberately made his tone businesslike, as if he was talking about a ship's route. There was too much emotion around. In him, in Herod, in the very room that enclosed them.

"I stole a camel and broke a branch from some bush. I rode all night, beating the beast and screaming at the stars."

"Steady . . . steady. It's done. Leave it behind. What are you going to do?"

"How can I think about that? I'm going to get away."

Herod's words were shrill, rising. Joseph pressed his shoulder.

"You cannot think yet. But I can. And you must listen to me, Herod. You will not run away. If you do, you will be dangerous. Those other men, who were they? Little men from little towns. Some musicians. Dancers. They would not dare tell of such an act by their king. Or, if they did, they would not be believed.

"But you—the King's nephew, the Queen's brother. People would believe you. Tiberius would believe you. Antipas would not allow that, cannot let you go.

"This is what we will do, what you will do. You will write a short letter to Antipas. You will tell him that when all the guests were leaving, you became entangled in the crowd and were carried outside. The night was beautiful, a camel was at hand. You decided to have the adventure of crossing the desert under the stars. When morning came, you were tired. It was too far to return to the fortress in the heat of the day. So you came to Jericho. Because you knew from our meeting in Jerusalem that I have been planning a visit to Tiberias, and you decided to accompany me.

"Antipas will know that you are lying. But he will also know that you have not fled, that you are with me. And he can be certain that I will not allow you to spread stories that might injure him. Because he and I are partners in a profitable business."

Herod drew away from Joseph. "Business is more important than murder. Is that it?"

"Don't be a child, Herod Agrippa. You're too old and too intelligent for that. I'll bring you paper and ink. Then I'll see about departure time from here. The sooner, the better."

"Joseph? Are you really going to take me to Tiberias?"

"It appears to be necessary. Write exactly as I told you. Afterwards, if there is time, you can have a bath before we leave. Antiochus will shave you. I like to have respectable company on my travels."

CHAPTER SIXTY-ONE

THE ROUTE JOSEPH TOOK TO TIBERIAS WASN'T DIRECT, BUT it was cooler, passing through hills that were well watered and green. More important, there were small cities, with excellent facilities for travelers, spaced close enough together so that no single day's journey was too long and tiring. Most important of all, these cities were among the group known as the Decapolis. They were under the direct control of Rome, almost totally Gentile, and would have no interest in the death of the Baptizer, even if it were mentioned to them.

The travelers did not enter Antipas' territory until the fifth day, when they reached the Sea of Galilee, about ten miles south of Tiberias.

"Is that the sea, Abba?" Ella looked at the deep blue waters and clapped her hands.

"It's called a sea, but it is like a bowl of water, compared with the real sea. We can certainly enjoy this, there are boats for hire. Then in a few days we will go to the beautiful marble city on the real sea."

Joseph was quite confident about the time they'd have to stay in Tiberias. For himself. He had many years' practice in masking his emotions, and he'd had to deal with people nearly as repugnant as Herodias. He was, however, worried about Herod Agrippa's stability. Antiochus had done what Joseph asked. In each of the Decapolis cities where they'd stayed overnight, Antiochus had taken Herod along on a tour of discovery of wineshops, food shops, gambling, and other entertainment availabilities. Philadelphia . . . Gerasa . . . Pella . . . Gadara—all had contributed to Herod's return to his customary feckless good humor. Now he should be able to maintain the pretense that everything was normal—both past and present.

The city that Antipas had built was directly on the sea, luxuriant with palms and flowers and fountains. An esplanade ran beside the water. Salome delighted in going there with Ella, in her cart behind Clip. They stopped often for the sweets and souvenirs sold by peddlers and to hold their faces into the fresh breezes. Salome was, Joseph thought, happy to be a child again, with another child.

Homer complained that Ella's exercise schedule had been cut short on every day of the trip and that now he had the time he needed but Salome was always there, talking a blue streak with Ella.

We won't be here long, Joseph promised him.

He said the same thing to Antiochus. In warning, not promise. The Galatian had gone off on his own, to explore the fishing villages on the sea. "And not for wineshops," he said emphatically. "I intend to get drunk on fresh air and not sour wine. I'll only be gone a few days, but I do need some time without Herod Agrippa."

They had arrived the afternoon before the Sabbath. Joseph had a strong suspicion that his presence in the palace was the cause of Antipas' devoted observation of the day of rest that followed, but he didn't care. The Sabbath always refreshed him, and he was tired. Travel with a baggage train was very different from travel with a mount or, simply, his own feet.

He looked down at the preponderance of gray hairs in his beard. It just might possibly have some connection with your birthday, he told himself. He hadn't mentioned it to anyone, but somewhere in the Decapolis he'd become sixty years old.

On the day following the Sabbath, Joseph and Antipas talked about the bronze smelting factory on Cyprus.

And the day after that, Antipas' scribe wrote two copies of the new agreement regarding the work that had to be done. Joseph and Antipas would divide costs equally. Joseph would manage the organization of workmen and check the quality of their work.

Everything had gone smoothly and quickly. Joseph was both relieved and glad. The bronze questions had really needed settling sooner or later, and now everything was done. He need not have been apprehensive at all. Herodias had kept to herself, other than greeting him with polished, almost convincing pleasure. Herod Agrippa had claimed to be working during the day at whatever his unimportant duties were. And at dinner, Joseph and the two Herods talked quite easily about people and places they all knew. Augustus Caesar was Joseph's favorite, but the others were most interested in King Herod, the father and grandfather they'd hardly known at all.

Joseph was quite willing to tell his anecdotes and to laugh at himself while doing so. There was that about growing older—a man had a larger collection of memories, and the distance to remember his follies with a certain fondness.

Antiochus returned for dinner on the fourth evening, which meant they would pack up and leave the next day. Caesarea was fewer than forty miles away. Possible to manage in one long day if everything went well.

Joseph was determined to see to it. There was still enough good weather left to sail from Caesarea to Cyprus, get the work plans started, and return to port before the first storms.

Ella would be able to see what the real sea was like.

* * *

The farewells did not take long, and Antipas' soldiers helped the cart drivers with the donkeys so Joseph's group was on the road when the morning was still fresh. A gentle sprinkling of rain had laid the dust on the road. Conditions were perfect.

Joseph and Antiochus rode side by side in companionable silence, leading their little procession. After a while Antiochus began to chuckle. "Funny how charming Herod Agrippa can be in memory when he sometimes irritates you so, in person."

"How much money did he get out of you?" Joseph was chuckling, too.

"A hundred sesterces. How about you?"

"A thousand."

Both of them had a good laugh at the other's expense.

"How did things go with Antipas?" Antiochus asked.

"Much better than expected. It's a good thing you came back when you did. He might have changed his mind about some of the things he agreed to if he'd had more time to think about them.

"Did you enjoy the fishing villages? And all the fresh air?"

"In fact I did stumble across a good local vintage. The fishing fleet was interesting. I went out one day with some men. The color of the water in the center of the lake is fantastic." Antiochus hesitated. "Joseph, a lot of people were talking about a local healer. They say—"

Joseph cut him off. "We've been through all that, Antiochus. You wanted to try the magician in Gaza, remember? Frauds. That's what these popular wonders are. You notice, they never stay in one place. They have to keep ahead of the people they've bilked."

"All right. You can stop steaming from the ears; I'll hold my tongue. The hills are starting to look menacing. Should I bring the dogs up front? The Galilean bandits hide out in the hills, and they love to attack the obvious rich."

"The drivers all have cudgels and swords. I feel safe

enough this close to the city. When we stop to eat, we might regroup."

They'd been on their way for a little over two hours when they saw the delay ahead. The road was clogged with people—farmers, by the look of them—arguing and shouting and shoving. Not moving.

"What's this all about?" Joseph grumbled. He dismounted. "We'll just push through and make room for the carts."

Antiochus joined Joseph. "Make way," he shouted. No one even looked at him. They were all shouting at a woman who was brandishing a staff and stabbing at people who got close to her. She was standing between two mounds of jagged rock, blocking a path that led up the hill behind her.

"You can fight the madwoman later." Joseph yelled at two men close to him. He reached out to move them aside. "Clear the road for my carts, or I'll turn my dogs on the bunch of you."

One of the men grabbed Joseph's arm. "You've got dogs? Turn them on her. He's up there, see?" The man pointed to the people on top of the low hill. "She won't let us get to him."

Antiochus closed his hand around the man's wrist and pulled him away from Joseph. "Blocking the road won't help you. Go around another way. We're coming through. If these people are friends of yours, warn them that I'm going for the dogs."

"I've come all the way from Damascus," the man said. "No woman and no dogs are going to keep me from seeing Jesus of Nazareth."

Joseph turned angrily to quiet the horses. "Go for the dogs, Antiochus," he said.

Antiochus was already running back to where the carts and Ella's litter were stopped. Joseph turned toward the crowd again, to warn them. "*Dogs!*" he bellowed. "Get out of the road or you'll be hurt." He didn't want to have to loose the dogs on these people. They were formidable weapons.

He'd hold their ropes, let the people see what they were capable of doing, Joseph thought.

Then he saw Antiochus. Ella was in his arms, holding fearfully around his neck. He was running, with long strides, as fast as any horse.

Joseph started toward them. "What are you doing?" Antiochus ignored him. He bent his head between his shoulders and butted people aside, making his way toward the woman with the staff.

She raised it, prepared to swing it against his head. Ella screamed. So did Antiochus.

"This child cannot walk. Let me take her to Jesus."

The woman grasped her staff more tightly. "He's tired. He gets tired, too, like other men. He's been up there since dawn. People never stop coming. He's got to rest."

Antiochus was weeping. "Please," he said. His tone was humble. "Please." He held Ella toward the woman. "She's never been able to stand. Her legs have never worked. She's such a good girl, so brave."

Ella wrapped her arms more tightly around Antiochus. He was frightening her with his intensity.

The woman smiled at the little girl. "Don't be afraid. I won't hit him if it'll make him drop you." The change in her was like sunlight emerging from a dark cloud. "He especially loves children," she said. "Step behind me and go up."

On the edge of the crowd was Joseph. Frantic. Calling, "Ella!" and "Antiochus!" and "Ella!" again. And yet again.

Then he saw them, on the hill, ascending by way of the narrow strip of green that zigzagged through sharp-edged boulders. He could see Ella's frightened eyes above Antiochus' shoulder.

Joseph didn't know anything—not what had frightened Ella, not why Antiochus was doing this, not whether the dogs had already been set free. He knew only that Sarah's little girl, their child, was afraid, and he had to get to her.

He became the young Joseph, the sailor Joseph, not the shipowner, and the road became a waterfront alley or pier. His hands became fists, or claws, and his feet and knees and elbows became vicious, knowing seekers of soft spots on the bodies that blocked his way.

He was hit in the throat, and he gagged, but kept going. Someone tripped him, and he fell. He got to his knees, fists striking out at anyone, anything that kept him from Ella.

The woman's staff end struck him in the chest. "No," she said.

Joseph grabbed the staff with both hands. "Yes," he said. They began to struggle.

"Abba! Abba!" It was Ella's voice.

Joseph searched for her with his eyes, looked for Antiochus.

"Abba!" The sound told him where she was.

"Abba!" Ella was laughing. And she was running, running down the hill.

CHAPTER SIXTY-TWO

"ELLA!" JOSEPH LET GO OF THE STAFF AND HELD OUT HIS arms toward his little girl.

The woman stepped aside. "Get on, you people," she shouted. "No sense waiting here. Jesus is gone." She turned her back on the curses that the crowd was hurling at her, to watch father and child.

Joseph lurched forward and fell. He'd been injured in his battle to reach the gate, but he hadn't noticed anything. Even now, he was unaware of the bruises on his body and face, and the blood streaming from a cut near one eye. He tried to get to his feet, but it wasn't necessary. Ella reached him when he was on his knees and threw her small round arms about his neck to hug him. But the sight of his face made her stop.

"Abba, you're hurt."

"It doesn't matter, my love. You're well."

"Isn't it wonderful?" Ella released Joseph, ran back and forth before him.

"A wonder," Joseph murmured. "A miracle." He looked upon his radiant, capering little girl, and his heart was too full to allow him thought.

Antiochus was hurrying down the path; he was dazed, like Joseph.

Only Ella and the woman with the staff seemed to be able to speak or think. "Where were you heading?" the woman asked her.

"To the sea, to Caesarea."

"You'll never get there today. You're not far from Sepphoris, though. Who's in charge of your travel?" She pointed at the string of carts that was approaching as the road cleared.

"My abba," said Ella. "But he's hurt. I'd better go get Homer. He'll know how to help Abba."

The woman grinned. "Whoever this Homer is, I'd best talk to him before he sees you. You wait with your friend and your abba. What is your name?"

"Ella."

"My name is Mary, Ella. Now, I'll go talk to Homer and send him to you." She looked at Joseph. Antiochus was stooping beside him, talking, his hands gesturing. "That one's not going to be much good to you for a while. Take this." She handed her staff to Ella. "Your abba's going to need something to help him walk. Do a little dance for me before I go."

Ella was happy to obey. Mary smiled. "Goodbye, Ella," she called over her shoulder as she walked away.

"Goodbye, Mary. Thank you for your stick." Ella held the staff upright on the path and ran around it in circles.

Antiochus told the story again and again. He never tired of telling it.

"Ella was holding tight to my neck because I was jouncing her so by my running. When I reached the top of the hill, I was breathless. I saw the man, walking away down the other side, and I could barely gasp 'Wait. Help.' He turned around. Jesus.

"Ella had stopped crying. Jesus asked her, 'Are you frightened?' and she said, 'No. Everything is all right.' Then he looked at me. 'Put her down,' he said, and I began to bend over, to set her on the ground. But he said, 'On her feet.' So I did. And she stood.

"She looked at her feet, then her legs, then at Jesus. And she threw her arms up in the air while she did a kind of hopping little dance. She was laughing. He laughed with her, then walked down the hill with the others."

Everyone at Arimathea marveled at the miracle. In the village and at the farms.

That was where they had gone, after Sepphoris. "We can't go to sea this year," Joseph told Ella apologetically. His knee was sprained, and he knew he couldn't be useful on a ship. Ella didn't mind, she said. She wanted to go to Arimathea even more. To dance on the grapes.

But it was too late in the year for the vintage, Joseph explained. That would have to wait until next summer, too, like the sea.

No matter, Ella assured him. She'd be happy running and playing with her cousins.

As indeed she was. There were more than a dozen children at the farms. Joseph's brother Amos was a grandfather of eight, and Caleb had five. Actually they had more, but not at the farms. Their daughters had married and lived many miles away.

Six families in three houses. Joseph began at once to remedy the crowding. Even though the farms were no longer his property, he still asserted his ancestral right to improve them. Within a week the existing houses were gaining additional rooms, and four new houses were under construction, the biggest one for him. If Ella wanted to visit her cousins, Joseph would see to it that she would have all the comforts to which she was accustomed and entitled.

Amos ranted. But only to Rachel, his wife. No one could be so heartless as to say anything to Joseph that might dim his radiant happiness.

Rachel, a sensible woman, told Amos to concentrate on getting the plowing done. She would be glad to get Joshua and his wife and his children out of the house. "That girl," she said, "insists on adding too many onions to everything I cook." She meant, of course, her son's wife.

Once the house building was well under way, Joseph left for Jerusalem and Jericho before the main rains began and the roads became impassable. He had to ride in the litter with his wrapped knee supported by a cushion. Ella rode with him sometimes, chattering merrily about what she had done with her cousins during the visit. But mostly she preferred to walk—or run—or dance—alongside the litter, or to ride on a horse or a donkey.

Homer watched her every minute. He was overjoyed, like everyone, by her healing. But he was worried about the strength of her legs and the possibility of an accident. He'd be glad, he admitted to Joseph, to get Ella back to Jericho and a regular routine of strengthening exercise.

He did not tell Joseph the rest of his intention. Once he was satisfied that Ella no longer needed him, he was going to buy Chloe's freedom and take her home to Greece, where both of them belonged and where he wanted Daphne, and any future children, to grow up.

Antiochus did not travel with them. Joseph had given the Galatian authorization to withdraw a large amount of gold from Stratos' strong room at Caesarea. Antiochus was to find Jesus of Nazareth and give him the treasure. "There is not enough wealth in the world," Joseph said, "to pay for Ella's healing. Tell him that whatever he wants, I will get it for him if it is in my power."

Ella's exercises quickly became more like play. Homer taught her at once how to use her legs in swimming, then how to "dance" in the water, doing underwater somersaults, forward and backward, using her legs, feet, and ankles for power and control. After that it was easy and logical to somersault outdoors, on the soft grass. Then cartwheels. Then gymnastics.

She loved discovering what her body could do. Homer

loved observing her steady, rapid progress. Not only for Ella's sake, but also for his and Chloe's.

Sometimes Joseph had to look away from Ella's antics; they seemed dangerous to him. Otherwise, he could feast on the sight of her. Just standing. Or walking.

Sometimes he woke, terrified, in the night, afraid that he had dreamed her healing, that it was not true. Then, like a thief, he would go quietly into the room where she was sleeping and fearfully tickle the sole of a foot. When she automatically jerked the foot away, Joseph thanked God.

He also thanked Him with sacrifices in the Temple. He arranged for one lamb and one offering of incense every day, whether he could be there or not. Using all his influence as one of the Sanhedrin, he was able to buy special music to accompany the sacrifice. Ella loved music.

The Sanhedrin was becoming, more and more, a place where men could air their worries and discuss them. The execution of John the Baptizer had become common knowledge. Not, Joseph was grateful, the details of its horrifying circumstances, but the deed was blamed, rightly, on Herodias' influence over her husband.

The Baptizer's followers were spreading his message throughout the land: The day of judgment was near, and the Messiah would be revealed. Soon.

Some of the followers were not waiting. Like the Baptizer, they were willing to accept martyrdom for their beliefs. In Galilee, it was reported, Herod Antipas was not offering trials. Executions were secret and widespread.

Pontius Pilate, too, was becoming ever more brutal and dangerous. Anyone prophesying the downfall of Rome at the hands of a soon-to-arrive Messiah was a criminal, an enemy of the Empire and its appointed representative. No one knew how many men had been executed or how many were in prison at the fortresses Pilate controlled throughout Judea.

At one meeting a judge brought up a new name. Jesus of

Nazareth. "It is said by some," he reported, "that this Jesus is John the Baptizer reborn. Antipas is fearful of him."

Joseph was able to correct that rumor easily. "I have personal knowledge of this man. He is a great healer. My own daughter was cured by him. My servant told me what he had learned about this Galilean. He has cured the blind, lepers, and the lame. That is what he does. Not baptizing and preaching the judgment day."

"Where can I find this man?" another judge asked eagerly. "My wife is beginning to lose her sight."

Joseph had to disappoint him. "I could not find him myself. Rather, my servant could not. I sent him with a reward for the healer, after my daughter's cure. But this Jesus moves from place to place, with no particular path or timing. My man heard he was in Tyre. When he arrived in Tyre, he was told the healer had gone to Sidon. In Sidon they told him the Decapolis. And so on."

Joseph held up the staff that leaned on the arm of his chair. "I wish I could find him myself. This knee of mine keeps reminding me that men of my age need a stick to get them up and down stairs."

Several other judges showed canes or other aids. They were all in the same predicament. The only thing to do was to mock their debilities, and so they did. The Sanhedrin Chamber echoed with laughter.

Antiochus had been extremely downcast when he had to report failure after almost two months of searching for the healer. He had thrown the heavy money belt on the floor at Joseph's feet. "Shackles of gold are no more comfortable than shackles of iron," he'd complained. "I'm going to get drunk, Joseph. I'm not accustomed to failure."

"Go tell Homer to give you a massage first. There's nothing wrong with feeling better. You can still get drunk."

"I hate it when you're right. A bath and a massage are exactly what I need. Oh—the reports from Caesarea are in the belt, too."

Joseph reached for them at once. He'd been out of touch with the rest of the world too long.

The most important news was the confirmation of Joseph's greatest apprehensions. The Emperor Tiberius was still shut away on his island Capri, and Sejanus grew daily more dangerous. Sejanus—the patron of Pontius Pilate.

The next Holy Festival would be the Feast of Lights. Joseph would have to pay a holiday visit to the palace while Pilate was in Jerusalem.

There was a single line of good news. At least, perhaps it was good. Berenice's stepson, Joseph's friend Marcus, was now a senator. That was a great honor. Joseph hoped that Marcus hadn't gotten the election due to any help from Sejanus. He would hate for Berenice's boy to sink that low.

Joseph had a cup of wine, at Pilate's urging, and a cautious, seemingly pleasant conversation about nothing at all. When he left the palace and walked out into the rain, he felt it was safe to shiver. He wanted to do so every time he looked into Pilate's cold eyes.

He set off to walk the few blocks to his house. Clomp, clomp, clomp his staff sounded on the wet stone paving of the street. Joseph began to smile. He had a joke to tell everyone in Jericho when he went there tomorrow. Ella had had Clip. He would name his staff Clomp.

There were handsomer ones he could get. Carved from rare woods, trimmed with gold, silver, even jewel stones. But this rough-hewn length of wood was more precious to him than any other could ever be. It was, in a way, part of the miracle of Ella's healing.

Ella giggled about Clomp. She liked everything to have a name. She had seen Clip only the day before, she reported, and had scratched his head for a long time while she talked to the little boy in the cart. Clip, cart, and chairs had been given to a child who had a broken leg that was healing too slowly.

"Did you see Aunt Abigail when you were in Jerusalem?" asked Ella. Family was important to her.

Joseph presented the news he'd been saving. "Yes, I did. She sends her love. And she is going to go with us to Arimathea to look at the new houses."

Ella jumped up and down. "When, when, when?"

"In about three weeks, when the rains are not too heavy."

Ella cartwheeled across the garden.

She cartwheeled down the street in the center of Arimathea village when they arrived there. Abigail clucked disapprovingly, to hide her laughter. "Naughty little show-off," she said. "It's a good thing you got rid of that Greek when you did, Joseph."

"I didn't get rid of Homer. He decided it was time to leave." Joseph remembered the expression on Homer's face when he learned that Chloe was a freedwoman, not a slave. The memory made up for the surprising hole left by the absence of Daphne. It was good that there was a two-year-old cousin at Arimathea to take the little girl's place in Ella's heart.

"Stop wheeling now, Ella," he called. "We're going to see the new house."

It was perfect, in Joseph's opinion. Plain stone block walls, with a flat roof and easy stairs to reach it. Built around a courtyard, in which the corner cisterns held plenty of collected rainwater. Large rooms, small rooms, store rooms, a special sheltered area for the dogs. Exactly what he had asked for.

Ella thought it was perfect, too. For Caleb's son Gideon and his family. "We don't need so much room, and they do, Abba. There are six of them, and only you and me and Antiochus, now that Homer and Chloe are gone."

Joseph gave in gracefully. Provided that Gideon would take care of the dogs. He considered it a more-than-fair trade. The original pair from Belerion were now proud parents and grandparents of an ever-growing family, even though he had given away puppies from every litter, in spite of Ella's objections.

After a whole-family discussion about the house, Joseph ended up with the small house where he and Sarah had lived. Nothing could have pleased him more. He walked through the familiar rooms alone, wrapping himself in memories.

"Your little girl looks more like you every day, my love," he whispered to the memories. "The same great dark eyes and tiny bird bones and raven's-wing dark hair."

When Purim came, with the village square music and dancing and noise making and costumes, Ella declared she had never had so much fun in her life.

She said the same thing when the whole family went to Jerusalem together and Abigail served her traditional Passover feast.

And again, when Joseph brought her back to Arimathea for the vintage. She danced in the grape-pressing cistern every day until her strong little legs were stained to the knee with grape juice.

"This really, truly is the best of all, Abba," she said every evening when he kissed her before blowing out the lamp by her bed.

The following year, for Purim, she made strings of raisins to wear around her neck, and stained her legs with wine she had purloined from the storage cave.

"I didn't use very much," she said when Joseph scolded her. "There's lots left for you and Antiochus to drink. I needed it for my costume. I'm the vintage dancer, you see."

The raisin necklace, suitable for eating, too, was so successful that Ella made them for all the cousins. On the trip to the city there was a noisy competition about who could arrive in Jerusalem with at least one raisin left.

The road became more crowded with families like theirs as they came nearer to the city. Joseph looked frequently at the sky, worried about the hour. A heavy storm—unprecedented at this time of the year—had forced them to shelter for a time under the carts. The final group to sacrifice the Passover lamb was always the largest. Therefore the slowest. Joseph was glad that Amos was the one who would be doing it, and not him.

"Until tomorrow's feast," Joseph said to the family. He took Ella's hand in his. "Let's go home to our house now."

"Oh, let her stay here with her cousins," Abigail said.

"Please, Abba?"

"Very well. Help Aunt Abigail with the feast. And no cartwheels in the kitchen."

Antiochus slowed his steps to match Joseph's as they climbed the steps. When they were on the highest level street, it was easier to walk, and Joseph clomped along with his staff at a rapid rate. He'd be glad to reach his quiet house, quiet garden, and a quiet slave to bring him a glass of wine.

A huddled figure crouched in front of Joseph's door leapt up and ran toward him when he came near. It was a woman, her hair disheveled, her face swollen and distorted by tears.

"Joseph of Arimathea?" she called out. "You remember me. I gave you that staff you carry. Tragedy has befallen us, and I need your help.

"He's dead! Jesus. They've crucified him!"

CHAPTER SIXTY-THREE

"WHAT ARE YOU TALKING ABOUT, WOMAN?" JOSEPH COULD hardly make himself heard through the mighty howl of rage and despair that poured from Antiochus' throat.

"Jesus of Nazareth! The Romans crucified him, and they won't let us take him down from the cross to bury him. We are only women. You are an important man, you can make them give us our Master. The day is almost ending; we must bury him. The Passover is coming."

Joseph didn't actually remember the woman, but that didn't matter. What she said was true. There was little time. He remembered only too vividly the slaughter in Jerusalem in Archelaus' time and the tormented cries of mourning throughout the night and day of Passover until the Holy Day was ended and the dead could be buried. Joseph had to act now.

Why the healer had been executed didn't matter either. The nature of this service for the man who had performed a miracle was pitiful. But at least it was something Joseph could do for the one who had done so much, so very much, for him.

Joseph struck Antiochus on his arm with all the force he could muster. "Your wits are needed, man, not your howling. I am going to Pilate. You get some men and a litter and an instrument to remove the nails. Take them—the woman will lead you there—to the place of execution. I will come, with Pilate's authority. Now hurry."

Joseph started toward the palace, stopped, turned. "Take some linen for grave clothes," he said. "Hurry, man!" Then he turned to hurry, himself, to Pontius Pilate.

"This man deserved to die," Pilate said coldly. "He has been—"

Joseph cut him off. The light was fading. "I know not, and I care not, Pontius Pilate. The dead deserve burial. Give me your seal and tell me where the execution took place. The time is short."

Joseph's manner was even colder than Pilate's, and had greater authority. Within moments he was on his way, escorted by Pilate's own men, with Pilate's scrawled and sealed authority to release the body.

The usual mob of the curious was gathered at the base of the low hill outside the city walls, called Golgotha. When they saw Pilate's men, they moved back to make room for them and began to disperse, afraid of what the soldiers might do.

Joseph paid no attention. He was looking ahead, and what he saw was heart wrenching. Three tall crosses with their piteous burdens stood stark in outline against the fading sky. The healer's must be in the center; Antiochus and the woman were standing at the foot of it arguing with a group of Roman guards.

Joseph looked up at the man who had given him the greatest happiness of his life; he'd never seen Jesus of Nazareth. So young! The healer must have been still in his thirties when he was killed. And tortured. The dried bloody stripes of the whip could be seen on his sides; his back must still be covered with open gashes. A larger gaping wound was gory on his side, staining his loincloth. Most pitiful of all was the healer's blood-streaked face. A wreath of thorns had been cruelly forced onto his head, ripping into his flesh.

So much pain. And yet . . . the face of Jesus bore an expression of peace beneath the blood and the lines etched by the agony of his death. Joseph could envision that face when it had smiled at Ella and presented her with the gift of a miracle. His heart turned over. Why? Why did this young man have to die? Why couldn't I have been in Jerusalem to stop it?

No time for such thoughts now. Joseph strode as fast as his knee would permit, holding out Pilate's authority. "This body is released to me," he shouted. Antiochus, the woman, and the guards all looked at him. "You heard me," Joseph said crisply. "Here is the authority. Now take this man down from the cross."

The centurion saw Pilate's guards as Joseph's escort. He barely glanced at the papyrus in Joseph's hand. "Ladder," he ordered his men, "and pry-bar."

Antiochus grabbed the ladder from the soldiers. "Don't touch him," he said. "I will bring him down." He placed the end of the ladder in the sockets cut into the rock. Its top rungs leaned on the horizontal bar of the cross, the wood of it stained at the spots where Jesus' wrists were impaled. Antiochus began to climb. "Joseph, I have my own prying bar. Take the soldier's and free the healer's feet."

The woman pulled on Joseph's arm. "Let me free him." But Joseph pushed her aside. He had a great need to do something for this man, even this ghastly service. "Help that woman," he said. Nearby an older woman was on her knees, bent over in suffering. The spike-nail that pierced the healer's crossed feet came out easily, so quickly that Joseph staggered backward several steps. He looked up. For the first time he saw the unevenly painted plaque nailed at the top of the cross. It said: "JESUS OF NAZARETH THE KING OF THE JEWS." Joseph frowned in puzzlement.

Antiochus had freed one arm. It lay limp across his shoulder, onto his back. He held his own left arm beneath the healer's freed one and across Jesus' back, supporting the body and the thorn-crowned head that lay on his shoulder. The pry-bar's notched end was easing out the remaining nail. It fell at Joseph's feet. He moved away from its cruel ugliness.

Antiochus descended the ladder slowly. Joseph wanted to urge him to hurry, there was so little light in the skies. But he could not fault his friend for cradling the dead healer and trying to protect him from further injury.

The woman who'd been kneeling was on her feet now, hurrying to the cross, her arms reaching up to Antiochus. "Let me hold him," she begged. "I am his mother."

While Joseph brought the litter and bearers, Jesus' mother knelt beneath the weight of his body, holding the torn head to her heart. The thorn wreath lay apart, thrown after she had lifted it from him. She was not weeping, only whispering wordless sounds of comfort, as to a hurt child.

"Mary, they must take him now," said the woman who had come for Joseph. Jesus' mother nodded.

Antiochus lifted her son's body from her arms and placed it on the litter.

"Quickly," said Joseph, "follow me. I have an empty tomb nearby. Antiochus, bring the linens and give me your arm to lean on. We must make haste."

The women held each other close, waiting in the garden area that lay in front of Joseph's tomb. Inside the roughly carved hollow in the rock, Joseph hurriedly spread out the linen sheets on the shelf cut from the stone inside the tomb. Antiochus carried the body of Jesus and laid it on the sheets. He straightened the legs and arms.

"Stop!" The woman was in the opening of the tomb, holding the staff. "We must get herbs and ointments for the winding sheets."

"There is no time, woman. After Passover you can bring

them." Joseph was folding a big square of linen across the healer's bloodstained brow. When it was done, he rested his hand for a moment on the clean cloth. "I never had a chance to thank you," he said softly. "From the bottom of my very being, I will be grateful to you for all the days remaining to my life."

He and Antiochus wrapped the sheets tightly across and around the body. Then they went outside. The sky was beginning to gray.

"Here," said Joseph. "Pull out the stake." Across the mouth of the tomb ran a channel cut into the rocky base. On a small rise to the left, the channel held the bottom of a tremendous solid wheel of shaped stone. A tall wooden stake placed in a carved socket held it away from the tomb. Antiochus snatched the stake away. With a heavy, thunderous noise the stone rolled down to seal the tomb.

"It is done," Joseph said with a great sigh. "In time." He looked at the dimming light. "We must leave. The path is steep and uneven, and it will soon be dark. At midday on the day after Passover, I will return with my servants to roll the stone away. Then we will do everything as it should be done. I'll bring fresh linens and myrrh and aloes.

"Come, now. Let me have the staff. Antiochus, will you help the women? The litter bearers can help me and carry the litter as well."

When they reached the road that led to the gate in the city wall, Joseph was able to catch his breath. He did not allow himself any emotion yet.

He approached the two women and Antiochus. "Lady," he said to Jesus' mother, "I would be honored if you would allow me to do something for you. May I offer you shelter in my house? Both of you."

Jesus' mother shook her head. "Friends expect me," she said. "I will thank you when we meet again."

Joseph bowed. "So be it." He looked at the other woman. "And you? Forgive me; if I knew your name, I have forgotten it."

"I will accompany Mary," she said. "I am Mary, too. Mary of Magdala. The Master's mother is Mary of Nazareth."

"Will you take your staff, Mary of Magdala? You must both be very tired."

"You need it more than I do, Joseph of Arimathea. Keep it."

Antiochus stayed where he was, between the two Marys. "I will accompany you to wherever you are going," he told them. "Lean on me."

"There is a house in the lower city where the closest followers of Jesus are staying," he told Joseph when he reached the house that evening. "Hiding, I should say; they are all frightened out of whatever wits they might have ever had. I took the women there. One of the men, named John, says that before he died on the cross Jesus told him to look after his mother."

"And the other Mary?"

"She launched right away into a violent denouncement of their cowardice in leaving Jesus after he was arrested. I thought I'd better leave, so I did." Antiochus was quiet for a few seconds, then he burst out. "I believe she was right. They are cowards. I wouldn't have left him."

Joseph looked at his friend. Never could he remember seeing the Galatian so passionate. "How did this Galilean come to mean so much to you, Antiochus?"

They talked late into the night. Antiochus tried again and again, but he could never put into words what he was feeling.

"You didn't see him, Joseph. Not when he was alive. I did. When I ran to him with Ella. This man was not like other men. I don't mean he looked different. He wasn't especially tall, or short, or fat, or lean. He was dressed like all the men around him, in rough country clothes, and sandals that were almost worn out. You would never have noticed him in a crowd.

"That is, not for the way he looked. But Joseph, there was something about him. All around him. Not a light or any of those magician tricks. What surrounded him was . . . the way he was inside. He was *good,* Joseph. There must be a better word for it, but I don't know what it is.

"Ella probably said it best, the way children can do. When he asked her if she was frightened, she said no, that *everything was all right.* That's what Jesus did. He made you—no, he allowed you—no, he somehow conveyed to you, inside you—that life is good, that you are good. Because he is good."

Joseph did not feel good at all. He could not forgive himself for not stopping the execution. "I can't even begin to guess how this thing could have happened. A man like the one you talk about, a man who heals people, who gives so much joy—what was he arrested for?

"And why wasn't I there, in the Sanhedrin, or at Pilate's tribunal, to stop it? I'll never forgive myself. He gave my daughter her dancing. I should have saved him."

The next day was Passover, with the feast at Abigail's. Joseph did not mention the death of the healer. Obviously none of the family had heard anything, because that name—Jesus of Nazareth—was never spoken.

Joseph did his best to match the high spirits of all the others. He didn't want to ruin this special occasion for them.

On the way home, Ella asked him why he was so sad. He hadn't fooled her. Joseph told her that his knee was hurting, and she accepted that. He was glad. He decided that he never would tell her that the man who had given her a miracle was dead.

It was barely daylight when a loud commotion at the front door brought Joseph out of his room. It was Mary of Magdala.

"You!" Joseph said. "I told you we'd meet at midday."

The woman was unaware of his rudeness. Her face was

transformed, her entire posture seemed acutely alive, almost vibrating.

"Joseph," she said to him, "Jesus has risen from the dead! I went to the tomb early, I couldn't wait until noon. The tomb is empty. He is not there. He is risen! I have seen him. The Master. He has come back from the dead!"

CHAPTER SIXTY-FOUR

"YOU'RE OVERWROUGHT," JOSEPH TOLD MARY OF MAGDALA. "Come. Sit down. Let me order you something to eat."

"Old man, are you deaf? Did you not hear the good news?" Mary was too ecstatic to sit. She was walking back and forth, her hands clasped or thrown wide apart. Talking. Talking, partly to Joseph, partly to herself. "This is the proof, and I am the testimony. Oh, thank you, Lord . . . it has transpired even as he said . . . but, oh, why did the suffering have to be so great? . . . Risen . . . risen . . ."

Ella heard the voice and ran into the hall. "Oh. I thought it was my cousins." Her disappointment was visible.

Mary smiled at her, then went to her and knelt, so that their faces were at a level. "Do you remember me?"

Ella nodded. "Your name is Mary. You gave Abba your staff after my legs got well. Is he with you?" She looked eagerly over Mary's shoulder.

Mary took her hands. "Jesus was killed," she said.

"Oh! How sad." Ella's eyes filled with tears. "Was that his name? Jesus?"

"That is his name. He is not dead."

Ella looked perplexed. "You just said—"

"I know what I said. They killed him. But he has risen from the dead. He will go now to his Father."

"How wonderful!" Ella's smile was open, natural, the smile of a child. "His father must be very happy."

"Yes. And all of us, too. Because when we die, we will join him, in heaven."

"But Mary, I don't want to die. I'm having such a good time."

"Dear child. You will not die, not for many, many years. Even then, you will not die. You'll go to Jesus and his Father."

"Is his father like him?"

"His Father is God."

"Who is God? A man on the hill with Jesus?"

Mary of Magdala looked at Joseph. "Have you taught this child nothing? What kind of parent are you?" Anger had eclipsed her radiance.

Ella spoke before Joseph could answer. "My abba teaches me lots of things. He's a very, very, very good abba. Don't you fuss at him."

Mary calmed herself. "I won't. God is Jesus' Father. Jesus taught me that He is my Father, too. He is everyone's Father in heaven, and He loves us."

"Like Abba loves me."

Mary was at something of a loss. She had no children of her own and no familiarity with the literal-mindedness of the young. "Yes," she said tentatively, searching for a way to explain infinitude to the little girl. "He loves you like your abba loves you, only much bigger."

Ella tried to help her. "Like Jesus loved me, you mean?"

"Yes . . ."

"I see. Yes, that makes sense." Ella nodded decisively. She looked at Joseph. "Abba, may I have a honeycake if I eat all my breakfast first?"

"And drink all your milk," he added automatically.

"And drink all my milk." Ella smiled at Mary, so close to her. "Would you like a honeycake? They're very good."

"Later, I think," said Mary. "You go have yours." She watched Ella run off. "She understands," said Mary with wonderment. "Jesus tried to tell us that. He said, 'Unless you change and become like children, you will never enter the kingdom of heaven.' I did not know what he meant, but now I begin to grasp the lesson."

Joseph offered a hand to help her rise. "I do not understand one word you have said since you entered my house," he said. "I hesitate to ask for explanations, because I doubt that I would understand them either."

Antiochus joined them. "Understand what? Why are you here by the door? Are you leaving to go to the tomb? I'll get the linens and herbs."

Mary of Magdala looked at him. "Of course. You don't know. We do not have to anoint the body. Jesus is risen from the dead. The tomb is empty."

Antiochus' face contorted. Anxiety, fear, hope, disbelief combined and conflicted and followed one another in his expression. "If only that could be so—"

"It is so. I tell you it is. I saw it myself, and I saw him. Jesus. The risen Lord."

Joseph walked toward the garden. "I need some air and some light and a bench to rest upon," he said with a decisive air. "Follow me, the two of you. I also need some clarity, if it exists."

Mary of Magdala thought for a long moment. "Where to begin?" she murmured, largely to herself. Then she took a deep breath.

"Joseph of Arimathea, do you agree that the healing of your daughter was a miracle?"

Joseph thought, too. "Yes," he said at last.

"Antiochus?" She turned to him.

"Yes," he said at once. "I was there, I saw him. Jesus. I felt the miracle that he carried about him."

"Yes," Mary whispered, "that's how it was." A special

silence of remembering connected her to Antiochus for a long moment.

She breathed deeply and became brisk again. "You may find yourselves talking to someone who knows my name, so I will tell you the truth of whatever you might hear. You can see that I am not a young woman; a few more years, and I will be forty.

"I come from a prosperous fishing village on the Sea of Galilee. I own more than half of it—houses, boats, land. I am a rich woman. This is because of an accident of inheritance. My father had no close male kin, and when he died, everything he owned came to me. I was sixteen years old. Spoiled, by my father. Educated, by my father, and you know what a shocking thing that is for a woman.

"As you can imagine, I was besieged by suitors. Some from as far away as Sepphoris. Jew and Gentile, old and young, rich and poor. If even the oldest and ugliest and poorest had had the wits to pretend—" She shook her head impatiently. "Ah, that's a tedious, irrelevant issue. The fact is, no one bothered to hide the truth: They all wanted my money. They would get control of it, and of me, when we married.

"I was intelligent enough to say no to every one of them. But that wasn't the end of it, it was only the beginning. Year after year the pressures went on. Not so many. The numbers dwindled. As they did, the pressure increased. More than one tried to rape me, get me with child so that I'd have to marry him.

"I defended myself. With words, with locked doors, with weapons. Most of all with hate. I hated all these men. Before long, I hated all mankind. Followed by womankind, children, animals, the whole world around me. I cursed them all. Hate. Rage. Fear. The desire to give pain. The pleasure when I did. Constant, ever growing, ever more powerful. I was possessed by devils of my own making for many years.

"Then Jesus came. I cursed him, too. Reviled him and his goodness. Cursed God and all His creation.

"Jesus cast out my devils. By talking to me, by praying for me. Most of all by standing there, in front of me, surrounding me with his forgiveness and the miracle of his love for everything that I hated. It cleansed me, set me free.

"I became one of his followers. He had given me life. Now, through his resurrection, he has given me—given all of us—the certainty of everlasting life. It is another of his miracles.

"I still have anger and continue to give pain through releasing it. I will have to struggle against it all my days. Jesus told me that. With compassion, and love, and humor. 'Your devils have left you, you can overcome the imps,' he said.

"So, men will say of me that I cannot be trusted or believed, because I was devil-possessed. You should not believe them, but you may. Such is the way of men. I hope you will be different."

She had talked for a long time. Now Mary of Magdala was silent, her eyes serene, her body relaxed.

"How did this terrible thing come to pass?" Joseph asked. He cared nothing about the story he'd just heard. He wanted to know what had happened.

Without visible emotion Mary told him. Jesus knew, she said, when his time had come. He led his followers to Jerusalem. Where the Romans would be, for the Passover Festival. Where the priests were, and the High Priests, and the Levites, the Pharisees, the Sadducees. His preaching, and his miracles, and the multitudes that followed him were already causing talk and rumor, alarming all those in power.

Mary's eyes glowed. "We entered the city through the Golden Gate. All along the road leading to it, men and women hailed him. 'Hosanna' they cried, and they threw their cloaks onto the road where he was going to pass. He was riding a donkey. They strewed fresh-cut fronds of palm, too, and waved palms in the air to salute him. It was a mighty day. The Messiah was come to Jerusalem."

Joseph stiffened. "Messiah." The word was dangerous.

Mary continued her account. In the days that followed, Jesus attacked those who were victimizing the worshipers at the Temple. The money changers' tables and scales, where pilgrims bought shekels, crashed into the pillars and walls of the colonnade when he threw them over. Then he attacked the sellers of the sacrificial animals that pilgrims bought with those shekels, for high prices. He released the pigeons, which were sold by servants of the High Priest Caiaphus, he drove the sellers and the money changers out of the Temple gates, shouting that they had turned the house of God into a den of robbers.

He preached, too, and daily crowds coming to hear him grew larger. His message was one of peace, not war, of fighting the power of evil within your own heart, not the outside powers of the outside world. Nevertheless, the people were calling him Messiah, according to their own beliefs of what that meant.

"And so he was arrested," Mary concluded. "I was not there. The men who were with him say that one of their own company betrayed him, bringing Temple Guards in the night to the garden where Jesus was, on the Mount of Olives. They took him to the High Priest, but we do not know what happened inside his house, in the night. From there he was taken to Pilate, then to Herod Antipas, then to Pilate again. Who condemned him to death."

Mary fell silent.

Joseph could understand now why the authorities had seen Jesus as dangerous. Passover was always a time when uprisings leapt from simmering to full boil.

But the healer was no Judas the Galilean, with his revolutionary movement, no bandit leader of armed men. There were other punishments, lesser ones, for disturbances like the attack on the money changers.

"I could have saved him," Joseph groaned. "If only I had been in Jerusalem."

Mary looked at Joseph in surprise. "No, you could not

have saved him. He knew he was going to die. He is the son of God, and he was sent to be a sacrifice. He is the Messiah. His resurrection confirms it."

Joseph made a sound of disgust. "Mary of Magdala," he said, "I am a Sadducee. I do not believe in any messiah, or in life after death. I understand and sympathize with your need to believe these things about the healer, because he made such a difference in your life.

"But—"

Mary leapt up. "Your deafness has not left you, I see. You've added blindness to it as well." She strode from the garden, stopped in the peristyle, and turned to look at Joseph again.

"I was letting my imps control me," she said. She even managed to smile. Her eyes moved to Antiochus. "And you?"

"I want to believe, but it is too much. That a man who could heal, could do so much good, who was goodness himself, that he would invite death. Such a terrible death . . ."

"I see. You will believe. Both of you. Go to your tomb, Joseph of Arimathea. Jesus' body is not there, but his spirit will help you.

"And listen to your little girl. She will help you, too. She has no imps to get in the way."

Later in the day Joseph and Antiochus went to the tomb. "Look," Antiochus exclaimed. "There are the grave clothes, Joseph, just as Mary said."

Joseph corrected his friend. "There are some linens, Antiochus. They may be different ones, or people may have taken away the body and left them. I know you want to believe this fantastic story of hers, but you've got to be sensible. The woman told us herself that she was 'possessed by devils.' That's the peasant's way of saying lunatic."

"She's no peasant, Joseph, and you know it. What about

the stone that sealed the tomb? Do you think her devils moved it?"

The stone hadn't been rolled back in its channel, an act of strength that would call for six servants. It was more than halfway across the garden, like a plate tossed from a table. Except that the great circle of stone weighed close to a ton, and there were no marks in the soft earth between it and the tomb.

Joseph found that disturbing. He found everything about Mary's story disturbing. Most of all he was deeply remorseful that he hadn't forestalled the agonizing death of the healer. The healer. He refused to attach any of those other descriptives to Jesus of Nazareth. Messiah. Son of God. Nonsense, Joseph told himself. He didn't say it to Antiochus. The Galatian was mourning.

"Let's go to Jericho and start putting this tragedy behind us," Joseph said to his friend. He turned his back and walked away from the tomb. Antiochus stood just inside it for a long time before he followed.

"I want to believe," he told Joseph after he got home. "I want to believe that the Jesus I saw and felt is not dead. I want to believe that I will see him and feel the miracle of him again, after I die."

Everything was blooming and beautiful in Jericho. Ella climbed the fig tree and picked the first figs. Joseph watched her strong, nimble legs moving surely from branch to branch with joy, and with a heavy heart. If only he'd been in Jerusalem to stop the execution.

At the next meeting of the Sanhedrin he learned that his presence would have made no difference. He had planned to introduce the subject of Jesus' death after all the regular business of the meeting was done, but it came up by itself. Or rather—even more dramatically—his son, Aaron, brought it up.

The case before the judges was that of a woman taken in adultery. She swore, on her knees, that her husband's brother had forced her against her will, and begged for mercy.

A majority found her guilty. Caiaphus ceremoniously tore his judge's robes, the sign of grief that always accompanied the death penalty. There was only one punishment for adultery; according to the Law, the woman would be stoned to death.

While they waited for the next case to present itself, there was the usual general conversation. Joseph heard Aaron say, "At least we won't have that Jesus of Nazareth interfering with the Law this time."

"What does he mean?" Joseph asked the men on each side of him.

While he was at Arimathea, he learned, there had been a different adulteress, also condemned. Jesus was teaching in the Temple courtyard; some Pharisees and scribes took the woman to him, with a challenge. Jesus had a reputation of befriending all kinds of undesirables, including tax collectors and known sinners and women. To trap him declaring defiance to the Law, the Pharisees asked him what he had to say about stoning the woman, following the Law of Moses.

What he said was "Let him who is without sin among you be the first to throw a stone at her."

"They were a cowardly lot," said Joseph's right-hand fellow judge. "Every single one of them just walked away, and the woman went free. To where we never discovered."

"Were you at his trial?" Joseph asked. Yes, said the stern judge. What was Jesus' crime? Joseph inquired.

"He'd been preaching in the Temple Courts. There was nothing we could do about that. But he had also been telling people that their sins were forgiven. By his authority. And we all know that only God can forgive sins. Then, when he was being tried, Caiaphus questioned him, saying, 'Are you the Messiah, the Son of God?' and this Galilean peasant answered him, 'I am.' Caiaphus tore his robe. There was only one possible sentence for such blasphemy."

Joseph knew that what the judge said was true. For such blasphemy only the ultimate punishment would suffice.

His conscience was relieved but not his bafflement. Why had the healer said such a thing? He had to know he was inviting his own death.

When he arrived at his house after the meeting, Joseph was dismayed to see Mary there with Antiochus and another man, a stranger.

"This is Thomas," Mary said. "He has been with Jesus since the beginning as one of the twelve chosen to be his disciples. He doubted me when I told him and the other disciples that Jesus was risen. They all doubted me. Later, when two of them saw Jesus themselves, they hurried to tell the others, and they, too, were not believed. Then Jesus came to them, in the house where they were all staying, and at last they believed what they had refused to believe from my mouth and the mouths of two of their own. All of them except Thomas, who happened to be away. All of them who had been with the risen Lord told Thomas, this intelligent creature in front of you. And what did you say, Thomas? Go on, tell them."

Thomas, a burly man with wisps of gray in his beard, hung his head like a child caught stealing sweets. "I told them that unless I saw the mark of the nails and the wound of the sword in Jesus' flesh, I would not believe."

"Go on, Thomas," Mary ordered. "Tell the rest."

He raised his head. Joseph saw tears on his face. And brightness behind it, from inside him. "Last night," said the disciple, "Jesus came to the house again. He looked at me. Not with anger. With that way he has of understanding and forgiving your weakness. He held out his arms. 'Put your finger in the holes made by the nails,' he said. I was frightened and ashamed and, at the same time, so joyful to see him that I began to weep. I backed away from the terrible evidence. He moved his mantle aside and I saw his side, with the great wound still fresh-looking. 'Thrust your hand inside, Thomas,' Jesus said. 'There is room for it.' I fell on my knees. 'My Lord and my God,' I wept. He looked on me with forgiveness. Then he said, 'Blessed are those who have not seen and yet come to believe.'

"That is what Mary wanted me to tell you."

Antiochus grabbed the disciple's thick, muscular arms. "Was he still in pain? Were the wounds still bleeding?"

Thomas looked at him with pity. "He cannot feel pain. Jesus is where there is no pain. He has crossed from this world of pain to heaven, where pain does not exist. That is what we know and what we believe. It shames me that I did not believe at once. He had told us that he would be killed and be buried, to rise on the third day. I did not believe him when he said it because I did not want it to be true."

"Well?" said Joseph to Antiochus when they were alone. "What are you thinking?"

"I'm ashamed that I didn't believe Mary the first time. It's small comfort that there is that man who's been as weak as I have been."

"What are you saying, Antiochus? Did this Thomas convince you that Jesus is holy, that he is the Messiah?"

"I know nothing about a Messiah, Joseph. I'm not a Jew. I've never had a god to believe in. What I believe—what I know—is what I felt when I was near Jesus. I felt the emptiness in me was filled. I will learn more about him, from those who knew him and his sayings. I will never know that emptiness again. It is another miracle that Jesus has done. I feel healed."

CHAPTER SIXTY-FIVE

ANTIOCHUS STAYED IN JERUSALEM; HE WANTED TO MEET THE other disciples of Jesus, to hear what they could tell him about Jesus and their time with him.

Joseph, therefore, went to Caesarea alone, except for the necessary guards. He appointed Barca host for the captains' dinner and presided, himself, over the party for the crew. The men were mostly strangers to him, and he realized how many years had passed since he was in charge of his shipping business himself. When had it gotten too big and too impersonal? He couldn't pin a notice on any particular year; he knew only that it was all very different. It seemed to have nothing to do with him.

At least the sea still wove its magic spell. Joseph did not need to go to Cyprus. He had sent a young man named Abram to oversee the improvements to the bronze factory nearly two years before. After the agreement with Antipas and the miracle of Ella's cure—

There it was again. Was this man Jesus going to keep entering his thoughts forever?

Joseph sailed to Cyprus on the pretext of a conference with Abram. In fact, he simply wanted to experience the freedom and excitement of leaving land and its complica-

tions behind him, to look at the wide waters and feel the invisible power of the winds.

The short voyage refreshed him, restored his energy.
When he returned from Cyprus, Joseph went straight to
Jericho to rejoice in its beauty and freshness and to see his
beloved little girl. In a bit more than a month it would be
time to go to Arimathea for the vintage and Ella's excitement when she danced on the grapes.

She could do that, because of the miracle—

Jesus, again.

"Listen to your little girl," Mary of Magdala had told
him. After he'd been at the Jericho villa for a few days,
Joseph decided to do it.

He watched Ella while she played with the two dogs that
hadn't been sent to Arimathea. They were still puppies, and
Ella's efforts to train them to obey mostly ended up in a
tumbling, face-licking failure.

"I give up for today," Ella laughed. She splashed water
from the pool onto her face and head, then sat cross-legged
at Joseph's feet, in a rare moment of inactivity.

"Tell me about when Jesus healed your legs," Joseph
said quietly. "Did he rub health into them, or just rest his
hands on them?"

Ella looked up at him, and she smiled. "Neither one. He
just told Antiochus to put me down, on my feet, and my
legs held me up without any wobbles at all. That was such
a happy time, Abba!"

"I know it was. After all those years, to have strength in
your legs—"

"No, Abba, no." Ella's interruption was urgent. "It wasn't
my legs working that made it happy. I mean, that was wonderful, but it came after. Jesus made me happy. All around
him there was this special feeling that went all over me,
outside and in. It made everything good. Even if my legs
had stayed the way they were, everything would have been
good anyhow."

"I don't know what you mean, Ella." Joseph felt a compelling need to understand what his child was telling him.

"It's kind of hard to tell, Abba. I don't know many big, complicated words." Ella shook her head, correcting herself. "No, big and complicated wouldn't be right, even if I knew the words. Everything was simple. Jesus was there, everything was happy and exactly the way it should be. Even me. Especially me. He loved me. Like you love me, Abba, and like I love you, only a lot bigger. Bigger than the sky.

"He didn't care if I was a good girl or a naughty girl. He didn't even care if I was a girl or a boy. It made no difference whether my legs worked. If I hadn't had any legs at all, or any hair, or even any eyeballs, it wouldn't have made any difference. He loved me, Ella, just the way I am.

"He loved Antiochus, too; I knew that, but I didn't think about it. I just knew for certain sure that there was happiness all around and that Jesus loved me.

"It's still there, whenever I want it. All I have to do is be quiet enough and make room for it inside, and it's all there again, just like before. I'm happy, happy, happy because I feel Jesus loving me.

"I wish you'd been there, too, Abba. You're not happy like me, I can tell. I wish you could be. It makes everything just right."

Joseph had tears in his throat. He opened his arms, and Ella climbed up into his lap to hug him. "I love you, Abba," she said. "Jesus does too, I know it. You'll see. One day you'll be quiet and have room inside, and he'll fill you up with happiness, until it's running over."

Joseph was quiet, and waited.

But what he felt was not what Ella was talking about. It was an unfathomable, inchoate need. For what, he did not know.

When next he went to Jerusalem for the Sanhedrin, Joseph sought counsel from a priest at the Temple. Not

Caiaphus, or Annas, or any of the priests who were fellow judges. He selected a young priest, newly invited to serve God in His Temple.

"I am driven by need," Joseph told him, "and I cannot give it a name. It is like a whirlwind in my heart; if it had sound, it would be a great noise as of roaring winds across the open sea. Yet, there is no noise, no direction, only turbulent power."

"It may be the voice of the Almighty," said the young priest. "If you were a younger man, I would send you into the wilderness where, it is said, He speaks to men."

I am not a young man, Joseph reminded himself. But if God wants me, I must go to Him. His blessings have been always with me. I cannot turn away from Him when He calls to me.

The Judean Wilderness was an arid area of yellowish chalk-like bluffs and ravines that ran between the River Jordan and the stony hills that rose to Jerusalem. The Wilderness extended south, beside the Dead Sea after the Jordan ended there. It was everywhere desolate, heat-baked and waterless, save for a few oases, widely separated from one another. Jericho was one of them.

To enter the Wilderness, Joseph had only to leave Jericho on the road to Jerusalem and, once Jericho was behind him, leave the road and walk southward, toward the Dead Sea.

He stood for a minute on the road, summoning all his courage. He was wearing an ankle-length, deep-hooded mantle over his linen tunic. The hood was to shelter his head and shadow his face, protecting him from the burning rays of the relentless sun. His sandals had thick soles as a barrier against the heat that collected in the sand created by crumbling chalk. A water skin hung from his shoulders, down his back. Attached to his belt was a wrapped packet of dates and dried figs and bread, and his left hand held his stout staff.

A new will and the account books for his property and the treasure he kept in the Temple were on the table in his bedroom.

Every preparation he could make was made. Now he had to step off the road and walk into the land where, it was believed, God spoke to those who sought Him.

Joseph breathed deeply. The hot, dry air felt burning in his lungs. Then he walked forward, along a dry wadi between fissured cliffs, until it ended in a bowl of sand.

The heat was like shimmering walls on all sides of him. Joseph walked slowly, giving himself over to the heat and the blinding sunlight reflected from the sands and the yellow hills. He knew that those who fought the Wilderness died of thirst, or the stings of scorpions; or else they went mad. Those who could become part of it survived, like the wild goats that lived on the cliff faces, eating the sparest wiry vegetation that existed in their crevices.

The Wilderness had no paths. A man wandered. Who could say where God was to be found? Joseph walked into patches of shade made by overhangs on the hills when he could, on level ground as much as possible, around hills, not over them. He waited until his thirst was raging before he slid the water bag off his shoulders, and when he drank the sun-heated water, he held it in his mouth for a long time before he swallowed. Water must be sparingly consumed. It could not be replaced, and without it a man would die within two days, perhaps less.

At night the sun plummeted behind the hills, and darkness came at once. The burning sands soon gave up the day's heat, and bitter cold filled the desolation. Joseph looked for a sheltered spot when daylight began to thin. Then he ate a mouthful of bread, a fig or a date, swallowed a mouthful of water, wrapped the fullness of his cloak around himself, and slept. He hoped for dreams. The Almighty appeared in dreams to some.

But not to Joseph. Not for four nights. He began to despair, and to grow angry. What self-delusion, what hubris, had led him to believe that God would speak to him, would care about an aged, dried-up, ant of a man in the endless wastes of this burning land?

"I am going back," Joseph shouted through cracked lips, in defiance of the terrible silence all around him. Not even the wind answered.

He made his way, on hands and knees, up the face of the tall hill that had sheltered his sleeping place. The sun was barely up, but he could get his direction from it, and a look to the north to see if there might be any landmarks stained a cruel red by the sunrise. He felt heartsick with failure and would have wept had he not been too dehydrated to produce tears.

The sun was behind him. Joseph turned to his right and began to climb down. His third step fell onto a jutting bit of weak, porous, chalky rock; it gave way, and he fell without control, half rolling, half bouncing, onto the sands below.

Nothing was lost. His staff had fallen nearby, his food was still attached to his belt, his water skin hung securely against his back.

He could not see the small tear in it, or feel the slow seepage of water from it.

He set off to the north. Back to his home and the life he knew.

Joseph was walking now, not wandering. The shadow his staff threw kept his direction true, until midday when there was no shadow. Joseph knelt on the sands. It was then that he noticed how swollen his once-sprained knee had become. He pulled his hood far forward and untied his food pouch. He would eat more now. He needed strength for rapid progress. He slid the water skin off his shoulders. And discovered that it was nearly empty, and the center back of his cloak soaked.

No panic. His fingers located the leak, and he folded the skin to move the remaining water away from it. Then he removed his cloak and sucked the seepage from its cloth.

When shadow from the staff gave direction again, Joseph

set off to the north. The water skin was tucked inside his belt, to guard the precious remainder. He could not have gone so very far in four days' wandering. Two days' purposeful walking should carry him back, and everyone knew that a man could last two days in the desert, even if he had no water at all.

He ignored the mounting pain in his knee as long as he could. It was swollen now to half the size of his head, and he had to slow his steps.

When he woke in the morning he could hardly move the leg at all. He had to drag it. North, always north, following the shadow of the staff.

At midday he squeezed the final drops of water from the skin and threw the bag aside. In mid-afternoon he realized that he had begun to follow the shadow as if it were morning. He was going back into the Wilderness.

Afire with pain, he hopped in a circle, holding to the staff, to head north again. At the first step, his knee gave way and he fell facedown onto the burning yellow sands. Consciousness slid away as he tried to crawl. North.

Lighthearted laughter woke Joseph. He sat up. Where was it coming from? It was familiar, so familiar.

"Joseph, my love, you look silly with your hair and beard full of sand. It turns them blond. All you need to do now is paint yourself blue, and you could be in Belerion."

"Sarah? Sarah, my heart, is that you?"

"Of course it is. Who else would find you attractive with a blue face?"

She was standing in front of him, not so far away, wearing her Celtic dress with the fern embroidery, holding her harp. Her dark braids hung long over her shoulders and breasts.

Joseph started toward her, eager for her embrace. Sarah began playing the song of their magic time at the base of the cliff of ferns. She was just out of reach, no matter how many steps he took.

"What are you doing here, Sarah? Wait for me, don't keep moving away."

"I'm only here for a visit, my love. We can't be together for a while yet. You have work to do before you die. Our baby needs you."

"Sarah! Sarah! Don't leave me." Joseph continued to reach for her, to follow.

She walked into one of the heat mirages, the apparent blue pools of water that drove men to madness. And then she was gone.

"Sarah!" His cry was broken by pain and thirst.

"You're bleating like a goat, my Joseph. Be a man."

"Rebekkah!"

His grandmother smiled at him. "You're not looking your best, Joseph. I understand how you feel, but you cannot let it stop you. Come on now. This way."

He staggered toward her, then crawled, despite the agonizing pain. He never knew how far, or for how long, or which found him first—the night or a blessed fall into the darkness of senselessness.

Now the dreams came. Terrifying dreams: Ella's baby legs limp across his arm; the Phoenician boy Ashibal holding his tangled guts together with his hands across his slashed middle; his father raising his fist in anger, then making a strangling sound and falling at his feet; the wet bloodstained head of the Baptizer on a golden platter in a spreading pool of blood that became a river, a cataract, an ocean . . .

Quiet, happy dreams: Augustus playing knucklebones sitting on the ground in his garden; Micah holding golden wine up to the light in a golden glass; tying sandals on the chubby feet of the little boy in Rome who was looking for the Messiah; Ella running, running, running down a green hill . . .

"Drink this. Slowly. I will hold it for you." A strong arm was lifting him to drink the cool water that was bringing him back to awareness. The water was fresh and sweet and cool; the cup never ran dry.

"Thank you," said Joseph when he had his fill. He sat up, twisted his head to find his benefactor. He felt strong, full of energy.

The man was already on his feet, walking away. "Follow me," he said, "the road lies ahead."

Joseph got to his feet and picked up the staff that lay beside him. The stranger was almost out of sight, turning at a hill, but he had left a trail of footprints in the sand. Joseph followed them quickly. There were drops of blood in the tracks that led through an opening between two rough yellow desert rocks. Joseph followed them.

On the other side of the rocks was the road from Jericho to Jerusalem. The man was not in view, not to the left nor to the right. The only thing Joseph saw was a milepost. It said that Jericho lay three miles away.

Nearly home, Joseph set off at a good pace, glad to be out of the Wilderness and danger.

He stopped. Abruptly. His knee was giving him almost no discomfort, and the swelling was gone. At his belt hung a pouch of fresh bread, still smelling of its baking, and a flask of light, delicious wine.

Joseph paid heed to what his heart was telling him. He was totally, undramatically happy. He sat by the signpost, leaning against it, while he ate and drank. Without thought, only pleasure and satisfied appetite.

When he reached the villa, Ella ran to him and jumped into his arms for a hug and kiss. Joseph held her tight.

After she wiggled to get down, he continued to hold her hand. "I met your friend Jesus in the desert," he told her. "He is just as you told me."

CHAPTER SIXTY-SIX

"YOU WERE READY ENOUGH TO LECTURE ME AND BRING Thomas in to talk to me, Mary, but when I came around to your way of thinking and wanted to ask you some questions, you had vanished."

Mary laughed at Joseph. "I came to my home. People do that, Joseph, even you."

Joseph looked around him. Mary's home was a big house on the edge of the village of Magdala. Like the other houses in the busy fishing village, it had a magnificent view of the beautiful bright blue waters of the Lake of Galilee. Unlike them, the windows of Mary's house were covered by a grid of iron bars. Its doors were closed, too, and barred, in spite of the summer heat and the refreshing breeze off the water. They were evidence of the fear she had told him about, and the intrusions and pressures that had tormented her to near madness.

Antiochus had traveled with Joseph. First to Arimathea, where they'd left Ella for the vintage and her favorite dancing on the grapes. Then into Galilee on the successful search for Mary of Magdala. He was in the village now, talking to people, learning things that might prove useful. Being Antiochus.

"And what did Ella say when you told her you'd come to believe in Jesus?" Mary asked Joseph.

He smiled, remembering. "She said 'I expected you would, Abba' as if it were the most ordinary thing in the world."

"She must know you very well."

That was a new and startling thought for Joseph. How could an eight-year-old child have any understanding of a man in his sixties? On the other hand, she was Sarah's child, too. And Sarah had known him better than he'd ever known himself.

He said as much to Mary. "Tell me about Sarah," she said. "I've been curious about Ella's mother."

"I could talk about her all day and all night, but I don't know that I could make you know her. She was a tiny little thing. I used to call her 'my sparrow.' But her heart and her spirit were as big as the whole world. She was a country girl. She loved the way the seasons changed, the way the green came in the spring and, equally, the way the brown came in the dry season. She loved everything around her. And everyone. Especially me, although I can't believe I deserved it. I followed my own wants, one time with a great hurt to her.

"You mustn't think, when I say Sarah loved everything and everyone, that she was a honey-sweet, meek and mild kind of woman. She could be very sharp with people. Again, especially me. But she wasn't rake-with-claws sharp. She would tease me, laugh at me with love in her laughter, and make me see what a fool or self-satisfied oaf I was being."

Joseph smiled, remembering.

"You loved her very much. Respected her, too, from what you say."

"I did. I still do. I always will. Sarah never seemed to get confused by the details of life, the thousands of little things, particularly the little things that seem big at the time. She could see through to the essential truths. My grandmother was the same way. The two of them kept me from being an even bigger fool than I was."

Mary got up to find cups and wine. "We will drink to your Sarah and your grandmother. I will even salute you, Joseph of Arimathea. I doubt you realize that you are a remarkable man. Most of your kind would mock the suggestion that a man should respect a woman or admire her for anything other than her ability to keep his house and give him children.

"That was one of the shocking things about Jesus. He really liked women. Not to bed them or to enjoy their admiration of him. He saw women as people, with minds and spirits and special strengths. He liked to talk with us, listen to our views, so often different from the way men looked at things.

"He was criticized for having women followers. I was by no means the only one. The men who followed him regarded us as a burden, unworthy to be treated as they were, to be talked to and listened to. It's nothing surprising that when I told his disciples that he was risen, they wouldn't believe me. Because I was a woman."

"Mary . . . Mary, your imps are showing." Joseph laughed gently. "They didn't believe two of their own group who'd seen Jesus, either. Resurrection is not an easy thing for anyone to believe, man or woman."

She glared at him. Then she relaxed. "Only children," she said, in grudging agreement.

Antiochus called through the window. "Will some charitable person unlock the door for a thirsty man?" Joseph let him in, threw the bolts again afterward. He knew Mary was afraid of her neighbors.

She brought another cup, for Antiochus, and food for them all. They talked until lamp-lighting time and long after.

Joseph resisted the most important thing Mary had to say. What he had to do—what they all had to do, she insisted—was to go and tell people about Jesus, his death, and his resurrection. She was urgent, stridently urgent, about his obligation to do so.

"Why do you think Jesus allowed himself to be crucified? Not just allowed—invited it? Because it is pleasurable to have spikes driven through your body? He suffered as no one should have to suffer because it was God's plan. His proof to mankind that God loves them. To a magnitude that only God can encompass. Tell me this, Joseph. Do you love anyone enough so that you would put Ella through an ordeal like the one Jesus suffered?

"Of course not. You are not God. How could you even begin to imagine the nature of the Almighty?"

Antiochus spoke up. "Jesus told them that, his disciples. The young one that he entrusted with the care of his mother told me what Jesus said: 'For God so loved the world that He gave His only Son so that everyone who believes in him may not perish but may have eternal life.'"

All three of them sat silent for a time, trying to comprehend the unthinkable sacrifice.

When Mary spoke again, her voice was calm. "We are among the very few who can bear witness. We have been given a gift beyond price to give to as many people as we can reach. We can tell them that there is life after death, that we know this. Not believe, but know. And that eternal life can be theirs, because Jesus gave his life for them. The Son of God. We ordinary people can show others the way to immortality. We can take away the fear of death. It fills me with awe."

"No one will believe us," Joseph cried loudly, in protest. "If they didn't believe Jesus, why would they believe anyone like me, or you two?"

Antiochus answered him, quietly. "We believed him. We three. I know there are others, but put them aside. Just consider. If each of us brings only three to belief, and each of those three reaches three, and that three, three more—it can move throughout the world. Jesus believed so; he must have. After his disciples were deaf to Mary's words, and to the testimony of two of their own, Jesus appeared to them, showed his wounds to Thomas. Finally, when they believed, he told them to go out to the whole world and tell the good news of this life and the message he brought from his Father."

"A slow-witted bunch, those men!" Mary said scornfully. "If Jesus trusts them to spread the news, he must know that it's not all that difficult to do."

Joseph and Antiochus looked at each other, then began to laugh. It was a surprise and a blessing to all of them, that laughter was possible at a time like this, when they were remembering and talking about something that, as Mary had rightly said, was awesome.

She didn't join in their laughter, but she did not disapprove. "It's good that you laugh," she said. "We have to remember, always, that Jesus brought a message that is joyful. The resurrection is proof of eternal joy with him and with God when the sorrows of life on earth are ended."

"Ella said to me that he made her feel happy, more so than she could have imagined was possible," Joseph said. "Not after her healing. Even before. His presence, she said, made the whole world a happy place."

"I felt that, too!" Antiochus added.

"And I," said Mary. "Always. I must remember that and hold the memory close. It keeps the demons away." She smiled sadly. "He said, near the end, that he was leaving peace with us. I'm sure he knew how much I was going to need it. I'm not a peaceful woman."

"Both of you know so much more about Jesus than I do," said Joseph. "I want to hear. I need to, so I can tell those who ask me. You were with him, Mary, you heard his words. You heard them from his disciples, Antiochus. Tell me."

Joseph learned about many miracles, some of them things he would not have believed if he had not been saved and restored in the Wilderness. Ella was only one of thousands that Jesus had healed. He had even brought some back from the dead. "How many loaves? How many fishes? Fed how many people?" The miracle that Jesus did when he created ample food for thousands from a few bits of bread and fish made Joseph's eyes bulge. He knew what masses of provisions he had to supply to each of his galleys for the meals of the crew while at sea.

He was shocked at the instances when Jesus broke the Law. But when Mary told him that Jesus was firm on the essential Law, he began to understand. Joseph himself was contemptuous of many of the refinements upon refinements, interpretations of interpretations, that teachers like his own son, Aaron, insisted on.

"Jesus told us," Mary reported, "that we must keep the commandments. We must not murder, or steal, or bear false witness. Also our fathers and mothers must be honored. Chiefly he emphasized, many times, the two most important. Love God with all your heart and soul and mind. And love your neighbor as yourself. All the law, he said, hung on these two."

"That's what Hillel said," Joseph commented. "He was a good man. Not like some teachers I know about."

Antiochus made a gesture to stop Mary's question before she could ask it. He knew that Joseph was privately lamenting what had become of Aaron.

Mary recounted one of Jesus' teachings to Joseph with a glint of humor in her eyes. "He told a young man who came up to him one day that he could not be accepted as a follower unless he sold all his many possessions and gave the money to the poor."

"'All?'" Joseph repeated, horrified.

Mary actually laughed. "Don't be quite so frightened, Joseph. You won't have to beg your bread. I fed him and his disciples with food I paid for. So did others whom I could name. What he said was that many men worshiped riches instead of God. All of us know that to be true. If you look inside your heart and find it to be true of you, you will have to choose. I expect you to make the only right choice."

Joseph became pensive.

"Do your looking on your own time," Mary said. "It is late, and we all need to rest. The main thing for us to hold on to is that the news we carry is good news. News that will bring joy to all who listen. We will be telling them of God's love. Love greater than the world has ever before dared to dream of. Love for even the least worthy of us, if only he will accept it."

Joseph intended to examine his fondness for his wealth and his pride in attaining it. But he was too tired to concentrate. He had heard so many new ideas, and each one of them would provide much to think about.

He stretched out in bed, grateful to be there. Before he fell asleep, he had just enough time to say the prayer that he had learned that night, the prayer that Jesus had taught his followers to say.

> Our Father in heaven, hallowed
> be your name.
> Your kingdom come.
> Your will be done, on earth as
> it is done in heaven.
> Give us this day our daily bread.
> And forgive us our debts, as we
> also have forgiven our debtors.
> And do not bring us into temptation,
> but rescue us from evil.

CHAPTER SIXTY-SEVEN

JOSEPH WOKE THE NEXT MORNING WITH WHAT HE CONSIDERED a brilliant idea. "Prepare yourself for a shock, Mary," he announced. "You are good enough to house and feed Antiochus and me, and I am going to relieve you of some of that burden. I was not always a shipowner, I was in my youth an excellent ship's cook. Therefore, today I will do the selecting and buying and preparation of our dinner."

Mary raised her eyebrows. "'Shock' is a mild term for my reaction, Joseph. I do have sufficient presence of mind to accept your offer, however." She handed him a basket for carrying his purchases.

He was gone for several hours. Antiochus decided, while he and Mary talked, that it was a good thing that Joseph was not there. And that he was a Gentile. When he asked Mary if she had any definite ideas about how she would begin to carry the news of Jesus' resurrection, she burst into a diatribe.

"I will not talk to the Jews! These chosen people of God, as they call themselves, are haters of woman. Schools are open and free to all—to all male children. Women are not considered worthy to learn God's word, or God's Law. If someone like me has a father eccentric enough to teach her to read the Torah, it is forbidden for her to read aloud in the synagogue, although the most stumbling, mumbling man is welcome to do so.

"And what is the center of Jewish life, of our religion, our special covenant with God that is our blessing? I'll tell you. The Temple! The Temple, where a tall closed pair of doors is magnificently mounted at the top of ceremonial stairs. *To keep women away from God*. Men can pass through. Men can see God's altar. Men can offer sacrifices to Him and worship Him. Men can witness the ceremonies.

"Women can stand aside to let the lepers pass into the special closed-off corner of the Court of Women that is reserved for them. Lepers. To the Jews, all women are unclean. As bad as lepers. I would gladly tell the women of the Jews that there is a savior, the son of God, who does not look down on women, who admires and accepts them for what they are—people, not things, not possessions, not servants and whores to the men who marry them.

"But to give these women hope would be to give them a dry, empty cup instead of water for their thirst. Because their men would be offended and angered by the women's belief that God's Son believes them worthy of notice. And the men would punish them. They have the power to do that.

"Women need to hear the message about Jesus. They deserve it. But I will have to find women who will not be put in danger by the news I bear. Someplace in this world such women must exist. I intend to go in search of them. I will go to Egypt first. Not so long ago a woman was ruler of Egypt. To me, that offers hope that a woman may be a freer creature there."

Mary was shaking from her wrathful emotions. Antiochus sat quietly until she became more calm. "I would like some water," he said in a casual manner. "Shall I bring you some?"

"I would like that," Mary admitted.

When their cups were empty, Antiochus told Mary he

would like to accompany her to Egypt. Before she could proclaim her independence, he told her what his hopes were. "I was bought as a slave by Joseph when I was no older than Ella. It was in Alexandria. He did it from pity and outrage when my owner offered me to him for an hour or more of 'entertainment.' Perverse, degraded, abusive 'entertainment.' From my earliest memories, that is all I know. The pain of beatings, of sodomy, of burning brands against my flesh or inside my bowels."

Mary moaned from the horror of what he was telling her. She stared, frozen, at Antiochus' handsome, strong face, the mouth from which the story was coming so calmly, the burning eyes that contradicted the calmness of the delivery.

"I am not as rich as Joseph," he was saying, "but I have stored up what some would call a fortune. I would like to use it to save those who are today what I was then and can never forget. I can buy those children, boys and girls both. Not all of them. Even Joseph's treasure could not do that. But I can save some, as he saved me. And I can do it in Jesus' name, and teach them about him, who sent me to them.

"When they have learned not to fear all people, I will find them instructors, to train them in skills, or in fishing, or in farming, or spinning and weaving—whatever will earn them a living when they grow old enough, and I set them free."

"I will help you," said Mary.

Joseph returned, a cloth covering the basket, and a suppressed delight curling his lips. He would allow no one in the kitchen with him. Unidentifiable odors floated into the room where Antiochus and Mary waited for the surprise he had promised.

He brought bread and wine to the table and ordered them to take their places. Then he emerged with a steaming bowl that smelled strongly of honey and pepper, which went to the center of the table.

"Two things before we eat," he said. "First I will give you a short prayer of thanks. And then, Mary, you will tell us again about Jesus and the Pharisees and the unwashed hands."

Mary and Antiochus exchanged glances, then closed their eyes when Joseph began to pray.

"We thank you, God, and your son, Jesus, for your manifold blessings, including this food that we are about to eat. Amen."

"Amen," chorused the other two.

"Mary," Joseph said, "the story, please."

"If that's what it takes to get food, so be it. Some Pharisees saw Jesus and several others, including me, taking a meal at an inn after we had walked many miles. There were no basins, so we had not washed our hands before we began to eat.

"The Pharisees pounced. Didn't we know about the Laws of clean and unclean? Did we not care that we were breaking the Law?

"Jesus stood and turned on them. They, the Pharisees, he said, had made so many Laws about food, about washing the inside of a bowl in one way and the outside in another, about what was clean and what was unclean, that a poor man with only one bowl, or with no water to wash it or his hands, would have to starve to prove himself law-abiding.

"Food was only food, he said, and was meant to be eaten. It could not defile, be unclean, because it went to the stomach and then to the sewer. It was not what went into a person from outside that could defile, it was what came out of him, from his heart, because it was from there that evil intentions came."

"Thank you, Mary," said Joseph. He was gleeful.

"What is in that bowl, Joseph of Arimathea?" Mary was suspicious.

"Honey and dates and almonds and barley—and pork," Joseph proclaimed with drama. "I've wondered all my life what it tastes like."

Antiochus roared with laughter, watching Joseph and Mary work up the courage to taste the food.

"I didn't find that particularly tasty," Joseph said when they had finished.

"It was quite nasty, Joseph," Antiochus said. "Most cooks use salt and pepper and onions to flavor pork."

Fresh figs and dates were welcome after Joseph's culinary experiment. While they were eating them, Antiochus told Joseph about the plans he and Mary had made for going to Egypt.

Joseph became very still as he listened. He had never imagined his future life without Antiochus as part of it.

"Have you any ideas about what you and Ella will do?" Mary asked him.

"Ella?"

"Of course, Ella. She is living testimony, the best there is. Not only the healing, but she felt the power of Jesus' presence."

"I'll have to think," said Joseph. "I haven't really begun. Yes, I did imagine the speech I could make in the Sanhedrin, but then I decided that would be a waste of breath."

"They'd probably flog you for blasphemy," Mary said. She wasn't bitter or angry. Her mind was already turned toward Egypt.

Joseph didn't hear her. In his mind there was another voice speaking, a young, timid voice. He saw again the little boy who kept losing his sandal, as he'd seen him when he was dreaming in his time of seeking in the Wilderness.

"Are you the Messiah?" the child had asked him at the synagogue in Rome. "My father says we are all waiting for the Messiah to come."

Joseph looked at the two whose mission called them to Egypt. "I will go to Rome," he said with certainty. "They await the Messiah there. I will tell them that he has come and what his joyful message is for all those who are longing for him."

CHAPTER SIXTY-EIGHT

ALL OF THEM HAD TO MAKE ARRANGEMENTS QUICKLY IF THEY wanted to use Joseph's ships for transportation. Mary told Joseph and Antiochus that she would meet them in Caesarea in thirty days.

Joseph hired three messengers in Tiberias to carry word to Stratos in Caesarea, telling him to keep two galleys in readiness for additional sailing after they returned to home port. Hired messengers sometimes never made it to their destination, but one of the three should get through. The distance wasn't great, and the road not renowned for danger.

"You could have used one of Antipas' couriers," Antiochus commented. "Why didn't you ask him?"

"I didn't want to see him. It would have meant a stay of several days, which neither of us would have enjoyed, and some hours at least with Herodias. Ever since the episode of the Baptizer's head, I have kept my distance. Herod Agrippa was smart to go up to Damascus and put himself under the protection of Rome's Governor of Syria."

Joseph and Antiochus rode a short distance ahead of their hired guards and talked quietly, so as not to be overheard, according to their habit. There was a great deal to be said, because they would be parting in thirty days, probably never to see each other again, after more than forty years of friendship.

Both of them found the separation impossible to believe and almost impossible to talk about. For Joseph it made the demands of his allegiance to the gospel of Jesus more actual and more painful than any prospect of abandoning his life of riches and power. He could conceivably regain that life, but he would never again have a friend like Antiochus. He was certain of that.

"Will you tell them at Arimathea, about Jesus and your mission to spread the gospel?" Antiochus asked.

"I have to, don't I? What kind of a missionary would I be, if I did not tell all the good news to my own family?"

"Shall I testify also?"

"I'll be grateful. In truth, Antiochus, I'm frightened. I don't know what to say. I have no eloquence, I'm accustomed to giving commands."

Antiochus tried to lighten his friend's spirits. "Keep in mind what we said in Magdala: Each of us has to convince only three others, and we'll have done a lifetime's work."

Joseph managed to laugh. "Can I count Ella?"

"Still the shrewd trader, are you? You won't get off that easy, Joseph."

"I'm afraid, Antiochus. It is not a familiar sensation."

"I understand. I feel the same. It will be easier when you are not so visibly a man of wealth, with guards to protect it, and you. No ordinary man trusts a man who clearly doesn't trust him."

"Are you really confident that the dogs will be an adequate substitute?"

"Better. I truly believe that. Men know what to expect when fighting other men. Dogs are unpredictable and unknown."

"And you're sure that I can control them?"

"I'm sure that Ella can."

* * *

At Arimathea Joseph's brothers, their sons and wives listened to his account of Jesus with the respect due to the head of the family. Then, in a carefully patient, unemotional manner, Amos spoke for all of them. "We are Sadducee, Joseph. You know what that means. We do not believe in a messiah, not with an army, and not on a cross."

In the village synagogue, the reaction was less controlled. "The true Messiah will deliver us from the Romans. And the landlords." When Joseph and Antiochus left the farms and the village the following day, they heard young voices shouting, "He defiled our synagogue by bringing a Gentile into it." A shower of rocks was thrown from a rooftop, barely missing them.

"Loose the dogs!" Joseph said. Antiochus stopped him.

"Remember the words of Jesus. 'If anyone strikes you on the right cheek, turn the other also.'"

Joseph groaned. "I cannot do this thing. I cannot hold to my belief, and I cannot follow his teachings."

Ella was sitting ahead of Joseph on the horse. She twisted her head to look up at him. "Abba, don't be sad. Jesus will make you happy. Just imagine that he's riding with us, and you'll feel good." She was so matter-of-fact that Joseph had to accept her conviction. For her.

"Try it, Joseph," Antiochus said quietly.

Joseph did try. But his mind saw the lifeless, defeated man on the cross, and his fearful melancholy deepened.

Then Ella began to nod sleepily. He put his arm around her to hold her safe, and for an instant he felt the support and safety of the strong arm that had held him in the Wilderness, lifting him to take the life-saving water.

His doubt vanished, and his despair. What he was going to do was right. Difficult, perhaps impossible. He might not find three who would hear him and believe. But he had to try. It was his mission. The most important and worthy thing he would ever do in his life.

* * *

Joseph stopped in Jerusalem while Antiochus, Ella, and the dogs proceeded to Jericho. He sought out Gamaliel, his fellow judge in the Sanhedrin and the grandson of Hillel.

"I have a great favor to ask of you," Joseph told the younger man. "You know that I am a shipowner. You have no way of knowing how my fleet operates." Joseph explained his half-share system to the young teacher.

"I am leaving Judea, and I do not know when I might return. Perhaps never. I would like you to accept my shipping income and distribute it to the poor and needy."

Gamaliel was visibly startled.

"You will do it? It will do good?" Joseph asked anxiously. He had counted on Gamaliel's acceptance.

"I must ask you, Joseph of Arimathea. Are you a follower of the Nazarene? It is said that you gave your own tomb for his burial."

"Yes, I am trying to follow his teachings and tell others about him."

"And you are going to give your wealth to the poor." Gamaliel was thoughtful. "I wish I might have met this Nazarene. His power exceeds what I have been led to believe. I was told that his disciples were poor men, Galilean peasants."

"I am not a disciple, Rabbi; only a struggling believer."

"Your struggles impress me, Joseph. To give away your riches for the memory of a dead healer."

"But he is not dead!" Joseph felt an unexpected strength. "He rose from the tomb, and he is with his Father, who is God."

Gamaliel looked at Joseph for a long, searching moment. "I envy you your passion, Joseph, even though I cannot share it. I will be honored to distribute your earnings. I am honored that you put your trust in me."

After his meeting with Gamaliel, Joseph went to the Temple, where he made a sacrifice of thanksgiving to God for the gift of a purpose and mission to give value to the remaining years of his life. The grandeur and beauty of the familiar ritual and music were soothing to Joseph. He realized, with anguish, that he would miss them when he left them behind.

But he still had many things to do, so he did not linger. He took part of his wealth from the Temple Treasury and went to his house. His slaves, many of whom were strangers to him, gathered in the atrium at his command. He told them that he was setting them free, with a purse of gold for each to use in his new life. "You may collect your manumission document and purse now. I have them here, on the table before me. Your rooms here will remain yours for another twenty days."

Their thanks and their questions took up much of the remainder of the day. Joseph then set out to do his hardest task.

In contrast to the slaves, his son was cold and angry. "I do not consider you my father," Aaron said. "You are unobservant of the Law, and I cast you out of my life long ago." He refused to let Joseph see his grandchildren, but he accepted the large sacks of gold Joseph gave him for their inheritance.

Joseph ate his dinner in the elegant wine and food garden that Micah had led him to. So long ago.

It is hard, Lord, Joseph said silently to Jesus. Or his Father. Or both. My past was full of richness far more valuable than gold. I will never see Micah again, or Eleazar, or Alexander, or Philo. Or Antiochus, my brother of the heart. My family is lost to me, except for my treasured Ella; also Arimathea is gone, with a lifetime of memories. Soon the Temple will be left behind, too. I pray that this sacrifice will gain your favor, and I beg that you will be with me in my mission. I need your strength, for I doubt my own.

He sacrificed at the Temple in the morning before he left for Jericho. When he was walking through the Court of the Gentiles on his way out, he saw a group of people gathered around a big, rough-looking man who was preaching. Joseph joined the crowd. Within moments he realized that the big man must be Simon, whom Jesus had named Peter. He was telling a rapt audience about the moment when Jesus was carried up to heaven. "He lifted up his hands and blessed us. We could see his holy wounds. His loving countenance rejoiced our hearts even while he was leaving us, because we knew that he was going home to be with his Father. I tell you, my brothers, that Jesus is your savior, too, even as he is mine. He paid for your sins with his sacrifice of his own life. He will grant you eternal life, if you will believe in him and accept him as your savior. I was with him, I followed him and witnessed the wonders he worked. Listen while I tell you of the blind man he healed here in the Temple Court . . ."

Joseph knew now that the call to Rome he'd found in his dream was right and good.

This eloquent, forceful, imposing man was a Galilean, with the distinctive accent of that region, an accent that was mocked by Jerusalem's upper city wealthy, the people Joseph knew.

But the men and women who clustered around Peter were not urban people, especially not from the upper city. They were country people, like Peter, and they could believe one of their own kind.

They would not have listened to Joseph of Arimathea, a man comfortable in a world that was closed to them, a man not at home in the world that was theirs.

In Rome, Peter's accent, his very language—Aramaic— would make him unintelligible. But Joseph knew their language. Not perfectly, but enough to make himself understood. He could, with God's help, do in that city what Peter was doing here.

Joseph felt greatly encouraged. He was eager now to begin his mission.

When he saw the marker that pointed to Jericho three

miles away, he could feel again the wonder of his Wilderness rescue.

When he reached the Jericho villa, Ella ran to meet him. "Are we going to Rome now, Abba? I'm so excited. I want to go soon."

"Soon, my Ella. I promise you. I want to go, too."

Packing was simple, because they were carrying as little as possible. Ella had her harp. Joseph had a capacious money belt and his staff. A soft-sided basket held extra tunics and sandals, plus a scroll Joseph had written to record the sayings of Jesus that he had learned in Magdala. And his scrolls from Augustus and Tiberius Caesar.

They were almost ready. Antiochus had introduced Joseph to the four dogs and trained them together in the few commands that were necessary.

When the word came that Pontius Pilate had arrived in Jerusalem to hold his monthly tribunal, it was time to act. Joseph went ahead of the others to Jerusalem; he bathed, then dressed, for the last time, in a rich, colorful silk tunic and mantle, to visit Pilate at his headquarters in Herod's palace.

Only the Roman Procurator had the power and the connection to Rome that Joseph needed now. He had to transfer the bulk of his fortune to the central imperial treasury in Rome. It was infinitely too risky to move that much gold, but Pilate could take possession of it and send—by imperial courier—the authorization to release to Joseph, in Rome, an equal amount.

Joseph knew that Pilate would "lose" some of the gold in the process. He also knew that Pilate would make no objections to Joseph's request, because of the "loss" that would end up in Pilate's own coffers.

Everything proceeded according to expectation.

Joseph donated a generous amount to the Temple, filled his money belt, walked—with Temple Guards—beside the cart carrying the gold to the palace, accepted Pilate's receipt and best wishes for a smooth journey, returned to the Temple for a final sacrifice of pure frankincense, then walked to his house.

Antiochus and Ella were waiting for him there, with the dogs and the packed baskets.

"Who's ready for adventure?" Joseph called to them as he walked through the door.

"We are!" they replied.

The dogs barked agreement.

Joseph changed into his simple linen garments and gave his silks to one of the few remaining servants.

Then the small group of adventurers said goodbye to Jerusalem. At Abigail's house the dogs were almost as noisy as her children and grandchildren once had been. She held Joseph close in her arms for a long moment.

"I am trying to hold fast to the story you told me, Joseph, about your resurrected Redeemer. The thought of seeing my mother Rebekkah again in heaven makes me want to believe. But it is hard."

"I know, Abigail. It is hard for me, too. Often. Yet I know it is true."

Abigail kissed Ella. Also Antiochus. "Leave now," she said, "before I start to cry. May God go with you."

"Amen," said Joseph. He kissed his aunt, and they left.

Outside her house, the house that had been his grandfather's, Joseph paused, to look across at the Temple's gold and white magnificence. He would never see it again.

Then he turned his face and his steps toward the Damascus Gate and the world outside.

The galleys were waiting in Caesarea. So was Mary of Magdala. Impatiently. Joseph gave Stratos instructions and authorization to deliver his profits to the head of the synagogue for transmittal to Gamaliel.

"Don't steal too much more than usual, my old friend," Joseph told the fat Greek. Stratos embraced him, blubbering with emotion.

On the quay, Joseph and Antiochus looked at each other, unable to say what was in their hearts.

"Get on with it," Mary scolded.

The men embraced.

"You have been more than a brother to me, Antiochus. I will think of you always."

"And you, Joseph, have proved to me that men can be good. I will always love you."

The ship for Puteoli left harbor with the galley bound for Alexandria a few lengths behind it. They were still close together when their bright striped sails rose and bellied and their oars were drawn in. Joseph and Ella stood amidship waving to Antiochus and Mary, who were waving to them.

Then the steersmen leaned in their sheltered pits. One to port. One to starboard. The ships settled on course. One north to Italy. One south to Egypt.

The adventure had begun.

CHAPTER SIXTY-NINE

THE JEWISH QUARTER OF ROME WAS JUST AS JOSEPH REMEMBERED it. He was oppressed by the decrepit tenements shadowing the congested streets. Joseph had made up his mind to live in the quarter, with the people he had come to, to tell about Jesus, the Messiah. But he couldn't bring himself to live in one of the cramped, high-floor apartments. He would look for one on the ground floor, with a courtyard for the dogs.

He had brought Ella and the dogs to Rome by water. One of his galleys to Puteoli, then hired space on a coastal trader to Ostia, and lastly, paid passage on a barge to the city itself.

Ella loved the sea, which gratified him, and the river delighted them both. There'd been a holiday atmosphere to the entire trip, a time for pure pleasure and no worries about future success or failure in his mission.

Now his spirits were low, his heart apprehensive. For the first time he was glad to have the four dogs. Even though they were docile and obedient and did not bark or pull against the ropes that leashed them, they were so fierce-looking that people made way for their passage in the streets.

Joseph asked at bake shops, wineshops, and food shops about available housing. Luck was with him. The ninth inquiry produced news about a new building, just completed.

The tenement was six stories high, the tallest on the block, and the cheapest, highest apartments had been rented before they were even built. The ground floor had two large apartments; Joseph justified taking the biggest, using the dogs as his excuse. He and Ella did not really need eight rooms for themselves.

The building was made of wood, with the smell of resin still strong in its uncured boards. Joseph knew that it wouldn't be long before the green wood would begin to warp, but the fresh smell was worth it, in his opinion. He had no idea how long they'd stay in Rome, so it would be futile to worry about future warpage. They needed a place to live.

Shopping for bedding was fun, Ella declared. So was buying pottery bowls and amphorae for wine and water and milk. Everything was exciting for her.

There was no kitchen. Roman law prohibited cooking in the tenements because of the constant danger of fire. Ella thought that buying their food at a cookshop, then taking it home to eat, was the most thrilling adventure of all.

Second best was the fountain at the corner where women got water, or sent their children to get it. The dogs obviously agreed with Ella. They drank from the basin of the fountain and panted loudly while she selected a thick meat stew at the cookshop for their dinner.

They had only to buy oil to burn in the pottery lamps, and the group from Judea could settle into their new home for the evening.

"Do the dogs really have to live in the courtyard, Abba? They might be lonely, and frightened in a new place."

"A little girl might be, also, is that perhaps what you mean to say?"

"I do usually have one at a time to sleep in my room, you know that. Ever since they were tiny."

There'd been several generations since those days, these

dogs were likely the great-great-grandchildren of the puppies Ella was talking about, and both she and Joseph knew it.

"Which one do you think needs to be with you the most?" Joseph asked seriously. He'd been with his daughter long enough, on their voyage, to learn how to enter into her games.

Ella made a show of giving his serious question equally serious consideration.

"Joppy," she said at last. "I'll tell him."

Antiochus had helped Ella name the young dogs. The names all began with J, because Joseph was their father—in a manner of speaking—and they were names of cities and rivers in Judea, so they'd remember where they came from. Joppa, Jordan, Jabbok, and Jericho had metamorphosed quickly to Joppy, Jordy, Jabby, and Jerry.

With the dog curled over her feet, Ella smiled at her father. "Thank you, Abba." She yawned. "What happens tomorrow?"

Although she was not yet nine years old, Joseph had designated Ella a full partner in their adventure. At Arimathea, he had had a long talk with her.

"Ella, I'm going to talk to you like a grown-up, because you will have to make a grown-up decision. I believe that Jesus and God want me to go to Rome. A little over ten years ago the Roman Emperor said that he was going to send many—a great many—of the Jews away from their homes and families in Rome. I was able to change his mind, and the Roman Jews were impressed. Because of that, I believe they will listen to me when I talk to them.

"I am going to tell them about Jesus, that he is the Messiah. I will tell them that Jesus rose from the dead, to prove that his Father, God, will give life after death to ordinary men, too.

"People will have a very hard time believing what I tell them. They might become angry, they may even try to hurt me, they might make me leave. You, too, if you are with me.

"But you do not have to be with me, Ella. You can stay with your cousins and your aunts and uncles, here, where you have such fun. You will probably be much happier here."

"Don't you want me to go with you, Abba? Would you rather go without me?"

Joseph answered her through a throat clogged with tears. "I would rather have you by my side than anything else I could imagine, my dearest child. But what I want is less important than what you want, in this case. It is your decision."

"I want to be with you. That's simple. You're my abba, and I love you."

And so now they were together. In Rome. In partnership. Joseph answered her question fully. Tomorrow, he told her, they would cross the river and go into the city. There were people there who worked for him. He needed to find out from them what recent news might be useful to know.

Then they would go to the baths. These weren't baths like theirs at home. These baths were full of people and entertainment. Music and jugglers and animals that could do tricks.

They'd do some sight-seeing, too, because there were many fascinating things to see in Rome.

That would make a long, busy day, and they'd be ready to come home and pick out the dinners for themselves and the dogs.

The day after that they'd go visit a Roman family. So that Ella could get to know some of her abba's friends.

And then, on the Sabbath, they'd go to the synagogue. To tell about Jesus.

"Now, it's time for bed. We're going to have a long day tomorrow." Joseph kissed his little girl goodnight. When she was sleeping, he sat by her for a long time.

Yes, Ella was full partner, but he had not told her everything. The visit to Berenice's stepson Marcus was much more important than he had made it sound. If anything happened to him, Joseph expected Marcus Emilius Flavius, Senator, to protect Ella and get her safely home to the family in Judea. He intended to talk to Marcus about that before inviting possible danger by talking in the synagogue. There'd been a few rocks thrown in Arimathea. Joseph could imagine far more deadly action in Rome.

Marcus and his family still lived in the house he'd inherited from his father, the house Joseph would always think of as Berenice's.

"Is this really Helena?" Marcus and his wife couldn't believe their eyes. They'd last seen Joseph's little girl when she was only two, a pathetic little thing with legs that had no life.

"She calls herself 'Ella' now, but she is the same."

"Who was the doctor, Joseph? He worked a miracle."

"Yes, he did. A true miracle. That's what I'm doing in Rome. Telling people about him."

"Well, then, tell me," said Cornelia. "We have our own little girl, too. I'm always worried that she might fall ill. She doesn't have Julius' sturdiness."

"His name is Jesus of Nazareth." Joseph felt uncomfortable. He hadn't come to Rome to preach to aristocratic Gentiles.

"Oh, in your country," said Cornelia, disappointed. "That won't do me much good in Rome."

For an instant Joseph wanted to tell her that it would do her unimaginable good, wanted to tell her, and Marcus, too, everything.

The moment passed. Marcus was talking about their son Julius. Marcus was legitimately proud of his boy. Julius had donned the toga of manhood earlier in the year, when he became fifteen, and he was now an officer in the Praetorian Guard.

The Praetorian Guard. Wasn't that . . . ? Joseph stopped his words.

Yes, Marcus said. Sejanus. The Guard was under his command. "The day will come," Marcus sighed, "when he tells me what he wants from me in return for Julius' acceptance into the Guard. I wake up every day of my life dreading it."

Cornelia shushed him. She was looking on all sides to see if an untrustworthy servant might have heard Marcus' words.

Joseph realized that everything he'd been told about Sejanus' increasing power was true. It wasn't safe to breathe a word against him, no matter how mild the comment.

"Cornelia," he said, "I'd be grateful if you introduced Ella to your daughter Flavia. She doesn't know any little girls in Rome. We arrived only two days ago."

When he had Marcus to himself, Joseph told him why he had really come.

Of course he would take care of Ella, Marcus said at once. But did Joseph really believe he was in danger? From what source? Was there anything Marcus could do to help?

"You are truly your father's son, Marcus. A noble Roman. He must be proud of you. I'm proud to call you my friend."

Joseph's praise embarrassed Marcus even as it pleased him. He was so flustered that he forgot to inquire more about Joseph's potential danger.

That suited Joseph perfectly.

Joseph and Ella left their apartment early to go to the synagogue. He knew he was going to have trouble finding it, no matter how often he asked directions.

And he was right. The service was well under way when they arrived. Joseph looked around him. He saw not one familiar face. Eleven years was a long time. Everyone had aged, including him.

When the moment arrived for anyone in the congregation to stand and ask permission to speak, Joseph stood. His mouth felt as dry as the desert.

"My name is Joseph of Arimathea," he said. "I come to you from Jerusalem. When last I was here, I was able, with the help of a friend, to effect the cancellation of a senatorial decree, that would have sent thousands of Jews to Sardinia."

Throughout the building there grew a chorus of whispers and murmurings. There were many who remembered him, many more who had heard of him.

Joseph raised his voice, to be heard. "I have a warm memory of a small boy, who kept losing his sandals . . ."

"That was me! I remember." A tall, strong young man had jumped to his feet.

"Sit down and be quiet, Samuel," said the man beside him. Samuel sat down.

"It is good to see you again, Samuel," Joseph said, with a smile at the enthusiastic youth. "You may also remember what you told me on that occasion. I never forgot it. You said that your father was expecting the Messiah to come soon.

"That is why I have come to you now. To tell you that the Messiah has come. Not in the manner that so many expected, but I can give testimony that he has come. His name is Jesus of Nazareth . . ."

As Joseph spoke, he could feel the growing confusion and dismay among the people around him. They would not harm him; he was the man who had saved them from Sardinia. But now they feared that he was crazy. And blasphemous. Some said nervously that he might bring down the wrath of God upon them.

Joseph felt someone pulling on his sleeve. He looked down into Ella's upturned face. It was glowing. "Abba, can

I talk to them? They don't understand what you're telling them, but my story is so simple."

Of course! Joseph told himself. Hadn't Jesus himself brought people to belief through his miracles?

"I ask you," he said urgently to the congregation, "to hear my daughter speak." He lifted Ella onto the bench where they'd been sitting.

In the shocked silence Ella's voice flowed like music. "My name is Ella," she said, "and Jesus healed my crippled legs by a miracle. From birth I had been unable to walk, or even stand. Now I run and dance because of him."

Everyone was listening.

"The important thing about Jesus was the happiness that was all around him. What it was, is what we call love. Love greater than the whole world.

"He did not touch me. He shed his love upon me, and I was cured. This love is called the Holy Spirit. It's everywhere. All around us. All you have to do is open your heart and let it come in. Then you can be as happy as I was when I was near Jesus. As happy as I am now."

She smiled radiantly at everyone, turning slowly on the bench so that she could see them and they could see her.

Then she sat down. Joseph sat beside her and embraced her.

While pandemonium filled the synagogue.

CHAPTER SEVENTY

TO BE PART OF A MIRACLE! EVEN THOSE WHO THOUGHT THAT Joseph—and probably his daughter, too—was crazy wanted to get close to Ella, to touch her hand, or arm, or proclaimed cured legs. Those who were certain that she was a fraud wanted to look at her closely, question her, trap her in her lies.

Joseph tried to protect her, to put himself between her and the reaching hands, the angry accusations, but there were too many people, coming at her from too many directions.

Ella remained amazingly calm, even when the pushing, touching throngs buffeted her and almost knocked her off her feet. She took hold of the folds of Joseph's cloak and held tight, standing behind him.

Samuel—of the lost sandals—and his muscular father appointed themselves guardians for Joseph and Ella. Shouting, shoving, threatening, they made a pathway through the chaotic scene.

From the back and sides of the mob, a small number of people, both men and women, watched. They were quiet, but concentrated, craning their necks in an effort to see this father and child who had lit a small flame of hope in their despairing hearts.

"Follow us," Samuel's father shouted to Joseph. He obeyed. The wild scene of reaching hands and shouting voices had shaken him. He reached for Ella. She took his hand and scampered along beside his uneven hurrying gait.

Their two rescuers led Joseph and Ella to a shuttered and locked tiny shop, through a low, narrow passageway beside it, and up a ladder to the single small room above that was their home.

"My name is Joel," said Samuel's father. "I will give you some wine. Please sit." He gestured to the two stools against one wall. Joseph was glad to accept. He lay his staff on the floor at his feet. It was slippery where he'd been grasping it. Slippery with sweat from his palm, the sweat of fear.

"Thank you," said Joseph. He was grateful for much more than the cup of wine Joel handed him, and Joel knew it.

"We won't talk about it yet," he said. While he and Joseph and Samuel drank, Joel talked about his cobbler's shop below and the sandals that he made there, as well as repairing all kinds of footwear.

Ella looked around the room, interested in the tools of Joel's trade that lay on a table and the long wooden flute that leaned against the wall in one corner.

When the men got around to the events in the synagogue, she offered an observation. "We should have had Jabby and Joppy with us, Abba. Then people would have kept back."

"Who are they?" asked Samuel. Ella explained.

"That would never do," Joseph said. "Animals aren't allowed in synagogues."

Joel held up a callused hand. "It's worth considering." He made his own suggestions. A congregation should know what to expect; he believed that it was the suddenness of Joseph's and Ella's messages that had caused such an excessive reaction. Perhaps an opportunity for questions should be given, too.

"I am assuming that you want your message to reach people, Joseph of Arimathea."

"But certainly. That is why I have come to Rome. The

Messiah told his followers to carry the good news into the whole world."

"Then you must make it possible for them to hear it. Many times, and in many ways. By the end of the day every Jew in Rome will have heard of what happened at the Synagogue of the Herodienses today. You will have many thousands who are curious about you. I suggest that you go, alone except for your dogs, to the heads of all the synagogues and talk to them about speaking there.

"They will know, too, about the breakdown in order today. They may welcome your dogs, if they are as well behaved as you claim."

"Of course they are!" Ella said emphatically. "My abba told you so, and he does not lie."

Joel smiled at her, and her vehemence. "Your abba will have to convince people that is so. His story is a strange one."

Ella looked at Joel with a child's directness. "Do you believe him? And me, too?"

Joel met her directness with his own. "I cannot believe either of you, not so soon. I am interested to hear more. That is a lot."

"Is that so, Abba?"

"Yes, it is. I am grateful to you, Joel. I believe that everything you have said here today has merit. Will you assist me?"

Joel became wary. "In what manner?"

"I have to learn about these other synagogues. Where they are located and how to find them. I can make no sense of the streets in the district, and the directions people give me are small help."

Joel relaxed into hearty laughter. He'd be glad to offer Samuel as guide, he said. He could spare his son's assistance in the shop for a day.

"And for a time today, too?" Joseph asked. "To show me the way back to where we live?"

* * *

When they were eating their dinner, Joseph told Ella how proud she'd made him feel. "Most children—no, most people would have been frightened when all the shouting and pushing started, with everyone trying to touch you."

"I was frightened, Abba. Except, you were there, and I knew you'd take care of me. Also I asked Jesus to help me not to be too scared. That helped too."

"Where did you learn about the Holy Spirit, Ella? I don't really know what the Holy Spirit is, though Antiochus and Mary talked to me about it."

"Mary told me the name. We talked about Jesus some in Caesarea, when you and Antiochus were doing some things about the ships. I didn't have to learn, Abba, I was lucky, because I knew what it felt like. I just didn't know what to call the feeling." She looked at her father. "Oh, Abba, I do hope you find out what it feels like. It's the best feeling ever."

"I will keep praying, and hoping, too, Ella. But for me, it is sufficient that I believe."

"I want you to be happy."

"I am happy, my daughter. And grateful for the happiness."

Ella had to settle for that. Still, she prayed earnestly that her abba might feel the sublime happiness, the divine love she was talking about, the extra-extra-extra big happiness, as she thought of it.

As Joel had foreseen, the heads of all the synagogues wanted Joseph and Ella to come and speak on the Sabbath. They also wanted them to bring the dogs. All four of them. Sometimes Joel or Samuel, or both, accompanied them, too.

The reactions of the congregations followed the pattern of their first appearance, with the difference that there was much less disorder. Shouts, objections, cries of "blasphemers," and insults, yes. But there was no pushing and grabbing at Ella. The four dogs were young, but big and fierce nonetheless. Their bared teeth and bristling backs kept her safe.

They frightened people so much that Joseph had to bring them inside the apartment to live instead of leaving them in the courtyard. Because there were people, like Joel, who wanted to know more about Jesus as Messiah. They came to the apartment, at Joseph's suggestion, to ask questions, and to talk, and to share the simple meal that Joseph provided every evening. They would not have dared walk through the courtyard if the dogs had been there. Inside the big apartment, they had no idea that the dogs were in the room that Ella had chosen for them, contentedly gnawing on the bones she bought from the butcher shop across the street.

"I feel sorry for the dogs," Ella told Joseph, "having to be shut up so people can come. I feel sorry for me, too, sometimes, Abba. They ask me the same things, over and over again. How many times do I have to tell the same story? We didn't even go out to see the lights at Hanukkah. There must have been so many, too."

Joseph owed Ella an apology, and an explanation. He made full apology and partial explanation. "I'm sorry, my Ella, I kept you in on purpose. The Romans have a festival of their own, called the Saturnalia, after one of their pagan gods. It comes at the same time of year as our Festival of Lights. The Roman festival is rough. People fill the streets, drink too much, get in fights, even attack and hurt strangers. I didn't dare take you out to see the lights. The district is not all Jewish, you know that. More than half the people living here are Gentiles. Pagans."

Joseph did not mention that the Saturnalia was a celebration of carnality and debauchery. Those attacked were usually women, and girls, who were raped.

Ella accepted her father's apology with good grace. But she had one quibble about his explanation. "Abba, I wish you would stop being so mean about the Gentiles. Jesus didn't ask me if I was Jew or Gentile. He just loved me and cured me. And Antiochus is a Gentile, but he loves Jesus and believes in his message."

"Very well. If any Gentiles come and ask about Jesus, we'll welcome them, too. Now, do you forgive your abba?"

Ella's hug was her reply. With her "I love you, Abba."

"I love you, too, my good girl. And I'll show you how much. Your birthday is coming soon. You'll be an elderly woman, nine years old. Would you like to go to the chariot races at the Circus Maximus?"

"Oh, Abba!" Ella cartwheeled across the big room.

The throngs at the fifty entrances to the enormous oval Circus were in holiday spirits as high as Ella's. She couldn't stand still, but jumped up and down at Joseph's side. It looked as if all Rome was there, in the bright January morning sun and cold, crisp air. There were seats in the stands for more than a quarter of a million. All classes, ages, nationalities mingled in the crowds.

"Joseph of Arimathea!" It was Marcus, not far behind Joseph and Ella. He was wearing his official senator's toga, with its coveted purple border. But his rank meant nothing outside the Circus. He had to wait with everyone else.

"Meet me near the ticket man after you enter," Marcus shouted. Joseph waved, and nodded his head in agreement.

As a senator, Marcus was entitled to seats in a special section, near the loggia reserved for the Emperor, his guests and attendants. Marcus invited Joseph to join him and his son Julius. "You get a better look at the races, and it's closer to the latrines. That offsets the risk of being hit by any fragments if a chariot goes out of control on the turn and crashes into the wall in front of you."

Joseph was more than willing to accept the favor. The tickets he'd bought would have put Ella near the finish line, but far from the excitement during the six earlier laps around the interior spina, the barrier that ran down the center of the racing area.

Twelve chariots competed in every race. Each chariot was drawn by four horses, driven by a specially trained and skilled athlete who wore the color of one of the four teams that were famous throughout the Empire.

"Do you favor any color?" Joseph asked Marcus.

"Green!" said the senator.

"Blue!" said Julius at the same moment.

"Which will you choose, Ella?" Joseph said. When she decided on red, that left white for Joseph. He wished he could make a wager, as he was certain Marcus and his son had already done, but he didn't want to introduce Ella to a new and potentially overly interesting pastime. Gambling had destroyed both women and men, he knew.

Once the twelve gates flew open, releasing the forty-eight gleamingly groomed, high-spirited horses, Joseph gave himself over to the blood-racing excitement of the speed, skill, and danger in front of him. It wasn't until three races were over that he calmed down enough to notice the spectacle of the viewers' excitement.

Marcus, he could tell, had gotten considerable amusement from watching him. "I should be ashamed of myself, but I'm not," Joseph told Marcus. "It would be hypocrisy."

"I envy you," Marcus said. "I should come less frequently, then I'd get more carried away." The fourth race had begun. Marcus gestured toward Julius. "He makes up for my faults. Who could say which one of them is the child?"

Julius and Ella were both on their feet, screaming encouragement to their chosen teams. His badge of manhood, the toga, had slipped from its careful balanced drape and was sliding to the floor.

Marcus gestured again. Discreetly. "Sejanus," he murmured close to Joseph's ear. "In Tiberius' loggia, but not quite yet on his throne."

For the first time in many years Joseph saw the man everyone feared. Sejanus was still handsome, but his cultivated noble stance had become undisguised arrogance and pride. He looked like the predatory animal he was.

The richly clad men and women around him were watching Sejanus more than they looked at the races. They were waiting for any glance or remark he might deign to bestow upon any of them, any indication of his favor. Or otherwise.

Joseph turned his eyes away from the chilling vignette. Power in ruthless hands was the most frightening thing he knew of, and he no longer had the protection of wealth and power of his own.

"He is co-consul with Tiberius now," Marcus muttered. "And Tiberius never leaves his island."

Joseph looked for a more uplifting topic. "Is the Lady Antonia well?"

Marcus smiled broadly. "Yes, thanks be to the gods. She's more tart-tongued and bony-bodied than ever. She's an inspiration, and she scares me half to death; every time I happen to see her, I feel like a boy with a dirty face and feet that trip over themselves. She always lectured me when she came to the house to visit Berenice."

"Do you think it would be acceptable if I called upon her? I've always admired her."

"You are quite the bravest man I've ever known, Joseph. Do visit her. I suspect that in fact she's rather lonely. She has outlived the era that molded her, when Rome's Republican ideals still had meaning."

"As they do to you, Marcus."

The gray-haired senator looked sharply at Joseph. "Too astute, Joseph. Don't tell anyone about such an idea."

"Forgive my impertinence, Marcus. And depend on my silence."

There were ten races scheduled for the short winter day. Halfway through the ninth one Marcus suggested to Joseph that they leave. "Even if we have to drag the young ones kicking and screaming. The crowds at the end are impossible to get through."

"Good plan. I'll bribe Ella with a sweet from one of the vendors in the Forum."

"I'll bribe Julius with a visit to the Senate. He has his eye on my toga . . . If he ever learns to wear his." Marcus' chuckle was dotingly fond.

They had almost reached the exit from the Circus building when Marcus suddenly grabbed Joseph's arm. "Get Ella," he said urgently. Joseph pulled Ella to his side. Marcus and Julius were bowing, so he bowed, too. Four women in belted gray cloaks and tall gray headdresses walked past them. Uniformed men marched in front of the women, and behind them.

"Who was that?" Joseph inquired after the little procession passed on.

"Vestal Virgins," Marcus replied.

"What is that?" Ella wanted to know.

Julius—his toga in place—answered her in lofty tones. They were priestesses at the Temple of Vesta, the goddess of the hearth and home, the mother of all Rome. "They keep the eternal flame in the Temple burning. It symbolizes the eternal future of the Empire, and it must never go out. Nothing is more sacred."

Ella did not appear properly impressed. "I meant, what is a virgin?" she said.

Julius turned scarlet. He'd been initiated into the joys of manhood, and he knew already that some of his fellow officers paid premium prices at the exclusive brothel that specialized in virgins. But he didn't know what to say to an ignorant little girl.

His father helped him out. "A virgin is a girl who hasn't married yet," he told Ella.

She frowned. "Seems strange to have somebody who's not married be the goddess of the home. What's a home without a family and children?"

Marcus looked at Joseph. "Your turn," he said.

"Symbols don't have to make sense in pagan religions," he said. That seemed to satisfy her.

Julius didn't like to feel deflated. When Ella was eating her honey-dipped dates in the Forum, he tried to retrieve his sense of superiority. "That's the Temple of Vesta," he said, pointing to a circular, columned building. "The eternal flame is in there. That's where the, um, priestesses live." He indicated another building. "They have everything they would possibility need in there. A bakery, kitchen, baths, pools of fish, lots of slaves, women to weave the cloth and make their clothes. They never have to go out, except to tend the flame."

"And go to the chariot races," Ella added.

"That's only if they want to!" Julius said. Exasperation made his voice rise. "And that's only the old priestesses. The young ones mostly just tend the flame, and the beginners don't go out at all. Every five years a girl gets picked to be a Vestal. She stays inside for ten years while the old ones train her, and then she gets to tend the flame for ten years. I guess that's why she wants to do things like go to the races. Being around little girls is a pain."

"Julius!" Marcus was stern.

Ella stuck out her tongue at Julius.

"Ella!" Joseph was shocked.

She made a pretense of guilt, then gave Julius a genuine smile and held out her sticky hand with two dates remaining on the palm. "One for you and one for me, Julius."

He accepted the peace offering, but he went to his father's side to eat it. "When do we go to the Senate, Father?"

Joseph and Marcus said their farewells, manfully containing their laughter.

"If we hurry we'll have time to take the dogs for their walk before it starts to get dark," Joseph told Ella. "You can wash your hands in the next fountain we come to, then hold mine while we're crossing the river."

It was a ceremony they had invented after Joseph showed her where he had tripped and gotten the scar that was hidden by his beard. Whenever they walked past the spot on the island in the center of the Tiber, Ella made sure that he didn't trip a second time.

CHAPTER SEVENTY-ONE

JOSEPH AND ELLA HAD BEEN IN ROME FOR A LITTLE MORE than three months when the days of the Purim festival arrived. They knew the neighborhood and most of their neighbors, and they joined in the dancing and singing and feasting in the streets with a joyful sense of being at home. It was still chilly at the end of February, but spring was definitely in the air, and the celebrations were truly felt by all those who lived in the cramped, smelly tenements and could now look forward to the outdoor life that was an important part of the Roman style. It made no difference that Purim was a Jewish festival. Everyone took part—Jew and Gentile, male and female, old and young.

Joseph observed the traditional rule that a man must get a little bit drunk. He was slow to wake when Ella shook his shoulder in the middle of the night. Then he heard the loud barking of the dogs and sat bolt upright in his bed. "Is there someone trying to break in?" he asked her. "Give me my staff. I'll stop them."

"No, no, Abba. Get up. Quickly. There's the smell of smoke. Something's burning."

Joseph woke instantly and completely. "Get dressed and get out into the street. Let the dogs out. I'll be right with you." He could smell it now, too. With the resin in its boards, the tenement would burn like a torch. "Hurry, Ella," he called after her. "Hurry." He felt around in the dark main room, found the precious scrolls and his staff, and hastened through the door into the courtyard.

It was a square of shifting shadow and light. Halfway up the building a window was bright with flame. "Ella!" Joseph shouted. "Ella, where are you?"

"Here, Abba. I'm all right." She appeared in the doorway of the tenement. She was dressed and held her harp in her arms. "I sent the dogs up the stairs to wake people up."

Now that he wasn't terrified about Ella, Joseph became aware of the sounds of barking and of screams and shouts from above.

"Good girl," he said. "Now, get out of the courtyard and down to the corner by the fountain. I'll take care of the dogs." Ribbons of flame were beginning to climb from the window up the outside walls. Joseph went back inside. "Fire!" he yelled. "Fire! Jericho! Jordan! Joppa! Jabbok! Come! Come! Fire! Fire!" He whistled for the dogs. He could hear feet pounding down the narrow wooden staircase. He whistled again, and called the dogs' names until thick smoke drove him outside. The dogs ran past him, and coughing people began to rush from the house.

"To the street," Joseph told them. "To the street. The walls will fall into the courtyard. Hurry. Hurry. To the street and away."

He heard the dogs barking with frantic urgency; he heard the ripping, sharp reports of igniting pitch inside the wooden wall of the tenement and saw the arc of a burning board into the courtyard. But there was still the sound of choked coughing from inside. Joseph hurried to find it. Three people were huddled together on the stairs. Below them small flames were licking at the stair treads.

"Come on, you can still get down." Joseph grasped his staff, pointed it up toward them, prodded mercilessly at the man's chest. "Grab hold," he shouted, coughing.

As if wakened from a nightmare, the man caught hold of the staff's end with one hand and the woman behind him with the other. She held tight to the child beside her.

Joseph jerked, then hauled on the staff as he backed toward the door. The three were drawn with him. Joseph saw the staircase explode into leaping flame behind them.

"To the street," he gasped. "And away."

The scene was as bright as daylight now, and the tenements were emptying. People carrying whatever they prized were streaming into the streets.

And from the corner where the fountain splashed, a troop of the night watchmen/fire brigade were entering the street, pushing the crowd aside. The Vigilum, as it was called, was a professional company of former soldiers, with the discipline and rapid action they'd learned in the legions before Caesar Augustus organized this vital new corps.

"Come," said Joseph to Ella. "Call the dogs. We can go now. Where, I don't know."

That night Joseph learned that everything he'd been told about Rome's Jewish community was true. No matter that his words in the synagogues had outraged and offended so many. The very men who had reviled him as a blasphemer were among the dozens who offered shelter to him and Ella, even to the dogs. The other dispossessed, all those Jews who'd had to flee the tenements, were offered the same. United by the Law of their forefathers, all Jews were one family and cared for one another in time of need.

Joseph and Ella finished the night in a tenement four streets away, with the bricklayer David, his wife Leah, and their five children, three boys and two girls, all younger than nine-year-old Ella.

David and his family lived on the third floor, in two small rooms. Eight other families, much like his, lived in similar apartments on the same floor. Fourteen families had one-room living quarters on the floor above. All shared the tiny airless courtyard at the tenement's base, with its single latrine.

In the morning Joseph and Ella rolled up the thin mats Leah had given them to sleep on. Joseph put them in the corner where the family's rolled mats were already stacked. He did not need to count them to know that two of the children had slept on the floor so that he and Ella would have the best comfort the family had to offer.

Leah was in the other room making breakfast. When Joseph saw her carefully measuring a quantity of barley from a covered pottery jar, he began to comprehend the importance of the government dole of grain that he had earlier considered an invitation to laziness. Leah stirred the barley into a large bowl of water, then spooned the cold gruel into small bowls for her family and guests. David, she told Joseph, in answer to his question, had already gone out. He left before sunrise every day to look for work wherever any building was going on. Many other laborers like David did the same thing. It was a hopeful omen that he hadn't come home yet; it meant that probably he'd been one of the lucky ones hired that day.

There was no trace of self-pity or complaint in Leah's conversation. This was life as she knew it. Hers and most women's that she knew.

Joseph ate every drop of the tasteless cereal. His eyes told Ella to do the same.

After he thanked Leah, Joseph told her that he and Ella were going to take the dogs for their morning walk. He'd look for an apartment of their own, too, he told her. Later he'd come back to report on his luck, or lack of it.

"You know you will be welcome for as long as you need to stay," Leah said. She was unaffectedly sincere.

Joseph and Ella walked a good distance, into a different neighborhood, before he stopped at a cookshop to buy food for himself, his daughter, and his pets. He was quiet, contemplating an idea that was taking shape inside his mind.

"What a good breakfast," Ella said happily. "Why don't

we take some of the bread and fish and cheese back to Leah? Milk, too. Her children don't have any milk."

Joseph tried to explain why generosity was sometimes an insult, because it implied the hospitality received was inadequate.

Ella tried to understand, but she could not. "If we can buy food and Leah can't, what's wrong about sharing? Isn't that what you and Antiochus were talking about—giving to the poor?"

"Yes, but without making them feel poorer by accepting what we give. Don't talk for a little while, I need to think. Come, we'll walk while I do. We've got to find someplace to live."

Joseph had always known that poverty existed. But he'd never been in its midst before, and he was shaken by the reality. Particularly the quiet dignity of its sufferers.

Ella was puzzled when her father looked at apartments like David's and Leah's, also even smaller ones. She was relieved that the one he finally took was a reasonably spacious four rooms on the second floor of a brick tenement house with a large courtyard. She did wonder why he was so uninterested in the selection of bedding and basic supplies, but she liked being able to make all the decisions herself. It made her feel grown-up.

"Now, Ella, you fix the bedcoverings, and put the pottery on the shelves, and fill the lamps and whatever else needs doing. Keep the dogs indoors with you. I'm going to tell Leah that we've found a place. I want to talk with David when he gets home, too, so I may be late getting back here. Don't worry. Then we'll give the dogs their walk and get some dinner."

"Abba, you have an odd look on your face."

Joseph hugged his little girl. "It's called responding to a challenge, dear daughter. It's what your old abba likes best of all things."

Joseph had found out how exorbitant rents were for even the smallest space. It was no wonder that a man could hardly afford to feed his family. Now he knew what to do with his fortune. He had moved it to Rome with the intention of giving much of it to the poor, and he'd made sizeable anonymous donations to all the synagogues, for distribution to the needy, but that hadn't been at all satisfying. He was only giving away gold, with plenty still left over. He wanted to do something himself, some work that would involve him and excite him.

And now he'd found it.

The next day he negotiated the purchase of the entire block of tenements that the fire had gutted. He was going to build new ones. Of brick. As safe as he could make them. And as generous in terms of space for people to live in. And decent, with running water piped to each floor, and the latrines there.

The rents would be what a man could afford to pay, not the maximum the landlord could gouge out of him.

The project would require all his ingenuity and all his energy. It was exactly what he'd been missing in his life for too many years.

He waved his arms excitedly when he described the scope of the enterprise to Ella. Her reaction rocked him.

"You said you were coming to Rome to tell people about Jesus, Abba. Why have you changed your mind?"

"But I haven't!" Joseph blustered. "This is my own way of doing what Jesus said to do. It's giving to the poor."

"Are you still going to talk in the synagogues? And let people come ask questions?"

"Of course. I'll only be working on the building project in the daytime. Never on the Sabbath. All that will be just the way it was before, except that I'll have to tell people about the different place we live now."

Before he went to sleep, Joseph knelt and prayed for forgiveness. Ella had seen to the heart of things. He had almost forgotten about his mission. That was supposed to be his chief concern, but it was a humiliating failure; not one person had made a commitment to the belief in the message Joseph preached. He knew his business project would succeed. He was good at business.

It was a good thing that Ella reminded Joseph about his mission because it was about to expand alarmingly. The drama of Joseph's heroics and the rescuing dogs had made the tenement fire an interesting story, not simply another of the tenement disasters that happened from time to time and occasioned no comment at all in Rome's fashionable society.

When it became known that the hero was a preacher of a new religion and that his daughter had been part of a miracle, Rome's bored wealthy classes began visiting the synagogue to see them and hear them speak. They were the latest novelty.

The most daring novelty seekers even went to Joseph's meetings in his home.

Leaders of the synagogues were angered by the influx of the curious. So was Joseph, especially in his own home. He was too tired in the evening, after a long day's work on the building project, to have his time wasted by frivolous, perfumed, and silk-clad men and women. Sometimes one of them would actually laugh at his account of the resurrection. "Come on, Preacher," the amused one would say, "where did you dispose of the body after you removed it from the tomb?"

Joseph longed for Mary of Magdala's presence. She would have known how to dismiss the mockers. But the only believer he had to talk with was Ella, and she always kept her serenity. "Remember about turning the other cheek, Abba. Even while a person's laughing, his heart might be listening to what you're saying."

And then it happened.

It was in the night's darkest hour that the dogs began to bark. Joseph took his staff and the dogs to confront whoever was knocking on the door.

He was nearly blinded when he opened it; the huge figure outside was holding a blazing torch.

Joseph shaded his eyes with his hand. "What do you want?" he demanded. Beside him the dogs were growling menace.

"Master, I want to follow Jesus. Will you help me?"

"Is this some kind of prank?"

"No, Master. I risk my life coming here. But I heard your message, and I want to worship the son of God."

Joseph quieted the dogs and backed away from the door. "I will light a lamp. Put out your torch and come in."

The visitor was a slave from the region of the Danube. He bore the name Rufus because of his red hair. He'd been bodyguard for his owner when the Roman youth had gone to the synagogue with some friends. Standing silently near the rear wall, he had heard Joseph tell of Jesus.

"My heart caught fire," said Rufus. "I want to know Jesus and serve him."

Joseph was deeply moved by the big man's simple statement. It rang with truth.

"What about your owner? What might he do to you?"

Rufus said he had to be back at his owner's house before dawn. If it were discovered that he was missing, he'd be called a runaway slave and reported to the Vigilum and the Guards. They would find him, notch his ears and whip him, then return him. If his owner chose, Rufus would be killed. Maybe that wouldn't happen, said the red-haired slave, because he was worth thousands in the slave market. But his owner was rich, and young, and hot tempered. He might enjoy seeing Rufus die, deem it an expensive entertainment.

"I will buy you from him," Joseph declared.

Rufus dropped to his knees. "Master, he would not sell me, but I do not fear death if I am part of Jesus. That is what you can do for me; that is why I came to you."

Joseph was humbled. "I welcome you in the name of our Lord," he said. "Confess your sins to Jesus in private, and I will baptize you as a token of God's forgiveness. Then we will pray together."

He went to get water, trying to remember the exact words Mary had used when she baptized him and Antiochus.

When he returned, Rufus was still on his knees. He had finished confessing, he said. Joseph's voice and hand were steady when he dipped water from the bowl and sprinkled it on the red hair of the kneeling man. "I baptize you in the name of the Father, and of the Son, and of the Holy Spirit."

He lowered himself to his knees, facing Rufus. "Repeat after me," he said, "Our Father in heaven, hallowed be your name . . ."

When the short prayer was over, Joseph gazed with awe on Rufus' glowing countenance. The huge man looked as if the torch he had carried had entered into him.

"These are the words of Jesus," said Joseph. "'I am the light of the world. Whoever follows me will never walk in darkness but will have the light of life. I am the resurrection and the life. Those who believe in me, even though they die, will live.'" He put his palm on Rufus' bowed head.

"Go in peace," he said.

CHAPTER SEVENTY-TWO

ELLA WAS NOT AT ALL PLEASED WHEN JOSEPH TOLD HER THAT he had hired a tutor for her.

"But it's getting warmer every day, Abba. I don't want to be cooped up inside with books and a writing tablet."

"You can have your lessons in the courtyard if you prefer. Or on the riverbank's green slope. The point is, I have neglected your education for too long. And also, I will soon be away most of the day once the building commences. You cannot stay alone."

"I could go to Joel's shop and help sell sandals."

"You've forgotten most of your Greek. You must get it back, and more."

"My Latin's better than yours."

"But you can only speak, not read. You need instruction."

"I could be more use helping Leah with her children than learning to write words I already know how to say."

"I am your father, and you will do as I say. Your tutor's name is Jason. He will be here tomorrow."

Ella giggled. "He sounds like another dog, with a name like that. I'm going to tell him so."

"It won't impress him. He is accustomed to impertinent students. His credentials are ideal."

Ella resigned herself to the inescapable. When she sighed to Joel and Samuel that she was having her last day of freedom, Samuel asked his father and Joseph if he could share Ella's classes. "You don't know how lucky you are," he scolded her. "I can do calculations, but that's all. I've always wanted to read and write."

All of a sudden Ella decided that she wouldn't mind having classes at all. "I wanted somebody to laugh with," she explained to Joseph. "Tutors never even smile."

Jason was the exception. Soon the riverbank rang with laughter even more than with conjugations and declensions. The classes were an unqualified success. Jason also added music to the curriculum. He played a double flute, Samuel the long flute, Ella the harp. Each taught the others songs, and they played together while Ella sang the words.

Joel and Samuel had talked often and long about Joseph's teachings since that first memorable Sabbath when they'd heard them. They were not impulsive men, this father and son. When they told Joseph they had decided to follow Jesus and his teachings, the announcement was not dramatic.

And yet, when they were baptized, everything about them was dramatically altered. The gift of the Holy Spirit transfigured their lives, filling their hearts to overflowing with happiness that they were eager to share with others.

They went with Joseph and Ella to the synagogues and added their testimony about the joy of believing to Joseph's and Ella's stories of their own experiences.

On one occasion Joseph saw Rufus standing in the rear while his owner snickered with friends. He wished he could ask the big red-haired man to add his testimony, too, but he knew he couldn't put Rufus at risk. It was a frustration. Rufus' eyes were alight with faith; Joseph knew he was longing to speak out.

If only my agents weren't so useless, Joseph thought. They'd had no difficulty determining the identity of Rufus' owner, but so far none of them had managed to get him to consider selling his bodyguard, not at any price. The problem haunted Joseph.

More so than he realized. He was appalled to hear himself blurt it out when he paid his call on the Lady Antonia.

"Please forgive me, my Lady," he said at once. "I don't know what made me tell you such a thing."

Antonia was as graciously patrician as she had always been. "There is nothing that calls for forgiveness, Joseph. You betrayed no names, made no disparaging comments about the slave's owner."

Joseph admired her more than he dared say aloud. She was showing her age in the deep lines on her face and the bruised-looking shadows beneath her eyes, but her spine was as straight as any centurion's, and she held her head high.

The woman with her was much less impressive. So much so that Joseph had already forgotten her name, and remembering names was one of his most reliable skills.

"Why do you want so much to buy this nameless slave from his nameless owner?" she asked, with small interest. "Have you fallen in love with him?"

Joseph was greatly offended, but he didn't let it show. Another of his skills. "It is a matter considerably more esoteric," he said. "We share a particular religious belief."

Antonia smiled. "Is it you everyone has been talking about, Joseph? I never considered such a thing. Are you really a Nazarene? Isn't that what these people are called? What in the world possessed you, that you would do such a thing?"

"I doubt that you want to hear it, Lady Antonia. It's a very long story."

"The best stories generally are," said Antonia decisively. "Tell it."

Joseph obeyed her command. When he finished, Antonia smiled. "I am glad that your daughter was healed, Joseph. I can well understand that it would have a strong effect on you. May your new belief bring you continued satisfaction."

Joseph recognized the dismissal. "You were extremely generous to grant me so much of your time, Lady. It is, as always, a pleasure to see you."

Antonia offered him her hand. "You are a good man, Joseph of Arimathea, and the world has fewer such with every day that passes. I am pleased that you came to see me."

Joseph bowed to Antonia's friend. "An honor to meet you, Lady."

She nodded. "Very nice," she murmured. She barely glanced at Joseph. I've outstayed my welcome by at least an hour, he thought to himself. That poor woman looks so hungry she might faint before Antonia orders refreshments served.

The buildings were rising with extraordinary speed. Joseph credited that—and their excellence in all ways—to David, the bricklayer. Joseph had hired him as personal assistant and construction overseer the moment he bought the property.

David knew, from on-the-job experience, which workers and material suppliers could be trusted. Joseph wanted the best, that had always been his way. David saw to it that Joseph got what he wanted; the bonus David delivered was dedication and pride in his workmanship that was contagious to the other workmen. Before the tenements were half-completed, other landowners were trying to bribe him to leave Joseph's project and come to theirs.

"What you must do," Joseph told him, "is start your own construction company. Work for yourself, not for whoever might hire you. Keep this crew you've assembled and you'll always be in demand."

David looked at Joseph with pity. "Forgive me, Joseph, but you don't know what you're talking about. You're a rich man, you can afford big dreams. I have fed my family and saved a bit on the steady wages you've paid me, but men don't start businesses on so little."

"Ha! So you say. Come to my place for Sabbath dinner.

With Leah and the children, naturally. I have a story to tell you about a boy from a farm who ran off to sea."

In late September Joseph celebrated the New Year at the Herodian synagogue and in his big new apartment in his big new building. He had invited the entire congregation to a New Year feast in the grand courtyard. Almost everyone came to enjoy the generous array of roasted meats and fish and breads and vegetables on the long tables set up in the courtyard. There were even bowls of carrots. When he was asked about the strange orange root, Joseph smiled. "They're in honor of my wife Sarah. We had a joke one time about carrots. I'm sure she is looking down from heaven and smiling now."

He showed the apartments with undisguised pride to all the guests. They were all rented, in all four buildings, but not yet occupied. Move-in day had been set for the day after the Sabbath.

When visitors moaned that they wanted one and couldn't have it, Joseph referred them to David. He had the ground-floor apartment adjacent to Joseph's. It was his family's home and the headquarters of his new construction company.

Joseph's apartment served two purposes, too. The biggest room was what people called the Home of the Nazarenes. Six more men and women had been baptized during the summer months. They met every week to celebrate their fellowship by breaking bread and drinking wine in memory of Jesus, as he had instructed his disciples to do. Although the bread and wine were symbolic of his crucifixion, the fellowship was a commemoration of his resurrection, and the small group celebrated with music, singing, and dancing.

"Agape" the tutor Jason named the celebration. "Love feast" was the meaning of the Greek word, for they celebrated their love of Jesus and of God, and of the gospel of the resurrection.

Jason had sought baptism after Joseph let Samuel borrow his prized scroll for reading lessons. In teaching Samuel the sayings of Jesus, Jason had become a follower of the man who taught those sayings.

Another of the celebrants was Antonia's friend, whose name was Lydia. Joseph had misread the hunger he saw in her face. It was a hunger for something to believe in, something that would fill the emptiness of life with too much luxury, too many lovers, and no purpose in living. The life that was typical of the Roman upper class. People who were unknowingly on the brink of cataclysm.

Joseph's informants passed on the rumors: Tiberius was planning to make Sejanus tribune, a position with even more power than the consulship he had been forced to resign in May when Tiberius himself resigned as co-consul, pleading fatigue; Sejanus was about to marry Livilla, the widow of Tiberius' son Drusus; Sejanus was plotting to kill Gaius, Tiberius' most likely heir; Sejanus was plotting to murder Tiberius and proclaim himself ruler of Rome.

Rumors were one of the chief entertainments in Rome. Informants had also reported that Macro, the Prefect of the Vigilum, was mysteriously missing. Possibly victim of another of Sejanus' murder plots.

Joseph saw no possible connection between the wide-ranging rumors. He was astonished—all Rome was astonished—by what happened in mid-October.

Macro had made a well-kept-secret visit to Tiberius on Capri. Sejanus must go, the Emperor had decided. He had informants, too.

Macro had returned in secrecy as well, with scrolls and instructions from Tiberius. On the evening of October 17, he passed on the Emperor's confidential oral instructions to his second-in-command in the Vigilum, and to the only man Tiberius trusted in the Senate.

The following morning Macro was waiting for Sejanus outside the Temple of Apollo, where the Senate was meeting. "I have just come from the Emperor," Macro told him.

He waved the scroll with Tiberius' seal clearly visible. "He's making you tribune. This is his letter to the Senate."

Sejanus went inside.

Macro acted quickly. He showed the Praetorian Guards on duty a second scroll. "I am now your commander. Go back to barracks; I'll be there shortly." Then he signaled the troop of Vigilum, waiting in concealment behind a tall hedge. They took the Guards' places, and Macro entered the Temple.

"A letter from the Emperor!" he announced. Sejanus hid his smile. Macro delivered the letter to the Senate officials, saluted, and then hurried to the barracks of the Praetorian Guard, to tell them that the Emperor had awarded them a special bonus for their loyalty, to him, the Emperor. "Sejanus," Macro said, "is being arrested at this very moment. And I am your new commander."

When the Senate official read Tiberius' letter aloud, the expression on Sejanus' face changed from hidden smile to frozen terror. He knew what to expect.

And it came. He was arrested, by the Vigilum troops, and taken to prison. Before sundown, Sejanus was strangled, and his body dumped on the steps of the Temple of Saturn in the Forum. By the time most people, including Joseph, heard the news, the formerly most powerful man in Rome had become a hideously mutilated corpse.

The body was left there for three days, to give the thousands who had feared and hated Sejanus an opportunity to invent additional mutilations, to piss on him, to defecate on what had once been his face, to carve bits of flesh or bone for souvenirs of his downfall.

The ghastly remains were then swept onto a dirty length of canvas, carried to the river, and dumped in, to be swept away from Rome altogether, by the Tiber tides.

The bloodbath had begun.

CHAPTER SEVENTY-THREE

JOEL HURRIED INTO THE ROOM WHERE JASON WAS GIVING A poetry exercise to Ella and Samuel. "Where's Joseph?" he asked.

Ella looked up from her efforts. "He and David went to look at a place where David might build his tenement."

"Do you know where that is?"

"They were talking about was it too close to the gate in the city walls."

"Good. That helps. Now, listen to me, all of you. There's rioting across the river, and it will break out soon over here. I've shuttered and locked the shop; everything's being looted. I want you, Samuel, to help Ella get all her biggest containers and go buy as much food as you can carry. Then bring her home and see that she locks herself in.

"Jason, you warn all the people in the buildings. Help Leah get food, too. It may not be safe on the streets for many days.

"I'll take two of the dogs and go after Joseph and David. Which two are the strongest, Ella?"

"Not Jabby, that's certain. She's going to have babies. I'll get Joppy and Jordy leashed for you."

"Quickly. All of you." Joel's urgency was clear, and they hurried to do as he'd ordered.

It was over an hour later that the sound of barking sent Samuel rushing to the door when the first knock came. Joseph and Joel were disheveled, and the dog's back was a ridge of bristling fur.

"Abba!"

"It's all right, my dear. David's taken Jordy to his home, and none of us is hurt." He and Joel swung the door closed against the noises of shouting and splintering wood in the street outside. The iron bolts slid into place with reassuring clanks of security.

Joseph smoothed the quivering dog's fur. "Good boy, Joppy, there, there, now. All quiet, all safe now." He patted the big head. "Good boy."

"The dogs may have saved our lives," Joel said. "The streets are swarming with looters and the mobs are drunk on the thrills of damaging anything and anybody they come across."

It felt strangely like the middle of the night for the next forty-eight hours. With the shutters bolted, the rooms were lit by lamps instead of daylight from the windows. Sounds of riot came and went outside while inside everyone worked hard to maintain a semblance of normality and calm. Jason gave lessons as usual. He, Ella, and Samuel played music to entertain themselves as well as people from apartments up the stairs within the locked building. The large supplies of food, wine, and water dwindled rapidly, shared with others who hadn't managed to stock up.

When the orgy of violence and robbery finally exhausted itself, all Rome was a shambles. The warehouses that held grain for the dole were empty, statues in the Forum were shattered, dead bodies sprawled grotesquely in squares and streets, and injured of all ages crowded the island in the river, waiting for treatment in the Temple of Aesculapius. Every shop of every kind had been looted and vandalized. Drunk stragglers adorned in stolen finery wandered aimlessly through the streets until they were arrested by Vigilum troops engaged in restoring order.

For weeks the cleanup went on. At the highest levels it included arrests, imprisonment, trials, and executions of Sejanus' close associates and family. His wife committed suicide before the Guard reached her to make the arrest. Some few were misguided, or terrified, or demented enough to fight the Guard instead of accepting their fate.

One of Joseph's informants was a slave trader patronized by many of Rome's prominent families. He brought the news to Joseph himself instead of sending a messenger. The reward, he knew, would be substantial. "That German slave you wanted—the one with the red hair—I've got him, but not for long. He was thrown in with a bunch I was buying. 'Use him for crow bait' the seller told me."

"Take me to him, and name your price."

Rufus' eyes were beginning to glaze. Death was at hand. He had carried out his duties as bodyguard. When the Guard came for his owner, Rufus fought them, three of them. His body bore a dozen sword slashes, most of them on the arms and shoulders, the deepest one on his right side near the hip. His head had a deep indentation near the crown where a sword hilt had finally felled him.

None of the wounds had been washed or stitched. Thickly crusted blood covered them, and crawling insects. The unmistakable odor of rotting was all around him. He'd been left where he fell, inside the gate to his owner's villa.

Joseph felt like weeping. Instead, he demanded, and got, immediate action. "A litter! At once. And men to carry it. Brush off those flies and cover him with a blanket. Take him to the Temple of Healing. I will accompany you." The slave dealer hovered uncertainly. "You'll get paid, you always do. Double if we reach the Temple before he dies."

Our Father in heaven, Joseph prayed silently, show mercy to your servant Rufus, who loves your Son.

At the Temple, a soft-spoken doctor told Joseph that

there was no hope. "Will you have us wash his wounds and prepare the body for burial?"

"I'll have you wash his wounds and close them with your needles. Myrrh, I want all you have. I'll replace it."

"'Myrrh?' The expense . . ."

"The expense does not matter. I do not appear so, Doctor, but I am a wealthy man. And this injured pagan is very special to me." The first, Joseph was crying inwardly, the very first who came to Jesus through me.

He remembered Rufus in the back of the synagogue, his eyes shining with the joy of faith; Joseph bowed his head into his cupped hands and sobbed openly.

No! He was feeling pity for his own loss, not for Rufus' pain. Joseph went to the pallet of the dying man and knelt beside it. He put his hand over Rufus' heart. The beating could barely be felt. It was slow and weak.

"Lord!" he cried aloud. "Even as you healed Sarah's baby, so, I implore you, bless this man with your grace. You saved me in the Wilderness, though I was not worthy of you. This man is all the things I was not, and am not. He is steadfast, Lord, and loves you with all his heart, and all his mind. Grant him life, Lord, I pray you. He is good, and deserving of your mercy."

The doctor tapped Joseph on the back. "You must move, if you would have us wash him." Joseph did not hear him. All his senses were concentrated in the fingers of his hand. They felt as if they were on fire and yet coated with ice at the same time. Insistent throbbing made the flame burn and the ice pierce his skin and the bones of each joint. He threw his head back, tears streaming from his closed eyes. "Thank you, my Lord Jesus," he whispered. "Blessed be your mercy and your holy name."

The throbbing was the powerful beating of Rufus' heart.

Joseph would allow no one else to bathe and anoint Rufus' wounds during his slow healing in the room that was his at the apartment.

He did permit everyone to visit the room in turn, to offer up prayers and thanks. For weeks Rufus remained unconscious. He could swallow the water and broth spooned between his lips, and he made low sounds of pain when Joseph and Samuel turned his big body when they washed it. But he showed no signs of life otherwise.

Until Ella noticed that his eyes were open and looking at her one afternoon while she sat with him. She smiled. "Hello, Rufus," she said. "Welcome back. My name is Ella."

"El-la," he echoed.

"You sound like you're dry as a bone. Here's some water. Try it from the cup; I'll hold up your head."

Rufus drank thirstily. "More?" he asked.

"Why not? The worst that can happen is you might throw up." Ella got more water from the ewer on a nearby table. "Abba," she called through the open door. "Rufus is awake, and I'll wager he's hungry as a wolf."

She was holding the cup to his mouth when Joseph rushed in.

"Bless Jesus," said Joseph.

"Amen," Ella added.

The big German's recovery was steady, but slow. Ella appointed herself his nurse and tormentor. "Now, this is something I know a lot about, Rufus. If your muscles don't get worked, they shrivel up and are no good at all. You've still got all those cuts on your arm healing, so we can wait a while up top. Your legs aren't cut up at all, and I know exactly what you have to do." She grabbed hold of one ankle, lifted, and pushed to bend his leg at the knee.

"You're very heavy," she fussed. "You'll have to help me. Come on, now. We're going to do this twenty times for each leg. Then I'll teach you about ankles and feet."

Rufus had lost a great deal of blood; lack of food had also weakened him; most debilitating of all, he had been flat on his back in bed for more than a month. He begged Ella to stop after four leg bends.

"What a crybaby," she responded. "Come on. Bend and lift your leg."

It didn't take long before Rufus was up on his feet and walking, simply to escape Ella's ministrations.

He walked—slowly—with Joseph and Ella to the temple on the island for the doctors to remove the stitches after the sword wounds were healed.

"You certainly weren't a crybaby about that," Ella told him with admiration. "I could hear you howling all the way out here. I wonder if that's what lions sound like."

When they reached the tenement, she offered him the reward that was part of their exercise regime. She fetched her harp, and together they sang Celtic songs. Rufus had taught her a number of new ones. He'd already known all those she had learned from Dosha, but Sarah's song of the fern goddess was new to him.

Rufus loved to sing. He had enthusiasm and volume to compensate for inability to carry a tune. Now, after the torment at the doctors' hands, he insisted that he deserved to sing each song twice.

"Once now, and the second time after you do your arm exercises," Ella said firmly.

"My body is healed near complete," Rufus said earnestly to Joseph. "I owe you my life and my freedom. What services do you require of me, Master? I will be happy to do all you ask and ten times that."

"I am not your master, Rufus. I've told you that before. Only God is your master, and His Son. They are my masters, also. Both of us serve them."

"That is my joy," Rufus said. His eyes spoke the same message. "Also, I want to serve you, and the little Ella."

"Here is your task, then. Be the older brother who guards her safety, and the son whom I wanted but never had. It will bring me great happiness."

Rufus knelt, kissed Joseph's hand. When he rose, Joseph embraced him. "Family," Joseph said.

Rufus repeated the word softly, tasting the sweetness of it. "Family."

Life in the poor quarters across the river from the city had recovered quickly from the damage of the rioting; there was much less there to destroy. On a day-to-day basis, what was happening in the center of Rome had no effect on the people of the Transtiber.

The downfall of Sejanus had left Rome leaderless. The Emperor remained distant, on his island refuge, present only in the infrequent letters he sent to the Senate.

Ambitious men sought power, competed for it, fought for it by fair means and foul.

The Rostra in the Forum, the platform for orators, was perpetually occupied by one or another would-be states-man. Romans greatly admired the art of rhetoric, and there was always an appreciative or insulting crowd to hear him.

On the floor of the Senate there were speeches, also. Many were attacks on fellow senators, accusations of com-plicity in Sejanus' schemes, demands for arrest and trial.

Week by week the prisons grew more populated. There were so many accused, and trials were lengthy procedures.

Joseph was surprised to receive a visit one day from Cor-nelia, Marcus' wife. Julius was with her. Marcus was not.

"Marcus doesn't know I'm here, Joseph. He's worried by my worries. But I can't help it. Every day, it seems, another senator is accused for no reason at all except that someone doesn't like him or wants to injure him for some personal insult sometime in the past. Marcus could be next. It mat-ters not a bit that Marcus always despised Sejanus.

"I'm frightened, Joseph. I've prayed to all the gods, given gifts to every temple. A woman I know named Lydia says that your god is one of great power and mercy. I want to beg for his protection, too. What do I do? Pay for a sacrifice? Buy a statue of the god? Build him a temple? I'll do anything you say."

Cornelia was near to hysteria or breakdown. Joseph barely knew Marcus' wife; he wasn't sure that he could help her. And yet, he thought of Lydia. She had heard him tell Antonia about Jesus, and it had changed her life.

"Come into a quiet room where we can talk, Cornelia. I'll get some wine and cakes. You, too, Julius. It is a pleasure to welcome you to my home."

This Julius was the boy who had shouted his throat raw at the Circus Maximus. He looked at least ten years older, although the races had been only a year ago. Joseph felt the weight of sorrow for the lost youthfulness of Marcus' son. Service in the Praetorian Guard must have exposed him to many horrors in this last year. Arrests, executions, street battles during the rioting. Becoming a man exacted a terrible cost sometimes.

Joseph poured wine for the three of them. "I am going to tell you a long story," he said. "It is a true story, my own experience, not a myth or a legend, like the stories about Apollo or Minerva or Venus.

"It began ten years ago, when my daughter was born. You remember how she was. Her legs had no strength . . ."

Joseph led Cornelia on the path of discovery and revelation he had followed himself. When he was done, he leaned forward. "So you see, Cornelia, Jesus is not a marble statue in a marble temple. He is our savior. He lives, through the Holy Spirit, within the hearts and souls of all who believe in him."

Cornelia burst into tears. "Joseph, I'm not looking for something or someone to believe in. I'm looking for protection against Marcus being arrested. If I say that I follow Jesus, can you promise that Marcus will be safe?"

"No, Cornelia," said Joseph gently. "That's not the nature of faith. It's not a bargain."

"Well, then, why did you make me listen to you talk on and on so tediously?"

"I'm sorry. I can do only one thing, and I will be glad to do it. I will pray for Marcus' safety."

Cornelia did not bother to say goodbye. "Take me home, Julius," she ordered, and she stood by the door, waiting for her son to open it.

Julius did so. He bowed to Joseph. "Thank you," he murmured, with an anxious glance at his irate mother. Joseph smiled, understanding the young man's difficulty.

He did not feel the depression of failure, as he had once done whenever a listener did not respond to the miracle of the resurrection. The message that was his mission was spreading. New followers were being added all the time. He had reached the three hearts that Mary of Magdala had named as his duty to the Lord. And more.

The only legitimate sorrow for him now was the failure of his own heart. He believed in the resurrection, he believed that Jesus was the son of God. Why could he not experience the happiness that Ella talked about with such simplicity? Why did he never feel the love of God, as he had known it for those few moments in the Wilderness? Was he unworthy?

Joseph bent his head to pray. For Marcus, as he'd promised. For himself, that he would find the gift of the Holy Spirit.

David's tenement began to rise higher than the city's wall a block away. Leah complained, not meaning it, that David knew the bricks in his building better than he knew his children.

Joseph admired his young friend; he was genuinely happy about David's success. And yet, he was wistful that the new tenement wasn't his project. He didn't have enough to do, no plans, no challenges. It was summer, the days were long, and hard to fill.

Summer was the sailing season. There were moments when Joseph's heart ached for the sight and the smell of the sea. Why had he given that up? It was his life, he was only half a man—less than half—without it.

Yes, he had his mission. But he wasn't needed anymore. The Nazarenes knew the story of Jesus' life and death and resurrection. They knew his sayings. They knew the happiness of God's love. They were telling others. The Fellowship was growing. Joseph had nothing special to contribute.

So he thought. But soon he was proved wrong.

The quiet man and woman watched for a long time without calling attention to themselves. Joseph, too, was watching. Ella and Samuel were trying to train the growing puppies that Jabby had delivered on schedule six months earlier. It was a never-dimming delight to see Ella running and jumping on her strong legs. The romping, tumbling puppies did not amuse him as much as they did her, however. It was a welcome distraction when he noticed the quiet pair near the gate.

"Are you looking for someone? Can I help you?"

The man spoke: "You are Joseph of Arimathea. My wife and I would appreciate an hour of your time, if that's convenient for you. Or, we could return on a different day."

"Not at all. In truth, I'm glad to get away from all this youthful energy. It makes me feel old."

The couple's smiles were dutiful. And nervous.

"Come inside with me," Joseph said. "We will have a quiet place to talk."

Their names were Martha and Saul. Their story made Joseph's heart swell with rage.

Martha began it. She had forced Saul to come, she said. He didn't want to do it because he worried that she might be insulted, shamed.

"I will do my best not to offend you," Joseph assured her. And her husband.

Saul picked up the tale then. They had married, he told Joseph, after a very long betrothal. He was apprenticed to a tanner, and they had to wait until he was able to work on his own, after the learning years, and earn a living. Martha was twenty, Saul twenty-four when they became husband and wife.

"We were not blessed with children," Saul said. He took Martha's hand in his. "So I was ordered to divorce and marry another, after ten years. I would not obey. I will never obey. Martha is my wife and I will not give her up."

He was forbidden to enter the synagogue, any synagogue, until he ceased to live in violation of the Law.

"We have been kept away from God for twelve years," Martha said. There were tears, and anger, in her voice. "From what people say, you worship God here in your home. Do you admit sinners like we two?"

"You have committed no sin!" Joseph was too angry to stay silent any longer. "God is love. He does not punish love."

Martha began to tremble. "How I wish that I could believe you."

Joseph got himself under control. His words were quiet, not alarming, when he spoke to the husband and wife about the Son of God.

The head of the Herodian Synagogue came to see Joseph three days later. No longer would Joseph be permitted to address the congregation, he said. Not unless he stopped consorting with sinners.

What was he talking about?

The man and woman who were living in sin had been to Joseph's "Agape." It was already common knowledge. No one who wanted to attend synagogue was permitted to talk with them or break bread with them. They were outcasts.

It was true, Martha told Joseph when he went to their tenement room. They had been pariahs in the district for a dozen years.

"Then we will leave Rome. I will lead my family, and

you and Saul, and any others who want to come, and we will carry God and His Son to some other city."

His blood was racing. Not from anger now. Joseph felt young again, and strong, and eager.

CHAPTER SEVENTY-FOUR

SAUL AND MARTHA WERE FRIGHTENED TO NEAR PARALYSIS BY
the thought of leaving Rome—more specifically, by the
thought of leaving the Transtiber district. It was the only
place they knew. Born there, of parents who'd been born
there, they had grown up considering the city side of the
river a far-off exotic land, visited perhaps once or twice a
year for holiday spectaculars or parades.

Joseph bullied them kindly, but adamantly. They must
leave now, when the days were long and many miles could
be covered before dusk. They would go north, he had decided. He did not know that part of Italy at all, and it would
be an adventure. He was thirsting for adventure.

There was an excellent road, well traveled and therefore
with minimum risk of bandits. Also, they would have
Rufus with them, and the dogs. Not all of them. Jabby was
large with a new litter. She would be given to David and
Leah; their children were already naming the puppies, although there was no way of knowing how many there
would be.

"Tell your employer that you will work only ten more
days," Joseph ordered Saul. "That is probably longer than
we should linger, but he is entitled to time for finding

someone to take your place. Select the strongest, lightest skin you have in the tannery, buy it, and give it to Joel. He will make you a money belt for your savings and some thick-soled sandals for you and Martha. You two will be walking more miles than you are accustomed to."

David was more than happy to accept the offer Joseph made him: "If you will be responsible for collecting rents and maintaining the safety of my tenements, David, you may have your own apartment rent-free. That is, unless you intend to move your home and business headquarters to your own new building."

David's grin was broader than any Joseph had ever seen on his face before. "I've been wondering how to put it to you, Joseph, that I wanted to keep my apartment here. The rents you charge are about half what I will charge in my own building. I couldn't afford to live as well there as I do now."

"So you accept?"

"Immediately. Before you change your mind."

"Some of the income will be needed for upkeep. Materials and so forth. The rest will be for the expenses of the House of the Nazarenes. I am going to ask Joel to take over the running of it."

"I am honored," Joel said. His manner was serious, and happy. "To do the Lord's work, to bring more followers to Jesus, will give meaning to my life."

Samuel startled Joseph by refusing to help his father. "I will go with you, Joseph, if you'll have me. The mission is important to me." He looked earnestly at Joseph. "I want the travel and adventure, too. Is that all right, or am I being selfish?"

Joseph clapped him on the back. "You're being a strong, healthy, eighteen-year-old man, Samuel. There's nothing wrong with that."

He said the same thing to Jason when the Greek tutor asked if he could join the travelers. Not in exactly the same words—he didn't know how old Jason was. It would be a genuine boon to have Jason along. Ella could keep up with her lessons, and the musical ensemble of harp and flutes would be a continuing pleasure. Even if Rufus insisted on singing.

Also, there'd be two more men now to deal with any difficulties along the way. And to carry part of Joseph's remaining treasure. It had dwindled considerably since it was transferred from Jerusalem, but the weight of the gold was still enough so that dividing it among the four would ease the burden that he'd expected to share with Rufus alone. Saul was already so nervous about carrying his little bit of silver that Joseph had kept the very existence of the gold a secret. It might terrorize Saul to know what an enticing target they were going to be for bandits.

Yes, everything was quite in order. Joseph's success with the tenement project was well known. When he arranged to have his treasure available, he'd allowed the government to extract from him his intention to build more tenements in the wealthy resort city of Herculaneum. He swore the man to secrecy, naturally. And expected him to sell the information. Naturally. So bandits would be looking for him on the road south, while he was heading north.

Only one small thing remained to be done. The young dogs. Tenants in the buildings were overjoyed to accept them. Everyone remembered that Joseph's dogs had saved hundreds from death by fire. But Ella was determined to have them perfectly trained before she left them, and Joseph didn't believe it could be done. Only eight days remained now before they were to leave.

Still, she was excited about the adventure, too. If she didn't finish teaching every one of the puppies to "stay," "speak," "sit," and "come," she would soon forget her disappointment.

"Come, doggie, come to Ella. Come on, now, stop teasing me like that. Come, sweet doggie, come. *Come!* I said."

The overgrown puppy had bounded out of the courtyard gate when a tenant opened it to leave in the early morning.

Ella's words were mild and affectionate, but not the tone she was using. She'd lost her patience ten blocks ago, her temper five blocks after that. Now she was really scared. The puppy was heading for the bridge over the river. Suppose it ran over to the city? She'd never in a million years catch it there. Ella ran full tilt onto the bridge. She could see her quarry ahead, picking up speed.

All of a sudden the puppy vanished. Where could it be? Ella breathed as quietly as she could manage after all the running, listening for any sound.

There was a rustling in the bushes somewhere. She looked over at the thick greenery. Yes, some leaves were moving. She ran to the place, dropped to her knees, and crawled into the thicket. She could hear the puppy whimpering. It was quite close.

She parted some branches and gaped at the scene in front of her. The puppy was busily licking the sores that dotted the head of a cowering, terrified little girl. She was making the whimpering nose.

Ella grabbed the scruff of the dog's neck with both hands and pulled it back.

"The dog won't hurt you," she said to the child, "really, he's just a puppy.

"What's the matter? Are you hurt?" Ella didn't know what to do.

Enormous dark tear-filled eyes looked at her, quivering lips parted, and a tiny, shaky voice said, "Help me." In Greek.

"Of course I'll help you," Ella said in the same language. I'll have to tell Abba he was right, she was thinking. He said I'd need to know Greek someday.

"What's your name? Mine is Ella."

"Claudia." Sniff.

"Claudia, you'll feel a lot happier after you blow your nose and get some salve on your head. Come on. I'll take you inside to the doctor." Ella reached for her, but Claudia scrabbled backward, deeper into the thicket.

"No, please, no, don't let them get me. They'll take me back there and lock me up." She was shaking with fear, and the leaves rattled all around her.

Ella settled herself more comfortably, sitting cross-legged instead of kneeling. She was intrigued. "Who's after you, Claudia? Who's going to lock you up?"

"Vestal Virgins," Claudia whimpered. "They pulled my hair and shaved it all off with a knife, and it hurt, and I cried, and they locked me in a room with no dinner until I stopped crying, they said. They're mean, mean, mean."

Ella was fascinated now. "You mean all those sores on your head are from knife scrapes?"

"Yes. It hurts real bad."

"I bet it does. How'd you get away?"

"The lock wasn't tight and there was a cart full of bundles, so I hid, and it went a long way, and then it stopped, and a lot of people were talking and shouting, and I was afraid, and I crawled out, and there were some bushes, so I hid."

"Good for you. Did they really, truly shave all your hair off?"

"Really truly."

"You definitely don't want to go back to the Virgins, then. What about your home? Where are your mother and father?"

"They gave me to the Vestals. They said I should be happy, that it was a special honor. They'd make me go back."

"The only thing to do, then, is for you to come home with me. But if they're looking for a little girl with a shaved head, you won't be hard to spot. Let me think . . ."

It didn't take long. Ella managed to unknot her sash with one hand, then tie it around the puppy's neck and to a limb. "That'll make you sit," she said.

Beside the hospital on the island, Ella had seen a row of

drying clothes on a neatly clipped flowering hedge. She ran
to it and grabbed one of the hooded robes worn by the doctors. It was grotesquely too big for Claudia but the hood
covered her head. "Hold up the bottom part so you won't
trip on it," Ella commanded, "and come with me. Hurry."

It was an exceedingly strange procession that wended its
surreptitious way through alleys and along the shadowed
sides of the tenements to the tiny leather-working shop that
Joel owned. Ella sighed with relief when she saw that it
was Samuel behind the counter. "Pssst, it's me. Can I go
upstairs?"

"Yes. But—"

"Tell you later. Hold on to this dog for a few minutes."
She handed Samuel the sash-leash and darted into the dark
alley where Claudia waited. The chid's enormous frightened eyes looked even bigger in the shadow of the deep
hood.

Ella grabbed her arm and pulled her to the ladder that led
to Joel's apartment. "Climb," she said. "I'll be right behind
you, Claudia. I won't let you fall."

Samuel didn't approve, but Ella bullied him. He carried a
formless bundle—which was Claudia hidden in the folds of
a cloak—to Joseph's apartment, while Ella walked beside
him, with a tight hold on the dog's new leather-strip leash.

He also promised to return the doctor's robe in secret
after dark.

Claudia ate and ate and drank four cups of milk before
she fell asleep in Ella's bed. She looked small and vulnerable in her little underclothes; Ella hadn't had time to find
anything for her to wear. The sores on her head looked
worse than ever. Ella had put oil on them, until Joseph
came home. He would know where to buy salve of balm or
myrrh.

She was, in fact, glad that her father and Rufus were out.
They might scold her as much as Samuel had. But what

could she have done? The little girl was frightened and alone and hurt. So she'd helped her. She looked at the worn-out, sleeping child and hummed a Celtic lullaby while she spread a linen cover over the girl and tucked it in around her shoulders.

Ella had just finished washing Claudia's bowl and cup when the watchdog Jordy growled deep in his throat. The loud knock on the door brought a louder growl. Ella rested her hand on Jordy's back when she opened the door.

"Where's your mother or your father?" The man at the door wore the impressive red-crested brass helmet of the Praetorian Guard.

"Why?" asked Ella in honest curiosity.

"Someone has stolen a valuable, and we are searching every building in Rome. It is better if an adult shows the interior of the house."

"You can come back later, or I'll be able to show you. My dog won't let anybody hurt me."

"I wouldn't hurt you, little girl."

"I didn't expect you would. My father told me always to say that to strangers."

The guard smiled. "Good idea. Maybe I'll get a dog for my little girl."

"Get her a puppy. They're much more fun."

"Perhaps I will. I'll look around if you and your dog don't object. House-to-house is easier if there's no need to backtrack."

"Come in, then." Ella looked with interest at the guard's impressive uniform. Julius must feel plenty pleased with himself when he dressed up like that.

The guard looked methodically over the big room, behind and beneath every table and couch. He did the same in Joseph's sleeping room, Rufus' sleeping room, put his hand on the latch of the door where the dogs slept.

"Stop," Ella said. He turned, suspicious. She ran to the door. "I'll open it for you. There's a mother dog in there, and she's very snappish because her puppies will be coming soon." She grinned at the guard. "Maybe you can get one for your little girl." She opened the door, crooning to Jappy. "Don't fret, sweet Jappy. This is a nice man, he won't hurt you. He's looking for something somebody stole." She stooped beside the dog and scratched her head. The guard was lifting the blankets on which the dogs liked to sleep.

"What got stolen?" Ella asked him.

"A little girl," he said. "She belongs to the Temple of Vesta."

Ella froze. Jappy whined at the fear she sensed in the fingers' sudden stiffening on her head. Ella caught her breath, resumed scratching.

"That'll do for this room," the guard said. "Do you want to close the door behind me?"

"Yes. Thank you," Ella replied. She saw him out. Her mind was racing.

The guard opened the door to her room. "Please be quiet as you can," Ella said. Her voice was steady, even though it was pitched rather higher than before. "My little sister is having a nap. She sleeps a lot. She has leprosy."

The guard was halfway to the bed, beginning to bend over. He straightened at once, backing away. Claudia slept peacefully, her bald, sore-covered head shining in the dim light.

In only seconds the guard was outside the door to the apartment. He had kept far from Ella and her dog.

Joel knew about Claudia. Samuel had told him. "Ella, you have no idea what you've done," he said gravely. "The Vigilum and the Praetorian Guard are searching every inch of the city."

"I know," Ella nodded. She told him what had happened earlier that day.

Joel was still laughing when Joseph and Rufus came in. It was, however, no laughing matter, he told them after they'd been told about Claudia.

"Vesta is the only goddess that still has any meaning to the Romans," Joel said. "What Ella has unwittingly done is as serious to them as the theft of the Ark of the Covenant to us Jews. You, Joseph, Ella, and probably everyone connected with you as a Nazarene will be tortured, then executed if the truth about this child is discovered.

"You cannot wait to leave Rome as you planned, Joseph. Send word to the others tonight that you'll be leaving at daybreak tomorrow.

"And be cautious on the road. Everyone leaving the city will be closely watched."

CHAPTER SEVENTY-FIVE

JOSEPH WAS AT HIS BEST WHEN RAPID THOUGHT AND ACTION were needed. He sent Samuel to get Jason. "Tell him to bring his travel things. He'll sleep here. So will you, Samuel. After you talk to Jason, get your things, too. I will go for Saul and Martha. It will reassure them. Joel, I'll be leaving you in charge a little sooner than we planned."

"Fine."

Samuel blurted the details of his other duty. "I'll bring my travel things after I return the hospital's washing. Will that be all right?"

"No, it will not," Joseph said briskly. "You will not go near the hospital. Joel?"

"I'll dispose of it right away. I will also bring food for tonight's houseful."

The eight voyagers left the apartment an hour before dawn. All of them knew what they were to say, in the unlikely event that they were stopped and questioned.

Jason was a Greek scholar traveling with his daughter, who was slowly recovering from a bad fall down the stairs some weeks earlier, hence her linen-bandaged head and broad-brimmed straw hat. Light still hurt her eyes, due to the head injury. Claudia would say nothing. Joseph and his daughter, both well-known figures, were traveling with their German bodyguard and three guard dogs for reasons connected to his trading business.

Saul and Martha and their son Samuel were going on vacation.

Joseph had already arranged the hire of one of the river barges to the port of Ostia. The river traffic was less likely to be of interest to the authorities. Rome was famous for roads, not water.

At the dock he eyed the large pile of baggage being loaded onto the barge. When time allowed, he'd have to do something about it. There was too much; Martha and Saul had been unwilling to leave behind any of the possessions they'd managed to amass during the twenty-two years they'd been together.

At Ostia, as Joseph had expected, there were a number of ramshackle small coastal traders, looking for cargo to any Italian port.

The group and their belongings became the cargo to Livorno, a hundred miles to the north.

When they were halfway there, Joseph changed the destination to Marseilles, the major seaport in Gaul. It was highly unlikely that the search for the missing Vestal would reach that far. And even if it did, by the time the communication arrived in Marseilles, the group would have long since departed.

Southern Gaul had been conquered by Julius Caesar nearly a hundred years earlier. Since that time, colonization of the rich lands had been constant. Big cities boasted baths, forums, temples, theaters, racing stadiums, athletic and gladiatorial arenas. The verdant countryside was dotted with villas owned by retired generals, senators, businessmen. Aqueducts led from mountains to supply water for the cities' fountains and baths. Rome's famous roads connected cities and towns. The entire region was thoroughly civilized.

Except that there was no synagogue.

Joseph was thunderstruck. How could he tell people about the Son of God when they did not know God?

"In many ways it will be easier," Jason told him. "As a Greek, I had no strong beliefs that were in conflict with the divinity of Jesus. Your synagogues were expecting a Messiah of a very different kind."

"And God? What did you learn of God from the sayings of Jesus?"

"That He loves mankind. Not that He would force Martha and Saul to part because they are childless."

Joseph experienced, for a fleeting moment, the all-consuming happiness of God's love, that mystical ecstacy combined with calm certitude that Ella talked about when she told of her healing.

"I will bring the good news to these people," Joseph said. "It will be pleasing to Father and to Son."

They were in the beautiful city that would later be known as Nîmes. Joseph had led the group from Marseilles to the nearby larger city of Arles. But it was the capital of the Roman provincial government, and he didn't allow any ideas of stopping there. Roman government authorities might have heard of the missing Vestal. Nîmes was an additional long day's journey, and everyone was weary of travel, but he insisted.

Now, he decided, they would stop. He found a simple villa on the edge of the city that had room enough for all of them, and a garden. "Of Eden," Martha breathed, after a lifetime of tenement living.

For her, life was happier than she had ever dared dream. She lost her timidity, took on the role of mother of the house, with Ella, now ten, and Claudia, nearly eight, as her children. The children she had so longed for.

Joseph hired freedwomen as cook and housekeeper. "The foods that grow and are eaten in this part of the world will be unknown to all of us, but not to local women," he said diplomatically. In truth, he wanted a better table than Martha knew how to prepare. When he accounted for the housekeeper, he was not being tactful; his words were simple, direct truth. "My Ella knows almost nothing about being a woman, she's been among men for too long. Your time and energies will be more important used for her education than for housecleaning."

It didn't take long for the household to find a rhythm and a routine. Ella, Claudia, and Samuel had morning lessons with Jason. The girls were taught weaving and sewing in the afternoon by Martha.

When she could catch them. Ella had introduced Claudia to the pleasures of running, tumbling, and tree climbing. Claudia taught Ella the little-girl games she had never heard of. Leaves and flowers created pretend banquets attended by pretend children represented by the well-behaved dogs, or simply imagination.

Ella had never had a girl to play with, to be friends with. Her cousins at Arimathea had been kind, but with close-knit ties to each other, they had little room for her in their lives. Even though Claudia was nearly three years younger, she knew more about being a girl than Ella. The two struck a good, shifting, balance of leadership. They quarreled just often enough to make reconciliation cause for celebration.

The men, too, found their lives full. Saul found work in a tannery; he was not happy when he wasn't working. Jason used the afternoons to copy, in beautiful, careful letters, the sayings of Jesus that were roughly inscribed on Joseph's precious tattered scroll. Samuel tended the garden with a passion that only another city dweller could comprehend.

Only Joseph found satisfying effort elusive. There was an open square in the center of Nîmes where ceaseless activity swirled in front of a magnificent marble temple that Augustus had ordered built to honor his two beloved grandsons, dead so tragically young.

Joseph stood on the temple's tall, wide stairs every day,

with Rufus in attendance and on guard. From that rostrum
he spoke to the people below, telling them about the resurrection, the promise of eternal life, the love of God.

Rarely, a scattered few would stop to listen. Never did
any stay for long.

Nonetheless, Joseph ended every oration with an invitation to come to him with questions or to join the Nazarenes
for their Sabbath "Agape."

He became more and more discouraged. Rufus' glowing
faith kept him going.

Jason, surprisingly, brought the first convert to Joseph.
Jason had been talking to the artisan who produced vellum
for manuscripts. Another writer, a young Roman
landowner, asked Jason what kind of work he was doing.
"Exciting," he said after hearing Jason's remarks. "I'd like
to know more about it."

As easily as that, the dam was broken. The young Roman
returned, with his mother, who then asked if she could
bring two of her friends.

One of those women said, with an elegant sniff of skepticism, that she personally considered miracles beyond reason.

"That is the nature of miracles, Lady. They are outside
everything we know. I will ask my daughter to tell you
what happened to her. She is not difficult to believe."

Ella's knees and elbows and face and hands were dirty
from playing outside. A leaf was caught in her untidy
plaits.

"You want me to tell you about Jesus? I'm happy to. Because he makes me happy all the time. I was a lot younger
when he made my legs well. It was four whole years ago.

"I didn't know who Jesus was. It was much later that I
learned about God the Father. Jesus was just a man, but a
special man. Because all around him—you couldn't see it,
you felt it—the whole world was a wonderful, happy place
to be. Even if your legs didn't work. That didn't matter.
What mattered was that everything was just right. He didn't

say anything to me, he didn't have to tell me anything. I knew about it, because I could feel it. He loved me. Just the way I was.

"He still does. I know that. Whenever I start to worry or get cross or even awful tired, all I have to do is remember to stay quiet for a minute and let myself feel Jesus loving me. I don't have to see him. I know it's him, because I felt it before when he was with me. And he makes everything just right."

The woman who'd doubted miracles looked at the grimy, plain-spoken child; tears filled her eyes. "Can anybody else be happy like that?"

"Of course," Ella said. "It's easy. Just be quiet for a minute and let yourself feel it. It's all around, all the time."

"May I touch you, little girl?"

Ella giggled. "You'll have to wash your hands if you do. I'm dirty all over. We've been making cakes out of mud." She held out her grubby hand. "Would you like to see them? I'll take you to the puddle we made for the bakeshop."

The woman clasped Ella's hand. "Thank you," she whispered.

"Joseph," said Jason quietly. "Ella is how you'll get people to listen to you. You're going to have to put her to work for Jesus."

"For Jesus? Of course, Abba, you know, I'll be glad to do anything I can for him."

The next day Ella went to the temple steps with her father. She took her harp along. As she played and sang a song Samuel had taught her, many people stopped hurrying about their business and stopped to listen. Her voice was clear, and sweet and plain.

"The Lord is my shepherd
I shall not want.
He maketh me to lie down in green pastures.

He leadeth me beside the still waters.
He restoreth my soul.
He leadeth me in the paths of righteousness
For His name's sake.
Yea, though I walk through the valley of the shadow of
death,
I shall fear no evil.
For Thou art with me.
Thy rod and Thy staff they comfort me.
Thou preparest a table before me
In the presence of mine enemies.
Thou anointest my head with oil.
My cup runneth over.
Surely goodness and mercy shall follow me
All the days of my life
And I shall dwell in the house of the Lord forever.

"That's a song about how it makes you feel when you stand still and quiet for a minute and let yourself feel Jesus and his Father loving you.

"I'll tell you about Jesus and how he made my legs well so I could walk and run . . ."

When spring came, Saul and Martha were upset because there was no way they could celebrate Passover in a synagogue.

"We will celebrate here the day after Passover, the day that Jesus rose from the dead. God set the Jews free of Pharaoh's bondage, and we celebrated Passover to commemorate it. But how much greater is His love that He set all mankind free of the bondage of sin and of death through His Son Jesus. That will be our new commemoration."

The garden and the main room in the villa were filled with long tables for the special Agape celebration. After prayers and song, the communicants broke bread and drank wine, as usual. Then they shared a feast of roast lamb and fresh spring vegetables. There were no bitter herbs.

More than a hundred Nazarenes shared feast and fellowship.

A week after, at the weekly Agape gathering, Joseph told the gathering that he would soon be moving to another city.

"You can select from among yourselves the ones who will perform baptisms and lead prayers. This house will be your home. Fill it with love, and the message of God's love.

"I will be carrying the message to others."

During the next five years, Joseph and his original seven companions went to five cities, each a day's walk westward from the previous one. The events in Nîmes were repeated, with variations that circumstances created by themselves. In Toulouse, the Nazarenes were more numerous, and more than half were slaves, or former slaves. The next place was smaller, but the fellowship numbers were larger. The fifth year was spent in Bordeaux, the great city of the province of Aquitania. Only sixty miles from the sea, the great sea, the Atlantic Ocean.

Joseph began to dream the same dream again and again. It was of Sarah, at the cliff where she sang the song that was theirs alone, then, in that magic time.

He woke from the dream filled with joy because Sarah was with him again. Then he realized that he was awake, in a world without Sarah, and his grief was agonizing.

He called Ella to him. "My dearest, sweet daughter, I believe that I am being called to carry the message to a community of Jews. To speak again in a synagogue.

"It is in the land of the men with blue skin. Do you remember the stories I used to tell you about them?"

"Oh, Abba, yes! I remember and I would love to go there. Can we, really, truly?"

Joseph hugged Sarah's baby who was no longer a baby. "It will be a difficult journey, but really truly I believe we can go."

CHAPTER SEVENTY-SIX

ELLA WAS SIXTEEN YEARS OLD NOW. "ALL GROWN UP,"
Joseph had said on her birthday when he gave her the jewelry her mother had once worn. Ella loved the gift, particularly the necklace of blue flowers, but she didn't like being
sixteen; it was too confusing. Her body was different,
strange to her. Not because of the monthly bleeding. That
was messy and inconvenient, but Martha had told her about
it before it ever started, so she wasn't scared when the
blood showed up the first time.

She didn't get stomachaches from it, either. Not like
Claudia. She'd started six months ago, and she carried on
as if she had eaten poison every time her bleeding started.

No, for Ella the unpleasantness about her body was the
way it had changed its shape. Taller. That was good. But
breasts—they ruined everything. Most of the things she
liked best couldn't be done anymore, not the way she'd always done them. When she ran, she felt unbalanced.
Climbing a tree, she bumped into branches that her body
never would have hit before the breasts grew. It hurt, too.

Martha told her to stop climbing trees. And other things.
"You're a young woman now, no longer a child. You have
to be less boisterous, less boyish. You have to change."

"I *hate* change!" Ella replied. Then she burst into tears. Why had she done that? She didn't know; she'd been completely surprised when it happened.

Change. Everything had changed, was changing. Samuel was gone. He had stayed in last year's city, to lead the Nazarenes there. And now, when they left Bordeaux, Jason couldn't be with them either. He'd "fallen in love," he said, with one of the new followers, a Greek slave, bought her freedom, and was going to marry her. He would stay and lead the fellowship in Bordeaux.

"In love." What did that mean? When Ella asked Jason, all he said was "You'll find out for yourself one day." When? How would she know when it happened?

Claudia just giggled when Ella complained to her about Jason's enigmatic remark.

Claudia! She had changed most of all. It had been so perfect, having another girl to be friends with. Before Claudia changed so much. She didn't want to be with Ella now, not nearly as much as she wanted to be with the new followers who'd come with them from Toulouse. Romans. Men. Gaius and Lucius. They were old, as old as Jason, thirty-four and thirty-six. Why in the world did Claudia hang around them and talk such nonsense about how wonderful it was to be Roman? She was like a different person when she did it, too. All big eyes and smiley and talking in a sweety-sweet voice that made Ella want to hit her.

At least Gaius and Lucius didn't pay much attention to Claudia. Ella got a disagreeable satisfaction from their lack of interest. She didn't like feeling that way, either. It was a new, a different emotion for her. More change. She hated it.

Lucius and Gaius were "on fire with the words of Jesus." That's what Jason said about them. They wanted to grab people on the street, practically, to tell them about the resurrection. Ella didn't understand it. When people wanted to hear about Jesus, it was always wonderful to see them become happy after they learned about him. Shouting at strangers didn't make them happy at all, as far as she could tell. Before Lucius and Gaius came along, everything had been nicer. Now it was different. Changed.

Ella didn't like anything about it. She used to be happy all the time. Now she had to remind herself, to realize that she was feeling restless, or upset, or irritated. She had to notice, to pay attention, before she could stop herself and tell Jesus she was miserable and make herself quiet for him to make her happy again. She was changing, too, and she hated that most of all. This was called "growing up," Martha said. Ella didn't like growing up.

The little band of travelers led by Joseph started out the week after the Agape celebration of Jesus' resurrection. They were not heavily burdened; years before, Saul and Martha had given their worldly goods to the poor. The accumulation that had meant so much to them in Rome had lost its value when they came to know the greater worth of the mission and fellowship of Jesus' followers.

The lengthening days of spring were fresh, and more beautiful with each one that passed. The glory of God's creation was all around them, and their hearts were light, as they headed north.

The seacoast was not Romanized. There were roads, but they were narrow and winding, as they had been for centuries. Roads built by the Empire's legions were straight. Rome recognized no obstacles. The wildness of the route was exciting. They were, obviously, going into the unknown.

And going slowly. Joseph set the pace, he was their leader, striding in front, testing the firmness of the footing with his staff. He looked just as the leader of a band of pilgrims should look. His hair and beard were white; they streamed and tossed in the winds from the sea. He was seventy years old. The dogs ran ahead of him, or dashed into the woods after small animals to satisfy their appetites for sport or for food.

The others followed, sometimes singing, generally in

pairs. Saul and Martha, now in their fifties, were nearest Joseph, followed by Ella and Claudia. The two Romans, Gaius and Lucius, brought up the rear, carrying the packs that held the group's baggage. Rufus was last, and most heavily loaded.

When they saw a village or a homestead, they visited it. Rufus kept the dogs at his side, and they approached slowly, so that the inhabitants would not be alarmed.

If they were welcomed, they stayed for a day or even longer, if the people were interested in the message they carried.

In every case, Joseph showed the inhabitants a piece of gold, indicating that he intended to pay for any hospitality offered. His treasure was hugely diminished, but there were still many coins in his money belt. Most of the time his money was refused. In this little-traveled part of the world, strangers were an exciting, welcome novelty. Only once did the glint of gold provoke an attack. Rufus loosed the dogs, and the assailants ran away. The others in the village were greatly entertained by the spectacle; once Rufus had whistled and the dogs returned to his control, they could laugh at the humiliation of the aggressors.

Spring became summer and then autumn. The forests were golden in the slanting sun.

"We will begin now to look for a village large enough to shelter us for the winter," Joseph said. Some days later they saw ahead a broad, fast-moving expanse of water, a river emptying its currents into the sea. "Exactly what we want," said Joseph. He led them in a prayer of thanksgiving, and then they turned their backs on the sea, to follow the river. Trade followed rivers, too. Joseph knew that a real town or city would be near the river's outlet. They came to it after only a day and a half.

The mark of Rome was on the ancient settlement. Rufus exploded with a barrage of Celtic expletives, words none of the others recognized. The huge redhead had been glowingly happy in the tiny settlements near the sea, at home again with Celts whose isolation had kept Roman influence away. After months among his own people, seeing the Roman temple that dominated the town was a maddening reminder of his long-ago defeat in battle and subsequent enslavement. But Joseph was their leader, and Jesus his teacher. Rufus tamed his rage and followed the others into the small city's narrow, crooked streets.

The noisy marketplace near the river was easy to locate; Rufus' glowering ended as soon as they entered its rowdiness. The voices were bargaining, shouting, talking in a Celtic tongue.

Joseph beckoned Rufus to his side. He needed help with the language for talking about finding a house, where, at what cost. After long conversations with many people, Rufus asked Joseph a simple question, in Latin. "How much are you willing to be robbed?"

Joseph chuckled. "Only as much as I have left. If the house is what we want."

It was not ideal, Rufus told him, but it sounded like the closest thing to what he knew Joseph liked. It was the never-used villa and vineyard of the Roman administrator of the region. The Roman's slaves worked in the vineyard, and a local wine merchant sent the absentee owner the income from his estate. It was just outside the city, near the Roman military encampment.

Joseph could buy the house, but not the vineyard. The merchant would sell it to him, and the owner would never know.

"Does the merchant have the right to do that?"

"No, but he has the power. It works out the same."

"Then we'll have a look at it."

Before day's end Joseph was the owner—more or less— of a startlingly out-of-place Italian villa in a Celtic community beside the heavily trafficked Loire River. The house was designed and furnished exactly like a nobleman's home on one of Rome's seven hills. It made Joseph laugh.

"We've walked many miles to end up where we started," he said.

"Walked, and sailed, too, Abba. It's more like Jericho than Rome." Ella felt a pang of longing for the simple days when she was a little girl climbing the fig tree in the garden of the Jericho house.

As soon as the small group of Nazarenes was settled into the house, Joseph proceeded, as usual, to establish his bona fides and cooperative relationships with the local authorities.

The military commander was both the most powerful and the easiest to manage. Joseph carried his scroll of citizenship when he presented himself, and it had the predictable, desired effect.

The seal and signature of Caesar Augustus! There was nothing more impressive in the entire Empire. Augustus was the unifying symbol and deity throughout the Roman world. The temple in this Celtic city was dedicated to him, as were temples in every Roman-controlled city throughout all the provinces and territories. Except Jerusalem, Joseph thought, with concealed pride. He also concealed his disdain for a people—no matter how powerful—that made a man into a god by a vote in the Senate. Joseph still cherished enormous admiration and respect for Augustus, but he had never for a moment considered the asthma-plagued, overweight Emperor as more than a man.

The camp was typical of Roman military establishments throughout the Empire. It had a tall wooden palisade surrounding it, and a deep ditch surrounding that. Entrance was through a guarded gate after crossing the ditch on a wooden bridge.

Inside, there was a geometrically exact grid of streets that separated precisely located tents into blocks of eight. An especially large tent had a block of space all to itself. It was the camp's headquarters and living quarters for the commanding officer.

Who looked at Joseph with awe after seeing Augustus'
seal. This commander was a young tribune named Severus;
his command was only a vexillation—part of a legion—of
four cohorts, just under two thousand men. They were
hardened veterans, unlike Severus, but they were only auxiliary troops, not real Romans. Severus felt slighted by the
general because his assignment was so undistinguished.

Also he suffered from a constant feeling of isolation. He
knew nothing about the Celts, including their language;
even worse, his troops came originally from Dalmatia, and
their language was equally foreign to him. It was a brilliant
concept—originally devised by Augustus when he first became Emperor—to augment the limited numbers of Roman
legions by recruiting from the population of captive lands.
These auxiliary legions were always used in areas of the
Empire far from their own homelands so that necessary
brutality in battle would not be vitiated by ties of kinship or
sentiment.

Severus—young and lonely and far from home—practically welcomed Joseph with an embrace. "Anything I can
do to make your domicile here more agreeable, I'll be
happy to do, Joseph of Arimathea. Anything. You have
only to ask."

Joseph took pity on the youthful Roman. "I will expect
you to dine with me and my company, Severus, as soon as
the household is organized."

"Gladly!" Severus looked as if he'd like to follow Joseph
that very minute, like a homeless stray.

The local man to cultivate was a Celt called Brigantius,
grandson of the chief of the tribe that had been conquered
by Julius Caesar's legions. Brigantius, unlike the population he governed, was thoroughly Romanized. He had been
sent to Rome as a boy, educated there, then returned to his
hereditary lands to make them "civilized." He was a thoroughly lazy and self-satisfied corpulent creature with perfumed hair and manicured soft hands that had never done a

day's work. Ostentatiously devoted to the worship of the Divine Augustus, Brigantius reacted to Joseph's proof of Augustus' regard with the same excessive respect and admiration that Severus had shown.

"We need not worry about him," Joseph told Rufus, "but he would do well to worry about those he governs, I expect. They must despise him."

"To a man—and woman, and child," Rufus reported to Joseph after he'd had time to make acquaintances in the city. "Befriend the tribune, and no one will care. They ignore him. But if you accept the friendship of Brigantius, you become their enemy."

They began the way they always did: Ella sang to attract the attention of the people in the marketplace, and then she told about her healing by Jesus. She sang Celtic songs here, not the psalms of David, and she told her story in the simple vocabulary that was all she could manage in Celtic. What she knew was oddly miscellaneous: the songs she'd learned when she was hardly more than a baby, plus some phrases and words from Rufus over the years, and finally the rudimentary conversation she had picked up at the villages and farmhouses they had visited during the months of walking the paths beside the sea.

It may have been that primitive, oddly accented, speech by a stranger was particularly intriguing. Or it may have been the oddity of a shapely young woman who spoke like a child and gave the unmistakable message that she was as untouched by life as a child. Whatever the reason, Ella's daily appearance on the steps of the temple quickly became an event that dozens of people always gathered to see and hear.

Many of them listened to Joseph, when he spoke after Ella finished. And some of them accepted his offer to answer their questions and tell them more about the Son of God in meetings at his house.

It seemed that the mission was finding success much faster than it ever had before.

Except that not one of those who came ever asked to become part of the fellowship of Nazarenes. Even after several of Joseph's meetings.

Gaius and Lucius, the fervent Roman men, were greatly angered. "Pearls before swine!" they proclaimed after every meeting.

Joseph managed to calm them. "Not every man is able to accept the gift of faith without a struggle. I myself . . ." He told them about his own intransigence even after the miracle that cured his daughter and after seeing the empty tomb with his own eyes. "It took the testimony of Jesus' close disciple Thomas about his own doubts to give me the vision to see how blind I had been." If Jesus had needed to be patient and understanding with his closest followers, surely their own group of Nazarenes could do no less with a people who were hearing Jesus' words for the first time.

Lucius and Gaius had to accept the counsel of their leader, but they did not find it palatable. They redoubled their urgent, loud preaching on street corners in the city.

Ella had no difficulty about the need for patience with the public. Her difficulty lay in finding patience to tolerate what she called Claudia's "silliness." Claudia called it "love."

It had been almost inevitable that the lonely young tribune Severus would be totally smitten by Claudia's big dark eyes, long curling dark hair, and feminine coquettishness. He'd been invited for dinner, as Joseph had promised, soon after Brea, a Celtic widow, came to work as cook-housekeeper at the villa, and Martha was satisfied that they could entertain guests adequately. The excellent food was wasted on Severus. He couldn't take his eyes off Claudia long enough to eat.

Since then Severus had found excuses to visit the villa three or four times a week.

"Do you think he likes me, Ella? . . . Really, really, really likes me? . . . Isn't he the handsomest man you ever saw in your whole life? . . . Should I wear my hair loose, or tied up with a ribbon? . . . Do you think he might come by today? . . . When is your abba going to invite him for dinner again? . . . Did you notice how broad his shoulders are? . . . Wouldn't you just love to feel his hair curl around your fingers if you touched it? . . ." Claudia was interested in only one thing—Severus—and she talked about him incessantly.

Ella had to bear it as best she could. Whenever she was in the house instead of the marketplace, Claudia followed her around, chattering, chattering, chattering.

Unless Severus was paying a visit. Ostensibly to Joseph. Then Claudia primped and preened and brushed her hair until it looked its shiniest and somehow—accidentally—walked into the room or onto the sun-warmed garden terrace or wherever Severus and Joseph might be.

"Oh, what a surprise," she would squeal. "Hello, Tribune, how good it is to see you."

"It turns my stomach!" Ella told Martha.

The motherly Martha was indulgently romantic. "Claudia is fourteen now, Ella. Many girls marry at that age."

And I'm nearly three years older, Ella thought. She found a corner of the garden where no one would see her, and then she allowed herself to cry, even though she didn't know why.

The cold wind that warned of winter's approach finally drove her into the house. It also accounted for her red nose and eyes. She was grateful for that.

Gaius and Lucius' aggressive preaching produced the first serious seeker after the meaning of Jesus' words.

"'Ask, and it will be given you; search, and you will find.' That's what these followers say that Jesus fellow said. What does that mean, anyhow? Ask for what? Search for what? Makes no sense that I can see."

The questioner was a newly retired legionnaire called Tastros.

"Is there something you can put a name to that you want from life?" Joseph asked him.

"A good reason to keep on living it," Tastros replied sharply. "I've done my twenty years in the legion with naught to show for it but the scars of battle, and now I'm thrown out, before I reach forty years of age, with my Roman citizenship and a patch of farmland as reward for my services." He spat on the floor and jerked his unaccustomed civilian tunic back onto his shoulder. "I got no use for the Romans, never did, and now that the cash bonus I was always promised turns out to be farmland instead, I hold them lower than ever. So what good is Roman citizenship to me, I ask you? Can I sell it for money to buy food? No, I cannot. Same with this farmland. I've been a soldier all my life; I don't even know where this place is that I'm now a landowner. Some no place desert or mountain most likely.

"So there's my question, old man. How am I going to support life and why should I take the trouble?"

Joseph clasped Tastros' shoulders with his two hands. "Those are exactly the questions that the message I bring you will answer. Come. Live here with us, share our lives, and in time you will, I am sure, share our belief and joy in the truth of the Son of God."

Tastros was suspicious. No one in his life had ever offered him anything without a cost attached. Yet, Joseph's unfeigned faith was so appealing that the old soldier agreed to "stick around and see if I can catch whatever sick craziness you've got."

The House of Nazarenes had its first new tenant. Would he become one of them?

CHAPTER SEVENTY-SEVEN

SAUL, WHO WAS ALWAYS THE MOST QUIET OF ALL THE Nazarenes, was the one who talked to Tastros about the message of faith and brought him into the quiet joy of fellowship. Everyone was surprised, except Martha. "Goodness shines from my husband if only you take the time to notice it," she exclaimed. "I've always known it and seen it and loved him because of what he really is."

Saul had found work at a tannery, as he did every time they stopped in one place for any length of time. He was happy to tell Tastros about his work, to show him how to do it, to describe the satisfaction he found in it. "You have an animal's skin. Rough, smelly, covered with fur or the sharp cut hairs left after shearing. You take this roughness, and you wash it clean. You cover the smell with a stink ten times worse. And then you wash it clean of that. Many times. Afterwards, you work with it, finding its strengths and weaknesses, using the strong, strengthening the weak. You smooth it, you bend it, you scrape it, you oil it, you grease it, you handle it, feeling it change under your touch. That's when you begin to love it, because you are creating from roughness a thing that is smooth and strong and beautiful and lasting.

"That is how to tan a skin. I have learned that the same is true of a man's heart and his soul. It needs long testing, long handling; it must know stink before it can reach strength and durability and beauty. It has to feel the master workman's touch and his love. That's what Jesus and his Father translate into for me, Tastros. I am the smelly hide. They are the masters. The Holy Spirit is that deep gleam that a supple, cured skin holds inside itself.

"Do you want me to teach you how to tan skins? And how to give your heart and soul into the hands of the masters for curing?"

Tastros worked with full effort at both apprenticeships.

During one of these lessons, he also told Saul the answer to the question that had been plaguing Joseph. Tastros mentioned it casually, not knowing how much it mattered. "You'll never get any of these townspeople around here to go along with your God and Jesus. The Druids won't let them."

Saul asked Tastros to talk to Joseph. Saul had never heard of Druids.

But Joseph had. In Belerion he'd had Druid interpreters, Druid teachers, even a friend who was a Druid Bard. He'd never found them to be hostile.

Because there wasn't any Roman troop there, Tastros said. Didn't Joseph know? The Roman Army, every soldier in it, had the Emperor's order to exterminate all the Druids because they practiced human sacrifice. Although, Tastros added, he didn't see what you could call battle except human sacrifice, and the Roman Army was proud of its record of killings in battle.

Joseph still didn't understand. If the Roman Army had exterminated the Druids, those fine scholars, as Joseph thought of them, then how could Tastros say that Druids were telling the Celts in this town what to do?

Oh, they weren't really wiped out, not by any measure. They'd been driven out of all the Romanized parts of Gaul, and some of Germanica. But there were still pockets of them in remote areas, like the territory just to the north. It was common knowledge in the camp—though not among the officers—that the Celts went to the Druids for doctoring and for judging arguments between them.

Joseph was intrigued. Would someone take him to talk to the Druids?

Not in a hundred years. The Celts would all say that there were no Druids in all Gaul. To protect them from the Romans.

Joseph thanked Tastros and let him go. There were many things for him to think about, to pull up from his memories of long ago.

Ella felt as if something or someone had kicked her in the chest when she walked into the room and saw Claudia and Severus kissing. They were so close, his arms so tight around her, it was as if they had made one out of two. What must that be like? What did it feel like to have a man's lips on your own? Unconsciously her fingers moved across her mouth. She turned and fled.

At the next meeting Joseph held with inquisitive people who'd been drawn to Ella's story of Jesus, he talked to them in a very different way. Instead of beginning with the story of Jesus' life and death and resurrection, he began with the ancient words from the Torah.

"God said, 'Let there be light,' and there was light. We all know the power of the light, the sun, that warms the earth and makes it give forth food for man and beast. Some people give the light a name. They call it Mabon. Others call it Sul. So also with many of the other things that were created by God. People give names to His wonders. Sirona for His stars, Taranos for the mighty sounds made by the storms God sends.

"All these things, with all the names that men have given them, are among the works of God. God has only one name, and that is 'God.' His wonders are too numerous to count. Of all his wonders, one is the most glorious. That is His Son. He, also, has only one name, and that is 'Jesus.' He is the one I tell you about."

Joseph's listeners were completely attentive now. By incorporating their Celtic gods and goddesses into his talk, he had become part of their world.

Later that evening when Joseph prayed, he thanked God with all his heart for the combination of events that had sent him to Belerion, where he had learned about some of the names pagans used for the gods they saw in the world of nature that enclosed them.

Within a month, there were a half dozen new Nazarenes. Every week that followed brought more people to hear about Jesus.

On her seventeenth birthday in January, Ella carried out a plan she had made. She went to the kitchen, where Brea was preparing dinner. As usual, Brea's son Harlyn was helping by bringing wood for the fire and water from the well.

Harlyn was about fifteen or sixteen. Ella neither knew nor cared about the exact number.

"Brea," she said, "I want Harlyn to help me with something. Can he leave for a little while?"

"Go along with Ella, boy," said his mother.

Ella led Harlyn to her room, closed the door. "I want you to kiss me, Harlyn. Put your arms around my waist, I'll show you how."

The boy backed away. His face was drained of color. "Aaaah," he cried while his hands frantically pulled on the door latch. When he got the door open, he ran as if the dogs had been loosed on him.

Ella crumpled onto her bed. Her fists beat against its cushions as she wept. What was it about her that was so repulsive?

*　　*　　*

Severus and Claudia married in February. According to Roman custom, they merely held hands and said "I wed thee" to each other.

Also according to Roman custom, Claudia had a dowry, which would be hers to live on if ever she and Severus divorced, as easily as they had married. Claudia's dowry was impressively large, and in gold. Joseph provided it, even though it nearly exhausted his treasure.

The loss of the gold didn't bother him. Soon he would be going to Belerion, in response to his dreams about Sarah. They still came to him in the night, filling his heart.

In Belerion, Joseph knew, he'd have no need for money. The Jewish community that he had established there must certainly have grown large by now. And Jews always took care of their own.

"Rufus, can I talk to you?"

"Of course, Ella. What do you want?"

"I want you to promise me two things. First, you'll keep this talk a secret for as long as you live. Second, you'll tell me the bone-bare truth if I ask you a question."

Ella's manner was extremely serious. Rufus gave her his promise with equal gravity.

Ella firmed her shoulders. Her hands were clenched. "What is the matter with me, Rufus? I have to know."

The big Celtic man was genuinely puzzled. "I don't know what you mean, Ella. You aren't sick, are you?"

"No! I never get sick, you know that. I'm talking about the way I look, maybe, I don't know. If I did, I wouldn't be asking you. Am I horribly ugly? Do I have an awful smell? What's wrong with me, Rufus? Why hasn't anybody ever kissed me? Or looked at me like I was somebody he'd like to hug and kiss?"

"Oh, Ella, I never thought you would concern yourself about such things. I can't believe you'd care. You've been touched by Jesus' miracle. You're holy. You're too special for anyone to ever consider profaning you that way."

Ella was thunderstruck. She couldn't speak. She nodded her thanks to Rufus and went to her room.

What he'd said had a dreadful logic to it. Why had she never realized that a miracle would, naturally, have to be paid for in some way?

She knelt in the corner, silent. It was a long time before Jesus filled the silence with love and contentment. Such a long time that Ella nearly began to fear that the wonderful sensation that she'd always found so easily might not come this time. That she might be punished for wanting to have been given a miracle for free.

When the happiness swept through her, Ella thanked Jesus and his Father. I'll try hard never to be ungrateful again.

CHAPTER SEVENTY-EIGHT

RUFUS WAS RELUCTANT TO LEAVE THE CITY ON THE LOIRE. Joseph saw it, and pretended not to. He knew that Rufus had found female companionship in every place that they had stayed, but he had never offered any information about his carnal adventures and Joseph hadn't asked for any. He was an old man now, over seventy, but he could remember the needs of the young, and Rufus was still in his twenties.

This was the first time Rufus had shown any signs of real involvement. Subtle, hardly apparent signs; nevertheless, Joseph loved the young Celt like a son, and he was sensitive to Rufus' moods.

It was a bizarre corollary that Joseph was so unaware of Ella's. He knew nothing about the girl's struggles with the same impulses that he recognized and accepted as normal in Rufus. He saw Ella's habitual happy nature and believed that she had not changed at all.

"We will have our big Agape feast in celebration of the resurrection, and then we will go north again," Joseph told the household. "Gaius and Lucius have agreed to stay and continue our mission here. Does anyone else wish to stay?" He was careful not to look at Rufus.

To his surprise, Saul spoke up. "You must help Martha

and me with a question that is disturbing us, Joseph. You have said that we will go, probably next year, to Belerion. We want to stay with you, to continue our mission for God and His Son. But we worry that the Jews there will make us outcast, as was done in Rome."

"I have given much thought to that," Joseph told Saul and Martha. It was true. He had speculated, and prayed many times for guidance. "It is my belief that there will be no such difficulties, particularly when they hear the good news we bring them. That is, as I say, my belief. I cannot be certain. It may be that we will have a fellowship separate from the synagogue and our brother Jews. I'm sorry I cannot answer your question more definitely."

Saul looked at his wife.

"We will go," Martha said decisively.

"I'll go, too, if you'll have me," Tastros said. "Saul and I can start our own tannery."

Now Joseph could look at Rufus. "Go," he said.

And so spring found them in procession again: Joseph leading, Martha and Ella behind him, Tastros and Saul following the women, and Rufus bringing up the rear, with the dogs.

The riverbank led them to the seacoast in two days. Joseph thrust his staff into the ground and held it for stability when he tilted his head up and back to feel and smell the strong wind from the sea. He opened his mouth to taste the sharp saltiness, closed his eyes to make the tasting stronger.

When he turned to the others, his smile was broad, and his lined face looked years younger. He lifted the staff, held it high, thrust it forward. To the north, toward Belerion.

The shoreline was increasingly steep, and rocky, and indented. Their progress was slower than ever before. But everywhere the wind brought the intoxicating scent of sea, and above them the sky seemed to rise higher and more blue as the cliffs soared higher above the deep, mysterious blues of the sea.

When evening came, they wrapped themselves in their

cloaks and slept in the shelter of ancient gnarled trees near the path. More than two weeks passed before they came upon a fishing village on a deep, sheltered bay. The path down to it was well trodden and easy to follow despite its steepness.

Curious villagers came to the foot of the path to see the strangers walking down. "Rufus!" Ella exclaimed, "They all look like your cousins." It was true. Every one of the villagers had bright carrot-colored hair.

They greeted Rufus as if he were, in fact, a cousin. The others were welcomed as well, because they were with him. At sunset the fishing boats came in with the day's catch, and an impromptu feast of hospitality began, which lasted well into the evening.

When Sarah came to Joseph in his dream that night, she brushed her lips across his brow and her hands smoothed his hair. "Rest, my love," she whispered. "Take a long rest beside your beloved sea."

Joseph did just that. The group stayed with the people called the Morbihand for nearly three weeks while Joseph told the villagers about God's creation of the world and His gift of His Son for the salvation of the world's peoples.

A great Celtic festival, Beltane, took place in the middle of the Nazarenes' stay. Rufus was almost in tears when he talked about Beltane celebrations when he was a boy. All Celts everywhere were joined on that night, he said. Celebrating here, on this rocky coast of Gaul, he could be joined to his family in Germania. That night the others in the group were able to see what he meant.

In the afternoon the entire village population climbed the path to the top of the cliffs. Another path led them up to a small hill to a great circle of immense upright white stones. In the center of the circle a tremendous pile of deadfall branches and tree trunks rose to a peak even taller than the giant stones.

There were many other red-haired people there, with groups arriving constantly during the rest of the day. The

Morbihand greeted these neighbors from all over the region with embraces, laughter, and happy tears of emotion.

Towards day's end torches were lit and a feast laid out on great stones that lay flat on the ground. A huge cheer greeted the presentation of a profusion of filled goatskins.

"Mead," explained the man standing beside Joseph. Joseph puzzled him by laughing long and heartily, repeating many times words that were strange to the man.

"Knees," Joseph was saying. "Weak in the knees."

The Druid appeared suddenly from the darkness that was falling. In his hooded white cloak, his face shadowed, he looked more apparition than mortal. Martha found Saul and stood close to his side. Tastros joined them, silently.

"Abba?"

"Yes, Ella, that's a Druid. I hope he comes to speak to us. If he does, use your Greek. They speak all languages fluently."

But at this moment the Druid was speaking Brythenic, the tongue of the Celts. He had pushed back his white hood, and his red hair was bright in the torchlight. He raised a bronze goblet high. "Beltane!" he shouted, then lifted his chin, opened his mouth, and poured foamy liquid from the goblet into it.

"Beltane!" The shout rose from hundreds of throats in a roar. Filled cups and goblets passed quickly from hand to hand and everyone toasted the holiday.

The Druid scanned the dark skies for a long moment. Joseph could hear the indrawn breath of all those close to him, discovered that he, too, was holding his breath.

Then the white-robed, red-haired priest snatched up one of the burning torches. "Beltane!" he shouted again; he ran to the mountain of piled brushwood and thrust the torch into it. A score of men did the same, running to the circumference of the pile, equidistant from one another.

In seconds the flames were climbing on and within the

wood. In minutes the bonfire lit the white stones and the area around them more brightly than noontime.

Everyone moved back from the heat and popping, leaping bits of flame.

"Beltane!" shouted the Druid. The long, full, flowing sleeves of his white cloak looked like huge pale wings when he spread his arms wide, facing the great inland darkness.

It was a moment before Joseph saw them. He was dazzled by the bonfire. But then, in the darkness, he saw a light. Another. And yet one more, then two, then a countless number. In every direction, as far as vision reached, there were bonfires, some so distant that they were only flickering specks.

Throughout the lands left to them, the Celts of the world were joined in a fiery celebration of life and brotherhood. The bonfire transformed the tears on Rufus' cheeks into drops of gold.

"I am called Cunomorus," said the Druid.

"I am called Joseph of Arimathea."

"You are welcome at our feast of Beltane, Joseph of Arimathea."

"I am honored to be here, Cunomorus."

"You travel?"

"To Belerion."

"Ah, yes. Your name is well known in the annals of Belerion. I will send word to expect you."

"I am grateful for your kindness."

They will be expecting us in Belerion. The thought sang in Joseph's head like music. He would have liked to buy one of the Morbihand fishing boats and set sail at once.

But the Morbihand had been extremely responsive to his teaching about Jesus, and that was his mission. All his life, Joseph had carried through to completion every major task he had undertaken. He would not change now. He would not abandon his duty to God and His Son.

Therefore, a little more than a week after Beltane, Joseph took his staff in hand to lead his small group up the path to the cliff tops and the seaside pathway north.

They visited a number of fishing villages, telling the inhabitants the story and sayings of Jesus. On the last day of October, the end of the year according to the Celtic calendar, they stopped in a town for the bonfire celebration of the beginning of a new year.

It was time to suspend their travels, for the winter, in the town. Rufus conducted the search and negotiations for a suitable house on his own. He had become, in effect, co-leader of the group now that they were in the Celtic world.

The house was different from any they'd had before. It was made of heavy, hewn-stone blocks, with tiny deep-silled windows to reduce the effect of the gusty winds that accompanied the storms of winter. Huge stone fireplaces dominated the main room and the big kitchen on the ground level. Small hearths high off the floor used the same massive chimneys for low-ceilinged big rooms above the living room and kitchen and for steep-eaved rooms on a third floor.

"You'll have the warm end of the main room for your sleeping room, Abba," said Ella. "The kitchen will suit perfectly for your meetings as well as for our regular living." The staircase was made of stone, too. It curved around a center well where the wind rose in a perpetual cold spiral. Joseph, old as he was, and with a bad knee, should by no means attempt to use it.

He flatly refused to give in to Ella's plans. "I will have the highest room, with the windows overlooking the sea. In clear weather it might be possible to see the mountain island Itkis from there."

They'd been in the house less than a week when Joseph was forced to submit to Ella's authority. He was carried down the stairs by Rufus, coughing and struggling for air to fill his congested lungs. Sickness had felled him in the night.

Tastros and Saul brought his bedding and the low bedstead that had rested under the eaves. Martha heated water in which she melted honey, fretting that she hadn't yet found where to buy herbs in the town market.

Ella gathered all the cushions and all the woolen coverlets from all the beds, fighting the frightened sobs that tried to burst from her throat. Abba couldn't die, not her abba. He mustn't.

I know he'll have eternal blessed life with you, Jesus, she cried inwardly. But not yet. Please, please, not yet. He wants so terribly much to go to Belerion. Let him have his wish.

Rufus helped her settle Joseph against the stack of cushions, covered by heaped woolens, beside a roaring fire.

Then he took control. "I will find a way to summon a Druid man of medicine, and I will buy more coverlets. It won't help if the rest of us get the sickness too, from being too cold."

"And herbs, Rufus. Can you find me some penny-royal and mint?" Martha was openly weeping, and wringing her hands. Rufus patted her shoulder. His eyes signaled to Saul, who led Martha into the kitchen where her weeping would be inaudible to Joseph.

"Tastros, we'll need a lot more wood for the fire. There's a stack in a corner of the yard outside."

"Will do," said the old soldier.

Rufus returned after an hour. He brought Martha's herbs, coverlets, and assurance that a doctor would arrive the following day.

None of them slept that night. They sat in the big room, listening to Joseph's desperate attempts to breathe, fearing every time that he might not succeed.

Ella wore her mother's blue necklace when she sat by her father, with her harp, playing and singing softly. The comforting psalm of David alternated with the song of

Belerion that Joseph so loved. Her heart prayed while she sang. It was the only thing she could do to ease her abba's torment.

> "From the winds they were spun
> the strings that shaped the music.
> From the stars she came,
> the goddess of the song.
> The cave it was her habitation
> Her couch was made of ferns . . ."

"My name is Galva," said the doctor. Ella stared. Galva was a woman.

"Take my cloak and bring me water and salt to cleanse my hands," the doctor ordered. She put her covered basket on the floor and loosened the belt around her waist. "You may goggle later, woman," she said, handing Ella her cloak. Then she looked at the others. "Someone find a low stool for me to sit upon, beside the sick man."

The basket contained phials of liquids, packets of powders, and an assortment of polished metal instruments in various shapes. Galva held one of them pressed against Joseph's chest while she put her ear to the other end of it.

Then, with terrible expertise, she lifted his head and slid a tube into his throat.

His breathing eased at once.

Ella ran to Galva, knelt on the stone floor beside her, and kissed the hem of the long dress she wore. "Thank you," she said.

The doctor wiped the tears from Ella's cheeks. "There is still much to do," she said, but she was smiling. "He will recover in time. If the rest of you are strong enough to take care of him. You must take care of yourselves first. Now, get an hour's sleep, and then I'll show you how to help me."

CHAPTER SEVENTY-NINE

WHEN THE ILLNESS WAS GONE, JOSEPH WAS THIN, PALE, wasted. "Now, Abba, you're going to eat whether you want to or not," Ella fussed. "And swallow that nasty medicine, too. If you are very good and obedient, I'll let you have a taste of honey afterward."

The household continued to revolve around their frail leader, but with joy now instead of fear. A succession of storms battered against the thick stone walls, but inside there was the warmth of the fire, and of love, and of laughter.

Rufus, Saul, and Tastros postured in the brightly colored wool trousers and leather boots that they were still trying to get accustomed to. Martha and Ella found their wool dresses both comfortable and practical, but they giggled foolishly whenever they took a swallow of the men's mead.

There were trousers for Joseph, too, when he was strong enough to begin walking across the room and to sit in a chair instead of lying in the bed. His were the gaudiest of all, yellow and orange lines criss-crossing one another topped by speckles of red, blue, and green. "Rufus!" said Joseph accusingly when they were presented to him. The rest of them howled with laughter. Even Martha. They'd been looking forward to this moment.

Joseph regained his strength with surprising speed. In little more than a week, when the day was cold but clear with a strong sun, he was able to go for a short walk outside with the dogs.

"The four old men," Joseph named himself and his four-legged companions. The dogs' muzzles had white hairs now, and their gait was slow, like their master's. The foursome became a familiar sight in the town whenever the weather was good. The butcher saved scraps for them. Including Joseph, who carried stew meat back to the house. "My boys and I can't trust our teeth against bones anymore," he joked.

While Joseph was out walking one day, Ella got the others together for an informal planning session. "We all know how Abba needs to be doing something," she said. "Walking with the dogs isn't going to keep him satisfied for much longer. Should we begin talking in the marketplace to find people to bring to him for meetings?"

They were discussing the where and how and who when Joseph returned. He made their discussion irrelevant. "I have bought a boat," he announced. "Tomorrow we leave for Belerion."

Some fisherman had told him that there was usually a spell of warm, clear weather at this time of year when the days were at their shortest.

His answer to all their protests was to swing the door wide and point to the bright clear blue of the sky. "I'm the sailor among you, and I have decided. If tomorrow's sky is like today's, we sail."

"The house—the fellowship—the Agape."

Joseph smiled at Martha's weak protests. "I gave a fisherman the house in trade for his boat," he said. "Each of us believes he got the best of the trade. It's the most satisfactory way to do business."

A little later Ella managed to talk with her father alone. "Abba? I don't understand. You talked so often, I remember, about the perils of winter sailing."

"True, that's true, Ella. For a trading ship on a long voyage. Our way is not long, though. Under two hundred miles. And there are secrets that I know about these waters. Out from land, in the sea, there is a strong current that could carry a craft all by itself. Also there is a prevailing wind from the southwest. It's strong and it comes from some hidden land, no one knows which one or where, that gives warmth to the wind.

"I will take the boat out until we catch that current and that wind. They will take us to the island I've told you about where the beach becomes a bridge from the mountain to Belerion."

Joseph took his daughter in his arms and held her close. "Ella," he said quietly, "the sickness forced me to understand that I am an old man. God's mercy has given me back my health, but who can say for how long? I prayed constantly when the air was hard to pull into my body, I prayed that I might complete my mission before I died."

He released Ella, then his two hands held her face while he looked into her eyes. "I know that I am called to Belerion, Ella. I must not miss this opportunity. Now, while I am well and strong enough to go."

Ella turned her head, kissed her father's palm. "I'll pack our things." She looked at Joseph with a teasing gleam in her eyes. "And you can just stop expecting me to forget your nasty medicine, Abba. That's the first thing I'll bring."

"Sarah's own girl," Joseph murmured when Ella left him. "More like her mother every day." The blue flowers around Ella's throat brought Sarah close.

There would be few hours of daylight, and they'd need every minute of them. Joseph herded the five people and three dogs onto the dock when the sky was still gray. They were all warmly dressed, with long, thick woolen cloaks on top of their wool clothing. The dogs, too, had the thickened coats of winter. And Martha had brought the extra coverlets Rufus had bought when Joseph fell ill. Together with a bas-

ket of breads and cheeses and a goatskin of Joseph's special
herbal drink—boiled, steeped and strained. The warmth of
it felt good held to her chest beneath her cloak in the cold
dawn air.

She—like the others—was shocked when she saw the
boat. It was so small.

Saul looked with approval at the folded leather sail at the
foot of the mast. He knew the strength of leather.

Rufus felt better when he saw the thick, sturdy oars. He
and Tastros would use them well.

Tastros regarded the wide, nearly circular, leather-
covered wicker-framed coracle with profound apprehension. He had never in his life been in a boat, and he could
not swim.

Joseph directed Rufus and Tastros to the thwart between
the oarlocks, with Saul between them. The plank seat in
front of the mast was assigned to Ella and Martha. The
dogs would lie at Joseph's feet in the stern, where the steering oar was moving from side to side in the tidal waters,
awaiting his guiding grip. Their baskets and bundles would
have to be wedged in wherever there was room. Martha and
Ella handed them down to the men, from the dock. "This
one we keep for us," Martha said firmly. She kept the
goatskin under her arm when she stepped fearfully into the
coracle. It was no longer bobbing on the surface. Their
weight had dropped it deep into the waves. The water
looked extremely close to washing over the boat's rim.
Martha watched the level when Ella stepped down to sit beside her.

"Excellent," Joseph announced. He used his staff as a
post to swing lightly down from the dock after he untied
the mooring line. Elation was in his supple movements.

"Oarsmen, to your work," he commanded, as he'd done
so many times over the years. "The sun is coming up."

Rufus and Tastros knew nothing about rowing. Joseph
hadn't thought of that. Their progress into the harbor was

jerking, halting, barely perceptible until the outgoing tide generously came to their aid.

Joseph let them bring in the oars. They did much better at hauling on the lines and raising sail after the tide carried the coracle past the harbor's headland.

The low sun stretched a golden carpet for them to follow onto sea. The wind and the air were cold. But they were on their way. And the sea was not coming into the boat. Martha cheerfully announced "Breakfast!" and bent to pass bread and cheese below the sail to the men behind. After some hours, when the sun was warm on their shoulders and the sky a brilliant blue, Martha began to relax.

Ella was loving every instant.

And Joseph, on his beloved sea again, was feeling the rapture of the salt wind on his face throughout every inch of his flesh and bone.

He felt the power of the current against the steering oar, dipped his hand in the wake, smiled when he perceived the slight increase in temperature. Just as he remembered. Slowly, gently, using the current's strength, he steered the boat onto course for Belerion.

The thick sail welcomed the stiff prevailing winds, and the tiny boat skimmed the sparkling waves as if it shared Joseph's desire and excitement.

When the sun passed its zenith and began to lose its warmth, Martha pointed out the bundles that held the coverlets. She wrapped Ella, then herself, scolded Saul until he bundled up, too, and persuaded Rufus and Tastros to do the same. There was no coverlet for Joseph, which bothered Ella, but when she looked at her father's radiant face, she kept quiet.

The wind that was taking them to their goal brought up the storm that hit in mid-afternoon. Its clouds covered the sun, giving Joseph a brief warning about what was coming from behind them. He turned, saw the wall of black turbulence, shouted as he turned back. "Shorten sail! Shorten sail!" His passengers didn't know what to do. He had no crew. And he could not abandon the steering to deal with the sail. The storm's winds were going to hit the broad leather square on every one of its parts.

"Get on your hands and knees," Joseph yelled. "Don't think, just do it. Put the coverlets over your backs and your heads and hold them out to lap the boat's rim. There's a storm about to hit, and you've got to keep the rain and waves out of the boat.

"Saul! Bring your coverlet to me. I'm going to need your help." Holding the waters out of the center of the coracle was going to demand superhuman strength, Joseph knew. Perhaps Rufus and Tastros could do it; certainly Saul could not. But he could bail out the water that did get in. Until his strength gave out.

Joseph put Saul in the midst of the dogs, seated, with the thick woolen coverlet around his body and over the dogs. There was barely time enough to show him how to use the wide, shallow, metal bailer before the fury of the storm struck.

The small craft was actually lifted from the sea for an instant when the cyclone hit the sail. It fell with an impact that threw Martha against Ella, Tastros against Rufus, Saul against the steering oar with such force that it snapped with a cracking sound that was lost in the similar deafening crackings of the lightning that was stabbing the sea all around them.

A louder crack, and the mast was snapped, dropping the twisted sail around its tip onto Ella and Martha. Joseph tried to shout to them, but the wind tore the sounds from his mouth and threw them into the blackness that had descended.

They were all at the mercy of the tempest now. Without sail, without steering, without light. They could only fight the torrents of rainfall and the foaming wave crests that were dumping a crippling weight of water upon them.

Rufus and Tastros held their arms outstretched, taking the assault on their backs, shoulders, and aching arm muscles, while clutching the edges of the coverlets over the coracle's rim with cold cramping fingers. The thickly woven wool quickly became saturated. The weight of it was greater than lead.

In the stern Joseph held the wool stretched across Saul until his arms had no more strength in them, then motioned to Saul to take the weight and pass him the bailing pan. They alternated, in that fashion, without need or strength for words. The dogs huddled together for warmth, trembling and whining and unnoticed.

There was no movement of any kind in the bow. The only ray of hope was that the heavy suffocating leather was proof against the waters.

Rufus and Tastros held the waters out with waning strength and mounting determination. Pain like swords made of ice stabbed their shoulder and arm muscles. Cramps made them scream. Their arms jumped in uncontrollable spasms, and their backs felt as though they were on fire. Delirium affected Tastros and he cursed the barbarian horde that he saw attacking them. Then he fell, unconscious, into the water swirling in the bottom of the coracle. Rufus was able to turn Tastros so that he faced up and could breathe. It drained the last shred of willpower and final reserve of strength from the big young Celt, and blackness filled his head. He fell across the body of Tastros. They had never known when the rain stopped. They did not now feel the diminishing winds.

Nor did the others. Joseph and Saul were bent into postures of pain, unaware of the whimpering moaning of the dogs or the licking tongues that tried to bring them back to life.

The sail covered the bow, as before, concealing any life that might remain there.

While the currents and the clashing waves tossed and spun the coracle like a damaged plaything discarded by the storm.

The night sky was clear and distant and strewn with stars

that sparkled like icicles in the moonlight. Beneath it the battered boat with its ghastly cargo of sprawling bodies was borne on the vagaries of tide and current upon the black waters of the sea.

It was the stillness that roused Joseph. There was no motion. And no sound. Not of wind nor of water. He raised his head. Fingers of rose and golden light were streaking upward into the gray sky. The dawn spread rapidly. Before it, a dark shape became a tall rounded hill. "Itkis," Joseph breathed. He rubbed the stinging crust of salt from his eyes. Yes, the dogs were there. And Saul. He was beginning to move.

But the others? Ella! Joseph's aching body found strength to call out. "Wake up! Answer me! Ella—Martha—Tastros—Rufus—are you there?"

In the growing light of sunrise he could see the sodden wool mounds in front of his knees. Yes, there was movement. But the heavy leather sail lay still. He grabbed Saul's shoulder with desperation. "Saul! Wake up, Saul. We have to get Martha and Ella free before they suffocate."

If it wasn't too late. Dear Lord, cried Joseph's heart, you healed her once, save her now, I implore your mercy.

The minutes that followed were frenzied, as Rufus and Tastros struggled free of the leaden coverlets, and the four men grappled with the weighty expanse of leather.

"Abba?" came a weak, muffled voice. Joseph cried out, in joy and thanksgiving.

Bright morning light made Sarah's necklace a vibrant blue on Ella's throat when she and Martha were set free to climb over the coracle's rim and onto the earth. Joseph embraced her. He was too emotional to speak.

Ella's arms hugged him with youthful strength. "I see it, Abba," she said, "I see Itkis. We're here, and we're safe."

Joseph looked around. The tempest had driven them ashore in a place that he'd never seen before. On all sides marsh and tide-bared gleaming wet soil stretched toward the waters behind them. There was no sand, no beach. The great hill ahead could not be Itkis.

"We were driven off course," Joseph told his exhausted companions. "This is not Belerion. We will have to find some people and learn where we are. Then, after we repair the boat, we will go there." His limbs felt too heavy to move. But it must be done.

"Find my staff for me, Ella. It's probably floating in the water inside the coracle. And get the dogs out. We'll climb this island in the reeds to get a good view. And to offer our prayers to God in thanks for safe landing."

Joseph led the way. One step, then another, and yet one more . . . two . . . three. Determination made it possible. "This is far enough for now," he told the others when even his fierce will could no longer move his legs. "We will rest here." He thrust his staff into the ground, used it to steady him while he lowered himself to his knees to pray.

He bowed his head. There was a multitude of thanks owing to God and His Son Jesus.

Joseph was unaware of the others, of their backing away from him, even of their soft, awestruck gasps. He did not know that, as they watched, his battered staff began to grow, to become thicker and taller. Before their eyes, branches grew outward from the staff, and on the branches leaves of a fresh green, holding among them buds that swelled, enlarged, and opened slowly into glowing, tender blossoms colored rose by the radiant dawn.

By the reckoning of calendars many centuries later, it was the year 39 c.e. The date: December 25.

CHAPTER EIGHTY

"ABBA," ELLA WHISPERED. "ABBA." SHE WALKED TO JOSEPH, put one hand on his shoulder. "Abba, Jesus has sent us another miracle. Look up."

Joseph did as she bade him. He saw a canopy of living beauty and, through the blossoms, the high blue canopy of sky. He stared at the softly stirring blooms. Flowering in December. "Miracle," Ella had said. It was true. "It is clear," he said, "that God has brought us to this place. It must be his plan that we stay. I am arrived where I am meant to be. And now I will rest."

Joseph lay on the cushioned turf beneath the flowering tree. He closed his eyes in blessed sleep.

The others followed his lead. Rufus joined Joseph beneath the limbs of the miraculous tree. Saul and Martha lay side by side, hands clasped, where they had witnessed the miraculous growth. Tastros was close by.

Ella, alone, did not give in to fatigue right away. The youngest, and the most agile, she ran back to the boat for Joseph's basket of scrolls, her harp, and Martha's goatskin of Joseph's herbal brew.

Then she climbed to the edge of the miraculous tree, dropped to the earth and into deep, restoring sleep.

*   *   *

"Wake up! Everybody, wake up." Tastros used his military voice, the one that gave orders that were instantly obeyed.

The others stirred, blinked; Saul yawned, Ella stretched.

Then they sat up. Hastily. As one after another, each of them became aware of what Tastros had been first to see. They were encircled by men who stood at arm's length from one another. Each of the men held a long sword, loosely clasped for the moment with its pointed end touching the earth in front of him.

Rufus jumped to his feet. The swords lifted, held tightly now.

One of the swordsmen wore a wide gold circlet around his neck and a headdress that looked like dulled gold. It covered his forehead and the crown of his head. Two horn-like conical ornaments extended from the helmet above his ears.

"You are Celt?" He stared at Rufus.

"Yes. You are chief of this country?"

"Yes. Why are you here?"

"A storm brought us."

The chief's gaze scanned the group, settled on Joseph. "You are chief?"

"Yes. I am called Joseph of Arimathea."

The chief was scowling. "Whence comes this summer tree? Did you bring it here?"

Joseph smiled at the bellicose man. "It was put here by God," he said slowly, quietly. "It is a miracle."

"Then you are magicians."

"No." Joseph shook his head. "We are only storm-wrecked, tired men and women. We do not even know where God has brought us. But He gave us this sign, this tree. It grew from a wooden staff I use to help me when I walk."

Joseph began to laugh to himself. It astonished the chief, his men, and Joseph's own followers.

"Why are you laughing, Abba?"

"Because now I don't have a walking stick." Ella began to laugh, too.

They had spoken Aramaic to one another, a foreign language to the Celtic chief. He glared at Rufus. "Tell the old man it is dangerous to laugh at Bodinnar."

Joseph understood the chief's words. He spoke to the angry man in Brythenic, the all-regions Celtic language. "I beg you to forgive me, Bodinnar. I meant no disrespect. I was not laughing at you." He explained that Ella was his daughter, and repeated their conversation. In Celtic.

Bodinnar looked at the beautiful, blossom-covered tree, then at the white-bearded old man lying beneath it, unable to get up. His blue eyes squinted when he understood Joseph's joke, then he broke into booming laughter.

The story moved from man to man around the circle, with loud laughter following.

"Have you hunger, old man?" Bodinnar asked Joseph.

"Very large, Bodinnar. Have you bread?"

The chief's laughter boomed again. He strode to Joseph, thrust his hand down in invitation. "I will be your walking stick," he said. "We have bread in our village."

Joseph took the proffered hand. "My companions hunger, too."

Bodinnar hauled Joseph to his feet as easily as if he were lifting a small child. "We have much bread, old man. All are welcome to the land of the Durotriges. You will answer my questions when your bellies are filled."

Rufus had been standing in tense readiness to attack the chief if Joseph was threatened. Now he confronted him. "This man is my master, Bodinnar. I will help him, not you." He put his thickly muscled arms around Joseph and lifted him, to carry him.

Bodinnar nodded approval. "It is good that a warrior cares for his chief," he said. "Follow me."

*   *   *

The village was the strangest kind of habitation that Joseph, in all his travels, had ever seen. It was like a gigantic anchored barge in the center of a wide marsh. Tremendous timbers sunk into the mud supported a platform of tree trunks flattened on one side, joined together with leather rope and pegs. The platform measured about two hundred feet by two hundred and fifty. The village on top of it occupied the center. It was surrounded by a tall, pointed palisade of tree trunks, small in diameter, and contained round huts, grouped in threes around beaten-earth courtyards, where the villagers lived, as well as buildings for other uses.

Bodinnar and his men took Joseph's group to the village in flat-bottomed boats they poled across the marsh. They landed at a jetty floating on the tidal marsh water, then walked up a ramp to the wood platform. Rising plumes of smoke beyond the protective wall were their introduction to the village. They soon discovered that every dwelling had its own raised stone hearth for cooking and warmth. And—more important at that particular moment—that the village contained seven stone huts designed specifically for baking. There was warm fresh bread in every home, together with a curiosity-laden welcome for the strangers.

The population of the village was nearly two hundred, including children. Before the day was over, every one of them had gotten a good look at the mysterious travelers and had heard about the miraculous tree. Everyone wanted to see it.

During the next ten days everyone did. Traffic was constant back and forth over the two miles that separated the village from the tall hill and the other areas of firm land that surrounded it in irregular formation.

Joseph thanked Bodinnar for the hospitality of the village, but he firmly refused the invitation to live there. "The miracle of the tree is, to me, a sign that we should make our homes nearby and that we should build a place of worship for the Son of God and his message to the world."

"But you can be attacked there. We have the marsh to keep enemies distant."

"Our Lord is a god of peace," Joseph answered. He told the Celtic chief Jesus' saying about loving one's enemies and turning the other cheek.

Bodinnar shook his head in disbelief.

"This is your god? I will never understand you, Joseph of Arimathea.

"But we will help you in your madness. A blooming rose in midwinter cannot be brushed aside. Your god is powerful, and we will try to take care of his people."

The marshes were a limitless resource for reeds and grasses and mud. The villagers taught Joseph's group how to build big circular huts like theirs. Ella celebrated her eighteenth birthday in her new home, a mud-caulked woven-reed hut with a stone hearth and chimney that she shared with her father and three elderly dogs.

It had no windows. A thick wooden door opened onto a sheltered courtyard for daylight. Martha and Saul had a hut, as did Rufus and Tastros. The six of them shared the courtyard that was sheltered from winter winds by the closely grouped huts.

A smaller hut stood a short distance away. This was the House of Nazarenes. It had no fireplace. The stone was used instead to make an altar. Joseph's scroll of the sayings of Jesus rested on it in a bronze box of beautiful workmanship, a gift from Bodinnar.

Other gifts from the Celts included furnishings for the huts and—most important—food for the months until they could begin to grow their own wheat and raise their own animals and become self-sufficient. Martha was all but feverish with anticipation. She had never really liked being subject to the tastes and choices of housekeepers and cooks.

All of them looked forward to the coming of spring. The landscape around them held lots of green, in the yellow-green marshes, the brown-green grasses of the flatlands, the fresh green leaves of the miracle tree that stayed thick on its branches after the flowers were gone. But the frequent rains were cold, sometimes with stinging bits of ice inside them, and a sharp wind blew steadily from the slopes of the distant hill that they planned to explore as soon as Joseph was strong enough.

He would have no difficulty about a walking staff. Except in the matter of selection. His joke about losing his support had delighted the whole village. Beside the door in his new home a tall basket of woven reeds held more than a dozen staffs given to him.

Joseph complained about the over-solicitude that kept him from investigating the Tor, the local name for the mysterious, solitary, tall hill. He was sure there was a secret attached to it. Bodinnar had been excessively emphatic when he advised Joseph to stay away from it. "Aren't you at all curious? Intrigued? Don't you want to find out what's there?" Joseph badgered Rufus and Tastros almost daily. Saul finally chastised him.

"We came here, Joseph, to teach the gospel of Jesus. We were given a miracle to prove that this is where we are meant to be. This is where we will stay. Already some come from the village to hear you speak in the House of the Nazarenes. Be grateful for the blessings of our safe arrival, for the grace vouchsafed to us in the miraculous transformation of your staff. And do what God brought you here to do."

"You are right, Saul." Joseph knew that it was true. Nevertheless, he went outside the courtyard often, to look at the Tor. What mystery lay within?

He had no way of knowing that the answer would come to him. Soon.

CHAPTER EIGHTY-ONE

BODINNAR SENT A FORMAL INVITATION FOR THE NAZARENES to come to the village for the Festival of Imbolc on February 1. The invitation was in the form of a song sung by a chorus of little boys, a salute to spring. The Celts considered the date the first day of the season.

Ella shook a glittering fall of frozen rain from her cloak. "First day of spring? In three days? I'll be glad if it comes true. Anyhow, the festival should be fun. Let's just hope it has a bonfire."

Indeed it did. And a feast. And unlimited quantities of mead.

Best of all, for Ella, there was music. A trio of white-robed Druid Bards accompanied themselves on lyres while they sang many, many verses of ancient tales of heroism and romance.

She approached the least impressive-looking of them when the applause and cheering finally faded. "Thank you, that was beautiful," she said. The Bard looked at her with interest. Her accent clearly identified her as a foreigner.

"May I ask you a question?" Ella continued.

"Of course. Were there verses you didn't understand?"

"Naturally there were. I don't know the legends. But

what I hope you'll tell me is where you get the strings for your instrument. I have a small harp, but its strings are broken. I miss playing it."

"You haven't been able to play at all?"

"Not even a twang."

"Would you like to try the lyre? I know how empty life is when one cannot have music."

He offered the beautifully carved instrument to her. Ella backed away.

"Oh, no. No. No, thank you very much. That's much too difficult for me. I just want to play my simple harp."

"I will give you strings. I have some with me, in case mine break. But the lyre is not so very different from the harp. All stringed instruments are much the same. Listen." He plucked each string individually, creating a staircase of tones that made Ella's heart ache with longing.

Oh, how she missed her music. It had always been her refuge from anything disturbing or distressing, and it gave her a lovely private place to be, where she could dream impossible dreams.

"Just one . . ." Her fingers plucked a thin, short string, producing a high singing sound of piercing beauty. "Oh." Her eyes filled with tears.

The Druid understood her emotion. He felt the same. What a pitiful thing, to be without music. "Sit here by me—what is your name? Ella? Good. Sit here by me, Ella. The festival is noisy, no one will hear what we are doing. Now, try the strings. Find the notes that you know from your harp."

Ella couldn't resist. She tilted her head to bring her ear close to the sounds, then pulled, released, listened to the lyre's voice. In a few minutes she became completely rapt, engrossed in the singing strings.

She had no conception of how much time passed. When Joseph touched her shoulder, she emitted a tiny squeal of shock.

"It is time to leave, my daughter."

"So soon. Oh, Abba, listen. I've found the song you like best." Her fingers made a plain, echoing accompaniment as she sang the song of Belerion.

> "From the cliffe they fell,
>   the words.
> From the winds they were spun,
>   the strings that shaped the music.
> From the stars she came,
>   the goddess of the song.
>
> The cave it was her habitation.
> Her couch was made of ferns.
> The night sky was her birthplace.
> Her father was the sun.
>
> White birds bore her on their wings
>   to her fern-filled home.
> Their beaks pulled softest down from their breasts
>   to weave her robes
> They fed her with their music.
> And named her in their songs. Lhuysa of the ferncliffe,
>   daughter of the stars."

"Thank you my dear. I have missed your singing."

"It will be fine again, Abba. This wonderful man is going to give me strings for my harp." She smiled gratefully at the silent Bard.

But he was different now. Still. Withdrawn. Even angry, perhaps. What had she done wrong? Had she damaged the lyre in some way?

"How do you know that song?" he said. The tone was icy. Ella's worry became indignation. How dare he? Couldn't she sing something for her father? Did every song have to be about battles and kings and pagan gods?

"Why are you so upset? It's a lovely song, a special

song. It was written for my mother, given her as a present by her music teacher. I love it, and so does my father."

"A gift to your mother? Who made this gift?"

Ella pushed the lyre into the Bard's hands. "Thank you," she remembered to say, and she turned to leave.

"Who?" the Bard insisted.

Joseph stepped forward. He put his arm across Ella's back, pulled her to his side.

"You are upsetting my daughter, and I resent it. Now leave her alone. I will manage to locate some strings for her harp."

"Sir. I must have an answer. How does your daughter know this song that no one is permitted to sing?"

"Not permitted? That's absurd. The song is innocent and tender. Like the young man who wrote it for my wife. His name was Nancledra."

Joseph led Ella away.

Many more people than usual came to the next weekly Agape celebration at the House of the Nazarenes. Joseph was overjoyed. Perhaps the promise of warmer weather was responsible. He'd tried the plank walkways over the marshes that villagers used to reach dry land, and he couldn't blame anyone who avoided the slippery, cold, windy outing. Only the chief, Bodinnar, had regular access to boats, it seemed.

Two nights later he learned the real reason for the increased attendance. The discovery was a frightening, dramatic occasion. Trumpets sounding brought all the group rushing out of their huts, out of the courtyard to see, approaching from the Tor, a column of torch-bearing Druids. The firelit hooded figures looked eerie. White robes, white hoods, hidden faces. They might have been specters.

Joseph's group gathered closely around him, together for warmth and for reassurance.

"Joseph of Arimathea," called a voice from the distance. "Is it you?"

"It is I," Joseph shouted to the unknown inquisitor.

The torchbearers moved quickly and silently closer. Closer.

"Joseph of Arimathea!"

Joseph raised his staff. "Here am I."

When the light of the fires was bright around the group, one of the hooded figures came forward. He carried no torch. A chain of heavy gold links hung around his neck and bore a gold sickle. They gleamed richly in the torches' leaping light.

"The Archdruid," Rufus muttered fearfully.

The figure pushed the deep hood back. Golden hair and a golden beard were like added regalia.

"Is it really you, Joseph of Arimathea?"

"It is." Joseph showed no fear.

"Fifty years. It is no wonder we are strangers. Joseph, it is I. Nancledra. Will you not welcome me?"

"Nancledra?" Joseph could find no trace in this golden wizard of the shy, handsome youth who'd been his interpreter and Sarah's music teacher. Had it really been fifty years ago, the magic time in Belerion?

"It is I, Joseph. Where is Sarah? She will know me."

The fire and the golden Archdruid blurred in Joseph's sight, through tears that filled his eyes. Yes, Sarah would have known. "She is dead," he said, "for many years now."

"Aaah! No." The sorrow in the Archdruid's voice was sharp. Its humanity made him real—a man, not a wizard at all. He truly was Nancledra.

"I know you now," said Joseph. "You are most welcome, Nancledra. Meet Sarah's daughter. This is Ella." He drew her forward.

Nancledra's jeweled white hands cradled Ella's face. "Yes. I see Sarah's eyes."

Ella looked at him with open curiosity. "Were you my mother's teacher?"

He smiled. "Of music, yes, but she taught me much more. About loving life, about courage, about laughter. She was an extraordinary woman, your mother." He released Ella, turned to Joseph.

"Word came to me from Gaul about you. You were going to visit Belerion again. Therefore, I was waiting for you there. I could hardly credit the next news I received. A man, a winter-blooming tree—I continued to await my friends; miraculous trees were less important.

"But when I was told of a beautiful young woman wearing lapis flowers on her throat and singing Sarah's song, I left at once, to come to you. It is good to see you again, Joseph. I have brought wine with the warmth of the sun in it. Invite me to your house. We will drink, and talk of the past, and, it might be, cry a little."

His retinue stayed in the courtyard after they deposited inside Joseph's hut the gifts that Nancledra had brought. They included a large, graceful bronze brazier and baskets full of charcoal to burn in it. Also, amphorae of wine, a jewel-studded gold ewer, and three huge golden goblets incised with Celtic swirling and interwoven ornamentation.

As Nancledra had foretold, he and Joseph talked, drank, and wept a little beside the warmth of the red coals in the brazier. Joseph learned that the Jews of Belerion were a large, ever-growing, prosperous part of the community. Isaac was still alive; "Patriarch" he was called. He had sent loving wishes for Joseph's happiness. "So long ago," said Joseph. Nancledra agreed, refilled the goblets. Ella had a few sips of wine from the one intended for her mother. Then she discreetly excused herself and went to bed, leaving them to their own memories.

The Archdruid, leader of all the Druids in Albion, was the most honored and respected man in the whole land. His wisdom and judgment were acknowledged as more profound and wiser than any other's. His power was incalculable.

It was hard for Joseph to believe that Nancledra had become this mighty figure. Particularly after Ella mentioned that his golden hair and beard were dyed that color. "He's as white as you underneath, Abba."

Joseph hugged her. "You are truly your mother's child, Ella. I can hardly wait to tell Nancledra. Sarah would have made exactly the same observation."

"The first thing Sarah would have noticed!" Nancledra exclaimed when Joseph repeated Ella's comment. His laughter was a kind of recaptured youthfulness. For Nancledra, and for Joseph as well. The early spring months found the two of them together often, at Joseph's hut or on excursions organized by Nancledra to places or to ceremonies that he believed Joseph, and Sarah's daughter, would enjoy.

Using chariots, horses, and drivers provided by the Archdruid's influence, they visited the nearby mountains and the soaring, magnificently colored caves within them where Druids from the region usually wintered, enjoying the constant mild temperature inside. They went greater distances, too. To the ancient circle of stones on the high plain called Salisbury, thirty miles distant. Even the Archdruid did not know the origin of the mighty circle, but he could—and did—show them that it was, in fact, a phenomenally accurate calendar. This was not one of the secrets of the Druids, so he could share the information. About many other things, he remained silent.

Even so, Ella and Joseph were privileged to see more of the inside of the Druids' world than any outsider had ever witnessed.

Ella's favorite was the Gorsedd, the meeting place at the head of a long avenue of the mysterious standing stones, where the contests were held among the Druid Bards. The music lasted for three days. On the fourth, students aspiring to become Bards held their own competitions and concerts. The grand climax of the entire festival and its conclusion was a performance by the Archdruid himself.

That ended, as it had for decades, with Nancledra playing and singing his most loved composition of the many hundreds he had written.

"The Song of Belerion"—"Sarah's song," he said to Joseph.

Following the Gorsedd, Nancledra took them to what Joseph proclaimed to be his favorite spot. This was a complex at the hot spring of the Celtic goddess Sulis. There were groves of trees with young tender green leaves, a large dining hall, kitchens, streets of stone-walled dormitories, gardens filled with flowing vines and shrubs and crossed by paths that were lined with benches for sitting in quiet enjoyment of the beauty and sweet scents. Best of all—and the reason for everything else—there was an immense stone-pillared pavilion that housed the spring. Mineral-rich water gushed forth year around, filling it with tangy billows of steam. The water temperature was 120 degrees.

Channels led water to baths, to basins with cups for medicinal doses taken many times a day, to tunnels beneath the dormitories for heating the rooms.

Joseph and Nancledra both groaned with pleasure when they lowered their bodies into the hot bath. Ella spent more than two hours swimming in the great man-made pool of springwater that had cooled.

"I visit the spring often in the winter," Nancledra told Joseph. "I recommend that you do the same. It's only a day's journey from you. Before we leave, I will make you known to the priestess who governs the complex. She will see to it that you never have to wait for your bath and that you have the best place at the table for meals."

Maen was a heavily built woman with thick blond braids. Her white cloak was made of linen, not wool, because she lived in a world of steamy air, summer and winter. She was deferential to Nancledra but in no way obsequious. To be a Druid was proof of superior knowledge and intellect. The

priestess need not bow before any man or woman, only to
the goddess she served.

An ancient road ran through the Sulis complex and continued to the southwest coast. It was known as the Fosse
Way, and passed by the Tor, visible for many miles before
they turned onto the track that would lead them to Joseph's
home, only four miles away.

It was near the end of March when they visited the
spring of Sulis for the first time. Returning, Nancledra's
driver pointed at the Tor and began to whip his chariot's
pair of horses to increase speed. A spiral of black smoke
was rising from the top of the hill, staining the blue sky.

Joseph and Ella were in chariots of their own, following
Nancledra's "Can't we hurry too?" Joseph asked his driver.
No, the man said. He drove Joseph to his home at a safe,
moderate speed, followed by Ella's chariot at the same
pace.

Joseph was fuming. He had persuaded Nancledra to
show him the Tor's mysteries when the Archdruid first
reentered his life. He knew about the grove of oaks where
Druid ceremonies were held, he'd seen the avenue of oaks
that led to the Tor, even the flattened ground on its top and
the ring of stones that marked the location of the festival
bonfires. But Nancledra had said nothing about signals.

That night, fire burned bright and tall against the dark
sky.

And the next day a continuous procession of the villagers
from the platform in the marsh moved past the new-leaved
miracle tree and the cluster of huts where the Nazarenes
lived.

They were going to the fortress at Hod Hill, Joseph was
told when he asked a family he knew. A signal on the Tor
meant danger. They'd be safe inside the walls of the fort.

"Should we go with them?" Martha asked.

Saul answered before Joseph could speak. "God and His
Son brought us here. They will protect us from harm."

Joseph went to the small chapel and knelt before the altar. He prayed that Saul was right. Why had Nancledra left without a word?

The black smoke was still rising from the Tor.

CHAPTER EIGHTY-TWO

TEN DAYS LATER, WHEN ELLA WAS HELPING MARTHA WITH preparations for the Agape feast, they saw the first group of villagers walking back toward the marshes. "Whatever the danger was, it looks like it's past," said Ella. "I know what, Martha! Let's invite all of them to our feast tomorrow. We've still got time to get more food."

On the day that the Nazarenes marked the anniversary of Jesus' resurrection, the chapel hut was crammed with people. Ella sang the psalm of David, and Joseph told the story of Jesus and his Father.

Then everyone went to the hill of the miracle tree, where Rufus and Tastros had put together tables and benches using all the furnishings from the huts as well as pieces borrowed from the villagers and planks of wood from an abandoned marsh walkway.

Six lambs were roasting over coals in a pit that the men had dug, together with a half dozen chickens and four basketsful of fish. Huge bowls of stewed onions, piles of bread loaves and cheese rounds waited on the tables. Nancledra's generous recent gift of wine promised plenty for all.

Joseph explained the custom of taking bread and wine in memory of Jesus. Then he bowed his head in prayer, thanking God for his bounty, and for the gift of His Son, and for the fellowship of neighbors, and for their safety. He broke bread into baskets that were passed along the tables and poured wine into cups that followed the breadbaskets.

One of the village women had just lowered her cup from her lips when she stood and shouted, "Look! Look at the magic tree."

The first buds were beginning to open into blossom.

"It saved us from the Romans," she cried. "Its god is a very mighty god."

It was weeks later that Joseph learned from Nancledra what had occurred. Celts in Gaul had signaled that a Roman army was massing there beside a small fleet of boats, in preparation for an invasion of Albion. "If danger had come near, I would have sent word to you, but it vanished."

No one knew why, but the soldiers had refused to enter the boats and sail across the narrow waters.

By the time Joseph heard the story, the tiny settlement of the Nazarenes had already begun to grow. From the nearby village on the marsh, from a similar one ten miles beyond it, from farms and villages alongside the Fosse Way, from other communities even more distant, people were moving to the place of the flowering tree and its god, who had kept the Romans away.

A wonderful time was beginning.

One of the first new buildings to go up was a hut with a bigger structure beside it, to hold a large cart and horses to pull it—a gift from the Archdruid to his old friend Joseph of Arimathea.

The hut was a home for the cart's driver and horse coper, a strong young man with light brown hair and dark brown eyes. His name was Lerryn. He arrived driving the cart, which he presented to Joseph. Then he presented Ella with the gift Nancledra had sent to her. It was a large assortment of strings for various musical instruments.

"I will be happy to help you string your harp," Lerryn said. "I am in my ninth year of study to become a Bard."

For three years, everyone in the growing village watched and waited for the romance between Ella and Lerryn to culminate in marriage. She was certainly old enough, and then some, all the women said. What was holding her back? Lerryn was good-looking, a good worker, a good musician, and would someday, most likely, become a Bard. Perhaps, someday he might even reach the rank of priest, the highest Druid ranking. Archdruid, no. Never. Lerryn did not have the special gifts, the leadership qualities. He was too quiet, too shy.

Nevertheless, he was obviously devoted to Ella. He spent every minute that he could manage with her. Why didn't she just scoop him up and make him happy? Herself, too.

What none of the other villagers understood was that Ella and Lerryn were already happy. As they were. They made music together, taught each other all the songs they knew. That is, all the regular songs. Lerryn explained to her that he was not permitted to tell anyone the words and music of the lengthy sagas that he memorized as part of his education toward becoming a Bard.

Ella replied that she wouldn't take the time to learn them if he begged her on his knees. "I like the ones you compose a million times better, Lerryn." They were ballads about beauty. The beauty of nature; the beauty of life; the beauty of love.

They shared many aspects of love, Ella and Lerryn.

They took long walks in the countryside, marveling over the endless variety of plants, of flowers, of colors, of shades of color, of clouds, of light and shadow and landscape at all times of the year.

They talked about their lives, their thoughts, their dreams. Ella told Lerryn about her love for Jesus and his love for all mankind, taught Lerryn the secret of silence and opening the heart to let Jesus enter. Then he, too, knew the miracle of heavenly love and the gift of the Holy Spirit.

Lerryn taught Ella what the Druids, what all the Celts, felt about truth as the ultimate good and the goal for which all men and women must strive. Ella learned to see and to feel the elusive perfection of absolute truth and to love it, as Lerryn did.

Most of all they shared their love for music. Each learned to play the instrument favored by the other. Then they taught themselves to play the rustic flutes that country people created from reeds. Each of them, both of them, made mistakes sometimes when they made music. Alone, or together. When either made a really foolish error, both of them laughed, and they shared the love of lightheartedness.

Both of them loved romance, that idealistic, unattainable, perfect communion between man and woman. In a way, they were trying to create their personal rainbow of romance, a shimmering, beautiful link between them.

Sometimes their joined hands, when they were walking, became a tingling, thrilling promise and invitation for a different aspect of love. When that happened, without a word or a look that might give the excitement a dangerous actuality, they untangled their fingers, as if neither had felt anything. Lerryn, because he needed to pour all his energy and all his heart into his pursuit of priesthood; Ella, because she believed that she alone had experienced the hunger for more physical contact and non-idealized love. She remembered what Rufus had told her. No man of integrity and sensitivity would profane the body that had been touched by a miracle of God.

While Ella and Lerryn spun their gossamer web of romance, both Rufus and Tastros discovered the deliriously, unreasoned, unplanned bliss of the ordinary, everyday love between man and woman. They met, fell in love, married young women who had moved with their families to the growing community.

Tastros built a new home for his bride. Rufus brought his new love to the hut he had shared with Tastros.

Each year the miracle tree bloomed in the season when the earth's growing things all wore the trappings of death. Joseph talked with all the Nazarenes, now numbering more than a hundred, and they decided to celebrate the annual miracle as the birth of Jesus in Albion. It had begun when Joseph and his companions and the scroll that carried the words of Jesus first touched the land. It was a nativity, a birth of the blossoming tree, of the message of God's love.

They celebrated the miracle with a feast of Agape, as they did in the spring when they celebrated the resurrection miracle. For the celebrations in the chapel, they decorated the altar with flowering branches, and a single blossom graced the table in front of each partaker of the Agape feast.

On these two days Joseph prayed most earnestly for the gift of the Holy Spirit, that all encompassing happiness that filled so many of the hearts and souls around him. There were instants of grace—at least he thought there were. But so evanescent was the feeling that he could not be certain. It burdened his heart.

To such a degree that he could not carry the burden alone. He asked those closest to him—Ella and Rufus—to add their prayers to his. "If I could know the Holy Spirit— really know it—before I die, my life would be complete."

Joseph was seventy-four years old when the wonderful time came to an end.

CHAPTER EIGHTY-THREE

NO ONE WAS EXPECTING ANY TROUBLE.

The winter had been mild. Joseph had enjoyed three trips to the spring of Sulis, Ella had celebrated her twenty-first birthday there, swimming in the tepid pool while Lerryn sat at its edge playing and singing the ballad he'd composed as his birthday gift to her.

The solid land around Joseph's community had been put under the plow during the years of growth. When the celebration of Jesus' resurrection took place, the fields already wore a green veil of new life.

Nancledra was an honored guest of the Agape feast. He and Bodinnar entertained everyone with the news from Gaul: The Romans were repeating the comedy they'd performed three years before. Troops massed on the coast opposite Albion were boasting that they would never set foot in the fragile, ill-built, wooden barges. There was a new Emperor in Rome, an old man that everyone laughed at and insulted to his face.

Nancledra, as usual, had been generous. The wine at the feast was a gift from him. So was the magnificent gold chain, very much like the Archdruid's own sign of office, that Joseph wore around his neck. The difference lay in the

medallion it carried; Joseph's was a gold cross, symbol of
the crucifixion of his Lord, incised with intricate interlocking Celtic circles, each centered with a representation of a
blossom of the miracle tree.

Following the feast there was joyous music and dancing.
Ella played the flute. But this one was made of silver, not
reed. Another gift from Nancledra.

"She is more like Sarah with every passing year," he said
to Joseph, and, as usual, they began to reminisce about
when they'd been young. With Sarah beside them.

A huge fire blazed on top of the Tor one night a little less
than three weeks later. Ella and Lerryn were the first in the
community to see it. They had arranged to meet to marvel
at the beauty of the stars that filled the dark sky.

Lerryn explained the fire. It was only a week before the
Festival of Beltane. People had been bringing branches and
winter's fallen trees to the fire circle for many days, building the tremendous pile for the bonfire. Some unruly boys,
he was sure, must have crept up on the Tor and ignited it as
a prank. "We'll stay out here and catch them when they try
to sneak back home. This calls for serious punishment."

"Like what?"

"Like gathering all the charcoal the bonfire makes and
then rebuilding the makings. They'll be aching all over before they're done."

"Lerryn! You sound suspiciously knowledgeable. Did
you play the same prank when you were a boy?"

"There were ten of us. It was Samain, though, not Bel-
trane."

The night passed, and no culprits came down from the
Tor. When the sun rose, a tall column of black smoke
marred the colors of dawn.

"It must be a real alarm," Lerryn said. "I'll get the horses
fed and ready to travel. You'll have to drive your father to
Hod Hill, Ella. I know he will say he does not want to go
without word from the Archdruid, but you must insist. Nan-

cledra is many miles away, I know. And if your father does not go, the others will stay here, too. I am confident that he will not want to endanger them. Speak to him. I must go to the oak grove and learn if the priests have orders for us students. They will be gathering there."

Hod Hill was an astonishment. It was by far the biggest, densest, most organized community Joseph had seen since he left the riverside town in Gaul to head north into the world of the Celts.

The hill was not nearly as high as the Tor, but it was as wide. Its top had been flattened, and the earth used to build tall, thick walls around its sides. They enclosed an area of approximately seventy acres of land. Each foot of it served a prepared purpose. Huts surrounded small courtyards. Bake houses, metal and pottery workshops, storehouses filled with grain, five wells, stabling for cattle, eleven latrines, chicken coops close by altars to sacrifice the fowl when supplicating and honoring the Celtic gods, and tower guardhouses at close intervals inside the perimeter of the walls—everything that was needed to shelter and support hundreds of people from the surrounding countryside waited in readiness for them at Hod Hill.

Ella stared, fascinated, at the warriors who were already grouped at the foot of the steep earthwork route up to the open gates of the fortress. Each wore a short leather kilt and a wide leather belt that held a gleaming longsword and a long, thick leather sling for propelling stones or sharpened metal missiles. Their hair stood out in long sharp-looking points from their heads. It was stiffened and bleached with lime and made them look like unearthly monsters. Unearthly blue monsters. Their skin had been colored.

At last she was getting to see the blue men she'd heard her father talk about. Their appearance terrified her, as it was supposed to terrify all enemies. When two of them demanded that she give up the cart and horses, she said not a word. She'd carry her father herself, if she had to, rather than argue with these warriors.

Joseph was more courageous about addressing them. "Who are the enemy?"

"Romans. They landed an army in the east during the night."

"I'll never understand wars," Ella complained to Joseph a week later. The blue men had returned the cart and horses to them, and she was driving her father home.

"There are a dozen or more different tribes in Albion," he explained. "They are all Celtic, but they consider themselves separate peoples, and they sometimes have wars of conquest, one tribe conquering another and taking its territories. The Catuvellauni are an especially aggressive tribe. They've been ravaging the eastern part of Albion for decades, selling the men and women they conquered to the Romans, for slaves."

The leader of the tribe had recently died, Joseph said, and his two sons were anti-Roman, not like their father. So the Roman Army had landed, fought a three-day battle with the Catuvellauni, killed one son, and sent the other one running away in defeat.

It seemed clear that the Romans had accomplished what they had set out to do, because they weren't even bothering to pursue the runaway Caratacus and his few remaining warriors. The legions had made camp and were settled in it. Quiet.

"They probably figure that Caratacus will be killed by the tribe whose lands he fled to. He's a danger to every other chief in Albion. Bodinnar is delighted at the prospect. So were the other two local chiefs I met inside the fort. They're never going to love the Romans. The Durotriges don't trust anyone, I'm afraid. But they're exceedingly glad that the legions have taken care of possible future threats to them from Caratacus. The eastern regions are distant and foreign in men's minds, but in miles they're not all that far."

"Well, I'm glad it's over. I'll be happy to get home."

"So will everyone else. The wheat needs tending, and the animals that were turned loose have to be collected." Joseph chuckled. "Also, there's the Beltane celebration tonight. No one wants to miss the feasting and dancing."

"Drinking, you mean. Men will do without food anytime, if there's plenty of mead."

"A celebration is justified, Ella. There's no war."

She grinned at her father. "Let's take a skin of Nancledra's wine to the festival, then. We deserve a celebration, too."

Joseph found that to be a fine idea.

Summer was as always. Bright days, sudden short showers to cool the air and water the crops. Lerryn was anxious about the upcoming competitions at the Gorsedd. If he performed brilliantly, he would receive the honor of the title Bard.

Ella listened to the works he had composed and assured him that they were brilliant.

About a hundred times a week, she laughingly reported to Martha. She was showing her age, Martha was, but Saul, who was nearly sixty now, looked exactly the same as ever. "That's because of the tanning," Martha sniffed. "His skin turned to leather a long time ago, and leather doesn't wrinkle."

Ella looked closely at Tastros, to check Martha's theory. "Maybe you're right," she reported to the older woman. "He actually looks younger than he used to."

Martha glanced, with an extremely casual air, at Ella. "Maybe it's because he's married and about to become a father. Being married and having children keeps a person young."

Ella pretended not to know what Martha was hinting. But, as soon as she could, she got away. She liked to make sure that she saw the others of the group as often as possible. The growing community, a more active community life, and the marriages of Rufus and Tastros had inevitably changed everyone's life; yet still, they had been so close, gone so many miles together, that she had a special affection for all of them. She even visited the out-of-the-way spot near a metallic-tasting spring where the dogs had been buried after each of them had died of old age.

Near the end of the summer, some hard-to-believe rumors came in from the east. It was said that the Roman Emperor himself had come to Albion to lead the victorious Army into the fortified city that had once been Caratacus' headquarters and tribal center.

That was unlikely, but not impossible to believe. Roman Emperors liked to be known as great generals. What Ella could not credit at all was the tale that he had brought a dozen elephants with him and had actually ridden on the back of one, seated in a little silk-draped pavilion.

She would have dearly loved to see an elephant, but the rumor had to be an invention. People—even emperors—just did not travel around with huge beasts as big as houses.

Another rumor—which did prove to be accurate—was much more upsetting to the men in the community. Bodinnar came over from the marsh village to tell them.

The Emperor—his name was Claudius—had made treaties with at least ten of Albion's tribes. In return for Rome's friendship and protection against their enemies, they agreed to pay tribute and taxes to the Emperor. One of the tribes was the Regni. Their territory bordered the southeastern boundary of the Durotriges. And their chief, Cogdumnus, had welcomed Roman soldiers into his headquarters, a town on the coastline. They were fortifying it and had a garrison of soldiers there.

Maybe it was a way of keeping Cogdumnus happy, speculated some Durotriges. The treaty said they'd protect him from his enemies.

Others had an even more hopeful theory. Maybe the Romans were preparing a safe place for their troops when they embarked for the voyage back to Gaul.

In any case, a close watch would have to be kept. And crops harvested at the earliest possible moment—for storage in the fortress at Hod Hill if they had to take refuge there from the Romans. Or the Regni.

The Emperor Claudius and his elephants had left Albion only a few weeks after they'd arrived. Now, at the beginning of autumn, the troops in the town of Regni pulled out, too, and returned to the east. Everyone in Joseph's community celebrated with a special Agape feast to thank Father God of the miracle tree and His Son Jesus for their safety.

Soon afterward there was another celebration. Lerryn had been named a Bard at the Gorsedd.

"I told you this would happen," Ella said to him. "I told you that you're brilliant."

Lerryn was ecstatic. Now he could begin the much more difficult studies that would lead—if he were truly brilliant—to the rank of full priest, of Druid.

It left a big hole in Ella's life when Lerryn went north to the secret academy where he would learn medicine. However, she reasoned, that lasted for only three years. And she'd be glad to have a doctor around when he came back. Her abba was feeling the cold in his bones more every winter. Someday she was going to have to face the truth: He was an old man and would not live many more years. Someday. But certainly not within the three short years of Lerryn's training.

And in the meantime there were the dependable pleasures and benefits of the baths at the hot spring of Sulis. She drove Joseph there after the Festival of Samain, the start of the New Year, on November 1.

The Druid priestess, Maen, moved another elderly man out of his big, warm, sun-filled room in the dormitory so that Joseph and Ella could have it. The evicted visitor could make do with lesser accommodations. He was not a friend of the Archdruid Nancledra.

"Will Nancledra come while we're here, do you think, Abba? He often visits after the New Year, too."

"I hope so, but I doubt it. The upset about the Romans has made all the Druids busier than usual. They have ceremonies in their oak groves where they sacrifice white bulls, to entreat their gods for their benevolence. Probably every oak tree in Albion will have some kind of ritual performed at its base before winter's done. Spring is the time when wars begin."

"Are you worried, Abba?"

"I will worry in April if it's called for. Now I'm going to cook my old bones until time to return home to prepare for the winter nativity Agape."

CHAPTER EIGHTY-FOUR

THE DINING HALL WAS MORE CROWDED THAN JOSEPH HAD ever seen it. Maen, naturally, put him in a spot sheltered from drafts and near to the kitchen so that his food would be good and hot when it reached him.

The special attention of the priestess caused considerable curiosity among the other diners. So did the great golden cross on Joseph's chest. Joseph paid no attention to the whispering, or the staring. He was hungry, and the rich stew smelled delicious.

When someone tapped his shoulder while he was eating, he was annoyed. "What do you want?" he said to the unknown blond man who was demanding his attention.

"My apologies, my apologies. If I could please ask your name?"

"Eat your dinner, Abba." Ella looked up at the intruder. "My father is called Joseph of Arimathea," she told him, and turned back to her own bowl. She was hungry, too.

Soon after they went to their room, there was a knock on the door. Ella went to see who it was. A tall, dark-haired, bright-trousered man was there, a lit tallow candle in one hand. He put his other hand across Ella's mouth.

"Shh," he hissed. "Don't give me away." He was speaking Greek. It made her curious. Ella decided not to bite his fingers just yet.

"You won't remember me, Ella, but your father will. I'm Julius, son of Marcus, the Roman Senator who's his friend. Let me in."

Ella stepped back to admit him. Under his fingers, her lips were smiling. She remembered Julius very well. At the chariot races in the Circus Maximus.

The first thing he had to explain was his presence. He was, in fact, a centurion in the Second Legion, the Roman force that had built the fort in the territory of Regni. His orders were to examine the Fosse Way for its entire length and then assess its condition as a possible route for movement of troops and supplies. Three of the Regni were escorting him, keeping his real identity secret. He'd had one of them make sure that Joseph was indeed who Julius thought he was.

Joseph winced when he heard about Julius' orders. He'd hoped the war was ended.

Julius shrugged. Lowly centurions weren't included in decision making, or even told what those decisions were. They were given orders, and they followed them.

He did know that the Fosse Way wasn't the only road being considered. Other disguised centurions were out in the countryside with escorts. "The commander of the Second is the most thorough man in the world. He looked at practically every stick of wood that went into building the fort. Some prefects are successes because they're flexible and quick-thinking under pressure. Vespasian has gotten his promotions by being overprepared. He'll know all about every track and path and bridge and stream in every direction from where he is."

Joseph was interested, but far from satisfied. "What do you think, Julius?"

The Roman soldier's face showed no emotion at all. "I don't think. I just follow orders."

Joseph felt the pain behind the mask. He changed to a happier topic. "Tell me about your family, Julius. How is my friend Marcus?"

Julius talked about his father with visible pride. Marcus was probably the most respected man in the Senate. The Emperor Claudius called him "the best example of what a Roman should be."

Suddenly Julius started to laugh. It took ten years off his tired, cold, old-man appearance. He looked even younger than twenty-eight, his actual age. "Joseph, you'll never believe who came back to Rome after you left. That wild man Herod Agrippa! Once Sejanus was out of the way, Herod showed up at Tiberius' palace on Capri. So did all the people he'd been owing money to for so many years, once they knew he had returned.

"You remember, he was best friend to Tiberius' son. Even so, the Emperor refused to cover Herod's debts. He put him in prison. The Lady Antonia came to his rescue. So then Herod put his mind to making friends with Caligula. Tiberius had already named him the next emperor.

"I won't even tell you about Caligula, Joseph. He was dangerously crazy. Nobody was safe around him. Except Herod. He could manage anybody." Julius' face lost its vitality again. His eyes seemed to be looking into the pits of hell. Then, quickly, he regained control and humor.

"Caligula was assassinated by his own bodyguard. Then good old Claudius was grabbed up and taken off to their barracks by the Praetorian Guard. They wanted to make him Emperor."

Joseph interrupted the story. "Who is this Claudius? The name's familiar, but I don't seem to remember him."

"That's Claudius exactly, Joseph! No one ever really paid much attention to him. He's Antonia's son, the one with the awful stammer, the one who wrote those history books."

Joseph remembered Claudius now. Drusus and Herod used to joke about him all the time, but at Berenice's funeral, it was the awkward, unattractive Claudius who had written the most beautiful tribute to her. Sensitive, yes. Tender, yes. But Emperor? A life-long laughing stock?

"I have trouble imagining Claudius as head of the Roman Empire," he told Julius.

Julius grinned. "So did the Senate. They were trying to think of anybody else, even talking about restoring the Republic. My father was in favor of that, of course.

"Who, do you suppose, took over and settled everything? Who else? Herod Agrippa. He appointed himself the go-between, dashed back and forth from the Senate to Claudius, and the Guard. Smooth as silk, slippery as a snake. He put some backbone in Claudius, and he rolled his eyes and shrugged and told the senators that he couldn't bear to think about what the Guard might do to people who went up against them and their choice for Emperor. Of course the Guard are twenty thousand strong and armed to the teeth.

"To no one's surprise, the Senate sent a very nice message, via Herod, to Claudius, asking him to become Emperor.

"In fact, Claudius is a good ruler. He claims that studying history all those years taught him what not to do. He spends the tax money on new aqueducts instead of on huge luxuries for himself. But the best part—the reason I told you all this—is about Herod. Claudius made him King of all the land that his grandfather ruled in his day! Herod Agrippa is the new Herod the Great."

Joseph rocked with laughter. "That boy always did manage to land on his feet, but this is the best yet. The rascal. Watch out, Israel. Your pockets are going to be picked clean, and Herod Agrippa will make you enjoy the process."

"That's almost exactly what my father said, only you phrase it better, Joseph."

The two of them smiled at each other, remembering the charming rogue.

Ella felt disagreeably left out. Julius hadn't even looked in her direction, nor had her abba.

On the other hand, she hadn't heard her father laugh so much in years. Julius was good medicine for him. There must be some way she could think of to keep him around, even if he did make her feel like a piece of furniture.

Perhaps Joseph was having the same kind of thoughts. "How long will you be here?" he asked Julius.

"I leave tomorrow. It's risky being around people."

"Do you go back to camp then?"

"Yes, I've already followed the road to its northern end. I'm retracing my steps now. I'll go back down to the coast tomorrow, then across to the camp."

"Disappointing. I'd like to have longer to talk."

Julius hesitated. "Actually, Joseph, I've wished for a long time that I might someday have a chance to talk with you. I brought my mother to you one time . . ."

"I remember."

"What you were telling her . . . I've thought about some of the things you said. Off and on. Not concentrating. They'll just pop into my head at odd moments." Julius shrugged. "Ah, well, so be it. I've got a job to do. No time for philosophy."

Joseph leaned forward. His tone was earnest, yet commanding, when he spoke. "Julius, there is nothing in your life now, or ever, that is as important as your eternal soul. I could not help your mother, but you make me hope that I might be able to help you. After you make your report on the road conditions, come to me at my home.

"It's unlikely that you'll be questioned by anyone. If you are, speak Greek. Say that you have been sent to me by my business agent Stratos. Can you remember that? I did, for many years, have an agent by that name. He is in Judea, in the port city of Caesarea. Greek is the common language there.

"Just repeat the names over and over again: Judea, Caesarea, Stratos, Joseph of Arimathea. It will make little sense to a Celt, but he'll possibly know my name. A Druid will speak Greek perfectly."

"But Joseph, I have duties—"

"In winter? I know enough about armies to be sure that they can be passed on to another. Say anything you like at the camp. Tell them you're going hunting for wild boar, or that you've met a woman. You'll know what will work best. The important thing is to come to me."

"I wish I could."

"Stop wishing, man, and act."

Julius' smile was a bit sorrowful. "You sound like my father."

"Then obey me, as you would obey Marcus. Now. This is how you reach my village . . ."

After Ella closed the door behind Julius, she scolded Joseph. "You were going to stay here for at least a month, Abba. I know Julius is entertaining, but—"

"The boy needs help, Ella. Help that I may be the only person who can provide for him. He is the perfect example of why I was sent to spread the message of Jesus.

"I can always return to the baths. I'll never again have the opportunity to help the son of a man who helped me greatly when I needed it. This chance meeting was sent by God, I'm sure of it.

"Tomorrow I will cook my bones thoroughly. The day after, we'll go home."

Julius was obviously shocked by the stark living conditions in the village, and Joseph's round mud-cemented hut made his eyes widen. Joseph was one of the most powerful, most wealthy men his father had known. Marcus had told many tales of Joseph that he had learned from Berenice. Julius himself had seen Joseph's entire block of buildings in Rome, and his huge apartment in one of them. How could a man accustomed to such a life be satisfied with so little?

That wasn't the only surprise he met. "You'll live here in

my house with me," Joseph told him. "It's already arranged that Ella will go stay with our friends Saul and Martha in the hut adjoining this one. You take her bed, there, in that part of the room, behind the screen."

"Doesn't Ella have her own house and family? My sister's younger than Ella, and she has three children. Did Ella's husband die?"

"She hasn't married. We have been on the move ever since she reached the age of womanhood. Until we came here. And there's a young man . . ."

"A Celt?"

"Yes, and more. He's well on his way to becoming a Druid. Right now he's at their academy for learning medicine."

Julius made awkward, jerking gestures of negation. "You must not let your daughter marry him, Joseph. You must have heard that the Roman Army is going to eradicate the Druids."

"Of course I heard that. In Gaul. But I cannot believe you know what you're saying, Julius. To drive a powerful, influential group out of a region like Gaul is despicable, but understandable. That's not the same as killing them. 'Eradicate' means destroy."

"That is what the orders are, Joseph."

"Have you been given these orders?"

"No, But all the men say . . ."

Joseph smiled. "There. That's it. Rumor. And rumor always magnifies.

"You'll find our living arrangements quite comfortable, Julius, even though you might doubt it at first glance. You are, to everyone here, a business associate who, unfortunately but logically, does not speak the local tongue.

"I don't intend to rush you, or preach to you. When you feel ready to ask questions, or to talk, I am here. Ella, too. She is, in some ways, even better at explaining the meaning of our belief than I am.

"Now to begin with important incidentals. A very fine

Gallic wine is stored in the tall amphora in the niche to the left of the hearth. Help yourself at will. You might pour some in the pitcher now, and we will salute your arrival."

"Didn't you love the gold goblets in a daub and wattle hut?" Ella was giving Julius a tour of the community while Joseph had his afternoon rest.

Julius eyed her curiously. Was she joking? Yes, she was. In a way. Not making fun of her father, or their home. Simply enjoying the humor of the contrast that had confused him no end.

"It made me wonder if I was seeing straight," he admitted.

"I wish I could have seen your face. Abba forgets that most people don't accept strangeness as readily as he has come to."

"He's a remarkable man."

"In every way." Ella looked into Julius' face. It was troubled; Abba had been right, as usual. "He cares for you very much, Julius. You have to believe that, right down to your toes. Many people go their whole lives without anybody caring—really caring—for them, in every way. He's happy to have you here, and so am I."

"You? Why?"

Ella slowly moved her head from side to side. "You poor thing," she said softly. "Has life made you question every kindness offered you? That's awfully sad."

Julius was embarrassed; he didn't know what to say. Ella extricated him from the awkwardness. "Over here," she said, with a small gurgling laugh, "is our miracle tree. It told us we had come to the right place."

The small gurgle became an outright shout of laughter. "Oh, Julius, I did it. It was too bad of me. I missed seeing your expression when you saw the goblets, so I got it to come back by dropping a miracle story on you. I can't even honestly say I'm sorry. You looked so funny!"

Her delight was contagious, even though it was at his expense. Suddenly Julius remembered an earlier walk with Ella, in the Roman Forum. He stuck out his tongue at her, as she had done to him.

Ella whooped.

Julius joined in. It felt foolish. And fine.

The three of them ate dinner together. While Ella soaked up the last of the gravy in her bowl with bits of bread that she ate with relish, she told Julius about Jesus healing her, as Joseph requested.

There was something beyond extraordinary about the naturalness of the circumstances for the supernatural event's recounting. Somehow it made it impossible not to believe what Ella was saying. She ended the story the way she always did. "All around Jesus, everything was happy, and it made me happy, too. Because he loved the world so much, and that included me. I knew everything was all right, was the way it was meant to be. Such a feeling, Julius. Even before my legs were fixed. That's what Jesus gives us. Inside and out, all around, things are as they're meant to be and he loves us, all the time . . ."

Julius was choked with emotion. He longed so desperately to have even the smallest part of what she had. Certainty. Faith. Happiness.

"Did Martha bake honeycakes today?" Joseph asked his daughter.

"She didn't have time. I made some, though. They're not as good as hers, but there's more honey in them." Ella smiled at Julius. "I've always had a sweet tooth." And she stuck out her tongue.

"So it really was a miracle?" Julius said.

Joseph nodded. "We should have died in the storm in the first place. But God made the storm so that it would carry us here unharmed. Then, to tell me that it was meant that we should be here, He transformed my staff into a flowering tree. In the depth of winter."

Julius could not doubt this man. But neither could be believe what he had heard.

"I know," Joseph said, understanding. "You'll be able to see the small miracle of it yourself. It will bloom next month, in the depth of winter, to mark the anniversary of our arrival. Then you'll find yourself nearer to faith."

"I want it so much!" Julius burst out.

"I know," Joseph said again.

Early in December there were two magnificently sunny warm days. Ella seized the opportunity to clean the brazier that held the warmth of glowing red charcoal close to Joseph's chair or bed around the clock.

Julius walked into the hut through the door wide open to the sun and stopped short, staring at Ella. She was smudged all over with charcoal dust. Hands, dress, chin, nose, cheeks—all had black blotches. She looked up when she heard his step, and smiled.

And she was the most beautiful thing Julius had ever seen in his life. When had he begun to love her? He didn't know. It seemed as if he had loved her all his life but had somehow not realized it until now.

"Ella." Julius found that the sound of her name was the sweetest music ever created. He said it again, for the magic of it. "Ella."

"What is it? Are you all right?"

Julius hurried across the floor, to kneel beside Ella. "You are so beautiful, Ella."

"Julius, are you running a fever?"

His smile was as bright as the sunlight. "The poets call it 'divine madness.' Ella, I love you. Could you possibly learn to love me? I'll do anything, be anything, say anything. Just tell me there's a chance that someday, somehow, you might return my feelings."

Ella had turned her head. She wasn't looking at him. "Have I offended you? Ella, I can't help how I feel. I love you."

She turned toward him. Tears had made clear tracks through the soot on her cheeks, were still brimming over and spilling into the tracks. "Julius? Are you making fun of me?"

"No! Ella, no, no, no. I love you. If it makes you cry, it breaks my heart to see you so unhappy. But it doesn't stop me loving you. Nothing can do that, not even you."

"Julius? Do you want to kiss me?"

"More than anything in the world."

"Even though my legs are all right?"

"What do you mean? I'm glad your legs are all right, but I'd still love you if you had fourteen toes and two pair of knees."

"Julius?"

"What is it, love?"

"Kiss me. Very hard, please, and for a long time."

Joseph found them kneeling still, embracing, when he returned home. Two radiantly happy smiles welcomed him, coming from two charcoal-smudged faces. He tried not to laugh at the sight, but he couldn't stop himself.

Julius and Ella weren't bothered in the slightest. They were in that state of bliss where the people and the world around them were shadowy and unreal. The only reality was the love in the other's eyes and the shared magic of that love.

Julius got to his feet. Ella hugged his trousered leg and transferred soot from her cheek to it. "Joseph of Arimathea," said Julius formally, "I beg the privilege, um, the honor of asking you to give your daughter to be my wife." Julius put his hand on Ella's head as if he could not bear to go another second without touching her.

Joseph hated what he knew he must say. "Julius, nothing would please me more than to see you and Ella married. But . . ."

"Abba! Don't say 'but.' Say 'yes.' I can't bear it if you don't say 'yes.'"

"My dear, I have to make the two of you use your heads. Julius is a Roman soldier. He has duties that—"

"Oh, Abba, that doesn't make any difference. Julius is going to stop being a soldier. He hates it."

"How did you know?" Julius stared down at his sooty beloved.

"Because I love you so much, and I could never love a man who didn't hate killing." The logic was more than a bit shaky, Joseph thought, but obviously the conclusion was correct. Julius was nodding his head.

Then he stopped agreeing. "But my father was a soldier, and his father, and his father's father. I was always meant to be a soldier."

Ella let go of his leg and stood to confront him. "Julius, that's dumb. You're not your father or his father or anyone else. You're you. Stop being dumb, please. I want an intelligent husband."

Julius looked at Joseph, a question in his eyes.

Joseph gestured denial. He couldn't make Julius' decisions for him.

Nonetheless, Julius needed Joseph's help. "I was a failure in the Praetorian Guard," he told Joseph. "If my father hadn't been who he is, I would have been executed for cowardice. I was one of the three ordered to act as Caligula's bodyguard and then murder him. He was a dangerous lunatic. Rome had to be rid of him. But I couldn't make myself use my sword. I just stood there, holding it. The others wanted my help, expected it, had a right to expect it. I failed them. I failed Rome. I am a coward, Joseph. My father arranged my transfer to the Second Legion because it was stationed in Germany and got me away from the stink of my name in the Guard and in Rome.

"A man cannot live as a coward. I must prove myself a man. I have to return to the legion."

Joseph considered for a moment. "Does a coward go unarmed among the enemy accompanied by strangers who may betray him at any moment, Julius? How many days were you on Fosse Way, how many miles?

"Is it an act of bravery to thrust a sharp blade into the flesh of a stranger, to rob him of his life? Is robbery courage?

"What takes the greatest strength and bravery in this world, Julius, is for a man to do what he believes is right, just, moral. For him to do what he believes wrong because another orders him to do it is not courage. It is evasion of private honor."

"But Vespasian will say to everyone—"

"Julius!" Ella had her grimy fists on her hips. "What's harder, telling your prefect that you refuse to stay, or staying even though you hate it?"

He thought, frowning. "You're right," he said finally. "Admitting to everyone that I cannot kill is more difficult than killing. I did my duty during the Sejanus riots and executions. I know I could kill, because I have done it. But no longer. I will go to my tribune to resign. Vespasian will not return before spring."

Julius looked again at Joseph. "When I return, I will ask you again to let me marry Ella."

"And I will give you my blessing."

Joseph asked God the Father, God the Son, and God the Holy Spirit to bless the marriage of Helena and Julius. The ceremony took place in the Chapel of the Nazarenes on the day of Nativity. Nancledra was there, his eyes misted by memories of Sarah. Ella was so like her. His gift, presented before the ceremony began, had been more precious than Ella realized. The blue, carved agate box had taken her breath away because of its beauty. She'd scarcely noticed the sprig of greenery inside.

The Archdruid lifted it out. Sunlight made the waxy berries glisten in their nest of leaves. "This is called mistletoe, Ella. It grows high in the branches of the oak tree. To Celts, it represents eternal life because its leaves remain green even in winter when the leaves of the oak have turned brown and dropped to the earth. I present it to you with the wish that your happiness may also have eternal life."

Ella did not know that mistletoe was sacred to the Druids, that she was the only woman who had ever held it in her hand, except for Druid priestesses. She thanked Nancledra with all her heart for the gift and for his thoughtfulness, rather than for the honor he had bestowed upon her. Ella carried flowering branches from the miracle tree in her arms. She tucked the mistletoe among the blossoms. The Agape feast that day was a celebration of the union of man and woman in earthly love as well as of the love of God and of His Son.

Joseph willingly gave his daughter, his most precious treasure, to Julius, but that was not the greatest gift bestowed upon him. Some weeks earlier Julius had been granted the gift of faith, of the presence of the Holy Spirit.

Joseph moved his things next door to the hut of Saul and Martha so that Julius and Ella could have their own home.

Ella delighted in complaining pathetically about the absence of the brazier. The delight lay in Julius' response. "I think I can find a way to make you feel warm."

Carnal love, in Ella's opinion, was undeniably the finest game ever devised.

"You're greedy," Julius accused.

"Do you object?" Ella knew the answer.

"On the contrary."

Just as sublime, in its own way, was the talking time, the secret-telling time, the dream-sharing time.

"Julius, if you could do anything—anything at all—what would you want to do?"

"You'll laugh at me if I tell you."

"What difference does that make? I love you most of all when I'm laughing at you."

"All right. Just don't guffaw."

"Tell."

"I visited a cousin of my mother's once. He had a villa and a garden and a farm and olive trees and a vineyard. In Tuscany. That's my dream. But I don't know the first thing about farming, Ella."

"Julius, I'll go with you in a minute, and I promise not to guffaw at your mistakes. But you have to promise me something, too."

"Anything. What is it?"

"I get to dance on the grapes as long as I want."

CHAPTER EIGHTY-FIVE

JOSEPH STOOD AND WALKED FORWARD EAGERLY THROUGH the spring wildflowers in the turf when he saw the Archdruid coming. He opened his arms to embrace Nancledra. "Perfect timing, my friend. We are just beginning the Agape feast in celebration of the resurrection of Jesus. Come, sit by me, and enjoy some of your own wine."

Nancledra held Joseph close, then stepped away from him. "My friend, my dear old friend, I come with a heavy burden. The Roman Army is on the move, Joseph. They left their fort at daybreak and at present they are attacking the defenses of our seaside fortress, Maiden Castle. They have ballistas, they are filling the refuge behind the walls with Greek fire. The screams of the dying can be heard a mile or more from the ramparts.

"Hod Hill will be next to fall. Within days. Unless the Romans can be stopped. Refugees from the lands north of Maiden Castle are running to Hod Hill now. The people all fear the gods are angry, and they demand that the anger be appeased.

"For Celtic gods, Joseph, the greatest dangers require the greatest sacrifice. I have to agree, and I have to choose the sacrifice most pleasing to our gods. It is the Archdruid's duty.

"My friend Joseph, I love you as if you were my brother, and yet you must be my choice. You worship a god foreign to ours; you bring Celts to your god and lessen their devotion to their own. You came to us from Rome, home of the enemy. I believe that your sacrifice will reverse the gods' anger."

Joseph signified his understanding and acceptance with a nod, as he looked into the eyes of his friend. "I have one question, Nancledra. What about my community here, my fellowship, my family? Will my sacrifice be enough to protect them?"

"Yes. Afterwards, we priests will lead them to our hidden places in the caves. They will be safe there until whatever is to come has come, and is done."

"Thank you, my friend." Joseph smiled. "Their safety is the only thing that matters. I am ready. By what means shall I die?"

"The signal fire on the Tor. You will be the warning to the countryside that the Romans are coming."

The two had been talking quietly, away from the crowded tables. Now Joseph went back. He lifted his hands in blessing. "In the name of the Father, the Son, and the Holy Spirit. Amen. I leave you now, my companions in the faith. Do not try to stop what is about to happen. Put your trust in Archdruid Nancledra and his priests. Do as they tell you." He looked at Ella, and his eyes gave a special message and blessing to her alone. Then he rejoined the Archdruid, unafraid.

Nine priests stood behind him. They came forward quickly. Two took hold of each of Joseph's arms; two seized each of his legs; the last supported his head when the others lifted him up.

The Nazarenes rose from the tables and pressed forward, Ella and Julius in front.

They watched the white-robed and hooded Druids lay Joseph onto a man-sized and man-shaped form made of woven reeds from the marshes. His arms extended outward, perpendicular to his body. Nancledra bent over him. "May you be blessed by your God as well as mine, Joseph," he murmured. And he placed a wreath of mistletoe on Joseph's head.

With silent dexterity the priests covered him with a second wicker form identical to the first, then lashed the two halves together with ropes of braided grasses.

The Archdruid walked forward, to lead the procession to the Tor. Three of the priests followed him, chanting incantations from their secret lore. The others carried Joseph the wicker man on a bier made of oak.

"What can we do?" Martha screamed.

Ella turned to her, to all the fellowship. "We can be with him to the end. That is all we can do. Let us follow."

Julius grabbed Ella's shoulders. "Are you as crazy as they are? I have sword and javelin in the house. I'll save your father."

She shook her head. "No, Julius. Did you see Abba's eyes? He is at peace. He has, at last, received what he has sought in vain. The Holy Spirit has entered his heart. Come, now. I want to be with him."

On top of the Tor the stone fire ring held a beautiful construction of interlaced branches surrounding the lower half of a tall pole of oak, carved with a design of spirals and chain-like interlocked ellipses.

Joseph, encased in widely spaced woven reeds, was lifted and placed upright on a support within the bonfire, then lashed to the pole.

Nancledra looked into his face, bowed to him in homage, then pointed to the bonfire. A tiny flame leapt to life, and in seconds the pyre was ablaze. A cloud covered the sun, making the burning seem brighter. Joseph's golden chain and cross were brighter yet.

As the flames and smoke climbed to him, he could be seen through the wicker enclosure. "Look," Ella murmured to her husband. She slid her warm hand into Julius' cold one. "Look at his face, Julius. He is happy in the love of the Lord."

The wicker cage caught fire and embraced Joseph with incandescence. It was no more radiant than the radiance of the Holy Spirit within him, as he embraced his ecstatic death.

EPILOGUE

The Roman conquest and occupation of the island nation of Albion changed its name to Britannia, then rapidly altered the patterns of life that its people had known for millennia. Cities with Roman design and government replaced tribal strongholds. Straight, paved Roman roads connected them. All this is recorded.

The spread of the good news that Joseph had brought to Albion was not recorded. Yet we know that it must have happened. For the Roman Emperor Constantine was crowned in the city now called York. And in the year 312, he made the Imperial proclamation that henceforth Christianity would be the official religion of the entire Roman Empire.

Joseph had met his death slightly more than two hundred and fifty years earlier. That is but a moment in time, in life everlasting.

A NOTE TO THE READER
FROM ALEXANDRA

Often people ask how much of a historical novel is history and how much is made up. This is what we know about Joseph of Arimathea: He is referred to in the gospels of the New Testament as the wealthy, powerful man who gave his own tomb for the burial place of Jesus of Nazareth. There is no description of him and no mention of his life or his family.

However, there is a legend of Joseph of Arimathea that is many centuries old, widely believed and reverently cherished. It tells us that Joseph was a man of the sea, a trader in the tin mined in the peninsula of England now known as Cornwall. Also that he and his companions brought the message of Christianity to England.

They came by sea and landed on a low hill among marshes. Joseph was carrying a staff, a lengthy piece of wood, which he drove into the ground for support when he left his boat. The wooden staff came to life, became a blossoming tree in the winter landscape.

Joseph and his group built a wattle-and-daub hut that was the first Christian church in England. This tiny church grew and developed and became Glastonbury Abbey, a magnificent complex of soaring stone buildings that included a cathedral acknowledged to be one of the most beautiful structures in the medieval world. Always associated with it was the flowering tree in its precincts, known as the Glastonbury Thorn. It was especially notable because it bloomed every year at Christmastime, in the dead of winter, as well as in the spring.

It still does.

The Abbey is now only a scattering of exquisite ruins, with Glastonbury Tor rising high and mysterious nearby in the flat terrain. Many thousands of people visit it every year and are deeply moved by its remnants of grandeur and by its legend.

At Christmastime, a budded cutting from Glastonbury Thorn is sent to the Queen of England, as was done for her predecessors on the throne for many centuries.

The gospels, the legend, and the Thorn were the beginnings of this novel. They drew me into the history of the era that produced Jesus of Nazareth and Joseph, who gave the tomb in which he was buried.

I was extremely surprised by many of the things that I learned. I suppose that you were, too, when you read the story I wrote. If you are a Christian or a Jew, you almost certainly thought that I had made dozens, or even hundreds, of mistakes.

They aren't mistakes. They are the surprises I discovered in the research I did.

For example: I never use the words Jesus Christ because "Christ" and "Christian" are terms first used after the date that the novel ends. And they were used in the city of Antioch, not Jerusalem. "Christ" was the Greek word for "messiah."

Also, the practice of Judaism was very different during the time that the Temple still stood in Jerusalem until it was destroyed by the Romans in the year 70 C.E., twenty-seven years after my story concludes. Synagogues had become widespread, but their practices were less formalized than they later became. Women were not separated from men. In fact, several synagogues in Rome left records of women as the chief officers of the congregation.

This was the time when oral tradition, the repetition of the words of such notable sages as Hillel, was being collected and put into written form. It became known as the Mishnah, the code of Oral Laws, and was completed about a hundred years after the destruction of the Temple.

Two hundred more years passed before the accepted version of the Gemara was finished. This is the collection of expanded interpretations of the Mishnah that provides much of contemporary Orthodox Judaic ritual and rules.

The oral tradition was also being gathered and recorded by the Christians, in the four gospels. Scholars place the date at between 65 and 100 C.E., with Mark as the earliest, John the latest. At the same time, Paul was sending his letters, epistles, to the Christian churches in the communities he had visited. The letters began as early as 55 C.E.

These developments all had as their setting the world of the Roman Empire. All the historic characters, events, and places mentioned in the novel did exist and did happen. We have no evidence that Joseph of Arimathea knew these people, witnessed these events, visited these places. Nor do we have any particular reason to believe that he did not. A rich, powerful Jew might well have done so.

Joseph's family, his servants, his friends, and the Celts are mostly my invention. Philo and Alexander were real. So was the doctor in Rome and the magician in Gaza. The sages Hillel and Shammai, the High Priests of the Temple, the family of King Herod, his counselors Nicolaus and Ptolemy—all played prominent, often dramatic, roles in the history that is the origin of many things that still guide and govern our lives today.

I enjoyed spending many, many months with them. I hope they were good company for you in the hours you passed reading their story.

Those of you who are curious to know more about the history and life of the time of Joseph will find the following books both useful and interesting:

Ausubel, Nathan. *The Book of Jewish Knowledge.* New York: Crown Publishers, 1964.

Connolly, Peter. *Living in the Time of Jesus of Nazareth.* Bnei Brak, Israel: Steimatzky, Ltd., 1993.

Day, John, editor, et al. *Oxford Bible Atlas*, third edition. New York: Oxford University Press, 1993.

Ellis, Peter Berresford. *The Druids.* Grand Rapids, Michigan: William B. Erdman's Publishing Co., 1994.

Klingaman, William K. *The First Century: Emperors, Gods, and Everyman.* New York: HarperCollins, 1990.

DAZZLING NOVELS OF SOUTHERN SPLENDOR

From Alexandra Ripley, author of *Scarlett: The Sequel to Margaret Mitchell's*
GONE WITHE THE WIND

- *CHARLESTON*
  (0-446-36-000-7, $6.50 USA) ($7.99 CAN)
- *FROM FIELDS OF GOLD*
  (0-446-60-249-3, $6.50 USA) ($7.99 CAN)
- *NEW ORLEANS LEGACY*
  (0-446-34-210-6, $6.50 USA) ($7.99 CAN)
- *ON LEAVING CHARLESTON*
  (0-446-36-001-5, $6.50 USA) ($7.99 CAN)
- *THE TIME RETURNS*
  (0-446-60-258-2, $6.50 USA) ($7.99 CAN)
- *SCARLETT*: The Sequel to Margaret Mitchell's **Gone With The Wind**
  (0-446-36-325-1, $6.99 USA) ($7.99 CAN)

AVAILABLE AT A BOOKSTORE NEAR YOU FROM
WARNER BOOKS

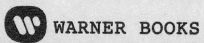

But, as soon as she could, she got away. She liked to make